Synchronization

More by Brooke Shaffer

The Timekeeper Chronicles

The Chivalrous Welshman

Time to Kill

Tick Tock

Windup

Stopwatch

Free Time

Leap Second

Imminence

Synchronization

Turning Point (Summer 2024)

The Hands of Time

In the Hands of the Enemy

The Hands Pulling the Strings

The Hand Holding the Knife (Winter 2023)

The Lone Wolf

Wolf Pack

Alpha Wolf

Lone Wolf

The Akari-Bearer

Bearer of Bad News (Winter 2024)

Singles

Of Saints and Sinners

Chasing the White Bear

Synchronization

Book Eight of The Chivalrous Welshman
The Timekeeper Chronicles

Brooke Shaffer

Black Bear Publishing

Copyright © 2023 by Brooke Shaffer

All rights reserved. No portion of this book may be reproduced, stored in a retrieval system, or transmitted in any form by any means—electronic, mechanical, photocopy, recording, scanning, or other—except for brief quotations in critical reviews or articles, without the prior written consent of the publisher.

Published in Michigan by Black Bear Publishing.

This novel is a work of fiction. Names, characters, places, and incidents are either products of the author's imagination or used fictitiously. All characters are fictional, and any similarity to persons living or dead is purely coincidental.

ISBN:

Hardcover: 978-1-953113-28-3
Softcover: 978-1-953113-29-0
eBook: 978-1-953113-30-6

For Reaves

Prologue
Self-Defense

Walter stared down the Hands as they looked down their noses under their shrouds at him and the small child clinging to his legs. He didn't like his son being bullied, and he wouldn't allow himself to be bullied either.

"If my son is not permitted to train early, there may not be an Apprentice to train in three years," he told them. "And you risk losing a Captain if you do not allow it."

"There are other Captain-trained Masters on your world," one Hand said.

"Yes, but what happens when word gets out, hm? Will they say that the Hands fear a small child? Will they say that the Hands fear even the probationary Timekeepers?" He gestured to Tommen, staring wide-eyed at the shrouded figures. "My son is no threat to you. But he faces a greater threat that has already harmed him and could even kill him if he is unable to defend himself."

They'd been going around in circles for well over an hour. The Hands said it was irregular. The minimum training age for humans had been set based on physical and mental maturity and capabilities. Walter's claim was that the outside threat was too great; they could make an exception. It was only basic probationary Banding skills, only used for getting away from the threat. The risk of Tommen accidentally revealing himself and his abilities to others was no greater than any other human Runner with ill intentions. And, being a child, he was more likely to master it sooner and refine his skills before his rebellious teenage years when he couldn't be made to give half a damn about anything but himself, his friends, and any girls he was fawning after.

"Very well," the Zero Hour decided. "You may teach him under the following parameters. Up until such time as he is of an age to become a probationary Timekeeper, he will learn only Fast and Slow Banding with the intent of escaping the threat, with no thought of doing harm. In the event that he acquires any residual abilities, he will not be permitted to hone or expand them. His primary Time education will be spent on knowledge. He will remain a probationary until the appropriate time when he may test for his Apprenticeship. His use of Time for self-defense does not grant him the privilege of testing until then. Furthermore, when his Apprentice review does come up, there is no reason he should not pass, as you say, with flying colors."

"I understand," Walter stated. "And I agree. Whole-heartedly. If I did not believe it necessary, I would not have brought it up in the first place."

The case was dismissed. As they left the Seat, Tommen asked, "Am I in trouble?"

Walter smiled and shook his head. "No, you're not in trouble. Not in the least. Actually, I think I'm the one in trouble."

"Why? For teaching me Speed Up and Slow Down?"

"Yeah. For that."

"Why?"

"Because that's something big boys learn, when they turn thirteen. But I decided you needed to learn it early, so you can stay safe from Tyler Freeman."

"Oh. Do I have to stop?"

"No, not at all. Actually, I want you to do it more. Just enough to get away, but don't be afraid to use it. I want to keep you safe."

"Okay. *Diolch, Tad.*"

He looked down. "*Croeso, mab.*"

Chapter One
A Dose of Punishment

Tommen hit the ground, rolled until his hands and feet were under him, and skidded to a stop. He looked up just in time to see a great rhino horn bearing down on him. He slipped to the side, but not fast enough as the enormous rhino man Berkloff snapped his head back and caught Tommen in the side, sending him flopping like a fish across the floor. With his head still spinning, Berkloff got under him with his horn and threw him another thirty feet.

He lay on the ground, stunned. The day was December 27th, about five o'clock in the evening at home. After getting off work at two, Tommen had gone home to fix himself some food, do a little channel surfing, and text his girlfriend to figure out when they were going to sleep together next. He managed to accomplish the first part, about getting some food. There were still huge containers of leftovers from Christmas dinner in the fridge, and he fixed himself a regular three-course meal from them.

Once that was finished, he went down to his room, intending to do something or other—he really couldn't remember—but when he pushed open the door, he found Julianna standing at the foot of his bed. Originally, he'd feared that Rifun had died and she was there to kill him. Instead, she politely informed him that Rifun had actually recovered very well in the last week and now wished to speak with him. Tommen couldn't decide which was worse.

He followed her to the Akarin fortress, now occupied by the Cult—ahem, First Order of the Akari. But rather than take him directly to see Rifun, she explained that there was something that had to be done first. All the other soldiers had already gone through, now it was his turn. Originally, he might have expected a debriefing, a congratulations, maybe some kind of undeserved medal. Instead of an after-action report or debriefing or awards, however, he was basically taken to court.

He was accused of cowardice in battle, which he certainly didn't deny. He was nearly accused of desertion, but that charge couldn't really stick, seeing how he had been in the second wave of battle, and he himself had accompanied the Faharoa—that is, Rifun—to the meeting with the Akarin council in which the Akarin surrendered. But cowardice, well, that was a fact. He thought he might have stunned the panel by not trying to deny it and make up some heroic story about him killing twenty men with a single blow. Actually, his honesty seemed to confuse them.

Nonetheless, he was sentenced to a beating. They couldn't really strip him of rank because he was already vaovao, the lowest man on the totem pole. He couldn't be sentenced to any kind of prison time because the prisons were kind of full of, well, prisoners, all the Akarin who survived and surrendered. Plus they couldn't just have a useless body taking up space and resources. Even the prisoners were put to work. And then there was that whole fact that he was the one who gave up the antidote to the Borelian poison and so saved the life of the Faharoa, going against even his own friend, Kayla, who'd been the one to stab Rifun.

In the end, he had to be punished for his cowardice, but anything beyond that would be left to the Faharoa. When looking for someone to administer an appropriate beating, the panel had to look no further than Captain Berkloff, the Korin with a real ax to grind. He was already bad-tempered, a perfectionist, eager to please his master. His youngest son, Kiffin, who had trained side-by-side with Tommen for months, had died in the battle. It was a great honor, certainly, but he was still dead. It was only made worse by the fact that Tommen was supposed to have been on the staircase with him when it was collapsed, but he'd been off stealing books from the Archives instead of actually fighting.

So Berkloff was extra enthusiastic about giving Tommen the beating he seemed to deserve. By the time all these thoughts went through his mind, he found that he was stumbling to his feet, only to be knocked aside by the rhino man once more. Berkloff had gotten down on awkward fours to fight him almost as a real rhino. But he was a humanoid, not an anthromorph, and could not go from all fours to upright and back again with ease. His lumbering gait was awkward and comical to watch, or it would have been, if Tommen had not been on the receiving end of that massive horn, or the keratin-like pseudo-hooves that passed as the man's hands.

He knew he had broken bones. He could feel them. But the events of the previous week as well as past events dictated that he get up, get away, fight back, do something, do anything. Anything was better than lying there waiting to be picked off.

Thankfully, Berkloff did not give him a full body blow this time, but it didn't take much to get him back down to the ground. Berkloff put his horn on Tommen's chest, effortlessly weighing him down. There was a time when such a position would have terrified him, and that wasn't to say he wasn't a little afraid, but just as recent events made fights with Tyler Freeman look weak and petty, so now did true battle make Berkloff's punishment feel like little more than time out at recess. He'd seen thousands of men killed, barely escaped being crushed under a collapsing staircase, barely escaped being crushed between floors, and watched as two sides faced off over a big red button that could have killed every single one of them.

Something must have shown on his face, or maybe something didn't show. Berkloff grunted and suddenly pushed down with his horn, effectively giving Tommen a perfect CPR compression, including a couple broken ribs and maybe even a broken sternum. He tried to gasp in pain, but his chest could not expand for his lungs.

"Stay down," Berkloff commanded, backing off and standing.

Obediently, Tommen stayed down, gasping for air and yet trying to keep his ribs from moving so they didn't hurt so much. He coughed and tasted blood in the back of his throat. Closing his eyes, he reached inside his body, Feeling out all the injuries. More broken bones than he cared to consider, including his sternum. One lung was bruised and that was where the coughing up blood was coming from, but it really wasn't anything too serious. His insides had been sloshed about a bit, but were otherwise in tact. His head hurt and there might have been a minor concussion, but certainly not worse than his skiing injury. The worst injury above his neck was a bruised cheek which was beginning to swell.

Taking a breath and calming himself down, Tommen Banded to heal what he could. The bruising and swelling, easy. Broken ribs, a little more difficult, a little more painful, but no different than letting them heal naturally as there was nothing any doctor could do for him. Bruised lung, same story. Once the pins and needles had passed, he felt around and did a reassessment.

His left arm, the one burned from shoulder to fingertips, that hurt like a mother. His elbow was sprained and his wrist was broken, he could tell. His collarbone was also sore. He right knee and ankle were pretty tender, too. Those were going to require a little more medical prowess. Time could condense the healing time needed, but it wouldn't magically reset a bone or reattach a damaged ligament or tendon.

So he did the next best thing. He reached and felt his left leg, Felt how everything was supposed to sit, supposed to attach. What did it look like normally? Then he returned to the right leg. He counted himself fortunate that the knee was only swollen, but everything was still correctly attached. The ankle was sprained, but once he maneuvered it into the correct position, he was able to Band and heal. His collarbone had a hairline fracture which was causing the nerves to flip out, but no doctor was going to touch that either. He set his arm where it would normally be held in a sling, and Banded.

The only thing he couldn't do was his wrist. He wasn't able to set it, and if he couldn't set it, he didn't want to Band it. It would have to wait until he got home. He could make up some probable story about slipping on the ice and wanting to tough it out, wait until it got really bad before going in. It would be just like him. Then, later, he could tell his dad all about it, how he was a disgrace to the Order army and was punished for his cowardice in battle. He doubted his dad would be too disappointed in him, actually.

"Stand up," one of the panel members ordered.

Tommen did so, gingerly testing out all his limbs, being gentle with his right leg until he was sure it was healed and could move normally. He approached the panel and stood at attention as best he could, keeping his wrist close to his body and forcing himself not to wince in pain.

There were five members of the panel, plus a few others: Berkloff, who administered punishment; a standby physician, ready with a medical kit, in case that punishment got taken too far; someone else whom Tommen figured to be Berkloff's antithesis, the one who doled out rewards instead of punishments, but that was only speculation; and Julianna.

"Tommen Forbes, your sentence for conviction of cowardice has been carried out," the head panel member—a hulking humanoid creature with four arms—told him, with about as much enthusiasm as relating what he'd had for breakfast. "This conviction and subsequent punishment will be noted on your record and can only be changed by the Faharoa or a designated agent."

"I understand, sir," Tommen replied.

"You have been able to heal yourself of most injuries. However, it is noted that some linger. Report to the infirmary for treatment. Dismissed."

"Yes, sir."

He left the recreational area, Julianna leading. There were twelve such recreational areas on the first floor of the fortress. According to some of the Akarin, those who were true Akari-bearers could use it as some kind of mind-reading holodeck apparatus. According to some of the Order soldiers, some of the Akarin had. Using the responsive nature of the recreational areas, some Akarin soldiers had conjured up infinite armies to scare the Order away. The nice thing was that it was only an illusion, and any of the phantoms that the Order cut down could be easily recreated. The problem was, it was only an illusion. Once the Order realized this, realized that the phantom soldiers couldn't leave the recreational area, they simply avoided going into them.

Three of the areas had collapsed in all the earthquakes and the fighting. One was currently being used for an impromptu military tribunal. Four had been turned into various wings of an infirmary. One was being utilized by various engineers and architects to safely test out reconstruction ideas without having to actually worry about more cave-ins. Two more were used as impromptu cells and quarters for Akarin prisoners who were too weak to fight or help with repairs, and were considered very little threat to the Order. The last area remained strictly recreational, open to any and all who needed to relax or blow off steam.

Julianna took Tommen to one of the infirmary halls, the walk-in clinic if it could be appropriately called such. The other wings were of varying specialty and priority, from fatal wounds and burns, to minor fixes and outpatient surgeries. Generally speaking, the physicians were skilled enough in Time and Matter that even some severe operations by human standards were reduced to outpatient surgeries. It made recovery time a lot faster, but it also accentuated the grave nature of the more serious wounds.

Some of the soldiers had been wounded without ever getting to the front line, Tommen knew. That was the magic of portals, specifically microportals. Open a microportal for a knife, slice through midair, cut an opponent's throat from half a room away. Shoot a bullet into thin air, open a portal to anywhere. They didn't have to be big, nor did they last long, and it was almost impossible to tell who did it or where they came from, or where and how to fight back. Tommen hadn't even been aware of the existence of microportals until the battle. Was that just something he'd been expected to know, or had it caught everyone by surprise?

It was a similar story with most of the fighting. Only those directly opposed to each other really did any hand-to-hand combat. Most of it was done from a distance. Time, Double Banding an opponent so they aged a hundred years in only a few seconds and dropped dead. Matter, taking the water out of an opponent and drying them up completely, or crumbling their armor. Energy, halting the flow of synaptic processes in the brain, putting an opponent at your mercy, if it didn't kill them outright. Was it any wonder he had fled?

And here he stood with a broken wrist. Even now, almost a week after the battle, with all their abilities to speed up healing, the physicians were still overworked and understaffed. From what little conversation Tommen was able to pick out, more than half of the physicians had stayed back in the ruins, waiting to be called after the battle was won, or ready in the event of a defeat and retreat.

He smirked. Sadurnon had been called out for their harboring of intergalactic fugitives. It wasn't as if they didn't know Rifun was hiding in one of their underground cities; he'd asked politely to use it and they had agreed. The Order had actively helped the Elif as a means of rent.

The only reason they got called out was because he, Tommen, had written a note telling about the attack. His dad had found the note and taken it to the human colony planet Tacaga, along with a whole host of other information he'd been leaking for the last couple months about the Order, its numbers, location, and all that. Tacaga, being technologically superior to Earth in every way, had gone to the Hands of Time. They exposed the actions of the Elif and had been granted permission to completely decimate the ruins and scour the rest of the planet for other Order strongholds.

They'd been too late to stop the battle, as had been the plan, but a few goods things had come of it. For one, the Order still only had one base of operations, instead of two. Second, now everyone was aware of the battle, not just the Order and the Akarin, which meant Rifun and the Order were back in the spotlight. Third, it put a black eye on the victory, because the Order had left its backside exposed. Now they were down almost half of their physicians, and their little refugee camp had likely been decimated as well, which really didn't go over well with public relations. And that wasn't even accounting for losing most of the elite ambony force because Tommen redirected the initial invasion portal so it hit a black hole and sucked them all through, or most of them anyway.

The best part was that there was no way to pin anything on him. No one would believe he had the strength to curtail the portal like that. And as far as giving away the location of the secret base? Rifun himself had said that some Akarin had joined the Order after the Akarin split. Some of them could have easily been double agents. As far as Tommen was concerned, he was in the clear on both accounts.

Eventually, a physician got around to him. He felt the bones in Tommen's good arm, did a little Feeling around—certainly much more gently than Tommen was capable of—reset the bones, then Banded his wrist until they healed. It hurt, and he cried out pretty good, but it was still better than having a cast for six weeks. He leaned against one wall, holding his wrist and gasping for air, not even bothering to try and maintain composure. That fucking hurt.

The only reason the pain lasted longer than sixty seconds was because of his arm. Because of the burn damage, it was hypersensitive. He'd learned to ignore the constant drum of pain that regularly fired off, but any time any new pain was added, the whole tidal wave moved through his arm and even his entire body. And, like a wave, it moved back and forth, growing larger for a time, and then mellowing out. It was a good minute or two before he was able to move and get going.

"Didn't you have a Funnel Band you developed for your arm?" Julianna inquired.

"I didn't want to mess with the physician," Tommen answered tightly. "By the time he released his Band, I was too slow to get it up."

"I bet your girlfriend didn't think so."

He blushed hard before his mind fully registered her words, and he followed her silently out of the infirmary.

The main floor of the fortress was originally dedicated to the non-essentials, like recreation. So far, only the recreational area had really been turned. The cafeteria remained in the same area with the same function, though the nutritional cubes had been replaced by real food. Tommen glanced in that direction, but said nothing. He was here for a purpose, and he had to fulfill that purpose. Maybe afterwards, if he was still upright, he would see about some lunch. Yeah, he just ate, but so what? He'd just gotten the shit beat out of him by a rhino. That was hungry work.

They emerged into the western corridor and made their way south. They might have gone north except the northwest stair had been completely collapsed. Looking back, Tommen saw that reconstruction efforts were presently concentrated in that area. If that corner could be stabilized, then relief efforts in all three remaining corners on all floors would be that much safer.

The southwest stair was unique in that it housed the only access to the lower portal room, which was now as heavily guarded as it was used, and the sub-levels.

The Lower Akarin had been holed up in the lower sub-levels. From what Tommen had heard, the Lower Akarin's biggest mistake was getting involved, trying to bring the fight into the open. If they'd stayed holed up in the lower levels, they would have been able to bottle neck the Order forces and hold them at bay, possibly indefinitely. But in exposing themselves, they had, well, exposed themselves, and went the way of the Upper Akarin. Now they were held in their own prisons. The second sub-level was the prison for those deemed a powerful threat, and the third sub-level was for the majority of the prison force. They were generally unhappy with the arrangement and could make a fuss, but they could just as easily be subdued. They were also used for a majority of the work force when it came to repairing the damage to the fortress.

Tommen followed Julianna up the southwest stair. The second floor was the common barracks. Unfortunately for the Order, the Akarin fortress, while nearly impregnable, was not built to house an entire legion of soldiers for an extended period of time. The entire fortress itself wasn't big enough to properly house all the soldiers and all assorted necessities therein. It could comfortably house twenty thousand for a short time. Cramped quarters and an even shorter stay could push it to a hundred thousand or so, depending on the aliens. When all was said and done, between the Order and the Akarin, they were looking at about a quarter million soldiers, give or take.

The fourth floor was officer barracks. That was where the higher officers like Berkloff were moved to, as well as what remained of the ambony. There was still some room left over after that, so some of the offices and meeting rooms from the third floor had been moved to the fourth floor, and part of the third floor had also been turned into barracks, mostly reserved for the afovoany and some of the lesser officers, like the instructor aides. The second floor barracks were primarily vaovao and afovoany. Space limitations meant that the lines were not so clear cut as they had been in the ruins, and the two groups were often housed together. Space limitations also allowed greater freedom for those like Tommen who were of Unengaged races and couldn't just disappear for weeks or months at a time to live among the Order.

Nowhere in the fortress was unscathed from battle. Cracks ran the length of the walls, ceilings and floors were cleft right down the middle, uneven and unsteady in places. Doors hung sideways on their hinges; most had been removed entirely. Everywhere, there were signs of reconstruction efforts. Braces and scaffolding had been installed, tools laid out, ready for the next phase of a restoration project. Large creatures with mighty strength held up or held back rock so it could be repaired using Matter and Energy. Small creatures, able to get into the tiniest cracks and crevasses, scoured through said cracks, looking for weak points or pointing out better uses for a particular tool or method.

It was a bit like magic, watching a bunch of wizards use their scepters to magically fit broken rocks back together. All it was, really, was using Matter to examine the composition of a rock and its surroundings, then using Energy to superheat the rock and essentially weld it back together. Every so often, Tommen and Julianna had to be careful to step around or otherwise avoid such work, as hot magma would drip from the ceiling or bubble up from the floor, like a bunch of tiny volcanoes.

The three major areas of construction were the northwest stair, first and foremost, then the other stairs, then the main floor and on up. The stairs were the pillars of the fortress; if they went, the whole place was liable to collapse. The closer one got to the northwest stair, the more uncertain his steps became. After that, it was a matter of strengthening the foundation and ensuring each successive floor was solid and secure.

For the most part, Tommen felt pretty secure on the second and third floors. They had seen a lot of action and a lot of bloodshed, but the cracks and crevasses were the least of the problems this place had, by way of renovation. And, the way he figured it, if a hundred thousand soldiers of all shapes and sizes could go glomping around without much issue, then he probably wasn't going to suddenly break the camel's back.

Now, the higher floors? Yeah, those made him nervous. The fourth floor itself wasn't too bad, but he had serious doubts about the ceiling, even with the added bracing. The sixth floor had collapsed into the fifth floor. Well, the floor of the fifth floor was the ceiling of the fourth floor, and the bowing of said ceiling made him very nervous. It looked a bit like a suspended tarp full of rocks; eventually, the tarp was going to rip open.

The fifth floor was a mess of rubble, with virtually no discernible features other than "where it should have been." Where the corridors branched off from the staircase was the only indication of said corridors. Other than that, it was like a bomb had gone off and the roof was suddenly twice as high as it should have been. With that loss of structural stability, Tommen wasn't keen on going higher. With the collapse of the sixth floor, all of the staircases became shaky and uncertain. Part of the northeast staircase had been destroyed because of it, and it was impossible to get to the eighth floor from the fifth floor, as it just ended, a gap up until the stair rejoined at the seventh floor.

The sixth floor hadn't been much of a loss, really. It had been a weapons cache. Small, personal weapons. Knives, guns, bows, things of that nature. But it was a shame that the fifth floor had been destroyed. It had contained the Akarin Archives. While not as big or dizzyingly impressive as the Wheel Archives, it had been more like a step into history with scrolls and old codex manuscripts, right there alongside true printed and bound novels. The foremost of these had been the Authored Books. Perhaps the only good Tommen had managed to do during the battle was save those Books, though he questioned whether it had been worth it as Rifun had confiscated them for his own ends.

Tommen swallowed as he looked over the edge of the staircase to the atrium, a straight shot to the main floor. That was a long way to fall. The staircases here were not like staircases on Earth. One staircase here was like four at home, so being on the fifth floor here was like being on the twentieth floor at home. That was a long way up, a long way to fall. He could feel Julianna's gaze, how she silently mocked him. He took a breath and continued up.

The seventh floor was perhaps the most frustrating one to have been cut off as it was the primary food store of the whole fortress. Right now, they were running off the cache on the first sub-level, but that wouldn't last long. The seventh floor was where it was at, and it was nearly impossible to get to easily.

Only the northeast stair went all the way to the eighth floor, so, on the southwest stair, Tommen and Julianna disembarked on the seventh floor and made their way along the south corridor to the southeast stair. Only a few people were on the seventh floor, large aliens capable of hauling the large containers of food and other nutritional sustenance. None of them really acknowledged Tommen or Julianna. Part of it may have been the load, as it largely blocked their view. Part of it may have been just the dull monotony of hard labor.

They bypassed the southeast stair and headed up the east corridor to the northeast stair. As they stepped out onto the platform, Tommen paused. On the one hand, he was glad to have a way up here that didn't involve manipulating Gravity to move enormous slabs of stone to walk almost straight up to the eighth floor just as a show of power. That didn't make the view any less terrifying as it was now the equivalent of falling twenty-eight stories—about to become thirty-two. It certainly didn't help when the stairs themselves moved with just their weight. He was about one-eighty, tops. Julianna, one-thirty soaking wet. So with a combined weight of just over three hundred pounds, and the staircase was wobbling, it was not a comforting thing.

The eighth floor only had one real room. It housed the inverter which kept the entire planet from tumbling into a black hole. As a side effect, it also made it so the fortress could bypass the temporal Energy of the Wheel in order to make it easier to open a portal in a specific location, that is, one of two portal rooms. The first was on the main floor that everyone knew about, but the second was an emergency exit on the eighth floor, just off the inverter room. Given that the only choices one had when trying to open a portal into the fortress was either a portal room or a black hole, blind portals were greatly discouraged. All in all, the fortress was strategically sound and nearly impregnable. Nearly.

The staircase ceased to shake when they stepped on the platform for the eighth floor. Tommen's stomach rejoiced at that, yet remained twisted for the fact of what came next. The last time he had seen Rifun, the man had been lying on the floor with a knife in his chest, bleeding and seizing violently. Tommen had given up the antidote to the Borelian poison in order to save this man who had killed his friend, tried to kill his father, stolen part of his hearing. All in the name of some no-kill vow? If anyone ever asked him what possessed him to do it, he could honestly say he didn't know.

Julianna stepped inside the inverter room, and Tommen reluctantly followed. Initially, he was stunned by the change. Before, it had been all business, a war room for the Akarin council to debate whether the time had come to push the big red button on the control panel. Now, it was decidedly...homier. A bed had been erected, a rug laid out on the floor. Some of the weapon racks had been moved to make room for chests, dressers, and tables of varying shapes and sizes. One corner had been sectioned off for reasons Tommen didn't want to think about. Overall, it looked more like some oversized office that someone had decided to convert, badly, into a studio apartment for someone to rent on the cheap. On one wall was an enormous board, half whiteboard, half pinboard. Some stuff was written on the whiteboard, a few notes on the pinboard, but it was all foreign to Tommen. Probably Malagasy, if he had to hazard a guess.

It wasn't as sinister as he thought it might be. There was no shark tank, no pack of Dobermans or Rottweilers, no trap door in the floor. It was just an apartment for a dude. With a big, red, world-ending button in the middle, but hey, every place has its quirks.

In the middle of it all was Rifun Ndolo himself. Tommen almost didn't recognize him. He didn't wear a Disguise, but a change of clothes did wonders. On a normal day, the man couldn't be bothered with much more than a hoodie and jeans. During the battle, he'd elected to wear Borelian battle gear. Today saw him in cargo pants and a button down shirt. The only indication he gave that he'd suffered a mortal wound was the gauze on his chest, visible against the fabric of the shirt. Otherwise, he did not falter, limp, gimp, hunch over, or show any kind of favoritism. Tommen might have said he looked a little paler than normal and maybe had a little trouble breathing, but that was only because he knew what to look for and why.

"You like it?" Rifun asked, looking around the room. "I admit, it's not my best work—certainly not as great as what I accomplished in the Wheel—but it's cozy."

He began walking toward Tommen who was still only a couple steps in from the door. As he walked, Rifun began unbuttoning his shirt, a small chore considering his missing fingers. He pulled the one side open and peeled back the gauze. A single line of stitches, about an inch and a half to two inches long, just off to one side of the sternum. Nothing gory, nothing scary, providing only slightly more interest than the twisted scar flesh surrounding it.

"Thought you might like to see the damage," Rifun said. "Or all that remains of it. There's a similar mark on my back. I'm told I have you to thank for giving up the cure for the Borelian poison."

"Um...yeah," Tommen said. He cleared his throat. "Yes, sir."

"Please, Tommen, you don't have to be so formal." He gently replaced the gauze, smoothing the tape on all sides. "Say what's on your mind."

Tommen made a tight sound, then asked, "You're not going to rape me, are you?"

Rifun paused and looked at him, his expression completely baffled. "Why the hell would I rape you? I wouldn't rape you. I wouldn't even hint a proposition, even if I were in a good mood right now." He shook his head, began buttoning his shirt back up, and walked away. "Believe me, Tommen, regardless if you had been the one to stab me or save me, I have no inclinations toward you. That's not how I get off." He leaned back on a dresser, elbows resting on top, facing Tommen. "Though it is a curious choice of topic. If I remember correctly, Christmas was the day you were supposed to finally get some." He grinned as Tommen blushed. "That's what I thought. But why is it that you thought I was going to rape you? Between getting stabbed by your friend and you subsequently saving my life, that I would somehow seek either retribution or amusement?" He shook his head again. "No. As I said, you have nothing to worry about there."

Relief flooded Tommen, though he was careful about making it too obvious.

"Now for the real question," Rifun went on, more serious now. "Why did you do it? I know you've at least fantasized about my death, probably numerous times. Julianna gave me one explanation, but I want to hear it from you."

Tommen took a level breath. "I will not kill. Julianna was going to kill Kayla. If I wanted to save her, I had to save you."

"Please, Tommen, we all know Kayla can handle herself. Barring that, she was certainly more than willing to die in order to kill me. And you knew that. I can understand that battle can take its toll, and you certainly saw some terrible things. But only a fool believes that he can save everyone."

"Then perhaps I am a fool. Because here we are. You're alive. And Kayla's alive."

Rifun grinned. "Here we are." He shifted his stance, Banded briefly, then continued. "I can also respect the notion of a no-kill vow. It works wonders for animal shelters, but is wildly impractical in war, for obvious reasons. Even conscientious objectors understand that in war, people die. Most often, those conscientious objectors have something of a moral compass, compassion for both sides, much to the dismay of their superiors.

"So here I am, once again, questioning your motives. I will give you credit. In the time that we've known each other, you've gone from being wildly predictable, to being just a touch unpredictable. I can respect that. At the same time, perhaps I myself am afflicted with a touch of survivor guilt, wondering why in the world you saved me.

"On the one hand, you could be a humanitarian who believes in saving as many as possible while the battle rages on, and, once the fighting is done, it's done. Kayla got in a cheap shot. The problem with this is that most humanitarians still believe in justice. They may have saved me in the hospital, but would happily deliver me to the electric chair once a verdict has been rendered. As you enjoy pointing out my crimes, I can't believe that this is the case.

"On the other hand, perhaps you finally chose your side. Perhaps some semblance of military order finally seeped into your brain and you discovered great respect for and loyalty to your superiors. I find this highly unlikely, however, seeing as you just took a beating for cowardice in the first wave. Considering that you took the time in the second wave to visit the Archives and take the Authored Books, I'm guessing you didn't do a whole lot of fighting or medic work then, either.

"On another hand, it could have been something reflexive, a child sitting in the corner while Mommy and Daddy scream at each other, all the while shouting, 'Stop, stop, please, just make it stop!' I find this explanation the most plausible. You want both sides to get along, want both sides to live and be happy, and you can't bear to listen to the screaming anymore, especially after the battle had already been won. Do I have that about right?"

Tommen elected to remain silent.

"He is learning," Rifun mused. He stood up straight and again approached. "Well, here's the thing. Mommy and Daddy aren't just screaming at each other anymore, they're going for the full divorce. In this case, Daddy is winning custody. And as in most cases, I have no problem with you, the child. I just can't afford to lose you to Mommy.

"To that end, you will be joining your vaovao friends on journal study nights. War is confusing, especially when you have no foundation of beliefs to either justify or rebuke it. You see me as evil; the Order sees the Akarin as misguided, if not evil. What does it all mean? I want to help you understand so that the next time Mommy and Daddy fight in front of you, you won't be the scared child in the corner, but can take a side."

"Your side, you mean," Tommen cut in. "Do I get education on Akarin beliefs as well? It would be a more well-rounded education. And if all they need is a small correction in order to come to your side and see the light, the flaws should present themselves. I am a huge skeptic after all."

He didn't like the man's expression. It was one he got when he was already five steps down that road and knew what was coming. "That you are. And while I appreciate the thoughtfulness of your suggestion, I don't think the Akarin would take it very well. You may have noticed, but relations are a little sour between us right now. Maybe wait a bit until things have cooled down and smoothed over, hm? And before you get all huffy over the rest of your Christmas vacation getting ruined, it won't be any time soon. It's hard to hold class in a collapsed fortress, so construction efforts naturally take precedence. This also means that regular training is also being put on hold, though you may still get called to help with some of the physical labor."

"Yes, sir. But if I may ask, if you were skeptical about me in the first place, why not send me to journal studies sooner?"

"Because, quite frankly, I needed a fresh perspective on things. You said it yourself, these people idolize me. You know what that makes them? Drones. All the same. When it comes to ideas, all we have is multiplicative idiocy. You were the outsider, the skeptic, the one who hated my guts and would do anything to see me dead, but have no power to effect anything to that end. But you also had a working mind, one that could come up with great plans that might be seen as service to me, while secretly trying to get me killed. All I had to do was flesh out these plans and run with them to the end, see how they might work, how I could turn them in my favor."

"And make yourself the good guy," Tommen finished. "Train me, when the Akarin wouldn't. Offer peace to the Akarin and have them make the first move."

"Exactly. Make no mistake, however. I am exceedingly grateful that you chose to save my life, but I do not in any way believe that you are loyal to me. You have to prove it to me. Over and over and over again. But before you can trust me and I you, you must have an understanding of what is going on here, what we believe, why we did what we did. Otherwise, it's just a centuries-old cycle of revenge. Someone has to be right."

"How do you know it's you?"

"Clearly, the Author has shown us favor here. And if that's not enough, well, we could stand here all day and debate theology. I figure to let more learned men than me explain things. Go straight to the source material, as it were."

Tommen immediately thought of Kayla, telling him to bypass everything and go straight to the Author. The journals, the Authored Books, the Order, the Akarin, children playing in the sandbox. Find the Author, find the material that matches it. Figure out what the Author really wrote and fuck the rest of them.

"Furthermore—and this is more of a bit of philosophy for you to chew on for a while—I want you to consider your actions against your plans. You seem to believe that the Order, the Akarin, and the Hands, all together could defeat the Borelians. As I've mentioned before, this is still genocide. That means people die. A lot of people. You're the one who proposed the plan in the first place; now you take a no-kill vow. The Borelians are still a threat. New Year's Eve is a pretty big target. If something happens then, what are you going to do? The Borelians are relentless, especially when they know they have the upper hand, which they do. Are you going to be the one to stand before their firing squad and tell them they have to leave? Are you going to make them?" Rifun took a step back. "As I said. Just something to consider over the next few days."

"Do you know what they're planning, where they're going to attack?" Tommen wondered.

"Sadly, since murdering all the Borelians in our ranks, I do not. I am not privy to such information. I expect that, while it may take some time as the aftermath of this battle gets sorted out, the Borelians will hear of my treachery. Of course, like Charleston Police, I'm already at the top of their Most Wanted list. A few more bodies isn't going to make much of a difference. Except this time, I've lost all my insurance. Isthim, General Misik, all of them."

Rifun casually shifted his stance. "It's a similar situation to the one between Tacaga and Sadurnon, wouldn't you say?"

Tommen felt the color drain from his face. "I...did hear there was a raid."

The man's expression was unreadable. "Did you really think you could get away with something that big? I will admit, it was very clever of you to use Tacaga—devoid of my influence—as a private conference center. I can only imagine the things you told your dad and Kayla. Oh, wait, I don't need to. Because Sadurnon is now lost to us. Seems this battle came none too soon, hm? Except I imagine you warned them about that, too. Perhaps they tried to head us off and arrived just a bit too late. I'm not entirely sure; I still have some catching up to do from the few days I was out. But rest assured, I will find out. Unless there is something you'd like to tell me now?"

Tommen took an even breath, let it out. "Honestly, I'm just tired of the fighting and the war and the threat of war. It feels like it's been a non-stop thing, ever since last year with the murders and the elections and everything else. Fine. You won your war here. Now that it's over, I'd like to get back home to Earth and figure out a way to stop the Borelians. And if—"

"Are you done?" Rifun cut in. "Let me spell it out for you. The Akarin are defeated. The First Order won. You went out on stage and made a scene, defying Kayla and saving my life. You will never not be part of the First Order. That's a hard thing to take in, which is why I am sending you to journal studies, so you do have an understanding. To that end, I also fully expect that everything we say and do will get reported back to your dear Daddy and Kayla. So I want a little something in return. I want regular reports on their progress in defeating the Borelians, whether it be cures for their poisons, planetary defenses, everything. And because I don't trust you, you are going to report everything directly to me. It's easy to lie to Berkloff when the man hates you and you can't please him one way or the other. It's much harder to lie to the man who holds reward in one hand and punishment in the other, and who can read you like a book. And whom you saved."

"Yes, sir. If I may ask, are the Borelians the next target?"

"I only said you are reporting to me. That doesn't mean you get a promotion. I'm having a hard enough time with inter-faction politics. If I do have something else for you, I will let you know. Dismissed."

Tommen nodded, turned, and made to leave. He hadn't gotten more than two steps before Rifun called to him again and he turned.

"And just so we're clear. I am grateful that you saved my life. Never think I'm not."

"Yes, sir," was all he could manage.

He started down the stairs. Okay, so, he was free to tell his dad everything that went on. Problem was, the battle was already over. Not a whole hell of a lot was going on. Construction, politics, all the boring clean-up. If the most exciting thing that happened was he had to come to a few extra classes to read some boring ass journals, well, intel would be limited, say it that way. He didn't expect that Rifun would bring him onto his secret war council and impart dastardly schemes which he could relay to underground intelligence. Probably the only reason he wasn't being punished even more for snitching and getting the Tacagans involved and everything else was because he'd saved Rifun's life.

Julianna caught up to him on the stairs somewhere around the fifth floor, or what remained of it. Despite there being a second portal room on the eighth floor, they were made to go all the way back to the main floor, to the main portal room off the southwest stair. He did not complain, however, lest he put his foot even farther down his throat. He really just needed to keep his mouth shut.

"Rifun will contact you when he is ready for you," Julianna began as they stepped off the stair onto the main floor. "It may be for physical labor in reconstruction, journal studies, or because he wants a report. The aftermath of battle is always messy and timelines are nebulous, so you may have to be patient."

"Well, I'm not exactly in a hurry," Tommen told her honestly. "If possible, I'd really kind of like to spend this Christmas vacation not worrying about me dying, my dad dying, or anybody else dying."

"I'll be sure to let the Borelians know."

With that sarcastic comment, she opened a portal into his bedroom, and he stepped through.

A few hours had passed. The house was quiet. His dad was gone to work. As his phone finally found signal off a tower, it gave a buzz.

"When can we get together again?" he'd texted a few hours ago. "When will you let me?"

Becky's reply had come in about an hour ago, but he'd been a little busy. And halfway across the universe with no cell signal. "Tommen, we've already stepped over that threshold. We can do it any time we want. When we won't get caught obviously. Come over, and if we want to, and we can, then it'll happen."

He liked the sound of that, actually. No more tiptoeing around the issue, pushing just a little more, toeing the line. As she said, they'd crossed the line. They'd both given up their virginity. Sex was theirs to explore now. Kind of like being married, but not really. They still had to keep it secret from their parents. But there was no more waiting. If it happened, it happened. Him and her, her and him, together. Joined at the hip.

He looked at the time. Even if her mom was off to work, her dad would be home from his practice by now, otherwise he would have gone right over. As it was, he could still probably Funnel Band the room. It would give the illusion of danger while removing any real threat. It was a tempting proposition, but he decided against it. For now, while they were still new and exploring, they would have to play everything super safe. He would pull out the party tricks later.

After a minute or two of consideration, he pulled out his phone and dialed his dad. To his surprise and relief, he picked up.

"Hello?" Walter wondered.

"Dad, it's me."

"I see that. Is everything all right?"

"Is it safe to talk?"

"Sure, for a minute. If you're really worried, speak in Welsh. What's up?"

"I got called to the fortress to speak with Rifun."

"Yeah? How's that son of a bitch doing?"

"Up walking around, no worse for wear, from what I can see. Same smirking asshole he always is. But he's basically given me the green light to talk to you. It's like Kayla said, I made a spectacle of myself, word gets around. He says the only thing he wants in return is updates on our progress against the Borelians, seeing how he murdered all of them that were in the Order. He also says he knows that we used Tacaga to talk, and that I'm basically the one who set them on Sadurnon and the Elif. The only reason I'm not being punished for it is because I betrayed humanity and saved his life."

His dad grunted discontentedly. "Well, I'm heading to Tacaga tomorrow morning once I get off. If you don't go, you won't have anything to give. If you do go..."

"Dad, he murdered his twenty best warriors and completely destroyed any future alliance with the Borelians. I don't think it's necessarily a bad thing if he knows. I don't really care if he knows. If he wants to destroy them, more power to him. And I never thought I'd say that."

"You may be right, but I'm still not a hundred percent. Rifun has proven himself more clever than we give him credit for. I think we should be careful."

"All right. I'll probably sit this one out then. One missed meeting won't kill me. I wasn't going to every single meeting before, either."

"Very true, and anyway, this one is meant to be a little more serious and higher up. Not exactly open to the public."

"Got it."

"I'll give you the gist when I get home. If he has to know what we talked about, you can give him a summary version."

Tommen nodded though his dad couldn't see. "That might work. Okay, mostly I just wanted to let you know that we don't have to be so secretive about it anymore."

"Good. It's a relief. And I'm glad you're home safe and sound."

"You've been saying that for the last week."

"And I still mean it. I love you, Tommen. I don't want to see you get hurt because of a psychopath."

"I don't want to get hurt because of a psychopath. Anyway, I'll let you go. See you in the morning."

"See you in the morning, kiddo."

Click.

Chapter Two
A Dash of Sugar

Sunday nights weren't usually too busy for the county boys. People had to be to work early in the morning, so antics and shenanigans, if there were any, typically tapered off about nine-thirty, ten o'clock. It made for an easy night for Walter who got off at the correct time, more or less. He punched out, but did not head home right away. Instead, he made a quick trip to Laura's apartment. His girlfriend, accustomed to being woken up at all hours on account of her work on the ambulance, was a light sleeper and an early riser. She wasn't too thrilled about being woken up at five-thirty in the morning, but it was one of the last times for a while that they would be able to have breakfast together.

Walking in the apartment, Walter saw stacks of boxes as Laura prepared to return to Minnesota to help care for her elderly father who had been given only a few months to live because of a multitude of health problems. Breakfast was uncharacteristically quiet. Walter wished he could find some way to lift her spirits a little; he hated to see her sad when she left. Laura assured him that breakfast with him did lift her spirits, and she was ready to skip ahead a few months, just get the whole thing over with. He didn't try to talk her out of it. He was the one who talked her into returning in the first place. It was the right thing to do. That didn't mean the separation was going to be any easier on either of them.

He left her apartment in a sullen mood and went home. It was a little past seven. The first thing he did, after taking his shoes and coat off, was go down the hall and push open the door to Tommen's room. The teenager slept, though he did not sprawl like he used to. Rather, he lay on his side, every muscle completely rigid, ready to fight. He did not twitch or yell or struggle, but that didn't mean he wasn't fighting the demons he'd brought back with him from the battle. Tommen hadn't talked about it, but Kayla had told him enough to get an idea of what had happened. Walter had never been in war; all his fighting came in bars or other, much smaller, slightly less violent affairs. These were demons he could not help his son understand or overcome. That was why he'd had to call a shrink. He wouldn't be available until after New Year's, but it was a start. Tommen denied it now, but he knew he needed help. He'd asked for that help; he was going to get it. Just not until after New Year's.

That was assuming the human race made it past New Year's. Halloween had been a huge target because of all the costumes and how easy it had been for the Borelians to blend in. New Year's would be an even bigger target just for the sheer volumes of people as they gathered in large areas. Times Square? A neon bullseye.

Tacaga had developed planetary defenses which they used to keep the Borelians at bay on their own world. They were working on similar measures on all human worlds, but it took time as each world had to be calibrated differently. They'd also agreed to hide a chemical engineer from Earth so he could work on solving the mystery of the Borelian poisons and finally unlocking the key to a universal cure. The preliminary data suggested it was as simple as glucose.

Right now, the question was whether they would get anything more than preliminary data. In the negotiations before any work had begun, Tacaga had claimed all rights to the cure, its production and development, its distribution, but most of all, its secrets. Tommen had basically announced to a huge audience, a huge swath of species, the preliminary findings. Maybe the findings only worked on humans; maybe they would be proven wrong, or prove to be more intricate than just glucose. But regardless of what the final results were, the foundation to get to those results had been compromised.

If Earth had any cards left to play, any leverage at all, it was the autonomy card. As a reward for their efforts to expose Sadurnon's treachery and attempt to wipe out the Cult—or the First Order as they were now calling themselves—the Hands of Time had agreed to grant Tacaga autonomy within the Time industry as their own separate planet and race, as long as the home world, Earth, would allow it. The idea was, Tacaga would continue its defensive efforts. Once the cure was proven, Earth would grant them autonomy.

It wasn't quite the trump card that Walter would have wished. The Tacagans were still the only ones with any secure planetary defenses. All they had to do was let the Borelians destroy all the other human worlds, then take the title of human home world all for themselves. So far, they were playing nice. Walter didn't want to jeopardize that, or make a bad situation worse.

He changed out of his blues and was just about to pull his shoes on when Tommen stumbled out of his room.

"Morning, Sunshine," Walter greeted. "Sleep all right?"

"Yeah, slept fine. I think." Tommen shrugged. "Got home, got taken, got returned, got dinner, got in bed."

"Sounds like the gettin' is pretty good."

"Are you off to Tacaga?"

"Yeah, I am. Going to meet a few others, and hopefully have some better answers than just sugar."

"Okay. Let me know how it goes."

"Do you have to work today?"

His son nodded."Yup. Three more days and that's the end of Bakery na hÉireann."

"Too bad. Maybe I'll stop by today before going to work. One last pastry for one last hurrah."

"You're going to be there all three days."

"I expect so." Walter stood. "I'll see you later."

"Let me know how it goes."

Tommen meandered off back to his room while Walter opened a portal to Tacaga and stepped through. It was easier, now that he'd been there multiple times. It was still more difficult than opening a portal to the Wheel, and that was saying something. The first time around, he'd put himself and Tommen in a river and passed out. These days, he could get to a safe location, usually within a mile or two of the capital city Lip, but it gave him some fierce vertigo, and he lost his entire breakfast. So much for home cooking; it didn't taste nearly as good coming back up. He really should have known better. Portal travel was always difficult; it didn't get "easier." Nevertheless, he picked himself up, stumbled, fell, got up again, shook his head, and made his way toward the main road.

When they'd first arrived, he'd assumed that there was absolutely nothing between the obscene mega-cities that the Tacagans called home. It wasn't entirely true. Aside from vast mountain ranges, great plains, and other assorted natural beauty, the planet was also littered with the ruins of their ancient ancestors. The ancient Tacagans, a splinter group of ancient Greek and Roman thinkers, had once sought to live in small communities as their atheistic utopia. When that proved too difficult to keep a hold on the people, to stem the flow of undesirable notions such as religion, they were gradually moved into the great metropolises they now occupied. Of course, that was stuffing two thousand years of history into two sentences. Walter was not here to examine the history of the Tacagans, though his inner explorer thought it might be interesting to investigate some of the ruins. The Tacagans were all holed up in their cities, so how would they know, really?

He traveled alone toward Lip, knowing he probably garnered plenty of stares from those on the high-efficiency bullet trains that connected the cities. Aside from being a pedestrian in the wilderness, he wasn't genetically engineered like the rest of them; he stood out with his brown hair, bushy blond mustache, and slightly overweight physique. In fact, when he reached the outer train platform, the other travelers cut him a wide berth, as if his wild genes might jump onto them like fleas and infect their perfect, optimized human bodies. That was all right with him. Every interaction he'd had with the Tacagans had been less than pleasant. The residents seemed to think themselves above their meager, pagan, Neanderthal cousins. Their every word, assuming they even deigned to speak with the Neanderthals, dripped with leering and sarcasm.

The bridge guards were the worst of these. They knew Walter by sight, even by name. They knew his business. Still they gave him grief at the gate, forcing him to basically do a whole song and dance, making him jump through a dozen hoops before finally admitting him. They probably would have made him wait while they called their superiors about him, except then their superiors would have been pissed. They couldn't be bothered with such a low life as an Earth human. His business was known. Let him in and tell him to be quick about it.

So Walter crossed the bridge into the city. There were no fossil fuels used on Tacaga; each city was powered naturally. For Lip, that meant drawing hydroelectric power from the Kominos River, as well as using the abundant solar, geothermal, and natural gas power available, plus whatever else they had invented—cold fusion, perhaps. Considering the city was the size of the state of Texas, it was a pretty incredible feat. The whole city, even the bridge, hummed with electricity and made the hairs on Walter's arm stand up. Or maybe that was his general anxiety about the place. He was fine with Charleston, but Lip had a population of four billion, and every single one of them thought they were better than him.

As had become the norm, the local peacekeepers were called to be his escort. It helped to minimize outside influences on Tacagan society and keep him from causing mischief. Because all the Neanderthal humans were so much more inclined to violence, after all. At the very least, Walter figured his escort kept him from getting lost in the massive metropolis.

There were no cars on Tacaga either. Walking was the preferred method of transportation in all the local neighborhoods. Transportation between neighborhoods in a borough was typically done on bicycle. Getting from one borough or another required the use of high-speed trains. They traveled over three hundred miles per hour at top speed and had zero loss of work or efficiency, meaning Walter never felt the train moving and had no run-ins with motion sickness.

Their destination was the governmental building, located about as close to the heart of the city as it could get. Once the cities had been established, their expansion had been planned out for centuries of growth and an exploding population. Everything was about optimization and efficiency. The only thing that the Tacagans developed to be clunky, awkward, and inefficient, was their government, and even then, it was only inefficient part of the time. When it came to building up Tacaga, everything was great. When it came to dealing with any other humans, slow and clunky and inefficient and red tape was the name of the game. Thankfully, it was a game Walter knew how to play.

The train station was located directly inside the governmental building, the platform leading into a lobby where he was checked in by more security. From there, it was a short jaunt down the hall to an elevator which Walter and his escorts took to Sub-Floor Delta.

The greater governmental building was pristine and high-tech, meant to show off every technological advancement and innovation and be the shining beacon of the Tacagan people, dwarfed only by the space center about half a mile away. The sub-floors—or Sub-Floor Delta, as Walter had never been to any of the other sub-floors—were not quite like those floors. Compared to Earth, it was still high-tech, about a hundred years more advanced in terms of look, security, and accessibility. For the building at large, it was, for lack of better term, the bargain basement. These were the things they considered old or outdated, regardless of whether they were still functioning, like how someone might throw away an old cassette player in order to upgrade to a CD or an mp3. There was nothing wrong with the cassette; it was upgrading in order to upgrade, because that's the way everything was moving.

As far as research labs went, Walter was no expert, but he figured the one the chemical engineer had been set up in was well-endowed. The lab itself was easily about three-quarters of the size of the high school football field, and half of it was dedicated to climate-controlled storage. Along one wall, six huge walk-in chambers with thousands of small lockers each provided precision control over any prolonged experiment. On the opposite wall, massive machines of all shapes, sizes, and functions he could not name sat quietly. If they were running, they were probably just as efficient as anything else on the planet and wouldn't make a peep. Only an occasional flashing light or a screen with scrolling data gave any clue as to its function or results. Along the far wall, between the climate chambers and the machines, were the traditional lab tables. Small refrigerators and ovens, sinks, safety features, all lined up with a smooth counter resting on top, overflowing with work and petri dishes and notes and everything else. In the middle of it all, cabinets and smaller machinery abounded, all of them precisely labeled, the countertops filled with more experiments.

The engineer himself, however, was not so clean or pristine as the building, and more resembled the scrambled countertops. He had the look of a man who'd been locked in his office and forced to work non-stop for weeks or months, throwing everything else to the wind. He was clean, only inasmuch as his work demand a clean, sterile environment, but his movements were less than fluid and graceful.

The escorts, with their duty fulfilled, departed without so much as an "Enjoy your stay." Walter stood outside the lab for a moment before pressing the doorbell. The man startled, looked around, saw Walter, froze, then nodded and gave a "one moment" signal. He finished up whatever he was doing, scribbled down some notes, huffed a sigh, and made for the exit-decon room. He did not wear the traditional white lab coat, but something much more form-fitting and better able to keep hazardous materials from eating into his flesh. He stripped off the suit and tossed it into some kind of laundry receptacle, then started the decon cycle. By the time he stepped out to meet Walter, he might as well have just walked out of a sauna.

"Yes, what can I do for you?" he asked.

"I'm here for the meeting," Walter told him. "The others should be here soon."

"Meeting. Is that today?"

"Yes, I'm afraid so."

"Oh."

"Are you not ready?"

"I have been ready for several days, but I think that was several days ago." He shook his head. "It's hard to remember when one day ends and another begins sometimes. I have so much work to do, and I sleep so little..."

"If you're tired, I'll Band you before the meeting so you can get some rest."

"No, that will not be necessary, but I thank you for the offer. Yes, yes, come down to the meeting room. Follow me."

Do Chien was easily a head shorter than Walter. A Vietnamese national, he'd been responsible for developing a number of chemical weapons for the communist government during the Vietnam War. He wanted to defect, but decided that it might be better to try to undo his work from within. He managed to smuggle out instructions on how to combat the chemical agents, even war plans on where the North Vietnamese were planning to attack next. The North Vietnamese found out. Because he had no family to threaten, they went after him directly. He escaped a number of government-sanctioned assassination attempts, and, after the war was over, he made his way to China, intending to head to the United States. But he found meaningful employment instead, using his skills to try and combat the smog hovering over Beijing and other major coastal cities.

Had he stayed in China and continued his work looking into the Borelian poison, he could have easily been accused of developing more chemical weapons. If the Chinese found him first, he could be accused of being a spy or secret agent. If the international community found him first, it could mean war with China from any number of nations. Moving him to Tacaga was by far the best move for everyone.

The meeting room was about thirty yards down from the entrance to the lab on the opposite side of the hall. It was big enough to hold a proper seminar for about five hundred people, but for now it was set up with only about thirty in mind. Glass tables were lined up in three rows, ten chairs in each row. The only indication that there was a screen of some form on the front wall was the black frame. Evidently, the wall itself was the screen, Walter figured. He didn't see a projector, but that didn't mean much.

He sat down at one of the tables, and the thing came to life in his spot. Greek and Latin letters showed him titles and menus.

"Do you understand any of this?" Walter asked. "Have you figured out their language?"

Do Chien tapped the wall inside the black frame, and the whole thing came to life. He answered, "I have learned some, and can manage simple communication. I can navigate the computers with few problems. Mostly, I use the translator. Which reminds me..." He dug in his pocket and tossed a translator to Walter. "You will need this."

Walter donned the translator. As he fiddled with the settings, a couple more people entered the room. Do Chien greeted them and handed out a couple more translators.

Today was a special meeting, to say the least. It involved all the higher-ups from all the human worlds. Walter was the first from Earth, but Mi Chin the Gatekeeper arrived moments later.

The people who had walked in right after Walter were Nakim and Loris from Sakaria II, a colony planet reserved for giants and other freaks of nature who, at one time in Earth history, had been in danger of being aborted or killed at birth, fearing that they were cursed by God or otherwise possessed by the Devil. Such was the reason for the "II" in its name. From what Walter understood, Sakaria was their word for "home" and the "II" represented a second chance, therefore, a second chance at home. These days, the inhabitants of Sakaria II came in four flavors: giants, dwarfs, other physical deformities, and normal. Rumors suggested that "normal" people were often discriminated against. Guess some grudges just went that deep, Walter mused.

The Sakarian representatives today fell in the giant category, both of them a solid nine feet tall, four hundred pounds or more of sheer muscle. To look at them, they were comfortable in their own skin, but wary of being in such puny company. Wisely, they sat in the back row.

The next envoy to arrive was the Vin Lay delegation. The residents of Vin Lay were of Oriental descent, and their history was often marked by new waves of immigrants from Earth. Originally starting out as refugees seeking asylum from the wrath of Genghis Khan, it had since expanded its borders to allow for those seeking to hide from the Killing Fields, the Vietnam War, North Korea, China, any Orientals looking for a new home. Sem and Lin spoke amiably to Do Chien, and cordially to the rest of them.

The Hlohi group was the only one Walter recognized, and that only because Kayla was with them, accompanying the liaisons between Hlohi and Earth's Region Four, District Nine, the unofficial District encompassing all the Native American tribes in North America. They sat with Walter at his table, and Kayla introduced Logan and Blake Wolf, Saul Wolf's brothers. Blake was there as the official Wolf Clan representative. Logan was there as the liaison between Wolf Clan and the rest of the Krydik who were now removed from their past history with Earth.

"Natalie would come, but she's elected to sit this one out," Kayla explained evenly. "New wife, going to be a new mother, she has other priorities."

Walter thought he heard an undertone of jealousy in her voice. Well, it would make sense, he supposed. Micaiah and Kayla had been trying to get pregnant before his death, and nothing ever came of it. Now she had to pretend to be happy for a friend who got what she never did.

Next up was the Aleisi representation. They were the real Pilgrims, Walter thought. Originally a group of Puritans seeking to farm and worship peacefully without the King of England or the Vatican breathing down their necks, they were a simple, if smug, delegation. John and Andrew greeted everyone peaceably, but their overall demeanor toward their fellows was a bit like the Tacagans'. The Tacagans disdained others for their belief in God. The Aleisi disdained others for their lack of belief in God. It was a no-win situation as far as Walter was concerned.

Ehani was an unusual world, more of a poor science experiment, what Hlohi might have looked like if things hadn't worked out. It had started out with good intentions, but the road to Hell and all that. Ehani had originally been populated with South American native tribes in order to save them from the Spanish and Portuguese, let them live their own lives however they wanted. The trouble came when the original planners thought it would be a good idea to throw in some African refugees, whether from the slave trade or general tribal warfare. Things did not go well. The Xalani were the original South American citizens, and the Etlawa were the African peoples. They'd made peace within their respective ethnic groups, but the two peoples still despised each other. Even now, their delegation consisted of two Xalani and two Etlawa, and they made no secret of their hatred for one another.

Following on their heels was Dorigis. Walter wasn't entirely certain of their back story, but he knew that their population was a mix of Scandinavians, including old Vikings, and Mediterranean peoples like the Greeks and Italians. Whoever they were, they were accomplished sailors and fishermen, which was good since their planet was ninety percent water. They were cordial and friendly with the others in the room, but, for lack of better description, a bunch of rowdy, bawdy sailors with each other.

The last group to arrive was the official representation of Tacaga, featuring Milay, the woman with the jet black skin, and Toros, the man with the pale white skin. Milay was originally from a city called Onis, near the equator, where it was optimal to have dark skin in order to withstand the harsh sunlight. Similarly, Toros was from a city called Hagin, far to the north where his pale skin was required in order to absorb as much sunlight as possible. They were optimally suited for their respective climates. Their smug superiority was noted by the rest in attendance and ignored.

The only worlds not there were the colony planets which had

been destroyed, Treman and Trebald. They were twin worlds, settled by thinkers and philosophers about four hundred years after Tacaga. Unlike Tacaga, the twin worlds did not discourage religion, instead encouraging their folk to reach for the heavens and get close to their gods. They were always in friendly competition, and had in fact planned it that way when settling two worlds at the same time. Always strive to outdo the other. Barring that, play the game of numbers. If one planet crashed and burned, be the twin that survived. Both planets had been comparable to Earth as far as technological advancement, though a decade or two behind.

Looking around, it was strange to think that everyone in the room was human, but they had such vastly different experiences. Even two humans on opposite sides of Earth, growing up, would have heard about the same basic history. Ancient Middle East, Europe as Christendom, the Chinese dynsasties, the Crusades, the Renaissance, Age of Exploration, American Revolution, the World Wars, the Cold War, and so on. Whatever the twists and bias were, the general history was still the same.

No one else here really had that. Tacaga had no concept of the Crusades or the World Wars—their history diverged around the time of Christ—and they would probably sneer at such events and call them the squabbles of superstitious children. Hlohi had not experienced the American Revolution, though their involvement in Earth politics was not entirely passive. Ehani was built on a variety of displaced peoples all looking to establish themselves and not have to flee anymore, but to make a stand and conquer. How would they have reacted to the Cold War? The Sakarians had left Earth when it was a spiritual crime to be born different and had never witnessed the Renaissance or any of the ensuing medical revolutions that said it was okay to be strange, and maybe some things could be fixed or prevented.

The room was full of humans, but they were all complete strangers.

"Why do I get the feeling that the time I'm about to waste here would have been better spent in bed?" Walter asked rhetorically.

"Believe me, you're not the only one," Kayla grumbled. "But this isn't something we can just put off, however much we wish it so. Treman and Trebald are proof of that."

"Have the Borelians said anything about that? Ha ha ha, look at us? Give us a million dollars and we'll release one prisoner?"

"Nothing," Mi Chin replied. "The Borelians rarely leave any kind of message. The graffiti is the most communication we have had, and there is no reason not to think that it comes simply from their supporters and allies."

"Keep us in the dark, make us wonder. Fantastic."

Up front, Do Chien was still messing with the presentation screen, skipping through menus with the speed and dexterity of a teenager. Then he pressed a button, and a new screen popped up. Walter did not read Vietnamese and trusted that the translators would render everything as it was spoken.

"Okay, everyone, please quiet down," Do Chien said, turning his attention to the audience who quieted quickly. "Thank you for coming to this meeting. I apologize for not being entirely prepared. I have been busy and lost track of time. My name is Do Chien. I am from Earth. I was born in a small country called Vietnam where I studied chemical engineering as it relates to the human body and medicine. I then moved to a country called China where I continued my work.

"As you may know, several months ago, I was approached by a Timekeeper who proposed the idea of researching the Borelian poisons. I agreed. This research soon turned dangerous. Because Tacaga is a safe and technologically-advanced world, I was smuggled here and allowed to continue my research in this lab, which I have done with, I believe, much success."

Kayla nudged Walter in the ribs and Banded.

"What's up?" he asked.

"Someone here isn't who they say they are," she murmured.

"What do you mean?"

"I mean, someone is wearing a Disguise."

"How can you tell?"

"A little trick we call Test."

"Do you know who it is?"

She nodded toward the Tacagans. "Him. Toros."

Walter frowned. "It would make sense. If the Tacagans view the Akari as a religion, then they're the last ones you would suspect for treachery."

"You want me to call attention to it? Expose him? He's keeping it pretty close to chest, but it only takes a good touch to break it."

"Can you tell who it is?"

"Rifun."

Walter grunted. "Leave it for now. If it is Rifun, I imagine he wants this information to give to his grunts. If he does, Tommen may hear something. Then we can see if he has any other plans in the works. We'll just have to be vigilant. We don't want to cause a scene, not with so many potential victims or hostages in such close quarters."

Kayla nodded. "Understood."

She released the Band.

"First I am going to address what is probably on everyone's mind," Do Chien continued. "How does the Borelian poison work, how much time do we have once we've been touched, and is there any true cure? Even better, is there any way we can protect ourselves?"

The presentation continued, moving into a very detailed picture of something. After a second of studying it, Walter realized it was a picture of a cell. Not a drawing, but a true, bona fide, up close, highly-detailed, 3D photograph of a cell. A bunch of labels began popping up.

"This is a cell," Do Chien went on. "We are made of billions of them, each of them with a specific function. Now, any given cell that is healthy, functions basically the same as any other. The function of the cell is to ensure adequate intake of glucose and oxygen, which releases energy for the body, and adequate removal of waste products.

"There are two types of metabolism where the cells break down glucose for energy. Aerobic and anaerobic. Anaerobic means the cell does not have the oxygen necessary to fully carry out its function. The glucose only goes through the first stage of metabolism, releasing a tiny bit of ATP—that's energy—and turning into pyruvic acid. Without oxygen, the pyruvic acid turns into lactic acid. A buildup of this acid inhibits enzyme function and can cause cell death and other long-term damage. Because anaerobic metabolism is dangerous and even fatal with or without Borelian poison, that's the only thing I'm going to say about that.

"Aerobic metabolism is the ideal. In a healthy cell, insulin attaches to the cell to make it open up for glucose. Glucose is taken into the cystol where it is broken down into pyruvic acid and releases a bit of ATP. When the cell takes in oxygen, the glucose moves into the mitochondria where it is converted into a large amount of ATP. As the available glucose in the blood decreases, the body taps the liver for glycogen reserves, to keep sugar levels within a normal range until your next meal. When no glucose is available, the body will convert other sugars and carbs into glucose. Epinephrine, or adrenaline, will stop the pancreas from secreting insulin and instead work to convert other substances into glucose.

"With the glucose and oxygen used up, the waste is taken out of the cell. The most common by-product is carbon dioxide, which attaches to the red blood cells, combines with water, and becomes bicarbonate. The bicarbonate then detaches from the cell and rides the bloodstream back to the lungs. There it reattaches to the red blood cell, combines with hydrogen, and dissociates into carbon dioxide and water which is blown off by the lungs. This is only done seventy percent of the time, but this method is what we are concerned with in this discussion.

"Also in your cells is a sodium-potassium pump. I am not going to go into as much detail about it, but its primary function is maintaining osmotic pressure within the cell itself. If too much sodium builds up inside the cell, water will follow, and the cell will rupture. Therefore, potassium is sucked into the cell in order to force the sodium out.

"Now then, the Borelian poison acts sort of like a virus, and I'll explain both the gas and the oil. First the oil. When the oil gets into your bloodstream, it tricks your cells into thinking that it is glucose. The insulin attaches to the cell, indicates to the cell to let it in. When it crosses the cell membrane into the cystol, if there is no oxygen, it may do some damage and kill the cell, but it will also die itself. If there is oxygen available, and both the oil and the oxygen get absorbed into the mitochondria, that's where bad things happen.

"First, the oil absorbs the oxygen into itself, depriving the cell of the much-needed gas. The mitochondria is the battery, the powerhouse of the cell, and the oil will use whatever power is available, combined with the oxygen and the sodium in the cell to replicate itself, essentially multiplying like a virus. Once it has sucked the cell dry of sodium, potassium is allowed into the cell through the pump. Potassium builds up in the cell to regulate the osmotic pressure, but instead of forcing out sodium, the oil is released back into the bloodstream to continue the cycle. The oil rides the bloodstream around the body, and once it reaches the blood-brain barrier, it's accepted in no question, again tricking the cells into believing it is glucose. The brain has no way to store glucose and so it needs a continual supply. Oil hits the brain, and different oils target different parts of the brain. That I will get to in a moment.

"Now then, the body's defense. With the oil destroying the cells, the cells aren't getting the actual glucose they need. The body goes into panic mode. The pancreas stops secreting insulin, buying a little bit of time as the oil cannot get into the cells as easily. Epinephrine is released to tell the liver to convert its glycogen stores into glucose. The glucose acts as a sort of antibody. In a normal person, the glycogen stores only last about twenty-four to forty-eight hours. Once the body starts tapping into its fats and proteins, breaking those down into glucose—which takes a lot longer than converting carbs—you're looking at a couple more days.

"If the glucose gets to a cell before the oil, the oil essentially dies. It has a very short time to pick a cell, get accepted, multiply, repeat. We're talking mere seconds, if that. A large dump of glucose, therefore, can head off an incidental touch. A small enough touch, and your own glycogen may be enough to stop it. This would be the case in second-hand touches, and possibly even the gaseous side effects, but more on that in a bit. Because most glycogen stores only last a short time, a sudden dump of glucose in an otherwise depleted body would have an instant effect. Yes?"

Kayla stood uncertainly. "What about the quick turnaround time? Walt was on his deathbed, but up and walking around by the end of the day after being given sugar, barring the actual, physical injuries. What about the tissue damage?"

Do Chien looked thoughtful. "I have yet to find a reason for the fast recovery, but I have a theory. Once the glucose hits the cells, especially a lot of glucose at once, that is a lot of sudden energy that is being released in the form of ATP. The cells become energized, excited, and there is a lot of repair work to be done. As I said, the oil only has a short time to find a cell and multiply. The oil itself may be killed off in only an hour, but there is still a huge chain reaction of energy going on, and the body goes into hyperactive mode, repairing much of the damage. And because I know someone is thinking it, no, I do not know why the injuries themselves are immune to Time.

"Now, the gaseous side effects. The Borelians push their oils through a second skin covering their bodies. I have discovered that where oxygen allows the virus to multiply, it is actually neutralized by nitrogen. Therefore, the high nitrogen content of Earth's atmosphere would render them almost nonexistent. Comparing our atmosphere to Brelix, the nitrogen content is considerably higher. It is also the highest concentration of the human worlds. Aleis is the lowest nitrogen concentration, so you would be more susceptible to their influence.

"That being said, any of the gases that you breathe and get absorbed by your mucous membranes will be considerably weaker. It is too weak to get into a cell to multiply, though it can still attach to a cell and get to the brain to affect the appropriate part of the brain. Once again, the glucose already in the body will head it off. If you are aware of the gas, it puts your brain into hyperalert mode which demands more energy which requires more glucose, which will effectively neutralize it completely.

"As for the Narcan, I have found it to be effective only with the blue oil for the simple fact that the Narcan protects the opiate receptors in the brain, which is what the oil attaches to, from receiving anything. It has nothing to do with the oil in the bloodstream, but it will protect the brain. If the brain is protected, it can still function to protect the body by releasing epinepherine to stop the flow of insulin and convert stores into glucose, which will, eventually, kill off the oil.

"The hasax flower has shown to be nothing significant in and of itself except as an extraordinarily high concentration of glucose, even more than refined sugar in the store. It has no complex sugar molecules; it is straight glucose which means it can go straight to work."

"What about the hasax oil?" Walter asked. "Have you been able to study that at all?"

"Only briefly, and the results were not the most promising," the doctor admitted. "The hasax oil is different from Borelian oil in that, rather than using the oxygen in the cells to multiply and everything I just shared with you, it actually affects the heart. The honey stimulates the cells to release an enormous amount of ATP which raises the heart rate and counteracts the effects. The good news, though, is that it is still, I believe, a viable weapon against the Borelians. The yellow cardiac ones may be less affected and could be called upon as physicians, but in the moment or in the heat of battle, it can do harm. Actually, it may be a more effective weapon because then it is not about glucose, but simply energy."

"Is there any way to test this theory?" Milay interrupted. "Can't you infect some of the Borelian oils with the hasax oil?"

Do Chien frowned and folded his arms. "Now we're getting into a gray area. See, in spite of all the climate control available in the lab, the Borelian oil, without the ability to spread and multiply, degrades very quickly. Nitrogen neutralizes it the quickest, but it will break down regardless. I estimate that since the acquisition of the first sample, it is only at about nine percent potency right now, which makes testing on it very difficult to do."

"Do you need more samples?" someone asked.

"How would we get them?" another person shot back.

"What would make it the easiest on you?" Kayla inquired of the doctor.

"Obviously, the easiest way to test it would be if it were fresh," Do Chien sighed. "The problem is, the Borelians are currently sitting quiet and merely sending out cryptic messages. I fear that once they decide to mobilize, the time for testing and theories will be long gone."

"What about capturing one of them?" one of the Ehani delegates proposed. It was one of the Etlawa.

"How would that be done?" one of the Xalani sneered. "Are you going to capture it?"

"There are over twenty different types," the other Xalani pointed out smugly. "Are you going to defeat all of them without getting touched even one time?"

"There are over twenty different poisons," one of the Dorogisi mused, a female Viking if there ever was one. "But many different types of Borelians. Most are single toxins. Some are bitoxic. But then there are the vodraks."

"One in a million," someone else said.

"So there ought to be at least twenty thousand out there to choose from," the female Dorogisi shot back. "The *vodraks* are either revered or feared, put in positions of great power and authority, or driven out completely. Look at Isthim."

"Are we really talking about this?" Andrew the Aleisi asked. "Doctor, there must be something else, some other way to continue your studies."

The doctor shook his head. "My studies on the oils have cleared this stage of research. The next logical step is a live test. Walter Forbes from Earth has already survived two Borelian attacks, which has provided a solid foundation for the study of the oils on a living human. All that remains is to study the oils as they are, fresh from the body. I understand that this is less than ideal, and perhaps you would wish to turn your attention to your defenses, but if you want more work on the oils, I need a live subject."

"Is there anything about the Borelians, physically, that we should know?" someone wondered. "If we end up in a firefight, what should we look for?"

"They're as mortal as any of us," Walter answered. "Heart, lung, head, all good targets. The horns are also a target. They are very similar to us, at least where it matters."

It was meager comfort, he could tell. The Borelians were able to be killed, but there was no silver bullet here.

"Is there any way to turn the oils against them?" Logan asked. "If nitrogen causes the oils to neutralize, what would happen if they were hit with a nitrogen bomb of some form? What about the salt? You said it needs salt as part of its replication process; what if we stopped using salt?"

"The human body needs salt to survive," one of the Vin Lay delegates said. "Lack of salt might kill the oil, but it will kill us."

Do Chien shook his head. "The oils have degraded too far; I can no longer use and test them reliably. I either need a living body, or, as may be safer, fresh samples. The good news is that most of the oils seem to work along the same lines. But just as the oils are mysterious, so the human brain remains a mystery as well."

"So you're saying that the only way you can continue your work," someone said, "is if you get oils or a living specimen?"

"That would be the summary, yes."

"How would that be accomplished?" one of the Dorogisi asked of no one in particular. "Either they come to us—which, as you pointed out, may be too late for more research—or we go to them—which would be like trying to steal a cub from a she-bear."

It was at that point that Walter tuned out of the conversation, for it was no longer a real conversation. It was speculation and curiosity and pleading and challenging and getting nowhere. He got what he came for, which was a solid answer on how the oils worked and how they could be combated. So far, the answer sounded like sugar. As for normal combat, they could be killed using conventional means. What more did they really need to know?

"What special considerations are there concerning the oils?" one of the Sakarians inquired. "On other worlds, humans are generally the same size. What about us?"

Do Chien dipped his head. "I would foresee that the giants of Sakaria may have greater resistance. By your own physiology, you may metabolize at a proportionally comparable rate and so your glycogen stores may deplete within twenty-four to forty-eight hours as expected, but based on sheer volume, you would have an advantage at heading off a minor incident or buying time to get help. That said, the dwarfs of Sakaria may find themselves on the opposite end of the spectrum. They may metabolize at a proportionally comparable rate, but sheer volume means they have less by way of defense.

"To that end, diabetic humans may have an advantage because the pancreas is dysfunctional or completely nonfunctional. Hypoglycemic humans who require constant sources of sugar would be particularly susceptible. On Tacaga, you've engineered yourselves to be optimally efficient. If you have the data on hand of this optimal efficiency, you could very well calculate how much time you would have, if exposed to the oils. And those of you from Hlohi or Ehani or Aleis, you may be in the best standing, though not by much, because you are still functioning as humans are meant to function. You haven't destroyed yourselves with genetic engineering or refined, processed foods. Your bodies may be the healthiest, the best able to withstand a poisoning. As for Vin Lay and Dorigis, your unique and highly-specialized diets may prove of use or a detriment, as I cannot determine. Of course, this is all only a theory."

This sparked some more back and forth, and a few what-if scenarios were posed, but Walter could tell the meeting was beginning to wrap up. None to soon, either, as he was plumb exhausted. He stifled a yawn and shifted position in his chair.

The Vin Lay were the ones to finally call an end to the gathering, citing things they had to do at home, both in terms of regular chores and passing on the information. The others reluctantly agreed, and they began filing out of the room.

"Want me to do something about our impostor?" Kayla hissed as the Earthlings and Krydik stood.

"Not just yet," Walter said. "Let me try something."

The Vin Lay were the first to leave, followed by the Tacagans. Then were the Ehani, the Aleisi, the Sakarians, and finally Walter. Once out in the corridor, he lengthened his stride and quickened his pace so he could catch up to the Tacagans.

"Toros, if I may have a word?"

The Tacagans paused and gave him a cat's regard. Toros looked at Milay. "Go on ahead. I'll deal with him." She left, and he turned his attention back to Walter. "Yes?"

"Mostly, I just want to thank you for opening up your lab here for our engineer, and sending the teams to install the defenses on each planet. It's a kind gesture, and it's nice to know that we can all set aside our differences for a common goal of not being exterminated or sent off to Borelian slavery." Walter held out his right hand as if for a handshake.

Toros' expression had not changed; it remained smugly repulsed by his inferiority. "You are...welcome. I trust our deal still stands." He looked at the hand and raised a brow. "Do you expect something from me?"

"Oh, no. My apologies. It's a local custom. A handshake, an expression of gratitude or brotherhood."

"I see."

Walter went for meek embarrassment. "I realize that you see me as inferior, and I'm probably carrying any number of foreign germs, but humor me for its own sake."

For a long moment, Walter was sure he wouldn't do it. Finally Toros extended his left hand.

"The other hand," Walter corrected gently.

Toros gave him a look and switched hands, reaching gingerly for him as if reaching for a dirty sock. He had almost no return grip as Walter clamped down hard. He put his left hand over Toros' hand, then gave a small compression at the base of his thumb, over Toros' index and middle fingers. Just as when Walter had worn a Disguise, the fingers were solid at a brief touch, but when he applied pressure, they vanished.

Rifun-as-Toros heaved a sigh and looked Walter in the eye as he threw up a Band around the two of them. "You figured me out."

"Lucky Kayla is still around," Walter replied smugly.

"Lucky indeed." Rifun shed his Disguise. "Not so lucky for me. First she stabs me in the chest, now she gives away my Disguise. She's a real nuisance, you know."

"Why are you here? To lay a trap to kill her?"

"Had the opportunity arisen, I will not say I wouldn't have taken it. The same way you would no doubt take the chance to kill me for attempting to kill you. Every man sees his own cause as noble."

"What cause are you advancing here by parading around as a Tacagan Governor?"

"The cause of information. I was dead, but now I live again, isn't that how it's supposed to work? Your son brought me back to life, and I'm grateful. But I want to know the what and how and why. The Borelians are coming for my people, too, and I want to keep them safe."

"So safe you led them into war against the Akarin."

"The Akarin chose their fate. I offered them peace, and they wanted none of it."

"And now you're on a humanitarian mission to rid the universe of evil."

"The thought had crossed my mind."

"No doubt in those last few moments before the darkness closed in around you. But now you're back. Why are you here?"

"As I said. Information."

"And what's to keep me from killing you right here?"

"The fact that you couldn't if you tried."

"Kayla almost killed you."

"I admit, she got the jump on me. And yet, here I am. Thanks to your son." Rifun went on before Walter could speak. "Now then, we could spend all day here, threatening each other, making demands, asking questions and beating around the bush. But I think that would get very old very fast for both of us. So let's cut to the chase. I'm here for information. Same as you. From past experience, you ought to know well that I'm not just going to stand here and monologue my evil schemes. I'm not even really in a mood to kill anyone right now. And seeing how my Disguise has been discovered, I think anything else may have to wait."

With that, he donned his Toros Disguise and dropped the Band. He resumed his air of Tacagan superiority. "You are...welcome. I suppose."

Then he turned and left, striding down the corridor to meet up with Milay. They spoke for a moment and vanished into the elevator, closing the door before anyone else could get on, like true self-righteous assholes.

"What happened?" Kayla asked, walking up beside Walter.

He relayed the conversation.

"It would make sense that he would want to be in on the information, but I think it's more than that," she mused. "This is Tacaga, where science and logic are as much gods as any god. You and Tommen exposed a weakness in his web of intrigue, a blind spot that he can't see. No doubt he's working to remedy that."

"I was afraid of something like that."

She let out a breath. "I hate to say it, Walt, but we might have to put him on the back burner for a short time. He's attacked the Akarin and won. Whatever his next major military or political move is, it's going to be a while because he has to build back his strength and numbers. He has to play politics with the Akarin for a while to try and win them over or else beat them down enough to subdue them and get them on his side. He has to reconstruct and strengthen the fortress. He still has to physically recover from a fatal chest wound. All of that is going to take time. New Year's Eve is in three days. If the Borelians are going to strike, that will be the time."

He grunted a reluctant agreement. "I know you're right. But what do we do about it?"

"I don't know." Kayla folded his arms and shifted her stance. "The travel warning in the Wheel has been lifted—yes, I know that it's a cautious lift and there's still a species-wide PSA about being careful and all that. But the point is, if there is a window of opportunity, maybe we ought to take it. Do some research in the Archives, see if we can't find a weakness."

"What weakness, though?"

"If I knew, we'd already be exploiting it. Rifun seemed invincible until he wasn't. Tacaga was his blind spot. The Borelians must have a blind spot of their own."

Walter let out a breath. "Well, regardless of all that, I have to get to bed. If you're going to the Wheel, be careful and let someone know all the details."

"Yes, Dad. I know." Kayla grinned. "Come on, Walt. Let's get you home."

Nothing sounded better at that moment. If not for strict rules about all outsiders coming and going outside of the city, he would have opened a portal right there, directly into his bed. Instead, he got on the elevator and headed up to the floor where the escort was waiting for them. In a way, having such a tight security detail made Walter feel important, as though he were an honored guest in need of the highest line of protection. In other ways, it made him feel like a dangerous criminal again, having to be guarded against any and all attempts at escape.

The Earthlings, the Krydik, the Aleisi, the Sakarians, the Ehani, all of them got on the train, the Tacagan escort spread wide around them. All of the foreigners got strange looks, but the Sakarians even more so as they stuck out, literally a head above the rest. Or maybe three heads, hunched over in a too-short cab, sitting in too-small seats.

Even once they got off the train, they had to have a walking escort seeing how they were too big for the bicycles. Walter and the others bid them farewell as they took off on bikes, heading for the bridge.

The ride was uneventful, but took twice as long, or so it felt. Walter handed off his bike and started across the bridge, practically falling asleep. He'd no sooner reached the other side than he opened a portal and stepped through to Earth. He forced himself to change out of his grungy clothes and brush his teeth before collapsing into bed, asleep before his head even hit the pillow.

Nightmares were nothing new to Walter, and yet he somehow never got used to them. He was having more good nights than bad lately, which he attributed to stress and having more pressing problems in the present than fears and worries about the past. Mostly he was figuring that he was so stressed out that he couldn't even reach REM sleep in order to be scared. It really wasn't a comforting thing to think about.

By the time his alarm went off, he was already awake, staring at the ceiling. He thought about calling Laura, seeing if they couldn't make a date to go out to lunch or dinner or breakfast one last time before she headed home to Minnesota. After a minute or two of batting it back and forth, he rolled over and grabbed his phone.

"Hi, Walt," she greeted, sounding as stressed as he felt. "You just get up?"

"Woke up, yes. Still making my way to the getting up part."

"Ah. Dreaming of me already?"

"What do you mean already? I've been dreaming of you for quite a while." It was a lie, but it sounded good, right?

"Big pushover. You're such a sap. What's up? Lamenting another day at work?"

"Is that what you call it? I call it sitting around not doing much and praying for something to happen."

"Well, it's an improvement over the ambulance barn, then. There I sit around and pray something doesn't happen."

"You working today?"

"No, but don't tell them I escaped or else they might drag me back for a shift that doesn't end until New Year's Day. And even then, I might be driving the bus all the way back to Minnesota, just in case I run across something."

Walter let out a breath. "Yeah."

"I know," she sighed. "As terrible as it sounds, I don't think I'll be gone all that long."

"You take all the time you need. Don't come rushing back on my account."

"Maybe I'll drag you up here at some point. How does spring break sound?"

"We'll see how things fall. It may not be so bad. There's every chance I'm going to lose Tommen to whatever fabulous vacation his girlfriend is going on, leaving me alone in the house. A little vacation all to myself sounds pretty nice."

"So there we go. Time to grow up and be your own man. Think you can handle it without your son there to hold your hand every step of the way?"

"Ha ha, very funny. Listen, I have to get up and around and get to work at some point today, preferably before the start of my shift."

"Yeah, and I still have to finish packing. Honestly, I wasn't even done unpacking from my last move here, which is kind of sad."

"Why don't I come by tomorrow morning after I get off? We can go to breakfast somewhere, and then maybe I can help you pack a little."

"That's sweet. Sure, that'll be fine, assuming you don't fall over on me."

"I can stay up a little later; I don't have to work tomorrow night."

"Lucky you. So I'll see you tomorrow morning. If I'm still asleep, just come on in and wake me up. I'm sure a cop like you knows a thing or two about getting through a locked door."

"I might. I'll see you then."

Click.

If that wasn't an invitation, he didn't know what was, and it was a long moment before he put his phone back on the stand and got out of bed. Tommen was at work and wouldn't be back until late. Only a few more days and Bakery na hÉireann would be no more.

Aw, shoot, he'd promised to be there tomorrow morning, hadn't he? Well, he could stop there before going to Laura's apartment. He didn't have to get anything, just stop in, say hi, wish Micah the best, all that jazz. Wasn't like his contributions or lack thereof would be noticed.

His mind was too full of stuff to be overly concerned with any one thing, his job least of all, and he walked into the precinct half in a daze.

"Evening, Walt," Kate greeted. "Ready for New Year's Eve?"

He faltered. "I'm ready for my day off tomorrow. Then I'll worry about New Year's Eve."

"I hear you. Listen, Vin called in sick, so we all got extra duties tonight."

"Hooray."

Vin called in sick, yeah right. Him and his wife just had their first child. His wife got six months maternity, courtesy of her employer. Vin got four weeks through the department. He'd taken his two weeks of vacation after the paternity ran out, and now randomly "called in sick." The joke going around the station now was that it was a bad idea to have kids because they came riddled with germs. Gary, who had six kids and cancer, declared that it must have been one of his little brats that gave him cancer. If he would have known, he would have stopped after number two.

Still, there was nothing to be done about it. Vin wouldn't be in, and the rest of them got hit with his chores, everything from area of coverage on the roads to miscellaneous clean-up duties around the office. Walter started his night with a large cup of coffee before grabbing the keys to his cruiser and heading out the back door. At least he was off probation now. Didn't make him any more important or any less the new guy, but it was embarrassing to have to ride around with another officer as though he were some rookie fresh from the Academy.

Although, whoever had the car before him must have been a rookie because the gas tank was below a quarter. Still, he made a note of it and, once his pre-inspection was finished, took it to get filled up. Yes, he was more than ready for his day off. Then he would worry about New Year's Eve. One thing at a time. And after New Year's? Not even going to worry about it right now. After all, there was no guarantee that he would even be around. If the Borelians had their way and did, in fact, invade Earth or launch some kind of super attack to devastate the human race, he might be spending January 1st on the auction block on Brelix.

Over his dead body.

Chapter Three
Pitchfork Mob

At some point during the night—some time between a standard traffic stop that turned into a near-deadly standoff when the van turned out to be a mobile meth lab, and a noise complaint that turned into a man beating and nearly killing his wife in front of their two year old son who had been the one to call dispatch—Walter decided it would be an excellent idea to take a quick trip to the Wheel for his lunch break. He told himself that it was for some intelligence gathering to see for himself what was going on, but he had also forgotten to pack something for his lunch.

Normally, it wouldn't bother him too much, but lately, he'd started to notice his dieting attempts. Aside from losing a few pounds and a couple inches, his stomach was a little cranky about it. Strange to think that even with Time slowing his aging, his body would still reject the idea of a diet, no matter how vain his attempts.

He was skeptical about visiting the Wheel, to say the least. Stepping through his portal, Walter wondered whether he ought to close it, for safety's sake. It would be the smart thing to do. At the same time, that would also make it so time passed normally at home again, versus stopping completely if he left the portal open. Even though he intended to make this quick, anything could happen, and he couldn't be caught away from his radio if something came down the line. Sorry to say, but service in the valley was bad enough; there was no way he would pick anything up in a separate dimension.

In the end, he decided to leave the portal open. The Borelians already knew how to get to Earth. They'd even been to West Virginia. Right in the middle of Charleston. Attacked its policemen directly.

There was really very little damage that could be done just by him leaving his portal open.

That wasn't to say he wasn't still skeptical, at least a little bit, but he forced himself to walk away. The faster he made this trip, the faster he could get home and get a move on. After all, time at home was stopped, but he was still active and moving, and it was hard enough to get through a shift as it was. At least he might get to sleep a little easier if he was a little more tired.

It was nice to have separate portal rooms now, so he didn't have to walk a half marathon just to stand in a mile-long line for the translator dispenser. He was able to get through pretty quickly now, comparatively speaking, and carry on with his business.

The last time Walter had been in the Wheel, things had been changed from Rifun's Shakespearean wonderland into some atrocious thing the kids were calling steampunk. Things had not changed since then. Apparently the intergalactic community approved of the decor and elected to keep it as is.

So, he meandered his way through what basically constituted an intergalactic junkyard, pieces and parts of all shapes, sizes, and uses put on display. Briefly, Walter wondered whether he could find used car parts here. Both his and Tommen's new cars were in good shape, but it wouldn't last forever, not in West Virginia. At least buying parts in the Wheel, if it could be done, it would only cost turns and not dollars, which would save them both money. Sure, Tommen's Apprentice salary was a pittance, but it wasn't doing him much good on Earth seeing how he never turned it in.

The closer he got to the main square, Walter noticed the crowds began to thicken. It wasn't necessarily a bad thing; it meant business was returning to normal as Merchants set up their tables and the customer base was beginning to grow once more. Actually, his curiosity lay more in the mood of the crowd. He was hardly an expert on alien body language and facial expressions, but agitation could be generally guessed at.

Every part of him said not to get involved. Walk away. Forget about lunch, go without, and get out of the situation. Well, maybe "every" part was too strong of a term. "Every part but one" would have been more accurate, and that last part was the police officer part, the part that told him to defy his innate instinct to run away and instead run into the fray, assess the situation, take control.

The problem was, that last part was a pretty strong force, even more so given that he was in uniform right now. No one else might understand, but he couldn't just walk away without bearing his own personal shame.

Knowing he was going to hate himself later for it, Walter followed the crowd. It wasn't a very fast-moving crowd, and he mentally compromised, saying that he would just go with the flow for now until he saw any reason to dive into the fray or retreat. Right now, he was just a spectator, curious as to the goings-on.

There was rarely any rhyme or reason to the Wheel. As Tommen had once crudely put it, if one could draw an accurate map of the place, it would be in the shape of a middle finger. Nevertheless, Walter might say he understood the layout of the place fairly well, enough to know a few shortcuts to get to the main square a bit faster, like taking a side road to cut out having to navigate a busy intersection.

Actually, he wasn't sure what his hurry was. If he was really concerned about leaving his portal open, he should have gone straight to the Archives and bypassed this completely, or as much as possible. As he neared the portal to the main square, he toyed with the idea of abandoning this little side mission completely, then decided against it. He was out of the loop, something was going on, and he needed to know what.

There was no breaking into the main square. In all reality, it was more of a sucking in of the gut and a tight squeeze with his back pressed against the wall, sliding into the room and taking his place in the back, straining to see and hear. Once he was able to assess the situation, he saw that most attention was turned to the Amphitheater. Was there no end to this crowd? Did he dare try to get even closer, maybe force his way into the Amphitheater and see what all the hubbub was about? Or did he squeak his way through the throng and head to the Archives?

Walter was not overly fond of crowds; too much could go wrong, and sometimes the worst part was friendly fire. He liked it even less when there was no way to tell friend from foe, and he had no visible backup. Even now, stuck in the fold, debating whether to approach the Amphitheater, he was assaulted with memories of the coup, being trapped in the Coliseum, the guards murdering anyone who tried to escape, the Hands and Grandfathers turning on one another, being marched away with the rest of the prisoners like sheep to the slaughter.

It was too much. He couldn't do it. And yet, even as he felt the terror, he also felt the anger. At himself. He had to stop letting everything get to him. He couldn't continue to cower like a child, hiding behind a blanket and a night light. He was here in, basically, broad daylight, in uniform, in a crowded room with a potentially volatile situation at hand. He had to man up, get in there, and figure out what was going on, what had everyone's attention.

Once again, he was faced with the reality of the crowd. He was only human, hardly the largest thing in the room, though he wasn't so small that he could just slip right through. So he was left to twist and turn and push and shove his way through, sometimes being carried, sometimes taking advantage of voids and spaces as they opened up. His heart hammered wildly in his chest.

He was momentarily relieved as a gap opened and he stepped into it, just inside the Amphitheater. He took several breaths to try and calm himself down before weaseling his way to the front of the crowd.

This close to the front, he could actually hear himself think as the throng itself was pretty quiet. He could hear someone up front talking, followed by a ripple of reaction, whether good or bad he could not yet discern. Eventually, though, he found himself in a position where the crowd really was just too thick, and even the species smaller than him could not snake their way forward. Part of him said to force his way through by any means necessary. A smaller part said that doing such a thing could not end well. Still another part of him said to run and get out before he got caught up in another coup or massacre.

In the end, he remained absolutely still, focusing on being aware of his surroundings. While the crowd was tense and a little agitated, it was not yet violent. There were murmurs and ripples of fear and disapproval, but he did not detect the undercurrent of panic that preceded a stampede, nor the undercurrent of rage that sparked a riot. Unlike the Coliseum, Time was allowed in the Amphitheater, and he saw very little use of it, or little use proportionate to a crowd this size. While some species were naturally gifted and others carried external weapons, nothing was presently drawn or being used that he could see, though there was a little muscle flexing, fur puffing, feather fluffling, that sort of thing.

But as he looked around, he noticed something a little peculiar. While he was no expert at alien physiology, he noticed that not everyone had a translator. While that might be fine for quick errands in the Wheel, it was extremely unusual for someone not to have one when in such an intense situation. Unless, of course, that person could naturally understand everything.

Micaiah and Kayla had once talked about how, through the Akari—or the Author—they could understand what was being said and be understood by others with the same Akari-bearer gift. Could some of those gathered here be some of the displaced Akarin? Sure, absolutely. Could such a thing be possible, that they could understand and be understood just because some Author said so? Understand, maybe. But if they could only be understood by others with the gift, then they would still need the translator to render their words, right? Of course, in a crowd this size, there was no reason to think that they would be able to address everyone, or even most of the group.

A gap opened up and Walter slipped into it without thinking. While still not at the very front, he was able to see through to the opening where it looked as though the Hands may have gathered.

"What consequences will Sadurnon face for their treachery?" someone demanded.

"The matter is being dealt with—" one Hand began.

"They cannot be permitted to stay in the Time industry!" another faceless someone said.

"But if they leave, how can the Hands keep an eye on them?" someone else rebutted.

"It is as it was with the Cult and the Akarin," a third stated. "No one kept an eye on them and look what happened."

"Yes, first the Akarin saved the Wheel after the coup, and now we have been attacked. The Cult is the enemy here."

"Both times the Cult has been in hiding. Perhaps it is good that they have made themselves known."

"At what expense, though? The only reason they have shown their colors is because they are strong. They will no doubt attack the Wheel again."

"If they were able to conquer the Akarin on their own, how much easier will it be with allies like Sadurnon? They have soldiers from many, many worlds. Surely some of them must be willing allies; the Wheel does not treat all worlds and all species well."

"And what about the unwilling ones? The Akarin were powerful enough to defeat them once. They may be conquered now, but what if they truly did become allied with them? We would be left all but defenseless!"

"Then perhaps we ought to welcome those who returned to the Time industry. They could give us useful knowledge."

"In the past, the Akarin knew well of the Time industry, but we did not know about them because they were so exclusive. We should make them tell us."

"And with the Cult now ruling over them, perhaps they could give us information on them, too."

Walter almost opened his mouth to speak, then reined himself in as he considered that his voice would be lost in the din. He was saved, however, by Sifura. He could not see her, but she had no trouble making herself heard.

"We already have information about the Cult of the Akari,

though they call themselves the First Order now. All this time, there has been an operative giving us information. This turn of events was told to us, but we lacked the speed to effectively head it off. It is the only reason we know about Sadurnon at all. There are more investigations going on, and we are receiving more information."

"Like what?" someone challenged.

Whoever it was, her tone met him head on. "Rifun Ndolo himself was wounded in the attack, stabbed with a knife laced with Borelian poison."

The mood of the crowd had begun to simmer, but her words disrupted that and caused a wave of confusion. Could they really hope it was true? Could it mean the end of the Cult? What if it didn't matter? Personally, Walter wondered how many of them knew that humans were working on a cure and had potentially found it. He wondered if anyone knew Rifun had already recovered and was out walking around once more.

"There is always a calm after battle," someone said. "If Rifun is wounded and his forces are weary after battle, now may be the time for us to strike and be rid of both of them!"

"How would we be any different than them?" another countered. "This is the Time industry. We buy and sell Time. Timekeepers are not military soldiers; we don't get involved in the affairs of others. If the Cult conquered the Akarin, that is their problem. Until they are a threat to us—"

"But they have already proven to be a threat to us."

"But they are not a threat now."

"Should we not anticipate threats?"

Walter did not hear Sifura, if indeed she spoke again, but he could feel the catch-22 involved. On the one hand, Rifun was dying from Borelian poison, perhaps spelling the end of the Cult. On the other hand, Rifun had recovered from the poison, stronger than ever, and could be on the attack. Throw in there something about his new mission to go after the Borelians—which Walter still wasn't fully convinced of—and then things would get twisted so that he was back looking for a new alliance with them.

He wasn't convinced that Rifun was a humanitarian looking to rid the universe of evil, but it not only took strength, cunning, and balls to dispatch a dozen Borelians single-handedly, it was a surefire way to paint a target on his back—or, you know, give the target that was already on his back a fresh coat of paint. That sort of deliberate act meant Rifun had something up his sleeve, and Walter actually found himself believing that it didn't involve the Time industry, at least not right now. Problem was, how did he discern the mind and plans of a madman?

"Rest assured," one of the Hands said, "that we are aware of the situation. We have intelligence on it. We understand the situation and we will take appropriate action as necessary in order to ensure the safety and security of the Time industry and all the agents and activities therein—"

"Is it true that Rifun himself killed the Borelian General Misik?" someone interrupted. "Is that how he was wounded?"

"Does that mean war with the Borelians?" another asked fearfully.

"Everything means war with the Borelians," a third sighed.

"And even so, it is not war with us," the Hand went on. "The Hands of Time and the Time industry will not intervene in the affairs of others. Whether it is the Cult and the Akarin, or the Borelians and the Cult, we will not get involved. We are interested solely in the well-being of the industry, the buying and selling of Time."

"Yes, but there is so much more out there," someone cut in. "Time is rendered useless at the hands of this...thing, this...Akari which they claim to wield. Whatever it is, we are powerless. Should we not defend ourselves against it? Should we not perhaps train in it ourselves? Maybe the Time industry ought to expand, to encompass our enemies rather than merely defend against them and hope to live."

"We are a business, not a government," another countered. "We do not interfere in the affairs of others. Our interests begin and end with Time. All current laws still stand, including those banning the use or mention of the Akari. And that is the end of the discussion on it."

Obviously, the crowd was too hyped up to merely nod their heads, turn, walk away quietly, and have thoughtful discussion on the way out the door. There was still more shouting and confusion and the desire to be heard and answered. There were more questions, more opinions, more doomsday scenarios, but overall, the pressure of the crowd began to thin a bit. Those outside of the Amphitheater moseyed away, and those at the back of the crowd inside the Amphitheater went about their business, albeit a bit more disgruntled than usual. Walter could breathe again, and he took a few steps back, far enough that he could spread his arms out and not jostle anyone.

So, that was the state of things. With the Zero Hour Revolution still pretty fresh in everyone's minds, now compounded by this secondary campaign by Rifun and the Cult to overthrow those who had saved the Wheel from him—and were subsequently banned, but, hey, details—and suddenly people were so afraid that they had no idea what to do. Rather than do their own thing and defend themselves, they wanted the Hands to defend them. What did they expect the Hands to do? Sure, they were automatically higher trained than the bulk of the Timekeepers, Harvesters, and so on, but they held no special superpowers. The people would be better off learning to save themselves.

But that was all political sentiment, lamenting about what ought to be. At least the meeting was over and things hadn't really gotten violent. It certainly had the potential to, but it hadn't. And he had a job to do. Already, he felt as though the whole of the Borelian army could have crossed back through his portal to Earth.

Before he could get three steps, he heard a voice.

"Walter Forbes!"

He turned to find Sifura walking up to him.

"I did not expect to see you here," she said, "but it is good that you are. I wish to speak with you."

Well, he couldn't say no. He nodded. "All right. Here I am."

"Come with me."

She turned and stalked off, lethal claws poking out of her tiger toes with every step. He followed her to what used to be a little African-style hut, though the steampunk monster appeared to have steamrolled the Amphitheater as well. Inside, he found several Hands already waiting.

"I thought I wasn't expected," he said.

"No, but your presence will be invaluable," Sifura told him. She introduced the Hands in turn, but damned if he would be able to keep them straight. He did notice, however, that they were often considered "lowly" Hands, or Hands of less importance because their representation was considerably small. Scientifically Primitive and Unengaged, Winking, Food Courts, things of that nature, ten in all. "We are the Hands chosen to keep an eye on the situation with Rifun and the Cult."

"Didn't realize there was a special committee for it."

"We are considered expendable," the Hand of Winking said. Even for an alien, Walter could hear the acid in its tone. "We are to gather information on the goings-on, but if anything happens, the rest of the Hands know nothing. We may be blamed readily."

"I see. So why call me here?"

"Regardless of what Churdik says, Tommen is our only direct link to Rifun," Sifura told him. "There are a few others who know the Cult, or the First Order, and the Akarin, and are willing to share. Some former Akarin, though they may be former, still feel protective of their secrets and do not share readily. But no one gets close to Rifun like Tommen and is willing to betray the information."

"What are you asking of him?" Walter asked warily. "He's already been through a lot."

"Right now, we are only asking what he knows. Our intelligence ends with the battle. After that, reports are scattered, confused, and conflicting."

Walter hesitated, but nodded. "Rifun is alive. He's not dying of the Borelian poison anymore. That was cured. He knows Tacaga was a blindspot for him, and he may be going after them, trying to gain influence there somehow."

"How was it a blindspot for him? It is a human colony world," someone stated.

"It is, but they broke over two millennia ago and want nothing to do with other human worlds. They are purely atheistic, hate anything even remotely religious, which includes the Akari, the Akarin, the Cult, all of it. Rifun had no influence there, and it was how Tommen was able to get the information about the attack and other goings-on to me in the first place."

Murmuring, conversing, silence. Sifura motioned for him to continue.

"Right now, it sounds as if Rifun is tied up with two things. The most visible problem is trying to gain the trust and alliance of the Akarin. At this time, he does not seem to want to destroy them, but use them. He has his own army and politics to deal with, on top of that. He probably won't be leading any grand campaigns in the immediate future.

"His second problem is that of the Borelians, both as a human and as the leader of the First Order."

"As a mere human, he would have had little support of the Order to go directly after the Borelians," someone mused. "Everyone fears the Borelians. But if he brought the First Order into their line of sight, he would have his entire army behind him to fight them. With the Akarin subdued, they may have no choice but to fight alongside him when the Borelians come calling. As well as the humans themselves."

Walter wished he could find a chair to collapse into. "And being the conquerer of the Wheel, former King of Time, conquerer of the Akarin, slayer of General Misik and a dozen others, he sets himself up to be powerful, feared, and beloved. A capable leader and warrior, assuming he can actually pull off a victory against the Borelians. And he has little trouble swaying others to his cause. Masses love victory and charisma."

"Then he will come for the Wheel once more," another Hand stated. "We should be prepared for the long term." He went on before Walter could protest. "We do not get involved in the affairs of others. If the Borelians have declared war on humans, we will not get involved. If the Order has overthrown the Akarin, we should not get involved. If Rifun is making plans to attack the Wheel again—"

"Then wouldn't it be better to stop him now, before he gets his strength and numbers behind him?" Walter cut in. "If it's not a matter of if but when..."

He trailed off. He sounded just like the crowd out there. Save us, save us. The Hands had no special powers. His better bet was protecting himself and his son. He wasn't Micaiah. He couldn't save the universe, and he wasn't dead. He couldn't let himself get wrapped up in Time politics again. Deal with the Borelian threat because that was here and real. Adopt the same policy as the Hands and don't interfere.

Problem was, he was still a sworn Timekeeper and kind of had to defend the Wheel if shit happened again. Maybe he should retire.

"Thank you, Walter," Sifura said finally. "You and your son have been very helpful. You are dismissed to continue your errands."

Her tone left no room for argument, and Walter left the little hut. He didn't like the sounds of things. It was too ominous, and yet far too certain. Things were about to change. Big time. This time, though, it would be exactly what the people wanted. And the people always got exactly what they wanted. That was the problem with mob rule. They thought they wanted something until they found out exactly what that meant.

And what did the denizens of the Time industry want? Safety, security, sure. But what they really wanted was power. The power to rule over all things, to stand on the high rock and beat everything back because everything that wasn't them was a threat to their safety and security which was held only by their power. They wanted Big Brother.

On the other hand, he could be reading too much into this.

Rifun was a definite threat. The Borelians were also a definite threat. Definite threats had to be dealt with definitely. Juggling the two was going to require finesse, not force.

He left the Amphitheater, pleasantly surprised to find that things had basically returned to normal. There were no mobs, riots, fist fights, or things on fire. People went about their business, going here and there as on any normal errand day. Runners were taken to the Judgment Wing, hungry folk went to the Food Court, and there was a ton of normal business to be conducted in the Amphitheater with the Hands. All was well for the moment.

Walter took advantage of it by heading to the Food Court to grab a bite to eat. He made it more of a fast food run than a sit-down restaurant, and was on his way soon enough.

One nice thing was that the Archives themselves hadn't changed, except to eliminate the need for separate chips; now, things got picked up and rendered via the translators. Of course, that didn't make it any easier to navigate the libraries upon libraries of information stacked within information. Walter searched and perused and followed a hundred paths looking for the right section. It wasn't that the information was difficult to find, it was that he could never find what he wanted, even at the much simpler library back home, assuming he ever got there more than twice a year.

Actually, he wasn't even sure what he was looking for. There wasn't exactly a marked section for "Borelian weaknesses" or anything of that sort. He started by browsing through volumes on Brelix, the Borelian home world.

Generally speaking, humans could survive on Brelix for short periods with no outside help. The nitrogen content of the atmosphere was lower, but so was the oxygen content. Borelians were more efficient in their processing of oxygen, and comparatively oxygen-rich environments like Earth only made them stronger and deadlier with their poisons. Brelix also had a higher concentration of other mixed gases with minimal or no known effects on humans. The reason for the greater variety of atmospheric gases had to do with the instability of the planet's crust, and earthquakes abounded, sometimes as many as a dozen a day around the world.

Looking at a map of the planet, Walter found a swath of land called the Land of Tujor, entirely uninhabitable because of the earthquakes and high volcanic activity in the region, believed to be the resting place of the god of death they worshiped. Similarly, there was another swath of land southwest of there called the Fertile Lands. Based on some geological and meteorological information Walter didn't quite understand, having to do with its proximity to the instability in the Land of Tujor, as well as its position along the only ocean on the planet, and a variety of other things, it was not only fertile land, but stable. It was the only part of the planet where earthquakes did not level cities and volcanoes did not melt the landscape. This was the location of Ancrath, the capital of Brelix, as well as a few other major and minor cities.

There were few maps depicting any other cities or towns on the planet. A few managed to eek out an existence in the center of major continents and landmasses, though they were primarily used as industrial centers for building ships and manufacturing weapons. Otherwise, the citizens, those who were not living in or around Ancrath training for the military or other things for the glory of Brelix, simply followed the earthquakes, or ran from them, depending on one's perspective. Mining for ore was considerably easier on Brelix seeing how all the metals just made their way to the surface eventually through the volcanoes, then broke apart conveniently in the earthquakes. Intentional drilling was strictly forbidden on the planet, for obvious reasons. And what they couldn't passively mine, they traded for or gained through war spoils.

Walter also browsed through a few anatomy tomes, though he found little of use. Heart, lungs, horns, nothing he didn't know already. As a joke, he looked up whether salt might be used as a defense, dry them out like snails. It did not appear so, as salt appeared to be used as a common spice just the same as on Earth, a nice little flavor enhancer added to most foods, or a barrel of it as a preservative.

Eventually, Walter found himself browsing through another section of the Archives, looking for information on Borelian culture, only to find precious little on the subject. Most Borelians were atheistic, or atheistic with common superstitious beliefs about Tujor and other silly things about good and bad luck. About ten to fifteen percent were true worshipers of Tujor and something called the Six Facets.

The planet was ruled by the Council of Ancrath which oversaw all planetary concerns; the major cities often ruled themselves with the minor cities being small protectorates, though in more of an economic sense than militaristic sense as the planet itself was unified. The ruling body of the Borelian military was called the Great Admirals of the Fleet, seventeen hand-picked generals of the finest order to rule over every aspect of the military. The liaison between the two was an organization known as the Holy Men of War. They were the link between the military might of the Great Admirals, the political and economic might of the Council, and the public will of the people. There was no more information on them other than that little bit, to Walter's dismay.

Brelix had two moons, both of which were used as strict farming colonies, populated and run by trusted prisoners, though still overseen by several military commanders and some part of the Holy Men which was not specified.

It was no secret that the Borelians had either claimed or conquered the other planets in their solar system. One was used as a prisoner of war camp and penal colony. Rocky, icy, with little or no vegetation to speak of, it was considered a death planet for slaves unlucky enough to be sent there. The rest were used as farming worlds.

The Borelians themselves did not farm while they were still in their prime. Nor did their elders really touch farming equipment. Slaves were made to do the work while retired fighters oversaw production, like a plantation owner in the old South. These retired slave owners were often the only source of pure Borelian artistry—culinary, canvas, music, all from the elders. While children and young adults might have a hobby, the true Borelian culture came from its older generation.

Walter leaned back and shifted position. Well, so much for a sixties flower power peace chant. Of the few systems the Borelians were able to reach with their ships, most worlds were claimed as slave-worked farming worlds. Only two were listed as allies, and only then because the inhabitants were a technological match, and their planets were uninhabitable for the Borelians for any number of reasons as well as rich with metals, minerals, and other goods which the Borelians traded for. So they weren't so much true allies as mutual acquaintances.

A long minute passed. Then another.

Then came the moment when Walter felt the fool.

He stood and did some more running around the Archives, looking up tidbits of information before returning all the tablets and finally heading out. He snaked his way through the main square, the marketplaces, and slithered into the portal room with the deft talent and grace of an overweight, retired ballerina. He almost forgot to return his translator, but was back on Earth soon enough.

Thankfully, it did not appear as though the whole of the Borelian army had walked through his portal to decimate the planet. Looking around his cruiser, the only footprints he saw were his own. He got back in the driver's seat and had just fired off a couple texts to Tommen when his radio screeched to life and he got called to a something or other. That something or other ended up being something of a drawn-out encounter, and he got back to his nightly boredom later than he really wanted. He dialed his son, hoping he was still awake.

"Hi, Dad," Tommen answered loudly, pointedly.

Something was up, that much Walter could tell right off the bat. "Everything all right?"

"Just fine. About ready to head off to bed."

"Slap happy then. Right."

"What did you find?"

"Well, it's either going to be a way to deter any New Year's Eve attacks, or it'll just speed up invasion. One or the other. Have you seen Rifun lately?"

"Actually...he is kind of standing right here."

That was not what he wanted to hear, and yet it kind of was. He took a level breath and said, "I need to speak with him."

It was a second or two before Tommen handed over the phone to Rifun.

"Walter, how are you?" Rifun's agitating voice came over the phone. "It's been, what, a few months, hasn't it? At least?"

"I don't know what you're planning tonight, but if something happens to my son—"

"Yes, yes, I understand all 'if you ever's and 'when I catch you's and all the threats that go with them," Rifun interrupted, sighing dramatically. "Please, save us both some time and get to the chase. You didn't want to talk to me just to threaten me."

"I'll threaten you as much as I please." It sounded childish, and Walter knew it. "But you're right. That's not why I'm calling."

"I'm all ears."

"Tommen told me you were saying something about going after the Borelians. How true is that?"

"As true as the fact that they are coming after us. Timelines have yet to be worked out, however, though with how quiet they have become and New Year's upon us, well, as they say, something's got to give. Why do you ask? You may not have heard, but there are unfortunately no Borelians left in my army; I do not have knowledge of their dealings."

"Doesn't matter. War is war, slavery is slavery, no matter which way you slice it. But I have an idea to put us on the offensive, maybe stun the Borelians into not attacking on New Year's, though it could also fully ignite this war or a full invasion."

Rifun's attitude did not waver from his smirking sarcasm. "And you're coming to me for help."

"Quite frankly, you're the only one either dumb enough or

brilliant enough to pull it off. Seeing how I don't think you'd pass up a chance to attack the Borelians and show off your limitless talents and brilliance—"

"All right, what's the plan?"

"The Borelians can't sow their own soil; Brelix is too unstable. Ninety-nine percent of their food is grown off-world. We may not beat them technologically, maybe not even in hand-to-hand combat. But we can hit them where it hurts. In their stomachs. Torch their fields, they have no food, they can't fight."

Walter liked to think he managed to stun Rifun into silence with the plan, and he went on, "I'm going to make some calls and get some people ready. I want to have a meeting tomorrow morning on Tacaga. Normally I wouldn't, but as much as it could send the Borelians scrambling, it could also be the catalyst for an invasion as they seek to take our food. Obviously, we're not the only human world, and the impact goes beyond our borders; I want the others to know."

"And you want me there?"

He let out a huffy breath. "I do. You're a genocidal maniac, but a brilliant one with an army. More to the point, your army consists of non-humans. If non-humans torch the fields, it could confuse the Borelians and stem the impending invasion."

Rifun was silent for a long moment. Finally, "Walter, if I didn't know you and Tommen were family, I would say that the odds of both you and your adopted son being so brilliant and conniving are astronomical. But we both know better. Yes, I'll be there. Even if the whole thing turns out to be a trap for me, it sounds exciting at the very least."

"Two missing fingers and half a heart don't seem to have slowed you down any."

"Very true, but then, what was that phrase you loved to parrot? Only injured, not helpless. Now then, if you will excuse me, your son and I have a few things to do tonight."

Click.

And that was that. Walter had just willingly allied himself with the man who had shot him almost point-blank, kidnapped his son, committed genocide, and done other unspeakable atrocities throughout the universe. Worse, if this plan went awry, he could have just handed over the human race to the Borelians.

Sometimes he wished he could turn back time, take a little more time to think things through. Sometimes he wished he didn't see the same impulsive patterns in his son. Sometimes, damn it all, he wished he could be a little smarter like Rifun, able to take a thousand plans and run through a thousand variations to pick the one that was the most advantageous.

Sometimes he wished he could go back and take that retirement. But would it really have made a difference whether or not he was an active or retired cop, when this was the fate of the human race and the potential for slavery to a hostile alien race? No.

It was the middle of the night, but now that he called this meeting, he had to actually set things up for it, which meant mustering the troops. Problem was, all his troops were not on Earth. But he couldn't very well go traipsing around on other worlds. His radio barely worked in the valley; there was no way he would get reception on other planets.

So he called and annoyed the hell out of Micah until he finally picked up.

"Fucking hell, Walt, the British better be coming this time."

"Not quite. I need you to go to Hlohi, find Kayla, and tell her to go to all the other delegates from the other human worlds. I'm calling a meeting for tomorrow—um, this morning. Eight o'clock."

"You called me at this hour to run errands for you?"

"I'd go myself, but I'm on shift. I can't leave my radio."

Micah groaned. "The things I do for you."

"In a few days, you won't have to worry about it anymore."

"I know. That's what worries me. What the hell am I going to do with myself? All right, all right, I'll go to bloody Hlohi and hope I don't get turned into a porcupine for being a white man."

"As long as you interact with Wolf Clan only, you should be fine."

"Should is a wonderful word. It's full of so much potential."

Click.

Walter leaned back in his seat. He felt as though there ought to be more he could do to facilitate things, but there wasn't as long as he was on shift. It wasn't that he didn't like his job, but sometimes, it just got in the way of more important things, like defending humanity from an alien invasion. Yeah, tell that one to his superiors. Excuse me, Kate, I need to put in for a couple days off. What am I doing? Oh, nothing special. Getting some house and yard work done, fixing up the car, saving the planet from being enslaved by a race of hostile aliens. The usual weekend things.

It was probably an hour before he got a call from an unknown number which turned out to be Kayla using one of the communal cell phones used by Wolf Clan operatives when they did time on Earth.

"Okay, Walt, Micah finally got in to see us. What's this meeting or plan he's babbling about?"

So he explained the plan again, carefully omitting the part about Rifun being the one to head the team to torch the fields.

"It's a dirty trick," she mused. "I'd chastise you for it if we weren't on the verge of invasion and possible annihilation."

"I don't know of another way, I really don't."

"Something is better than nothing."

"Since Micah is cranky the day before his grand closing, would you mind visiting the other colonies and letting them know about the meeting? What time is it there on Hlohi?"

"Indian time." He grunted and she laughed. "I'd say it's about noon. Yeah, I'll grab Blake and Logan and we'll make the rounds. See you in a few hours."

And that was that.

Surprisingly, he got a call from Tommen not long after that, but it seemed to be driven partially by curiosity and partially by insomnia. Walter hated to think that his son, who wasn't even a legal adult yet, was already having the nightmares of a veteran. It wasn't right.

A short time after hanging up, he got called to a breaking and entering which turned out to be a teenage boy trying to get back into his own house after sneaking off to see his girlfriend. Thankfully, Walter was able to talk the father out of a good whoopin' by relaying his own experiences with Tommen. He still wouldn't have been surprised to find that Tommen and Becky were sleeping together, but he instead picked out the story of catching him and his friends out smoking weed and swiping booze. Was it illegal? Yes. Was it sinister? Hardly. Punish the crime, but don't reward the thrill.

Walter was still pretty sure the kid was in for a good switchin' out behind the wood shed once he left. *Spare the rod, spoil the child. Parenting isn't about fun and games and being friends.*

Other than a couple of speeders, the rest of the night passed uneventfully. Walter punched out more or less on time and headed home, the drive being equally as boring. He was thankful for the rare moments of boredom, really. A time of peace and quiet before the shit hit the fan.

The house was quiet when he arrived. He slipped his shoes off, hung up his coat, then went down the hall where he pushed open the door to Tommen's room.

Well, he wasn't sprawled out like a lounging teenager, but he wasn't quite as rigid as he had been lately. Maybe that was a good sign. Things were starting to look up. The memories would never really leave, but the terror could be held at bay, at least for a little while.

If only I could be so lucky, Walter thought as he retreated to his room, stripping off his uniform and tossing it in the dirty laundry. At the very least, once New Year's was over, he had a couple days off. Assuming they weren't all carted off into slavery, it would give him a little time to consider things and come up with a real plan of action.

He went out to the kitchen to scribble a quick note before fully retiring to bed. It was one of those rare nights when he managed to slip quietly into sleep rather than linger at the edge of consciousness until the demons came and dragged him down into a nightmarish hell, and he woke up feeling almost refreshed. He sat up and found Tommen in the doorway, looking as though he'd just crawled out of bed after a bad night's sleep.

"I'm the one who had a long night," Walter commented. "So why do you look as bad as I feel? Did something happen?"

Tommen shook his head. "No. Couldn't sleep. Slept like shit when I did."

"Well, give me a few minutes to get up and around, and then I'll tell you the plan."

His son ducked out of the room, and Walter moseyed his way here and there, the bathroom, his closet, and finally out to the kitchen where Tommen stared at a bowl of cereal, as if entirely unsure what to do with it.

"Do you think you can go today?" Walter asked.

Tommen sighed but nodded slowly. He'd brushed his hair and generally gotten ready, but his whole posture and demeanor was ragged. "Yeah. I can go. What's the plan?"

"Something came up earlier during our initial investigation into the Borelian poisons. I didn't think anything of it until I went to the Archives and ran across the same information, just a little more detailed.

"Borelians aren't farmers. They don't spend their days picking tomatoes under the hot sun. Their elderly might, but not the majority of the population. Anyway, not the point. Ninety-nine percent of their food comes from slavery and outside sources. What's the fastest way to torture someone? Deprive them of something their body desperately needs. Even if they have stores, they can't last forever."

Tommen rubbed his face and absently picked up his spoon. He still didn't dig into the cereal. "I don't follow."

"As I said, Rifun is the only son of a bitch crazy, stupid, and brilliant enough to pull it off. He's going to lead an attack on one of these food sources and burn it to the ground."

There was a long moment of silence. Eventually, Tommen figured out the purpose of cereal and how to use a spoon, and he started in on the food. Hunger quickly made itself known, and soon he was pouring himself a second bowl. A minute later, Walter got his own bowl and spoon and helped himself.

"What's on your mind?" Walter asked.

Tommen shrugged. "Not much. I mean, it's a logical plan. It really is. Basic necessities trump technological superiority any day. I mean, what would happen if another Dust Bowl hit the Plains? What if we woke up one morning and ninety percent of the corn and wheat crop had been decimated? It seems almost rude, until you consider the alternative."

"Believe me, I wish we weren't at war. If the entire Borelian race wasn't against us, wasn't hostile and set on the conquering of the universe, I wouldn't even suggest it, for the sake of the civilians. Unfortunately, I don't believe there are innocent civilians in this, not on their side. Besides, we're not looking to win and conquer, just survive. I'm hoping that this sends a message."

"Oh, it'll send a message. It's just a matter of what message it's sending."

"As you said. It's either this or a very unpleasant alternative. Something is better than nothing. We have to try."

Chapter Four
Mission: Possible

It hadn't been a dream, then. It had been real. Except this time, it was better. The first time had been slow movements and questions, each wondering what the other felt, expected, wanted, needed. This time around, some of the weird awkwardness had gone, allowing them to be a little more open with each other.

This kind of openness resulted mostly in Becky's uncertainty, both about the dull, lingering pain from the first time around, as well as her complaints about getting a rug burn on her back. Her bed was too short to do anything together comfortably, and it squeaked obscenely, so they did it on the floor. Tommen couldn't say he really had any complaints, but he was torn between indulging his own pleasure and worrying about her beneath him, compounded by the awkwardness of the first time in his car, and he almost wasn't able to finish. And that did not help things.

He withdrew and sat back against her bed, heart racing. Peeling the condom off his cock and tossing it in the trash, wrapped in a few fabric scraps, he lay down beside Becky on the carpet.

"Was it as bad the second time around?" he asked, getting up on one elbow so he could kiss her.

She opened her eyes. "Actually, no." She kissed him. "It was better. Not by a whole lot, I mean, it wasn't just super awesome amazing. But it was better."

"Good. And no rug burn?"

"I don't think so."

She sat up on the fabric scrap she'd placed beneath her, inspecting for any residual blood, in hopes that she wouldn't stain the carpet and have to explain it. The seats in Tommen's car were leather, which had made clean-up a breeze, though he still got light-headed thinking about the blood. It hadn't even been that much, certainly far less than anything he'd seen in the fortress. She'd assured him it was completely normal, a true sign of a virgin for women. Men, well, that was more determined by their awkwardness, and he'd hit the bullseye. He'd played dumb and asked if it could be her monthly cycle, and then she'd schooled him on that, saying that because of her dwarfism, she didn't get monthly cycles. If she got her period four times a year, that was a lot. That was also good, she said, because then she wouldn't make him wear a condom every time, either. He was leery, but decided not to argue the point. Sex felt good. It felt damn good.

"So there," he told her. "Just in case the first time was a dream or a fluke or whatever, you are now officially consummated."

She tossed the fabric in the trash, leaned back on her elbows, and kissed him again. "*We* are consummated. And I don't think the first time was a fluke. Or a dream."

"That's a good thing, I guess. Personally, I'd like to get through this awkward stuff."

"Time and experience, my love. Learning each other."

Well, that experience wasn't going to be compounded any more today because he was spent. Another thing he'd learned: sex took a lot of strength and energy. He reached for his boxers, then stood on wobbly legs to pull them up. Once he was all dressed, he flopped back on her bed and stretched out as much as possible, relaxing as Becky crawled up beside him, fully dressed, and nuzzled into the crook of his arm, resting her head on his chest.

"I think I could get used to this," he murmured.

"The sex?"

"Well, yeah. The sex, obviously. And having you here curled up beside me, small and warm and beautiful. Hard-working and exceptionally brilliant—"

"Okay, what do you want?"

"Nothing. Just kind of speaking my mind, saying what I like."

She raised a brow and looked at him. "Ah. I see." She rested her head back on his chest. "I think I could get used to it, too. It was less painful this time, and there was some pleasure in there."

"I don't want to hurt you or anything."

"I know. And I'm pretty sure it's normal. Okay, you're stuffing a banana into a baby carrot-sized hole. It needs time to adjust."

Now things just got weird. "If you say so."

She grinned and shifted position so she could kiss him once more. "Point is, you're still going to get some. And so am I. Just probably not today."

"Probably not."

Aside from him needing a short resting period, there was the point that her mom was right downstairs, fast asleep seeing how she worked the night shift. They didn't need to wake her up. Becky's dad wouldn't be home until after Tommen left for work, but regardless, they definitely didn't need him finding out. Not if Tommen still wanted to have a dick at the end of the day. Jews were famous for their circumcision; Tommen didn't want to find out what else they could do down there.

So they lay in her bed, talking about school and work and how happy they were that the holidays were almost over. With Christmas over, most of her family had gone home. The Jewish side typically stayed home during the day while Dr. Polski worked, but made frequent trips over in the evenings to celebrate Hanukkah. Neither Becky nor Tommen saw a lot of action over New Year's, though he was sure his dad would have all kinds of stories to tell once he'd slept off his shift.

As if reading his mind, Becky asked suddenly, "Do you think your dad and his girlfriend are sleeping together?"

"I don't know," Tommen admitted. "I mean, my dad's kind of a stickler, and he's always on me about it—"

"About you sleeping with his girlfriend?"

"Ha ha. No, about sleeping with you. So he could be all uptight about it. On the other hand, he's still a man. Hasn't gotten laid in at least forever—that I know of—and he really likes her. I guess it's equally possible that they're being hypocritical about it. Why?"

"Well, it's just that. The hypocrisy. The whole, 'We're adults, and we have jobs, and we live on our own, therefore, we're automatically more responsible than you.' The only part there that isn't subjective is being adults. What if one of them lost their job, or both? I mean, she lives in an apartment, so they can't even use the own your own house excuse. What if they were suddenly homeless because of economic disaster?"

"You've given this a little too much thought, methinks," Tommen said.

"Oh, probably, but it really bothers me."

"What bothers me is that, as it stands, I would be homeless, too, if there was some economic disaster and my dad lost the house."

Becky shook her head. "No, I wouldn't let that happen. You could come stay with me. Sleep at the foot of my bed. And your dad. He could take the couch. With all five of us working, we would probably make the monthly house payment."

"Four of us working. I've only got, like, three days left of work."

"Do you have any prospects or interviews?"

"Only one, and he's not going to get a hold of me until after the first."

"So you'll have a few days off. That'll be nice, won't it?"

"It will. Means I can come over here any time."

"Any time we're not in school. That resumes after the first, remember?"

He sat up and stretched. "Yeah, I remember. But not until the fifth." He turned around, kissed her, then got off her bed, reaching up until his fingertips just brushed her ceiling at its peak. At three-foot-nine, the best she could do was either fold her arms and pout, or stand against the wall where the ceiling was much lower.

"All right, smart aleck," she said, poking him in the ribs to get his arms down. "I guess I probably need to feed you something before you run off to work."

"Sex and a sandwich?" he wondered playfully.

"Keep it up and you can make your own ham on rye."

"I already do. Try again."

She swatted at him and headed out of the room. He followed her down to the kitchen. There was no such thing as a quick meal in the Polski household. There were no microwaveable, instant meals, no processed lunches, no fake foods, and the only frozen vegetables were the ones that couldn't be grown in the area, such as pineapples. Everything that wasn't home grown was at least fresh, local, organic when possible, and always kosher. Even the snacks were elaborate and took no less than twenty minutes to prepare the first time around. Due to a number of grandkids having peanut allergies, peanut butter was nowhere to be found in the house. And even that would not have been the stuff out of a jar, but a bag of peanuts that Mrs. Polski would lovingly grind down herself into creamy, nutty delight. Food was taken very seriously in this house.

Once again, Tommen wasn't going to complain. Sex, food, a damn good paycheck coming his way from the holiday bonus, no school, no training, life was good. Of course, this kind of shangri-la never boded well for him, but he was going to enjoy it while it lasted.

They ended up watching a little TV together before he headed off to work. Bakery na hÉireann was in its final days of business, which meant pickings were getting slim. Micah wanted to get as much product used up as possible before locking the doors. So while flour and sugar were still daily necessities, the extras and toppings started disappearing. Blueberries, raspberries, cherries, one by one the flavors would disappear, unless a large order came in that could justify running to the store to pick something up quick.

"How's it going?" Micah greeted as Tommen punched in.

"Better than you can imagine," Tommen replied. He hadn't told Micah about the sex and had no plans to, but sometimes he wondered if the younger twin was able to pick up on things like that, just by demeanor. Maybe it was just limited to twin senses. Of course,

Tommen was so new to sex, he probably had a big dopey grin on his face that gave it away.

"So eager to leave the bakery and get a move on?" Micah asked.

"Well, I doubt you've changed your mind any, so...yeah, I guess so."

Ever since Saturday, the day after Christmas, Micah had been almost back to his old self, upbeat, personable, far more agreeable than Micaiah, even when he had to do paperwork. Maybe the thought of striking out on his own was finally showing its appeal, and he was ready to make a new life for himself. Or maybe he'd just gone insane and now everything was absolutely happy and hilarious.

The day passed uneventfully, all things considering. The holidays were over, people were coming to terms with the business closing, and they were slowly migrating to other bakeries. After they got the five-for-one special on pretty much everything. It was liquidation time, and people were loving it.

Nevertheless, Tommen was able to close on time, and he made it home without incident. His dad was gone to work, but he'd left a note on the kitchen table detailing plans to go to the Wheel to run a few errands that he'd understandably fallen behind on because of the travel warning. But he promised to make it quick and take every precaution. Tommen fully understood that things weren't automatically safe just because the Hands said so, but did his dad really have to get so sentimental?

He made up a plate of Christmas leftovers. It could have been Hungarian, Polish, Jewish, or some crazy blend of all three, he didn't know, or really care. Mrs. Polski was a phenomenal cook, and he was glad to know her. Even now, almost a week later, they reheated perfectly, just as if they'd come fresh from the oven.

Despite the impressive remodel done earlier that year, the kitchen was still extremely small, and Tommen ended up taking his meal into the living room where he plopped down on the couch and reached for the remote. Now that Christmas was over, programming had mostly returned to normal, though there were a number of marathons of shows counting down episodes until the new year. Some of the movie channels had also picked up on this as movie series played out until the new year. In all reality, though, the holidays and the countdowns really provided a better selection of TV entertainment than he might normally find, and he was faced with the rare dilemma of having too many good options to choose from.

He texted Becky.

"Want to come over and watch a movie?"

"I could probably manage a few hours away from my sewing machine," she replied after about ten minutes.

It was still another fifteen minutes before she actually arrived, and by then, the movie had started. She crawled up on the couch and sat between Tommen's legs, bowl of popcorn in her lap.

"Sorry, my mom wanted to talk to me about something," she said, shoving a handful of popcorn in her mouth.

"Anything I should know about?" Tommen wondered.

"She's not suspicious, if that's what you're asking. No, she wanted to double-check that I'd gotten some scholarship essays turned in before the deadline tomorrow night. Which I did."

"Ah."

"What about you? You're dual-enrolling; you can still get scholarship and grants and stuff."

"I know. A couple of the easy ones, I already applied for. But some of them require essays and other things I'm not good at. I'm kind of putting them off as long as I can."

"Do you want help? I'm no English major, but I am better than you."

"Rub it in, why don't you?"

"Do you want the help or not?"

He sighed. "I probably should...But can we wait until after the movie?"

"I think we can do that."

The movie didn't actually end until midnight. Nevertheless,

Tommen pulled up one of his scholarship essays—or what little he had of it—and let her peruse. It didn't take long for her to find his first mistake, and it all went downhill from there. He corrected what he could do easily, but some of her suggestions he just made notes of and said he'd get back to them later.

Before either could say anything more, his phone chimed. It was his dad.

"Made it back."

"Anything interesting?" Tommen asked.

"More than you know. I have a few things I need to do, but I'll call you shortly."

"Okay."

"Your dad?" Becky guessed.

He nodded. "Of course. Now that he works nights, he doesn't bother me at school, but he bugs me half the night."

"He worries about you."

"I'm seventeen. Not seven."

"Who's had his hearing busted and his arm burned in the last year."

He gave her a look. "Thanks for the reminder." And that was just the stuff she knew about.

"I'm just saying."

"Remember when we first met, when you asked me why I was so miserable, and I said that I wanted to be judged for who I am, not who I was, and move on? It really doesn't help when you point out everything that's wrong with me. Do I constantly point out your height or your shoes or anything like that?"

She put her hands up. "Okay, okay, I'm sorry." She let out a breath, and her expression became unreadable. "Does this mean sex is out of the question?"

Tommen raised a brow. "I thought good little Catholic girls didn't get horny?"

"Little Catholic girls are probably the horniest girls you'll meet. Good ones just won't tell you about it. Now come here."

Twice in one day? Okay, so technically it was two different calendar days, but it was the same time period of being awake. So, twice in one day? Yes, please. He was more than happy to oblige, and this time it was in a proper bed. His bed. Not the backseat of a car, not the floor, but the bed. Not only that, but she even seemed to enjoy it, which made him even more excited.

It was nearly one o'clock when he walked her home. Her mom met them at the door, thanked Tommen for his gentlemanliness, and invited him in, which he declined. It felt insulting to do so, but Mrs. Polski did not flinch or get offended. Instead, she said she understood, wished him a good night, and closed the door.

Yup. Today was a good day. He got sex not once, but twice. Work hadn't been half bad. He got sex twice in one day. Even though his dinner had been leftovers, they were probably the best leftovers on the face of the planet. Sex happened twice. He got to cuddle with his girlfriend and watch a movie. Plus he got to start and finish his day with sex which was getting better with each encounter. Hot damn, now that was what he called a good day.

He got home, kicked off his shoes, and went to the fridge to scrounge up one last morsel of food before going to bed. He didn't really want a whole, full meal, just a light snack. Sex was exhausting, and he needed to refuel. In the end, he found a leftover container with only a little bit left in it. It wasn't one of Mrs. Polski's delectable dishes, but something his dad had made. Fried chicken and mashed potatoes by the look of it, which was fine with him.

Once he'd finished his food, he made for the bathroom to brush his teeth and go about his normal, nightly routine. And to think, in just a couple days, he would have some time completely to himself. No work, no school, nothing at all to occupy his time. It was strange think about, and kind of sad. But it would be the vacation he needed, certainly.

Naturally, it was not to be, or that was Tommen's first thought when he walked back to his room and found Rifun on his bed. He still wore a button-down shirt, and while Tommen could see the gauze had been removed, he could tell the stitches were mostly still in place, only just begun to fall out.

Tommen opened his mouth to speak, but was interrupted by his phone, the call from his dad. He gave Rifun a smirk of his own as he answered the call.

"Hi, Dad," he said loudly, sarcastically.

There was silence on the other end for a moment. Then, "Everything all right?"

"Just fine. About ready to head off to bed."

"Slap happy then. Right."

"What did you find?"

"Well, it's either going to be a way to deter any New Year's Eve attacks, or it'll just speed up invasion. One or the other. Have you seen Rifun lately?"

"Actually...he is kind of standing right here."

Tommen could tell that was not what his dad wanted to hear as he took an even breath and said, "I need to speak with him."

Tommen blinked, then handed over the phone to Rifun who raised a brow then put the phone to his ear.

"Walter, how are you? It's been, what, a few months, hasn't it? At least?" Pause. "Yes, yes, I understand all 'if you ever's and 'when I catch you's and all the threats that go with them. Please, save us both some time and get to the chase. You didn't want to talk to me just to threaten me."

Tommen could not hear the conversation, nor did he want to ask for him to turn on speakerphone. Anything that was said, his dad could relay at a later time. Nevertheless, the conversation must have been intriguing as Rifun's expression went from smirking, lackadaisical, devil-may-care, to thoughtful, calculating, scheming.

Finally, "Walter, if I didn't know you and Tommen were family, I would say that the odds of both you and your adopted son being so brilliant and conniving are astronomical. But we both know better. Yes, I'll be there. Even if the whole thing turns out to be a trap for me, it sounds exciting at the very least." Pause. "Very true, but then, what was that phrase you loved to parrot? Only injured, not helpless. Now then, if you will excuse me, your son and I have a few things to do tonight."

He hung up, then handed the phone back to Tommen.

"What was that all about?" Tommen asked.

"Your dad will tell you about it in due time, I expect," Rifun said, opening a portal. "Most likely tomorrow morning once he gets home. Given the task he's laid out, I am suddenly inclined to make this a very brief trip tonight."

Tommen couldn't have heard better words, and he stepped through the portal into the fortress. He noticed, that as Rifun came through, the man seemed to have a lot harder time of it than he normally did. The man who had manipulated Gravity in order to move huge stone slabs to create treacherous makeshift stairs, now had trouble doing a comparatively ordinary task like opening and walking through a portal.

"Julianna said your pulmonary artery had been severed," Tommen ventured. "How long does that take to heal?"

"Longer than a week and a half," Rifun countered irritably, though his words held very little malice.

Tommen turned to head into the main fortress, the southwest stair, when two things happened. First, he spotted Julianna just walking into the portal room. Second, he heard something large and heavy hit the floor behind him. By the time he turned to investigate, all he saw was Rifun standing there.

"Are we going?" the man asked.

"You're still having seizures," Tommen stated suddenly. "Julianna has to cover them up because otherwise you'll look weak in front of your men, and the Akarin. You can't risk mutiny or an overthrow. But Borelian poison is fixed in Base Time and you've been cured of that, which means these are naturally-occurring, maybe a side effect of the poison that could stay with you."

"And you're a perceptive little brat with a big mouth," Julianna hissed, moving to stand close to Rifun.

Right. Thinking before speaking. He still had to work on that. Fortunately for him, it was the worst rebuke he got for the time being. Julianna glared at him, and Rifun seemed more concerned with continuing on and getting wherever it was they needed to go. Tommen made his way out of the portal room, then stepped aside to let Rifun take the lead. Had he not been present, Tommen never would have guessed the man had just had a seizure, the way he carried himself. All was back to normal. How much time did he have to take in order to get that way? Ten minutes? Half an hour? Longer? Judging by his reaction to Tommen's statement, Rifun was perplexed by this turn of events and generally unsure how to handle them. Were they permanent? Would they go away in their own time?

Tommen tried to think if his dad had suffered any such effects from either of the Borelian poisons that had touched him, but couldn't come up with anything. All wounds had to heal on their own, and by the time the pink poison wounds had healed, his dad was back to his old self. As for the blue poison wounds, that was impossible to tell because that recovery had been intertwined with his addiction recovery. Maybe there had been side effects, but they were either too closely tied to the wounds themselves to be distinguishable, or else...could they be more latent, something that wouldn't show up for some time? Wouldn't that be just perfect? But then, it had been a year since the warehouse; surely any dormant side effects would have been noticed by now. Right?

There were just too many unknowns. Tommen felt as though he were swimming in a sea of murky unknowns. Borelian poison, Borelian war, the Order and the Akarin, a whole new chapter of things that had never been done before, and he was right in the middle of it. Could he just skip to the end and read about the details later?

Looking around, reconstruction seemed to be...happening. It wasn't super fast, nor did it appear to be going seamlessly, but it was happening. Most of the damage to the first floor had been minimal, and to look at it, things seemed almost normal again. There were still a few small cracks here and there, and some repairs were more obvious than others, but overall it was looking pretty good. The second and third floors were still sorely in need of more repairs, but those, too, were coming along.

"With any luck, we'll have things back to normal by the end of January," Rifun said as he stepped off the stair onto the third floor. "Of course, some of that depends on these new developments from your father."

"What developments?" Julianna asked.

"Something we'll discuss after our meeting with young Tommen here."

Tommen was pretty sure he saw a Band encase the two of them, but he couldn't tell the strength of the Band, nor how long they were really in it. They could have exchanged a few words, or held an entire conversation; there was no way for him to know once the Band was dropped and they continued moving. Of course, it only frustrated him more to know that Rifun knew something he didn't, and his dad wouldn't be able to tell him until morning, after Rifun made whatever plans he needed to make.

He ended up following them to one of the meeting rooms. Once he was inside, Julianna shut the door behind them.

"All right, to answer the question that is no doubt on your mind, we're here to discuss your performance during the battle last week," Rifun began half a second after the door clicked shut. He leaned back against a table. "Quite frankly, it was even worse than pitiful. You are absolutely useless. Medic, soldier, doesn't matter, you are useless to us in a fight."

Tommen wasn't sure whether he ought to have been discouraged, offended, or relieved. Discouraged, because he didn't want to admit that it was true. Offended, because he didn't want it to be true. Relieved, because if it was true, maybe he could get out of future soldiering activities.

"The good news," Rifun went on, "is that we are restructuring how we do things. The Order must now carry its own affairs as well as manage those under them, the Akarin. We're no longer single-mindedly training for war, but must also branch out into politics, religion, culture, work on a blending of our two peoples that we may become one, that we may forge a new identity and become even stronger.

"That said, this new restructuring allows for far more opportunities for those like you who are terrible at soldiering. I've given it some thought, and I may have an idea where we could use you. I thought about setting you up as an English teacher. Comparatively speaking, it's easy work. You don't have to teach them to write essays or anything sophisticated, just get them started with the basics and hand them off to other teachers. You would be a huge hit because, after all, you are human and a native English speaker—yes, I know it's a foreign language to you, me as well, but they don't need to know that.

"And then there is menial labor. A cook in the cafeteria, bed pan scrubber in the infirmary, those sorts of things. Before the battle, I would have handed you over without a second thought as a means of teaching you humility and submission. But I think you've learned that lesson well enough.

"Instead, we—Julianna and myself—came up with a mission for you, something that blends what you need with what you want. Think of it as gaining valuable work experience before ever applying for the job you want most in the Time industry. And we both know it's not Timekeeping."

Tommen gave him a look. "Scouting?"

"Exactly. Not to worry, though. You won't be going alone, but with an experienced group of people. They'll get you through the local customs, politics, all that. At least, to an extent. There is no telling where this could lead. You may very well reach worlds untouched."

"Where am I going? What am I doing?"

The thought of being able to go out and do some Scouting thrilled him, even as he mentally beat himself for tripping and falling right into Rifun's trap. Give him what he wants, tell him what he wants to hear, play on his secrets and desires, pull the strings just a little more. A huge move they couldn't do, but a little nudge, a little at a time, and he'll fall off the cliff on his own.

"Your mission," Rifun continued, his tone growing more serious, "is to find Richard's third journal. Julianna can give you the details as to when she last had possession of it and what happened, and there are several rumors you may wish to investigate as well regarding its location."

"Richard's third journal?" Tommen echoed.

Julianna nodded. "The Book of Philosophy opened everyone's eyes and minds to the existence of the Author and the greater universe; it kept the Cult alive for over a hundred years. The Book of Abilities strengthened the loyal followers and gave them the power they needed to overtake the Akarin.

"The Book of Commands is what's missing. It details the more day-to-day affairs of conducting business internally and externally, especially in dealing with the Akarin. I have quite a bit of it memorized, but just as the Akarin draw strength from the Authored Books, so the Order will be strengthened by having all the journals together. It will also provide a more solid, reasonable basis for our claims, far more than just hearsay and rumor. If we conduct business with the Akarin according to the details set out in the Book of Commands, then we will be without fault according to our own rules."

"Why send me to find it? If I'm going with a group, then it's not like I'm your only hope."

"You're not," Rifun told him bluntly. "Quite honestly, I'm trying to find a job for you where you aren't rendered useless and menial. I'm trying to give you a career, not a day job at a bakery, as it were. If you think you want to be a Scout, or something like it, this will be an excellent test to see if you have what it takes. You are the spearhead of the search; you are responsible for gathering information and following leads. You just also happen to have a safety net at your back for social niceties, political dealings, and the ever-possible threat of violence. This time around, you are the hero. You have a sidekick, or a posse. You call the shots. You are the one chasing the priceless artifact."

It sounded fantastic, like a dream come true. He would be able to go out and explore the universe, but he wouldn't be alone; he would have the means to survive an alien culture and get through whatever he needed to in order to complete his mission. He would be the one in charge, doling out the orders. His underlings would report to him with "yes, sir" and "no, sir" and "right away, sir" with no questions asked, unless he specifically requested counsel. Which he would do. He had no illusions that he was an end-all fountain of knowledge and information. On Earth, he might have that kind of ego, but that cocky well dried up as soon as he left the atmosphere.

"Furthermore, if you pull this off, you will have standing among your peers. Human, hero, globetrotter extraordinaire. You may even become more of a celebrity than me. It will also serve as a solid foundation for future assignments as you learn to navigate the tricky details of cross-cultural niceties. In the process, you will learn many essential skills for the Scouting lifestyle. More than just politics and religion, we're talking about picking up languages, wilderness survival on a strange planet, and general ethnology, reading others without making a scene.

"You're right; you are not our only hope. You're not even our best hope. But we want to give you a chance to prove yourself, to make an investment, both for us and you. You don't want to be a soldier, and I don't want to throw you in the kitchens. We're giving you a lot of leeway and extending a lot of trust to give you this opportunity."

Somewhere in the back of his mind, Tommen could picture a carrot and him walking over a cliff trying to get to it. In the front of his mind, however, he saw a dream come true. Going out into the universe, exploring, treasure-hunting, calling the shots, proving himself to be useful and resourceful. And finding one stupid book? Hey, he stumbled across one already, maybe he could go two for three. At least this time, he would be able to see if there were any Time traps in the immediate vicinity.

"I can see the wheels turning," Rifun goaded. "He wants to do it. But he's uncertain. What if the others in the group don't listen to him? Is this some kind of test? What if I fail? A cowardly soldier, a useless medic, and a worthless treasure-hunter. How can I show my face after three strikes?"

"I'll do it," Tommen cut in. Even as he said it, he knew it was giving in. It was a more regal way, perhaps, of calling Marty McFly a chicken, but it was the same damn thing and it still elicited the same damn reaction.

"Excellent." The man straightened, his expression saying that he was glad the meeting was over and that things had gone exactly how he wanted. "Well then, I have many other things I need to do today. Julianna will give you the rundown on how to begin tracking the journal."

"Wait, I have to do this now?"

"Quite frankly, I would hope not. There are a few things you need to learn before you just go gallivanting off across the universe. Surely your experience with Sifura taught you that much. Normally, I'd say you got lucky, but seeing how this is all unfolding makes me think the Author had this planned all along."

And isn't it strange how it unfolded in my Books and not your journals? Tommen was half a breath from saying it out loud, then caught himself before he found himself doing something very unpleasant, or having something unpleasant done to him. Instead, he watched as Rifun left the room in his normal confident stride, leaving him and Julianna alone in the meeting room.

"The last time I had the journal," she began, "I was in Boston. I gave it to a Merchant named Andrew O'Dell for safekeeping. He in turn gave it to another Harvester named Nathan Wilde who took it off-world to somewhere I do not know. I lost track of him after that also, so I have every reason to believe his intentions were malicious. You may start with either of them."

"And no one ever made any mention of it, like, during or after the coup?" Tommen wondered. "I mean, shit like this doesn't just disappear, especially when, you know, the whole Cult gets put center stage. Someone has to know something."

"You're right. Someone has to know something, but whoever this someone is, they're not saying anything. As I said, malicious intent. Your job is to find that someone and get them to talk, if not hand over the journal completely."

"So this is less of a treasure hunt and more of a *Godfather* style shakedown, is that it?"

Julianna's expression was a brick wall. "Your job is simply information and retrieval. As for the rest of it, I suggest you utilize the different members of your team."

Tommen didn't like the twist in his gut as he asked, "So who's on my team?"

Now she relaxed a little and folded her arms. "Well, that's the thing. I was very happy to let you know and send you on your merry way. But whatever your father told Rifun, he's put the whole thing on hold until after New Year's. Obviously, this doesn't mean a whole lot since New Year's Eve is literally tomorrow. I suppose it gives you a little time to prepare. Mentally prepare, anyway. The good news is that there really isn't a time limit on this one, not like your mission to save your father. Obviously, we want this done as quick as feasibly possible, but we're not going to give you some kind of arbitrary timeline."

Well, at least he had that going for him. It would be nice to have a mission where he could work at his own pace, set his own hours, work around his schedule of school and work and home that was otherwise pretty fixed. He could take the time to do research before running off to a strange world, and he would be able to go a little slower and really absorb and appreciate a foreign culture rather than just eating their food, sleeping in their beds, and leaving the next morning without even so much as a good morning kiss. It would be a nice breath of fresh air, really.

Whatever plans Julianna had originally laid out to tell him about his mission and where and how to begin, they had been derailed by Walter contacting Rifun. So a three-hour meeting had been cut down into about a thirty minute meeting, and soon enough, they returned to the portal room where Julianna opened a portal back into Tommen's bedroom and sent him home.

Before being interrupted by Rifun, Tommen had been getting ready for bed, but without the strength-sucking exhaustion that normally plagued him after a long day at school, a long day at work, a long night at training, plus all the stress he carried on top of that from a variety of things. He didn't have school, work hadn't been bad, training had been brief and non-physical. Even with two rounds of sex thrown in, he found that he couldn't quite muster up enough fatigue to get him to want to sleep, not after this latest turn of events.

He lay in bed for a short time before reaching for his phone and dialing his dad who picked up on the fourth ring.

"What's up, kiddo? Everything all right? Normally you're gone longer than that."

"Yeah, fine," Tommen told him. "Whatever they had planned, they had to cut it short because of whatever you told Rifun. So...what did you tell him?"

"I've called for a small meeting tomorrow on Tacaga, and I want him there. I have a plan, and I fully believe that he's the only one crazy, stupid, and brilliant enough to pull it off."

"What's the plan?"

"It will be easier to explain it in person. Get some sleep, and I'll be home in the morning."

"What time is the meeting?"

"Our time, it'll be about noon, twelve-thirty, somewhere in there."

"Great. So I sleep now, then when I wake up, you'll be asleep. I have to work tomorrow, too."

"Not until two. Besides, I think Micah would understand."

"Wait...I'm going?"

"Of course you're going. And after I'm finished telling you my plan, you can tell me what sort of antics Rifun is up to now that he had to take you tonight."

"Got it. All right, I guess I'll try to get some sleep. It'll make tomorrow come faster."

His dad seemed to falter at that, but wished him a good night and hung up. Tommen understood his hesitation; he understood it far better than he ever wanted to. For Walter, it was his years in prison and fear of the dark. For Tommen, it was the terror of battle, the far too acute realization that any moment could be his last and he may never actually see the face of his killer. He didn't like the thought, and he certainly didn't like that feeling of helplessness.

It was over a week since the battle, and most of the details were gone, the memories faded. He could conjure them up in stunning detail with hardly a difficult thought or second guess, and he fought the tidal wave pressing at the doors of his mind, ready to flood his sleep with nightmares and paralyzing fear.

The problem was, he could only really keep his guard up while he was still awake, still conscious. Sleeping required him to be unconscious, and as soon as he hit that threshold, when the terror waited for the last lock to unlatch, his sense of fear and self-preservation kicked in and he jolted back to full wakefulness. This was fine for the first hour or two, but as his clock ticked by, almost time for his dad to get off work, and he still hadn't gotten more than a heavy doze, it was not only frustrating, but he was seriously exhausted and unable to find meaningful sleep.

So he reached out. It was a strange thing, to essentially cast his consciousness, his Energy out into the world, riding the Energy that encompassed every molecule, every atom in the universe, looking for someone to influence. Most often, it was manipulating the Energy in the brain to appear in dreams. This was possible only because the brain was actually more active during REM sleep than being awake, and it took a considerable amount of Energy to do what he needed to. Supposedly, extremely skilled Akari-bearers could influence the waking mind to see visions or some such thing, but he didn't have that kind of talent yet.

His dad was awake, so that was a no go. Tommen ventured

toward Becky and found her having some kind of weird dream that involved being on a lake with a horse, a jet ski, a ladder going up to a helicopter, and a bunch of potted plants. He couldn't make heads or tails of it. He might have tried to influence the dream a little, then backed off. Becky wouldn't understand that it was a real thing, and he didn't want to make any mistakes that might bring her into one of Rifun's sick games. She needed to be protected in her own little box, safely tucked away from Time, the Akari, all of that. It was bad enough she'd almost been carted off to Borelian slavery during the Halloween attack.

He left her and continued on. It wasn't necessarily a fully conscious, astral sort of thing where he walked around looking for sleeping people to fuck with. It was more a matter of will, with a slight hint of lucidity. For example, he didn't so much think, "I want to go see what Micah's up to" so much as he had an inkling and then he was basically there, swimming in some kind of murky blackness, like the bakery but having no electricity. He wasn't there for long, before an alarm clock was going off, ripping into the tail end of a dream he could not quite make out. Tommen held onto a thread of sleepy consciousness as Micah groaned and fumbled for his alarm clock, breaking free as the younger twin sat up and rubbed his eyes, ready for the day, more or less.

He couldn't say just what happened or when, but Tommen figured he must have slept at some point, even if he didn't have any dreams of his own. He didn't hear his dad get home, and when he did finally pull himself back together and open his eyes, daylight was filtering in through his curtains. Looking at his clock, it was about eleven. Even if he'd gotten to sleep before five, six hours, while not horrible, still wasn't great, considering that what sleep he did get had not left him feeling rested.

Grudgingly, he pulled himself out of bed, went to the bathroom, then made his way to the kitchen where a note on the table interrupted his foraging.

If you get up before eleven-thirty, Band me, please. -Dad

Yawning, Tommen made his way to his dad's bedroom and did just that, giving him a good six hours or so before he woke up on his own.

"I'm the one who had a long night," Walter commented, yawning and stretching. "So why do you look as bad as I feel? Did something happen?"

Tommen shook his head. "No. Couldn't sleep. Slept like shit when I did."

"Well, give me a few minutes to get up and around, and then I'll tell you the plan."

Despite having felt left out the previous evening and desperately wanting to know what kind of plan was in the works, Tommen now found himself rather unenthusiastic about the whole thing. When would they get back to plans that involved skiing, going out to dinner, seeing a movie, staying up late, things like that? Couldn't they just put off this whole war business for a while? Next week, next month, maybe next year—a full year, not the new year that was coming in only a couple days.

But just as time waited for no man, neither did war. It was here, and they had to do something about it. So Tommen got out a bowl, a spoon, the jug of milk, and picked out a cereal. It wasn't much, but it helped to wake him up a little. His dad was out soon enough.

"Do you think you can go today?" his dad wondered.

Tommen nodded slowly. "Yeah. I can go. What's the plan?"

His dad still seemed uncertain, but continued anyway. "Something came up earlier during our initial investigation into the Borelian poisons. I didn't think anything of it until I went to the Archives and ran across the same information, just a little more detailed.

"Borelians aren't farmers. They don't spend their days picking tomatoes under the hot sun. Their elderly might, but not the majority of the population. Anyway, not the point. Brelix is too unstable for standard farming practices. Ninety percent of their food comes from slavery and outside sources. What's the fastest way to torture someone? Deprive them of something their body desperately needs. Even if they have stores, they can't last forever."

Tommen rubbed his face. "I don't follow."

"As I said, Rifun is the only son of a bitch crazy, stupid, and brilliant enough to pull it off. He's going to lead an attack on one of these food sources and burn it to the ground."

Chapter Five
Conference Call

Blind portals—those that bypassed the temporal mechanisms of the Wheel and the Order fortress—were about ten times harder to open and about twenty times harder on the body, or that's what it felt like anyway. Given how awful normal portals to the Wheel could be, going directly to places like Tacaga was hardly a picnic, and Tommen felt like puking his guts out when they landed. The first time he'd come with his dad, they'd ended up in the middle of the river. Thankfully, they'd made enough trips and were coordinated enough now to at least step through on dry land.

Comparing to Earth, the capital city of Lip was situated about where Kansas might be, and it was high summer. Tommen could feel every degree of it, and his body struggled to adjust from beginning of winter to height of summer. At first, it felt pretty darn good. Then the reality of it started to creep in until he was sweating buckets and longing for a lake to jump in. He might have jumped in the river, but that was decidedly frowned upon by the Tacagans. The good news, though, was that the Tacagans rarely strayed too far from their cities or roads, so as long as they were out of sight of the local authorities, he could dip his feet—and maybe his whole body—in the water here and there. The gate guards gave him stern looks as he passed through, but he simply shook his wet hair and carried on.

"As amusing as it is," his dad said once they were out of earshot of the guards, "we probably shouldn't actively try to antagonize them."

"Should I go back and offer them a towel to wipe the small splatters from their faces?" Tommen asked smartly.

His dad simply sighed, rolled his eyes, and shook his head, all while trying to fight a full smile.

As expected, their escort was waiting for them on the other side of the bridge, not two steps into the actual city itself. The local peacekeepers were all plainclothes, not even a lapel pin to tell they were peacekeepers. Nonetheless, they seemed to get the same escort every time—although maybe it only seemed that way, given their heavy use of genetic engineering and possibly even cloning—and Tommen was getting to know the faces, if not the people.

On the whole, Tacagans were a bunch of stiffs. But a couple of the peacekeepers had warmed up to them, much to the chagrin of the supervisor.

Dermos was the newest peacekeeper on the force, a true rookie fresh from the academy, and he'd been completely surprised by the escort assignment. Normally, assignments involving outsiders were given only to veterans on the force, those who couldn't and wouldn't be influenced. Apparently, since he'd warmed up to Tommen, Walter, and the others, his supervisor had requested he be taken off the escort, but was denied. The reasoning was that first, escort details were traditionally absolute; second, that meant involving another peacekeeper and it was better to keep these things under wraps, especially with the sensitive nature of the dealings; third, if Dermos was kicked off, he was a liability to tell or else have his own thoughts about the outsiders and outside world. He wasn't ready for that yet, or so they said. If he was to be exposed to the outsiders, it would be done in a controlled environment until his resilience could be tested. When Tommen asked why he'd been selected in the first place, Dermos simply shrugged and said sheer chance, probably a mistake that got overlooked until it was too late.

The other friendly Tacagan was Yeros. Or Geros. Tommen had a hard time deciding between the two as the sounds seemed to be blended—like trying to pronounce "gyro" correctly, which was also a Greek word—though he leaned more on the side of the g. Geros was younger than Walter, about forty years by appearance, though he still sported the body of a thirty year old body builder, or maybe a retired soldier. His general disposition seemed to be frowned upon by all of the peacekeepers, but especially his supervisor. His attitude was pretty relaxed, completely unconcerned with the opinions of others or the way things had been done for the last dozen centuries. He would do his job, do it well, but if he didn't like something or wanted to try something different, no one was going to tell him otherwise. He wanted to talk to the outsiders and generally make nice, though he was still far from casually friendly, and he would do so on his own terms with no regard for protocol or social custom.

Walter had told Tommen and the others to take advantage of the friendliness, though not in a mean way. The Tacagan Governors were very good at propaganda and pushing the idea of a perfect human utopia. Chat it up with Dermos and Geros and any of the others who were less than frosty, and get an idea of the real Tacaga. They didn't have to ask about military strategies or anything like that, but figure out their grunts and grumbles about their lives and slowly paint a picture of the man behind the curtain. How stable were things? How did they work? Did they work? What were the shortcomings?

More spy work was all Tommen heard. It wasn't meant to be an active thing, an interrogation, but he wasn't interested in the passive thing, either. He was tired of secrets and spies and everything of that nature. He just wanted everything out in the open.

They rode bikes from the edge of the city to the nearest train station. The train was something Tommen never got used to. Running at one hundred percent efficiency, the train could travel at over three hundred miles per hour, and yet its occupants never felt a thing. No jerks, jolts, thumps, thuds, or anything at all. Simply get on, sit down, wait until all passengers were seated, wait the five or ten minutes for the ride, get up, get off. No swinging around on poles or hanging from handle bars.

The train station they stopped at was literally inside the governmental building, and it wasn't far from the elevator. Everything on Tacaga was about efficiency and optimization. The location of the train station and the elevator was specifically designed for the fastest, most efficient flow of people to and from wherever they were going in the building. In all actuality, it worked very well. Like the train, the elevators also worked at one hundred percent efficiency, and they were in the basement in no time at all.

The lab that the engineer worked in was a dream for any scientist, and Tommen found himself staring through the glass walls at all the cabinets and cupboards, the tables full of astounding instruments that could be used to do amazing things, all so full of potential. Some things he knew, some things he didn't. All of the larger machines were alien to him, but that only made him dream all the more. The things he could do in there. Was it possible to do some kind of apprenticeship under the engineer? A few hours after school, learn some real, hands-on material? Hey, saving the universe was pretty hands-on and kind of necessary.

Of course, he'd only really seen the engineer once or twice. On the rare occasion that he did come to Tacaga, interactions were often limited, or else under the supervision of the Governors, or else with the Governors and not the engineer, or else he just wasn't invited into the room but told to keep an eye on things outside. To be invited now into this incredibly high-stakes, high-risk, classified meeting was extraordinary, maybe even on the same plane as Dermos being selected for escort. It just didn't happen.

The meeting room down the hall, while high-tech, really wasn't anything to write home about, Tommen thought. A meeting room was a meeting room. Tables, chairs, lectern, projector, or variations thereof. The engineer was already there, fussing needlessly over small details, probably trying to make busy work. He looked up as they entered the room.

"Walter, why have you called this meeting?" Do Chien asked, sounding equal parts curious and concerned. "I have heard only that you may have a plan of attack."

"I didn't want to give away too much information before everyone could be assembled," Walter told him. "Quite frankly, this is more of an announcement than a discussion, but we don't have time to waste on the post office. We need everyone here, together, at one time."

"You heard about the attack on Ehani, then."

Walter stopped short. "No, I didn't. What happened?"

"Four thousand taken, ten thousand dead," the engineer reported. "Mostly Etlawa, but a good portion of Xalani, too."

"Think it might persuade them to unite for a common cause?"

"If the Borelians do not, nothing will."

Walter nodded grimly and turned to Tommen. "You can have a seat here in front. I think you're going to be a bigger part than you realize."

Tommen nodded. "I have a good idea. And I want a front row seat."

He sat dutifully, initially unaccustomed to the arrangement. Normally, he was the one in the back corner, the kid who never raised his hand, never volunteered any answers or other information, never got excited about anything except the bell to dismiss the class—all of this with exception to his science classes, and even then it was a fifty-fifty shot whether the class was interesting enough to warrant his eager attention. Now he was sitting in the front of the room, ready to go. He couldn't say he was excited to be present, but he had a better understanding and appreciation for the severity of the situation and the mission at hand.

He watched his dad and Do Chien discuss how to use the sort of special touchscreen smart board high-tech projector and display getup. There was some back and forth, technical difficulties, language barriers, more technical difficulties, frustration, and then that moment of joy and relief as everything came together exactly how it should, followed by that moment of trepidation as one hopes that everything stays working as it should.

Being surrounded by such vast advanced technology, Tommen had to do a double-take when a couple of Amish-looking men walked in the room. Suspenders, jackets, hats, beards, he half-expected them to bring a plate of potatoes to some Thanksgiving feast. He was even more surprised when they started speaking English to him. They introduced themselves as John and Andrew, from Aleis, a traditional, Puritan- or Amish-like planet. After that whole colonization thing, disagreements with European royalty, and skirmishes with the Indians didn't quite work out. They took a seat several rows back on the other side of the room. Tommen Banded himself and his dad.

"So, they're, like, Pilgrims?" he asked. "Honest to God Pilgrims?"

"A few centuries removed, but yes," his dad answered. "They've carved out a good living for themselves on Aleis."

"They probably don't get along too well with the Krydik, then."

"Each has their own world with no need to go to the other. They get along just fine. But, like most, they have very little in common."

Tommen glanced back at the men, looking sorely out of place, like the Flintstones in a Jetsons' world. "Do they even use Time?"

"Minimally, if at all." His dad continued before he could say more. "Tommen, a lot of the colony planets are populated by displaced people groups. Those who volunteered to leave—like the Tacagans, the Trebaldi, and the Treman—are in the minority. When given room, everyone gets along fine. It's the push and shove of too many people and not enough land to go around for everyone to live how they want that causes problems. We can discuss it later if you want, but for right now, we have a mission to complete."

"You say that as if we don't have the ability to magically bend Time to our will," Tommen said smartly.

His dad just gave him a look, and he released the Band.

As the delegations made their way into the room, Tommen could pretty well guess the story for each of them. Vin Lay, Orientals escaping Genghis Khan, Pol Pot, and others. Ehani, tribal groups seeking refuge from European slavers and conquerers. Judging by their general demeanor, each one wasn't too thrilled about having the other around, and one was forced to wonder whether they had really given up their own slaving. When he asked his dad about it, Walter simply said that some cultural differences couldn't be reconciled, and the South American Xalani and African Etlawa were an easy target for the Borelians.

The Sakarians were another easy guess: humans with physical deformities who, at one time, may have been considered cursed, and left to die. Their delegation today consisted of a giant nine feet tall and a dwarf a third the size. Tommen found himself less repulsed by the dwarf, but that was probably thanks to Becky. He also discovered what it was probably like to be her when he compared himself to the giant. He tried to do this all discreetly, of course. Staring seemed to be a rude gesture across the universe.

He had a harder time trying to pin down a story on the Dorigisi. Scandinavian and Mediterranean sailors, the lot of them, but what led them away from Earth was anyone's guess, it seemed. They sat one row behind and to the right of Tommen. While they were still waiting on the last delegations, he twisted around to speak to them.

"So, what led you off-world?" he asked, figuring the worst they could do was tell him to fuck off. Actually, judging by their bulk, the worst that could happen was they snapped him in half and used his bones as toothpicks. But their light-hearted demeanor toward each other didn't quite jive with that thought.

"Dorigisi originally come from many worlds," one brutish man said. He was easily six-foot-six, three hundred pounds of sheer muscle. "The Scandinavians were the first, the Vikings fleeing the forced Christian conversion of Charlemagne. Then were the Mediterraneans, fleeing the Black Death. Finally, the Islanders, fleeing those who would conquer their islands. And so, we are a sailing people."

Tommen nodded. "I can tell."

"Yes. Do tell. You may be a sailor yourself."

He shook his head. "I don't think so. I'm a mountain kid. But why do you say so?"

"Look around here." The man swept his arm widely around

the room. "We are all human, yet no one talks to each other. We are too far removed, or so some would say. You are brave to bridge the gap between us, speak to us without fear, ask a direct question without knowing how we may react. So a sailor braves the waters without knowing what may lay beyond."

"Don't listen to him," the woman of the delegation said. She looked like she may have been a Mediterranean-Scandinavian blend, with the Mediterranean olive skin and Scandinavian bulk. "He is right, but he'll preach to you all day long about the seas and the ships. He would have you think our oceans are endless. They are not. We have mapped them entirely and traveled them countless times; we have ports and trade cities. While a great percentage of our population sails or rows in some fashion, whether to work or as a hobby, others stay on the land to tend the crops and build the houses."

"Oh," was all Tommen could find to say.

The woman raised a brow and pointed at him. "And I have even seen a mountain. There is a chain of islands that was once a solid land mass. Then there was an earthquake and the mountain range split into four land islands and many smaller ones." Her expression turned unreadable. "The tsunami that resulted from the earthquake, unfortunately, destroyed a city two hundred miles away. But such is life."

Tommen's attention was taken then as Kayla and the Krydik delegation sat down beside him. He recognized Blake. Judging by the familial similarity, he figured it was safe to guess that the third member was Logan.

"Hey." Kayla flashed him a grin. "Long time, no see."

"At least a week," Tommen replied.

"Life treating you all right?"

"Could be better, could be worse."

"Yeah, same here. What's this cockamamie plan your dad's cooked up now?"

"I...don't really know. I got the gist of it, but I don't fully understand the details."

It was only half a lie. He knew Rifun was involved in some way. But he figured his dad had a way of tactfully introducing him versus just blurting it out and having the whole thing spiral out of control before it even started. Tommen was going to say more, but Kayla suddenly stood and went to speak with Walter.

As Walter, Kayla, and the Ehani delegation—both Xalani and Etlawa—had their own private conference before the meeting at large, the Tacagans walked in and took their seats, in the front of course, at the other end of the row, as far away from all the unevolved humans as possible. They did not speak to any but each other, and no one spoke to them.

The private conference ended and Walter stepped to the front.

"Good morning," he began. "Or whatever time of day it is for you at home. My name is Walter Forbes, from Earth. I know I originally called this meeting, but first I would like to give the Ehani a chance to speak."

There was some uneasy shifting as one Xalani—with chocolate skin and coarse black hair—and one Etlawa—with jet black skin and almost no hair—stood together at the front of the room. The Etlawa spoke first.

"My name is Tambu, from Ehani."

"My name is Xoris, from Ehani," the Xalani introduced.

"Late last night, there was an attack by the Borelians," Tambu went on. "Eight thousand Etlawa were killed, three thousand taken away to slavery. Two thousand Xalani also died, and a thousand more taken away. The Borelians relied on their superior weapons and the element of surprise. The only reason more were not killed or taken was our use of Time. But we know they will return. They will take more and they will kill more."

And that was that. They sat down. The two groups did not argue or bicker, though they did exchange a few nasty looks. The rest of them could only hope the two peoples were more resolved to fight the common enemy. It would be a good start, at least. Too bad fourteen thousand had to be sacrificed for it.

"Thank you," Walter said, stepping up. "Have there been any other attacks, or any other news that we should know about before we begin?"

No one spoke, though a number of uncertain glances swept around the room. Except the Tacagans who remained as impassive as ever.

"Very well. I've called you here because I would like to propose a plan of action. On Earth, it is very nearly New Year's Eve. If you don't know, that is a huge event. Millions of people gather in certain places all around the world to celebrate the new year and turning the calendar. If you take nothing else away, know that we are talking millions of people in one spot. They will be reckless, careless, and usually drunk or otherwise incapacitated and unable to defend themselves in any way.

"This will be quite possibly the largest target the Borelians have been presented with so far, or the largest that they will be able to attack." He gave a look to the Tacagans as they shifted snootily and turned up their noses. "If they do, it will only be mop up from there. We will not be able to fight back. If we can't fight back on a large or small scale, it will be open season, and the Borelians will have no reason to not swoop in and take all of us. But if we fight back now, before it gets to that point, it may give the Borelians enough pause to leave us alone long enough to come up with a slightly better and more effective plan. Or it could spark a full invasion of all worlds, which is the only real reason I called this meeting."

"Sounds like you went ahead and made the plans anyway without consulting anyone and have simply called us here to witness either your brilliance or, more likely, your stupidity," the male Tacagan Governor, Toros, sneered. "Why have you really called us here?"

Tommen saw a momentary flash of a Band slip between Walter and Kayla. Oddly enough, he had a pretty good idea what it was about. His suspicions were confirmed as Walter took a step back and said, "Well, would you care to come and explain things, then?"

Although his face was different, the smirk was still the same. The female Governor got a bewildered expression on her face as her counterpart stood and made his way to the front of the room. Her bewilderment turned to horror as Rifun shed his Disguise, an impostor all along. He looked back at her once and winked. She clearly had no idea what to make of it as her lips parted but no sound came out.

It was unnecessary anyway as the rest of the room made enough noise. Shouts, outrage, fits of fury and roars of disbelief. Tommen flicked his hearing aids into quiet mode and took it all in. Kayla and the Krydik were perhaps the calmest of the group, though their expressions were of undisguised hatred. Tommen watched Kayla send several murderous, threatening looks at Walter who kept his gaze firmly fixed on some blank spot on the wall.

Eventually, however, the noise quieted down. Rage can only be kept up for so long before it is replaced by exhaustion and, in this case, curiosity. Okay. Rifun was here. Why was he here? What was his purpose? What were his motives? Why had Walter brought him here?

"Thank you for the fanfare," Rifun began, bowing. "In the event that you simply went along with the mob and do not know who I am, my name is Rifun Ndolo, from Earth, former King of Time, and Faharoa of the First Order of the Akari and, more recently, the Akarin." He gave a look to Kayla who shot daggers at him with her eyes.

"Why have you brought him here?" the Mediterranean Dorigisi woman asked Walter hotly.

"I came of my own free will, thank you," Rifun answered. "Quite frankly, I have enough on my plate recently that only the sheer ingenuity of the plan and the challenge even got my attention. And as Walter has so kindly put it, I'm the only one crazy, stupid, and brilliant enough to pull it off."

"The plan is simple," Walter went on before anyone could interrupt. "The Borelians don't farm. They rely on slaves to tend their fields. Brelix is too unstable to allow for much, if any, agriculture, which means it has to be done off-world. Ninety-nine percent of their food is gotten this way. The idea is to go to one of these worlds and torch their fields, decimate their food supplies. We can't beat them on the battlefield, but if we can make the home world a higher priority, we may be able to get them off our backs for a short time.

"And it won't be humans pulling this off, either. We're the brains behind the operation, but we don't want to paint an even bigger target on our backs. Rifun's army is comprised of a multitude of species. Whatever Akari talents he and his army possesses—which you can debate amongst yourselves afterwards, the point is, it's more than just Time—it may be enough to get them in the door, do a hell of a lot of damage, and get out. It draws the Borelians back home, does not implicate humans on the whole, and his army may be able to fend off a retaliatory strike. If not, well..." Walter looked at Rifun and shrugged. "No skin off my back if it goes south for him."

Tommen saw stiff nods from Kayla and the Krydik.

"How do we know he won't turn on us?" someone asked.

"If I wanted to do that, I would not have to come here for this dog and pony show," Rifun informed him. "As Kayla and Tommen can attest to, I no longer hold any sway or pull with the Borelians. Not since the Wheel, and especially not since I murdered General Misik, among others, to get them out of my army before they became a problem. I am as much a wanted man as anyone here, though for more egregious reasons than simply being human."

"Yes, but why him?" another inquired. "Surely there must be others. The universe is a big place, after all."

"Crazy, stupid, brilliant, and with access to an army with enough power to have taken over the Wheel and the ones who overthrew him afterwards," Walter answered bluntly. "I'm not a fan of it either. He tried to kill me, tried to kill my son. But we need to use the resources available to us. If he's willing to send a team out to do this, I say let him. No humans will be involved. If the Borelians do know or find out that they're Cult—or Order, or whatever you're calling yourselves these days—then it will be seen as Cult activity. They've already got a bone to pick with them, so we ought to be in the clear, let the two of them fight it out. But I can't guarantee anything.

Like I said, if there was zero possibility that the Borelians would take out revenge on any of the human worlds, I wouldn't have called this meeting because we're looking at less than a day to get this done."

More grumbling. Rage mixed with discontented reasoning. He had a point. Tommen slowly let out a breath. Once again, Rifun was being set up as the hero.

Tommen found himself forcibly sucked into a very strong, tight Band, spearheaded by Kayla. She glared at him menacingly. "Did you know about this?"

He made a tight sound in his throat as he opened his mouth and answered, "I...yes. Yes, I did."

He fully expected her to go raging she-bear on him. Her posture certainly said she wanted to. But she restrained herself. "Why didn't you say anything?"

"What would you have wanted me to do? You think I could have just told Rifun to sit this one out? My dad talked to him about it before I could. They already had this in the works. I was just as in the dark as you were for the details."

Kayla continued her angry stare for a moment longer before throwing him out of the Band and releasing it.

"How do you expect to pull this off?" one of the Vin Lay asked grudgingly.

Rifun's expression turned into one Tommen had come to know as satisfaction, pleasure that his audience had submitted to him. He went to the front wall which also doubled as the smart board projector screen. An image came up of a planet. From above, it looked as though it had a very dense atmosphere and the surface, what could be seen of it, was rugged and not very friendly.

"Brelix is one of eleven planets in their system." As he spoke, the map zoomed out until it showed a more textbook drawing of a system. He began pointing and gesturing. "The Borelians are able to easily reach any of these planets, so they are easily-defended from above. Because the Borelian ships are either there constantly or can get there quickly, these worlds are populated and worked by the slaves they trust the least. Keep your friends close and your enemies closer." He shot a look at Walter.

The map zoomed out and moved to a neighboring system. "This is the Theridan System, or so they call it. It's their closest neighbor. Of the eight planets, five are under Borelian control, one is uninhabitable, and two are allies inasmuch as neither one can conquer the other, so it's more of a stalemate. The Borelians are always on the lookout for enemies looking to supply their slaves and try to start an uprising; these worlds will also be well-defended."

Another zoom out and move to a third system. "The Othmin System will be the target. Nine planets. Two uninhabitable, one struggling to tame their planet's wilds, but all under Borelian control. There are no enemies in the same system, which means they're not expecting their upstairs neighbors to smuggle in weapons. It is also farther away than the Theridan System, which means it takes longer for reinforcements to arrive. Two of the enslaved worlds are mediocre at best, as far as farming and production goes. Enough to make it worthwhile to generally farm, not good enough to invest a whole lot of new infrastructure.

"The other four are lush farming utopias. Because of isolation, distance, and how useful these planets are, these worlds are worked by the slaves the Borelians trust the most. That means fewer slaves because they are more hard-working, more efficient. And fewer guards."

"Wouldn't it be better to attack one of the worlds with the less-trusted slaves and the enemies to hand?" one of the Sakarians inquired.

Rifun shook his head. "No. Those worlds do not contribute as much to Borelian food supplies. They are rugged, difficult worlds. More prison camp than farmland. It may start some kind of revolt, maybe spark a skirmish between them and their neighbors, but they would only have to dispatch a few additional resources to put it down and get everything back to rights. It may not even register as a real or uncommon problem. For all we know, such revolts could be a fairly common occurrence, in which case we have accomplished nothing.

"By going after a major food source, we can cripple them for a longer period of time. It may not start a slave revolt there, but if word gets back around to those outer worlds—through the chain of command and daily soldiering news—and those slaves hear about it, that someone managed to attack a major Borelian stronghold, it could start a chain reaction. Maybe, maybe not, I would consider it icing on the cake."

"If the slaves on this world truly are loyal, what if they attack you?" someone asked.

Rifun shrugged. "It means they have little or no Time training. What do you think is going to happen? I may be in this to help humanity, but I'm not going to tell my men to back down if someone attacks them. Besides, the fewer loyal slaves they have, the fewer drones we have to worry about."

"So what exactly is the plan?" Kayla wondered coldly. "Torching one corn field isn't exactly going to put them into a famine."

"You're right. But torching a couple thousand corn fields might. It will at least get noticed. I have enough men prepared to hit every major field and forest. They'll start in the minor fields and surrounding areas to draw attention away from the fiasco hitting the main areas. The details you don't need to know. I've tried to include as many different species as possible to confuse the Borelians and not focus the attention on any one species. Furthermore, as much as I would love to be there and burn the planet myself, I will refrain from going so there are no humans involved whatsoever. This should not come back on Earth or any human planet. If it does come back on anyone, it will be the Order."

"And what do we owe you afterwards?" Logan challenged, sounding very much like Saul in that moment. "I have a hard time believing you're going to be that selfless."

"Seeing how we're on a tight schedule and we all have something of a vested interested in the success of this mission, how about we leave discussion of payment for afterwards?"

There was some uncomfortable shifting in the room, but no one really wanted to press the issue. While it was disconcerting that Rifun was going to hold off on demanding payment until afterwards, it only brought the attention back to the fact that they just didn't have time to negotiate this. It was a bad day when their only hope of survival came from a psychopathic maniac.

Was he really their only hope, though? Maybe now, considering the short notice. But what about afterwards? If they did manage to buy themselves a little time, could they put out something like a Help Wanted ad?

Position: Savior of humanity. Job description: Helping us beat the Borelians. Pay: Negotiable. Tommen let out a breath. Rifun was probably their only hope. Crazy, stupid, and brilliant. Humanity was doomed one way or the other. If they weren't standing on the Borelian auction block, they'd still have Rifun sitting over them one way or another. More than that, if they did end up defeating the Borelians, Rifun might just find his way back into the Seat of the Hands.

Fucking hell.

"So you just expect us to trust that you're going to do what you say you're going to do?" someone was saying.

Rifun folded his arms. "Quite frankly, I've never not done what I've said I'm going to do. You just don't always like what I say I'm going to do. I am many things, but not a liar. If I say I will or will not do a thing, I will or will not do that thing. If I say that I have men ready and willing to go out and attack the Borelians, you can rest assured that they will do just that."

"How do we know you won't betray us and strike up some kind of bargain or alliance with them?"

"I'm sorry, there must be a Sound Shield in here somewhere. I have no influence with the Borelians. In case you haven't noticed, I am no longer in charge of the Wheel. They consider it a breach of contract. Furthermore, I murdered one of their leading generals, and only just barely. Let me tell you something, it's no walk in the park to tangle with a yellow Borelian in hand-to-hand combat, trying to kill him while you're vomiting blood. Some call me a coward, I call it saving my skin when I can, but I don't enjoy picking fights I don't think I can win."

"You do think you can win, then?" another person asked.

Rifun said something to Walter which Tommen couldn't catch. Judging by his dad's expression, it was some comment that he reluctantly agreed with.

"Yes. I do think I can pull this off. Whether we win the war in the end remains to be seen."

"What do you want from us, then?" Logan asked stiffly. "Not as payment, what do you expect us to do while you're off on this noble, selfless quest of yours?"

"I detect a hint of sarcasm in your voice. As to your question, I expect all of you to sit down, shut up, and stop whining. I'm doing you a favor. Don't send advance word to the enemy, don't try to help, don't try to sabotage my men, and carry on with your New Year's celebrations as planned. Or, seeing how Earth is the only one with a major holiday today, go about your normal business. As most of you have said in one way or another—and I'm sure all of you have thought it at least once—you wouldn't care if I died or if my men failed and were sold into slavery themselves. You hate us. Quite honestly, you have nothing to lose at this point by trying."

"Our dignity," someone said.

"The alternative is Borelian slavery. Dignity has nothing to do with it. Now then, we could stand here all day going round and round in circles, making threats, looking for assurances, and absolutely nothing would come of it. The only thing that I can promise is that my men will do it, and they'll do their damnedest to cause as much damage as possible. No humans will be involved. If it comes back on anyone, it will be me and the First Order." His tone was irritable. "Now then, if we're done with the threats, insults, and mindless questions, I have work to do."

"I have a question," Kayla said icily. "Why the hell don't you just die?"

Rifun's expression turned unreadable, though it resembled amusement. "If you are referring to the fatal chest wound, I don't know except that perhaps the Author kept me alive so that I can help save humanity from this impending doom. After all, if there were others out there you could call, I think you would have done it by now." He gave another sweeping bow just for her. "Until we meet again, Aklaq White Bear." He winked. "Balabinov."

Only Tommen and Blake's quick reflexes kept Kayla in her seat. Rifun smirked and left the room, head held high.

"I swear to Almighty God, the next chance I get..." Kayla growled. "And anyone who tries to interfere is going with him."

She did not look at Tommen, but her words were cold daggers aimed straight at him. His grip loosened a bit and she wrested away from him, standing angrily and storming out of the room. The Wolf brothers whispered to each other, their posture saying they were debating whether to go after her. Or that's what Tommen told himself. If that was their debate, they obviously decided it best to let her alone.

"Why would you do this?" one of the Dorigisi asked of Walter. "Why would you put our fate in that man's hands?"

"Because I don't know what else to do," Walter answered hotly. "I don't see anyone else coming up with ideas. Trebald and Treman are gone. Ehani has been attacked. The rest of you, if you haven't been attacked already, you will. Maybe you all are content with sitting around and waiting for the invasion, but I'm not. I've survived Borelian poison. I want to know why and how. Earth humans are the ones who discovered a cure for the poisons. Earth humans are the ones looking for ways to beat our enemy. I'm forced to wonder what the hell the rest of you are doing with your time. Defenses aren't enough. No wall lasts forever. We have to take the fight to them. That's what I intend to do. Do I like asking Rifun for help? Do I want to ask him for help? Not in the least. But we can't do nothing. We have to take what help we can get. Now then, unless someone has something constructive to add, I think we can consider this meeting adjourned."

Tommen was the first to leave, mostly because he was hoping to find a bathroom somewhere in the compound. He nearly wet himself when he walked out the door and heard Kayla's voice.

"I hope your dad knows what he's doing."

She stood with her back against the wall, just outside the door, arms folded.

"Believe me, you're not the only one," he found himself saying. "But he does kind of have a point. I mean, he probably would have gladly asked you guys, except...well, there was that whole defeat thing."

"Tommen, we were expecting some kind of New Year's attack even before the battle. Why not ask us then?"

"Political turmoil?"

He could see her grinding her teeth, displeased with his answer, even if there was an element of truth to it. Everything was happening at just the wrong time. Finally she pushed away from the wall and dropped her arms, just as Blake and Logan exited the meeting room. "I'm going back to Hlohi. We'll take care of things there. Let me know if you don't die."

She pushed past him, and she and the Wolf brothers made for the elevator. He watched her leave, unsure how he felt about the whole exchange.

What if he had let Rifun die? Would they still be having this discussion? It was unlikely they would have as much help; the Akarin hadn't exactly been human-friendly beforehand. If she, a human, had killed Rifun, and he, Tommen, had let him die without giving up the antidote, it was highly unlikely that the Order would have offered any help, regardless of their own standing with the Borelians.

Maybe there was an Author out there somewhere who recognized that they would be screwed if Rifun had died. They didn't want to ask him for help, didn't want to be in his debt or anywhere near that bank, but they needed his crazy, stupid brilliance. But did that mean that Rifun and the journals were right, and the Akarin and the Authored Books were wrong? Certainly any omnipotent being could do whatever the hell he or she wanted to do, but when speaking of such high stakes, was it really smart to give the enemy that much credit? Just where was this story going? How did it end?

More to the immediate crisis, did that mean that there really were no other options? Was there no one else out there—in the whole, bloody universe—who could stand up to the Borelians in the same way, and were willing to do so, not only for themselves, but for a foreign race they knew nothing about and were inferior in probably every way? The honest answer was probably...no. No one was coming to help them. The only ones who could were ruthless, reckless, bloodthirsty mercenaries led by a madman.

Tommen walked back into the room where most of the delegations were immersed in their own private grumbling sessions. Most of the translators had been removed, making each conversation relatively private, but Tommen kept his in just so he could keep an ear out for anything strange or otherwise interesting or noteworthy. His dad was in deep conversation with the Tacagan Governor, so he picked a corner and waited, observing the room and keeping an eye on things. If his phone would have worked, he might have browsed the Internet a little to give himself some cover; his watching over the room and its inhabitants wasn't exactly discreet.

No one came to speak to him. And while he did not see anyone obviously whispering and pointing like he might see at school—the passive aggressive way of letting someone know you're talking about them while still pretending to be discreet about it—his paranoia said that they were talking about him. And why not? His dad was the one who just proposed a veritable alliance with Rifun. Tommen was also a known associate, whether by choice or duress, didn't matter because he'd publicly saved the man's life. Just what were they up to, the three of them?

It was a disconcerting thought, really, that Rifun could manipulate those he'd wronged the most and get them to need him and ally themselves with him. Tommen let out a breath. He had to find a way to get out from under the man's thumb. The problem was, the only way that seemed plausible involved, well, getting more involved. Getting closer to slit his throat in the night, as he had once put it. Tommen had little desire to get close to the man in any sense, and if saving his life in front of all his men didn't win him some points, he doubted anything he did would.

By now, some of the groups were breaking up and leaving. Most of the delegations pointedly ignored Walter or cast him dirty looks. The only ones who seemed any kind of thoughtful or curious or even hopeful, were the Vin Lay. They graciously thanked Walter and Do Chien for their hard work and best attempts at saving humanity. Once they had gone, the only ones left in the room were Tommen, his dad, and the engineer.

"That went better than expected, actually," his dad declared, sighing. "I was fully prepared for a riot. Even some rotten tomatoes or other vegetables."

"We are treading very dangerous waters, forming an alliance with that man," Do Chien said worriedly. He sighed but nodded slowly. "And yet, as you said, we must use all our available resources. If he is willing to help, then we cannot turn him down out of our own sense of pride or self-righteousness, for none of that will matter if we are standing on the auction block waiting to be sold."

"Agreed. And I didn't bring this up in the meeting just because it's a side issue that I didn't want any input on, but they also have orders—or a request, I should say, I suppose—to capture a *vodrak* or else obtain oil samples from as many Borelians as possible, so you can continue your work."

The doctor looked uncertain. "I can see why you didn't want to bring that up, and yet, while it would let me continue my work, is that really wise? Perhaps if we found equal footing in this war, but right now, they still have all the advantage. *Vodraks* are either revered or expelled. What happens if they kidnap one who is revered?"

"Then I guess Tacaga gets a stunning opportunity to show off its planetary defenses."

"So, assuming this works," Tommen interrupted, "and they

burn all the Borelian corn fields and whatnot, stave off an attack tonight, when are the Tacagan teams supposed to finish up the defenses on Earth?"

His dad folded his arms and shifted his stance. "Well, there was a little back and forth about the whole thing after you gave up the antidote—apparently union-like influence isn't limited to Earth, much to our dismay—but the teams are back working on it. They're predicting March 1st as their online date, assuming they can still keep it quiet and fudge enough classified documentation to keep global governments satisfied. If someone goes sniffing, it could be longer."

"How difficult is that going to be? To keep it quiet."

"It's the government. What they should know, they don't, or they say they don't. What they shouldn't know, they can't keep their noses out of while still saying they don't care. Could go either way."

It wasn't reassuring.

"Anyway," Walter continued, "I need to get some more sleep, get ready for work. Tommen, you have to go to work. I think it's time we were heading home."

They said their farewells to Do Chien and left the laboratory floor. They waited at the elevator for half a second before the doors opened. To their surprise, the escort was not there, but Rifun was. Cautiously, Tommen and his dad got in the confined space and waited for the doors to close.

"So," Rifun began, "here we are. The question is, why are we here, really? Do you honestly believe you need my help?"

"If I didn't think so, I never would have asked," Walter told him sternly.

"I see. But you would still like to see me dead, whether by your hand or someone else's, you don't care."

"You deserve it."

"Well then, here I am."

Walter shook his head. "I'm not an idiot. I learn from my mistakes. You'd lay me out flat without breaking a sweat. Even Kayla proved that you have to be taken by surprise."

"Then why continue to hold a grudge if you can't act on it?"

"Do I really need to remind you of your crimes?"

"Seeing how you seem to enjoy recounting them every time we meet..."

"Then why do I need to remind you again? How do you not understand why some people might be a little irritated with you?"

Rifun shifted his stance. "Everyone loves to make the conversation about me. While I'm flattered, let's consider you for a moment, you and your little hero gang. You took two of my fingers, killed my business partner, killed my lover, took my kingdom, tried to foil an attempt to rescue my friend, and stabbed me in the chest with a poisonous knife."

"You ordered the deaths of millions, if not more."

"And as I have pointed out to Tommen, you want to do the same thing to the Borelians. So who's really in the right here? I could point out any number of men that you yourself have delivered to the grave. Did you ever get what you 'deserved' for it? Did you bow your head meekly so they could put a rope around your neck? No, you ran. You escaped. And now you play cop in an effort to scrub your record with deeds, rather than justice."

"You murdered billions of innocents in cold blood."

"Hardly. There are always casualties in war. Sorry to say, they're not always the enemy soldier; sometimes there are civilians in the mix. But if you are going to apply that logic, then walk into any VA clinic and indict the men sitting there with hollow stares and shaking hands."

Walter shifted and folded his arms. "Do you regret what you did, then?"

"I regret that it had to happen, but I don't regret that it did. When Casey Oldman ousted half the city department, do you think he wanted to do it? Do you think he wanted to be so short-staffed, some of his guys were pulling twenty-hour shifts until replacements arrived? He regrets that it had to happen, but he doesn't regret that it did. He removed his greatest rivals and was able to bring in his buddies. The political fallout was great, but for now, the whole department is one body under one chief, not divided between squabbling captains and other higher officers. What good is a takeover if your enemies are allowed to remain where they are with all their disgruntled followers ready to stab you in the back and maybe even get more people killed out in the field when solidarity really matters?"

"A hostile takeover of the Wheel."

"So indict Genghis Khan. Indict the Christian Crusaders. Indict the Muslims. Indict China. Indict Great Britain and Spain and Portugal conquering the world and its native peoples. Indict France; I certainly have. Indict every civilization in history. The only reason you think I'm the bad guy is because you were on the sorry receiving end and I was overthrown in the end. History is written by the victor. You ought to know that. But who are you to judge which side is right? Micaiah collapsed a lot of portals in the Wheel which isolated us there. Isolation breeds paranoia. Cut off from the Wheel, you could concoct all sorts of terrible things I was doing hiding in my castle. Cut off the from the Wheel now, because of the Borelians, you can concoct all sorts of terrible things going on, when nothing has really changed because humans aren't much of a presence, never were."

"You murdered—"

"Then I guess I'll just call off my men from torching the Borelian corn fields. Granted, one act in itself will not cause the downfall of their civilization, but if it works, humans are going to be jumping on this idea, and others. And just think, you would have been the mastermind behind it all, if and when the Borelians start dying—from starvation, from battle, doesn't matter. And then what, hm? I never actually killed anyone in the Wheel during my reign. I may have given the order, but I never touched anyone. This all goes down with the Borelians, what separates me from you, hm? Is it because of our preconceived notion of evil, that the Borelians are a blight that must be wiped from the universe? They see us the same way. We're enemies; it's what happens. Same with the Order and the Akarin. History is written by the victor, and the Author is one who decides the victor.

"Dust and logs, Walter. Given the state of things and what I listed earlier, I might be a little irritated with you." Rifun lifted his right hand for emphasis even as he released the Band he'd erected around the elevator car. "But I've decided to forgive and put it behind me for the sake of this little endeavor we've got going on." The elevator stopped at its destination and the doors opened. Rifun stepped out first. "Now if you'll excuse me, I have some corn fields to burn."

By the time Walter and Tommen stepped off the elevator, he was gone. They met up with their escort halfway to the train station and boarded quietly.

"I feel like I should have said something," Tommen mused as the doors closed and they sat down.

His dad shook his head. "No. Being quiet was the smartest thing you could have done. You've already drawn enough attention to yourself as his associate. It was good to stay quiet and let me take some of the heat this time."

"I don't like being quite 'that' associated with him. It was bad enough when he got stabbed, now this."

"I know. As a last-minute notice, it may be the best we can do. If it works, maybe we can buy ourselves enough time to find more allies who aren't him."

Tommen nodded wordlessly.

"What's on your mind?"

"Tell you when we get home."

Tommen could see his comment made the escort uncomfortable, as they shifted in their seats and merely cold gazes turned absolutely icy. Still, their short train ride came to an end and they disembarked, each man grabbing a bike and starting off into the streets.

Clouds had gathered over the city. Once they got to the bridge and could look north up the river, the clouds turned absolutely black, and a wall of rain made its way closer and closer. His dad suggested they hurry, and Tommen readily agreed. The gate guards never gave them any trouble on the way out, and today was no exception. As they crossed the threshold into open country and made their way to their usual portal site, it began to sprinkle, and the flat wall of rain was less than a mile out. Thunder rumbled overhead and a lightning bolt touched down on the water. Walter opened a portal with Tommen lending strength, just as he'd been taught to do. The two of them stepped through just before the bulk of the storm hit them.

The first thing they did upon arriving home was grab a couple towels to generally pat themselves dry. They hadn't gotten soaked, but neither wanted to be wet when they went out into frigid temperatures.

"All right," his dad said, tossing his towel in the washer. "You said to wait until we got home. What's on your mind?"

Tommen shifted uncertainly, then asked, "If you got the chance to kill him, would you? If he was laid out before you and completely helpless, would you kill him?"

"Are you asking generally, or making a specific request?"

"Asking generally."

"Quite honestly, I'm not sure. If it involved a fight, war, something in the heat of the moment, I probably would. But I'm not a cold-blooded killer anymore, or that's what I tell myself. I really don't know how to answer that question. Why?"

"You're right that he has to be taken by surprise, but there is one thing that does take him by surprise."

"What's that?"

"The poison that Kayla used on the knife was a toxin called urlo. It causes headaches, seizures, that sort of thing, and it made it a little difficult for the physicians to heal him physically. But that was a week and a half ago, and he's still having seizures. Julianna has to cover them up so he doesn't appear weak in front of his men, but he does have them. I don't know if they'll go away in time or what, but while he's down, he's helpless."

His dad folded his arms. "Are you sure?"

"I haven't actually seen it myself. Like I said, Julianna has to cover them up by Banding him. The way I figured it, Borelian poison is immune to Time and he's already been healed, so this has to be some naturally-occurring side effect."

"Interesting."

"So, would you do it? If he'd had a seizure on the elevator, without Julianna to cover it up, would you have killed him?"

Now his dad faltered a bit. "Probably not. He's still our best bet at surviving New Year's Eve."

"And what if, afterwards, we can't find any other allies, only him?"

"Then maybe we can turn this around. You know about his seizures and how hard he's working to cover them up. If he's worried about his army abandoning him because of it, maybe we can use it as blackmail. We'll keep it under wraps from his men and we won't kill him if such an opportunity arises, but he answers to us. Similarly to how he was trying to use me and you against each other, threaten to kill one to gain the cooperation of the other."

Tommen frowned. "He's not afraid of death, but he's not going through the trouble of hiding it for nothing. It's a small bit of leverage, but it might be enough to nudge him one direction or the other going forward."

"We'll need to think it through a little more before actually trying anything, but it's something to keep in the back of the mind." He glanced at the clock. "But for right now, we both have to think about our respective workplaces. I'll see you in the morning."

Chapter Six
Stranger Discussion

Walter went to work feeling not a little anxious. It was easy to pass it off as general anxiety and resignation over having to work New Year's Eve; certainly he wasn't the only one groaning about how they weren't going to get off until noon. But he was the only one worried about an alien invasion. Well, to be fair, he didn't exactly take a poll of his coworkers to find out. Eric was a little questionable on the sanity part; he could easily be worrying about an impending alien invasion.

"Evening, Walt," Kate greeted from her desk as he walked by her office. "Ready for a fun-filled night?"

"That starts tomorrow, doesn't it? When everyone is hungover, pregnant, and miserable?"

"Ah, you sound like you've done this before."

"Only from the city side, and that's about as much excitement as I can take."

"Well then you're in for a real treat."

"That's what I'm afraid of."

She stood and moved around her desk. "The good news is that just for safety and because it always ends up this way, we go in pairs. Never fails, you're going to get at least one call where you need a second person. Most don't escape without having two calls like that."

Walter nodded. "Sounds good to me. Do we get to pick our teams or has the teacher assigned them already?"

"Teacher's assignment. You'll be out with Vin."

"Assuming he doesn't call in sick."

"No, he's here. I've already seen him. I think he just went to the bathroom. Anyway, better get out there before the crazies come out to play."

"What are you talking about? The crazies are already here."

He grabbed the keys to a cruiser and was just walking down the hall to the back door when he ran into Vin just walking out of the bathroom.

"Hey," Vin said. "Did Kate tell you?"

"We're on assignment tonight," Walter said, nodding. "She told me."

"Cool. You got keys?"

"Right here."

"Sweet. Let's go."

From the half dozen times Walter had ever interacted with Vin, he had a pretty good idea what the guy was about, and he wondered why Kate had put them together. Vin was active, flamboyant, a bit of a smooth-talker, and excellent at moving quickly in order to make himself look busy in order to get out of chores or other responsibilities. According to some of the others, when his back was against the wall, he was an excellent officer. Problem was, he did everything he could in order to avoid being in that situation and pawn it off on someone else.

"So, I went to the casino today," Vin was saying. "Wife said I could take fifty bucks and go have fun, so I did. You know what happened?"

"You lost every penny?" Walter guessed.

"Nah, man, I won me five hundred dollars."

"And I'm sure you bought your wife a diamond ring and your new son a gold pacifier."

"Not quite. Oh, Tammy got her fifty bucks back and I picked up a couple packages of diapers, but I went and had me a couple drinks, too. Expensive ones. You ever had a forty dollar glass of beer?"

"No, and I don't intend to, but I imagine it tastes the same as a four dollar glass of beer."

"Damn right it does, but it's the psychology of it, you know? I had me a forty dollar beer."

Walter did not reply. He didn't need to because Vin kept on trucking.

"Oh, and I got me a lead on a job. Not, you know, replacing the department or nothing, but as a side gig, you know? Make a little extra cash to take care of the kid. Kids are expensive, dude. Course, you know all about that, don't you? Anyway—"

"What's your son's name? I don't know that I ever heard."

"Barnabas. Barnabas Oliver."

"Uncommon name."

"Tammy wanted something a little unusual. As luck would have it, both her dad and granddad have unusual names. Barnabas is her granddad, Oliver's her dad. Worked out perfect."

"Sounds like it. How old is he?"

"Gonna be three months next week." Vin jabbed him in the ribs. "Got any advice for me? You know, old pro to newbie?"

"Old pro? Just how old do you think I am? And anyway, I only have one kid."

"Yeah, but still a kid. How was it for you?"

Walter raised a brow. "I don't have any newborn or infant experience." *Or none that I'm proud of, nor that I can logically explain.*

"But your son—"

"Is adopted. I got him when he was eight years old. Hit me up then if you want advice."

"So...you were never married?"

Long before you were born. "No."

"And you were a cop when you got him? How the hell did you manage that with the courts?"

"Tommen is my nephew. His pa was my younger brother."

"Oh, one of those. Abuse? I mean, if you don't want to tell, that's fine, it's none of my business." His tone said he wanted it to be his business, regardless of what Walter thought about it.

"He died. Carbon monoxide poisoning. Him, his wife, their kids, all except for Tommen who had run away and was out of the house that night."

"Aw shit. Dude, I am so sorry. You know, I had a buddy back in high school—"

Walter was mercifully saved by the radio squawking and sending them on some domestic dispute call. No weapons involved—yet—and no physical altercation—yet. By the time they arrived, the verbal argument had turned into a shoving match that was just about to turn into full fisticuffs. The men were too drunk to know better than to be afraid of the blues, and Vin didn't appear smart enough to keep his motormouth shut and very nearly caused a fistfight himself.

Walter was the one who got the situation back under control, writing both men a ticket for public intoxication and telling them that if he came back, they'd be spending the night in a cell. He called a cab for one and the other had his girlfriend help him back inside the house. Once all was clear, Walter and Vin vacated just as soon as they possibly could, stopping in a quiet alcove a couple miles down the road to finish up the paperwork. But when Walter put the car in park, he turned to Vin.

"Now, maybe it's because I'm new or I don't work with you a lot, but—"

"I know, I know," Vin said, rubbing his eyes. "I let myself go too far and it was unacceptable. I could have made a bad situation worse, I understand."

"Do you? You've been on the force for, what, four years? Cops develop habits over time, a way of doing things. I don't think that was the first time you've let your mouth go."

"It's not. I'm trying to be better about it, I am. I was doing better, and then the baby came and life is super hectic. I mean, kids change things, but babies change things a lot because they're so darn small and helpless and it's a lot riding on my shoulders. Then Tammy and I had an argument before I came in and it's New Year's Eve... I'm sorry. I'll do better."

"I don't know if you're into prayer, meditation, happy place, whatever," Walter said sternly, "but you need to find whatever works for you. Yeah, it's New Year's. It sucks. Believe me, I would much rather be sitting at home right now. But we're here and we need to act professionally because, obviously, no one else is."

Vin nodded. "I understand. I get it. I'll try to do better."

Walter felt as if he were giving a scolding to a rookie ride along, not a four-year veteran of the force. Vin should be telling him how things were done out here on New Year's Eve. Nevertheless, his piece was said. All that remained was to see how the rest of the night went. He rummaged around for a pen, sorted the paperwork, took a drink of coffee, and hoped he could do more than get comfortable before the next call came down.

Apparently his had his hopes set too high. He'd no sooner written "We" than the radio squawked and an overworked dispatcher came over the high band, telling them about some drunk and disorderly going on at one of the local backwoods bars. Information was scarce, but dispatch quickly moved on to the next caller in line.

"Okay," Vin said. "I know, I gotta keep it reined in. It's New Year's Eve, everyone is going to be drunk and disorderly and argumentative. Most of them probably won't even remember it in the morning. They just wake up in jail and wonder what the hell happened."

"Do you always pep talk yourself like this?" Walter asked.

"I was just letting you know that I am totally focused for this one."

"Let me know by showing me."

That got him to shut up at least. Walter kept his mouth shut and his thoughts to himself, telling himself that he would handle the situation alone if he had to, and he wasn't going to babysit this guy. How he had survived this long was a mystery.

The bar wasn't too far away, but by the time they got there, a pretty good fight was brewing. According to witnesses, two dudes—who supposedly had never met before in their lives—had been drinking and got into a game of billiards. The bets started out with drinks. Then with cash. One of the guys was kicking butt and collecting a ton. Not every game, but enough. Finally the challenger who was losing says game over, no more cash, no more drinks, he surrenders. The winner says he has one more thing he can bet, and that's his hot girlfriend. Loser says no way in hell, but the girlfriend, who is equally as intoxicated, says to go for it.

Well, winner wins yet again, demands his prize. He forcefully kisses the girlfriend, starts stripping her right there in front of everyone, the pool table his location of choice. Girlfriend goes along with it, loser gets pissed. Then it comes out that the winner and the girlfriend used to date in high school and had rigged the whole thing. Girlfriend knew the loser was terrible at billiards and the winner great, so they concocted a little scheme to get back together, humiliate the loser, and apparently have sex in front of everyone.

To the absolute shock and awe of everyone gathered, the loser boyfriend was not too thrilled with this, and where he was terrible at billiards, he was excellent at fighting. The winner, well, he was pretty good at fighting, too. By the time Walter and Vin arrived, the men had taken it outside and were tussling something fierce on the ground in the wet, muddy parking lot. Vin offered to call for backup. Walter's first instinct was to tell him to stop being a coward and get in the game. Then he considered that backup might be more than a couple minutes away, and he agreed even as he stalked up to the two men. Using some of his experience in bar brawls both from the criminal and police side of things, as well as a few clever Time tricks, he managed to subdue both men on his own.

That is, until the girlfriend decided to get rowdy and try to jump him from behind. The only reason he wasn't taken completely by surprise was because he heard her coming across the parking lot. He got her down as gently as he could seeing how she was a woman and not very big, but it still wasn't good enough. Self-defense be damned, both men became upset that he'd touched the girl they were fighting over. One managed to jump his cuffs while the other struggled to his feet to try to...headbutt Walter to death? He wasn't sure. He didn't care. He was sick of this game. He was too old for this shit.

Thankfully, the girl stayed where he'd put her so he could deal with the angry boyfriends, putting all three of them in the backseat of the cruiser with the girl between them to hopefully keep the beatings to a mere tongue-lashing. No sooner had he closed the door than backup arrived. Kate was the first one out, followed by Gary.

"Oh, sure, now you show up," Walter said, breathing heavily. "Where's your respect for your elders?"

"In the fact that we showed up to help, not kick your ass," Kate replied jokingly. "All right, what do we got?"

He explained the situation. Kate nodded along and decided to take the winner boyfriend. The loser and his girlfriend could have a nice awkward ride to the jail. Walter was more than happy to oblige, and they all made their way back to the office, meeting up afterwards in the break room for coffee, donuts, and a quick first lunch.

"Sometimes I wonder how the human race has advanced so far," Walter mused.

"No shit," Gary agreed. "But then, more advancements are made during war than peacetime. A lot of wars have been started over women."

They made a bit of small talk before packing up and getting ready to head back out.

"Kate, do you mind if I speak with you privately for a second?" Walter asked once Vin had left the room.

"Sure. In my office."

He followed her to her office and shut the door. Before he could speak, she beat him to it. "I know what you're going to say. Vin is pretty damn useless."

"How has he lasted four years on the force?"

"Finesse, charisma, the ability to charm his way out of responsibilities and punishment, and because his rich uncle is on the board. As long as Vin is on the force—barring a definite illegal act or other unethical behavior—we get whatever the hell we need. Otherwise, we'd still be running the Panda Police at half a million miles. Ask the fire department and the ambulance, too. Vin's cousin is on one, his other cousin with the other. Problem is, we asked for a knife and got the spoon."

"Why did you assign him to me? Or me to him?"

"Quite frankly, because I'm hoping you rub off on him. You're a go-getter. But maybe that's the problem. Maybe I need to assign him a rookie so he's forced to do something, show someone the ropes."

Walter shook his head. "He'd just make the rookie show him what he learned, offer no help, and give a lecture about it afterwards. There's always a way out of doing work. Always."

"Well, here's a tip. And since I'm in charge tonight, you can blame me if it gets back to Mr. Rich Uncle. Give him orders. I don't care that you're the new hire. He needs it. Give him orders, make him do something. If he complains, tell him to call me and I'll tell him the same thing. You did an exemplary job subduing three guys—well, two guys and a girl—on your own, but you shouldn't have to, not when help is literally ten feet away and half your age."

"You had me until that last bit."

"I'm serious, Walt. He wants to look good. I want him to work. Find me some way to get both out of him." She sighed and shook her head. "Come on. Better get out there before something too terrible happens."

Walter followed her out of the office and met back up with Vin, saying, "Why don't you drive this time out?"

Thankfully, the man didn't seem to have a problem with that. Maybe he thought he was going to star in some movie where a cop does a slow, heroic drive-by, pushes his sunglasses down a little, then resumes his cruise.

They didn't even make it out of the parking lot before they were called out for a vandalism. That resulted in half a dozen MIPs and Furnishings for a group of nineteen to twenty-five year old guys egging and spray painting someone's house.

This was quickly followed by a sexual assault case where a man, fully sober, tried to rape his drunk girlfriend. That turned into a small fiasco because the girlfriend, understandably, only wanted to talk to a female officer and female medics. Problem was, females were not only a minority on both ends, but all presently busy with other calls, and it took the better part of an hour just for one to become available. Then it was another forty-five minutes before Kate arrived, looking haggard and still running from her last call. Walter stopped her, got her calmed down, then let her in the front door to meet her victim.

He simply stood by on that one, making sure that only women went in the house. Once they were all packed up, the ambulance transporting the woman to the nearest hospital, Walter and Vin were on their way once again.

It was only ten o'clock.

As if the general anxiety around the New Year's shenanigans wasn't enough, Walter also had the extra fun of worrying whether any call was going to turn out like the trailer. And if that wasn't bad enough, he also had to worry about whether Rifun's plan—and by Rifun's plan, it was really his plan—would work, and whether it would stem the invasion or speed it up. Well, he didn't have to worry about it, seeing how he could do nothing to influence it now and he would be as powerless as the rest of them to stop a full invasion, but worry he did.

Most of the calls they responded to were public intox, usually resulting in stupid things like drunk driving and vandalism, occasionally spilling into the realm of domestic or sexual assault.

Walter did his best to follow Kate's orders by giving Vin orders, and he did his best to word them in such a way that the man would have no choice but to do some kind of work other than calling for backup and mopping up afterwards. Sometimes he was successful. Most of the time, Vin still managed to finagle his way out of doing anything really difficult or otherwise resembling work.

By about midnight, Walter had had enough and stopped giving orders. Let the man be the backup and mop up; Walter would handle everything on his own if he had to, just as if he were out on his own. Maybe if he stopped including Vin, then the kid would notice. But if not, just carry on like normal.

Between midnight and two was when things really started ramping up, especially the drunk driving and ensuing accidents as people left their parties and headed home, or went from the party to the after-party, sometimes with no break in between. The first accident Walter got called to for backup, a van into a tree, the driver and passengers—those who weren't ejected and unconscious—were still drinking and smoking their weed. They panicked when they realized what happened, then drank and smoked some more to try and forget about it.

Vin was again conspicuously absent from the crash site itself, but Walter carried on. He couldn't even be mad, really. Even just from a preliminary overview, he could see at least one fatality, possibly two. If a kid like Vin couldn't handle work, he probably couldn't handle death very well either.

And that wasn't the only fatality that night as their next call was a suicide. Sixteen year old male whose only new year's resolution was to kill himself. He managed to accomplish that within the first hour of the new year. It wasn't a pretty scene, either, an overdose or a hanging or something of that sort. This was the full 12-gauge in the mouth, head completely missing. Walter found he couldn't blame Vin for running out of the house to get sick; he felt a bit queasy himself.

The only thing that saved them from being there for the next eight hours was that the wife was related to or good friends with another one of the officers who came over right away and promised to take good care of the scene. That didn't mean there wasn't a shit ton of paperwork to do on it still, but they managed to get out of there a little after two.

"Why don't we head back to the station, get something to eat and drink and calm down a little?" Walter suggested. "You look a little pale."

Strictly speaking, Vin looked paler than Tommen, and he was still shaking. He looked at Walter. "You can look at something like that and still suggest we get something to eat?"

"Fine, don't eat. But get some water, anyway. And sit down for a few minutes to collect yourself. If you want, I can call Kate, see if she'll let you go home. I can call a CISM counselor, too."

Vin shook his head. "No, no, it's okay. I'll take the water and maybe a combat nap, if that's all right with you."

"You need it."

They returned to the station. Walter went to the break room to fill his coffee thermos while Vin stumbled down to the bathroom. They stayed there for a good twenty minutes. Walter got caught up on some of his paperwork, and Vin collected himself until he was slightly less annoying than he had been at the start of the night. Whether it was because he'd found some yoga zen mantra to calm himself down or it was a screen, Walter couldn't tell, but he did make a note to talk to Kate about getting the kid some help for it.

They started back out and managed to make it almost a mile and a half before getting their next call. Thankfully, it was an easy one. Actually, it was one they got on a routine basis. Widow White was calling because she heard something and thought a prowler was going to break into her house and steal her jewels. What she was hearing, most of the time, was the music from her nearest neighbor, half a mile up the road. That guy knew how to party, and he made sure everyone in a five mile radius partied with him.

On their way there, they made a pass by Mr. Jorin's house. Sure enough, the guy and two hundred of his closest friends were still partying like it was 1999. They might stop by there on their way back to check in and say hi and make sure everything was all right. But for now they scooted on down to the Widow White. Walter saw the flutter of a curtain as she looked out her window.

"Why don't you talk to her and I'll take a look around," Walter said. Vin readily agreed.

It was an easy enough task; the old lady was vicious with her tongue, but she was generally harmless. Vin skipped up the steps to the porch to meet her, his carefree, charming, ignorant demeanor of more use than Walter's gruff appearance and blunt attitude. So he clicked on his flashlight and went looking around the property.

Memories of the trailer flashed through his mind, and he looked back at Vin more than once. What if this was another trap? It was easy to slip into the same-old, same-old attitude with a same-old, same-old call. What if the Borelians were taking advantage of that?

But to what end? Why go through the trouble of setting up another single-victim incident, or maybe two or three, when they had places like Times Square they could pick from? It didn't make sense from any standpoint.

A stick cracked. Walter threw up a Band and looked around, shining his flashlight here and there. He didn't see anything. He told himself it was a deer. Or maybe one of the widow's cats.

"Boo."

The voice came from behind. In one less-than-fluid motion, he whirled around, drew his gun, and aimed. He was half a second from firing before a deadly grip sliced through his Band and clamped down on his right wrist. His grip faltered just enough that another hand was able to break the grip on his gun and snake around his left arm. He managed to confuse his attacker a little; instead of trying to pull away from the grip, he put his full weight behind a sudden shove. Rather than stumble back, however, his attacker went low, releasing his left arm and instead twisting around to grapple at his old right thigh injury. When Walter's leg reflexively jerked, his attacker went in for the takedown, crumpling his knees and getting him on his back.

But instead of continuing the fight, his attacker released his wrist and moved off several feet, chuckling. Walter knew that antagonizing laughter anywhere.

"You son of a bitch," he hissed, getting to his knees, finding his gun, and reholstering as he stood. "Did you enjoy that?"

"I have to admit, I did," Rifun said, still grinning. "I have to make sure you're still alert. After all, New Year's Eve is a pretty hectic night for you, isn't it? I saw your bar brawl earlier, and I will say that I was thoroughly impressed. I hope you get a commendation for that."

Walter brushed sticks and leaves from his uniform. "Why are you here? Is this another trap?"

"Not a trap that I know of, certainly not one set by me. Now, whether or not I was Mrs. White's potential prowler is another matter."

"If you wanted to talk, you could have just called."

"Yes, but I had to get you alone somehow."

"Great. Here I am. What do you want? Did your plan work?"

"Your plan, you mean. And yes, it worked. Seeing how my men were only ordered to start the fires and not to put them out, I imagine that most of them are still burning. It makes California look like a matchstick."

"Good." Walter nodded.

Rifun put a hand to his ear. "Do I hear a...?"

Walter sighed. "Thank you."

The man did a sweeping bow. "You are most welcome." He straightened. "Now then, I'm sure we'll all want to get back together for group therapy sometime soon to discuss what happened. We can also discuss the matter of my payment. Obviously, I am not speaking of monetary compensation, but favors and the like."

"Your payment," Walter interrupted, "is your secrecy."

Rifun raised a brow. "I'm sorry, I don't understand."

"Tommen told me about your seizures."

Now he folded his arms and shifted his stance uncomfortably. "What about them?"

"If you have to cover them up, it's because they're naturally-occurring, outside of whatever may have been done to you by the Borelian poison which was cured. You cover them up so as not to look weak, but also to minimize your vulnerability. If you dropped right now, you would have no defense if I decided to kill you. You don't like being helpless. How many people out there in the universe want to see you dead? Word gets out about your seizures and that vulnerability, and you'll have assassins practically at your doorstep, just waiting for you to go down. Not to mention what your men might think about you, their fearless leader, shaking uncontrollably, pissing himself on the floor."

Walter continued before Rifun could interrupt. "Payment for your services is keeping that secret. Only Tommen and I know—aside from Julianna and whomever else you've told, that's beyond us. We're willing to keep it that way. If you make a move against either of us or try to pull anything clever, well, Kayla might get a second shot at her revenge."

"And what's to keep me from killing both of you?" Rifun countered. "Men kill for information all the time. I have no real need for either of you. Neither of you is essential to anything I'm doing. You're not particularly useful anywhere else. You are special only to each other."

"Because you may be a cold-blooded killer, but you don't do anything senselessly. Kayla and a lot of others know that. You kill us, they'll go digging, looking for the reason why. It's only a matter of time before they figure it out, too. As it is, it may be only a matter of time before your little secret gets out anyway, just the luck of the draw when they decide to hit. But it won't come from me or Tommen."

He didn't like it when Rifun grinned. "Now you're negotiating. And what is it you expect from this little bargain?"

"A little cooperation would be nice."

"Cooperation? This does sound interesting. Please, explain."

"You seem pretty eager to go after the Borelians, maybe as a human, maybe as the Cult leader, whatever it is, you're in. You may or may not have heard, but there are rumors in the Wheel that you're gunning for the Zero Hour again, having taken out your greatest opponent."

Rifun nodded slowly. "Ah...I see...and you want me to make some special announcement or other spectacle that lets everyone know that I'm not, that I'm going after the Borelians solely. In fact, you want me to make a big deal about perhaps allying myself with the Hands, a joint venture as it were. Just as your son proposed, a three-way alliance between the Order, the Akarin, and the Hands, all joining noble forces and defeating the scourge of the universe, like a bad novel and worse movie.

"It's an interesting proposal to consider, and yet I have already rejected it. Even if we did do such a thing, rid the universe of the Borelian scum, we would merely devolve back into our petty arguments soon afterwards. I am not a destroyer, Walter; I am a conqueror. I do things my way. And before you say anything, it has worked out for me in the past, and I expect it will continue to work and get back on track now that I have, as you said, defeated my greatest opponent."

He shifted his stance, his tone turning serious but with a slightly nervous waver. "Now, as to the matter of my seizures, certainly the secret to end all secrets. I will make an effort to get the word out that the First Order is going after the Borelians. Anyone asks, we have a mutual interest alliance, the Order and the humans, brought together because I am both. I won't claim that you are my allies in the same way that Sadurnon was, we just happen to be working toward the same goal. Similarly, you will not seek to conquer or otherwise overthrow me and the Order. You're not going to storm my castle or sell the fortress schematics to the rebel alliance. If you do, well, Earth will see an invasion; it just won't be the Borelians.

"Furthermore, I expect you to not only guard my secret, but defend it. If Julianna were unavailable, such as right now, I would expect that you or your son would shield me if something happened."

"And about not going after the Wheel or the Zero Hour?" Walter asked, folding his arms.

"Let me put it this way, Walter. I've already conquered the Wheel once. I've conquered the Akarin. If I defeat the Borelians, what is the Time industry really going to do about it, even if they do discover my secret? I put the First Order in that position of power with that track record and no further enemies—or no credible threats is what I should say—they will fight to hang onto that power, regardless of whether I'm alive or dead. I am merely the cornerstone of that empire, the Founding Father if you will. I get them where they need to be, and they take it from there."

Walter shook his head, but could not deny it. More to the

point, there was nothing he could do about it. So far, Rifun was their best chance at defeating the Borelians; they just didn't have the ability to go it alone. Tacaga had the planetary defenses, but they couldn't huddle in their safe spots indefinitely. Eventually, they had to fight back.

"Well," he said at last, "it's like you said. I imagine we'll need to have a debriefing to discuss what happened and how to proceed. Perhaps in the next day or two, try to analyze how the Borelians are going to react. Once they've put out the fires."

"Indeed." Rifun shifted his stance, grinning. "See, this is more what I envisioned for that day at the warehouse. A little give and take, a little understanding—"

"You know why I couldn't do that. I stand by my decision."

"Hm, very well." He shrugged.

"And besides," Walter went on, "you made the first move by taking Tommen and killing Bravo Team. Yet we still won. And if you and I had been fighting instead of Isthim, none of that would have happened either."

Rifun gave him a knowing look. "And yet here we are. But that little saga took Tommen across the universe looking for a flower which has spawned this incredible endeavor to find a cure for Borelian poison."

"That would have happened anyway just based on this war."

"Would it have? The Borelians had it out for me as soon as I was overthrown. Because I associated more with the Order, their chances of declaring full war on the human race was smaller. Not negligent, but minimal, considering Micaiah, a human, led the charge against me. But searching for—and finding—a cure for the poison is a treasonous offense to the Borelians, a guarantee for war. So then we weigh the scales." Rifun put his hands out and shifted them up and down. "Tommen keeps his dad but forfeits the human race. Tommen loses his dad, and the chances of war are greatly lessened."

"If there is a chance of war either way, I think he's glad he chose me over the human race," Walter said smartly. "And besides, it may help us to be rid of the problem once and for all."

Even as he said it, Walter knew he'd just walked right into Rifun's trap. Agreeing with him. Getting on the same page or same wavelength. Alliance. Now that they were there, he was obligated to go along with it, including shielding Rifun's seizures from the general public.

Say one thing for Rifun. The man knew how to control a conversation. Probably would have made an excellent cop in another life. Or a politician.

"I'm glad we see things eye to eye," Rifun said. "Now if you'll excuse me, I have a few more things to take care of this evening."

With that said, he opened a portal and was gone, leaving Walter alone on Widow White's property, looking for a suddenly nonexistent prowler.

After a minute or two of consideration, Walter returned to the house. Vin and the widow had evidently gone inside, and Walter let himself in, knocking lightly and announcing his presence, mostly so the widow didn't freak out thinking it was the prowler, causing Vin to shoot first and ask questions later.

He found the two of them in the little breakfast nook having coffee and cookies, their conversation about how good new babies smell, obviously referencing Vin's newborn as well as a new great-grandson for the widow, born just a few weeks ago. Vin looked up as Walter entered the room and stood.

"I see you were acting as a bodyguard," Walter observed dryly. "No sign of any prowler, just the neighbors up the road with their loud music and louder partying."

"Those boys should turn down that loud music," the widow huffed. "They'll be deaf before they turn forty."

"I think that's why they turn it up so loud is because they are deaf," Vin told her lightly.

Nevertheless, Vin thanked her for the coffee and cookies, and Walter assured her that everything was fine, but if she felt uncomfortable, she could always call them back. The widow was kind enough to top off their thermoses and send them with half a dozen cookies each. Then they got in the cruiser and backed out of the driveway.

"I can tell you're thinking something, Walt," Vin said. "I know I probably screwed up—"

"Shut up, Vin," Walter interrupted. "Just stop talking. It's fine to make nice with people and win a little PR, but you let your guard down. For one, your back was to the door and windows. If something had happened to me and an armed intruder had gone in—and he would not have announced himself as I did—you would be dead. Assuming you did encounter such an armed intruder, maybe you wouldn't be. Because nothing I have seen tonight makes me trust you or think that you're going to have my back when something goes down. Did you just sit back and watch while I took on the bar brawlers and the girlfriend?"

"I called for backup."

"That takes fifteen seconds. I could have used help."

"You subdued them on your own."

"That's not the point. What if I hadn't been able to? When would you have jumped in? When one of the guys pulled a knife? A gun? When I'm on the ground getting the shit beaten out of me? Wouldn't it have been better to get in sooner before it got to that point? Four years on the force, and you act like a rookie ridealong. I don't trust you, Vin. I would not put my life in your hands. I would almost say that I still like you, but I know that's how you've been able to get by. Charming, personable, funny, and with a little local government safety net."

"That's not true! My uncle has nothing to do with this!"

"The fact that you even understand the reference tells me it does."

Vin faltered. Then, "Fine. I'll ask him. I will have him show that I'm a good officer."

"No one can show that but you. And I am far less than confident in that right now."

The young man hesitated as they pulled in the driveway of the raucous party. "What do you want me to do here?"

Walter reached for the door handle. "Just stay here."

The sudden presence of the cops jarred the partygoers. Not a few of them—most of them underage, Walter suspected—decided to make a hasty exit. A few of them just turned their backs to him, trying to hide whatever it was they were doing. A few, who were so drunk they could hardly stand up and Walter was afraid they would puke on his uniform, either tried to fight him or proposition him, sometimes both at the same time.

He found the owner of the property and party host snoozing away on the couch, vomit on the floor, half-naked girl drunkenly riding his hips. Long story short, Walter woke the man up, had words, ended up arresting him for drunk and disorderly, furnishing alcohol to minors, solicitation of one minor, statutory rape of another, and assault on an officer. After dumping him in the cruiser, he and Vin cleared out the party pretty quick, calling in several more officers to assist with arrests and other citations.

What officers weren't at the actual party got dispatched to any number of drunk driving accidents that ensued as partygoers tried to flee the law. So they were not only charged with a DUI—among MIP, furnishing, et cetera—but fleeing and eluding and resisting arrest.

By the time the whole clusterfuck got sorted out, it was just before five o'clock. Walter headed to the break room to top off his thermos one last time. As he did so, he noticed Vin speaking with Kate. She nodded and motioned something, and they headed in the direction of her office. So there was every chance that he was going to start off the year unemployed. But he meant every word he said, and to the best of his knowledge, it was all true.

Not five minutes later, Sheriff Williams walked in the door. The man looked as though he hadn't slept a wink, and he broke into a yawn halfway into his "Good morning" to Walter. He made for the coffee and filled up his mug.

"Please tell me that it was so boring last night that you all sat around the office playing poker," he murmured.

"Strip poker at that, and wow-ee, Kate is a looker," Walter told him. At the sheriff's look, he said, "No, not really. It's been busy as hell. Non-stop running around. If you can make it out of the parking lot before getting a call, you're lucky."

"Shit." Williams yawned again. "Well, that just means that I'll have enough paperwork waiting on my desk that I can tape it together to fashion a mattress and a blanket."

"No, you should go for a tent. Then you can put a Keep Out, No Girls Allowed sign on there."

"Hm...problem is, there aren't enough girls to make it an effective sign. I have to keep you boys out, too."

"Keep Out, No Underlings Allowed?"

"Hey, works for me. All right, guess I better get my day started at some point. The sooner I start, the sooner I can leave, right?"

"Permission to go home, sir?"

"Denied. And your sarcasm is noted. I'll see you later, Walt."

The sheriff left the break room and moseyed down to his office. Vin was still talking to Kate, so Walter sat down at an open desk and finished up some of the paperwork he'd begun at the start of his shift but never really finished. Just with the way the night had been going, he knew he wouldn't be off until six or seven, maybe later depending on how the morning went with the day crew. On the one hand, it meant good overtime. On the other hand, that was a long shift, plus he had to work the next night, too. Even with Tommen to Band him, that was still a long shift, sleep, and another long shift, with no break in between.

"Walt."

He looked up as Vin called his name.

"Sheriff wants to see you."

Walter got up, stretched, and headed down to the sheriff's office. He wasn't worried until he saw Kate in there with him; then he knew he was in for it. He walked in and closed the door without being asked.

"All right, Walter," Sheriff Williams sighed. "What the hell happened tonight? I know what Kate and Vin told me; let's hear your side of things."

So he gave them the unedited version of events and his thoughts that went with them. He could see that neither of them liked what he had to say, but they couldn't deny it either. It was the same look he probably had when allying himself with Rifun. He didn't like it, but he couldn't deny it was his best option so far.

"Walt, you do realize that what I told you earlier was to be in confidence, right?" Kate said.

"What do you want me to say? Yeah, sure, it's fine. Let's have an officer who does no work, has no professional police instincts, will probably get someone killed one of these days, and can't be touched because his uncle owns the department? It's like I told him earlier. What if I hadn't been able to subdue those three people? When would he have jumped in to help? Or Widow White, having a nice cup of coffee and completely exposing himself and having little or no concern for his partner? And that was just tonight. In four years, how much has he been able to dance through and skirt by? I don't trust him, and I sure as hell wouldn't want him on my team in a firefight. And you can't tell me he was completely clueless about his uncle, assuming what you told me is true."

"It is true," Williams answered. "But we can't just turn down that kind of funding."

"So the department has become dependent on him."

"Walt, you're used to the way city works. The city has a lot of people, a lot of rich people, a lot of tax money coming in. How do you think they managed to afford Casey Oldman and his band of cronies? You don't leave New York for a forty thousand dollar pay cut. But in county, things are different. People are leaving. Okay, in the mountains, if you're not rich, you're in poverty. The rich are moving to the city or just out of the mountains, out of the state entirely. The poor, well, those who do pay taxes don't pay much. Before Vin's uncle, we were on the verge of our officers having to literally buy their own vehicles to use as police vehicles because the budget wouldn't allow for new vehicles or maintenance of the old ones. All the old man wanted in return was a spot for his son and nephews.

"Yes, we know he's more useless than a bag of dirt. We figured that out in the first three months of his employment. That's why he got the easy assignments, the patrols, the animal control, things like that. It kept him on the force to please his uncle, and it kept him out of our way.

"Then the whole fiasco at city happened, and we lost a lot of guys to Casey. We had to bump up Vin's responsibilities, but we knew he couldn't just step into the role. That's why we put him with more experienced officers, like you tonight, in hopes that you might be able to show him a thing or two. You're experienced, direct to the point, and I know you've had your share of rookie ridealongs to train. Maybe it was our fault for not explaining this sooner, so you understood our goals."

"It would have been nice to know that I wasn't going to have reliable help before I started out tonight, yes."

"Well, regardless, the cat's out of the bag. Vin's going to go crying to mommy and daddy and rich uncle, I'm sure. And I'm going to hear about it." Williams went on before Walter could speak. "You're not fired. Quite frankly, I don't see Vin lasting very much longer after this little revelation, and I'd still rather have you than him. I can't reprimand you for insubordination since Kate mentioned she put you over him tonight, and I suspect you're a bit of a hard nose when it comes to training rookies and dealing with lazy officers. However, as I've already told her, I will be reprimanding her for upjumping you without my knowledge or permission. Just something to think about for the remainder of your shift. Dismissed."

It had the intended effect, Walter thought. He immediately felt guilty about getting Kate in trouble for his actions, and he hurried back to his cruiser, feeling a bit like a teeny-bopper who wants to have a temper tantrum while still trying to maintain composure and not be a crybaby.

Thankfully, he didn't have to be out long, and the most he got in was a speeding ticket before returning to the precinct and handing off the cruiser to the sleepy-eyed first shifter. He did not see Vin, and his customary farewell to Kate was met with a cold reply. He punched out and headed out to his car. Instead of going straight home, however, he made a detour to Laura's apartment. She had gotten off shift the same time as him and they pulled in the apartment parking lot at the same time.

"You look like your night was about as dull as mine," Laura said, breaking into a yawn. "Want to come up for some coffee?"

"The coffee might be a bad idea, but I'll come up," he told her. "We can swap stories."

They went up and made breakfast using the last few ingredients in her fridge. A pancake for each of them, two sausage links each, an orange to share, two single-serve pints of milk, and a few strips of bacon to fight over.

"Long night?" she guessed.

"You have no idea."

So they shared their stories of the night. At least Walter had a variety of things to share. Laura's calls seemed to fall into three major categories: drunk, result of drunk driving, and domestic assault victim. Then he told her about the rest of the night and the squabble with Vin and that whole debacle.

"Well, it's kind of on them," Laura mused when he was finished. "I mean, if I'm working with a new guy, I kind of need to know, 'Hey, he's new.' Or, 'Hey, he's not too confident or competent and your better bet is to take lead.' That way I'm not depending on someone I can't count on. At the same time, it sounds like you kind of gave the kid hell."

"It's been a long night," Walter sighed, rubbing his eyes. "And I didn't like being paired with an idiot without knowing why we were paired or why he was an idiot. If they would have told me right off the bat, it would have changed completely how I did things tonight. Now I got my road sergeant in trouble, may have contributed to the loss of yet another officer—in all reality, having a guy to do the low-key things is great because it frees up the rest of us—and may have caused a small financial meltdown for the county police."

"Bad luck just follows you wherever you go."

"Thanks a lot."

She stood, went around behind him and started rubbing his neck and shoulders. He let out a breath. "That could be a dangerous thing."

"Oh?"

"Make me too comfortable, I might just fall asleep."

"I got about as much sleep as you did. You can crash here if you want." She bent down and nibbled his ear a bit. "Would you prefer the couch or the bed?"

Oh, *that* kind of crash.

"Mm...I don't think that's such a good idea."

She stopped nibbling but remained close to his ear. "Why not? It'll give you something to remember me by. Give me something to remember you by. A little whetting of an appetite while we're apart." She gave another small nibble.

"Wouldn't the anticipation alone be enough? Besides, what if something happened?"

"Please, Walter, I've had three kids and a hysterectomy."

He chuckled. "That's not what I'm talking about." He turned to face her. "What if something happened where we couldn't get back together? I don't know what, but something."

"Then at least we shared this."

"Yes, but if we can't keep it together, it's not worth sharing in the first place."

She straightened and took a step back, her expression looking as though she'd been slapped. He stood and kissed her. "I love you, Laura, but I'm not going to disrespect you. You are beautiful and amazing, there is no doubt about that. And I'm sorry that you have to leave, and especially the reason you have to go. I do hope I can visit over spring break and I hope that we can get back together once everything is taken care of. But not before then."

Laura took a shuddering breath and nodded. "Okay. You're right. You're right, I am such an idiot."

"No, you're not. You're afraid. You want to be loved and comforted. But that's not how I'm going to give it to you." He pulled her close. "We'll see each other again. When everything is taken care of and the dust settles, then we'll talk."

She nodded again. "Okay. I'll be waiting."

"I'll let you get some sleep, and I'll be by Saturday before you leave."

She agreed and saw him out the door. Walter walked away with mixed feelings. Hurt, curiosity, pity, and a certain sense of pride that after all these years, he could still get it up.

Chapter Seven
New Year's Eve

Tommen never really understood how much the bakery meant to him until it was time to leave. Sure, he'd already left once by technicality, but this was leaving and never coming back, not even for a visit. This was locking the door, turning his back, walking away, and leaving. Forever. As in, this was it. This was the last time he would walk in, punch in, grab an apron, and walk over to the production schedule. It was the last time he would go rummaging for utensils and supplies, ripping open bag after bag of flour and sugar and mixing them according to one of dozens of super secret recipes.

Yeah, it was possible for him to go work at some other bakery, but this was, like, his bakery almost. He'd been here forever, often complained about how long he'd been working here. This was his first job. The twins had been his first friends, his first bosses, his crazy uncles for years. Now it was all coming to a close.

He might not have been so sentimental about it except this wasn't how he wanted it all to end. Going to college, fine. The twins going dark, fine. One twin being murdered and the other giving up? Not fine.

He'd already gone over this in his head multiple times, actually. Micaiah was dead. Kayla was gone. Micah was coming back around, but his mind was made up. This was it. Say sayonara.

"You look like a chicken," Kyle said, jabbing him in the ribs as he walked through the kitchen. "All broody and stuff."

Tommen rolled his eyes and grinned. "Ha ha, very funny."

"You're not going to cry on us, are you?"

"Not planning on it."

"This really getting to you that much?" Kyle started rummaging in a drawer for something.

Tommen shrugged. "This was my first job. Micah and Micaiah were my crazy uncles. I didn't think it would get to me, but I'm kinda feeling it. You know, it kind of feels like a family business that's going out of business."

"Maybe he should sell it to you, that way you can work here forever and ever."

"That's the thing, though, is that I wouldn't really want it. And anyway, they would have to go dark and..." He shook his head and went back to his dough. "I've already gone through all of this. It was inevitable."

"Just the circumstances." Kyle nodded. "I get it. Believe me, I get it."

"You're not still beating yourself up, are you?"

"It's hard not to, man. I mean, in all reality, if it hadn't been Cai, Micah could have just as easily been the one in the office. Or me. Or Jenna. We're both smart enough to know it wasn't just a run-of-the-mill robbery, and Rifun could and probably would have murdered whoever had been in the office at the time. Or maybe taken out Cai some other way."

"Well, there is some truth to that."

Some truth, yes, but Tommen had a hard time believing that Rifun was as much of a loose cannon as he once thought. He could murder without conscience, yet everything he did was calculated. If Jenna had been the one in the office, Tommen would place a bet that she would have lived. Maybe the safe would have been robbed, maybe not, but she would have lived. Why? Because she was unimportant. She had no bearing on Rifun's plans. Micaiah, on the other hand, was a serious disruption, an obstacle that had to be removed.

Of course, that begged the question, what were his plans now? So far, everything felt like a means to an end. Maybe Rifun still longed to be King of Time and subduing the only opponent who had bested him thus far was just one stop on the road back to that throne. The next logical step might be the extinction of the Borelians, but without the Akari, any opponent, no matter how great, was at a distinct disadvantage.

What did he tell his men, then, the ones who were going to set fire to some Borelian corn fields? Was it all "part of the plan"? Did they do it for the glory and honor of the Order? Did they do it for some monetary compensation? A promotion? Out of the goodness of their hearts and love for the universe? Out of some sickening lust for death that even the battle with the Akarin had not satisfied? On the other hand, could the men Rifun picked be the ones of questionable loyalty or skill, the ones who, if they were killed or captured, were no great loss to the Order overall?

Tommen shook his head. He had to stop thinking about it and worrying over it. What was done was done. The plan was in motion, no turning back now.

Were they out there already? Setting fires, leaving long lines of gasoline for the fire to follow and destroy as much as possible? Was there any fanfare, any fighting? Or was it kind of a more severe form of ding-dong ditching, set the fire and run? Did they go after homes and buildings, too, or just the fields?

He glanced at the clock. Just after six. They would have to be out there now, or just about. They had to have enough time to cause enough damage to get the Borelians' attention and call them back from wherever they were ready to launch their invasion, assuming that was what they were about to do.

He set one pan in an oven and squeezed out the last of the red icing onto a cookie. He had a few more pans to make and then that was it. Supplies were scarce, and anything left over after the official list had been completed would be by experiment only. There might be enough to properly bake some product, but it would be in two's and three's, not by the dozen. Anything leftover at the end of the night was theirs to take home if they wanted it.

"How are things out here?" Micah asked, walking in and looking around, his gaze saying he was sorry to see it all go, too.

"Just about done," Tommen reported. "And I'm not even Banding."

"Yes, I can see that. Or not see that." The younger twin sighed. "Well, carry on, I guess. Get it used up however you can."

"That's the plan. You found a place to stay yet? The new homeowners take possession on Monday, don't they?"

"They do. And to answer your question, yes, I have found a place to stay. It's temporary for the time being, until I can actually get looking around, find a job, build a life."

"Still going to pass yourself off as your own kid?"

"Doing the math, I'm going to have to be my own grandkid."

"Still going to look for your brothers and sisters and nieces and nephews and all them?"

"Oh, I've already found them. Social media is a wonderful thing. Yeah, we've been in touch. Actually, I will be arriving as a student, studying abroad in Ireland for a time. A couple of relatives are already studying, so they said they would show me around campus and help me out and whatnot."

"Cool. What will you study?"

"I haven't decided. Either mechanical engineering or forensic science."

"Oh. Nice. I never pegged you as that type of person."

Micah laughed. "Well, let's just say that I want to get as far away from baking as I can for a while."

Tommen grinned. "I don't blame you there."

He finished up icing the cookies and took them to the front case where a short line had formed. Compared to previous years, they were pretty dead for New Year's Eve. Yeah, everyone wanted some kind of sustenance between work and New Year's festivities, but the bakery was closing, and everyone knew that the last day of any business was slim pickings. Several people seemed surprised that Tommen was bringing out any fresh pans, and one asked if they really were going out of business. Everyone reluctantly confirmed that this was the last day, Tommen explaining that they were just trying to get product used up and there were only a few more pans left to come out for the evening.

By six-thirty, the store was empty and even the parking lot was pretty sparse. Across the street, the pizza place was stuffed more than their stuffed crusts. When Tommen went out front for some fresh air and to take a look around while he had a minute, music was blaring from somewhere and the bar half a block down the road was already filling with people. Like birthdays, Tommen wondered what made New Year's so damn special. Hooray, we made it another full revolution around the sun and didn't die. Let's all get wasted and take our chances that we won't survive the first six hours of the new year. And if we survive that, we'll spend the next revolution around the sun regretting the choices we made in those first six hours.

But it was what it was. Tommen went back inside to find Micah putting out the last pans of product.

"Call it a hunch, I think we're taking these home with us," he said.

"There is that possibility," Tommen agreed.

He followed Micah back to the kitchen where he'd pulled out most of the remaining product. Also on the counter was about four pounds of flour, two pounds of sugar, a cup of baking powder, four eggs, and a myriad of various ingredients and garnishes all packed in smaller and smaller leftover containers.

"Take what you want," Micah told him. "I don't think I'll be taking any with me to Ireland."

While Kyle took most of the leftover baked goods, it was more to be polite than anything. He was heading back to California and wanted to travel as light as possible. Tommen felt guilty about the rest, not because he was taking the most, but because it probably wouldn't get used. The eggs, yeah, those would get cooked up within a day. But he and his dad really didn't do a whole lot of baking.

"Kyle do you think you can manage if we take a quick trip?" Micah wondered.

"I don't know," Kyle said, sighing sarcastically and

dramatically shifting his stance. "A couple plates of cookies and a few brownies are a pretty huge target for thieves. One guy might not be enough."

"I'll take that as a yes."

"Where are we going?" Tommen inquired.

"To get some coffee. Gather some of this up, put it in a bag here, and hang onto it."

Tommen did as he was told, not considering until a minute later that Micah was referring to the South American coffee farmers that they traded with. About once a week or so, the twins gave the farmers the bakery's day's end goods, and, in this case, some raw ingredients, to help feed their families, and the farmers gave them coffee straight from the hand of God.

In the same way that it was a huge leap from Charleston to Lip, so it was again going from Charleston to some unknown village in South America. The heat was intense, made even worse by the load he was carrying. They landed somewhere in a jungle and followed a game trail a quarter mile out to a dirt road on the side of a cliff. Donkeys and llamas pulling carts vied for space on the road amid cars and trucks, and still they walked. Tommen could feel his shirt sticking to his back and wished he had at least a pair of sandals.

They walked up the cliffside road, departing just as soon as they could, following a smaller path up to a village overlooking a vast valley. On the other side of the village, on solid ground, tucked behind a wall of trees, coffee plants lined the hills for miles. Several children stopped whatever game they were playing and ran to meet them, while another child ran off into the village. Micah entertained the children for a minute or two until an older man, perhaps sixty years old, came to meet them.

"Ah, Micah Durvin, you did come," he said in heavily-accented English. "When you told us you were closing your bakery, we thought it was all over."

Micah shook his head. "One last delivery, Hector."

The product was handed off to younger men and children.

"And who is your friend here?" Hector inquired.

"This is Tommen. He's been working for us for, what, seven, eight, nine years?"

"Ah, so, the mystery boy of the cave. They told me stories about you."

"Oh, jeez," Tommen said. "I'm afraid to know."

The man laughed. "All of it good, I assure you."

"How are things here?" Micah asked. "I would imagine your remote village is pretty safe from the Borelians."

Hector gave an indifferent shrug. "Does it matter? We work the coffee plantations here, we work the fields there, either way, we are a slave to our work. The only thing that changes is who is over us. The great government of Peru, or the great government of Brelix. It makes no difference to us. That is not to say that I would go quietly. Here, we have friends, family, God. There, it is only death and despair. We will fight if necessary."

"Hopefully it won't be necessary. We have a plan and it's being carried out right now. Either it will buy us time or it will speed things up."

"As I said, it makes very little difference to us. You in the big cities who concern yourselves with television and the Internet and other frivolous things, you would not survive the transition to slavery as well as we would. But, as you said, hopefully it will not come to be."

Micah thanked him, wished him well, promised to visit from time to time, and left, Tommen a step or two behind.

"He's a fun guy, isn't he?" Tommen said, careful not to point or make it obvious who he was talking about.

"We live in different worlds, come from different places. His primary concern is his village, his family, and I don't blame him. Our concerns typically range from not being thrown into Borelian slavery to finding the cheapest gas station. He's always prioritizing. We aren't. That's how we get caught off-guard so easily. It's also why he's right. The more you have stripped from you, the harder it is to cope. The only thing that would change for him is the crop he grows. For us, me and you, how much would we lose?"

Tommen let out a breath. "Everything."

"Exactly."

The walk back down the road, down the cliffs, was considerably easier than the walk up, both in terms of going downhill and not having a load to carry.

"I thought he was a Time Agent?" Tommen said suddenly.

"He was," Micah replied. "He elected to be Suppressed so he could raise a family. The other coffee farmers we traded with are more actively involved."

"So maybe not so much for him, but why don't the other farmers take all their people to the Wheel to feed them? Or bring food back? Not like there's a food shortage in the Food Court."

"They don't take people in because it would be too great a shock, and they don't want to create a bunch of new Time Agents. They don't bring food back because they don't want to be accused of stealing. When you live under drug lords and oppressive regimes, the one who has nice things and plenty of food becomes a target. They just want to lay low. That's not to say that they don't do that from time to time, but they can't make it a regular thing."

"Oh."

They reached the game trail and turned off, heading into the trees just far enough to not be seen so Micah could open a portal. Within seconds, they were back in the bakery, the sudden blast of comparatively cold air stunning Tommen momentarily. Gradually, he adjusted to the temperature and humidity change. Once his tactile senses got themselves sorted out, he was comfortable again. Then he began to cool down a bit, and he realized that all the product was out and the ovens, which were the primary source of heat in the kitchen, were shut off. When he moved to the front counter, the furnace took over and he was warm again.

From what he could see, all was well and quiet on the storefront. No major catastrophes had occurred in the last hour or so. Kyle returned from taking out the trash. While he washed his hands, he also prepared the mop water.

"How were things?" Tommen asked half a second after Micah did.

"Good and...good," Kyle answered, pushing the bucket into the dining room to start mopping. "More customers than I thought there was going to be, fewer than you'd probably like since there is still product left in the case. I wasn't sure quite what you wanted to do with it, so I left it. Trashes are done, tables are cleaned, everything is clean. Just mopping and...half hour to close. Then three more hours until the new year. Woo hoo."

"Hey now, calm down, I can't stand your excitement," Micah told him.

With the store empty and ready to be completely abandoned, the three of them gathered at the bar to watch some of the New Year's celebrations going on in Times Square. The news anchors were gushing about all the social progress made in the country over the last year—because obviously during a drinking festival, everyone really wants to talk about politics. They talked to random people in the crowd, interviewed famous people performing or speaking on stage.

They also talked about the heightened security at the square, how they were taking every precaution after the Halloween attacks and other threats by In Jezik. Apparently the silence of the terrorist group was more frightening than the actual attacks, especially since they had been so effective. They talked about how they'd pulled in all the active duty people, the reserves, the Academy, dogs, federal agents, and a number of other things they were not at liberty to disclose. They interviewed the New York City Police Commissioner who gave some vague, rehearsed, politically correct statement that, in the minds of the news anchors, seemed to be worthy of a Nobel Peace Prize.

"I never thought I would say this, but I'm glad they're still talking," Micah said. "Annoying as hell and I kind of want to punch them all in the face, but as long as they're talking, the Borelians aren't invading."

"Going to stay here all night, then?" Tommen wondered.

"Nah." Micah got off the stool. "I can just as easily watch this at home." He sighed and looked around. "Guess it's time to lock it up and throw away the key."

The thought was sobering as he flicked off the TV and took the remote into the office. The desk was the cleanest Tommen had ever seen it as all the papers were gone and the computer was gone. Micah locked the office door, locked the front door, then followed Tommen and Kyle out the back door, locking that as well. And just like that, their shift had ended and Bakery na hÉireann was no more.

"Take care of yourself, Kyle," Micah said, extending a hand. "And don't let me hear anything about you getting into Running again, all right? Else we're going to have a talk, and it won't be a friendly one."

"Yes, it will, because you're likely to be there with me," Kyle replied, taking the hand and giving it a firm shake. "Keep in touch, dude."

After giving similar departing pleasantries to Tommen, the California surfer dude walked down the alley and disappeared around a corner.

"You especially are not allowed to be a stranger," Micah told Tommen. He faked him out by offering a handshake and then pulling him into a full embrace that lasted only a second or two. "You take care of yourself, too. And your dad. Look out for each other. And if you ever get the chance, kill that son of a bitch Rifun. Give him my regards."

"And Kayla's," Tommen added.

"Definitely Kayla's." Micah nodded. "Listen, assuming we don't get carted off to Borelian slavery tonight, I'll probably stop by when I'm on my way out. But if I miss you for whatever reason, know that it's been awesome. I've enjoyed working with you and watching you grow up. I've enjoyed being your crazy uncle."

"Crazy uncle is getting sentimental, methinks."

"Maybe a little. But I mean it. Don't be a stranger. You ever find yourself coming across the pond, look me up."

"I'll be sure to ask for Micah Durvin, grandson of Micah Durvin."

"Something like that."

And with that, they got in their respective vehicles and drove away. Neither would be coming back the next morning to meet a production schedule or start preparing for the next major holiday. The bakery would sit quietly, waiting for its new owner.

Half a block from the store, Tommen's phone buzzed, signaling a text. He Banded and checked; it was Becky.

"Watching the countdown?"

He typed back, "Watched it a little at work, but that's about it."

"Want to come over and watch it here? Are you off yet?"

"Bakery na hÉireann is officially closed. I'm off."

"Aw, I'm sorry."

"I'll come by. Long as there's food."

"When is there not food?"

Food, girlfriend, possibility of sex, yeah he might be inclined to show up for a party he'd never indulged in before. "On my way."

He released the Band and made his way through the city. There were some festivities going on downtown, and he cut a wide berth around some of the more heavily congested areas, reaching the bridge in good time and returning to the peace and quiet of the south side of the river. From there, it was the same trek as normally going home, but he stopped about half a block away.

Unlike Thanksgiving and Christmas, New Year's was a decidedly more demure affair. Uri and Andrew, Becky's oldest siblings who were in their forties and fifties, were there with their wives. Their grown children and younger grandchildren were nowhere to be seen, which made Becky and Tommen the only ones under forty in the house.

"Hello, Tommen," Mrs. Polski greeted as he walked into the living room. *"Boldog új évet!"*

"Happy new year," Tommen replied meekly.

The same countdown was on TV. Mr. Polski was talking to his

two sons, and the wives were speaking between themselves. Becky was curled up in one of the armchairs, but left her post when Tommen walked in. She gave him a huge hug and practically dragged him back to the armchair, like a child dragging a parent to see some thing. He sat down in the plush chair and Becky crawled in his lap.

His sense of arousal warred with his equal desire for the food on the coffee table. It was far less formal than a sit-down dinner, but Mrs. Polski didn't just run to the store to grab some chips and dip. No, she made everything herself, and it in no way resembled your typical Super Bowl party platter. Homemade potato chips broke off in homemade dip, and one dish was filled with something like a homemade Chex mix. Tommen counted fourteen dishes on the table, including six different dips.

"Yeah, I know what you're looking for," Becky said. "I know why you really came here, and it has nothing to do with my amazing company and conversational skills."

She got off him, grabbed a plate and loaded it up with a little bit of everything. Like her mother, she felt the need to name and explain every dish as he sampled it. He only paid small mind to her, instead focusing more on the food and the screen. It wasn't that he particularly enjoyed the obnoxious news anchors, but like Micah said, as long as they were talking, Earth wasn't being invaded. So nightly news did have its purpose, he supposed.

"So, Tommen, how was your last day of work?" Mr. Polski asked. "The bakery was closing today, wasn't it?"

Tommen nodded and swallowed his food. "Yeah. No, it was pretty quiet. Micah got a little sentimental as we locked up and said our goodbyes."

"What's he going to do now?"

"He's moving back to Ireland, going to pursue a degree, reunite with the rest of the family, that sort of thing."

"Well, it will be good for him," Mrs. Polski said, bringing in a new dish of snacks to replace one that had gotten low. "I'm sure you and your dad have been very good friends, but I think he needs more familial support after what happened to his brother."

"What is he going to study?" Andrew inquired.

"He hasn't decided completely. Either mechanical engineering or forensic science. But the most important thing he said is that it's not culinary."

That elicited some chuckles and the older men began to reminisce among themselves about their days in school. It started out as college, then slowly devolved into reminiscing about high school and middle school and elementary school, how different things were back then and so on and so forth. Tommen tuned them out and returned his attention to the food on his plate, which Becky had somehow managed to replenish without getting off his lap or otherwise disturbing him. He suspected her mom may have had a hand in such a ploy, but neither of them gave anything away.

Ten o'clock rolled around. Tommen made an excuse to go to the bathroom where he texted his dad.

"Anything?"

"All quiet on the Earth front," his dad replied. "You?"

"Watching the Times Square broadcast. Nothing suspicious that I can see. As long as the anchors are talking, we're still safe."

"That's one way to think about it."

"Any word from any of the other worlds?"

"Not a peep."

"Okay. Well, I'm at Becky's house for their New Year's party. It's pretty low-key. But, like I said, broadcast is still normal."

"I expect we'll all hear about it if something happens. Be good."

"We could be enslaved tonight and you're worried about me and Becky?"

"We could be enslaved tonight. Why shouldn't I worry about you and Becky?"

Okay, he had a point. "Fine. Yes, we're being good."

"Make sure it stays that way."

Tommen sighed, put his phone away, washed his hands, and rejoined the party. He refilled his plate before sitting down and getting comfortable again.

"That's your fourth plate," Becky observed. "Does it ever end? Or is your stomach a black hole?"

"It's a black hole," he told her casually, taking a chip and making a large scoop in the dip. "But I will give your mom credit. She knows how to take a mundane snack and turn it into a meal."

He made an imaginary tip of the hat toward Mrs. Polski who grinned and shook her head.

As the night wore on, the drunkenness and debauchery of the Times Square party became more and more obvious. At the start of the broadcast, even in the background, the crowd was excited, milling about, taking pictures, taking selfies, taking videos, enjoying the bands and speakers, and casually enjoying a drink. Now the drinks were starting to add up and the antics became more flagrant. Smiles were too big, laughter was too loud and inappropriate, movements were wonky, and the whole mood of the crowd went from polite, to loose, to few or no inhibitions. Tommen knew there was typically a five second delay or more on the broadcasts so that anything terrible could be cut out before it aired live, but not everything could be edited out every time, and on more than one occasion, Tommen saw inappropriate touches, grabs, and other interactions, shielded only by a few people and a quick-thinking producer.

"Honestly, you would think some people would have a little more respect for themselves and others," one of the wives complained. "This is New Year's Eve, not a strip club."

Taking the hint, Andrew grabbed the remote and turned it to the New Year's *Star Wars* countdown where Episode Six was about halfway through. A small graphic in the corner of the screen gave the countdown. Well, if the Borelians invaded, that would certainly be a good reason for the government to interrupt all broadcasts to bring everyone an important announcement, right? Alien invasion was a pretty good reason, right?

Maybe not. First, they would deny it. Once they realized it was true, they'd want to stifle the media so as not to cause a nationwide panic, maybe even shut down the Internet so people couldn't upload to social media. After that, they would want to politicize it and find someone to blame for the invasion. By the time they got done bickering—and maybe they sent out the head of housekeeping to talk to the aliens in the meantime and keep them busy—the human race would be enslaved.

But the countdown continued, *Star Wars* plodded along as the rebel forces and the Ewoks defeated the greatly superior Empire, and Luke turned Vader to the Good Side and defeated the Emperor. Commercials ensued, thus delaying the end of the movie. It was a little before eleven-thirty. The movie itself ended about ten minutes before midnight, then cut to the hosts or producers of the channel, all dressed in costumes or other nerd gear, ready to ring in a Nerdy New Year.

The TV was switched back to Times Square where the news anchors were getting all hyped up over, in Tommen's opinion, sliced bread. He got himself another plate of food.

"Have you ever considered becoming, like, a competitive eater?" Becky asked. "Because I'm pretty sure you could do it. With zero problems."

"I'm sure I could, too," he agreed. "But I have higher goals than that."

He fully expected Dr. Polski to jump on his statement and start grilling him about his life's ambitions, but the doctor wasn't paying attention to him.

The clock ticked down, Times Square got all kinds of excited and everyone began counting down together. Ten...nine...eight...seven...

Tommen ignored it. The ball lit up, the 2015 lit up, fireworks went off, people cheered, people cried, people kissed, people drank, Tommen took his last potato chip and scooped up the last of his dip.

Uri and Andrew and their wives got up, stretched, walked around the house a bit. Tommen made himself a last plate of food before the dishes were taken away, most of them empty or near enough. Once the dishes were clean and put away, the visiting couples wished their parents good night, happy new year, and departed. Dr. Polski announced he was going to bed, and his wife said she would probably join him shortly.

"Doesn't your mom have to stay up, like, all night so she can keep going on third shift?" Tommen asked.

Becky shook her head. "No, my mom is one of those people who really only needs three or four hours of sleep, and it really doesn't matter when she gets them. She could stay up forever. I think she sleeps just to be polite, and so my dad can get some before he goes to sleep."

"That was more information than I was hoping for."

"I know."

They wished her parents good night as each retired, then sat and watched the after-drop partying of the Times Square crowd for a few minutes. It wasn't much to see, really, just the anchors interviewing more random people about their resolutions and goals and dreams and plans and other fuzzy things. The only reason Tommen was interested was for the impending invasion. Even if the Borelians wanted to wait and totally master the dramatic timing of invading right as the ball dropped, said invasion never happened. And, if he wanted to be honest, it was already a full day into the new year for places near the edge of the meridian. Japan, China, they'd celebrated New Year's forever ago. The United States was pretty slow to get there, in all reality, so any invasion could have come at any time.

But it never did.

He was pulled from his almost trance-like state by Becky's dramatic yawn and stretch in his lap. Then she curled back up and looked up at him like a puppy looking for a belly scratch.

"Are you ready for bed, too?" he asked.

"I suppose so," she mused.

"Is that all you want?" He bent and kissed her on the lips, on the neck. One hand went under the back of her shirt to unclasp her bra.

"Well, we're certainly not going to do it here in the living room," she told him, her voice low. "Follow me."

She went first to the kitchen for a glass of water before proceeding upstairs, Tommen close behind. She stepped normally while he stepped as light as he could. There was no telling whether her parents were actually asleep, nor how deep they normally slept. But then, half the thrill was the prospect of being caught. That thrill would quickly diminish, however, if and when Dr. Polski got his hands around his throat, but Tommen figured he had a few tricks up his sleeve that would help him get away if need be.

"I could feel you all night," she told him, undoing his belt and zipper. "Are teenage guys really that horny?"

He swept her up and put her down on him as best he could with her pants still on. "You tell me. Are teenage girls really this horny?"

She kissed him. "Take my clothes off and find out."

He found out all right. He found out good. Becky buried her face in a pillow several times to keep from getting too loud, but she assured him it was all good.

"Getting better all the time," she told him once they were done. She lay back and rested her head on his chest. "So, what are some of your new year's resolutions?"

"I don't know," he admitted. "I've already crossed off my big one from last year."

"Losing your virginity?"

"Yup. After that, there wasn't a whole lot left. I got my license, got a car. There's not much else to do until I get to college, I suppose."

"I see."

"What about you?"

She shrugged. "Same, I guess. Can't resolve to do a whole lot when the first eighteen years of your life are determined by the government. I know I'm going to graduate high school. I know I'm going to WVSU. I gave up my virginity. I don't drive. The only resolution I have is an ongoing one to keep my blood sugar and weight in check."

"So there we go. We have fulfilled our life's ambitions before we are twenty years old."

She gave him a look. "Uh-huh. Right. I think we'll have more goals than that in the future."

He almost asked, Like what? Then decided he didn't want to know the answer. The sex was good, and he didn't want to leave on an awkward note. So they cuddled a bit until they admitted defeat and the need for sleep. Becky saw him to the door and he drove the last half block home, walking in the door at two o'clock.

He grabbed himself a quick snack from the fridge and went down to his room where he plugged in his nearly-dead phone and texted his dad.

"Anything?"

"Nothing," his dad replied. "If the Borelians were planning an attack, maybe our first strike stopped it. If they weren't planning an attack, well, maybe this small show of force will keep them off our backs for a short time."

"Think it's safe to go to bed?"

"No less safe than staying up, I think. If something happens, I'll come and get you."

"Got it."

"Has Rifun visited at all?"

"No. I just got home, actually. All quiet."

"Polskis are real party animals, huh?"

"You were at their Christmas party; you ought to know how it goes."

"Fair enough. All right, hopefully I'll see you in the morning. Night, kiddo."

"Night, Dad."

Tommen headed off to the bathroom to get ready for bed, returning to find, no surprise, Rifun sitting on the end of his bed.

"I take it the mission was a success?" Tommen asked.

"We're sitting here, aren't we?"

"How did you manage to pull it off?"

"Very carefully."

"I know, I know, not a promotion."

"No, but with a new year and a new ruler comes some new rules and new ways of doing things." Rifun got off the bed. "We are going to discuss your place in the new way of doing things, as well as some leads for your assignment. I apologize that it got put on hold, but your dad made me an offer I couldn't refuse."

He opened a portal to the fortress and Tommen followed him through. The portal room was still heavily guarded, and the guards gave Rifun a veritable king's acknowledgment; all it lacked was a bow and a ring kissing.

Looking around, the southwest stair appeared to have been fully restored, not that there was a whole lot wrong with it, certainly not as much as the northwest stair. But the staircase itself had been stabilized and repaired, the cracks sealed and solidified, the rocks worked and reworked until it was as if there had never been any damage at all. As they approached the staircase, Tommen looked down the west and south corridors. The northwest stair, what little he could see of it, was still a chaotic mess, but progress was evident as the first floor was almost passable. The southeast stair looked to have normal operations underway.

Heading up the stair, the southwest corner of the second floor also looked sturdy and structurally sound once more. No cracks, dents, dings, or scratches. Actually, looking at it, the stone even looked a bit polished and shiny.

The third floor was less than stellar, though better than the last time Tommen had visited. Most of the major crevasses had been reduced to less scary cracks, and a lot of the stabilization measures had been removed and placed on the fourth floor. Little work appeared to have been accomplished from the fourth floor up except to stabilize the ceiling in order to minimize any shifting from the collapsed floor.

"Once the northwest stair has been repaired and the first three floors made solid, then work will begin on this mess," Rifun told him, as if reading his mind. "I expect we'll be done around mid-February, around the same time the Tacagans ought to be finishing with Earth's planetary defenses. Then we can really get this show on the road."

"What show is that?" Tommen dared ask. He went on before the man could speak. "Yeah, I get it. Just a vaovao, not privy to that sort of information."

"Now you're catching on."

"Where's Julianna?"

"Gathering some information and a few supplies you're going to need to begin your task. She will join us later."

Tommen remained silent after that, following Rifun through the fourth floor, making their way to the northeast stair. They did not go by the main corridors, but instead navigated the smaller hallways that served as a more direct route. During the battle, the Akarin had used this maze of hallways to ambush and confuse the Cult forces.

Despite the repairs and stabilization efforts, Tommen was still anxious about the northeast stair, and he stared up at the gap in the floors and the huge stone slabs that covered them. Rifun walked on confidently, not waiting for him. Taking a breath, Tommen reluctantly followed, making sure to step where Rifun stepped and stay a short distance behind. If shit happened, he wanted time to react. If Rifun fell off the stair to his death in the atrium below, Tommen was not about to follow him.

"I'm thinking about keeping the slabs," Rifun said, glancing back. "It gives something of a dramatic effect, don't you think? And it limits access to the eighth floor even more. I think it will let me work in privacy a little more if I don't have to listen to the comings and goings of those looking for the food stores on the seventh floor."

"I suppose so?" Tommen replied uncertainly. "I mean, I guess it makes sense?"

It would also serve as a kind of drawbridge. If the armies come looking for your head, you only have to pull the wire to fell the slabs and isolate yourself long enough to escape out the back door.

They stepped off the slabs onto the eighth floor. The first thing Tommen noticed was that he wasn't huffing and puffing, or not as hard as he normally might. He was getting stronger, increasing his endurance. He was growing accustomed to this godawful thirty-two floor climb. Rifun appeared a bit winded but that was all.

The room remained a combination of an office and a bachelor pad. On one side, all business. White board filled with notes, pinboard stuffed with pictures, clippings, notes, and other assorted items. Desk with more papers and assorted office staples including a computer of some form. Briefly, Tommen wondered if this place had some kind of intergalactic wifi. More to the point, could he tap into it somehow?

The other side of the room, a cozy apartment for a single dude. Mattress with minimal frame, sheets immaculate and ready for the military inspection. Dressers arranged so they sort of sectioned off the area for minimal privacy while also acting as overflow desks for all the work being done in the room. The only things really missing were a mini-fridge, a microwave, and a TV. Another part of the room had been fully curtained off, and Tommen deliberately avoided thinking about what could be in there, even if it was probably little more than a bathroom. Evil ruler of the universe or not, a dude needed privacy to go.

"So I take it Julianna isn't your roommate," Tommen observed casually.

"Indeed she is not," Rifun replied, rifling through several papers, gathering one here and there into a stack. "She prefers her accommodations elsewhere. Speaking of which, how are you and Becky getting along?"

"Fine. I spent New Year's Eve at her house."

"Yes, this I know. I was at your house earlier looking for you. When I saw you were still down at her house, well, I decided to come back later and give you two some privacy of your own."

"Why do you spy on my sex life?"

"I don't spy on your sex life. I spy on you. Tonight, the two just happened to coincide. Not my problem you didn't go home right after the ball dropped."

Tommen rolled his eyes, even if Rifun couldn't see, though he suspected he still could. "And you bringing me multiple boxes of condoms, among other things, isn't spying on my sex life?"

"Not spying on it. Enhancing it. There's a difference."

"How would you like it if I spied on your sex life?"

Rifun turned, brow raised. "Do you really want to know what my sex life is like?"

Tommen opened his mouth, paused, then said, "No, actually I don't."

"Good answer." He went back to his papers. "Now then, if I can just find one...more...thing..."

In the midst of his rifling, Rifun opened a cabinet door, behind which Tommen saw the Authored Books. They appeared neat and organized, unmolested in any way. Then the door was closed. Rifun looked around a bit more, finally finding whatever thing he was looking for and adding it to the small stack of papers in his hand. Was it just fate that all business offices had to be clutter bombs?

"Now then, this is a list of..."

He trailed off, staring at the papers in his hands, blinking rapidly and occasionally shaking his head as if to clear it. Then he collapsed into full seizure.

Chapter Eight
Reorganization

Tommen looked up from his reading as Rifun stirred. About an hour had passed since the man collapsed into seizure. It had lasted about a minute or so, and after a brief arousal back to semi-consciousness, the man had lapsed into slumber. Reluctantly, Tommen had used Gravity to get him into his bed, then took the time to go snooping around the room. He didn't read Malagasy, and his French was as bad as his Spanish, so anything important or damning was lost to him. He ended up going to the cabinet with the Authored Books and picking out the first of Rifun and Cassius' novels. Since then, he'd just been reading quietly, waiting for Rifun to come back around.

He couldn't say quite why, except that he was still torn over what happened at the victory, his supposed no-kill vow, the success they'd had against the Borelians, and the twinge of pity he now felt. At first it was simply pity to watch a powerful man seize on the floor, completely powerless to stop anything that might befall him, like an assassination attempt. That pity was only amplified and mixed with confusion as he read through the Book.

"*Inona...?*" Rifun rubbed his eyes, tried to sit up, lay back down, put one arm over his eyes and the other under his head.

"You're blind?" Tommen asked.

Rifun turned his head and lifted his arm just enough to look in Tommen's direction. "What?"

"Your Book. It says here that you're blind. Or were you blind and it got fixed?"

"I'm not blind," he sighed. "Or not in the traditional sense."

"You took a pickax to the head."

"Yes, I did. It damaged part of my occipital lobe which is responsible for seeing and interpreting visual input. My eyes are still perfectly healthy. They can still see and send signals to the undamaged part of my brain which tells me what I'm seeing, but I can't physically see it. It's called blindsight."

"So...all the shit with the Zero Hour Revolution...the battle with the Akarin...you did all that blind? You couldn't see any of it?"

"Not like you do. My eyes can see everything that's going on and my brain can perceive it, similar to how you can close your eyes and picture something in your mind, like your house for instance, but the connections for me to physically see it are gone."

"There's nothing you can do to fix it?"

"You should know better than that. Time does not heal all wounds. As for Matter and Energy, aside from me not willing to let anyone that close to my brain, there are too few Akari-bearers who even approach that level of skill. The brain is a delicate thing. I figure that if I've managed to accomplish everything I have without full sight, well, no need to go messing with it and lose what little I have left. After all, would you ever have guessed that I have such an injury, just from your past interactions with me?"

"Never in a million years."

Rifun sat up, rubbing his eyes and head and neck as if he'd slept terribly and woken up with a migraine. "So there you go."

"That's where the seizures are originating, isn't it?" Tommen guessed. "Something about the Borelian poison triggered something in the damaged part of your brain."

The man nodded and stifled a yawn, staring at nothing as though truly blind. "Yes. It's terrible because I can feel it, right before it hits, that buildup of pressure. The aura, it's called. And it's like being struck by that pickax all over again just before I black out."

He stood slowly, took the book from Tommen's hands, and went to replace it in the cabinet. Then he stretched a bit, rolled his shoulders and neck, Banded briefly. By the time he turned back around, he appeared almost back to normal.

"Now then, we were here to discuss how things are going to work in the new First Order and where your place is in all of this."

Before he could get much further, Julianna walked in the room, notebook and papers in hand.

"Am I late?" she wondered, her tone suggesting she didn't much care.

"No, we were just starting," Rifun answered.

She paused, looked at him, looked at Tommen. A look passed between her and Rifun, but Tommen did not see any kind of Band. Julianna spoke first.

"Very well. I suppose I will leave these here and come back a bit later, then."

She dropped off her load on the corner of the desk and left the room.

"Does she know about your blindness?" Tommen wondered.

"Of course she does. Anyone who has read the Books knows. And while I understand that it may come as a bit of a surprise, I don't understand your fixation with it. Once again, it's not blindness as you traditionally understand it. For example, I can see that you have your hands shoved in the pockets of your blue jeans. Your shirt is blue and green and you're wearing something of a spring jacket—certainly not heavy enough for the chill of winter—which is black and gray. Your hat is worn out and you prefer fingerless gloves because 'homeless' is the new black I suppose. You could probably stand some new shoes, but maybe wait until spring so they don't get chewed up so bad from the snow; start fresh.

"So, let's cut the obsession with something you didn't know about until an hour ago and never would have guessed at because it makes very little difference one way or the other—"

"Except, if it's the cause of your seizures, wouldn't you want to try and fix it? Kill two birds with one stone, stop the seizures and restore your sight."

"Are you volunteering?" Rifun was growing irritated. "We're here for a purpose, and enough time has been wasted already."

"Yes, sir."

Tommen stood at attention as best he could. Despite training under Berkloff for months, he knew he was still far less skilled than most recruits fresh out of boot camp, simply because Berkloff was dealing with a few dozen species. Under a real human drill sergeant who dealt only with humans and knew how to make greenhorns come to attention, he probably could have snapped to attention so fast, sparks would fly.

Of course, his other flaw was that he couldn't focus as well as a recruit fresh from boot camp, nor could he quite pretend to. His mind was too distracted, now more than ever. He was going to have to look into this blindsight thing because it seemed to defy everything he knew about blindness and brain injuries. There was no real reason to disbelieve it, but the fine line between moderate head trauma with a one-in-a-million condition, and permanent, retarded brain damage if not death, was stunning. The man seemed to scrape by with only centimeters to spare. A few more centimeters lower in the chest, and Kayla would have ripped out his heart. A few more centimeters into the brain, and he could have died or been rendered an idiot.

Did that mean that Rifun and the journals were right, and the Author's preservation of his life was ongoing proof? Was there another force at work, trying to do or undo all the work? Could there be multiple authors? As much as Tommen hated to admit it, he kind of needed to get a look inside the journals. He knew what the Authored Books said—or his Authored Books, anyway. Maybe it was time to look at the opposite side of the coin.

Was that going against Kayla's suggestion to find the Author and then pick the side best corresponding? Maybe, maybe not. His goal in that had been to speak to Chandler about it. Problem was, he hadn't seen Chandler in at least forever. Hard to talk to a guy who never visited, didn't call or write letters or even send a Hallmark card. Lacking guidance, Tommen had to go with what he knew and what was available to him. Wasn't as if Kayla had stuck around to help him. She just lectured and left. Granted, helping her people defend themselves against the Borelians was pretty important. Apparently more important than saving that one lost sheep. But then, while searching for the one might be nice, if the ninety-nine still in the pen are being assaulted by wolves, well, you can't just leave them or else you'll have only the one sheep. Was he getting too philosophical again?

He brought his mind back around to the present, though he was still unable to really focus. So, here and now, with Rifun facing him, the man's eyes could see him and relay the information to his brain where he could perceive the nerve impulses but not consciously see what he was seeing? That just didn't seem possible. It would be like him, Tommen, having some kind of brain damage where he was unable to hear, and yet his ears and everything were structurally sound and still sending signals to his brain where he couldn't actively hear and yet he still knew what was going on. It just sounded preposterous.

"Now then," Rifun began, interrupting his thoughts, "most of this I expect you will learn in journal studies, but I'll give you a brief rundown anyway. Before the first Authored Book, the Akarin had only scraps and fragments and oral history. Then a Book appeared. It was called *Wolf Pack*."

"The Krydik," Tommen stated.

"Their origins, anyway. The appearance of the Book caused massive upheaval among the Akarin. No one quite knew what to make of it. Some were offended that it focused on such an undeveloped, nobody species. Some were offended that it focused on an undeveloped, nobody people." He said the words with some disdain. "Many left the Akarin. Some were absorbed back into Time while others formed smaller splinter groups. Some are still in existence today and each one might lean either more toward the Akarin or the Cult in their sympathies.

"Obviously, neither the Akarin nor the Cult have ever really been widely accepted, instead being seen as the two largest splinter groups off of the Time industry. So to the Time industry and greater universe, we're typically peaceful toward the outside world but huge rivals with a blood feud. On one hand, meek and mild, minding our p's and q's and generally not causing too much trouble. On the other hand, huge military factions with only domination on our minds.

"Part of this was caused by the disappearance of two of the journals. The Cult's only identity came from the Book of Philosophy. It shed light on the big questions of the universe, but each man was left to fend for himself in his own cultural identity, which sometimes conflicted with the Book of Philosophy.

"Once the Book of Abilities was discovered, we were able to fortify our military. You've clearly seen the result of that. The problem is, while it unified the army, it did nothing to bring in outsiders who may have been unable or unwilling to fight. You would be one of those, by the way. And it only further cements our image of being nothing more than religious fanatics.

"The main reason we want to find the Book of Commands—other than Julianna's sentimental reasons—is that it will help form a unified identity among the First Order members. Anyone can be a soldier, speaking more figuratively. And while it's nice to have a general consensus on the bigger questions that all men ponder at one time or another, it does very little to help, comfort, and strengthen in the day-to-day activities of life.

"Our goal is not to be an army or a group of philosophical thinkers, but a culture, a way of life, centered around the Author and the journals. If we can do that, I have little doubt that the Akarin will come to join us."

Rifun picked up a few papers. "That said, we're restructuring things around here so they are distributed among the three journals. Different departments as it were. The Philosophers will be based on the Book of Philosophy. They will be responsible for studying all three journals, ensuring correct interpretation, and teaching English."

"They're the priests, the one in charge of all the religious instruction and institution," Tommen interrupted. "Those in the department headed by the Book of Abilities are going to be your soldiers and other military aspects. The Book of Commands is going to be your culture group, but only inasmuch as it still follows the teachings of the journals, which the Philosophers will relay to them. You're setting up a theocracy."

"Good old George Washington and the American Founding Fathers set up the American Constitution based on Christian values. Did that make them a theocracy? Or was it simply a system that made the most sense and was widely understood at the time? They didn't exclude anyone. It was simply a matter of, If you want to come here, you will assimilate. Bring your food, bring your music, bring your traditional clothing, but don't expect to sacrifice your child on an altar. No different. Freedom does not automatically mean anarchy.

"And, as many have pointed out in the Time industry, how do you plan to unify thousands of species from hundreds of planets? For the Time industry, it was greed. For us, it's simply the bigger things in life."

Rifun handed him a sheet of paper. "I don't often get to do this, hand things out. For most species, it's just impractical. But for you, I'll make an exception. It's a flow chart of how things are going to work out, basically what I just told you."

It looked like a very nice, well-thought-out, sensible flow chart with clear labels and as many straight lines as possible. There was just one problem.

"I can't read this," Tommen said, handing it back. "It's Malagasy, right?"

Rifun took the paper and looked at it, then shrugged. "Fine, so you don't get a flow chart. The point is that you will be in the Culture department, whom I have decided to call the Artists. For the purpose of your mission to locate and retrieve the Book of Commands, I've decided to put you in the Archeology division of the Interculture set. It could change, it could dissolve, but for the moment, that is where you are going to be. The good news for you is that you are no longer under Berkloff's instruction. Yes, go ahead, sigh with relief, you can thank me later."

It was a relief. Not under Berkloff anymore, nowhere near the army or any kind of soldiering. He was going in the Culture department, into Archeology. Not exactly his first career choice, but it was something new and interesting and exciting. This was going to be like Indiana Jones, following old clues and conspiracy theories, outwitting that one nemesis in a race to claim the golden artifact. He was probably exaggerating it in his own mind, but it sounded cool.

"If I'm not under Berkloff, then who am I under?" Tommen wondered. "Julianna?"

"Through a series of twists and turns, yes. But your...immediate supervisor, if you will, is Gadora te Vil no, an Arowa from Pawom, 03-06-11-60-58. I will introduce you to her next time you come here. She is currently away, and there are still a few things that need tying up before I give you the green light to run off to other worlds.

"But, in the meantime, I would highly suggest you familiarize yourself with the journal, what it is, what it looks like, who had it, where it is rumored to have gone, the whole works. And for that, I have Julianna. Seeing how she seems to have wandered off, I suppose I will have to bring her back."

"No need for that," Julianna said, walking in the room. "Trust me, I didn't wander far."

She cast Tommen a pointed look, as if he might have been at fault for Rifun's seizures. A Band enveloped her and Rifun for just a moment. When it finally dropped, he looked irritated and resolute, and she appeared grouchily pacified. Tommen wished he could have heard the conversation, but knew he never would. Despite his new mission and all the ego-stroking praise they heaped on his head, he was still treated as a child among adults, or a traitor amidst loyalists. But still, passing up two perfect opportunities to murder the man the universe hated had to count for something, right? At least a pat on the back, an attaboy, even a biscuit?

He waited patiently for Julianna to reshuffle her papers, converse privately with Rifun again, do some more unknown shuffling and organizing, then finally turn around to face and address him, looking very much the part of the schoolteacher ready with the ruler at a moment's notice.

"I will tell you what I know for sure," she began. "Then I will tell you some of the more credible rumors, and I have a list of some of the more dubious ones.

"The year was 1847. Without going into details of a story you already know, I crossed the Atlantic with Cassius and Rifun. In order to keep the journals safe, I scattered them, intending to return to them but severely underestimating the power of both the Time Portal as well as Cassius himself. One I left with the Cult of the time, and they kept it safe. The third I hid in the cavern when Cassius turned on me. The second, I gave to a man named Andrew O'Dell whom I believed was a supporter."

She handed Tommen a stapled stack of papers containing a full profile on Andrew O'Dell. An Irish native, much like the twins, with coppery hair and full beard. As far as quick information went, he was born in 1643, exposed to Time when he was twenty-eight, chose to forsake his Timekeeper exposure to pursue a career as a Merchant, and reached the rank of Auctioneer before being identified as an Akari-bearer in 1717 and forced into hiding. Or that was the official record. There were also a number of handwritten notes, most likely Julianna's, detailing more of his history and movements, up until World War I when he finally gave someone the slip and went into the unknown universe.

"At some point, he gave the journal to this man, Nathan Wilde, a Harvester."

She gave him a similar profile for said man. A born and bred Brit, Nathan Wilde was one of the early settlers, rumored to be one of those who'd given Time to the Native Americans and led to the founding of Hlohi. He was never identified as an Akari-bearer, though he was listed as a Runner around the same time as Andrew O'Dell and disappeared.

"So..." Tommen began. "No one has seen or heard from these

guys in almost a full century?"

"As I've said before," Julianna sighed, "someone knows something, but that someone isn't saying anything. Even the Books thus far are silent on the matter. Now then, I have a few credible rumors that may be worth investigating.

"The first is, admittedly, a bit dated, but it is the most solid lead I have found. It comes from 1965 our time. Supposedly it was spotted in a shady marketplace on a world called Maronet, coordinates 02-08-16-43-96-06-13, home to the indigenous Mishim and their contentious would-be conquerors, the Lilir. At the time, the marketplace was home turf to what we would consider a crime lord or mob boss, called Arshoni the Slayer, a Mishim."

"How do you consider this a solid lead?" Tommen interrupted.

"The Mishim and Lilir have little love for one another and are always looking for ways to best each other and so settle their numerous territorial disputes. Neither race is Openly Engaged, preferring to remain as Engaged Privilege, with the crime lords in control of who has that privilege and who doesn't. So when someone gets wind that Arshoni the Slayer might have found an edge over the Lilir even greater than Time, well, eventually, word gets out."

She handed him a piece of paper with a summary of basically everything she just said. Tommen was grateful, as he had not thought to bring a notebook and pencil with him.

"The second most credible rumor comes from a Turitian outpost in Quadrant One, Parsec Four, Sector Eleven, System Fifty-Two. In 1971, the journal was reportedly given to Commander Dira as a gesture of goodwill in a newly-formed alliance between the Turitians and Kolkath. The only reason I consider this rumor credible is because, supposedly, around the same time, there was heightened interest in the Cult of the Akari and the Akari in general among the Turitians, though little came of it."

"But how would it have gotten from Quadrant Two to Quadrant One?"

"I don't know. That's what we're hiring you to find out. Not that it particularly matters, but it would be interesting to see what kind of journey the journal has taken across the universe, know whose hands have held it and tried to decipher its words."

Again she handed him a summary of the rumor.

"The third rumor comes shortly thereafter, from 1975. A Psiaco pirate captain named Titik was rumored to have pillaged it in a raid on a royal emissary near coordinates 03-01-16-13-09, a planet called Chilip. I believe the planet to be unrelated, just happened to be where the ships crossed paths. But it is information to keep close to hand."

As each credible rumor got more and more vague, the notes got shorter and shorter, Tommen saw as she handed him the third piece of paper.

"And these," she said, giving him a few sheets stapled together, "are the less credible rumors. Obviously, the less detail there is, the less credible it is. Though some of the detailed ones are pretty sketchy, too. I will leave you to peruse at your leisure and decide what's worth pursuing and what isn't."

Glancing over everything, Tommen was suddenly hit with the magnitude of his mission. He was in charge, which meant he had to tell everyone what to do. More to the point, he had to decide what was worth doing. He had to decipher these notes, go over the history and the people and the events and decide what sounded logical and what was total bullshit. He was the leader, which meant he had to actually start leading, and lead in the right direction. The search might take them all over the universe, but he had to make sure it was a path worth following. The shortest distance was a straight line, so he had to make sure their path was as straight as possible without a ton of detours and unnecessary sightseeing.

Shit.

"So...who's on my team?" he wondered, trying to sound confident and ready to undertake his new mission.

"Come with me and I will introduce you," Rifun said.

Tommen followed him out of the room and back down the slab stairs to the main staircase. Other than repair efforts still fully underway and focused on the northwest staircase, he couldn't really see that anything was especially different about how things were getting done.

"Accommodations and other arrangements are still being decided and settled, so it will take time to get used to them and have them memorized," Rifun was saying as they descended. "The first floor will remain the same. Portal room, cafeteria, non-essentials, but with the addition of the infirmary. That will become a more permanent installment. The fifth floor, once it has been recovered and restored will go to the Philosophers. I think it will give them a nice quiet place to do their studying and learning and teaching. Once you begin your journal studies, that is where you will go. Think of it like going to college and having to find the correct room in the correct building on campus.

"The seventh and eighth floors will remain the same as they are now, emergency stores and my quarters. Other than that, the rest of the floors are still being shuffled and decided. This fortress was not built for this large of a population. Those like you who come from Unengaged worlds or otherwise have families that need tending will most likely be sent home at the end of the day. I'm sure that breaks your heart."

While Rifun continued to speak, Tommen found his mind drifting back to their earlier conversation. The man was doing all of this blind. He avoided obstacles and interacted with others with no problems whatsoever. Somehow he couldn't see but because the problem was in a small part of his brain, he was still able to perceive? How did that work? Tommen made a mental note to look up that "blindsight" thing when he got home.

He also recalled that the supposed injury was on the left side of Rifun's head. Walking on his left side, Tommen Banded and gave Rifun a quick once-over. He didn't touch his hair or actively look, but maybe he could find the small bald spot that the long hair covered up. He couldn't see anything right offhand, but the man had thick hair anyway. He released the Band.

"Looking for the injury?" Rifun asked, glancing at him briefly. Without slowing, he reached up and moved a large lock of hair to reveal a twisted and scarred bald spot at the back of his head on the left side. "Right here. It's not a hole per se, not a direct shot to my brain; some of the bone fragments haphazardly grew back together. But no hair will grow there."

"Oh."

"I still don't understand your fascination with it. You certainly don't appreciate people staring at your hearing aids."

Tommen felt his cheeks grow red. "I don't know, it's just...I guess I'm trying to picture the whole being blind but still able to perceive."

"If I asked you right now to picture your house, your bedroom, your dad's room, the living room, the kitchen, could you do it? Do you know how to get around it, all the little nooks and crannies? Same concept, except I do it in real time. I can't see it, but I can put together a blind mental image of my surroundings, or whatever I'm looking at. It's difficult to explain, but I've made it work in the last hundred years."

Tommen was ready to say something more about the seizures, then decided against it. Little bits of information at a time, figure out how to put them all together. He'd just been given a huge chunk of information about a very big vulnerability of Rifun's; he didn't need to screw it up. He needed to do some research, find out how it worked and how to potentially exploit it.

It seemed almost a cruel thing to do, looking for ways to exploit a crippled man's weakness. But was Rifun really crippled? Had he used his cunning and prowess to advance the good of the universe, he would be heralded as the crowning achievement of humanity, the ultimate testimony to disabled and disadvantaged people overcoming whatever shortfalls initially set them back. Even if this blindsight thing was true, Rifun was no invalid begging for change on the streets.

What if it wasn't true? Tommen hadn't gotten very far into Rifun's story. The man himself could have lied about not having his sight fixed. He could be using it to mess with Tommen's head, make him second guess everything, throw in a little needle of pity. Dependence on his brilliance, pity for his disability, it was a good way to throw off the hounds of war and the vehement cries for his blood. Confuse the authorities long enough and he might be able to make an escape into safer territory.

They made it to the third floor, what used to be primarily meeting rooms and offices. Most of the construction here was complete, the last fixes being finished up, tools being taken to the mad scramble of construction at the northwest stair. They stepped off the staircase and began making their way through the corridors and then to the smaller hallways. "Smaller" was a relative term as even the smallest hallways were still easily twice the size of the halls at school.

"You know these halls pretty well now," Tommen observed casually.

"Of course I do," Rifun replied. "I want to know what my enemies know so it can't be used against me a second time. Tell me, have you ever read *The Art of War*?"

"Sun Tzu? I've glanced through it a couple times."

"You're not going to be a soldier, but it is still a useful read. Maybe if you find time between school, work, and this little Easter egg hunt of yours, you can borrow a copy from the library and do a little more intensive study of it. Never know what you might learn."

"Yes, sir," was all he could say.

"Now then, you will have several individuals with you. If we come across any, I will introduce you. Otherwise, I will tell you their names and introduce you later.

"Your political boni is—"

"Boni?"

"Short for *manamboninahitra.* Literally it means officer or dignitary, but for the non-English speakers among us, it simply means any kind of teammate in any sense and is easier to say. In this instance, you would be considered ekipitarika, a mishmash of *ekipa* and *mpitarika* meaning team and leader respectively. Or it could be ekiboni.

Quite frankly, I can't keep up with all the colloquialisms going around, and I've lost the will to try and correct it. Language evolves, after all. As long as they learn English well enough to read the journals, I'm not going to stop them from using any other language however they choose."

It was difficult to read his true disposition on the matter, whether he found the use and abuse of his language amusing, flattering, or insulting. After a moment or two, Tommen decided he didn't care.

"As I was saying, your political boni is an Arowa named Sisith. He will be your guide to the world of power for each place you travel to, how the government functions, who's in charge, shadow governments, back door dealings, all the juicy stuff that makes *The New York Times* look like an honest middle school newspaper.

"Next is your cultural boni, a Dimica named Rorion. She will be your guide to the niceties and social customs of your travel destinations, including proper greetings, good and bad gestures and body language, and so on. You will obviously be pegged as a tourist wherever you go, but you don't need to offend the locals more than absolutely necessary. She will also give you a bit of a TV travel guide to local customs, festivals, music, food, and so on, in the event that you do end up with some sightseeing time on your hands. And actually, here she is now."

The alien they approached was humanoid, about seven feet tall with no hair and large, mostly black eyes, but its most striking feature was its skin. From a distance, it appeared scaled dark blue and black, like some kind of lizard. Up close, holding a normal conversation, Tommen saw that it was covered in what looked like a layer of water, about an inch deep, all over its body, with no leaking or dripping. It moved and rippled almost like normal skin, and yet it looked like water. Tommen tried not to stare.

Rorion was like most of Rifun's followers, attentive to her master and eager to please, though her general demeanor spoke of experience and more deeply rooted loyalty than what bright-eyed new recruits had going for them. She accepted the mission with dignity, though Tommen suspected she'd known about it before he had.

"I will see you later," Rorion concluded, making a decent attempt at a bow toward Tommen. "I look forward to beginning our mission."

Like Rifun said, she would obviously be pegged for a tourist, but she had the gestures and the mannerisms down well enough to be thought polite and civilized.

Rifun dismissed her, and he and Tommen continued on their way.

"You will also have a linguistics boni. Naq is a Yakik; it's a race universe-renowned for their ability to recognize even the smallest patterns and predict outcomes. They can predict economic forecasts for a century, election results, even the local weather, with ninety-nine percent accuracy. To that end, they can also assimilate languages very quickly by reducing them to a series of vocal and grammatical patterns. So even if she is unable to go into a place speaking the language, give her an hour or two and she'll be talking like a native."

"Did she predict the outcome of the battle, or tell you how to win?" Tommen wondered.

"As I said, Yakik can recognize and exploit even the smallest and barest of patterns."

Tommen took that to mean yes.

"Your journal and Akari boni is thoroughly familiar with the journals, their teachings, their rumors, and, most importantly, their unique secrets. Ilit will be able to tell you whether a journal is real or fake, should someone claim to possess it, and give you details on many of the rumors Julianna briefly told you about."

"I thought the journals were Imprinted? Wouldn't only an Akari-bearer be able to do that—and undo it?"

"And yet, the Akarin could easily produce a fake using similar techniques."

"How will Ilit know if the journal is real if it's been missing for over a century?"

"He has great knowledge of the journals. He ascended to such a point in his studies that only Julianna herself could educate him now. She trusts him. That is all you need to know."

Tommen had his doubts, but elected not to press the matter. He was getting good at that, he thought, keeping his mouth shut. He seemed to acquire more information that way.

"The last boni you have at your disposal is, for lack of better term, the bodyguard, Emet the Siboxi. His social and political value is limited; his sole job is to ensure that if things get hairy that you all get out alive. He's not an idiot, grunt, trigger-happy meathead, however; he is very discerning of the situation at hand. He's not going to jump in and start swinging just because someone got a little testy. But when he does start moving, I suggest you get out of the way. A speeding train is hard to stop and harder to take down."

Tommen had never seen a Siboxi, but he liked what he was hearing so far.

They circled the third floor, then moved down to the second floor and the first floor, doing the same thing each time, finally stopping in the southwest staircase near the portal room.

"We found fewer of your teammates than I would have preferred," Rifun mused, "but I think you have enough information to keep you busy for a while. You know the bonis you will have, and you have some rumors to chase and vacations to plan. Once you believe you have a direction you'd like to go, let myself or Julianna know and we'll gather everyone and tell you how to proceed. Do you have everything?"

The man was out of his element, Tommen reflected. He'd gone wandering semi-aimlessly through the fortress and had only found one person he'd been looking for, wasn't sure of the location of the others, had some small dissertation on the state of the language among his men, hadn't been entirely prepared for this meeting at all, and he'd made up a flow chart. A *flow chart.* Tommen had seen his office getup, but Rifun just wasn't a sit at a computer and print out flow charts kind of guy. He was the go-do person. If he had some semblance of a plan in his head, never mind written down, that would have been astounding. While Tommen could understand mild disorientation from the seizure, he'd Banded himself back to rights, right? It certainly couldn't have caused all the office and paperwork confusion beforehand.

Maybe it was because he'd been moved from warlord and general of the army to political leader. Suddenly, it wasn't all about winning wars and conquering foes. It was, as he himself had said, about forging a new identity in the social, political, and religious realms, not only for his people, but for and with the Akarin. He'd gone from the battlefield to a desk job. A PR job at that.

Still, Tommen made no comments out loud, just flipped through his papers a bit, trying to look busy and interested in his new mission. He was interested, certainly, but he had no idea where to start. Even if he knew where to start, he wasn't sure how this was going to work out exactly. Were his boni teammates under orders to listen to him? Would they follow him willingly otherwise? How would he have to prove himself to each of them, knowing that they came from different cultures which may have very different ideas about good leadership? He could barely get his classmates to listen to him when he got put in charge of a group project.

Yet he said none of this out loud, instead following Rifun to the portal room where he was sent back to his room like any regular night. He couldn't decide if it was way too late or way too early, but three o'clock in the morning was not the ideal time to be doing anything, much less planning an intergalactic vacation. He tossed the papers on his desk and kicked off his shoes. He'd been almost in bed before Rifun came calling. He removed his hearing aids and slid into bed now, and the last thing he remembered thinking was that he probably needed to wash his bedding pretty soon because it had been a while.

Daylight was streaming in through his windows when he blinked awake from a dreamless sleep. His whole body ached, but he really couldn't say why. Walking around the fortress hadn't been all that strenuous, in actuality. Work certainly hadn't been anything special, except for the whole closing part. The Polski party had been relatively tame. He didn't think the sex had been that rough, but what did he know? Maybe it was just the stress about not being abducted by aliens and sold into slavery. He sounded like a loon.

It was almost two o'clock. He'd slept half the day away. That was fine with him. He needed a day off, anyway. Grudgingly, he sat up, stretched, and got out of bed. He inserted his hearing aids while he moseyed around the corner to the bathroom to begin his day. By the time he got around to going out to the kitchen for food, it was past two-thirty. It was after three before his dad roused from his bed and made it out to the living room where Tommen was watching TV.

"So, we survived the night," his dad observed sleepily.

Tommen nodded. "We did." He looked at him. "Do you have to work?"

"Yes, but they're having me come in at eight."

"Too much overtime?"

"Too much overtime, a small thanks for working a dreadful holiday, and other workplace politics. This time, though, I'm the one who set off the fireworks. Intentionally."

"Ouch. That doesn't sound like you."

"It needed to happen. How was your night?"

"Well, Bakery na hÉireann is officially closed, which means I am officially unemployed. Polski New Year's party was a fraction of their Thanksgiving party. And I got taken to the Order fortress."

"Rifun bragging about stopping the Borelian invasion?"

Tommen shook his head. "No. Actually, it started out with him having a seizure. While he was down—which included about an hour-long nap—I decided to read through his Authored Books."

His dad shifted in his recliner and folded his arms. "All right. Find anything interesting? Any Achilles heel?"

"Not Achilles heel. Achilles head. Dad, Rifun is blind."

Walter raised a brow. "Do explain."

"According to his Book, he was on some chain gang, got in a fight with another prisoner, and the other guy put a pickax through his skull. It damaged part of his brain that processes visual input, but not all of it. I'm not sure how it works, but his eyes can see, his brain just can't fully interpret the signals. He called it blindsight. Anyway, point is, he's got a hole in his skull."

"You're right, that is interesting. But I don't see—"

"That's why he's continuing to have seizures," Tommen went on. "Something about the Borelian poison triggered something in the damaged part of his brain. He basically admitted that the seizures are here to stay."

"Once again, a fascinating bit of information, but I don't see how it helps. Unless the bone never healed over the hole, which I doubt, it's only going to be twice as strong in that part of his skull. You're still looking at a regular headshot. And even so, if you're trying to kill someone, go for the overkill, not the just enough."

"No, but I did have another thought. That is, Rifun claims to have had his Books for a while. Every time, there are two copies. One shows up for the person being written about, and one in the Akarin Archives. Kayla had to have known about Rifun's Book. Why stab him in the chest and not in his head?"

Walter shrugged casually. "Rage of the moment? A chest shot would have been easier to pull off and would have happened much quicker. Trying to pull off a head shot like that would have required much more coordination and it would have put her at a cross stance with his arm. Besides, she laced the knife with Borelian poison which was supposed to have killed him anyway. I don't know that it would have mattered much."

Tommen frowned and let out a breath. "Okay, I guess you're right."

"Still, it's good to know. Maybe do some more research on this 'blindsight' and see if there isn't some way we can use it to our advantage. Oh, and that reminds me. Before he visited you, Rifun also paid me a visit."

So his dad explained the brief encounter, including the "negotiations" in which Walter and Tommen kept Rifun's seizures quiet and defended him if necessary.

"What do we do now?" Tommen wondered. "I mean, we're going to go out and look for allies other than him, right?"

"Of course, but we have to do it discreetly. And we have to be absolutely sure that they are as strong or stronger than him and won't turn on us and try to enslave us. We already have one begrudging ally, we don't need two. Assuming we can find such an ally, then we can take all these little secrets and start spreading some rumors."

"Sounds like a plan to me. Where do we start?"

"Well, I imagine there's going to be a meeting soon to discuss what happened, or didn't happen, last night. Earth is safe, but I want to know if the others are, too. There's going to be some fallout, some discussion, some blaming, and probably a lot of questions about Rifun going forward and how much we owe him and so on."

"Will I be there for this meeting?"

"No, not this time. Actually, the only reason I wanted you there for the last one is because I expected him to try and use you in some way, make you a pawn. I was a little surprised that he himself stayed out of things, and part of me thinks he may have gone anyway in some fashion. But that will all come up, I'm sure."

Tommen shifted uncomfortably. "Actually, he did give me a mission of sorts, but it doesn't have anything to do with the Borelians. It was the whole reason he took me last night."

He relayed the mission bestowed upon him, from the goal of finding the journal to the solid story behind it, to the rumors, to his team and how he was generally supposed to go about things, the whole works. As he spoke, he could see his dad's expression growing grimmer and grimmer.

"I suppose to say that I don't want you going would be both obvious and unnecessary," he said when Tommen was finished.

Tommen shrugged. "Honestly, I don't have a problem with it, and there's one reason why. If I find it, we have instant leverage over the Order."

"That's what worries me. It's too obvious, too perfect. Rifun isn't going to entrust his Holy Grail to someone of questionable loyalty, regardless of how you saved his life. There's something more at work here, some other end game he has in mind. I would tread carefully."

Tommen sighed and rolled his eyes. "I've been treading carefully for so long, I don't think I would know how to tread carelessly."

"Good. Keep it up." His dad got up out of his recliner. "In the meantime, I think I'm going to make me some breakfast or lunch and do a bit of loafing before going in to work. You want anything?"

Tommen stood and followed him to the kitchen. "When do I not?"

Chapter Nine
Same Stuff, Different Year

Tommen came awake into a groggy consciousness, fumbling for his alarm and slapping it off. He pulled the blankets up over his head for another minute or two before untangling himself and moseying his way out of bed. Who knew that just four days of staying up late and sleeping in could wreak so much havoc? And that wasn't even counting how his Time and Akari mischief was starting to mess with him.

Halfway through his morning routine, his dad walked in the door, home from work. He wasn't exactly the most popular guy at the station these days, and his demeanor reflected this as he huffed into the seat at the kitchen table and worked on his laces.

"How was work?" Tommen wondered as he fished around for something to eat.

"Nonstop thrills," his dad answered sarcastically. "Just another day of being the guy who may have shot the county's gift horse in the mouth." He shook his head.

"You're not going to be fired for it, are you?"

"No, not likely. But that doesn't mean they won't keep me as the rookie for a little while longer."

"They put you back on probation?"

"Not officially, but they sort of treat me like it. I understand where they're coming from, I do. The county isn't rich and everyone is scrambling for what few tax dollars there are. But I don't like so much money and influence coming from a single person. It's not right." Walter kicked off his boots and stood. "But maybe I'm a little too old-fashioned."

"No more than me, and I'm the Chivalrous Welshman," Tommen told him smartly.

His dad paused, sighed, patted his shoulder. "You're a good man, Tommen." And he headed down to his bedroom.

Tommen got ready in silence after that. How did normal people go through life with so much stress and still find it within themselves to keep going? Normal life was hard enough without throwing Time into the mix. War, colony planets, cults and religious factions, political turmoil, alien abductions. Some days it all seemed surreal.

He shook his head, finished off his peanut butter toast, grabbed his backpack and keys, and headed out to his car. Normally he might have complained about having only a one-car garage, but they'd worked out a system. Tommen pulled his car out and moved his dad's car inside in the morning, and vice versa in the evening. So it was that Tommen's car wasn't frozen solid, and his dad's car could thaw out a little during the day.

His first stop was Becky's house. She wasn't waiting at the curb, but appeared as soon as he pulled up, shuffling hurriedly across the snowy walkway.

"Oh, good, your car is warm," she said, shivering and shaking the snow off her mittens. "Nothing worse than sitting in an icebox."

"Do that often, do you?" Tommen wondered, pulling back onto the road.

"Very funny, smart aleck. Got your new job yet?"

"Um...no, not yet. The guy hasn't called me back yet."

"Think he will?"

"I don't know. I hope so. I guess if he hasn't called me back by Friday, I'll call him back or keep sending out applications and stuff."

"You can always come work for me. I don't know that I want to expand my business to include employees, though, so I'd have to pay you under the table."

He grinned even though she couldn't see. "We can do it

anywhere you want and I won't charge you for it."

"Hardy har. Fine, no job for you. You're probably an illegal immigrant anyway. You and your dad."

"Yup. Better benefits that way."

"When did you get glasses?"

Tommen grinned. He wore the Time glasses his dad had given him. He didn't tell her any of that, but he did explain that they were color-correcting glasses so he could now see in full color. Becky geeked out and wanted to see them, so he handed them over for the remainder of the drive.

The second stop before school was at the house of Will and Eli Shaw. After an accident involving fireworks left Will blind, he and his little brother had transferred to South Charleston High School. Tommen gave them a ride every morning and sometimes in the afternoon.

"Morning, guys," Becky greeted as the brothers got in.

"Morning," Will replied, unusually awake and optimistic. "So, good news. Because of my good behavior over the holidays and stuff, I'm now off house arrest, thanks to my probation officer. He put in a good word for me."

"That's great, dude," Tommen said. "Good for you. How's your community service?"

"With the way my schedule is, I should be able to get it done by spring break. Honestly, I'm feeling kind of good about it so I might see if I can't bump it up a few hours each week and get it done sooner. And actually, if I do that, then I have a little wiggle room if I can't do a day because of court or a doctor's appointment. But if I do get it all done before spring break, there's a dude says he'll give me a job, try to help me stay busy and make some money."

"What's the job?" Becky wondered.

"Dude works for a publishing company, but it's not the standard print publishing, it's all the extras, especially audiobooks and, get this, braille. Said he'd love to have a blind kid on staff who can proofread the braille since his sighted braillists tend to go cross-eyed after a while, can't pick out some of the minor mistakes. Or that's the gist of it. Likes my voice, too, so he might have me going the other way, braille to audio."

"Sounds like a good gig."

"Yeah. Starting pay is pretty nice, too. And if I work with Mrs. Wendell and can get scholarships and stuff to go to school for English or journalism or something that, you know, relates, he said he'll give me a nice raise."

"Good for you, dude," Tommen told him. "See? The world isn't ending."

It was like watching himself for a third party perspective. Will had gone from miserable and cynical at the beginning of the school year to eager and hopeful now. Life had changed, yes, but it wasn't over. His blindness had made him uniquely equipped for this braille-audio job.

As usual, Tommen dropped off Will and Eli at the front curb of the school, then went around to find a parking spot. He and Becky traded secret movements and gestures before getting out of the car and going inside. Becky gave him back his glasses and wandered off to her locker. Once he'd dropped off his things in his locker, Tommen went to find Will at his.

"What's up?" Will wondered.

"Got a question for you," Tommen said, leaning against an adjacent locker and folding his arms. "Know that I don't mean to insult you or anything, but I was wondering if you'd ever heard of a condition called blindsight."

"Blindsight? Can't say that I have, but it sounds like an oxymoron to me. What is it?"

"Supposedly, it's a condition where the eyes are perfectly healthy but the part of the brain that processes the visual input is damaged. The person can't physically see, but some part of the brain can still process the information and let that person...see? Like a mind's eye picture without actually seeing anything. Or that's how I understand it. Someone I know—I wouldn't exactly call him a friend—

says he has it, and he showed me the part of his head where something big went through his skull and damaged that particular part of his brain." A lie, but oh well. "I mean, I never would have guessed that he was blind, and I'd never heard of such a thing before. I was wondering if maybe you had."

Will shook his head. "Nope. Never really applied to my situation, I guess, because, well, you can obviously see that my eyes are not perfectly healthy."

"Well, I was just wondering if you had."

"Sorry, dude. Listen, I have to go talk to Mrs. Wendell. I'll see you at lunch."

"Roger that."

Tommen moved off as Will skated toward Mrs. Wendell's office, his white cane gliding along the floor. He returned to his own locker three seconds before Becky appeared.

"It's nice to see Will getting his life back on track," she commented.

"It is good," he agreed.

"I think everyone needs a nosy little dwarf in their lives."

"Sorry, I'm not sharing you with him."

"Good to know. But then the question becomes, where can we find another nosy little dwarf for him?"

"I think," Tommen said, mussing her hair, "with everything going well for him and things turning around, he can find his own girlfriend without your help."

"You think?"

"I know."

She sighed. "If you insist. That's not to say I might not make some subtle hints and recommendations, at least on the female side."

"How do you know he's not already dating someone, like from his old school? Quarterbacks are still a pretty hot commodity."

"Because he's never mentioned anything like that. And you know how hard it is to keep secrets and information from me."

He thought about saying, I don't know about that. Then he

figured it would only compel her to be more nosy to learn his secrets. He didn't need to bring her in on any of that. Instead he opted for a more neutral, "Don't I know it?"

This seemed to please her, and he left it at that.

It was a little annoying to have one semester split up by Christmas break, just for the fact that it was so hard to get back on track. First period Spanish, no one remembered jack shit from the previous chapter, and that was assuming anyone realized they were back in school seeing how there was more conversation about all the fun over Christmas than anything school-related. It didn't help that Mrs. Perez was half the problem, going on about her trip to Ecuador.

To that end, she had a whole new batch of conversations for them to listen to and analyze and dissect and rearrange and try to replicate. At least the conversations were authentic and not a bunch of scripted parrot talk for them to repeat over and over again with no clue what they were saying or why. Reasons why Spanish III was better than Spanish I, though Tommen still only took it because it was required. He much preferred his own Welsh or Irish, or Hebrew or Hungarian or Polish. Damn. Maybe he ought to start listing this shit on his resume when he sent out applications. Maybe he could forgo all this entry-level stuff and get a job at the UN or something. Was there a need for Welsh interpreters? Maybe not, but if he got good enough, Hebrew had to be high on the list, right? Become an interpreter in the military or something? Tour overseas a little, sit in on diplomatic exchanges, meet high-profile people, if someone asked about his job actually be able to legitimately say, "I would tell you, but then I'd have to kill you"?

Well, it probably existed only in his head, anyway. He leaned back in his seat as they got started on the actual lesson with only about twenty minutes left in the class. Then the bell rang and they were off again.

He found a substitute waiting for them in Algebra, as Mr. Keller was not yet back from vacation; supposedly his flight had been delayed and he was, even now, rushing to get back home.

Of course, that just meant that the entire class was a blow off, and everyone basically did their own thing. Tommen did some of his writing in his notebook, perused the Internet a bit on his phone, texted Becky once, and was surprised when she texted back.

"Is your class as exciting as mine?" he'd written.

"Ten times more," she replied. "Half the class isn't even here, so it's basically just doing whatever."

"Mr. Keller isn't here, so it's basically the same thing."

"Why do they even bother coming up with lesson plans for today? Why do they even bother having school? Why not just call it a snow day automatically and not waste everyone's time?"

"Because then we would just have the same problem tomorrow."

"So, do you enjoy writing?" a new voice wondered.

Tommen clicked his phone screen off as the substitute walked up to his desk. "Huh?"

"Your notebook there. I'm not exactly a globetrotter, but that doesn't look like English or Spanish to me."

The sub took a seat in the desk in front of him which was normally occupied, but the assigned student was off on the other side of the room.

"It's just writing," Tommen said, closing the notebook. "Just to pass the time and stuff. A little stress relief, too, I guess."

"What about?"

"Historical fiction. Appalachian history."

The man nodded. "I'm from New England, actually, grew up in one of those little fishing villages that seem to attract ghosts and murderers and horror stories like a magnet."

"My parents and uncle immigrated here from Wales. My older brother was born there but was really little when they came over."

"First-genner, then. Very good. What do your parents do?"

Tommen blushed hard. "Um...well...they died. All of them. Carbon monoxide. I was raised by my uncle."

"I'm sorry to hear that. How old were you?"

"Eight."

"Aw, that's terrible. But. At least you were able to stay in the family."

"Yeah."

The man shook his head. "I'm sorry, I seem to be an expert at bringing up bad memories in people. Heh. Makes you wonder how I got to be a substitute teacher, eh?"

"No, it's all right."

"Your last name is Forbes, isn't it? If I remember from roll call."

"Yeah."

"Tommen Forbes. Are you that kid from the camp—"

"Up in Wellspring? Yup, that's me." Tommen rolled up his coat sleeve to show off his burned arm.

The sub nodded. "Yeah. I had a niece in the younger kids' camp, her first year. I was a little skeptical since I knew a bit about the history of the camp, its ups and downs. But it's good to know that they hire good counselors like you to look after the kids."

"Thanks. I think?"

The man clapped him on the shoulder—his left shoulder, causing sharp pain to start zinging from his shoulder to his fingertips and back again—and stood. "It's a compliment. You're a good man. Your uncle ought to be proud."

And he moved off to talk to another group. Tommen sat in his seat, stunned. That was the second time today someone had told him he was a good man and that his dad-slash-uncle was or should be proud of him. He wasn't complaining, but he was suspicious. When coincidences started popping up, or when a bunch of good things in a row started happening, the paranoia bells started going off. He texted his dad.

"You awake?"

No answer.

Well, it was only ten o'clock, after all, even if it seemed later. Twenty minutes later, the bell rang and the mass that was the student body shuffled off to third period.

For Tommen, that meant English, the bane of his existence. He paused at his locker, as if he could put off the class for so long, he would just be excused. But it only gave Becky an extended opportunity to drop by and give him—well, his waist—a huge hug.

"And why isn't Little Miss Studious rushing off to her next class?" he asked mockingly.

"Oh, please. It's going to be just like this all day," Becky said, rolling her eyes. "I mean, just look at the halls. They even look emptier from all the kids still gone. The only ones here are the poor kids whose parents couldn't afford expensive, exotic vacations."

"Aren't you one of those kids with the rich parents?"

"Mm...by technicality, I guess. But if we'd gone on vacation over Christmas, we couldn't do anything over spring break. And my parents have to put aside a little extra since it sounds like we're going to have a stowaway this year." At Tommen's expression, she rolled her eyes again and said, "You, dummy. If you're interested and can get time off whatever job you find, they're totally willing to bring you along. I mean, there will be stipulations and stuff, but you can come."

"Um...where?"

"How about we talk about it at lunch? Why don't you think about some of the places you'd like to go? It'll give you something to do in your dreaded English class."

Oh, right, that. That awful thing that was going to consume his time for the next hour or so. Sighing, Tommen grabbed his things and slipped in the door to his class just as the late bell rang. He managed to get in his seat half a second before the teacher looked up and counted him late.

English was spent actually doing English stuff, not talking about vacations or goofing off because half the class was gone. Only a couple people were missing, but they had things they needed to do, like analyze history and themes and racism and write essays about all three. Because no one had anything better to do with their time, of course. Chapters were assigned, papers were handed out, worksheets were handed out, homework was given. Then they all went down to the computer lab to start on their essays, and they would be turning in the first draft by the end of the week. Have fun, kiddos.

Thank God lunch was next. A shitty class followed by man's saving grace. Tommen traded his books for his lunch sack and met up with Becky at her locker before heading to the cafeteria.

"Okay, so, I'm seeing...I'm seeing...a turkey and cheese sandwich," she said jokingly, putting her hands up to her head like a TV medium.

"Not quite," Tommen told her, sitting down at their usual table. He dumped out the lunch bag. "Ta da!"

"Oh my gosh, he changed it up! What is this?"

"This...is what we here in the mountains call French toast. I don't know, in California they might call it cultural appropriation for toast to be associated with the French, but—ow!"

He smiled and put on a good face even as his left arm screamed in pain from a playful punch. He took his dish to the microwave to reheat the food. By the time he returned, Will and Eli had joined them.

"Becky here says you brought something other than your ham on rye with mustard," Will said. "What the hell, man?"

"Oh, you know, new year, new resolutions," Tommen replied, shrugging even though the blind man couldn't see.

"Nah. Same shit, different year."

"Something happen this morning when you talked to Mrs. Wendell?"

"I told her about the job and everything, you know, going to school for English or journalism or whatever, and she said she'd look into courses to take and scholarships and everything. But she also said that other than scholarships for disability and being a minority, I was probably SOL on having my college paid for because I never gave two shits about my grades except to keep them up enough to be able to play football. I mean, I had a sports scholarship lined up, but that got retracted, obviously. On top of that, most scholarships require essays and shit. Dude, I can barely write a letter to my grandma. How can I convince people to give me money, especially this late in the game? I'm supposed to have all this lined up already, but I feel so far behind."

Becky shifted. "I might be able to help with that. I'm already kind of helping Tommen with his essays. Maybe we can all get together and have an essay party."

Will shook his head and gave a look in Tommen's general direction. "If that's what you two do for fun, I don't know that you'll ever have sex."

Tommen elected to remain silent on that one and instead started in on his lunch. He supposed there were worse things he could be accused of, though he'd never actually been accused of being boring. He wasn't sure how he felt about it. On the other hand, Will could be joshing him and totally suspected that he and Becky were having sex. He didn't dwell on it for too long, however, lest he somehow give himself away. He didn't mind people knowing that he was sexually active, but Becky had higher standards for herself. Let it be known that she was sexually active, and all sorts of unwanted attention would suddenly come her way. Was that a double-standard? It wasn't as if it would be difficult to guess who he was sleeping with if it became known that he wasn't a virgin. Either it was Becky, or else he was cheating on her. Maybe he was overthinking things.

Somehow, while he'd been lost in his own mind, Becky had made arrangements for the three of them to meet up at Will's house and go over scholarships and essays and other un-fun English-y things. Neither male wanted to do it, but they did want to knock a few thousand dollars off their college tuitions. They were saved from having a pre-essay party discussion by the bell signaling the end of lunch. Trash went in the big gray bin, and Tommen took his paper sack back to his locker to trade for his Psychology books.

Nothing much had changed over Christmas break, except the teacher, who was already certifiably crazy, now had a huge batch of conspiracy theories to preach about. He'd had his theories before break, of course, but now he had new, rock-solid evidence that Christmas was a conspiracy. It wasn't about Christians changing pagan holidays, no, but it was intentionally placed near New Year's in order to facilitate excessive drinking and other memory-wiping activities so the government could carry out various nefarious activities and experiments. That's why he would not touch any alcoholic drink between December 1st and January 31st, because he wanted to be alert when such activities took place.

Tommen tuned much of this out, silently noting one of his previous conspiracy theories that alcohol itself was not a beverage enjoyed by humanity for the last ten thousand years, but another government conspiracy to control the masses. Prohibition had been the response of the select few who'd uncovered the conspiracy, and the government sent disposable, private agents—by the names of George Nelson and Al Capone, among others—to get rid of these protesters.

The man wasn't stable, say it that way. Why he'd been allowed to teach psychology was beyond anyone's comprehension. Why he'd been allowed outside of any mental institution was a conspiracy theory in itself. Several of the students wondered whether the name he gave and they all called him by was his real name, or something he'd come up with in order to throw off whatever phantom government agents were following him.

But for as crazy as the man was, it kept his students alert, and class was never dull. So he had that going for him. Tommen didn't feel particularly enlightened or educated by the time he left, but he didn't feel like melting into the floor, either. He was halfway to his locker when he felt his phone buzz for a text, but he ignored it for the time being.

He did not see Becky at his locker and headed off to Chemistry without incident. As soon as he walked in, his attention was taken by a huge diagram on the board with a title reading "New Seating Chart!" Because why not?

Tommen found himself sitting at a lab table across from Julie, the special needs sophomore whose name he'd drawn for Secret Santa. She was actually very smart, but completely socially inept. For those who knew her and understood this, accommodations were made, and life was reportedly very nice; she never had a bad word to say about anyone and would help anyone in any capacity she could. For Tommen, though, he wasn't sure how to respond to her. Of all the things to not teach in school, understanding and interacting with special needs people was one of the most glaring deficits, in his opinion.

For the longest time, his opinion had been held only of those like Julie who had mental problems. Lately, though, his definition had expanded to include those like Becky, who was sharper than a filleting knife, but just a little different physically; and even those like himself or Will who had hearing or vision problems. They all gravitated toward each other because no one else did. As if being blind or being short or having hearing aids suddenly made them super weird and untouchable. Maybe he was just being cynical. Most people were very nice and understanding. But the cruel words of one moron could sometimes undo the kind words of a thousand nice people.

"I requested to sit by you," Julie said suddenly, interrupting his thoughts. "I wanted to, because you're nice."

"Do you have any glowsticks left?" he wondered politely.

"One. I'm saving it because it's special."

"Oh. What makes it special?"

"Because it's white. All of the other ones are colored, but this one is white." Then she named off several chemical compounds that the manufacturers must have forgotten to include to give it a color. "So it's rare. That's why I'm saving it."

"What are you saving it for?"

"I don't know yet. But I'll know when to use it."

She never stopped smiling, and Tommen found himself a little more at ease. To be so excited over something he considered simple and cheap, and to not be fazed by what he considered greater concerns, it was nice. As the teacher went up front to begin roll and make sure everyone sat where they were supposed to, Tommen figured that Chemistry might not be so bad this time around.

That thought only lasted into the first half of the lecture. He had a good table partner, but class was still class. He didn't mind Chemistry, and he was grateful that they were finally getting out of the same kiddie building blocks they'd been going over for the last seven years just reworded more and more sophisticatedly, but that was the reason the first year of college cost so much and was so unnecessary; it was because high school curriculum was a joke. Teach them something useful, if they must teach them anything at all.

Tommen got off his mental soapbox before he got too carried away. Just a year and a half left and then he could move on to something he really wanted to do. Actually, not even that. One more year. He'd decided to go with a full two semesters of high school his senior year, and then enter the spring semester of college. That way, he could be fully free and clear of high school and his idiot classmates while still getting the dual-enrollment discount. One full-time semester of college was still more doable than a couple of part-time semesters. He could handle it, he was sure. Wasn't like he didn't have the ability to make all the time he needed to get homework done.

And just like that, the day was done. Julie wished him a good afternoon and headed out. He gathered his things and followed the crowd into the hall, snaking through the throng to his locker. Just as he was zipping up his bag, Becky joined him.

"I guess since you don't have to work, you can take a lady home," she said.

He paused. That's right. He didn't have to work. The bakery had been closed for a few days now, and yet his first instinct was to get in his car and drive there for a shift. He nodded. "Yeah, I guess so. What about Will and Eli?"

"Will is riding the bus to wherever his community service place is today, and Eli has sports practice. Just me and you."

Well, he wasn't going to argue with that. They made their way to the parking lot, but elected to wait in the lobby a few minutes. The buses were pulling out and there was a huge line to get out to the road. It wasn't worth sitting in a cold car for that kind of a wait.

So they talked about all the fun of being back in school. The work was hard, teachers were crazy, and somehow they had to balance their jobs in between, to say nothing about their relationship. Once the crowd had thinned some, they headed out to his car.

"Your house, then?" Tommen wondered.

"Do you still want help on your scholarship essays?" Becky asked.

He grumbled a little. "Yes. I don't want to do them, but I need to save up some college funds somehow."

"When does your dad leave for work?"

"Four, usually. Why?"

"I may have picked up a little something to try. If you're interested."

"I could be. What is it?"

"A surprise."

Damn, but she was good, and he wanted her all the more for it. He managed to quell his thoughts by the time they reached his house, but the primary factor there was that his dad was still home; he couldn't just walk in with an obvious erection like a neon sign saying, "We're going to have sex later."

"Hey," Tommen greeted as they walked through the living room.

"What's on the agenda for today?" his dad inquired, one brow raised.

"I have two scholarship essays due by the end of the month and I am nowhere near ready? So Becky is here to help."

"Did you get my text?"

"Um..." Oh, right, his phone went off earlier, didn't it? "If I did, I didn't check. I haven't really been on my phone lately. Why?"

His dad shook his head. "Nothing. Something we can talk about tomorrow. Unless this 'essay writing' is going to be going on all week?"

"We can always talk in the garage."

Becky excused herself to go to the bathroom, and the men took the hint to move it out to the garage.

"What's up?" Tommen wondered, encasing them both in a Fast Band. "Word from the Tacagans or Borelians or what?"

"There was a meeting today, on Tacaga, to see how the Borelians are recovering from the attack, and to try to predict what their next move is going to be."

"Was Rifun there?"

His dad nodded. "He was. In summary, it goes like this: The Borelians don't appear to suspect human involvement. It's unclear whether they suspect Cult involvement. It sounds like they pulled back a good portion of their forces to the three systems they control. Sounds like most of the fires still aren't out."

"So that's a good thing."

"It is, for now, but there's no telling what they're going to do next. We got lucky with this one hit, but now we have to be careful how we go about things."

"Why? We found a weakness; let's exploit it."

"Pearl Harbor was a serious blow to the United States in World War II. We weren't involved up until that point, and when we stepped in, we brought the war to a decisive close. We, Earth, humanity can't be on the receiving end of a similar retaliation by the Borelians."

Okay, so he had a point. "What's our next move, then?"

"With the Borelians pulling back their forces to deal with the fires, we can't attack them so directly so soon."

"What's Rifun doing in all of this?"

"For the moment, he's in agreement. And that might have something to do with protecting his own interests."

"His seizures."

"That's right. But he's also trying to play the Tacagans. Now that they know what he's capable of with his Disguises, they're like a couple of wolves circling each other. I don't know what his intentions are there or how the Tacagans are going to react; I just hope we get our planetary defenses before it all hits the fan. As for the overall plan, I honestly don't know. I'm not exactly consulted for war strategies."

"If you were, what would you tell them?"

His dad huffed a sigh, his mustache twitching. "We got them pulled back by attacking their home territory. If we went after some of their allies, we may weaken their standing when they venture out again. But we would have to be discreet, or else we just end up with more enemies ourselves and a very deadly alliance with their sights set on us."

Tommen rubbed his eyes. "War is complicated."

"Yes, it is. And to that end, do you have a job yet? Interview, schedule, anything of the sort yet?"

"No, not yet."

"Good. Thursday is your first appointment with the therapist."

"Dad...I said I'm fine. Okay, it's been a couple weeks, school is back in session—"

"This isn't a discussion. You're going. That's all I'm going to say about that."

Tommen sighed. "Yes, sir."

"Good."

He dropped the Band. Becky would expect them to talk for longer than three seconds, after all. "Have you talked to Laura lately?"

His dad faltered a bit. "I did talk to her this morning. She made it back to Minnesota, staying with her parents to take care of her dad."

"How are things looking?"

He shook his head. "Not very good. The way they're talking, if I do get up there to visit over spring break, it'll be for his funeral."

"That sucks."

"So, that's where that stands."

"Ouch. Just...that really sucks. Tell her I'm sorry, next time you talk to her."

"I will. All right, get back to your essays. And make sure that's all it is."

Tommen rolled his eyes. "I know. She has to get home to get her homework done, too."

His dad didn't buy the flimsy excuse, but said nothing more as they retreated back into the house which was actually heated. Walter paused. "It's a strange thing, seeing you twice in one day. If it's not school, it's work for one or both of us."

"I'm not the one who passed up retirement," Tommen told him.

"Oh, sure, rub it in."

Tommen headed down to his room and fired up his computer. A minute later, Becky walked out of the bathroom and joined him. It didn't take but fifteen seconds for her to begin critiquing his essay.

"Does it really matter all that much?" he whined, about halfway through.

"Yes, it does. You aren't the only one looking for these scholarships, and they'll use any excuse to throw your paper out. You have to look and sound professional, excited, educated, and worthy of all the cash they're throwing your way."

He groaned but said nothing more as his dad poked his head in the room.

"I'm heading off to work, kids."

"Bye, Dad," Tommen sighed.

"Not going so well, huh?"

"I'm going to need every day between now and January 31st to get this thing up to par, at least if she has anything to say about it."

"I do have something to say about it," Becky told him smartly.

Walter nodded. "All right. Well, be good."

"Yes, Dad."

His dad Banded the two of them, gave him a look and another warning, then released the Band and headed out. Tommen heard the car leave and zoom off down the road. He couldn't get two words in before his phone rang.

"Checking up on you already?" Becky teased.

"Never know."

Tommen recognized the number, and it took him a second to answer. "Hello?"

"Hi, is this Tommen?"

"Could be. Who's calling?"

"This is Chris from Rock Construction and Remodeling. I was calling to find out if you are still interested in the job and when we can meet for an interview."

"Oh. Yeah. Sure, I mean, I'm interested. I guess the only thing I've got going on is school. And a doctor's appointment on Thursday."

"Great. Why don't we meet tomorrow, then?"

"Works for me."

"Excellent."

Chris gave him directions to his office, confirmed the time, and hung up. Tommen still sat there like an idiot for a minute or two before finally setting his phone down.

"Tommen? Tommen? Earth to Tommen? Are your antennas still receiving signal?" Becky asked, poking his hearing aids. He shook his head and moved out of the way.

"Huh? Yeah. No, I'm good."

"Got a job interview at the construction place?"

"Yeah, tomorrow after school."

"Sweet. Although, once again, I won't be able to see you a whole lot."

"For right now, it sounds like it's just a weekend gig. No point in me showing up to a site at three if they're going to be done at five. That kind of thing. Summer, yeah, there will be a ton of work to do."

"Well, it's good news, anyway." Becky grinned. "And I think it calls for a little celebration."

"Ooh. Do I get to see the surprise now?"

"You get to see it, touch it, feel it, move with it..."

An hour and a half later, they were still naked in his bed, talking, cuddling, laughing and carrying on.

"So, really," Tommen said. "You can't drive, and it's too cold to just walk to the local porn shop to buy stuff. Where did you get it?"

"The Internet has everything," Becky informed him. "I order stuff all the time for my sewing business. Just one more box in with the rest, no one is the wiser."

"Then the question becomes, did you overnight it, or have you had it for a while? It's been hardly two weeks since Christmas."

"I've had it as long as you've had the condoms in your shirt drawer. I suspect it's a little harder for you to sneak stuff in and hide it, so you had to have had those for a while, too."

Tommen felt his whole body turn red. "Maybe."

"I also use prepaid cards, so I can keep better control of my spending and so I don't have to answer any uncomfortable questions."

"Yes, but once again, I'm a guy. You're the good little Catholic Jew."

She shrugged. "What can I say? It's a gift."

He kissed her, she put one leg over his hip, and they did it again. They lay in bed for another ten minutes or so afterwards until they conceded defeat to hunger. Essays forgotten, they got dressed and headed out to the kitchen to see what they could scrounge up. It was seven o'clock before Tommen took Becky home, and when he returned, found that very little had gotten done by way of his essays. But sex, man...that was a winner.

Soon enough, he found himself trying to make sense of Becky's notes and corrections. The easy things he could handle: punctuation, spelling, little things like that. When he got to the notes about rearranging words and phrases and sentences and considering his voice and this, that, and the other thing, that was where he got lost. Why was it so hard to convince people to give him money? He was poor, dammit. Half-deaf, child of a single immigrant parent. Why did he get no weeping media sensation where his story would be broadcast to the entire nation and people from all across the country would send him money? Why did he have to do this the hard way? He wasn't even entirely sure what a euphemism was.

"Is your mission to find the journal going to take as long as these essays?"

Tommen looked behind him to see Rifun sitting on the edge of his bed. The man continued, "I enjoy a good romp as much as the next man, but there is still work to be done."

"I thought there was no time limit?" Tommen wondered.

"There isn't, but if you're just going to spend all your free time having sex, I could just as well assign this to someone else."

"No, I'll get to it. I haven't been able to get to the Wheel is all. My dad is reluctant to take me, and since Micah and Kayla are gone, I really don't have anyone else. You just pop in and out whenever you feel like, so it's not like you're a very reliable taxi—"

"Would you rather open the portals yourself, then?"

Tommen stopped. "Open...the portals myself, what do you mean?"

"Instead of relying on others for a ride, maybe I ought to cut the crap and show you how to drive yourself. Give you your other set of keys as it were. I know you've been shown how to lend strength. It's not a huge leap from there, just ripping a hole through Matter and Energy, connecting two points in the universe."

"Nothing difficult about that, is there?"

"Not at all. Come with me. Let's try something easy to start."

Reluctant yet curious, Tommen got up. He followed Rifun through a portal to the fortress.

"I realize this is a difficult place to go because of the Wheel interfering, but if you train difficult, the rest ought to be easy. The only thing tougher than this is opening a blind portal. Now then, we're here. Take us home."

"How am I supposed to do that? Just will us there?"

"Mm...to an extent, yes. You know Earth's coordinates?"

"1-11-5-4-38."

"Very good. Now, I'm going to let you in on a little secret. It's much easier to open portals as an Akari-bearer for the simple fact that you understand the properties of Matter and Energy, not just Time. The Time industry views portals as a matter of sheer power and a little magic. But we know better. In the same manner that you feel inside yourself, now feel outside. Don't just touch the Matter around you, but the Energy. Feel your exact position in the universe. Now feel the exact position of your bedroom. You walk from one place to another and may not notice a difference here or there, but each place is unique. Think of it as how you perceive the passage of time. Others feel hours, minutes, maybe seconds. But you notice more than that. So it is with the portals."

Tommen did as he was bid, but still couldn't shake the feeling that he was supposed to be cross-legged on the floor with a bunch of incense and chanting "ohm" or something similar. Feel his place in the universe, and then feel his bedroom. Right. He knew there was a difference; there was a huge difference. The gravity was different, the air was different, even just the feel was different. This was a fortress that had seen a lot of blood lately. His room was, well, his room. It was warm and familiar, and he'd shared his bed with Becky.

Suddenly, it was as though he'd been punched in the chest. He stumbled back several steps and fell on his seat, stunned as something resembling a broken portal flashed and then sputtered out, like a candle. Rifun walked over and offered him a hand.

"Not bad for a first try," he mused as Tommen got to his feet, ignoring the hand.

"Did I do it?" Tommen asked.

"According to your girlfriend, you did it two or three times."

Tommen gave Rifun a look, but the man just smirked for a moment before answering, "For a brief second, yes. It wasn't very big and it certainly wasn't stable by any means, but you've got the idea. Do it again."

Taking a breath and steeling himself for any more physical surprises, Tommen tried again. This time, he was able to see and hold his tiny portal for a full second before being forced to drop it. He again sat down, sweat pouring down his forehead and dripping off the end of his nose.

"Holy shit," he breathed. "That really is difficult."

"Did you think your many-decades-experienced Captain,

Lieutenants, and Faharoa were lying?" Rifun wondered casually.

"Did I at least get it to the right place?"

"Given that it wasn't much bigger than a box of cereal, it's hard to say. One more time, then, just for kicks."

Grudgingly, Tommen got to his feet one more time, this time accepting the hand that was offered. He tried to focus himself more this time, root himself where he was and really think about where he wanted to go, feel it as much as possible, before trying to open the portal.

Once again, it wasn't much bigger than a cereal box, but Tommen was able to peek through it long enough to see that it was his bedroom. Then the portal snapped closed and he went down a third time.

"I'd say you're getting the hang of it," Rifun mused. "And, in all reality, that was a very easy portal to open. You're standing in a place you've been multiple times and you're trying to go somewhere that is intimately familiar, never mind that you're trying to fight the pull of the Wheel. I suspect future portals to other, less familiar places, will be much more difficult. But for a first attempt, you did well."

"If that's a compliment, I'll take it," Tommen breathed. He wiped his brow. "Construction is going to look so easy compared to this."

"Indeed it will, especially if you throw a little Gravity into the mix."

"And get thrown in the loony bin? Or have the other guys thrown in the loony bin? Thanks but no thanks."

"I'm not talking about magically lifting huge stones or trusses or anything like that, or not necessarily. I'm simply talking about making it easier on yourself. Why have trouble hauling around bags of concrete? Let Gravity take some of the weight. Why let yourself get boxed in for two fifteen minutes breaks and one measly half hour lunch break? Extend them out. Take time to rest and relax, gather your strength. You'll be the star employee in no time."

"If I do stuff like that, it'll be to save my back and my sanity, not necessarily to draw attention to myself."

"Not at first, but you will, one way or another."

Tommen rubbed his face and stood on rubbery legs. "Are you going to make me stay here all night until I can show myself the door?"

Rifun shook his head. "No. You need time to process things, think things over. And you have to be up for school tomorrow. What kind of teacher would I be if I cut into your education like that? We'll continue this training for a bit until you can at least get yourself to the Wheel to do research for your mission. As for the blind portals to other worlds, we'll leave that to the more skilled on your team, hm?"

"Hey, sounds good to me."

"Excellent."

Having had his ass kicked three times already by portals, Tommen was in less than stellar condition to go through yet another one, and he stumbled to his bed without so much as a "good bye" or "thank you" to Rifun, which didn't bother him any.

He crawled into bed and lay down, rubbing his eyes and willing himself not to fall asleep. It was a dumb thing to do, and he removed his hearing aids and set them on the charger, knowing he would inevitably fall asleep after the night he'd had. He'd actually learned how to open a portal. And he'd done it. It hadn't been very big or very stable, and it had completely kicked his butt, but he had physically opened a portal. That was Journeyman level training right there, and he was still only an Apprentice, at least by Time standards. To that end, he didn't have much of a comparison other than his dad showing him how to lend strength, but he thought it might have been easier doing it Rifun's way because, as the man had pointed out, he was able to use the other elements like Matter and Energy to form a fuller, more complete picture of what he was doing.

Maybe he could ask Kayla about it the next time he saw her. Ask her for a little explanation, a little tutorial, show some deference to her and her version of the Akari, and try to get back on her good side. And he would obviously have to ask his dad for a little more training, a few pointers to make it less strenuous. Although, there was nothing easy about opening any portal. But he would ask anyway, just to be sure.

Tommen figured he must have fallen asleep at some point, because the next thing he knew, his alarm was going off.

Chapter Ten
Studies

Tommen woke, feeling as though he hadn't slept at all, and he ached something fierce, like a sore reminder of his days of fighting with Tyler Freeman. He rolled over and slapped off his alarm, then dragged himself out of bed, grabbed his hearing aids, and began his day. He met his dad in the kitchen.

"How was your shift?" Tommen asked.

His dad slipped off his second boot and stuffed the pair among the rest of the shoes. "Long to begin with, but it was quiet enough this morning that I got out on time."

"Anything unusual, of the Borelian or Time or other extraterrestrial variety?"

"Nothing that jumped out at me. Gabriel reported that he turned over one Runner who happened to wander into his neighborhood, but that's about it. How was your night?"

Tommen hesitated for half a second before explaining his adventures. Yes, Rifun had taught him the very basics of opening portals. No, he hadn't mentioned anything about the meeting on Tacaga or the attack on the Borelians. Yes, he was still expected to track down Richard's third journal. No, that didn't make him privy to Order plans or other goings-on; he was just the grunt. A grunt with a very important task, but a grunt nonetheless.

"Well, if he's still willing to bargain for secrecy on his seizures, he has every incentive to play nice with us," Walter mused.

"True, but what if that changes?" Tommen wondered, shifting his stance. "What if he finds some way to stop the seizures, or maybe he decides to let everyone know, play it up as something wonderful about the human race? I don't know, but just something where we don't have that bargaining chip anymore."

"Then we play it where it lies. Truth be told, I've been mulling over the same possibility. The fact that he hasn't done it already tells me that he's having a hard time coming up with such a lie, or a cure, as the case may be. And if he was waiting for some event to throw in some theatrics about it, I would think the attack on the Borelians would have been a pretty good stage for him. All of this to say...I've got nothing."

"So what do we do?"

"Right now, you're going to school, and I'm going to bed. As I said, they don't exactly consult me on battle plans. Going forward, Earth's stance and all diplomacy goes through Mi Chin as the Gatekeeper. If it has to come down further, it may go to the Regional Managers, but it won't reach us."

"So they just expect us to sit tight and let them do everything? We're the ones who brought this to attention and got us where we are."

His dad chuckled. "Exactly. We're the reason we are where we are, and we're the reason all of this is happening. Feelings about you and me specifically are mixed, but it still won't get this low, not unless something major happens where more manpower or firepower is needed." He held up a hand. "I know. I get it. It's frustrating. I don't enjoy being kicked out of the war tent any more than you do, but believe me when I say everyone has a vested interest in this because we're all targets, and not well-defended ones at that."

"Is there anything we can do?"

"I only said we got kicked out of the tent. That doesn't mean I won't be eavesdropping and making their business my business. But you let me worry about that part. What you need to do is try your damnedest to learn the Cult and how it's operating now. Obviously things have changed, and you're the only reliable source of information we have. Their numbers, their strengths, their movements and operations, and especially their leader. We have the advantage right now, and we need to milk it for all it's worth."

Tommen nodded. "I can do that."

Walter let out a breath. "Good. Well, in that case, I'll let you continue whatever you were doing, and I am going to get some sleep. What are you doing after school?"

"Oh, um, I have an interview for a job."

"What kind?"

"Construction, remodeling, that sort of thing."

His dad nodded. "Good. It'll definitely be a change from the bakery."

"Kind of what I'm hoping for. And maybe I can stop being such a skinny white kid."

"Well, I don't know that that'll happen, but we can hope for the best."

"Dad..."

His dad's eyes glittered with amusement as he again wished him good day and good night and headed off to his bedroom. Tommen sighed, shook his head, and finished getting ready for school, pulling up in front of Becky's house just as she was walking out the door.

"I thought you'd never come," she said, climbing in.

"You can see my house from your living room window," he pointed out. "You knew I was awake and getting ready. What did you have to worry about?"

"I don't know. Maybe you've been up all night puking from food poisoning. How am I supposed to know?"

"If that was the case, I would text you and let you know. Same as Will and Eli because they have to catch a bus in that scenario. Otherwise, I'm fine."

Becky sighed. "Truth be told, I had a nightmare last night. About Halloween. I was in the ash and dust and everything, looking around, hearing people running and screaming and calling for help, but the part that scared me the most was that I couldn't find you. I couldn't call out, either, because every time I opened my mouth, I just gagged on ash and everything else."

"I'm sorry."

"Do you still have nightmares about Halloween?"

"Sometimes," Tommen answered truthfully. "Usually I can wake myself up, though."

"Must be nice. I can't do that."

"I would hug you if I could, but I'm kind of driving."

"That's okay. You can hug me when we get to school."

They picked up the brothers, Eli coughing and hacking the whole way, but still fairly alert. Actually, Will didn't sound too much better, but he didn't feel like being cooped up in a sick house, or so he said. Tommen made a mental note to find some hand sanitizer and wipe down everything in his car at the end of the day.

"How did you get sick?" Becky asked. "You both sounded fine yesterday."

"Something going around at the garage that my mom brought home," Will said stuffily. "Kicks your ass, but she says it goes away pretty quick."

"She didn't get sick?"

"Dude, she's got an immune system made of steel. She could walk into the CDC, break all their vials of the worst diseases on Earth, and walk away without so much as a sniffle. Obviously, me and Eli didn't inherit it."

"Yeah. Listen, you'll have to ride the bus home, or, you know, whatever after school. I have a job interview to go to."

"Cool, man. That construction job you were talking about?"

"Yes."

"Cool. Yeah, I'll just ride the bus home. I don't have service today, and even if I did, I don't think I could make it."

Well, at least he was honest, and they spent the rest of the ride into school listening to Will sniffle, snuff, cough, and clear his throat. Occasionally he got a word in for a conversation, but mostly he was just sick. He got out of the car at the front curb like normal, a little hesitant with his head as cloudy as he reported it to be.

"I thought we'd never get rid of him," Becky said as Tommen pulled away and looked for a parking spot. "I feel like I need to take a bath in sanitizer or bleach or something."

"You're not the only one," Tommen agreed. "It's like, dude, seriously, stay home for a day. Lock yourself in your room if you don't want to hang out with your brother."

"Or lock your brother in his room."

"That, too." He parked and turned off the car. "Okay, time to make a mad dash for the inside."

It was a joke and they both knew it; Becky did not "dash" anywhere, not in her clunky, orthopedic shoes. She hurried the best she could, but they still landed in the school cold and shivering, brushing the snow off their heads and laughing for no reason that Tommen could think of. They parted ways and headed for their respective lockers. As Tommen approached his locker, he saw Will heading for the office, backpack in hand, head down. Turning around and going home, then. Good, the guy needed it. But did he really have to spread his germs all over Tommen's car before he realized he shouldn't be in school?

Still, he didn't complain. Wasn't as though Will would have seen him looking. He was going home and that was all that mattered. Didn't change any of Tommen's plans seeing how he had an interview after school anyway. He shut his locker door and went to meet Becky.

School was fairly normal, or what passed as normal so soon after Christmas break. The remaining rich kids returned from their luxury vacations to Cancun, Hawaii, Florida, or wherever they went to burn cash. A few of said rich kids were in Spanish with Tommen, and Mrs. Perez was more than happy to indulge their tales of poor little rich kid who could only go to Cancun, as long as they did it *en español*. Tommen simply flicked his hearing aids into quiet mode and scratched away in his notebook of stories.

Most of those who had been stranded at airports, like Mr. Keller, had also returned. Being new and having been gone for an extra, unscheduled vacation day, Mr. Keller felt as though he'd lost a whole week's worth of teaching time and so sped through two lessons and heaped on as much homework as could possibly fit in a backpack. Tommen could have easily Banded and gotten it done, or gotten a head start anyway, but he didn't. He wrote down the assignment, then promptly ignored it beyond what he could get done in class, which wasn't more than writing his name on the paper.

In English, Tuesday was his day to be in the library on the computer, and he sent up a silent, nebulous prayer of thanks for hybrid classes. He didn't know what he would have done if he'd been forced to sit in the classroom the whole fucking time. At least on the computer, he could work at his own pace and research what he needed to know and wanted to know without disrupting "The Schedule."

He normally sat next to Will who would flip through his CD case of all his courses, brushing his thumb over the little braille labels until he found the one he needed. Once they got settled in and started on their respective work, they would inevitably start talking and goofing off, but only when the librarian wasn't looking. With Will gone, Tommen was suddenly faced with a very long, very dull class.

He plugged away at it, slowly, wondering when in the world he was ever going to need this, like most of the student body. Thinking critically was good. Being able to analyze something, catch details, and see subtle undertones of...something, was also good. But did it have to be taught with boring books from a hundred years ago? Why couldn't they think critically about current events and have debates that meant something? Why couldn't they analyze real legal contracts and find where the loopholes were? Why was it so damn important to be able to read a book and understand themes and stuff? With exception of these arbitrarily-declared "classics," most books would be pushed aside within ten years of being published, regardless of how awesome they were at the peak of their popularity.

Briefly, Tommen wondered what would happen if he chose his Authored Book for his next free reading book report. Could he do that? Would his teacher think he'd written it under a pseudonym? Would she think it was some kind of prank or mockery? Would he be congratulated or failed?

He leaned back in his seat and stretched. He could hardly focus. Part of it was because English really was just that boring. The other part was because he was too distracted by his new mission.

It was probably foolish on his part, but he'd packed Julianna's notes in his folder, and he brought them out now, tucking them strategically in with some of his other handouts and homework so they could be easily hidden and tucked away if necessary. In case Banding wasn't enough, you know.

The first and most credible lead took him to a crime town to meet with a mob boss. Because why not? Did he really expect to go to a humble country village with honest, hard-working farmers? Not with that much power at stake, that was for sure. But at least the lead that took him to meet with royalty and impressive dignitaries sounded way cooler and a little safer. It would be a little easier to explain to his dad, "Hey, guess what, I went and met with Queen Aronet of Turit today" versus, "Yeah, I met with Arshoni the Slayer in some creepy back alley on Maronet." The first one, his dad would chide him and tell him to be good. The second one, he'd probably have a heart attack, but only after lecturing him about staying out of trouble.

Tommen rubbed his eyes. He needed to get to the Wheel and do some research, but he didn't trust his portal abilities worth peanuts, and he really didn't want to go back to the Land In Between. Certainly, since escaping, it didn't have the same ominous foreboding of eternal separation going for it, but it had still been a huge pain in the ass to get back.

On the other hand, if he did end up back in the Land In Between, he'd have an opportunity to talk to Chandler again, seeing how the man had apparently taken a vacation from dream-stalking him, or sending his animals to dream-stalk him. It felt like forever since Tommen had seen the White rabbit. Even though it was annoying as hell, now that it had all stopped, Tommen felt a little abandoned. Sometimes he missed the sarcastic humor and dry wit in which Chandler and his animals wrapped their sagely wisdom;

certainly it was more palatable than listening to some dude stand high on a pulpit pointing menacingly at everyone in the crowd without stopping to consider the three fingers pointing back.

Did he dare—God help him—pray? Could he ask Chandler to come back? No, that wouldn't work. Chandler was no god, but he seemed to be pretty close to one. So the question then became, did Tommen ask the Author to send Chandler to him, or God? If there was an Author, did that mean there was no God? Did they work together? If he was really, honestly, truly in a novel with an Author, could there still be another God out there above the Author? Was this multiverse theory? Would God listen to him if he was just words on a page? Or was it all just a metaphor?

Tommen pushed the notes back in the folder pockets and laid it on the desk. He let out a breath. This was all way more philosophical than he wanted to get today. And those were just the Big Questions; he didn't even want to consider where the journals or the Authored Books fell in this Author-God-universe-multiverse conundrum. Maybe he should skip talking to Chandler for now. If he was going out into the universe to look for the third journal, he didn't need to have any existential crises in the middle of a shady town ruled by the mafia.

The bell rang none too soon. Tommen quickly logged off, swept up all his things, and made for his locker, arriving half a second before Becky.

"So, how does it feel to be back in government-run daycare?" she teased as he grabbed his lunch and they started down the hall toward the cafeteria.

"Same shit, different day," he answered, shrugging.

"Are you really that excited for a new job? Do you really just want to go to work?"

"At least it pays."

"School pays, too. I mean, you need a high school diploma for just about everything besides McDonald's. And it helps you get a good job."

"Good job according to who? What's wrong with the trades?"

They claimed their normal seats at their normal table. Becky studied him as she got out her food. "Thought you wanted to be a super physicist?"

"I know, and it's still super cool and I love the idea, but I enjoy physical work, too. It'll probably be what pays my bills while I'm drowning in student loan debt."

She let out a breath. "Well, you're not wrong there."

"Tired of sewing yet?" he joked.

"I've been over sewing for a while now; I'm ready to be done. But, like you said, have to pay the bills and definitely have to pay for college. It's the only way I'm going to get away from sewing."

"Still want to be a geneticist?"

"Please." She waved a hand at him around a mouthful of food. "I've wanted to be a geneticist since I learned what genetics was."

"Why not dual-enroll, then? Get a jump on your degree. It's going to take a little longer than two or four years, I think."

"True, but like I've said before: taking a ton of AP classes in high school means I can cut out a lot of unnecessary college courses. I'm already here and already have to go through the motions, might as well make them count. Shaving off one or two semesters of college is easily more inexpensive than dual-enrolling now."

"Oh." Tommen went back to his food, leftover chili.

Becky shifted in her seat. "That's not to say that what you're doing is wrong. Personally, I enjoy school and it doesn't bother me to take the extra classes and the extra work. But you, you hate school. It's good for you, but spending half your life in school isn't for everyone."

"Nice save."

"I try."

Eli joined them, and Tommen noted how he was starting to look a little sick, too, a little pale, a little sweaty, and he even admitted he felt a little fuzzy in the head.

"If half the school gets sick from whatever this is, I'm blaming you," Tommen told him.

"If half the school gets sick, means they shut down for a few days so everyone can go to a doctor and so they can sanitize the school," Eli countered. "I'm doing everyone a favor."

"How is getting everyone sick doing us a favor?"

"Means you get to stay home, sleep in, not work, eat whatever you want—"

"And be so sick, you can't enjoy any of it," Becky finished. "Doesn't sound like much of a favor."

Eli shrugged. "Well, I'm here now. Will already did whatever damage he was going to do. Time to see what happens."

"Right." Tommen nodded uncertainly. "Well, stay away from me, at least. I have an interview and I don't need to walk in looking like I'm about to keel over."

Considering how fast Eli had gone from healthy with his usual banter, to sick and getting sicker, Tommen was afraid that he might just walk into the interview looking like death, because he didn't already, apparently. He washed his hands twice after lunch and again between classes, and still he asked to be excused from each so he could go wash his hands again. He constantly used Matter to Feel inside himself, wondering if he would know if he had any foreign germs, and, if he did, if he could somehow will his immune system to fight it off or just dispel it himself.

These thoughts plagued his mind even as he pulled out of the parking lot at the end of the day and started following the directions on his phone to get to the main office of the construction company.

He'd heard that everyone feared interviews, no matter how skilled or talented, but he wondered if his level of fear was normal. Maybe it had to do with the fact that if he blew it, he didn't have the bakery to fall back on. If he didn't get the job, he would still be unemployed and he would still have to go back to the job boards and keep looking. It was disquieting.

He had changed in the school bathroom before leaving. Now he sat in the parking lot and looked himself over, wondering if he was too informal for an interview or too formal for construction work. What a conundrum that he next expected to have. It was like the summer camp all over again.

The office was situated about half a mile from the city limit in the shipping district, actually not too far from the warehouse where the shootout had occurred. Immediately upon entering the office, Tommen felt overdressed and conspicuous. The room was clean, but bare. Beige walls may have been white at one time, and old industrial carpet had been worn to tatters. An enormous whiteboard was covered in messily scribbled notes, and a corkboard spilled dozens of papers onto a cluttered desk where a computer from no later than 2003 hummed away next to a printer, which was just as old and clacking away noisily as it spit out page after page of some kind of schematic. The chair behind the desk was empty.

Tommen stood there, frozen, unsure what to do or where to go. The wall to his left had a door that was partially open, but there was a hallway to his right. He was saved by the appearance of a man who went to the desk to scoop up the papers from the printer.

"Can I help you?" he wondered, suddenly struck by Tommen's presence.

"Um, I have an interview with Chris?" Tommen told him.

"Okay. Yeah, I'll get him. It might be a minute, we're kind of busy. What's your name?"

"Tommen."

"Cool. Yeah, um..." The man looked around, then swung the office chair out in front of the desk. "You can chill out for a second. Like I said, we're super busy and it might be a minute."

The man strode off, leaving Tommen alone with the chair. Did he sit? Was it a test? Were they looking to see if he would be lazy and play around on his phone? Were they checking to see if he could stand it? Would they think he was just trying to be a tough guy? Could it really be just a courtesy thing? From the look and sound of it, they didn't get too many visitors.

After a minute or two of waiting, Tommen sat. He looked at the whiteboard, tried to decipher the notes. He did some Feeling, looking for any foreign germs. He played with his glasses a bit, flicking them through the different modes even as he still tried to get used to having them on his face constantly.

Finally a tall man in dirty jeans and paint-spattered T-shirt walked in the room, hand extended. Tommen stood and took it, forcing himself not to wince in the man's bone-crushing grasp.

"Tommen, right? I'm Chris, nice to meet you."

"Thanks for seeing me," Tommen replied, hoping it was the right thing to say.

"Sorry for the delay, we've got a big project and trying to keep up is terrible. Anyway, let me grab another chair and we'll have a chat, hm?"

So it was that Tommen ended up sitting in the comfortable office chair while Chris found a rusty folding chair which he clunked down behind the desk and sat in without complaining.

"So, the other day I was thinking to myself how I knew you, or where I'd heard your name before," Chris began. Tommen's stomach twisted, unsure where this was going. "And then it hit me that there is—or was, I should say—an interior designer in the area named Kayla Durvin who was married to your boss at the bakery. Your name came up a few times." He grinned as he noted Tommen's expression. "All good, I assure you."

"How do you know Kayla?" Tommen found himself asking.

"Oh, she sent us a lot of business once the design portion of a project turned into actual construction or remodeling. Yeah, it's too bad what happened. Anyway, why don't we start off by telling me what you think or hope she told me about you."

"Well, I hope it went something along the lines of a loyal, hard worker with a halfway decent sense of humor."

He was sure he was done for, and Tommen tried to keep his thoughts reined in as the interview went on. He didn't have any experience in construction; he counted himself lucky he knew how to use a hammer, a screwdriver, and a drill. Remodeling, well, he knew a little more about that just from helping his dad, but that hadn't been anything major. They hadn't moved any drains, knocked out any walls, or done anything extreme. A few new pieces of furniture, a few new coats of paint, a new floor, and that was all. And he was a science geek, not exactly tradesman material, to say nothing of his skinny physique, whereas both men he'd met in the office so far had probably been star linebackers in high school and college.

He wasn't even sure whether he ought to have been afraid or relieved when Chris finally called for an end to the interview. It hadn't seemed very long, but what did he know? Was that a good thing? Maybe he was exactly what the man was looking for and fishing around would just be wasting time. Maybe he wasn't anything like what the company needed and they were wasting time anyway, so it was time to cut the losses. Maybe he was overthinking things and just needed to shake the man's hand, thank him for his time, and go about his business before his thoughts made their way to his face.

"I have a few more interviews to go through, but I'll let you know by next Friday, hopefully," Chris said. "I hate to seem rushed, but we're busy. Stay safe out there, roads are treacherous."

Tommen thanked him and watched the man disappear back down the hall. Then he returned to his car and sat in the driver's seat for a minute while it warmed up. His phone buzzed. Becky.

"How'd the interview go?" she asked.

"I'm pretty sure I blew it," he replied. "Guess it's back to the job hunting board."

"It couldn't have been that bad. You looked good, you smelled good, and you're only seventeen. No one expects you to be a master interviewer or employee of the year. They expect you to be young, dumb, and lazy. The fact that you aren't means that you'll stand out."

"It's construction. Manual labor. Who would apply for a manual labor job and expect that they're going to be sitting around?"

"You want an honest answer?"

"No, I can take a guess."

"Even if you don't get the job, it doesn't necessarily mean that there's something wrong with you. If he's got one opening and ten applicants, nine guys are going to be turned away. That's how it works. It just means you weren't the best fit for his needs."

"Yeah, yeah. I'm going home to get something to eat and get started on my homework."

"Does that include some of your essays?"

"If I get to them. I'll text you to come over if I need help."

"All right, fine. Erase all my excuses not to work on my own homework, why don't you? I'll see you in school tomorrow. Love you."

"Love you, too."

Tommen stared at the last two texts, then deleted them. He didn't need his dad snooping through his phone and finding anything questionable. On the surface, his dad might pick on him about dating a girl. Then would come the lecture on love and sex and honor and respect and being good and everything else. Then the tighter security would follow, which would no doubt be a more coordinated effort between his dad and her parents to ensure that they were being good. Was sex really such a big deal?

By the time he got home, his dad was long gone to work. Rifling through the fridge, he made himself a sub before going down to his room to start his homework. It wasn't even eight-thirty before Rifun showed up.

"I'm surprised," he said, propping up a couple pillows and laying back on Tommen's bed. "You're alone. No sex today? I thought for sure you'd try for a month-long streak."

Tommen looked back at him, brow raised. "Yeah? I'm surprised you're not seizing on the floor right now. That seems to be a fairly regular occurrence for you these days."

He fully expected some sort of reprimand, but Rifun merely said, "They've been improving lately, I think. Thanks for asking."

"You cured them?" Tommen spun around in his chair.

Rifun chuckled humorlessly. "Only if you consider midazolam and tarka root tea a cure. Bitter stuff that, and the most godawful aftertaste. Takes an hour for it to go away." He shook his head. "But I'm not here to talk about me."

"More portal training?"

"Perhaps on the way back. I don't need you throwing yourself into a black hole. Actually, tonight you will begin your journal studies. You'll be joining about sixty others as they study the Book of Philosophy. Not the most exciting read, admittedly, but it will provide a foundation, a bit of an explanation, and it may help you figure out some of your own Big Questions." Rifun sat up. "Come on, then."

Tommen sighed but obediently followed Rifun to the fortress. The collapsed northwest stair had been stabilized and rebuilt on the first and second floors, and other repair efforts were speeding along nicely it seemed.

"When this all gets done, journal studies will be on the fifth floor with the rest of the Philosophers," Rifun was saying. "But for now, you'll join the others in here."

"Here" turned out to be one of the old recreational halls. It had been sectioned off into a number of smaller rooms and reminded Tommen of pictures of old one-room schoolhouses that had curtains to divide them into the different grades and everyone could hear everyone else's instruction and goings-on. He was dropped off in one of the sections without even so much as a "have a nice first day of school" and left to fend for himself.

Immediately, he noted that he was the only human present, and he counted only seven humanoids out of sixty to seventy beings. Most of them seemed as socially awkward as him, new, uncertain of protocol, unfamiliar with everyone else in the room. Tommen didn't peg anyone as being the instructor, and he didn't see any kind of textbook to grab and review.

A few more aliens filtered into the room, but it was a good ten minutes before anyone moved to any semblance of order. Once again, Tommen found himself in with the grunts, those with no order, no discipline, and no clue of what was going on. He fell into that pool, too, but it felt a little insulting. He found himself wishing for more portal training so he could take himself to the Wheel and get a move on with his scavenger hunt. At least there he was among experts and professionals in their given fields; he could count on them to do whatever it was that needed to be done without waiting for orders or reassurances. He might need a little reassuring, but being among professionals would be easier to handle than being in the midst of grunts. Greatness breeds greatness, right? He'd be a regular Indiana Jones by the time they actually found the journal.

The instructor for the class was an Arowa, something resembling an eel mixed with a Chinese dragon mixed with a bear, and that was a generous description. He introduced himself as Tarith, one of the instructors for the first class of the Book of Philosophy. Supposedly there were six different levels for each book. Also supposedly, the first classes were meant to be audio-oral only while some of the grunts picked up on and improved their English, but because there was a human among them, Tommen was designated as the reader of the day's passage.

Feeling very conspicuous, he moved to the front of the room and took the paper he was handed. This was as bad as English class, he thought, having to get up and read something aloud. Could be worse, though. At least this was something someone else had written and not his own original work, which would only make it more embarrassing.

He wasn't sure what he was expecting from the Book of Philosophy. Maybe start out with "In the beginning, the Author wrote the words and the story." That would be ironic, wouldn't it? But if there was an Author and a God, would that make it blasphemy? Was it blasphemy to write Jesus as a lion in a fictional land? Where did allegory end and arrogance begin?

Instead, the first passage from the Book of Philosophy read a bit like a grocery list, or maybe a genealogy. Short, easy, declarative statements. Was this actually how the Book of Philosophy began, or was this Rifun or Julianna simplifying things for those who didn't speak English well? Given that the book was written in the 1800's, even he, Tommen, might have a tough time following along with the freakishly long sentences, weird grammar, and archaic vocabulary. Maybe this simple stuff was for the best.

And he couldn't say that he found anything sinister about it, really. It started out with the first words ever written in a story by the Author—that is, "One day"—and so spawned the universe, or that was the simplified version. Then it went into a long line of characters declared Beloved by the Author: Kalian, Rebecca and Thoreau, Faith, Tobias, Half-Face, Strikeslayer, Shadow-Come-Reaping, Allison, Jack and Carmen.

Tommen was interrupted as Tarith called on another student with a question. "Yes?"

"Do we have these stories? Are they Authored Books?" the student asked.

Tarith shook his head. "We must take care not to confuse the journals with the Authored Books of the Akarin. The Authored Books are good stories to read and have some element of truth to them, and it is good to have a well-rounded view of the universe, but the words of the Author in these journals is what we live by. You will do some study of the Authored Books in the fifth and sixth classes, but for now, we will study only the journals. Tommen, continue."

The reading concluded with a split between two Beloved characters, Allison and Carmen. The Author was ready to release her first Book and so chose Allison. But Carmen became jealous and so devised a scheme to get back at the Author and destroy Allison.

Even as Tommen read, he couldn't help but wonder why the Author had any problems with her characters at all. She was the Author, all powerful over her works, in charge of the backspace key as much as the letters. What was the problem? If someone did get unruly, throw the book in the fire and delete the computer file—or whatever the cosmic equivalent of such things was.

Homework proved to be an easy assignment. They had to memorize the first words written by the Author and name all the Beloved characters in order. In the next classes, they would be going over each of the Beloved characters, why they were called Beloved, what little was known about their stories, and how they contributed to knowledge of the Author and Time and the Akari.

Tommen left the class with mixed feelings and a strong desire to talk to Chandler again. Was there any way he could seek him out? If he reached out with Energy and started poking around where he thought he remembered Chandler's cave to be, could he find him? Could he annoy the man enough that he would have to come talk to him?

"So, how was your first day of school?" Rifun asked, coming alongside Tommen as he left the recreation hall.

"Less sinister than I was expecting," Tommen answered honestly.

"You were expecting ritual sacrifice and fervent prayers to Satan?"

"Well, no...I mean...I don't know?"

"As I said, the Book of Philosophy isn't the most exciting thing out there to read. The Book of Abilities is much more fun, but you won't get to that until the third level, being an Artist and all."

"Where does the Book of Commands come in?"

"Julianna is teaching from what she remembers, but it would really help if we had the real thing. Assuming you find it, then we already have a plan and a schedule."

"Teach me to open portals. I want to be able to go to the Wheel whenever I need to. I'm sick of this ridesharing business."

Rifun grinned. "I thought you'd never ask. Come on. Let's start in the portal room and get you home safe and sound first. Then we can work on portals to the Wheel."

Trying to open a portal back home was less grueling than the first time around, though not by much. But, with Rifun lending strength, he managed to get one open and stable enough for them to pass through. Once it snapped closed, Tommen flopped on his bed for a good five minutes before recovering enough to even think about attempting a portal to the Wheel.

"You're a quick study," Rifun observed from his seat at Tommen's desk. "Keep up the good work. Now then, about that portal to the Wheel."

Grudgingly, Tommen sat up and rubbed his eyes, a headache splitting his skull. Well, he'd asked for this, hadn't he? Dumbass.

"Excellent. Now then, there's really no trick to this as far as opening the portal or going from a place to the Wheel. Think of the portal you opened here. That's a bit like swimming upstream. Opening a portal to the Wheel is like getting swept downstream in a rushing current, and stepping through the portal so it gets locked in is like being caught in a fishing net at the proper place."

"On a scale of one to ten, how bad is that analogy?" Tommen asked smartly, breaking into a yawn at the end.

Rifun smirked. "Open a portal and find out."

Well, he had that coming, didn't he?

"Oh, and one more thing," Rifun said. "Here, the fortress, any solid place, those are places on the banks of the river. The Wheel is more like a certain spot in the river itself."

"And the self-destruct inverter in the fortress is like a bridge, is that it?" Tommen asked.

"Mm, think of it more like slightly-submerged slippery stepping stones. They help, but are by no means a complete bypass. But we're getting off-topic. Open a portal."

As Tommen prepared himself to open portal and tentatively stepped out into the universe to do so, he found the analogy surprisingly accurate. Then he felt a little resentment toward Rifun for not giving him such an analogy in the first place, because having the mindset of fighting a current almost made it easier to bear. This time, though, instead of fighting the current, he went along with it. He quickly discovered that the river was not clear, and it felt as though he smacked into rocks and logs and all sorts of debris, but he still moved with the current.

The portal sputtered to life. Where traveling from the fortress to home was indeed like fighting a strong current and slogging up the opposite bank, this was more like trying to wrestle a huge sheet of wallpaper knowing he had to just get one small area stuck properly before he could smooth out the rest.

Yeah, that analogy didn't work quite as well.

The next thing Tommen knew, he was on the floor looking up at Rifun who held out a hand. Groggy and uncoordinated, Tommen reached for it, got up on wobbly legs, and crawled into bed on his stomach, tossing his glasses on his nightstand and burying his head under his pillow, willing himself not to throw up.

"Well, I've seen worse first attempts," Rifun was saying. "Keep practicing and you'll be on your way in no time."

Tommen rolled onto his back, keeping his pillow over his eyes. "Could me or my dad get in trouble for learning this? This is Journeyman-level stuff."

"And you were an Apprentice long before you were an Apprentice. I see no reason why you can't be a Journeyman before becoming a Journeyman. Besides, you're not learning Time. Time would have you opening portals by rote memorization as it were. This is the Akari, the critical-thinking and application side of things, utilizing Matter and Energy to make things much easier."

"I'd hate to think what it would be like to open a portal with only Time."

"The good news is, you won't have to find out. But I think we've made enough progress for one day. You look like you could use some sleep, and with that virus going around, the last thing you want to do is weaken your immune system."

"How do you know about—never mind. You already said you spy on me."

"While that is true, I'm actually investigating a different angle."

"What, like, biological warfare from the Borelians?"

"Is it impossible?"

Tommen let out a breath. "No, I guess not. But why this particular virus? Will just said his mom brought it home from work but she's fine."

"His mother also has an incredible immune system. I've been tracking it since it got my attention. Four hundred people have been hospitalized from it, with potentially thousands more too poor or too stubborn to see a doctor. Hospitals are calling it a severe flu strain, but I'm a little skeptical. Nothing you need to worry about yet."

"Will was sneezing and coughing all over my car. Eli was getting sick by lunch. Everyone in school has been exposed. How do I not worry about it?"

Tommen cried out in pain and threw his pillow across the room as Rifun jabbed him in the thigh with a needle and depressed the plunger, sending cold green fluid into his body. "What the fuck, man?!"

"Call it a vaccine if you will, but it's for Borelian pneumonia. As common as a cold on Brelix because of the turbulent surface and atmosphere and fairly common on most of the slave worlds. If the Borelians can pre-infect their targets, weed out the weak and boost the immunity of the strong, it saves them a lot of time and trouble down the road. Obviously it moves very quickly. New Year's Eve may not have been about invasion, but infection. Spread the virus far enough and fast enough, start a global pandemic, kidnapping and invasion becomes ten times easier."

"Do you actually sit down and think about this stuff, or does crazy come naturally to you?"

"What's your favorite saying? It's only paranoia until it's true?"

Tommen just sighed. "Okay, fine. Let's say this is the Borelians and they're giving everyone space pneumonia. What are we going to do about it?"

"You mean, what if your friends and girlfriend all end up in the hospital? Well, if there was some way we could stop time long enough to smuggle some entirely untested, unproven, non-FDA approved medicine into the hospital—"

"Fine, I get your point. How are you going to get enough for that many people, though? And where did you get that syringe, anyway?"

"What, you thought I just told my men to burn everything and forget the rest? No. I'm more thorough than that when it comes to taking down my enemies. Why don't we just leave it at that, hm? You're exhausted from a long day at school, training, studies, and conspiracy theories. Assuming you don't come down with space pneumonia as you call it, I expect I will return soon to continue your portal training. Then you will be free to travel at will."

Tommen didn't even want to think about that. He knew when Rifun left, but still he kept the pillow over his eyes. For a long moment, he just lay there. His thigh burned something awful. Was it possible the Borelians were going for bio-warfare? Sure, but it didn't seem to fit the mantra of violent and hostile and war-like. Those words seemed more reminisce of brutish, hulking warriors who couldn't form proper sentences and wielded clubs and spears. This was far more sophisticated, far more subtle, and far more effective. The Borelians had perfected their warfare and slave trade and gotten it down to a science. It didn't matter that they had no space fleet to back them up during an invasion. By the time it actually got to that point, their prey would be so weak, there wouldn't even be much of a fight.

Only paranoia until it's true, but he couldn't just go running off and spouting conspiracy theories at the hospital. They'd cart him off to the psych ward. But what if Becky got sick? Diabetes made her more vulnerable. How fast would it ravage her body? How would Tommen contact Rifun to get the medicine if indeed it was Borelian pneumonia? Eli went from zero to sick in only a few hours. What if Becky was sick at home right now? What if she skipped school tomorrow and was in the hospital by the end of the day?

He shook his head. He couldn't let his imagination run away. Whether it was an ass-kicking strain of the flu or space pneumonia, he couldn't give in to the same hysteria that the general public would. He got his regular flu shot and Rifun just gave him pneumonia meds; he would be one of the few healthy people available to keep the masses calm in the event the sickness spread. He had to be a man. He had to be a leader. He had to stay calm.

He went to sleep.

Chapter Eleven
Candles and Animals

Tommen knew he was dreaming, just for the sheer fact that there was no snow in the forest he found himself walking through. Once he realized it was a dream, he was able to stop walking and look around. He couldn't see the sun, but long shadows snaked every which way, making discerning the finer details of the landscape impossible.

He froze as something moved. A bush rustled and a twig snapped. It was classic horror movie, and Tommen almost expected a sudden hand on his shoulder, only for it to be his dad or Becky or some other familiar friend. But the sounds just echoed, bouncing from tree to tree, making it impossible to tell where the sounds actually originated.

Tommen stayed where he was, torn between the desire to stay still and hope danger passed him by, and run and try to make it out. His instincts told him to stay. He was prey here, and most predators had a chase instinct, to pounce if their target fled. If he stayed still, the predator might get bored and leave him alone. Or it could pounce anyway, take out a target that was too stupid to know the danger it was in.

But it was only a dream, right? Even if someone was walking in his dreams, tweaking them, forcing them to be frightening nightmares, it was still just a dream. He could wake himself if it got too scary or dangerous. Compared to some of his nightmares about Halloween and the fortress battle, this was pretty mild.

His heart leapt into his throat as another stick cracked and there was more rustling, this time closer. The undergrowth was thick, but not so dense that Tommen wouldn't have been able to see a bear or a mountain lion or anything big. Whatever this was, it was smaller. Maybe a wolf or a fox. Or just a young bear or young mountain lion. That was also very possible.

He took a step back as a bush not four feet away rustled, but an instant before the animal appeared, he knew who it was.

"Rabbit!" he exclaimed as the fluffy White rabbit tumbled out of the bush.

Well, he still wasn't wearing a dinner jacket or crying about how he was late for a very important date, but he was holding a small candle which gave off more light than a candle that size had any right to. Tommen was about to say more when the rabbit pointed at him with a menacing paw.

"I don't enjoy reconnaissance missions, thank you," he said irritably. "Personally, I think Chandler should have just fessed up and kept you out of here. But no, he's all, 'We can't change the future. This has to be done.' Don't get me wrong, he's a nice guy, and we're obligated to do the Author's work, but sometimes, you humans are simply exhausting! Do you understand that?"

"I'm sorry...I think?" Tommen offered. He shook his head. "I've been wanting to speak with him, but I don't exactly know how to contact him."

The rabbit sighed. "That's because you can't." He gestured around. "In places like this, only the Author can hear you. She's the one who decides how you get out." His tone became irritable again. "This time, it looks like I'm the one who has to drag your sorry hide back out."

He turned to hop away, but Tommen stayed where he was and asked, "Does that mean you're mine?"

The rabbit paused and looked back. "Your what?"

Tommen shrugged. "I don't know. Kayla said that if an animal is 'mine'—whatever that means—then eventually he'll tell me his name and stuff. Considering how much I've seen of you and the fact that you're the one here to 'rescue' me, does that make you mine?"

The rabbit turned around. "You put a lot of emphasis on 'you're' as in, I'm the one here and not someone else, Yawi, for instance. Do you think a rabbit can't handle himself in here?" He stood up on his hind legs again and pointed once more. "Let me tell you something, human, one little rabbit can go places wolves and bears can't, and I have more power than even the biggest, baddest, most threatening—"

"You're evading the question."

For a long moment the rabbit simply glowered at him. "Come on, human. We better get going before it gets completely dark."

With that, he turned and hopped away. Tommen followed, picking his way through the brush. Every so often, he caught a glimpse of white fur, but mostly he just followed the light from the candle.

Chandler couldn't hear him? Why the fuck not? Chandler had little problem going wherever he wanted. Or did this go back to the free will thing again? Tommen thought back to his last dream where the rabbit had told him that if he entered the forest, Chandler and the White animals could not follow. But one forest was the same as any other, right? What made this one different?

On the other hand, if Chandler, the man who could cow Julianna at his mere presence, couldn't go in the forest, what sort of evil power lurked in there? What was so great that only the Author could hear him? Did this line of thought make him nuts? If he hadn't physically met Chandler, seen and touched him, Tommen probably would have dismissed all of this as a bunch of kooky dreams. But he'd met Chandler and he'd seen Yawi on multiple occasions, even if not lately. The wolf had probably gone back to the Krydik.

"Do all the White animals talk?" Tommen asked conversationally, still following the orange glow.

"Yes," the invisible rabbit replied. "Some are more reserved than others."

"Not you, obviously."

"I'm what they call...the honest one, for humans who need

more of a hard nose approach to things."

"I'm not sure how to take that."

"With a grain of salt. Or two. Now hush. We're nearing the edge of the forest."

Tommen was ready to ask why that mattered, then decided against it. The rabbit was already cranky enough; he didn't need to get another earful from it.

And yet, as they neared the edge of the forest, it seemed to get lighter and darker at the same time. Lighter, because he could see the light beyond the trees, almost midday in a forest nearly midnight. But there was also a certain darkness surrounding the doorway as it were, like a living shadow. Twenty feet from the midday field beyond the forest, the shadow took the shape of a great cerberus, blocking the path and looking down at the tasty snacks before it.

"You're a long way from home, little one," the beast said in a rumbling voice, lowering its heads to look at the rabbit.

Tommen might have peed a little, but the rabbit simply got up on its hind legs to address the creature. "No, not far at all. I'd be there now but you're kind of in my way."

"The one you take with you—" said the middle head.

"—he cannot go," finished the head on the right.

"Chandler has called him and the Author has permitted it," the rabbit informed them.

"He made his choice!" the left head snapped.

"He made a mistake. He did not know better."

"Then that is his own fault and the fault of those around him," the right head growled.

The rabbit took a step forward. "The ones whom the Author calls, you cannot stop."

He waved his candle at the cerberus which lifted its massive heads and took a step back. All three pairs of eyes rested on Tommen who felt his blood run cold.

"Maybe—" said the middle head.

"But only if they choose to follow," said the left.

The three-headed dog, easily as big as a shipping freighter, lowered its heads to give Tommen a close inspection.

"So, human—"

"—what will it be?"

"Do you really want to cross us—"

"—just to follow a little white rabbit—"

"—and a crazy hermit?"

Tommen glanced at the rabbit; its expression was impossible to discern. Finally he swallowed hard and nodded. "Yeah. Yeah, I kinda do."

The cerberus heads lifted to the trees and barked laughter.

"He kind of does."

"How adorable."

"How sweet."

The heads lowered.

" 'Kind of' does not work here," the right head told him. "Everything that isn't white is black, however much you try to paint it gray."

The dog looked back at the rabbit. "He's made his choice. He doesn't know what he wants. And shame on you and the fiery one for not explaining things better."

The cerberus lifted its heads as if to laugh again, but the only sound that came out was a yelp as the rabbit threw its candle at the beast. It did not go out, but when it hit the ground, the thick, dry undergrowth began to smolder until flames sprang forth in a sudden inferno. Tommen recoiled, pulling his left arm close to himself.

"Run, Tommen!"

He hesitated for only a moment, looking at the flames as they spread. The cerberus, confused and enraged, was stamping around as if to put out the fire. Finally he spotted the white rabbit and darted after it. He dodged massive paws and closed his eyes before running through the wall of fire.

He ended up tripping over something, but when he finally came to a stop after tumbling head over ass, he found himself looking up through tall grass to a bright blue sky. His burned arm hurt like a bitch, but he didn't seem too worse for wear otherwise. He just got sitting up when he was back down, and it took a moment for the pain in his face to register. He sat up a second time.

"Did you just punch me?" he asked the White rabbit.

"Paws, human," the rabbit said, waving his little front paws in the air. "Rabbits have paws. I couldn't punch you if I wanted to, which I really do, by the way."

"You carried a candle and threw it at that thing. That takes more dexterity than just paws."

"Either way, I didn't punch you. I kicked you. For being a stupid human. Have you learned nothing? Only white can be white. Anything less than white, even a pretty gray, isn't white. And if it isn't white, it belongs in there." The rabbit pointed toward the forest, a good eighty yards away.

Tommen rubbed his face and stood to look at the forest. He saw evidence of the fire and there was still some smoke, but the flames appeared to have been put out. "So far, everything I've seen and done has been real. A little strange, but real. There's always been an explanation of some form. But Cerberus isn't real. That's Greek mythology."

The rabbit shrugged. "The darkness takes any form it pleases. Sometimes it's big and scary. Most of the time, though, it appears small and harmless, looking just like everything else. Besides, in a world dictated by the Author, who are you to say what's real and what isn't? And as you have seen, big power can come in small packages."

"Yeah. Thanks for saving my ass back there."

"Well, don't make me do it again." The rabbit moved past him, muttering, "Stupid human."

Nevertheless, the rabbit's mood seemed much improved now that they were out of the forest. Tommen's heart rate and blood pressure slowly returned to normal and his arm stopped throbbing.

They walked for a good five minutes before cresting a small hill. The rabbit continued on, but Tommen paused. This was part of a small parking lot, the one where he'd taken Becky at Christmas. If he was right, the city was just on the other side of the trees. Looking behind him, the field and the forest had gone, replaced by more mountains, everything crusted with snow.

"Wait, what?" He looked around some more. "How did that happen?" He shook his head. "Never mind, I know how it happened. I'm still dreaming."

"Are you?" the white rabbit wondered. "If dream-walking is simply traveling the Energy current to get to a place, what makes you think you couldn't go traveling elsewhere, say, in the in-between dimension?"

"Is that what this is?"

"Of course not, stupid human. You're dreaming. And yet, we do travel far and wide in our dreams, do we not?"

Tommen mulled over the rabbit's words as they made their way through the familiar forest of home, abandoning the trail and moving along a game path until more familiarity began to unfold. As they made their way up a rocky cliff, he recognized the cabin built from a cave.

"Hey!" the rabbit called. "I got him!"

They went up to the cabin, but there was no sign of the man.

"Hey!" the rabbit shouted again.

"I can hear you."

The voice came from the forest and Chandler appeared a moment later, bearing a basket and a burlap sack, both looking rather full. Several knives sat on his belt. Tommen had a flashback of Saul going out into the forest to hunt with his handmade bow.

"We were held up by one of the Shadows," the rabbit told him. "They tried to take him, but I distracted it with a bit of fire."

"A bit?" Chandler raised a brow. "Well, no matter. I expect I will be making more candles soon enough. Did he come of his own free will?"

The rabbit sighed dramatically and grumbled, "He gave them a gray answer."

Chandler frowned. "Then they will come for him again."

Tommen folded his arms. "Why? I mean, I wanted to leave, I guess—"

"There's the gray. You guess."

"—but if the Shadows hate the light, why would they come here for me?"

"The Shadows hate the light, but they hate losing what's theirs even more. Just because you drag someone to a place of light does not mean they truly want to go, nor that the darkness will not follow." Chandler looked down at the rabbit. "Take your burrowers and others. You know what to do."

The rabbit gave a salute and a "yes, sir" and bounded off as if hounds were on his scent. Once he was gone, Chandler simply motioned for Tommen to follow him inside the cabin cave where he set down his things and revealed the fruits of his gathering. In the basket, plants still fresh, even in the snow. In the burlap sack, a rabbit which he set to work skinning.

"Does the White rabbit know you have that?" Tommen wondered.

"The Whites see themselves as separate from their common kindred, for they are not truly animals. They have no quarrel," Chandler replied.

He skinned the rabbit with the speed and skill of a man who did it almost every day, and Tommen found himself a little jealous.

"Here's something I don't understand. Why can't you go into the forest?"

Chandler looked up briefly from his work, though his hands never stopped moving. "What makes you think I can't?"

"Because the rabbit came to get me."

"Yes. The Author told him to."

"But why not you? And what about the whole, 'Only the Author can hear you' bit? I mean, it's only a dream, right? And you were pretty badass in the in-between dimension."

"Is it only a dream? Or perhaps a metaphor?"

"Metaphor? For what?"

Chandler's expression turned unreadable, though there was some of the familiar irritation that seemed to run in the Wolf family. "Why did you want to talk to me?"

"Because Kayla told me to."

"Why?"

"Because the First Order is creepy and the Akarin are self-righteous even in defeat."

"And...?"

Tommen let out a breath and sat down. "And I'm confused. Everyone claims to know the Author and have the Akari and this and that, and I don't know who to believe. You seem to lean more toward the Akarin, but I don't remember you ever declaring for a side."

"The only side is for or against the Author."

"But who is she? The Akarin say to read the Books, the Order says to read the journals. And there's probably some other group out there who says something else. I don't understand. And then, yesterday or last night or earlier or whenever it was, the Order starts talking about Beloved characters? Who the hell are they?"

Chandler answered without missing a beat in preparing his rabbit. "The Cult regards the so-called Beloved characters as special 'chosen ones' if you will. They believe that these particular characters progressively shaped the knowledge and views of the Author and use of the Akari until the split between Akarin and Cult, and that Richard is the final Beloved character meant to put things to rights."

"So who are these people? Kalian and Rebecca and Tobias and everyone else?"

The man shrugged. "Simply people. With their own stories. Not much is known about them because, although their stories predate us, they also haven't been written yet."

"That makes no sense."

"As I said, all a metaphor. And sometimes metaphors can be like jokes. Try to explain it too much and make every aspect fit perfectly and it loses its nuance and deeper meaning and humor."

"How do they fit into the Akarin, though?"

"The Akarin are split between them, actually. Some regard them as mere fictional works. Others call them the Invisible Author Tales, those where the Author is never mentioned, but much can be learned about her through that."

"And how is it, really? Like, what are they, how do they fit?"

"In the end, the Akarin have the right of it."

"Which one, the fictional works or Invisible Author?"

"Both. They split over nuance. As I said, all metaphorical."

"Why can't you explain the metaphor?"

Chandler finished preparing the rabbit and put it over his fire. As he added more sticks to the coals to coax the flames back to life, he answered, "I could, but faith discovered is more powerful than faith explained. You will figure it out through guidance and discovery, not instruction and ritual."

"You're not much of a guide, you know that?"

The man smirked, all Wolf. "The path you have chosen is the more difficult one, but I fully believe that you will be stronger for it in the end."

Tommen sighed and rubbed his face. "Okay, fine. More mystical riddle prophecy bullshit. Can you give me some direction on this mission Rifun's got me on? He wants me to find the third journal. Personally, I'm all for it, but like my dad said, he wouldn't entrust his Holy Grail to someone of questionable loyalty."

"Indeed he wouldn't," Chandler said, almost accusingly.

"What, are you saying I am loyal? Fuck no! I don't want anything to do with the guy."

"Don't you?"

"No."

"Then why do you still go to him when he calls, like a loyal hound? Why save his life? Why undertake this mission? Why do any of it?"

"Because he will fucking kill me and the people I love if I don't."

Chandler let out a breath. His posture became one that Tommen quickly recognized as one that Dr. Polski got when he was imparting wisdom to his kids, grandkids, or other interested parties.

"Tommen, if Rifun has to threaten those you love, it means that he knows he can't threaten you."

"But he's more powerful than me in pretty much every way."

The man sat down again, cross-legged, looking Tommen in the eye. "You've seen the power of both the Order and the Akarin, both of whom claim to wield the Akari. Only one of them does. The Akari is separate because of its use of Faith. Simple Faith. Sorry to say, but the Cult lacks faith in the Author and the Akari. They put their faith in the mission. Conquer, rule, authority. Their fourth element is not Faith, but Force.

"Consider the rabbit and the Shadow. The Shadow was vastly more powerful in Force. Yes, it could have killed the rabbit and you. But the rabbit had Faith."

"No, the rabbit had a candle," Tommen interrupted.

"Is not light a metaphor as well? One little rabbit conquered a huge Shadow. David against Goliath. Because of Faith. Rifun is immensely powerful, yes, in Force. He conquered the Wheel of Time because they lack both Force and Faith. The Akarin defeated him because of greater Faith. But in their own arrogance and pride, they lost Faith in the Akari and the Author and instead turned their thoughts inward until there was little left to stop the Cult from conquering them."

"What does that have to do with me?"

"You have Faith and don't even realize it. It's been there, dormant, for a long time, but still there. Rifun recognized this and mistook it for Force. The choices you will have to make in the near future will determine whether this little seedling of Faith turns into true Faith or only Force."

Tommen leaned back on his elbows. "I get the whole Faith part. But why is the other one called Force? Is that a *Star Wars* reference or something?"

Chandler grinned. "No, it's called that because you have to force yourself to believe a lot of bullshit in order for it to work. Keep your Faith pure and you will recognize it the more you read the journals."

"So you think I should continue reading them? Why not just tell Rifun to fuck off and run for the hills?"

"Small Faith will only carry you so far. As I have said, you have chosen the more difficult path. And as Kayla has told you, the Faith of a skeptic is greater than the Faith of someone who knows nothing else. You will learn and train and it will be difficult as you walk in many worlds. In one world, you will be shown Force and told that Faith is inferior. In another world, both are scorned as a dangerous fairytale. In a third, the choice between passive compliance or the break in the metaphor."

"Have I ever told you that you make a better prophet or mystic than a guide?"

Chandler shrugged. "I've heard worse."

"Kayla said the two of you have had disagreements."

"That is true."

Tommen had hoped to get some kind of story out him about it, but the man volunteered nothing.

"So where does the human alliance with the Order come into this? What role do the Borelians play?" Tommen inquired.

"It is simply reaping what has been sown. Ignorance, arrogance, apathy. The overall situation is fairly straightforward. As for the alliance with the Order, self-defense is not wrong, but beware the cost of prolonged relationships."

"I was afraid of something like that. Is the sickness going around really from the Borelians?"

Chandler dipped his head. "It is."

Tommen gave him a hard regard. "I find your straight answers suspicious. What's going on?"

"These are things that must be known. But if you would rather have more riddles and—"

"No, no. That's fine. I'm down with the straight answers. Just a little spooked by them. But I'll take them while I can get them." He shifted position. "Okay, let's talk about my mission. Do you know where the journal is, or maybe a good, solid, honestly credible lead?"

"Such knowledge, the Author has not given to me."

"Do you know anything about it?"

"I know that it will be as a wolf in sheep's clothing and catastrophe will follow."

"Why did Rifun give the mission to me? Or was it the Author giving it to me so maybe I could destroy it?"

"I don't know what the Author has in store, but I can tell you that Rifun chose you because you're new, young, naive. You have not yet realized what it means to have Books."

Tommen huffed a sigh. "So what do you want me to do? Tell Rifun no? Okay, great, he can't threaten me so he threatens the ones I love. I'm still a weakling compared to him. And if I don't do it, he'll find someone else. He has no shortage of lackeys who would jump off a cliff if he told them to. But I have you. Help me make this not a catastrophe. Make me like the rabbit. Okay, he hates recon missions, but he can still walk in the dark forest without being consumed by it. Help me navigate both worlds."

Chandler leaned back and grinned. "So I shall do to the best of your ability to listen. Now then, would you care for some rabbit?"

Tommen raised a brow. "Um...would I actually be eating it? I mean, I'm still dreaming, aren't I? Or have I learned to teleport in my sleep?"

"Does it matter? Do you want some or not?"

"Well, I'm not going to say no."

Dream rabbit or not, Chandler knew how to cook. Of course, seeing how he couldn't exactly just go down to the grocery store and pick up a few things—oh what was he saying? The man lived in the in-between dimension. He could walk into the Oval Office and face no repercussions. He chose a survivalist lifestyle because the Author apparently commanded it and it was what he knew from his old life way back when. This was no inconvenience for him.

"I see your arm has healed well," Chandler observed.

"Oh, um, yeah." Tommen pushed up his sleeve to reveal the twisted, scarred flesh. It was mottled pink and white and there were still tiny pinpricks of dark brown and black on his fingers that made it look as though a pen had exploded near his hand. He flexed his hand as best he could, tried to make a fist but was only able to with the help of his other hand and gritting of his teeth. It was his index and middle fingers that were the problem, able to move and curl a little but not fully and certainly not without pain. He took another bite of rabbit. "I never did thank you for helping me, both with my injuries and the escape."

"No thanks is necessary."

"I guess I never really considered that maybe you had been hurt collapsing the Time Trap and the cave. Could you have been hurt in that? I mean, you took the fireworks for that purpose, right?"

Chandler nodded and wiped his mouth. "Yes, I did. I could have been hurt. I could have been killed, in fact, seeing how I was sitting in the Matter shift between dimensions with that much raw Energy around me. But all is well."

They ate in silence for a bit, finishing up the rabbit and moving on to some fruit and vegetable preserves Chandler had stashed away.

"So what do you do for fun?" Tommen wondered. "When you're not defeating Shadows, saving my ass, and dispensing riddles, that is? Do you have any hobbies, weird collections, anything like that? I see you make candles, but I imagine it gets kind of lonely."

"Not as lonely as you might think. The Whites provide as much company as I can normally stand. With the rise of the Cult over the last couple years, my hobbies have been pushed aside for more practical activities."

"But what are your hobbies? Besides candle-making."

Chandler grinned and shook his head. "I enjoy collecting feathers, though that is a more passive activity. I also make pottery." He turned and gestured to all the pots on the shelves and in the little nooks and crannies. "I made all the pots and dishes you see here. And painted them."

Tommen gaped. "Holy shit."

But had he really expected anything less? Wasn't as though the man didn't have time to perfect his craft. Still, to look at the pots, they were damn near perfect, the sides smooth and gently curving, not lumpy or misshapen. The paint was pristine, the lines elegant, straight or curved as they needed to be, not wavering as from an infirm hand. The ones with little pictures painted on them were astounding.

"How long does it take you to make each one?"

"It depends," the man replied predictably. "The smallest ones will take a day to shape. I don't use a potter's wheel, but craft everything the old way."

"Where does the clay come from?"

"I make it. Making pots like these is a lengthy process and requires much patience and care. If I cannot give the time and care to a piece I do not immediately require, I will not make it. Such is how it is with the Cult."

"Oh."

"But priorities must be arranged sensibly."

Tommen let out a breath. "Well, you're not wrong there." He shifted position. "I feel like I should be tired, except this is a dream—or I hope it is, or else I'm fucked when it comes to waking up for school tomorrow. I don't know. Should I be getting home or just chill here or what are your plans?"

Chandler shrugged. "I make few plans. They usually end up changing."

"I know the feeling. But I'm serious, like, how does this whole thing work, anyway?"

He didn't like the expression the man got. It was all Saul. Smirk, sarcasm, scheming little mind. Chandler stood and closed the short distance between them. Tommen leaned back warily. Chandler squatted down in front of him, reached out, and said, "Wake."

He no sooner touched Tommen's forehead than Tommen sat

bolt upright in bed, his alarm screaming at him to wake up. His initial reaction was fear, until his brain realized he hadn't had a nightmare. Then it was confusion over whether he'd actually been dreaming or literally returned to the in-between dimension to speak to Chandler. He certainly didn't feel tired, as if he'd been hiking and then visiting for hours, and yet his stomach told him that the rabbit and preserves had been both real and delicious.

Groaning, he lay back down, rolled over, and hit the button on his alarm clock, very nearly knocking off a perfect little handmade pot with a lid, not much bigger than a teacup. It was painted with thick lines of bold red, deep black, and pure white. Beside it was a folded up piece of paper. When he touched it, he found that it wasn't paper, but a very thin weaving, like papyrus. He unfolded it and read the message, written in fine, delicate handwriting.

When you make your choice is when the war really begins, but the Shadows are not the only beasts out there. Take a pinch of these and make with tea or burn them in a candle when the nightmares overwhelm you. -Chandler

Curious now, Tommen set the note aside and opened up the pot which turned out to be stuffed full of some dried herb. He didn't recognize the smell, but it was not unpleasant. Actually, he wanted to try a bit now just to see what would happen, then decided against it. He had little doubt that the nightmares would return soon enough, assuming a visit from Chandler could keep them at bay for more than a night. Then he could find out what the herb was and how it worked.

He pushed his blankets aside and blindly reached for his hearing aids, momentarily confused at their absence until he recalled that he hadn't even taken them out before crawling into bed. Annoying, but not the end of the world as he tossed them on the charger and Banded them until they were fully charged in only a few seconds.

His dad walked in the door just as he walked in the kitchen about ten minutes later.

"Morning, Sunshine," his dad greeted gruffly.

"Morning yourself. What's got you all grouchy?" Tommen

wondered. "Bad night on the town or bad night in the office?"

"Both." His dad set his boots aside. "Good news, though, I have tonight off. Which means I'll be there to make sure you check in with the doctor."

"Doctor? Oh, the shrink." Tommen let out a breath. "Right. Yeah. That's today, isn't it?"

"Yes, it is."

"Dad, I'm fine, I promise. Everything is going back to normal again."

"Not good enough. You're going to the initial session, and then we'll see what he recommends. He's also a Time Agent, so you can speak a little more freely than you would with a normal psychologist."

"You want me to tell him about Rifun and the Order and the Akarin and everything else?"

"I imagine he'll want to hear all about it, but part of it is dependent on you and building trust and a relationship with him. It's not just about diagnosing the problem but working through it."

"Why aren't you a shrink? Sounds like you've got the basics down."

His dad gave him a look. "I already offered, but you refused. You told me you need help, now we'll find out what kind of help and how that's going to work."

Tommen sighed, but there was no getting out of it. His big mouth had gotten him in trouble again. Well, maybe it would do him some good with the shrink. And who knew? Maybe he could convince the shrink he was fine. He just had to remember to keep his mouth shut in the future. Therapy only helped as long as no one else found out about it. Thankfully, Tyler Freeman was gone, but that didn't mean he couldn't rear his ugly head again if he got word through his younger brother Ricky who was a junior with Tommen.

But with that, it meant he couldn't tell Becky either. He had no doubt of her support, but he also had little doubt that her mouth was bigger than his. She may not intentionally blab about him seeing a shrink and actively try to hurt him, but one off-handed comment and word would spread. This time last year, Tommen had been that kid who'd been kidnapped, held for ransom, and almost lost his dad. For the staff, he'd been placed on a suicide watch. He didn't need to again be that kid, this time a survivor of the Halloween attack and now seeing a psychologist for that along with all his other past traumas both real and rumored.

There was just no way to win, it seemed. No matter what he did, he was always that kid in school. In Time, he was again that kid who'd defied the Hands, snubbed the Borelians, almost caused Time civil war and had helped instigate a Borelian declaration of war again humans. According to the Akarin, he was that kid who'd saved Rifun's life. According to the First Order, he was that kid who was both a coward but still the Faharoa's favorite, now being sent to find the third journal.

In some naive past life, Tommen might have been flattered to have so much attention. These days, it just made him feel ill. It made him feel old. He didn't want the attention, but neither did he want to be invisible. He just wanted to be normal. Wake up, go to school, complain about school, complain about homework, go to work, complain about work, hang out with friends, have dinner with his dad, putter around online, stay up way too late, and get way too little sleep. Rinse and repeat.

He wished his dad sweet dreams and was met with a sigh and a raised eyebrow. Then he grabbed his peanut butter toast, backpack, and headed out to swap cars in the garage. Before long, he was slinking down the road to Becky's house where she hurried out to meet him.

"Well, at least you're still feeling okay," Tommen said as he pulled away from the curb.

"My head's a little fuzzy and I was starting to cough this morning, but I'll be fine," she told him. "I took some day meds before I walked out the door and I have a few tablets I can take at lunch if I need to."

"Eli went from zero to sick in just a few hours. Are you sure?"

"Yeah, I'm fine. Mrs. Shaw isn't the only one with an incredible immune system."

"Please tell me you're being sarcastic."

"Of course I am. But really, I'm fine. Let's go."

As expected, the Shaw boys were out sick. Heading to school, Tommen Banded several times so he could look back and check on Becky. Other than her eyes being a little red, she appeared no worse for wear. Whatever meds she took must have been pretty good because she didn't cough, sniffle, or sneeze the whole ride in.

"Sorry to say," she said as Tommen found a parking spot, "but I don't think there's going to be any sex for a bit while I'm sick."

He glanced back at her. "I won't say I'm not disappointed, but I'm not arguing. Besides, our relationship is more than just sex, right?"

She cleared her throat sickly. "Yeah. It is."

While she claimed to value his health by not holding his hand on the way in, that didn't stop her from touching the door handle before him, and he made a dramatic excuse to go to the bathroom before going to his locker. Of course, he should have predicted that she would beat him to his locker, and he found her making hand prints all over the front of it.

"I don't think you're that sick if you can keep up your usual antics," he told her, spinning his lock and opening the door.

"Aw, you really think so?"

"I know so. Listen, I've got a test coming up that I kind of haven't studied for. At all."

"Want me to quiz you?"

"No, I kind of want to just study on my own quietly."

Her expression was equal parts puzzled, hurt, and too sick to care about either. She nodded, rubbed her eyes, and made some excuse about finding a corner to nap in until first period. Tommen said he would see her at lunch, then slammed his locker shut without taking anything, and made for the bathroom.

He headed into one of the stalls, but stopped there. He was no expert at opening portals. He'd only done, what, one that hadn't collapsed and landed him on his ass? But what was the worst that could happen? If he was successful, he was successful. If not, he landed in the in-between dimension and could speak to Chandler.

Becky was sick. If it was Borelian pneumonia, he needed to find the cure and get it to her before things got out of hand. Who knew how many others were infected because of Will and Eli? If it spread as fast as Will claimed, could Tommen have given it to his dad who would take it to the precinct? Could his dad have some kind of immunity to it because of his exposure to two Borelian poisons? Were the illnesses in any way related to the toxins, or were they completely separate entities?

Between his anxiety over just opening the portal, plus added anxiety about potentially getting caught—he wasn't sure why, seeing how he was locked in a bathroom stall and no one was likely to bother him except if they intended to rape him, which wasn't actually out of the realm of possibility in this school—the best he managed was an unstable little blip, enough to show that he could have gone where he needed to if he had been able to open the portal correctly.

It was an exhausting process, and Tommen took a second to Band and collect himself. He knew he'd just been trying to open a portal. Anyone else, seeing his redness, breathlessness, and sweat would probably have other thoughts. Once he'd recovered and calmed down somewhat, he dropped the Band, flushed the toilet, stepped out of the stall, washed his hands, and carried on like normal.

Tommen returned to his locker, grabbed his books for first period Spanish, and headed to class a little early. Mrs. Perez was at her desk, entering grades and sorting through homework papers.

"Buenos dias, Tommen," she greeted.

"Jó reggelt," he replied in Hungarian. Then, in Hebrew, *"O hu 'boker tov'?"* (Good morning. Or is it 'boker tov' [Good morning]?)

She sighed dramatically and shook her head, but was smiling the whole time. "You are determined to speak every language but the one we're learning."

Tommen set down his books. "Yes, but think of it this way.

You're teaching one language. By the time I graduate, I'll be speaking five, not including English. You've more than quadrupled your success rate with me. You should take pride in that."

"If it keeps you studying and learning something, I guess I should."

She coughed some, then reached into her purse for a cough drop.

"You sick?" Tommen tried to keep the question light and not let the dread bleed through.

"Oh, I have Eli Shaw in my Spanish I class. He went home sick yesterday, but not before coming to class. Probably gave me whatever he's got. But what can you do? It's January. Tis the season to be sickly."

"Fa la la?"

"Very funny."

He left the room and meandered through the hall a little bit, listening to the din of activity and generally trying to be observant without being the obvious security guard in the corner. He heard the usual chatter and gossip and people still going on about extravagant vacations.

But he also discovered that there was an advantage to his hearing aids pushing sound at him indiscriminately. He heard the little noises, from the obvious coughs and sneezes, to more subtle throat clearing, scratchy throats and congested speech. Few comments were made about it except to be passed off as, "Yeah, our family gathering was huge and my little cousin Timmy was sick, so he probably gave it to me" or "There were a ton of people in the airport, so someone was bound to be sick and passing on germs."

He never heard anything specifically referencing one of the massive New Year's parties such as Times Square or something similar, but he didn't really expect to. New Year's at Times Square was a novelty, an opportunity. Few families with the means—at least in this area—would trade one cold and snowy place for another cold and snowy place, not unless there was some kind of exotic skiing involved.

Switzerland, for instance. Not impossible for someone to have gone to Times Square, but he found it unlikely.

Even so, how did it help him? The virus was out there, and it was spreading quickly. So far, it sounded like a bad cold, maybe the flu. Suck it up, suck down some fluids, keep on trucking. What would it turn into? What did the middle and later stages of this virus look like? How would it affect those who did contract a simple cold over the holidays? How would it affect people whose immune systems were less than stellar for one reason or another? When did the CDC get involved, and what could they really do to help? How would it affect the planetary defenses? What if the Tacagan teams got sick? Did the Tacagans have the medical technology to produce a cure, or was that as heavily guarded as the straight Borelian poison antidote? Just how had Rifun gotten his syringe of the stuff? How much more did he have?

He returned to class when the bell rang, sitting in his seat and pretending as though nothing were wrong. Up front, Mrs. Perez popped another cough drop, took a long drink from her thermos, finished up whatever she was doing on the computer, then headed to the front of the room to begin the day's lesson, which started with collecting the homework from the previous night.

Several other classmates were also in the beginning stages of sickness. Given how Mrs. Perez loved interactive activities with conversation and culture and everything else, everyone in the room would be infected before the end of class. Everyone in the school would have been exposed to the germs by the end of the day.

Rifun was only going after the Borelians because they posed a direct threat to him and the Order. He'd given Tommen the medicine because he was technically part of the Order, and still some kind of weird pet project. But what about the rest of humanity? Population in chaos is easier to conquer because there is no direction and the people crave order of some form, whether it's freedom or oppression. Such was the logic behind bio-warfare from the Borelians, but that didn't mean Rifun might not take advantage of it somehow. The man was powerful, but he was also the most unpredictable wild card they had, and even their so-called leverage against him with his seizures was tenuous at best, growing weaker by the day if he'd found some kind of cure or at least management for them.

They needed a plan. They needed a lot of plans. Then they needed to figure a way out of the corner they'd painted themselves into.

Fuck, he needed therapy.

Chapter Twelve
Shrink and Expand

Tommen arrived home from school to find his dad waiting for him in the kitchen.

"Ready to go?" Walter wondered.

"Not really," Tommen said, mostly just stalling. He blanched. "Do I have to?"

"You brought it up in the first place. You need it. You need to talk to someone who understands Time so you can explain what's going on." He went on before Tommen could interrupt. "You're going to the first session. We'll see what he recommends from there. It's only an hour or so. Fair?"

Tommen ground his teeth and sighed. Then, grudgingly, "Fair."

To make a point of it, his dad drove him.

The doctor was fully licensed and accredited, but wasn't exactly in practice in Charleston, or anywhere in West Virginia at all. He was originally from Vermont which was where he was exposed to Time. He was a Master Timekeeper now, with little desire to advance his Timekeeping career. Rather, his goals were more humanitarian. He became a licensed psychologist in both the United States and Canada and so worked with Time Agents who were struggling with issues they couldn't speak of to anyone else. He was presently located in Kansas, but made the special trip at Walter's behest.

So they did not meet in a quaint office setting with pretty office plants and calming earth tones and paintings, but in a park about thirty miles south of Charleston. Parks and other rest stops varied in their style as far as upkeep and amenities went. Some were little more than rain shelters while others were just short of motels with showers, decent vending, and even some mats to sleep on. The one they approached now was somewhere between the two. The building was small but clean with a single snack machine, a drinking fountain, and a deck with a picnic table overlooking the western mountains where the sun now set.

The man himself bore the appearance of being in his mid-forties, thinning hair cut short, transition lens glasses to cut down on the blinding sunlight beating down on the patio table which he'd cleaned off and dried. His teeth were crooked, Tommen noted, and one had a partial filling, but he did not appear ashamed by any of it as he shook both their hands with a firm grip.

"Thank you for coming," Walter said. "I'm sorry you had to drive all this way in these conditions."

"No worries," the doctor assured him. He looked at Tommen. "Good to meet you, Tommen. I'm Doctor Anderson, but you can call me Harold if it makes you feel better. We'll have a little chat and see where we ought to go from there."

"Wait, so, is he coming with us?" Tommen asked, looking at his dad.

"No, but 'we' still constitutes you and me. Would you rather sit out here or inside? Or anywhere you want."

"I'll let you two alone, then," Walter said, stepping back a few feet before turning and disappearing around the corner.

Tommen was immensely uncomfortable with the whole thing, and while he wasn't a fan of sitting at a cold picnic table in the middle of winter while the sun went down, he didn't want to go wandering around the immediate vicinity looking for a quiet corner. They were just two dudes talking, not secret lovers looking for a fuck spot.

"How much are you going to report back to my dad?" he began, sitting down and focusing on his hands.

Anderson shook his head. "Unless you talk about harming yourself or others, this all stays between you and me."

"So if I told you something, like, my girlfriend and I are having sex—which my dad would probably stripe me for—you wouldn't tell him."

"I couldn't even if I wanted to, legally speaking. And I wouldn't anyway, as it would be a terrible betrayal of trust. Surely you can appreciate that; your dad tells me you have the nickname The Chivalrous Welshman."

Tommen shrugged. "I guess so. Not that it does me any good. Got my ass kicked multiple times because of it in school, and I may have helped save the life of the universe's most wanted mass murderer. How's that for chivalry?"

It was a long sixty minutes. Or maybe it was more like ninety. Either way, too damn long and too damn awkward. There were a number of long silences as Tommen tried to size the guy up, tried to determine whether the doctor could be a double-agent going to report back to Rifun, or just a nice guy wanting to help out. He didn't like the idea of spilling his life's sob story, regardless if the man was a Time Agent and would understand a good portion of it. Part of it felt petty and childish to go into something that, even to his ears, sounded like, "When I was seven, I wanted a pony, but I didn't get one." Other parts felt like admitting, at best, cowardice, or, at worst, something highly illegal or severely questionable. Still some parts felt like giving up, as if he ought to have thicker skin and deal with everything on his own. He probably should have. But for as much as he'd told himself that he could convince the shrink to give him a clean bill of health, he found that he just couldn't do it, could barely get up the will to try.

Seeing how they'd just met and were starting from scratch, Tommen was willing to bet that they'd made a ton of progress that day, more for the fact that he'd spoken honestly at all. It hadn't been much, at least from his point of view, but if his dad and Micah and Kayla and Rifun could all read him like a book, then someone who was trained to read people like books probably had little difficulty picking him apart from the inside out.

How was it that everyone seemed to look right through him, but everyone appeared to him as brick walls? What was he missing?

What was he doing wrong? If his Psychology teacher wasn't such a freak himself, would the class be more meaningful, more helpful? Should he see about adding Psychology classes to his college roster?

As the minutes dragged on, Tommen dreaded what kind of diagnosis the doctor was going to come up with. Depression would be the most obvious, but what if he threw in some kind of curveball? Even with his knowledge of Time, what if the doctor came up with something like bipolar disorder? Bipolar depression was said to be a bitch, at least according to the girls at school who'd been diagnosed with it. Would his constant fear and paranoia land him a paranoid schizophrenia label? God knew how that was going to go over if the kids at school ever found out. But was it really paranoid schizophrenia if it really was true, that there was a psychopathic cult leader stalking him and trying to manipulate his life? Fuck, he sounded crazy even to himself.

What would his dad think about all of this? People went to the doctor hoping to get a clean bill of health—or else get told their symptoms are very minor—but always secretly dreaded that it was really something bigger—a headache turned into a brain tumor, back pain turned into cancer, sore muscles turned into arthritis or some muscular wasting disease. What if Walter was hoping for an easy fix but then found out his son had bigger problems? He'd already been chained down once because of Tommen's fighting at school. That had gotten cleaned up. Having a son who was depressed or nuts was a little harder to shake. Would he blame himself for not doing more sooner to try and help?

Another thought occurred to Tommen, as they wrapped up and went inside for a minute to warm up. Could he just hand the doctor his Authored Books? Was that allowed? What would the doctor think? Where did he stand on the Akari-Akarin-Order business? On that same note, though, did he really want to give his Books away at all? It sounded as though he didn't have a choice in the matter. Once they hit 2017, those Books were going to be available for everyone to see and read. Most would think them fiction. Tommen still wasn't sure how he felt about that. It was his life. Who was spying on him and what gave them the right to just document shit like that? Why had the Author chosen him? What made him special and why did she feel the need to poke her little Tommen voodoo doll viciously and repeatedly? Hadn't his life been hard enough before the whole soccer fields incident?

"Well, in all honesty, I think my dad may have fallen asleep in the car," Tommen said, blowing on his hands to warm them up. "I'll go wake him up."

"I'm rather disappointed in your lack of faith in me," Walter said, walking out of the bathroom. "I think I've been working nights long enough that I can keep going for a little while. I would have already been on duty for a couple hours by now."

"I don't think you're as nocturnal as you think you are."

Walter looked at the doctor. "How did it go?" He went on, "I understand, you can't tell me anything, but what can you tell me?"

"PTSD. Classic depression," the doctor answered simply.

"What?" Tommen wondered. "I'm not depressed. I don't feel like killing myself or anything."

"Depression comes in many different flavors. Seeing how we've had only one conversation and it wasn't exactly your life story, I am both unable and unwilling to make a greater determination beyond that."

"What do you recommend?" Walter asked.

Tommen shook his head. "I'm not taking any pills. I'm not crazy. I'm not depressed."

The doctor shifted his stance. "I don't believe pills would be of any great help in this instance, and I don't recommend prescriptions based on the preliminary results of a single session. I would like to continue to speak with you, Tommen, once a week if possible."

"But I'm trying to find a job. It's probably going to be an unpredictable schedule."

"I understand that, and if that ends up being the case, then we may not have a set schedule, but have to plan from week to week.

There is also the fact that, as we are both Timekeepers, we are able to condense one hour into only milliseconds."

Reasons why normal shrinks were looking preferable to this one.

"So are you suggesting same place, same time next week?" Walter asked.

"An indoor locale might be preferable. Winter isn't exactly the best time to go strolling around in an outdoor park."

"Well, you're not wrong there."

"And before I forget, Tommen, here's my card with my personal cell number." The doctor handed him a business card. "If you need anything, don't be afraid to call or text me. Day or night."

"Yeah, sure." Tommen pocketed the card, mentally debating whether he wanted to add it into his phone.

He was less enthusiastic about hashing out details for the next session. Somehow, it felt like he'd lost. He hadn't been able to convince anyone that he was fine, least of all himself. If he was already depressed, this sure wasn't helping anything. It was only made worse when the doctor said he worked on either six- or twelve-month commitments from his patients, for reasons both practical and financial. If Tommen was going to keep coming, he was in this for the long haul. That would give his classmates plenty of time to find out.

More to the point, what if Rifun found out? What if he thought Tommen was giving away secrets and saying all sorts of things—what things he wasn't sure, but things nonetheless? The man would have no qualms about killing the doctor. Would he do it to protect himself and exert even more control over Tommen? Given his claims about caring for his pupils, would he actually encourage it? There was a lot of talk going around these days about mental health and getting help; would Rifun be on that bandwagon as well? If so, he would more likely recommend someone in the Order for a therapist, but would it help Doctor Anderson any, at least to spare his life?

Maybe he was overthinking things. Maybe he was fully deserving of not only the depression label, but paranoid schizophrenia as well. He almost didn't realize when the conversation wrapped up and they were preparing to go their separate ways. His dad might not have noticed his distraction, but Tommen had a feeling that the doctor would have seen everything, maybe even read his mind and would use it as some kind of starting point next week. Next week? When was the next appointment? He hadn't been paying attention.

His dad took the driver's seat again, and Tommen tried not to sulk as he got in next to him. It was probably five miles before his dad spoke.

"So, how did it go?"

"Okay, I guess," Tommen answered evasively.

"I'm not asking for a play by play. What do you think? Are you willing to let him try and help or is it going to be a huge waste of time?"

"I just don't want him to get hurt, too."

"Afraid Rifun will find out?"

"Yeah."

"Well, maybe that's something you ought to bring up. I think he might appreciate a little warning if there could be a threat against his life, and it might help to—"

"I know. I get it. Talk about it. Work through it. Sunshine and roses."

His dad gave him a sideways glance but said only, "I'll take you next week, too, since I know I have the night off. After that, though, I'm trusting you with the responsibility. Don't play hooky on me."

Normally Tommen would feel offended that his dad was treating him like a child and try to reassure him that he was very nearly an adult and extremely responsible besides. Now, though, the thought of playing hooky held some appeal.

He still wasn't sure how he felt about the first session; he hadn't quite processed it yet. He wasn't exactly falling over in uncontrollable sobs, grateful to spill his life's woes to a stranger. But neither was he offended or disgusted. Neutral might be the term he was looking for. He was neutral about it. Like talking to strangers on the Internet, even though everyone was faceless, some measure of rapport still had to be built.

"You're quiet over there," his dad observed after another ten minutes or so. "Anything you want to talk about to me?"

"No, not really," Tommen answered honestly. "Just trying to figure out what just happened."

Now that he'd thought about it a little, he could honestly say that not a lot had happened. He'd been too busy trying to evade the questions and size the man up to do much real conversing. In the moment, it had seemed logical. Looking back, it felt cowardly and childish. He trusted his dad to try and help him the best he could, do his research, and find someone he believed could help. He wouldn't have just gone to the yellow pages and eeny-meeny-miney-moe'd a name.

Did that make Tommen a bad person, then? Sure, it may have been a little childish to have done what he did, but he really didn't need this much help. Maybe a yellow-page therapist would have been just fine, no need to go through the hassle of getting a referral, writing a petition, and submitting an essay on why this doctor ought to see this patient.

Speaking of essays, he needed to get a move on with his scholarship essays if he even wanted a chance at some money. Damn it. He took out his phone and texted Becky.

"I'll be home in ten to fifteen minutes and I could really use some help on these essays." He added some appropriately distressed and frustrated emojis. "Some of your corrections are confusing."

"I guess I could come over for a little bit, as long as you have chicken soup or something," she replied after a minute or two.

"Your incredible immune system isn't so incredible?"

"Obviously not. Or you can text me your questions, if you don't want to get sick."

"You rode in my car and made little sick hand prints all over my locker today. I think if I was going to get sick, that would have done it."

"Yippee for you."

"Do you want to come over?"

"Not really. I kind of just want to stay in bed. I won't be going to school tomorrow, though, that's for sure."

"Okay. Maybe I'll try to figure it out on my own and text you if I have questions or something."

"I'll try to answer them, but I might fall asleep, too."

"That's fine. Feel better, okay?"

"I will eventually."

And that was the end of that.

"Telling Becky all about your appointment with the shrink?" his dad wondered.

"Not unless I want the whole school to hear about it," Tommen scoffed. "I don't think she'd explicitly tell someone, but word would get around. I would just as soon keep it to myself."

His dad's sideways glance was unreadable, but he did not push the issue. Tommen decided to sidestep the whole thing by asking, "You're not feeling sick, are you?"

"As in, cold and flu? No, can't say that I am, though half the department sounds like they have one foot in the grave. Why, are you sick?"

"I'm not, no, but there's something going around and it sounds pretty severe."

Again with the odd sideways glance. "Someone bring Ebola back from an exotic Christmas vacation?"

Tommen grinned. "No, I don't think so. At least I hope not."

"Do Rifun or the Borelians have anything to do with it?"

"Only in our house does that topic ever actually come up as a possibility. Conspiracy theories are wonderful things, aren't they?"

"Tommen."

He sighed. "Yeah, sort of."

His dad frowned. "Okay, let's hear it."

Tommen shifted in his seat. "So, Rifun dropped by last night and said that a New Year's Eve attack had occurred, but it wasn't impending invasion or anything like that. It was about infection. It's some kind of, I don't know, space pneumonia. I guess it's super common on Brelix and Borelian slave worlds. The intent was to infect the human race, weed out the weak and save time and resources down the road on slave health care. Any ensuing pandemonium because of it would only be a bonus because it would make enslaving humans that much easier."

"Say one thing for the Borelians, they're not dumb," Walter mused. "If indeed that's what happened."

"Well, the good news is, there's a cure. Rifun had his men who were torching the fields also grab some of the medicine for it. He gave me a shot of it—involuntarily, I might add—and so far, I'm the only one who hasn't gotten sick."

His dad grunted. "I wonder if any of the other worlds have experienced something similar."

"I don't know. Honestly, I would think not."

"How's that?"

"Depending on the percentage of survival and the immune systems of the other humans, it could wipe them out rather than weaken them enough to enslave. Earth and Tacaga have the population and the technology needed to resist the Borelians, maybe fight back. Get rid of us, the others might just surrender."

"Maybe. Maybe the Borelians gave the other worlds different sicknesses, that way we can't collaborate cure efforts, and it's harder to cure ten separate illnesses versus just one. But, once again, that would be brought up at one of the Tacagans' super secret meetings." He bit off the last few words.

"Still not invited back into the war tent?" Tommen asked.

"No, but I'm not selfish enough to keep this kind of information to myself. If it spreads quickly and could be deadly, then we need to stay ahead of it while the CDC tries to play catch-up. It could get interesting. I'll pass it along to Mi Chin."

"That's it?"

"At this point, it's all I can do. But, if you can get more information about it from Rifun, it might prove useful. How many medicines did he get? How much?"

"I don't know, but I'm sure I'll see him again. Although..."

"What?"

They arrived home, Walter pulling up to the garage door where his car would sit outside until morning. They hurried inside.

As Tommen flipped on the kitchen light and sat to take off his shoes, he answered, "Rifun's been teaching me how to open portals. It's a pain in the ass, but I can physically do it. Small ones, and only one has been successful."

"Asking for pointers?"

"Something like that." Tommen relinquished the chair. "If space pneumonia is that common and widespread, there might be a chance that the Archives in the Wheel has the answer for the cure." *And I really need to get going on my journal tracking. Is there anything going on right now that isn't of the utmost importance?* "If we find it, I don't have to ask Rifun. If we don't have to ask Rifun, he can't hold it against us."

His dad nodded. "I like your idea, even if I am less enthusiastic about going to the Wheel."

"We have to do something. At least this time, it doesn't involve charging halfway across the universe on a hunch and a prayer."

"That it doesn't," his dad laughed.

"What was the name of the guy who helped with the hasax cure?"

"Monsieur Alexander LaPouir, but he's a botanist who studied the flower and its cultivation, not necessarily the medicinal properties."

Tommen tucked that information away for later use, even as he shrugged and said, "Oh. Okay, fine."

"But Do Chien might be happy to have a slightly easier project to work on for a bit."

"There aren't any other really smart guys out there we can ask?"

"Oh, I'm sure there are, but Do Chien has access to the Tacagans' technology, which they don't easily share. I don't think they would be too keen on opening up to a second Neanderthal."

"Then why don't they do it themselves?"

"Because they would ransom it. It's all politics and bullshit."

"What about the whole, 'Help us and we'll let you be autonomous'?"

"That card can only be played so much. As you said, if space pneumonia is so common, and there is a cure to be found in the Archives, there's no need to hold it over the Tacagans. We should be selective in our use of the autonomy card."

Tommen couldn't deny his dad's logic there.

"So," Walter said, standing, "did you want to start on portal training?"

"Um, well, maybe not right this second. I kind of have to work on my essays. Becky's sick and can't come over to help and explain her notes, so I have to figure them out on my own."

He felt his skin turn red even as his dad nodded and headed into the living room. "Fair enough. I'll be up all night, anyway, so just let me know when you want to practice. I'll Band you so you can get some sleep before school tomorrow."

While there had been many a night where Tommen was grateful for the ability to bend Time and so be able to stay up later than normal working on projects or other shenanigans, it also frustratingly eliminated the ability to plead fatigue. He couldn't say that, well, he had to be up early for school so he couldn't do such a thing tonight. Maybe tomorrow. His dad would just smile politely, nod, and remind him that with Time, there was always time.

So he reluctantly slunk off to his room and opened up half a dozen unfinished and grammatically atrocious essays. The easy stuff like punctuation he knocked out quickly, but it didn't make him feel much better considering the number of marks still scribbled on the pages.

After an hour or so of editing, printing, comparing, editing again, and hoping he interpreted Becky's corrections correctly, his activities wandered in a different direction, and he found himself logging into the Time Agent database. As an Apprentice, he couldn't do much more than open basic profiles of all the Time Agents on Earth, but it was all he really needed to do as he narrowed his search by Region and District.

It was getting late in West Virginia, but western Europe would be going about their normal morning routines. Tommen Banded so he could slip out of the house without having to explain himself, then dug out his phone. The good news about paying his own phone bill was that he didn't have to explain things like international calling.

"Bonjour?" a male voice answered questioningly on the other end.

"Um, *bonjour,*" Tommen said awkwardly. Of course. When calling France, people are going to speak French. Duh. What if he didn't speak English, though? "Is this Monsieur LaPouir? Do you speak English?"

A sigh. Then, in a heavy accent, "Yes, I do. Who is calling?"

"Tommen Forbes, Apprentice Timekeeper, Region Four, District Four."

"Why is an Apprentice from so far away calling me?" His tone was one of wariness, not amusement or irritation, as one might have expected.

"Because I have a few questions for you."

"Your father is Walter Forbes, yes? He asked me to research the hasax."

"That's true, but it's not why I'm calling. I'm calling because you were once Rifun Ndolo's Master."

Silence. It stretched out so long, Tommen might have thought the call had been dropped or his phone died. Finally, a slow, *"Oui, j'etais.* I had his Apprenticeship stripped from my record in the Wheel, and my Mastership was stripped from his. I wanted nothing to do with what he was becoming—or has become. He did not argue. I don't know if he even noticed or cared. How did you find out?"

"It was in his Authored Book."

"Bah! The Books, the journals, the Akari! It consumed him."

"But it is true."

"I was his Master, *oui*."

"What about his injuries? Is he blind? Why train him?"

Now Monsieur LaPouir faltered. "He is not blind as you and I understand it." He paused and seemed to search for the words. "He was imprisoned in Madagascar on a chain gang, going through a field to break up the hard clay soil so it could be farmed. Another prisoner, who was a Timekeeper—a Runner, I should say—attacked him. He took a swing at Rifun's head with the pickax. I tried to intervene before blade met flesh, but was just too late. The pick did not bury itself far into his brain, but far enough. When he woke up in the hospital, he was blind."

"Completely?"

"Completely. There was nothing that could be done for him, so he attempted to return home to his mother who had died while he was in prison, and his abusive stepfather chased him away. Now, you must understand, in African countries, especially in those days, family was everything. A rich man with no family had less than the poorest man in the world. I found him on the streets, took pity on him, taught him Timekeeping, tried to give him some sort of purpose in life. As he healed from his wounds, he also proclaimed that his vision had been restored. While this is cause for celebration, yes, I think he may have taken it just a little too far."

"What do you mean?"

"You must also understand that the Malgache at the time were undergoing a cultural shift, a revolution of sorts as they tried to be independent of France. European Christianity was scorned and the peoples returned to their traditional animism. He had very little love for Christians, and his animism seemed to have failed him. But religion can bring comfort, so I told him the legends of the Akari. Legends, myths, bedtime stories, something to give the training a little more mystical feel. Obviously, technology in the Wheel was far more advanced to us a century ago than it is today. It frightened many people. Using the Akari legends made it a little more familiar, more personable. Some have likened it to the Holy Grail."

"I've heard it referred to like that."

"I fear he may have taken it too far. Young men who have lost everything and have no purpose will latch onto anything. Usually foolishly. With everything going on in Madagascar, the restoration of his sight, he took it all and twisted it into some kind of savior complex, rising through the Timekeeper ranks. He fought in World War II and was wounded again, but continued afterwards to fight for Malgache independence. But the Malgache lost the war. He was captured by French soldiers and imprisoned for a decade. In that time, he was tortured frequently within an inch of his life, burnings, electrocutions, any horror you could imagine; he has very little normal skin left on his body. But he refused to open a portal and flee because he saw himself as the savior of his people. The last time we spoke, he told me to leave and never come back."

"And you've never thought to mention this to anyone? Zero Hour Revolution, attack on the Akarin, anything like that seem important to you?"

"*Pourquoi?* So I could be charged and hanged beside him, guilt by association? Certainly not. I wanted nothing to do with him or his actions before the revolution, and even less once I had heard what had happened. We have not seen or spoken to each other in decades. I would prefer to keep it that way."

Tommen rubbed his eyes and shivered in the cold. "What do you know about him? Any weaknesses? What about the hole in his head from the pickax?"

"I could not say. Such an injury...the bone may be weak there, but it is more likely reinforced. As for anything else, there is nothing you can do to him that his torturers did not do a thousand times worse. That is a fact. But the greater miracle would be getting close enough to him to strike a blow. He is very powerful, both physically and in Time, and whatever it is he believes his Akari powers can do. I do not believe in the Akari, but he has certainly found something out there. I do not need to tell you that he is a dangerous man."

"What does he want? What's his end goal here?"

He could imagine the Frenchman shrugging. "What else? Power. Oh, he says he wants to bring about world peace, and maybe in some strange way he thinks he can accomplish this, but only if he is in control. Put another way, he wants to be God and reshape the universe in his image."

"But why? I mean, who would want that?"

"Only a man with permanent victim mentality and the power to get what he wants. Rivotra has indeed been wronged in many ways, but those wrongs passed on many years ago. Yet he still carries them around. No matter how much power he gains, even after the Zero Hour Revolution, he will always play the victim because of invisible adversity. When he was overthrown, he took it as another wrong against him, another tally mark in his victimhood. The only thing he is a victim of is his own ego and self-loathing, his lust for power. And he is very good at getting others to feel the same way about themselves and follow him."

"He sets himself up to be the hero. He offered peace to the Akarin knowing the council would reject it. It sows discord into the troops, sets up their own victim mentality after the defeat, wins him converts. Not all, but some. He offers to help humans with the Borelians because is crazy, brilliant, and stupid, and because we're all victims of slavery if we don't do something."

"*Exactement*. He does not even realize that in the Zero Hour Revolution, he sought to destroy the very thing that gave his life meaning after leaving home."

"And the Cult?"

"A cult of victims to lead, with the power to do anything he wants. He could be the most powerful man in the universe right now, but it's not enough, because he still sees himself as the victim. Only when he is the last one standing at the end of the bloodbath will he rest. And he will probably die trying to get there. I fear to ponder how many more he will take with him to the grave."

"Then why not stop him? Or help me stop him? Turn the tables. There has to be a way."

"I imagine there is a way, but I do not know it."

"You think...you think maybe the Author has a bigger purpose here?"

LaPouir scoffed. "If there is an Author, he or she is clearly a sadist who's only in it for money and cares nothing for his creation, what he puts us through. I understand that all good stories have conflict of some sort and a lesson to be learned, but some days, I wish for my greatest conflict to be what to eat for breakfast. This is the least of my problems right now, and if there is an Author, I resent him for it."

Politics and religion, two subjects usually best avoided, and Tommen managed to hit both in a single conversation. "Um, right. Listen, I have to get to bed and you probably have stuff to do today. Thanks for talking to me."

"I only wish I could be of more use. If you do try to cross Rivotra, I will be certain to come to your funeral. *Adieu*."

Click.

Tommen was not comforted by the man's parting words, but he told himself the shiver was from the cold. It was a lie. Or a partial one, anyway. He put his phone away and headed back inside. His Band-exit forgotten, he walked in the front door. His dad whirled around in his recliner.

"How—?" His dad shook his head. "Never mind, I don't want to know. What were you doing outside?"

"Um...nothing, really."

"It's below freezing, and you were doing nothing?"

Tommen hesitated for a second. "I called Monsieur LaPouir."

"Oh, really? And what happened to working on your scholarship essays?"

"LaPouir was Rifun's Master when he was going through his Timekeeper training."

That gave his dad pause. "I don't recall seeing that on his record."

"He said he had it erased because he didn't want anything to do with Rifun, didn't want the guilt by association label."

"Makes sense, I suppose. Did he have anything of interest to say? Anything of use?"

Tommen shook his head. "No, nothing. Just telling me what we already know. Rifun's got a lot of ego and a lot of power to back it up."

"Worth a shot. How did you find it out if he had the training erased?"

"It was in Rifun's Authored Book."

"Can't hide anything from the Author, right?"

"Not if she wrote it." Tommen moved into the living room, heading for his bedroom.

"You believe it, then?" his dad wondered behind him.

"I...I believe in something. The Akari. Some kind of Author. Whether it's Kayla's or Rifun's or something else, I still don't know for sure. But I intend to find out."

His dad's expression was unreadable, though surprise was definitely in there. And why not? For years, Tommen had sneered at religion of any form, and now he was on a mission to find out more about this mystical Author that everyone seemed to claim was on their side. He found himself hoping for another visit to or from Chandler, though somewhere deep down, he knew the visits would more likely be few and far between.

He returned to his room and again opened his essays. He stared at them for a while, texted Becky, got no reply, told himself she had just fallen asleep, mused over his essays some more, then eventually closed out of the program. He was never going to get these stupid essays done. Writing was hard. Editing was worse. Scholarships and college seemed like such small things compared to everything else going on. Eventually, he wandered out to the living room where his dad was reading a book; the TV was off.

"This is new," Tommen observed.

"I decided to stop at the library," his dad said, placing a bookmark and setting the book on the stand. "They made me get a new library card. Said they expire after five years."

"A terrible thing, I'm sure."

"Ready for some more portal instruction?"

"I guess so. Not making any progress on my essays right now. Why does writing have to be so hard?"

"Because good writing gets you stuff, like money."

"I know, I know. Can we do some portal training to take my mind off it?"

His dad nodded and got up from his recliner. "What have you learned so far?"

The question was honest, yet grudging. Walter was teaching Tommen things appropriate to his rank in Time, the things an Apprentice ought to be learning. Rifun was teaching him things far beyond his rank in Time, things far beyond Time itself, even. Tommen could see it frustrated his dad to not be teaching his son himself, to be bested once again by this lunatic.

Nevertheless, Tommen demonstrated his paltry portal abilities. He managed a slightly more stable peek into the fortress, could do a pretty good portal to his own room, but when he tried to get to the Wheel, he again found himself on the ground, dazed and confused. Blindly, he reached out and found his dad's extended hand. He got to his feet long enough to get to the couch and lie down, migraine pulsing behind his eyes.

"Overall, I'd say you're not doing too bad, considering portals aren't normally taught until you reach Journeyman rank," his dad told him. "But I think you might be overthinking it on the portal to the Wheel."

"What do you mean?" Tommen asked, his voice muffled by the pillow on his face.

"The Wheel has the monopoly on portals, so any other portals are fighting the current. The Wheel also has the technology to hold a portal, which you already know. I think you're trying to force something that doesn't need to be forced. Finesse. Move with the current, and as soon as the Wheel has a hold on your portal, let it do most of the work to get it open. Then walk through and let it take the reins."

"But watching you and the twins, opening a portal to the Wheel always looked like an exhausting pain in the ass."

"It is, which should tell you something about how unnecessarily hard you're working. Do you want to try it again?"

Tommen let out a breath. "Give me a minute?"

His dad nodded and went back to his book. Tommen took the pillow off his face, but kept his eyes closed. Once again, he was working too hard, using the wrong tool to get the job done. Using a mallet to drive in a finishing nail as it were. Hey, that was a construction reference. Wasn't Chris supposed to call him about the job? Oh well, maybe he hadn't gotten it. He wasn't really surprised by it, but he had hoped to minimize his time between jobs—that is, the time between paychecks.

On the other hand, if he got really good at his Timekeeping, maybe he could advance a little more quickly, increasing his pay just by increasing his rank, plus help himself more by being able to turn in Runners. If he got good enough and ranked up fast enough, he might not even need a day job.

He mulled over his time with the Order. So far, he hadn't seen anything resembling a paycheck. Did they get paid? It was a pretty tough gig if they didn't. Yeah, let's all go to war and get nothing for our efforts! Sure, new digs and the thrill of conquering one's foe was nice, but to take nothing home at the end of the day? No monetary spoils? That could be pretty hard on morale. Maybe he would ask Rifun about it later.

After a few more minutes of consideration, Tommen sat up, rubbed his face, and nodded to his dad to try again. Less force, more finesse. Less force, more finesse. How was it that he always seemed to overdo everything that needed to be done gently? Less force, more finesse. Ha! Less Force, more Faith.

Before he knew it, he was on his ass again, but the portal sputtered to life, revealing the portal room in the Wheel. Without thinking, he went through the portal, feeling as though he'd been holding onto some kind of tether that now snapped. He sucked in a breath of air but still went to his knees, then his face. When he finally sat up, the room spun, but he could make out his dad also stepping through the portal, weary, but no worse for wear.

"Well, it wasn't as stable as I would have preferred it to be before walking through, but you got the job done," he said mildly. "Good job."

Tommen let out a breath. "I don't even know what I did."

He knew it was a lie as soon as he said it. With Time, it was about rote memorization and brute strength. For the Order, it was about Force. But somehow he'd tapped into that little bit of Faith. Faith in what, though? The Akari? The Author? The faith and hope that he could do it right without sending himself and his dad into the Land In-Between?

He picked himself up and looked around. Yes, they were in the Wheel, no doubt about that. There was only one place in the universe that was this fucked up.

"All right, let's go back," his dad said, breaking into his thoughts.

"Shouldn't we go to the Arena and stuff?" Tommen wondered. While he was certainly eager to finally get into and train in the Arena, he had other things he needed to do, too. "And what about looking up the cure for space pneumonia?"

"We'll do that, but I want you to practice your portals a few more times first. Once you get good at it, then we can double our efforts in the Archives because you won't have to wait for me every time." Tommen mentally added the unspoken, Or Rifun.

Conceding his point, Tommen and his dad walked back through the portal. He knew how awful it felt just going through. Being the creator of the portal, though, that added a whole new level of discomfort. It was like taking back the reins on a stubborn goat and trying to force it to move. But goats, when stubborn and forced to move, did not always walk calmly. Sometimes they would jump, try to surprise the handler and make a run for it. That was what this felt like. Pulling, pulling, trying to force, using all his strength, and then a sudden release. Sort of like sex, but with far less pleasure.

He didn't know how he made it to the couch, only that he did. Judging by his dad's demeanor, sitting and reading, he must have passed out for a short time.

"How long was I out?" Tommen wondered, sitting up and rubbing his eyes, debating whether he was going to throw up.

His dad looked at his watch. "Half an hour? You want to try again or go to bed?"

"I just want to go to bed."

"Sleep tight."

Tommen stumbled down to the bathroom to hastily brush his teeth and get ready for bed. A little cold water and normal routine helped to perk him up some, enough that he was able to take out his hearing aids and get into bed without collapsing like a drooling idiot. Friday. One more day and then the weekend. He wasn't sure what he expected to be doing seeing how he did not as yet have a job and all his friends were out sick. He did not get a chance to ponder for long before sleep claimed him.

He jolted as the ground shook and a loud noise blasted his brain. He turned around and saw fire, smoke, and a huge cloud of ash and debris raining down. His skin began to burn from the hot material and he instinctively crouched down, pulling his arm close to his body. All around him, he could hear panic and confusion, people running, screaming, and yet he saw none of it. It was if he stood alone in a cloud of dust and ash.

Then something huge began to take shape, a great dark thing that blotted out what little light there was. A moment before it emerged, Tommen could feel the ground shake and hear the snarls. He stood, spun, and started running all in the same motion, tripping over himself and almost unable to get away as a huge paw came down where he'd been just half a second before. Slobbering jaws snapped an inch from the back of his head, three of them taking turns, trying for a little Tommen treat.

As he ran, the ground began to slope. A little at first, and then a lot. Then he was turning, running up the fortress staircase. He could hear the sounds of battle, felt pushes and shoves and the wind of a weapon coming too close to his body for comfort, but again he saw nothing. The ground did not shake, but he wasn't about to stop and find out whether the Cerberus Shadow was still after him.

"Here! Here!"

Tommen skidded to a stop for just a moment, long enough to look into a dimly-lit room where something small was motioning for him. "In here!"

He skidded to a stop and ducked into the room. Outside, he could still hear the sounds of battle, but they were distant, muffled.

"Thanks," he breathed, looking around. "Who are you?"

"Friends," came a voice.

As his eyes adjusted to the dim light, Tommen could make out movements. Whoever the aliens were, they were small, the largest looking no bigger than a cat, and they were all shapes and sizes.

"Well, thanks for saving me back there," he said finally.

Everyone in the room froze as the ground began to rumble. A bulge appeared and moved through the room, scattering the small aliens. It disappeared for a moment, then reappeared, growing bigger just off to Tommen's right until the ground broke. An orange glow appeared followed by a White gopher. The little aliens hissed in rage, and Tommen saw that they were Shadows also, having a form, yet not a definite one.

"Run, Tommen!" the gopher said, chucking a candle into the middle of the Shadow horde.

Tommen did not need to be told twice. He stood and ran from the room. As soon as he hit the doorframe, he came flying out of his nightmare, sucking in a breath but unable to make a sound. He grabbed his chest as if it would release the tightness, looking around, trying to tell himself all was well even as he struggled to figure out what was off.

Then he realized he could see. His room wasn't dark. Glancing at his nightstand, he found a candle, flame burning steadily. His clock said it was a little before four. Still a few hours before he had to get up for school. But did he dare go back to sleep?

Next to his clock, his phone blinked, signaling a message. Body still tight, Tommen grabbed it and turned it on, navigating to his texts. A message from Becky.

"Too sick to go to school tomorrow. Probably best to stay away over the weekend. Parents are starting to get sick, too. Might go to the ER tomorrow or Saturday. Will let you know. Love you. Hope you don't get sick, too."

Tommen sent a reply, then lay back in his bed. The sheets were wet, and his body was shaking and sticky with sweat. He stripped down to just his boxers and lay on top of the blankets. He still felt warm.

It was quarter after four before he sat up again, exhausted but too afraid to go back to sleep. The candle still burned steadily, its progress slow. Beside it was the pot with the herbs Chandler had given him. Just a pinch, the note had said, to make with tea or burn in a candle. Well, how nice of Chandler to have dropped off a candle tonight, as if he'd known what would happen. Maybe he had. Maybe that was why the gopher had been sent to rescue him.

He really just wanted a normal day. Tommen carefully dropped a tiny pinch of the herbs into the candle flame, watching as the flame turned colors. He grabbed his color-correcting glasses and watched it go from orange to blue to green to purple to yellow and back again. Maybe it was a distraction. Maybe there was some kind of medicinal effect being released by the thin tendril of smoke. Whatever the case, it put him back into a dreamless slumber.

Chapter Thirteen
Myth

By Sunday night, Tommen did not get a call back on the construction job. He batted around an idea, whether or not he wanted to call and ask about it, unsure if it would be seen as rude, figuring there was no harm in trying. As it turned out, most of the crew was sick, including Chris. No one was doing anything right now, and no one was being hired in, either. He was still a possible candidate, so until he heard for sure or decided to pursue another offer, don't count it out just yet.

So he wasn't being ignored, and not having a job freed up a little time for other things, like his essays which still sat destitute on his computer. Wasn't as though he could ask Becky for help. She and her parents had gone into the emergency room the previous evening, only to find that half the city and surrounding area had the same idea. News was starting to pop up about this mysterious disease. On the official, PR side of things, doctors were calling it an influenza-pneumonia combo package. Two diseases for the price of one.

But then there was the in-the-know crowd. Walter talked to Laura who confirmed it was pretty widespread in Minnesota, too. Her family was terrified it would hit them and infect her dying father. By all accounts, the progression of the disease was not pretty. It did appear to be a type of pneumonia, but a strongly mutated one. Traditional antibiotics were effective at buying time, but there did not appear to be any real "cure."

In the United States and other developed countries, natural survival with good home care—staying home, washing hands, drinking fluids, and getting fresh air in the house—was rated at about eighty to eighty-five percent. Survival with hospital care was rated at ninety percent, though it took longer just because there were so many sick people in one place. The survival rate in third-world countries with little or no healthcare or basic hygiene was in the twenty to thirty percent range. But the numbers fluctuated constantly. The disease moved so fast, if someone didn't jump on it and begin treatment, it could progress and kill in three to five days. They weren't even two weeks into the new year and thousands of people around the world had died, a couple hundred of them in the United States. The CDC and WHO had put out an official PSA to up the hygiene routine, get checked out at the earliest signs of sickness, and stay away from crowded places.

Monday morning, all the schools in and around Charleston, including South Charleston High School, made the announcement that there would be no school for the week. Too many staff and students were out sick. Everyone who was sick should go see a doctor, and those who weren't sick should stay home. The school was going to be deep-cleaned, bleached, sanitized, so it was more sterile than an operating room. Of course, the lost week was going to be made up at the end of the year. But for the moment, hey, extended vacation, anyone?

At the precinct, everyone was being shuffled around and pulling longer shifts to try and cover for those out sick. Walter was working with second shift guys who had to stay long, and he had to stay long to help cover part of first shift.

This left Tommen alone. His dad worked, Becky was sick at the hospital, Will and Eli were sick and staying home to try and beat it. The only time Tommen had contact with any of his friends was when they were lucid enough to have half a conversation via text or social media. Most of the time, though, they seemed to be sleeping or too sick to think straight.

"So if you have the magic cure, why not distribute it?" he asked Rifun.

It was Wednesday night. Tommen was just finishing up the

first draft of his last essay, dreading that the only thing to do now was edit and polish. Rifun dropped by and now sat on his bed.

"Quite frankly, because I've been asked not to," Rifun replied. "We had a meeting on Tacaga to discuss things. Seems as though only a couple of worlds have been infected with a Borelian disease, or only a couple are admitting to such weakness. I made mention that my men had acquired the cures to these diseases, but was told, to paraphrase, 'Fuck off.'" He shifted position. "It's a fascinating thing, actually. Tacaga has been hit the hardest, not because they lack the technology to synthesize their own cure, but because they pack into these enormous cities. Lip itself has a population of four billion. Eighty percent of them were infected by the end of the first day. Even now, I don't know that there isn't a sick person on the planet, except Do Chien who is locked away in his little laboratory."

"What kind of disease are they battling?"

"Nothing too serious. It spreads quickly and mutates even faster, but it's hardly deadly. It's more to incite panic among the populace than truly kill, if you know what I'm saying."

"That's Tacaga, though. Why not ignore them and distribute the cure here? People are dying. Why don't they want the cure?"

"Oh, they want the cure. They just don't want to get it from me. They don't like owing me. Besides, who doesn't love a good plague now and again? Helps cleanse the population, I think."

Tommen shook his head and shut down his computer. "Whatever. Why are you here tonight?"

"I know you've been doing more portal training with your dad. I just want to see how it's progressing."

"And journal studies?"

"Once a week. Just because you can pick up on it easily doesn't mean others can. Some are still struggling with the basic sounds of the language. Memorizing 'one day' is as difficult as writing an essay for them, never mind getting the names right. Be patient and show me what you've done so far. Can you go to the Wheel?"

Physically, yes. He didn't have much problem with that. He

could get a portal open and go through. It kicked his ass and he could only do it once before crawling into bed like a mewling child, but he could do it. He could also go to the fortress if he really wanted to, but not after going to the Wheel; it took too much energy and he didn't need to put himself into a black hole. Rifun merely watched him, making no comments or snide remarks and offering no critiques or pointers.

After three demonstrations, Tommen was in the bathroom, bent over the toilet, offering up his dinner. He slogged back to his room and curled up in bed. Rifun moved to the chair at his desk.

"You are certainly a quick study and an excellent student besides. I trust, then, that there will be no further delays in your expedition of which you are the leader?"

Tommen sighed into his pillow.

"No school, no work, no sex, what better things do you have to do?" the man continued, his tone mocking.

"I'll get on it," Tommen promised. "Just as soon as this migraine goes away, which will most likely be tomorrow morning."

"Good lad." He could hear the squeak of the chair as Rifun stood. "I will still come to fetch you for journal studies, however. I don't want you to play hooky on me, nor do I want you to land in a black hole. I do recognize that going back and forth to the Wheel can be trying. With that, I congratulate you on your progress and bid you farewell and sweet dreams."

He may have done a dramatic bow; Tommen did not lift his head to find out. Indeed, it was another five minutes before he dragged himself out of bed to turn off the lights. Only when he pulled the blankets up did he consider that maybe it was possible to reach out with Energy and just cut the electrical current so he didn't have to try and get up. Would that short out the circuit and cause a fire? In this house, anything was possible. Maybe it was for the best that he just did things manually.

He slept and woke on his own terms, which was actually pretty nice. He didn't recall having any nightmares, and his migraine had gone. Rolling over, it was a little before nine.

By the time he got around and made it out to the kitchen, his dad still wasn't home, which wasn't a surprise. If he got home by noon, it would be an early day, the way things had been going lately. So Tommen made up his own breakfast, watched some TV, and even got a little editing done on his essays. Maybe he would get something for his troubles after all.

It was eleven o'clock before he pushed himself away from his computer and considered his options. He really needed to get going on his research into the journal, before Rifun assigned the mission to someone else. Chandler might accuse him of being loyal, and Rifun most likely had some sinister plans for when the journal was found, but Tommen was determined to surprise both of them.

He ended up surprising himself first by even making it to the Wheel in one piece. As he pulled himself back together and made his way to the translator dispenser, he reflected on how it was like getting his driver's license all over again. He no longer had to rely on his dad or Rifun or anyone else to go where he wanted or needed to go. He had freedom now. What's more, he didn't have to explain himself. He didn't have to tell anyone why he was going to a place; he could just do it. To an extent, freedom meant secrecy. Yes, yes, rights and responsibilities and all that, but he was free. He could look up the cure for space pneumonia without Rifun knowing. If he searched hard enough, he could probably find something his dad wouldn't want him to see—a space Kama Sutra for example.

He was also free to come to cash in his turns and explore the marketplaces. The wares marketplaces were not nearly as vast as the Time marketplaces, but goods were always rotating; there was bound to be something interesting he could now buy without his dad's permission.

Tommen wasn't sure how much time he spent roaming. He could do that, too, now, if he wanted. He could look and see and roam and explore without being bound by someone else's timetable. Rifun was right. No school, no work, no sex, he really didn't have anything better to do. He could do whatever he wanted. He didn't even have to do journal research if he didn't want to.

Problem was, he kind of wanted to. He wanted to know what it said, what was so special about it, and how he could prevent Rifun and Julianna from getting their hands on it. But if he wanted to do that, he had to find it. In order to find it, he had to figure out who had it and how it got there.

It wasn't until he reached the Archives that he remembered there had recently been a travel ban in effect in the Wheel, and the odds of the Borelians honoring some invisible agreement not to kidnap humans from the Wheel was a roll of the dice at best. Tommen scolded himself for being so careless about his own safety and vowed to be more watchful in the Archives, where it was very easy to hide and even easier to get lost.

It was nice to not have to grab a chip anymore, though he briefly wondered how the Archive secretaries felt about their jobs being automated. Well, just another sign of the times, he supposed, moving through the lobby into the dizzying tessellation beyond, the universe's largest library.

How did he even want to go about his search? His most credible lead took him to a place run by a mob boss. Did he want to start with the name of the mob boss? The history of the city or region? Did he want to play it safe and look up the inconsequential stuff about the planet and dull statistics?

Well, if the journal really did go there, and if it would have been seen as such a game changer between the warring parties, there was every chance that someone had to write about it in some sort of history. Might as well start there.

Maronet was home to five different races living scattered and intermingled across eight continents. The only two Tommen saw to concern himself with were the Mishim and Lilir.

The Mishim were traditionally clan-based. Each family chose from themselves a head who represented their interests to the clan at large, and the families lived together in these clan units, ranging in size from four hundred to four thousand members. In times of war or other hardship, the family heads would appoint three from among themselves to oversee the clan and make it through the hardship.

On the opposite side of the social spectrum were the Lilir, arguably the strongest and most militaristic race on the planet. Traditionally, the Lilir had no families. Offspring were property of the state, raised to be soldiers or other needed professions, all for the advancement of Lilir. A bit like the Borelians, Tommen thought.

With the clash of races and values and societal structure came the rise of the crime lords. The Lilir had been able to conquer most of Maronet because of their use of Time, but in some of the outlying regions where the higher-ups were less of a presence and reinforcements were a distant dream, the Mishim were able to keep the Lilir at bay and even absorb some of the Lilir's military tactics, and the Lilir found a little freedom from their rigid, militaristic, totalitarian societal structure. Both sides had crime families and mob bosses and a lot of hatred to go around.

Tommen perused several historical volumes, looking for any mention of a sudden shift in power or explicit mention of the journal. His most reliable information came from a brief biography of Arshoni the Slayer himself. According to the text, while a successful mob boss, his hold on his territory against the Lilir was quickly unraveling. Then, one night, a mysterious stranger approached him claiming to have the power to overthrow the Lilir for good. Money changes hands, goods are delivered, and within a month, half the city is destroyed by an earthquake. Arshoni the Slayer is killed in the earthquake, but from then on, the fight between the two groups is decidedly more even.

It wasn't a lot to go on, really. How was he to know whether the earthquake was from some mishap trying to learn the Akari, a natural phenomenon, or something mechanical? Looking at a geological dissertation, tremors weren't especially uncommon in that particular city. And if the Lilir were at a disadvantage for higher commands and reinforcements, it would only make sense that the Mishim, who were more accustomed to doing things on the fly and organizing at a moment's notice, could take advantage of a chaotic situation, choose their leaders, and get the jump on their conquerors.

He moved on to the second rumor, the Turitian outpost. Turit was Openly Engaged, but at the time of the alliance, Kolkath was Unengaged. Indeed, they were only Scientifically Advancing, much like Earth. Supposedly, they had been communicating with the Turitians for some time through crude, basic means—like how NASA sent out simple messages through space, hoping for a reply. The Turitians even helped the Kolkath build their first spaceship and what might be likened to the International Space Station.

When the Kolkath finally made their first extended, manned trip into space, the Turitians were there to meet them and show them around the neighborhood, figuratively speaking. Once the Kolkath established a regular space travel program, they sent a group of diplomats to meet with Turitian Commander Dira and give them a huge load of gifts. Among monies, artifacts, and other things of great monetary and cultural value was a book, said to be a valuable religious text from a distant peasant region.

Tommen liked this rumor, if only because he had little doubt that diplomats and commanders and new alliances probably kept better records than a mob boss from a questionable planet. Even better was that the story continued, in another text, and tied into the third rumor.

Most of the goods went into one museum or another, and any money went into the treasury, but Dira apparently took a liking to the religious text, for she kept it with her, reading it and reportedly educating the men under her in its words.

Tommen paused. The journals were Imprinted so that only those trained in the Akari could read them. How had Commander Dira learned to read the journals? Had one of the Kolkath shown her? More to the point, in teaching her Imprint, was she one of the Cult or one of the Akarin? How had Julianna not known? Tommen took an even breath. His dad and Chandler were right; there was something more going on here.

He continued reading. Commander Dira later accompanied the Turitian royal family on a diplomatic mission to Sren, in Quadrant Three. Before they arrived, they were attacked by the Psiaco pirate Titik. The Turitians took heavy damage and were forced to pay a huge ransom as Titik took the prince hostage for a short time, but they arrived at Sren safely otherwise.

Other than the earlier mention of Dira keeping the journal with her and telling her underlings all about it, no specific mention of it was made in the pirate attack, neither before nor after. Maybe Commander Dira hadn't even taken the journal with her on the royal mission. Maybe she had indeed lost it to Titik and counted it as a casualty of war. Whatever the case, no mention of the journal could be found anywhere after that, and Tommen shut down the tablet he was reading.

That would be where he wanted to start. He needed to find Commander Dira and ask her what she did with that journal, or religious text as the case may be. Maybe it wasn't even the journal they were looking for, but it was the most credible lead he had so far. The rumor of the journal was nearly forty years old, yet, as an Openly Engaged Civilization, Commander Dira and several of those involved in the diplomatic mission and pirate attack were still alive.

He turned his research in a new direction, focusing on Turit. It was a tiny planet, a marble, really, a fraction of the size of Earth with a population of only ten million, homogeneous Turitian. While some considered it unified, there were four countries, one on each continent, and a royal ruling family overseeing each. Digging deeper, Tommen saw that they functioned a bit like Tacaga, where each continent had a specific task or duty designed to improve the economy and quality of Turit as a whole. One country oversaw agriculture, another the military, another industry and innovation, and the smallest continent was in charge of the culture and history of the planet and its people. Unlike Tacaga, where every city's task was absolute, there was some bleed among the Turitian continents. There was some innovation done within the agriculture, some military in the innovation, and culture and arts throughout. Case and point, Commander Dira was from the agricultural continent, but chose to pursue a military career.

Overall, while Turit itself was somewhat strict on its societal structure, their presence in the greater universe was amiable and generally non-threatening. They were usually more than willing to lend a helping hand for races trying to break into space, and they were big into trade relations. Apparently, the space station outposts they had littered around their system were considered Turit's fifth continent, dealing in all interstellar commerce and trade, which included Time Capsules. Despite the Hands of Time keeping the Turitians on a short leash with their markets, Runner activity was still high there.

The Turitians had little love for Rifun and his Zero Hour Revolution as it supposedly strangled their markets, but they suffered little more than economic hardship. Supposedly, there was to be some kind of trade deal in place with the Turitians which spared most of their Time Agents from execution, but Micaiah collapsing the portals in the Wheel and isolating the Cult put a halt to those plans. They were upset, like most of the universe, but seemed more neutral about it than most species. All of this according to what Tommen was reading.

He leaned back and rubbed his eyes. As much as everyone mistrusted the secretaries and ripped on the Scouts, they were also the source of all the information in the Archives. The Scouts brought in new information from new worlds, and the secretaries had to keep it accurate and up to date. That was no easy task considering the information ranged from the microscopic to the giant; everything in the universe, quantified and cataloged.

So then why was the Wheel itself so fucked up? Doing a mindless browse through the map on a random tablet, Tommen couldn't find anything about the physics or mechanics of the Wheel, how it worked the way it did, how the secretaries kept it working so smoothly, how Micaiah could have collapsed the portals or how they were rebuilt, and especially nothing about how it could be redecorated from sci-fi to Shakespeare to steampunk in the space of a year.

He also couldn't find anything on the Akari other than legends both familiar and wild. If not for the Faith element, it might have been quantifiable, but how did one quantify faith? How could one reliably factor in irrational views and beliefs of the universe? To that end, it was simply relegated to religions of the universe, even though Tommen had seen it in action, doing impossible things. Were his wild dreams to visit Chandler and all the White animals and the Shadows part of that, too? Was that quantifiable? Testable? How about visiting Chandler in a dream, only to wake up and find something had been dropped off in his room? Could it be that Chandler, in the in-between dimension, was visiting him and so influencing his dreams so they could speak?

Tommen sighed and rubbed his eyes. So many questions, too few answers, and that wasn't even going into the journals or anything else. He needed to get back to work, focus on a task.

He had a safety net of intelligent crewmen at his back, who were well-versed in politics, languages, and local customs, but he didn't want to rely totally on them. He wanted to appear intelligent, able and willing to do his research and make the effort to stand on his own, to be able to do or say the right thing because he'd discovered the information on his own, not because he had to look to one of his groupies for the most basic niceties.

Generally speaking, Turitians were very proud of their country duties and respected others in their duties. A farmer was not looked down upon for being a farmer, a soldier was proud to be a soldier, and so on. Family was said to be held in the utmost importance, though Tommen had a difficult time understanding how the family structure worked and who was involved. It certainly wasn't limited to mom, dad, and kids, but neither was it mandatory to include any of them. Well, for now he would just look up the major components; the nuances he would leave to his groupies. He didn't have the time to get too in-depth, and he really didn't want to fuck everything up by pretending to know something he didn't.

Besides, he wasn't going to be on the streets talking to common people; he would be dealing with the higher officers, the military, the royal families. A handshake on the street was nice, but he needed to learn to bow or whatever it was the upper crust did to say hello.

The Turitians were humanoid, but they made linebackers look anorexic. Huge, bullish creatures, their heads were something of a cross between a goat and a bear, with maybe a dash of frog thrown in, judging by the skin texture in the picture. Their hands more resembled paws with only four fingers, but it was difficult to say for sure. Those in the army wore armor, as might be expected. The common folk, however, wore little more than a belly band cloth, which seemed strained over an abdomen that seemed more befitting of a gorilla or a grizzly bear. No pants, but no obvious genitalia either. They also had stubby tails, like a goat. Their legs seemed disproportionately small and thin, given the size of the upper body. Tommen read that their way of life demanded far more upper body strength than lower, which he found unusual, but decided not to argue until he'd seen them for himself.

The good news, he figured, was that because they were Openly Engaged, they would be more approachable and understanding than Sifura's people, or the D'Bok people for that matter. He didn't have to bullshit about the translators or the technology or any of that.

As far as niceties and social customs went for those a little more well to-do, it seemed the appropriate thing to do was turn to one side. An inferior approaching a superior was to turn to the right, a superior approaching an inferior turned to the left. So Tommen would be turning to the right. The one being approached could respond in a number of ways. If his target turned in the same direction, it was a gesture of equality, and they could speak informally. If he turned the opposite direction, it was a gesture of hierarchy, and all other social customs must be observed. If he did not turn at all but remained facing Tommen, it was a gesture of great superiority, and Tommen would have little or no room to speak at all, but would simply listen, like getting called into the office at school for a lecture from Layman. If the one being approached turned his back, game over, no more audience would be given, and they would be escorted off the premises, willingly or not.

There were a number of other turns and gestures that could be made under a variety of circumstances, and Tommen had trouble memorizing them all. Standing behind him facing him had more of a familiar, parental meaning. Standing behind him facing away from him could be interpreted as a gesture of goodwill, brotherhood, turning and exposing one's back, or it could be interpreted as a gesture of conspiracy for ill will, that neither could look upon the other's face. It could also be seen as a modified version of simply turning and walking away.

There could be a whole class just based on Turitian body language, Tommen thought as he returned the tablet feeling as though he hadn't learned anything. Just as well that he would have his band of heroes with him to save his ass. And this was stuff that was already known. And he wanted to be a Scout and have to figure it all out for himself on a totally new and hostile world? Maybe he ought to reconsider his career path.

Tommen did a quick search and found a bit of information on Captain Titik and the Psiaco people at large. They were Engaged Privilege, though not for lack of knowledge about Time. Turned out that they had literal Time Academies where Masters taught Apprentices and Journeymen the same as any regular school. Every District had a school which was overseen by the Captain and his Lieutenants, which were in turn overseen by the Manager, and so on. The schools were considered very elite, and only those who showed special promise were invited to study.

Titik himself had been a student at one of the schools. He'd been bright and promising, but prone to causing trouble. Given the nature and structure of the schools, they were low security facilities. One night, Titik and three others had simply vanished, only to show up years later as space pirates. They'd honed their skills on their own a bit, but were still only about Journeyman level. They easily preyed on vessels belonging to Unengaged worlds, but usually fled from their own people. What possessed them to attack the Turitian royal emissary was anyone's guess. But if the journal had been the target, the kind of power the Cult promised might have broken through any misgivings Titik had about his opponent.

But that was all speculation, and Tommen didn't want to get too far ahead of himself on his research. Maybe it hadn't been the real journal. Maybe it hadn't been stolen; Dira just kept it quiet in order to avoid attracting more attention to it. He needed to take this one step at a time.

Now the problem was that he seemed to have backed himself into a corner. He could get to the Wheel any time he needed to do research. He could get to the fortress whenever he needed to contact Rifun or his groupies. He had his mission and both Rifun and Julianna were breathing down his neck about it. He had a plausible lead that needed to be investigated. What he didn't have were any more excuses why he couldn't carry out his mission. There was his fear of the unknown and approaching an alien race—the royal family and a high-ranking commander, anyway—to ask them if they'd ever been involved in the Cult of the Akari, but that was tempered by his excitement to get out and do some intergalactic exploring.

Then there was his fear of what would happen if he did find the journal. A wolf in sheep's clothing and catastrophe will follow, that was what Chandler had said. If he didn't do his task, Rifun could assign it to someone else easily. Tommen had to do this. He walked in both worlds and at least had a chance at destroying the journal, or using it as some kind of leverage. But there was still the small whisper of doubt that said it wasn't so straightforward. Chandler might question his loyalty, but few would accuse him of being loyal strictly to Rifun, and Rifun wouldn't send him out when he already had a group of qualified minions ready and willing to go out on the hunt. Something was up, he just knew it.

It didn't change his mission any, however, and he had nothing else with which to stall. Either he went to Rifun and told him to rally the troops, or else the mission would get reassigned to someone with less moral confusion. Should he see about sending a note to Commander Dira, let her know that they were coming and try to get an appointment, or would that all be taken care of as soon as he said the word? How did all of this work?

He stalled a bit longer and meandered through the rows of tablets. Unlike a traditional Earth library where one might be attracted to an interesting title or flashy cover, the tablets in the Archives were all the same. The only way one could get an idea of what could found in them was by examining the registry at the end of each row. He did this a couple times, but soon grew bored. He needed to get something done, even if that was helping to advance the cause of a madman and his cult. He just had to hold out hope that, in the end, he could destroy the madman and his cult. Was he being naive?

His otherwise slow departure from the Archives was suddenly hastened as he spotted a set of familiar horns down one aisle. The Borelian did not look up or give any indication that it had noticed him, but that didn't mean it hadn't. Tommen moved along quickly, making for the exit.

He was suddenly overwhelmed by a sense of déjà vú, and he looked around to see if any Grandfathers were after him. He didn't see any, nor did he see any Borelians or hear any significant movement. Maybe the Borelian really hadn't noticed him. Maybe he was just being paranoid. Either way, he didn't want to take any chances. Sorry to say, but with Rifun and the Borelians feuding, Rifun wouldn't be able to save him if something happened. No one would be able to save him if something happened and he was captured by the Borelians.

Tommen left the Archives no worse for wear and no mob of angry Borelians or Grandfathers on his tail. No one raised an alarm, and this time around, there was no need to overturn any Merchant tables in the marketplace.

He returned home unscathed and flopped on his bed. He was only an Apprentice, but learning Journeyman skills. Learning more than Journeyman skills. How did the Hands feel about all this? Did they even know? They had to. There was no way they couldn't. His Apprentice review had been hard enough; what would they do for his Journeyman review? Could they deny him advancement because of his activities with the Akarin and the Order? Would they have him arrested and his clock broken?

He didn't know if he slept at all, but he stirred when he heard the garage door open and his dad entered the house. Tommen waited a minute or two before dragging himself out of bed and going out to meet him.

"Long night?" he wondered.

His dad looked run ragged and about ready to fall over from exhaustion. He sighed and rubbed his face. "Half the guys are out with this mystery flu-monia going around, your space pneumonia as you call it. The rest of us are pulling longer shifts to try and make up for the lack of coverage. Personally, I don't think that's necessary because just as we're getting sick, so are a lot of other people, which means call volume is down. Have you heard from Becky at all since she went to the hospital?"

"Not really getting better, but not getting worse, either," Tommen answered. "I texted Eli. He says he's feeling better, but Will isn't doing too great."

"Any word from Rifun?"

"Says he has the cure, but the Powers That Be have told him not to distribute it. He suspects they just don't want to get it from him specifically. Tacaga's got their hands full with their own infectious disease so they're not going to do anything for the rest of us, not they were going to anyway."

Walter grunted disapprovingly. "Pride goeth before the fall. Humans were too concerned over who had the cure that—never mind. I don't blame them, but I do. Maybe I'll go to Tacaga and speak to Do Chien about a cure. It's a lot to ask given how much work he's doing already, but if there is already a cure for this Borelian pneumonia, it can't be too difficult to replicate elsewhere with the right tools."

"And you're feeling okay?" Tommen asked.

"For now, yes. We'll see how long it lasts." Walter set his boots aside and stood, stretching weakly and making for his bedroom, Tommen following.

"Do you want me to Band you so you can sleep for a while?"

His dad hesitated for a moment, laying out his gun and taser and other assorted tools on the bed before slipping off his belt. Finally, he nodded. "That would probably be for the best. Give me a good eight hours, then let me go from there. What's on your agenda for the day? You didn't just get up, did you?"

"Would it matter if I did? No, actually, I, uh, I went to the Wheel. Got started on my research into the mysterious third journal and its disappearance."

"Oh? And where is my globetrotting, adventurous, teenage son going off to?" Walter's tone was difficult to judge.

"Turit. 01-04-11 – "

"Yes, I know the place. Rather, I've heard of it. The Good Samaritans of the universe, or so they're called. Why would they be in with the Order?"

"They may not have known what they had, if it was incidental. But I am going to have to talk to one of the royal families and some of their highest-ranking military officers."

"So just a light vacation with a few friends, right?"

Tommen grinned. "Absolutely."

"Have you been practicing your bows?"

"I wish it was that easy. The Turitians have this whole system of turns and gestures, and it's just wild how it changes from place to place and class to class."

"Welcome to Intercultural Studies 101."

"How do you do it? As an officer and stuff?"

"I've forgotten a lot of what I was taught just for the sheer fact that I don't go asteroid-hopping all that frequently, but there are some blanket rules to observe when presented with a vastly different culture."

"Oh? Like what?"

"One, never pretend you're not a tourist. You will always be a tourist. No one likes that arrogant guy who thinks he knows everything there is to know about a place he's visited once. Two, always do research beforehand if you have the time and resources, which you obviously do. Three, with that in mind, ask sensible questions and do it respectfully. Don't be the tourist asking directions to all the most touristy spots in town. Get as informed as you can be, and ask questions along those lines. And always assume the one you're asking has the information you want and won't part with it for a moron."

"Why can't regular tourists follow those rules?" Tommen asked sarcastically. "I mean, how many times in the bakery did people ask me for directions to the bridge when it was, like, half a mile away? You could almost see it, if not for the hotel in the way."

His dad shrugged awkwardly as he pulled off his uniform shirt. "Well, you can't fix stupid. And anyway, we're just a couple of peasants serving kings." He rolled his eyes. "But that is how you're going to have to approach this, especially if you're meeting royalty or high-ranking military."

Tommen sighed. "I know, I know." He paused. "You met a president before."

"Nixon, yes. You want to know how I approached him?"

"Yeah. I mean, it's not like meeting the Queen of England, but still pretty important. What led to you meeting Nixon, anyway?"

His dad waved a hand. "Oh, it wasn't anything special, really, more of an opportunity than a planned meeting. I was living dark at the time in order to avoid the draft and stay out of the Vietnam debate. It was only a couple months before Watergate broke, and I was visiting Washington, D.C., just to look around, never been there before, figured why not. And that day, Nixon just happened to be out and about with the D.C. police officers, trying to show some support for the cops, who were not very popular at the time, as you might imagine. When he was done talking to them, he gave a short speech, then went to meet some of the people. I happened to be among them, one of the last. I think we exchanged all of four sentences, and he went on his way. Can't say I was impressed, either at that time or after Watergate, but I can say that I have met a president."

"Oh. So, it wasn't, like, secret meeting in the Oval Office or anything."

"No, not at all. Nothing like that. Sorry, kiddo." Walter tossed his dirty uniform in the laundry and his gun and assorted weapons and accessories in his safe. "All right, guess I should try to get some sleep." He gave Tommen a look. "Don't let me sleep too long. You still have your doctor's appointment tonight."

Right. Back to see the shrink. His dismay must have shown because his dad went on, "It's good for you. And as long as I think you're going to play hooky on me, I'll keep taking you myself. Got it?"

Tommen rubbed his face. "Fine, got it. You get in bed; I'm going to run to the bathroom first. Then I'll be back to Band you."

His dad nodded and pushed back his blankets while Tommen meandered to the bathroom. He told himself he didn't want to go back to the shrink, though a small part of him said he did. He wanted to talk to someone, he wanted it to be a professional, he wanted it to be confidential. He wanted to say what was on his mind. But did it really have to be so obvious? Some days, it felt as though he walked around with a huge neon sign over him that said, "Mentally unstable and seeing a shrink! I'm crazy!"

It was a foolish, childish, paranoid thought. He knew he needed it, but even that bothered him. He didn't want to need it. He wanted to handle things on his own. Problem was, handling things on his own had brought nothing but catastrophe. Reading about it in his Authored Books certainly wasn't helping matters.

He was still debating whether he wanted to mention all of that to the shrink. He was still pondering the potential consequences of mentioning the hold Rifun still had over him. Then his thoughts wandered to Chandler and his words of wisdom. If Rifun was threatening those he loved, it was because he couldn't threaten him. He was too powerful. But how did he tap into that power? He was still having to be rescued by furry woodland creatures for fuck's sake. Sarcastic furry woodland creatures at that. Maybe he was crazy. Maybe he did have a neon sign hovering over him that read, "I'm crazy!"

He returned to his dad's room, Banding his dad from outside the room, not even looking in on him until the eight-hour Band was released. It was possible to tell the quality of sleep he'd had just by looking at the sheets, how torn up they were. Tommen glanced in his own room at his own bed, almost equally torn up. Like father, like son, he supposed.

There was still some time before he had to see the shrink. With his dad yet sleeping, Tommen decided to head to the fortress to make his report. No point in delaying the inevitable.

The portal to the fortress was more difficult to make, though whether that came from trying to overcome the pull of the Wheel or the fear of falling into a black hole if he did it incorrectly, he did not dwell on too long. All he knew was that he made it in one piece.

Construction seemed to be moving right along, and life seemed to be back to some semblance of normal on the first three floors. Of course, Tommen wouldn't know what normal life looked like around the fortress now, but he thought it looked normal. No construction, no armies, no fighting, no quarantine. People walked to and fro with a purpose, but not in any way that resembled frantic or urgent. It was a bit like a shopping mall, the overall atmosphere.

This idealistic fantasy was broken as he watched a scuffle from afar. He couldn't make out the words exactly, though he caught the word "Akarin" a few times, and several words which made no sense to him, but judging from the reaction, might have been some kind of racial or religious slur. So the Akarin and the Order weren't getting along so well. That was to be expected, but it was also a little sad. Why couldn't everyone just get along?

He navigated through the construction on the fourth floor, making his way ever upward, the crowds thinning, his strength waning, his senses on high alert. Sometimes, he would hear a noise just right, and it would make him jump, thinking that he was about to be attacked by some enemy soldier. Other times, he only thought he heard something, but would look and find nothing there. That scared him more, if he wanted to be really honest about it, the fear of going crazy, of having that battle follow him wherever he went, like Beaumaris Gaol for his dad.

By the time he reached the sixth floor, he was exhausted, and there was still more to go. The eighth floor seemed so far away, but he dragged his sorry hide up the stairs, all the while thinking that if the Akarin were so much more powerful and advanced than Time and the Hands, why hadn't they invented elevators yet? Even the moving platforms from the Archives would work.

Reaching the top, Tommen rested a moment and Banded so he could collect himself before knocking on the door to Rifun's chambers. He heard a muffled, "*Hiditra,*" and pushed open the door. He didn't know what "*hiditra*" actually meant, but figured he would find out soon enough.

Rifun stood at his whiteboard. With his crippled right hand, he awkwardly held a paper. With his uncoordinated left hand, he deliberately scrawled out some notes on the board. He still wore a button-down shirt and cargo pants, which meant this was probably going to be his new "look" for the time being, though the long, loose hairs were more evident on the nicer shirt than they had been on the hoodies. Had his face not been plastered all over national and even international news, with his casual demeanor, he could have easily walked down any street and been any regular dude. Tommen even noticed a thermos off to the side on the desk, the logo too faded to tell who it was supposed to advertise. The man glanced at him briefly as he scribbled out his notes.

"Good morning. This is a surprise. To what do I owe the pleasure?"

"I've figured out my starting point for the third journal search," Tommen told him, feeling every bit the traitor he had been when he gave up the cure for Borelian poison. "I don't know how this all works or who needs to do what, but I figured I should let you know."

"And I appreciate it very much." Rifun finished his notes, set down the paper and the marker, then picked up his thermos and took a long drink. "Where is your search beginning, pray tell?" He took another drink, his expression saying he wasn't enjoying its contents all that much.

"Turit, with Commander Dira."

"I see. I do recall that being a plausible lead." Rifun nodded. "Very well, I will pass word to your team and get them all preparing for the trip. When do you want to leave?"

"Tomorrow morning. Ten a.m. or whatever time that is here?" Tommen actually hadn't thought about that and just picked out what he thought was a good time. "Or do they need more time to prepare? Like, twenty-four hours or whatever?"

"Make it ten p.m. and that should be sufficient."

Rifun took another drink and grimaced, turning away as if to hide it while pretending to look for something else among his paperwork.

"Is that your seizure tea?"

"Tarka root tea, yes."

"So you haven't found anything to actually cure the seizures?"

Rifun gave him a look. "You seem oddly interested in it. Afraid of losing your little bit of leverage over me? Are you going to run back to Daddy and tell him if and when I do find a cure? What is it going to change, I wonder? Only a few people even know about it. Everyone else thinks I have sinister intentions with the way I've been negotiating lately." He took a drink, shook his head, set the thermos aside, and folded his arms as he leaned against the desk. "Your determination to outsmart and-or kill me has turned into stalker-level obsession." He dropped his arms, grabbed the thermos, and walked elsewhere in the room, grabbing this and that and setting it in a pile. "No matter. It's only your sanity being affected. I shall simply carry on with my day. And I will let your ekipa know that you are ready to proceed with your mission."

"Oh. Okay. Thanks, I think. I guess I will be back tomorrow at ten p.m."

"I should expect so. You may want to get here a little early, though, because every team loves a good pep talk, and an outline of the plan for when they get to Turit."

Plan? He had to come up with the plan? He thought he was supposed to be making a plan with them. Together. Go team. Oh, shit.

"Right."

Tommen turned to leave, but paused and looked back when he got to the door. "You don't happen to have any of the Borelian pneumonia cure on you, do you?"

"Has your darling girlfriend fallen ill?" Rifun did not look at him.

"And my friends. And a lot of people in the city. A lot of people around the world. It's become a global thing."

"I believe I stated that no one seems to want my help in this. I have no reason not to oblige."

"Fine, so don't give me seven billion doses. How about five? Or ten? Just so I can save my friends."

Now Rifun looked at him, his expression unreadable, but cold. "If your little trip to Turit proves fruitful and you do find some evidence of the journal or its further whereabouts, I may be inclined to hand over a couple doses."

It was a test, but this time, Tommen knew he could pass. He wasn't trying to outsmart Rifun this time, at least, not yet. He still had to talk to Chandler about what to do if and when he did find the journal. But for now, he just had to play along. To that end, he dipped his head, thanked Rifun, and headed out of the room and down the stairs.

Tomorrow at ten o'clock. He'd probably make it nine, just to be safe. And somehow, he had to come up with the plan to get in and talk to Commander Dira and the royal family. How the hell was he going to do that? Was that something he'd been expected to know, or was that another test on Rifun's part, to see how ready he was to lead?

Well, he was going to treat it as something he had to do, which meant he was going to be busy as fuck the next twenty-four hours. Good thing his dad was off tonight so he might be able to Band his sleep. Coupled with the non-passage of time while he was in the Wheel, he might get a few things done.

Problem was, first he had to survive his second session with his shrink.

Chapter Fourteen
Delegates and Diplomacy

Now that Tommen knew what to expect, his second session with the psychologist was a little less daunting and probably a little more productive. He still didn't divulge his life's sob story, but he was getting there, he thought. In the end, he did mention the possibility of Rifun threatening the shrink or his family or friends and so on. The shrink thanked him for the info, promised he would keep it close to hand, then turned it into a talking point, because he was just that good at his job. The second session was much less stressful than the first, and Tommen left feeling not quite as terrible as the first time around.

"So, can I trust you to keep coming back on your own?" his dad wondered about a mile down the road.

Tommen nodded slowly. "Yeah, I guess so. It's not all bad."

"For now, I'll take your word for it. I'm glad to see you're willing to go." Pause. "What's your first step in finding the third journal? When are you leaving to meet exotic princesses and slay dragons?"

"Ha ha, very funny. We're leaving tomorrow at ten p.m. I have to be there at the fortress at nine so I can give them a pep talk or something and lay out the plan."

"What is the plan?"

"I have no fucking clue. I'm a nobody kid from an Unengaged world, and I have to get an audience with a high-ranking military official and the royal family. How do I do that?"

His dad gave a casual shrug. "I don't know. How do you do that?"

With more research, apparently, and Tommen soon found

himself back in the Archives. As was to be expected, it was hard to get an audience with the upper crust. They had lesser royalty and lords and such deal with complaints from the common folk while they themselves dealt with more international matters, if such things could be called international matters. Tommen had his doubts, but did not say anything aloud; it wouldn't have done any good. But, he did notice that the royals were always willing to meet with leaders of other worlds and peoples.

It didn't take much to figure out how one head of state could meet with a Turitian royal family, though it involved more clever maneuvering than he had ever done so far.

Sending messages within the Wheel or between worlds was about as simple as using the post office. Write a digital letter, specify the recipient, and a messenger secretary would ensure the letter got to that person as promptly as possible, no muss, no fuss. The problem came with the verification of the identity of the sender. Nothing could be sent anonymously; everything was double-checked via DNA scanner, similar to the one used in the translator dispenser.

Tommen was careful in how he crafted his message, every word reminding him of how laughable his English composition skills were. He used his Time watch to double-check the daytime discrepancy between Earth and Turit, looked over his message two or three times, then finally handed it off to the secretary.

He fully anticipated that the secretaries read all the mail that went through. He fully expected that his message would send up some serious red flags. He fully hoped they did something about it.

Then he returned to Earth to go about his normal day, puttering around the house. He texted Becky, getting promising replies that she was starting to feel better, might even return to school next week. Similar story with Eli as he was on the mend, but Will wasn't responding to treatments, and the doctors were looking at more extreme measures.

"When can I expect you back from vacation?" his dad asked as he pulled on his boots.

Tommen shrugged. "I don't know. I hope it doesn't take very long, I mean, I'm hoping the message I sent gets us in pretty quick."

"Well, if anyone comes asking, you weren't feeling well, and with this pandemic going around, you're just going to stay in bed. No visitors."

"Fair enough."

His dad sighed and looked at him. "Just be careful."

"I will."

He tried to put on a good face, but he felt a nervous wreck, and he spent most of his dead time in the evening pacing, wondering what he was going to say, hoping his plan worked so he didn't look like a moron in front of his team. Even when he finally stood before them later that night, he was almost sure they could see or smell his fear and unease. What if the Turitians didn't get the message in time? What if they rejected his request for an audience?

"Tonight we'll be going to Turit, Quadrant One, Parsec Four, Sector Eleven, System Fifty-Two, Planet Twenty, Region One, District Three," Tommen began, forcing himself to speak confidently. "We will be meeting with the Turitian royal family Jalar and High Commander Dira. Our primary goal will be to determine whether the religious book they had in their possession was indeed the third journal, and to learn its fate. It was rumored stolen by the Psiaco pirate Titik, but we must be certain that this is what happened. I trust that you received word of our mission in good time and had a chance to do the appropriate research on your own. We will be expected, and I want this to go as smoothly as possible." The second part was true, the first up for speculation. "Are there any questions? I will do most of the talking and negotiating, but I am counting on each of you to fill in the gaps in my knowledge of their cultural and societal practices."

Had this been a group of immature high school kids, there would have been whining and complaining and "Who made you the boss?" These people, though, they simply agreed. They had been given orders to follow him, so follow him they would. He just had to make it so they would follow him because he was likable and capable and not just because Rifun told them to.

As the Akari boni, Ilit the Qalik was tasked with getting them from place to place. At first, Tommen couldn't remember quite why he thought he recognized Ilit until he recalled that when he'd gone before the Hands for his dad's illness, one of the lower judges had also been a Qalik, humanoid, with mottled green and yellow skin, and vine-like hair.

Emet the Siboxi was their bodyguard, and also the one to lean on if extra strength was needed to open a portal. Tommen had expected a giant, hulking beast fifteen feet tall with arms like tree trunks that could rip apart trees and rocks with no effort at all. Rather, Emet was about five-foot-six, but a stocky five hundred pounds with skin like granite and so black it made Will look white by comparison. He didn't say much and wore only what he needed to carry an assortment of weapons, but Tommen had little doubt of his strength in a pinch.

Rifun wished them all well and happy hunting, then stepped back so Ilit could prepare himself to open the portal. Tommen felt his stomach turn. This was really happening. This was the first leg of their adventure. Here they were, great heroes of legend, off on a quest of epic proportions to find a long-lost mysterious artifact of unknowable power. Would there be ancient curses and booby traps somewhere along the way? Tommen found himself hoping so, even as he knew he would probably be the first one skewered by poison arrows because he stepped on the wrong stone in the corridor.

Ilit went through the portal first, followed by Rorion the Dimica, Naq the Yakik, Tommen, Sisith the Arowa, and Emet bringing up the rear. Surprisingly enough, Ilit's portal was one of the smoothest, least traumatizing portals Tommen had ever been through. It was still difficult to recuperate as his body tried to collect itself and realign with the different Matter and Energy going from one place to another, but the overall trip wasn't bad. He wasn't nauseous or gasping for breath; he certainly wasn't passed out drooling on the floor. The worst that overcame him was a little dizziness and shortness of breath, as if he'd tried to run any kind of distance, but it all passed within sixty seconds and he was upright once more. Looking at the others, they seemed to be in similar states of recovery. If anyone took the journey hard, it was Rorion who was kneeling on one knee. As she put one hand on a knee to push up to a standing position, Tommen saw that where her hand touched, her watery skin not only rippled but changed colors, blue and light blue and stunning aquamarine. Then it was back to normal.

"Is everyone all right?" Tommen wondered.

His *ekipa* gave murmurs and gestures of affirmation. He nodded, momentarily forgetting where they were and what they were supposed to be doing. Then he recalled that he was the leader. He was the one giving orders. Fuck.

"Rorion, where are we?" he asked, looking around.

The Dimica didn't miss a beat. "We're in the quola section of the governmental center, home to the royal family and highest ranking officials. Ahead to the west is the road to the srile section where the higher lords and ranking Time Agents reside. To the north are the gardens and recreational areas. Behind us, to the east, are offices, archives, and libraries. To the south is the reception room where we will meet the royal family. It is also used as living quarters."

The whole area was paved or laid in brilliant, shining stone, black with gold and silver designs, lavish and excessive, each road wide enough for a six-lane highway. All around, buildings no more than two or three stories tall—five at the most for a single southern building—glimmered gold in the light of a sunrise or sunset. Enormous domes sectioned off the north area, the east area, and the south area. The western road was open, tall street lamps glittering gold with gold and iron fences lining the path. A similar set of domes could be seen a few blocks away. Outside the domes and fences, rocky countryside gave way to enormous mountains on the south side, white peaks nearly invisible in misty clouds. Sloping, rocky countryside sprawled out to the north where a white sun was blocked by hills but provided a stunning halo effect that nearly blinded Tommen in the half-second he glimpsed it.

Even as he thought it, his left arm began to sting and he found himself short of breath, as if he were standing in a sauna. He could tell most of the others looked uncomfortable as well. Emet did not seem fazed, but Rorion seemed to be having the most difficult time as wrinkles began to appear in her watery skin.

"The heat and ultraviolent light is too intense for us," Tommen stated. "We need to find shelter."

He no sooner finished speaking than he headed south toward the reception room. Looking around as he did, Tommen saw that no one else appeared to be walking about freely, though he did see several pods that may have been something like self-driving cars. They moved along specific inlays in the black streets, as though along an electromagnetic rail.

The whole square was massive, at least the size of several city blocks. Tommen was not very athletic, though most of the others appeared to have some semblance of physical fitness, however it looked for their particular species, and he felt sorely out of place. He forced himself to keep up and not show weakness, but this was driven primarily by the burning in his arm and the sweat soaking his shirt. So much for looking cool, calm, and presentable for royalty. He was going to walk in looking like a beggar.

They reached the southern dome and had no problems pushing through the energy field to safety. The air cooled and everything appeared easier on the eyes through the golden lens. Tommen rolled up his sleeve and inspected his arm. Only the tips of his fingers had actually been exposed to the UV rays, and they were pulsing as if he were still holding them over the flame on the stove. As for the rest of his arm, because of the burn damage, some parts up his upper arm and most of his lower arm and hand didn't sweat, making it more susceptible to overheating and edema. It had only been a short run, in all reality, and the coolness of the interior of the dome was quickly taking away the worst of the pain.

"Are you injured?" Ilit inquired.

"Pre-existing condition," Tommen replied, sliding his sleeve back down and shoving his gloves in his pockets. "But I'm fine." He looked around. "Which way?"

He thought the domes protected specific buildings, or that the complex would be all one building, when in actuality, it sprawled out more like a college campus. Buildings were set here and there, connected by pathways and interspersed with art and architecture. The only thing that really jumped out at him as being of potential royalty was the tall five-story building set about where he guessed the center of the dome to be.

Feeling the moron for not looking up this somewhat important information, Tommen started in that direction. No one objected. He told himself that it was because he was right, and not because they were as clueless as he was, and any guess was as good as any other.

Under the dome, everyone walked about freely, and the only pods to be seen were at stations at specific points along the outer edge of the dome. True to form, the Turitians made NFL stars look anorexic. Each one wore a wide belly band. Some were simple bands made up of a solid color or simple pattern. Others were lavish with streamers and glitter and patterns and jewels. A few had a second band going up around one shoulder. One even had a third band going around the chest, and the whole thing looked as if it had been decorated with the crown jewels themselves. No one stopped them or questioned them, no one made any gestures that Tommen saw, but there were plenty of stares

"What's the significance of the bands?" Tommen inquired. "Is it about status?"

"Among royalty and leadership, yes," Rorion answered. "A single, solid colored band is often that of a servant; single patterns are messengers and servants of distinction. Streamers indicate power, the patterns and decorations symbolic of the territory which they oversee and where they rank in terms of leadership. The shoulder bands are symbolic of military rank and power. The bands with the shoulder and chest band attached are indicative of the highest military status along with great honors. The streamers and decorations tell which battles and wars they fought and which honors were bestowed upon them."

So basically, everyone in the military bands was high brass. He expected nothing less, being in the capital among royalty, after all, but it was intimidating. Tommen was a failed soldier and a failed field medic. If things didn't go well here, he'd be a failed diplomat, too. Then where would he be? Not in Rifun's good graces, that was for sure.

The five-story building was surrounded by what Tommen figured would be considered impressive gardens, though they looked more like overgrown weed patches in his eyes. Here, there were fewer servants and more people of rank, those with veritable grass skirts for the number of streamers coming off their bands, including those with two or even three bands. They walked purposefully to and from and around this building which, up close, looked about the size of Tommen's high school. Smaller than he would have expected from a royal palace, but impressive nonetheless.

There were no windows to be found on either the north or south sides, the walls instead being adorned with marvelous carvings and paintings of people and events that meant nothing to him but everything to the Turitians. The east and west sides of the building, however, were nothing but windows, it seemed. In some places, they were simple, clear windows that could be looked through on either side. In other places, especially higher up, they were mirrors, perhaps one-way mirrors. In other places, dazzling stained glass depicted more people and scenes whose significance was lost on the group of tourists below.

"Many of these are depictions of the hero Ilar," Rorion said, as if reading his thoughts. "He is said to be the one who fought for the royal family during the dark times eight hundred years ago, ending the Division and bringing all of Turit under one system, one rule. It has been modified slightly since his time, but he is credited with starting the Turitians on the path to peace, space travel, and involvement in Time."

Tommen nodded without saying anything. Turitian Jesus, got it. It was a good thing to know, really, so he didn't accidentally insult him or take his name is vain or something.

"Are the Turitians religious?" he wondered.

"Turitians are largely naturalist, though some incorporate animism into their daily lives and have a vague belief in a creator. There has not been a concrete, widespread, organized religion in four hundred years, though small pockets of old religions can be found in outlying, country regions."

"Say one thing for farmers, they don't give up easy. What about the Akari?"

"There was an interest in the Akari about forty years ago, but it was a brief movement. It died down for a time. After the Zero Hour Revolution, many Turitians have become indifferent to it at best, suspicious or hostile at worst."

"Sisith, what do we know about the royals and top commanders? How do they feel about it?"

"Annoyed, but not openly hostile," the Arowa reported. "They were promised exceptional trade deals for their outposts with Rifun's ascent to power in the Wheel, but it was not delivered upon. However, the Turitians are known to be a very patient people and may be willing to listen if we have something to offer them for information on the journal."

Tommen almost asked if they had something to offer the Turitians, then refrained. He was the one in charge of the team. He was Faharoa's favorite. He was utilizing his team's strengths, but not asking them for permission to negotiate. He would have to be very cognizant of what, if anything, he promised the Turitians, and not overstep his bounds. On the other hand, if he was speaking for Rifun, it would be Rifun's problem to deliver on whatever Tommen said.

The main entrance to the royal building was on the east side, and Tommen knew this only because of two enormous statues reaching all the way to the fifth floor. One he assumed to be Ilar. The second he wasn't entirely sure.

"That is Dern, Ilar's greatest adversary during the wars," Rorion explained. "He was the only opponent Ilar could not beat. In the end, because of dissent among his own men, Dern surrendered to Ilar. He was named Commander General of the Turitian army under Ilar who was the first king. They ended up becoming best friends. Rumors say they may have been lovers as well."

"Okay, that was more than I wanted to know," Tommen cut in. He glanced at the Dimica. "Is there anything you don't know, or are you just a walking encyclopedia?"

"I have been tasked with being your cultural boni and explaining things to you. I try to anticipate your curiosities and questions and explain things as we go. Given that we are in the capital city outside the royal building, there is much culture here, often the things of utmost importance that will have great bearing on how the Turitians conduct business, whether they realize it or not. If you want me to stop—"

"No, I'm not saying that. Actually, it's kind of neat. I was just wondering is all." Pause. "Where do we rate in terms of approaching the servants?"

"As an off-world diplomat, the only ones we are considered inferior to is the royal family and their highest commanders who will be with them to receive us. All others, we are superior approaching an inferior."

That was a turn to the left, right? Or maybe the right? His other right? Shit, he forgot. Maybe he could sneak off to the Wheel to look it up real quick. Would that be seen as inappropriate, either to his team or the Turitians? Messing up in front of a servant might make them laugh at him or confuse them, but he could shake it off. Fucking up in front of the royal family? That carried a little more weight. He would never presume to think himself superior to them. Meeting with the royal family, they probably expected their guests to have a tiny inkling of social norms, which included the correct turning procedure.

"Turn to the left," Rorion offered quietly.

Tommen just nodded once without looking at her.

The inside of the royal building was no less astounding than the outside, but that might have just been Tommen's first-time impression, the same way the tourists in Charleston marveled at the capitol building or the bridge over the Kanawha River, when it was just an ordinary Tuesday thing for him. But, he thought, the royal building interior was still impressive.

At least part of the first floor was two stories tall, the ceiling vaulted with carved, painted domes depicting more people and scenes. Because there were no windows on the north or south side of the building, direct sunlight was sorely limited. Somehow, though, the paint used on the interior was reflective metallic, and colored light danced around the room like a disco. The floor itself was white and nearly blinding except for Tommen's glasses smartly turning into sunglasses. A shelf ran along the entire wall about eight feet up, some unknown light source offering up another ambient dimension.

In the center of the room was another painted carving, this time of some fancy design, perhaps the royal seal, if they had such a thing. More designs graced the floor perimeter. Most of the doors had carved pillars of some form or another with generic designs, leaves, and flowers. A few had carvings of people; whether they were all Ilar or different historical figures, Tommen did not know. Maybe later, when they weren't pressed for time, he would ask Rorion or just do his own research. As it was, they had a time to keep.

Turitian reception was very reminisce of Earth reception: a desk with a poor, tired, overworked receptionist sitting behind it. The band it wore was a single band with a simple design. A messenger or servant of higher standing.

"Naq, are you ready?" Tommen inquired.

"I am," the Yakik replied. She was a small thing and put Tommen in mind of a fennec fox, but when he'd done a little research on her people, he found incredible complexity in the parts of their brains that processed patterns and abstract thought, and even greater fine-tuning in their sense of hearing and in their vocal chords, making them able to mimic an array of sounds that would be impossible for a human. It was like comparing a human's nose to a dog's nose, how complex and finely-tuned the Yakik were.

Suffice to say, Tommen had little doubt in Naq's ability to assimilate the Turitian language and interpret back and forth if necessary. He was less than confident in his ability to speak, to sound both confident in himself and his mission, and actually convey what he wanted. Nevertheless, he approached the Turitian receptionist, telling himself to walk like a leader, talk like a leader. Pick a role model and imagine what they would say or do. Now imitate that. Easier said than done.

As they approached, Tommen suddenly realized that he had zero clue of the names of the royal family. He knew the family name was Jalar, but he didn't remember any specifics. He couldn't say King George or Queen Elizabeth or any of that. What was the queen's name? Ariel? Arya? He almost forgot to turn to signal his approach and intent, trying to keep his back straight and chin level as he turned to the left. The servant stood and turned the opposite direction, then knelt. After a second, they turned back to face each other.

"We are here to meet with the royal family Jalar and Commander Dira," Tommen told the servant. "The emissary from the First Order of the Akari under the direction of Faharoa Rifun Ndolo. We ought to be expected."

"You are expected," the servant replied, Naq interpreting in addition to the translators. "You will be escorted to waiting quarters, and I will tell the royal family and the commander of your arrival."

A lower servant was summoned and given orders to take Tommen and the rest of the "emissary" to waiting chambers. These chambers were located on the third floor of the building in a quiet, dimly-lit corridor on the east side. The outer wall was stained glass. With the light of about two dozen candles flickering around the room, it was like a glittery disco ball in the room.

That wasn't to say it wasn't comfortable. Everything was plush and oversized. Well, it was oversized for Tommen; he suspected this was pretty standard furniture for the Turitians. He sat down, every part of him wanting nothing more than to dive onto the velvety sofas and jump on them like a bratty little kid.

But at least he'd gotten them in and hadn't made a fool of himself or the others. The way things looked, he appeared professional, competent, and at least a little culturally sensitive. No one had chastised him for improper gestures or turns. So far, all was well.

"Everyone doing well so far?" Tommen wondered, looking around at his group. A good leader concerned himself with the welfare of his team, after all. He didn't want to be an aloof, egotistical jerk.

"Very well, thank you," Rorion replied politely.

"I am also well," Ilit answered.

The others gave varying answers of affirmation. Tommen turned to Sisith. "So, what are we looking at politically? Anything of note or intrigue?"

"High Commander General Dira was awarded her fifth Commander General commendation, making her the most decorated Commander General in living memory and the second-most decorated since the hero Ilar. She is virtually untouchable by any court or law and the only superior she has is the royal family. She is, however, beloved by all, and her record is utterly pristine."

Go into politics; the media and the opposition will find some kind of dirty laundry. Tommen did not say this out loud, however, merely gestured for Sisith to continue.

"The royal family Jalar is the second-youngest dynasty on Turit, arising through an unlikely marriage three hundred years ago to an inventor from the industrial complexes of the third continent. While relations are good among all the royal families, the family Jalar is still looked down upon as it was not established either by the hero Ilar or through other, more noble means."

"Who is part of the royal family? Who will I be talking to?"

"The core royal family is comprised of Queen Aronet, King-in-Waiting Luril, Princesses Nit, Roda, and Nish, Elder Lord Baro, and Younger Duchess Pary. The only ones who are blood relatives are the queen and Princess Roda."

"How does that work?" Tommen wondered aloud.

"Turitian family structure is decidedly complex—" Rorion began.

"Stop. Sorry. Thinking out loud. Unless it's important, I'll just stick with names and titles and worry about family relations later."

The Dimica did not appear offended, merely nodded and stopped talking.

Tommen looked around and fiddled with his glasses, switching through the different modes: infrared, x-ray, and so on. He always started his sweep of the room by looking at his group, just to get an idea of what he was looking at in order to identify life forms. He didn't expect to find anyone hiding behind the curtains necessarily, but he might pick up some interesting anomalies, anyway.

The room appeared clean, and he switched back to normal lenses. Then he took his glasses off, squeezing his eyes shut as if he suddenly stared into a bright light. He'd gotten too accustomed to the color-correcting lenses that his eyes didn't know what to do when he went back to his regular, bland deuteranopia. Well, that wasn't entirely true; it wasn't as bad as he probably made it out to be in his mind.

"Sisith or Rorion, what's the protocol on keeping your guests waiting?" he asked, hoping he sounded appropriately irritable without dipping into the whiny toddler begging his mom to hurry up in the store. "Are we being snubbed in some way?"

"In general, only the military is strictly observant of time," Rorion answered. "Most Turitians regard it with some measure of fluidity. That's often the reason why they are allowed to continue their Time practices, because they 'don't take Time seriously enough to be a threat.' "

In other words, they could be waiting a while. In a moment of dry humor, Tommen half-expected to see the Bat or the Day walk through the door to tell him that the Hands were ready to speak with him. He took an even breath. It didn't take any effort at all to recall his horrifying Apprentice exam. Supposedly the Journeyman exam was plain potatoes, comparatively speaking, but that didn't make him feel much better.

Tommen tried to stay dignified, but he had a hard time figuring out what that looked like. He wasn't anyone particularly important back home. He wasn't raised to be a snob, expecting to be waited on hand and foot. Yeah, he was normally "that guy" for one reason or another, but that just made him want to be more invisible. How did he pretend to be something he wasn't? More to the point, was it a good idea?

"Rorion, what do the Turitians expect from their guests as far as demeanor and personal presentation?"

The walking encyclopedia was ready with a reply. "Aside from the appropriate turns and gestures, the Turitians expect you to represent yourself as you are, within the boundaries of being the best possible representation of your species. Anything otherwise may be perceived as deception."

Tommen nodded thoughtfully. So if he wasn't descended from royalty and well-versed in the ways of the universe, that was all right so long as he still conducted himself appropriately for the situation. Sounded doable. At the same time, it sounded almost like a trap. Being given permission to be less than stellar—especially in front of royalty—was too good to be true in his mind.

He didn't have time to dwell on it for very long before another servant came to fetch them. Tommen checked and double-checked his turns and gestures, then followed the servant out of the waiting chambers, his loyal posse following him. It was still surreal to think that he was in charge. He was leading them. They were waiting for him to tell them what to do. They didn't argue with his decisions and they were more than willing to help and answer questions.

Something was up, or else he was dreaming.

The reception room was located on the fifth floor. Like every other advanced civilization in the universe, they had yet to invent elevators, and Tommen Banded momentarily once they reached the top floor so he could catch his breath. Fuck, he was out of shape. He needed to exercise more. Maybe he should think about taking up track in the spring, or just go out and jog in the morning or evenings. One cold thought about the snow waiting for him at home squashed that idea. Maybe he could go to the gym and get on a treadmill. Either way, this on-a-whim excessive walking business was not working out for him.

The servant took them to a set of almost completely round doors that looked as though they were made of solid bronze, and spoke to a couple guards. Tommen glanced at Naq to see if he could discern an underlying motive based on her body language, but unless it was obvious, he had a decidedly difficult time in reading alien body language. And if he could have been able to see it, so could the Turitians, and he highly suspected she was more disciplined than that. All of this passed through his mind in only a second or two. Then his attention turned back to the task at hand as the guards apparently liked or agreed with whatever the servant said. The servant made some more appropriate turns and gestures, then stepped out of the way so the guards could open the massive doors which were apparently much heavier than Tommen initially gave them credit for.

The Turitian royal reception room was not quite what Tommen was expecting. He'd envisioned a long, grand ballroom with a red carpet streaming down the center leading to a throne of gold. Or a throne of swords, that worked, too. The queen would be there with the prince at her one side and her commander on the other. He would kneel—or, you know, turn—and she would bid him rise and speak his piece.

In actuality, the room wasn't much bigger than Tommen's entire house, and very poorly lit, all things considering. While small lights and candles provided ambiance, the main source of light came from a skylight, an enormous stained glass mosaic with no discernible pattern or picture that he could see. In the center of the room was a round table, the dappled colors making it impossible to determine what the table actually looked like. Fifteen chairs sat around the table, four of them empty.

Tommen approached, then paused and made his turn. Across the table, two Turitians stood. Both were vividly decorated. They turned opposite him, then bade him sit. He chose Sisith, Rorion, and Naq to sit with him. They all had translators, but he wanted someone with a more intimate understanding of the language, who could explain nuance where mere technology could not.

"Welcome, Tommen Forbes, emissary of the First Order of the Akari," one of the Turitians greeted. "I am Queen Aronet. This is High Commander General Dira."

"Thank you for agreeing to speak to me," Tommen replied as graciously as he could, immediately doubting whether he should have said "me" or "us." "Me" because he was the diplomat, and his groupies were just groupies here to help him, not negotiate for him. "Us" because they were all here together at the table. Didn't matter now, he supposed. He went on, "I realize you may have reason to be suspicious or upset."

"An agreement was broken," one of the other Turitians at the table stated. "And your last ally was raided by both the Time industry and your own people, the humans. What do you bring us today?"

"I seek only information. In exchange, perhaps we can repair some of the damage that has been done and perhaps yet deliver on some of the trade agreements." God, he sounded more and more like Rifun every day.

"What information do you seek?" another Turitian inquired.

"High Commander Dira. Approximately forty Base Years ago you accompanied the royal family on a diplomatic mission to Sren and were attacked by the pirate Titik. Is this true?"

"It is," the commander replied. Say one thing for the Turitians, they were either just that patient, culturally, or they were masters of poker.

"It is rumored that at the time, you had in your possession a book of some form. A religious text, a journal, something of the sort, and it was taken or destroyed in the attack. Rumors state that it was a gift from the Kolkath. What was this book, how did you come to have it at the time, and what happened to it?"

It was impossible to read the commander's expression, both for alien physiology and the poor lighting in the room, but if Tommen had to pick a word based on what little he could see and hear in her voice, he would say thoughtfulness. She made several gestures of unknown significance.

"I do recall this. Ambassador Fili of the Kolkath gifted the journal to the Turitian royal family Jalar. His claim was that it was a religious text found in an old monastery of a religion no one practiced anymore, though some scholars still studied the language therein for historical and cultural purposes. Queen Aronet gave me permission to study the language a bit and learn to read the book. I found it fascinating, and I admit I may have been overzealous. I did take it with me to Sren. After the attack at Chilip, I was unable to find it, but we had taken heavy damage from Titik's ships and pirate crew. I thought it had perhaps gotten lost or destroyed. I sent a word of apology to the Kolkath. There were words, but all is well."

Tommen didn't expect her to admit to causing strife between their peoples for such a thing, and he let the whole thing slide. What was important was that she'd had a book of some form.

"And," she went on, "now that I think about it and the memories have been refreshed, you seem to speak this language as well."

"I do?"

What actually surprised him more was that he was speaking English. Any time he had the translator, he usually tried to speak Welsh. Of course, that was typically when he was on his own or with his dad. Speaking to others who didn't speak his language, he resorted to English, such as speaking to Rifun before coming on this adventure.

"You do. I remember it."

"Did they teach you anything else about the book? Anything in particular about the text itself?"

Dira made a negative gesture, the Turitian equivalent of shaking one's head. "No. The Kolkath scholars taught me the basics of the language, and I patiently learned more from there."

Tommen would give her the credit for the discipline and fortitude; it had taken him years to learn English and he still sucked at it. That reminded him, he still had to work on his essays; the deadlines were coming up quick. No, he had to be focused on the here and now and worry about everything else later.

If Dira only had to learn the language, that meant the words hadn't been Imprinted. Even if she'd had a copy of the journal, it wasn't the original journal, which was what they were after. It might also explain why the Kolkath had been so chill about her losing it. That didn't mean Tommen and his group wouldn't still check out this Captain Titik and see what he had to say, but it was no longer a priority. They might have to shift their focus to the Kolkath instead.

"That is all I know about where it came from and what happened to it," the commander finished. "May I inquire as to your interest in it?"

"It wasn't a Kolkath holy text," Tommen answered. "It belonged to a very prominent member of the Order. But you did not know, and it matters not. We will move our search elsewhere."

The Turitians exchanged looks and gestures. Tommen glanced at Naq who appeared to be studying them intently. Then a male Turitian spoke.

"Then, as we have given you all the information that can be known about this book, perhaps we can turn our attention to matters of trade?"

Oh, shit. Now he had to actually negotiate.

During Jazz Festival in Charleston, there was always a huge flea market. Part of it was more of a multicultural thing. You had to bypass all the teenagers selling the same jewelry, bad photography, and egotistical self-expressive art, but it was there. It was where the immigrants sold their traditional wares: scarves, spices, wood carvings, kites, and assorted cultural good luck charms and religious icons. One of the most prominent themes of the multicultural section of the flea market was the cultural desire to bargain. Only in developed countries it seemed did one pay what the seller asked for. Everywhere else, it was the thrill of the bargain, the negotiating, seeing just how good a deal you could get.

Tommen was sorely inexperienced. He'd gone to the flea market a couple times. On the rare occasion that he could afford something—or, more accurately, the rare occasion that he got over his stingy money management to actually buy something—he only did the bargain banter once, maybe twice, and he always played it safe, or what he considered safe. He knew he was losing dearly, but he just always had this image of an angry shop owner chasing him away, throwing things at him and waving a knife or something, telling him to get out and never return.

"I am afraid that, as I was not present during the original negotiations, my knowledge is limited. Tell me your side of the story." That sounded good and diplomatic, right? Get both points of view in order to make an informed decision and a mutually beneficial agreement.

"The original agreement stated that while Rifun and the First Order was in power, that we would be granted jurisdiction over all outposts and would be permitted to expand our sales of Time Capsules without fear of prosecution or punishment from the Timekeepers or Grandfathers. Furthermore, we would be the unofficial head of the Scouts. 'Unofficial' because Scouts are notoriously rebellious against anyone who claims ownership of them, though we would have the final say and power, similar to being the Hand of the Scouts."

Ouch. That was a heavy offer, and not a bad one for the Turitians, either. They already had the outposts and the markets; it was simply a matter of giving them permission to operate as they wanted to—something the Hands wouldn't do, but Rifun would, probably for a little larger cut of the profits. Giving them control of the Scouts gave them more power and influence to expand their markets and bring in new recruits for the Order.

"You understand the circumstances which made honoring that

agreement more difficult?" Tommen asked.

"We are aware of it, yes," Queen Aronet replied gracefully. "We Turitians are a patient people and willing to give second chances on defaulted agreements and contracts, hence why we are here today. However, as the Elif have already been hit hard by the Time industry for aiding the Order, we are faced with the decision to look out for ourselves unless you have something greater to offer."

"Perfectly reasonable."

"What are Rifun's plans? Where does he stand in terms of plans and power?" a male Turitian inquired.

"Within the last month, Rifun has managed to overthrow the Akarin, the ones who deposed him in the Wheel. He now has a more fortified base and a stronger army. He is currently working to bring all the peoples together, rest his men, and be ready for his next move, which will most likely be against the Borelians."

Murmurs.

"He plans to move against the Borelians? He allied himself with them," Dira objected.

"Yes, and they are not as patient and forgiving as you are. They are enraged, over the broken contract and the research for a cure for their toxins. They have declared war on both the Order and against humanity itself. I realize the latter is not your problem, but the former may be if you wish to have further dealings." He continued before anyone could object further. "I realize that your first instinct may be to wash your hands of this and walk away. I would not blame you. But you are a formidable people on your own. Combined with the First Order—who has overtaken the Time industry and the Akarin—we are stronger together.

"The Borelians control three systems and dozens of planets. Their space armada is nearly unmatched. What could you do with those worlds if they were freed? If you don't want the worlds, fine. You could build an outpost in each system; at least one has neighbors you can sell to or even compete with.

"Furthermore, having that kind of status, being part of the force that defeated the Borelians, the scourge of the universe, you gain notoriety and surely other worlds will come to you for alliance, protection, trade. Become more than an ally and immerse yourselves in the First Order and gain even more. I don't want to overpromise, but there are great possibilities here."

"Including a great possibility of death," Dira mused grimly. "Once one moves against the Borelians, there is no compromise, no third option. You win or you die. Worse yet, you may be enslaved."

"So far, everyone has said the Borelians are too big to hit. I say they're too big to miss. We've already launched one attack against them and burned one of their slave worlds. They are still scrambling to recover. What else can we do?"

The Turitians glanced at each other, making gestures. It was Queen Aronet who spoke after several minutes of muffled deliberation.

"Your proposal is bold and intriguing. We must consider the matter carefully. We do, however, thank you for coming to meet with us in an attempt to repair relationships and renew contracts. You may tell Rifun that we will contact him when we have rendered our decision. If he asks when he may expect an answer, you may kindly remind him that we are, as you said, a patient people."

Don't call us, we'll call you. Tommen felt his hopes sink, even as he was wailing at how unfair it was. He could barely negotiate a price at a flea market, and he was here negotiating intergalactic war alliances with foreign diplomats? How was this supposed to work again? Were Rifun and Julianna trying a more subtle approach to getting him killed? Show him the carrot and he'd walk right over a cliff to get it.

The Turitians then made a gesture dismissing the group. Tommen and his posse made the appropriate return gesture and stood to leave.

"One more thing," Dira said. The group paused. "You are yet young, Tommen, but you are fearless, a credit to your people. You may take that as my personal compliment."

"Thank you, Commander Dira."

With that, they left the reception room, first escorted by a guard, then a servant beyond the doors. They passed another group of Turitians in the corridor. The next group seeking the time of the royal family? The servant took them back to the main floor and left them there to their own devices. Tommen waited until they were outside before speaking.

"So, how did it go, really?" He looked at Rorion, Sisith, and Naq.

"All turns and gestures were appropriate in our interactions," Rorion reported. "The gestures they made among themselves suggest they are immediately divided over the offer you made. Some think they should go forward. Some think the deal should be modified. Some think they should back away. However, they are all intrigued by it, and they are all grateful that the Order has contacted them again and wishes to resume relations with them."

Naq made a motion which Tommen had learned meant agreement. "All vocal communication concurs. I heard no evidence of treachery or double-meaning."

"And politically?" Tommen wondered, looking at Sisith.

"Politically, their farming regions have the most to gain with the offer of the worlds, the military and innovators the most with the offer of new outposts, the artists the most with the expansion of influence at all. There will be support from all sides. As to which way they will decide, I cannot say."

"They will agree," Naq said simply. "Their patterns of gestures, movements, and some of their vocal articulation strongly suggest an agreement, at least among those who were present. How it will go over with the other royal families and population at large remains to be seen."

But first there was the problem of seeing how well it went over with Rifun. Tommen had basically just promised the Turitians at least one planet and rights to build at least one outpost, all without the consent of the one who would be doling out the spoils at the end of the day. So approaching the Faharoa at the conclusion of this mission—or this leg of the mission anyway, seeing how they had made virtually no progress on the journal—was not as objective as he would have hoped. Originally, he'd hoped to just say, yes, he'd found concrete evidence of the journal, or no, he hadn't. This had not been part of the plan. He found Rifun just leaving his quarters and heading down the stairway.

"Back so soon?" Rifun wondered, motioning for Tommen to follow him back down the stairs which he'd just so painstakingly climbed. Again. "That's either really good news or really bad. Seeing how you're not calling me for bail money, I'm hoping it's good news."

"Well...good and...yet to be determined," Tommen said haltingly. He felt his face turn red. "On the one hand, I did get more information on the journal and its possible whereabouts."

"And on the other hand?"

"The Turitians wanted to renegotiate the deal you made them before the Zero Hour Revolution. It was on the spot, and I was unprepared."

"What did you tell them?"

"I told them that if they went in with the Order to help overthrow the Borelians that they might get one of the Borelian-controlled planets and the rights to build another outpost...?"

Rifun stopped in his tracks and Tommen nearly ran into him. Rifun turned.

"You promised them a planet and an outpost?" he echoed.

"Um...yes."

The man studied him for a moment, then continued on his way. "At least that's all you promised them. Leaves some for the rest of the species I'm trying to get to help us."

Tommen silently let out a breath and hurried after him. "So...I did good?"

"You didn't do bad, is how I will say it. Where are you heading next?"

"Psia, or that's where we'll start. We'll be searching for Captain Titik."

"I see. Very well. When do you expect to leave?"

"Um, I want to do a little research first. I mean, I did some on Turit and the Turitians, but it just didn't feel like enough. I want to give myself time. Plus I have school and everything else. How about I just let you know?"

"Fair enough."

"Oh, and the Turitian royal family Jalar said they will be contacting you about...my...offer. Yeah."

"I will await their call, then. If there is nothing else?"

"No, not really. Just giving my report."

"Which I appreciate."

"What about the medicine for the Borelian pneumonia?"

"You'll get it. You are free to go."

Tommen did so, if only because he wasn't sure what else to do, and because Rifun's behavior was both uncharacteristic and worrisome. He wasn't sarcastic, uptight, scheming, smirking, manipulative, or narcissistic, lording his superiority over everyone else, i.e. Tommen. He seemed aloof, disinterested, taking in information and filing it away for later rather than jumping on it, working it, trying to make it advantageous to him and his plans. Even his reaction to Tommen's bungling negotiations was oddly muted. It was frightening. Either something was going on with him, or something bigger was going on, in which case Tommen wanted to be free and clear, and he got home just as fast as he could.

All appeared normal as he stumbled through the portal into his room and clawed his way to his bed. Fucking hell, too many portals in too short a time, and that wasn't even counting the two portals he'd opened himself. His head pounded wildly, and his eyes felt tired and swollen. After a few minutes of consideration, he got up and dragged himself to the bathroom.

He was sunburned to shit, red all over, everywhere his skin had been exposed to the harsh ultraviolet rays of the Turitian sun. Carefully, he peeled off his coat and gloves and pushed up his sleeve to inspect his arm and hand. His arm still felt abnormally warm, but did not seem any worse for wear. His fingers, however, where they had been exposed, were red and blistered. He shook his head in disbelief, shifting his stance a few times before rummaging in the drawer for a needle. He lanced the blisters. They weren't bad, not much worse than normal wear and tear as from a shovel or something similar, but they might as well have been amputated as he also dug out a small bottle of alcohol and began spraying them down before Banding a little to speed up the healing.

Ten minutes later, he was still in bed, face-down in his pillow. His fingers had stopped throbbing and he had stopped cursing, but that was small potatoes compared to the rest of his aches and pains, from going up and down the fortress stairs, to the portals, to the stress of suddenly becoming an intergalactic, high-profile negotiator.

The next thing he knew, he was halfway off the bed, his sense of falling screaming at him to wake up and get things to rights. He scrambled back and righted himself, breathing heavily and rubbing his eyes. His clock read just past noon. Grudgingly, he picked himself up and headed for the bathroom, momentarily confused why the door was locked until he heard his dad's gruff, "Wait a minute or find a tree."

"But there's snow outside," Tommen replied smartly.

"Well then you don't have to go that bad."

It was a minute or two before the door opened.

"Where have you been? Aruba?" his dad asked.

Tommen ran a hand through his hair, wincing at his itchy, burned scalp. "Turit. Their sun went nova or something, destroyed the planet except for where the Turitians have been able to build domes. Discovered that in the first three seconds of standing outside unprotected."

"I see. Anything interesting happen? Meet any princesses? Slay any dragons?"

"Met with the queen and the High Commander General, among others. Basically promised them a planet and an outpost."

"Sounds like a story."

"Oh, it is. Can I go to the bathroom first, though?"

His dad stepped aside. "I think there's some aloe in the bottom drawer if you need it."

He did need it, though he Banded a little more to help the healing along. The pain was less this time, and he went out to the kitchen where his dad was making a sandwich from a leftover pan of meatloaf.

"You want some?" he asked.

"Sure, I could eat." Tommen grabbed a plate.

"Turitian bug gut surprise just not part of your palette?"

"We didn't get offered food."

"Too bad. So what happened?"

So Tommen recounted his encounter, from Turit's landscape, to its lethal sun, to the cities, the buildings, the sights and sounds. By the time he actually got around to detailing the meeting with the queen and the others, he was on his third sandwich. He slowed down a little when he got to the part about the negotiations and promising planets and outposts and all that.

"You sound like quite the up-and-coming diplomat," his dad commented. "Do you think you can get the Tacagans to agree to help us a little more?"

"Causing problems again?" Tommen wondered.

"Oh, nothing out of the ordinary, I think. I'm heading there tomorrow morning after I get off and I'm going to talk to Do Chien, get the state of things. I'm sick of the politics and the bullshit. He's the boots on the ground, the only pair we've got. We need to get more."

"Agreed."

"Do you want to come with?"

"As fun as it sounds, I think I'll pass. I really just kind of want a couple days to relax, goof off, and worry about normal stuff like school."

His dad nodded. "I understand. I wish that's all you had to worry about. Is school resuming this week?"

"I don't know. I haven't heard that it's not."

"How are Becky and Will and them?"

"Still sick. Becky and Eli are getting better, slowly. Sounds like Will isn't responding well to treatments. Because of the whole pandemic thing, there are no visitors allowed with exception of his mom."

"What about Rifun and his miracle cure?"

Tommen shrugged helplessly. "He just said that he would get it to me. Didn't say when or where or anything like that, but I'm hoping it's soon. I don't want to see anything happen to Will."

His dad nodded. "I know." He stretched in his recliner. "Any plans today?"

"Nothing beyond what I've said."

"Worrying about normal things?"

"Yeah."

"Great. Then you can go out and shovel the driveway. And maybe help out some of the neighbors. If Polskis haven't been home or are too sick to shovel, I think they would consider it very kind of you."

Tommen sighed but did not argue. After all, snow was nothing.

Chapter Fifteen
Area 51

These days, Walter had very little trouble getting to Tacaga and into the city Lip. The gate guards no longer questioned why he was there, at least while he was standing right there. The police escort remained as silent as ever, with exception of Geros and Dermos, but they weren't exactly chumming up to him. Their task was only to deliver him to the governmental building, which they did, and then left for their next assignment, as mundane as ever. As a cop, Walter understood.

He was also grateful as he could then move freely about the building, at least as far as the elevator that took him to Sub-Floor Delta. Then it was a short jaunt down the corridor to the laboratory where Do Chien diligently did his work. Or, in the case of today as Walter approached, slept on a small mat in one corner of the room. Walter Banded him for a good nine hours, releasing when he saw the doctor stir. The man looked around, saw Walter, and scrambled to his feet.

"I'm so sorry, I didn't know I would have guests today," he said humbly, hurrying to the decon unit and going through the process of exiting his laboratory.

"No worries," Walter told him. "You looked like you needed the sleep."

"How can I help you, Mr. Forbes?"

"Oh, I just came to offer my amazing company. I hope it's better than the Tacagans' and all the political bullshit otherwise."

Do Chien grinned. "Kind company is always welcome, but I have much work to do." His expression faltered.

"Something tells me not all is as cheery as I would hope."

The doctor removed his translator, and Walter did the same. Then, in heavily-accented English, "The Tacagans are up to something. I don't know what. The Governors visit me more and more, always asking about the cures and my experiments."

"Isn't that to be expected? Aren't they infected, too?"

"They don't ask about the widespread sickness. They ask only about the poison cure, if there is a way to negate the sugar."

"Negate it?"

Do Chien nodded severely. "Come with me."

Walter was less than enthusiastic about the decon process going into the laboratory, but he was rather excited about finally getting inside to see the work in action. Once safely in the lab, Do Chien handed him a white coat, a hairnet and a beardnet to cover his mustache. Then they headed over to the back wall where the doctor flipped some kind of switch and opened a secret second hallway. It was like something out of a spy movie. What Walter found beyond the wall was less so.

"It's a prison," he stated.

Four cells on either side of the hallway with another one at the very end. Three were occupied.

"When Rifun's men torched the Borelian farming world, they also took it upon themselves to capture some of the slave masters." Do Chien paused in front of one of the cells. "This one, Danik, she is *sidakvar udo*, disjunct bitoxic. This one—" He turned around. "—refuses to tell me her name, but she is *sidakvar batil*, adjunct bitoxic. And this one..."

They moved to the cell at the very end of the hall. "This is Tarma. She's a *vodrak*."

If there was any good news to be found, Walter figured, it was that they did not appear to be obviously mistreated. The two bitoxics did not pay either of them any mind, just sat or stood and dwelt on their own thoughts. The *vodrak*, however, Tarma, she watched them like a hawk, pushing her colors slowly she they knew just how deadly she was. Walter saw one of her horns was broken and healed over.

"So what was the point of bringing them here?" Walter dared inquire.

"I am supposed to test cures for each of the poisons," Do Chien answered levelly. "It is decidedly dangerous and difficult to do, but comparatively speaking, it's the easiest job I have."

"You're experimenting on them."

"I have been asked to find ways to kill them, yes."

"I assume you're not talking about bullets." When the doctor hesitated, Walter continued, "I understand we're at war, but we don't need to torture them. We're working in self-defense. Even if it comes down to killing every last one of them, at least we can be humane about it."

"Humane genocide," the Vietnamese chuckled.

"We're not Nazis."

"You're right. We're the Jews and the gypsies and the gays fighting back against the Nazis. Difference is, at least everyone in World War II was human. The Borelians, you may have gathered, are not human. We need to understand their physiology. I have learned all I can from the material available in the Wheel. It's good, but noticeably lacking in anything of real use to us." He went on before Walter could protest. "Believe me, Walter, I am the last one who wants to do this. I am still ashamed of my actions in Vietnam. But my work there makes me uniquely qualified for the work here.

"I am not doing this because a small man in a big castle wants to dominate the other castles around him. I am doing this because not doing it means the extinction of humanity. Tell me, Walter, having been exposed to Borelian poisons and sickness on multiple occasions, would you kill any or all of these here? Right now, would you shoot them? Kill them humanely, as you said?"

Walter sighed. "I've been exposed to enough poisons to have taught me a lesson or two. Considering this one is probably plotting our deaths a hundred different ways, I would say so, yes."

Do Chien reached into a pocket inside his lab suit and brought out a gun. He held it out to Walter. "Then do it. The glass is not bulletproof. You're an expert marksman. Shoot them dead." Walter gingerly took the gun. "And when you're done with that, shoot their children." Walter looked at him. "It's all the same. All humane."

Do Chien continued, "That's what we are facing, Walter Forbes. We face extinction. In inciting this war, you and the others have called for total genocide. Or slavery. Torture will never be okay. Killing children and suckling babes will never be okay. But it is necessary. Not because we have some misconceived notion of superiority, but because they do." After a moment of tense silence, the doctor added, "You know, this could have all been avoided."

"How is that?"

"If your son hadn't found the hasax flower. If you had died. Then everything would have simply gone back to normal."

"There is no guarantee of that. The Borelians could have declared war on humanity anyway when Rifun broke his contract with them. Then we never would have known about the hasax and the cure for the poisons. If anyone is at fault, it's Rifun for ever getting in league with them." Walter handed the gun back to Do Chien. "Fine. Damned if we do, damned if we don't. Just remember that they are living, sentient beings, too."

"Believe me, they never give me a chance to forget."

Walter stalked out of the corridor, the alarm bells ringing in his mind. Everything decent in him screamed that this was wrong, yet the logical part of him said that it didn't matter. The Borelians would enslave and destroy the human race if they didn't do something, and that might involve some killing techniques that were less than humane. If they couldn't get close for hand-to-hand combat, and if the Borelians used Time well enough to render standard rules of warfare laughable, then they needed some other advantage. The only way to get that advantage, prior to actual, physical engagement, was through a little experimenting.

But still, experimenting on—well, they weren't human, but living, sentient creatures, it went against every ethical code he knew. Mice, monkeys, those he had little problem with as long as they were being otherwise cared for. In his mind, even an enemy of war deserved some measure of respect and dignity. Poking and prodding and unspeakable torture just didn't happen, not for civilized people. They were better than that.

"So what have you discovered through your experiments?" Walter asked levelly.

"You mean, have I found anything to justify my work?" Do Chien wondered. "Yes, I believe so." He walked over to a table, shuffled some papers, and produced one in particular. "I know you cannot read Vietnamese, but I will explain. Each toxin, while cured by glucose, also has its own unique weakness, shall we say. For blue, respiratory, it was naloxone, or a similar inhibitor. I am still testing my theory on bronchodilators, but I want to get a preliminary on each poison before going into any one in depth."

"Makes sense. What have you found?"

"Yellow is circulatory manipulation. Depending on how it is used, the effects may be lessened via blood thinner, as long as the victim has no open wounds. Similarly, an AED does wonders."

The doctor went through all the colors perceivable by humans, and Walter did his best to take notes. Some colors were easier than others to deal with, it seemed. Purple, emotional manipulation, was most often controlled through sheer will of self-control. Orange had no known effects on humans because it dealt with extraneous organs they didn't have. Green seemed pretty absolute as it dealt with one's inner sense of time; once the damage was done, it was done. Nevertheless, Walter scratched away. It was when Do Chien started going through the eleven imperceivable colors that he faltered.

"Urlo seems to be a roll of the dice on its side effects. They seem to range from red to purple to pink to ith; I can't find any real pattern to it. But the poison itself causes seizures. I haven't been able to study whether they are permanent or if they go away after a time, but they seem to be tempered by normal seizure medication—midazolam, lorazepam, things like that."

Walter decided it best to keep his mouth shut. Instead, he

asked, "Is there any way to tell which color is which just by looking at it?"

Do Chien reluctantly shook his head. "No. Some colors appear more on the blue side of our spectrum, other closer to silver, but I have not found any definitive way to say 'This is urlo' or 'That is ith.' I'm sorry."

They finished up the notes and Walter tucked everything away in a pocket. It wasn't the real reason he'd come today, but it was helpful nonetheless.

"Is there anything else I can help you with?" the doctor inquired as he reorganized his papers. "Since you don't come to the meetings, I can only assume you are either uninterested or uninvited. Given your visit today, I think the former is unlikely."

"That is true. Do you know anything about the diseases the Borelians have unleashed on us?"

Do Chien shrugged. "Pneumonia on Earth, a cold on Tacaga, stomach flu on Dorigis, fatigue and joint swelling on Hlohi."

"Do you have any cures or ways to synthesize them?"

"I have the resources, but not the time. I am only one man. Besides, I have heard that these diseases have a very high survival rate when treated properly. Yes, yes, I know, not everyone can treat it properly. But for those in the third world, if this doesn't kill them, something else will. This is my mission, Walter. I am working on the bigger picture, trying to keep humanity out of slavery. Sometimes, it means ignoring lesser diseases. Sometimes, it means doing a little questionable experimenting. If your ethics have a problem with it, come to the meetings and tell them. I do as they tell me."

Walter did not miss the unspoken, "Not you." He took it as a dismissal. He thanked the doctor for his time, politely offered to bring him something—comfort food, a cup of coffee, a memento from home—was turned down, then grudgingly went through the decon unit to escape the laboratory, collecting his notepad and phone on the other side.

At the last minute, Walter considered that he probably should have asked when the next meeting was scheduled. Maybe he would show up and express his ethical concerns. But could he really? This was the war version of having a belligerent suspect rushing at him with all drug-induced intent to kill. In a split-second decision, Walter would put his own life over the suspect's life. He would put his partner's life over the suspect's life. Was it fair? Maybe not. Maybe the guy just needed a chance to talk and get his act together. Maybe, maybe, maybe a thousand different scenarios. But in the moment, it was his life or the suspect's.

The Borelians were on a mission to kill and enslave. There was no reasoning, no peace treaty, no compromise. All or nothing. The lives of humanity versus the lives of the Borelians. All the way down to the last child, perhaps. Their entire civilization was moving against humans, against the rest of the universe, even. It was sickening, but this was the way it had to be.

Walter got on the elevator, his thoughts swinging back and forth. On the one side of the pendulum, yes, full steam ahead, figure out what it would take the kill all the sons of bitches in one fell swoop. On the other side, no, stop, this isn't right, there has to be another way, a path to peace. One made him sound like a madman Nazi. The other made him sound like a naive idealist. Was there no middle? Even as he thought it, he knew there wasn't.

He stepped off the elevator and had no sooner turned toward the train station than a voice spoke behind him.

"Captain Forbes."

He turned to see a Governor striding toward him purposefully, the woman with pitch black skin, Milay. If her frown got any deeper, it would fall off her face, Walter thought wryly.

"Governor Milay, what can I do for you?" he wondered cordially.

Her expression said, "You can do nothing for me that I cannot do for myself, you stupid Neanderthal."

What she actually said was, "I want to have a word with you, which you may take back to your Gatekeeper."

"Of course."

"Come with me."

She did not give room to argue as she turned on her heel and swept down the hall. Walter quickly caught up to her and followed her to something of a sitting room. Books lined one wall opposite a magnificent painting of someone very important, he was sure. Furniture was plush and deceptively antique. She took one chair and he chose the other, the glass table lighting up with a hundred different menu options. Milay tapped a few buttons, and the table turned off.

"We, the Governors, have concerns," Milay began, and Walter bet that if she'd had a glass of wine, she would have been swirling and studying it like a true snob.

"Does it have anything to do with your prisoner test subjects down there?" he wondered.

"So the engineer did show you. Yes, it does have something to do with that."

Walter shifted in his seat. "Well, as you enjoy pointing out, we are guests in your home. If you want them gone, all you have to do is say so."

"As true as that may be, our concerns run deeper than that. Do you understand all the different Borelian toxins?"

"I can't say as I have them memorized, but I've heard of all of them."

"There is a color called thar. The toxin is associated with telepathic manipulation."

"Yes, that sounds right."

Milay heaved a sigh. Dumb Neanderthal couldn't read her more sophisticated mind. "Captain, all Borelian toxins, while toxic to everyone else in the universe, are also applicable among the Borelians themselves. The doctor believes that the orange 'extraneous organ' toxin may have to do with a secondary organ in their endocrine system, or with the toxin system itself. Either way, something they may be afflicted by. What does that tell you about thar?"

Walter blinked. "Are Borelians telepathic?"

"When we heard of Do Chien's findings, we asked him to look into it."

"How can you do that? Monitoring brain waves?"

"There was that, but we also wanted to know the physiology of it. Let's just say that we started out with five prisoners."

Walter felt his stomach lurch. "What did the good doctor find?"

"They are telepathic. It's not so sophisticated as holding conscious conversations, but they are able to relay brief messages, impressions, directions..."

"What's the range of this telepathy?"

"We don't know. But rest assured that if they are able to send messages beyond their cells and across the universe, the Borelians will come. Rifun may have done all he could to throw the hounds off humanity's scent for the attack, but this will leave them no doubt."

Walter ground his teeth. "Then why not kill them?"

"Because *vodraks* are rare, and this may be our only real chance at studying all the toxins at once."

"But if it brings the Borelians straight here..."

"What do you want, Walter Forbes? Do you want a good offense, or to hide under a rock? We have our planetary defenses. I've been informed that the defenses of the other worlds, particularly Earth, ought to be functional within a month."

He sighed and studied her, trying to read her expression and body language. "What is the real purpose of this meeting? What message do you want me to take back to Mi Chin?"

"If the Borelians do come, our first priority is ourselves."

"You would call your engineering teams back? What for? You literally have billions of people on your world."

"The planetary defenses work in such a way that we are completely shielded, completely insulated. No portals may be opened in or out, and we will not leave our people stranded on any other world."

"What do you suggest, then? You keep your technology locked down tight, so we can't continue the work ourselves. You would leave us to die or become slaves?"

"I am only here to inform you of the situation, Captain, not tell you what to do."

Of course, the only time the Tacagans did not dictate to their lower brethren was when it involved leaving those lower brethren to die. How considerate of them to let the meager Neanderthals choose death on their own terms.

"Is there anything we can do?" he asked evenly. "Either to speed things up or...what? We need to figure something out."

The Governor studied him for a moment. "I really don't know that you have much left with which to bargain, Captain. Autonomy is a nice bargaining chip when the threat is still across the field. Now that it's here, it won't matter. If we get destroyed, your autonomy means nothing. If you get destroyed, home world authority will most likely fall to us anyway. So really, we have no reason to help you."

"How about your inner sense of right and wrong and compassion for your fellow man? As I've said before, what moral code do you use to establish yourselves as better than everyone else?"

"The genetic code, Captain."

Walter raised a brow. "Must be nice to be able to blame everything on something other than yourselves."

"The soul is a myth, and we are getting off-topic. Now then, what is it that you want?"

"How about we start with planetary defenses? Now that we have a rough idea of the diseases and toxins and their cures, I would say our bigger concern is making sure we don't actually have to use them, which means keeping the Borelians off our planets."

Milay nodded once. "Very good. I can tell you that as long as Tacaga is safe, our engineers will continue to work on the planetary defenses of all human worlds. With the understanding that Earth will grant us autonomy when it is complete. And when I said that the genetic code makes us superior in every way, we also have extensive reports detailing how we have engineered ourselves to be not only better, but separate from mere *Homo sapiens* like you. We call ourselves

Homo perfectus."

Walter leaned back in his chair and made a motion. "Sorry, I couldn't hear you over the sound of your ego. What was that?"

Her expression was not amused. "That is the deal."

"Yes, yes, we made this deal already. I understand it. Last I heard—Mi Chin's dealings in your meetings notwithstanding—Tacaga will be granted autonomy once the defenses are in place. It seems to me that the question is whether those defenses will get in place if you call your dogs back home before they are complete. How can we ensure that if you won't leave them stranded and you won't teach anyone else how to continue the work? Sounds to me like you're just putting on a show, biding your time until your lesser Neanderthal cousins are wiped clean from the universe. Do I have that about right?"

"Captain, we've had this argument many times in many different forms. You humans are simply too sentimental. Sometimes you have decent ideas, or ideas founded on decent principles, but this has now become a matter of practicality."

"Practicality and survival. You want to dump us, save your own skin, and leave us to die. But you ought to understand better than anyone that we don't give up that easy."

"Indeed you don't, which is why we're here. And once again we have come full circle. You argue philosophy, I argue practicality and basic negotiation. Give and take."

"Hard to bargain with someone who doesn't care whether you live or die."

"Entice me."

"Have your teams stay on the other worlds and finish the defenses, even if the Borelians come and attack Tacaga."

"That's our give. Now what's our take?"

Walter wasn't actually sure. He didn't have much authority over anything, and Mi Chin could always override him. "If your teams become stranded but finish the work, you don't get autonomy." He put up a hand as Milay moved to speak. "You don't get autonomy. You get home world authority. That will allow you to declare yourselves separate and you can hand over home world authority to any other human world you choose, Earth or not."

The Governor sat back and studied him. "Now that is an interesting offer. Don't just give us power over ourselves, but everyone else, too. Give us the power to take the power away from you. See, the problem with that, though, is that with Treman and Trebald gone, all the other colony worlds are exceptionally primitive. They would just give the authority right back to Earth. Then where does that leave us? I'm afraid I cannot accept. Perhaps I will bring it up with Mi Chin at the next meeting." She stood. "Thank you for your time, Captain Forbes."

She left without so much as a handshake. Walter watched her go. She'd been fishing for something and he hadn't given it to her, but what could she have wanted? More to the point, why hadn't she outright demanded it? Sure, Tacagans were self-righteous, but they never passed up an opportunity to make other lesser humans look bad and wave around their flag of intellectual superiority. Playing some invisible mind-reading game was not their style.

Walter stood. Well, what did he know? He was just an occasional visitor, after all. He left the room and again headed for the train station. This time he was not stopped, though the escort fell in around him like Secret Service.

"What are your opinions on other humans?" Walter asked, not expecting an answer. "I mean, asking the governing body is one thing, but what's the word on the street? What do the common people say?"

"You're strange," Dermos blurted before one of his superiors could stop him. "You're not engineered, less than perfect, but you seem to be okay with it."

"Oh, yes, I am truly flawed, but that's okay."

"Why?"

Before Walter could answer, it was as if the whole train car became covered in a shadow as the other members shifted and stared at him, their mood going from annoyed but passive to actively ready to pounce and kill. They feared his answer, feared he would say something religious, something along the lines of, "God made me just the way I am and that's good enough for me." They were afraid of infectious ideas, something that, given time and care, would cause an upheaval of their entire society.

Walter had no desire to get carted off to a dark cell, so he simply answered, "Maybe one day when you're off work, we can go out for a beer and have a chat."

Dermos looked perplexed by his answer, but accepted it.

"Far as I'm concerned," Geros cut in, "you're a bunch of misshapen, hairy humans that we have to parade around for no good reason at all except at the request of the Governors. But hey, it's a job, it's a paycheck."

Other than that, Walter got nothing. So there were those who were genuinely curious, those who couldn't care less, and those who would kill to protect their fragile way of life. Had he really expected something different? Had he expected them to huddle around his feet in quiet glee that their illegal pastor had finally been smuggled into the country to preach to them in spite of the threat of death? These guys were the threat of death in those cases. These were the guys who raided homes and carted those illegal pastors off to dark cells to be tortured for their beliefs.

The train ride suddenly took on a darker meaning, and Walter was more than happy when the doors opened. The escort took him to the main street where they all grabbed bikes and started off toward the bridge.

Walter really didn't mind the bikes. He'd never done a lot of it, maybe because he'd learned it so late and so never developed that childhood excitement, that first sense of freedom. But he'd grown to enjoy it as they navigated the wide streets. For all his misgivings about the Tacagan government and their authoritarian stranglehold on their people, they had accomplished a number of things that Walter wished could be taken back and implemented into Earth society.

When they reached the bridge, Walter's police sense kicked in before his mind could fully register what was happening, and even then, he couldn't make sense of it. People were running, yelling, all of them racing off the bridge back into the city. Some grabbed at their arm or neck or side, others limped, some just let head wounds bleed freely.

Blood. People were injured. Something was happening on the other side of the bridge and it was driving people into the protection of the city. Walter dropped his bike and jogged uncertainly toward the chaos, then stopped. His escort abandoned him and raced past him toward the bridge.

Misgivings or not, people were in danger, and he had a good hunch who was on the other side of the bridge. Well, if it was one thing he knew, it was chaos and trying to help people. He ran to where the peacekeepers had set up some kind of operation on the bridge. Five of them looked to be working cover fire while three more got the injured and confused up and running in the right direction. Dermos and another young gun made sure everyone crossed over into the city proper. Out of nowhere, emergency medical personnel—or what Walter took to be emergency medical personnel—began setting up shop for quick transport-quick turnaround.

One man stumbled across, hand at his neck. When he fell, his hand jolted, and he began bleeding anew, an obvious arterial bleed. Walter jumped in and clamped down on the wound. Half a second later, three medics knelt around him.

"Arterial bleed," Walter reported.

"Who are you?" one demanded.

"Step aside, Neanderthal!" another barked.

Stunned, Walter did not fight back as they pushed him out of the way and went to work on their patient. Why the hostility toward someone who was just trying to help? Was it even worth the blood on his hands now?

He stood and was nearly knocked over by Dermos as he ran past. The rest of the peacekeepers seemed to be congregating for a conference of some sort. Well, what was the worst that could happen? Walter approached, getting close enough to hear without trying to get all chummy as if he was part of them.

"The military is assembling. As soon as they arrive and Dermos brings the bikes, we ride to the nearest station and we have to activate the shell. Other cities are confirming they will do their part as well."

"Is there anything I can do to help?" Walter asked, hoping he sounded both willing and humble.

"I advise you to go home," the lead peacekeeper told him, the first time he'd spoken to Walter in all the times he'd been coming to Tacaga. "Once the shell goes up, no portal may be opened. You will be stuck here."

It was then that the military arrived. At first he couldn't figure out why their uniforms looked so darn bright and even shiny. That could get a man killed, easily. Then it occurred to him that looking from the bridge into the city, it was pretty bright and shiny because of all the technology and the look and feel of the buildings and architecture. It was both camouflage and distraction. Only half of them had weapons, one unarmed person was paired with one armed person, and it took a second for Walter to realize that the unarmed person was a Timekeeper, using Time to augment the armed soldier's abilities as well as confuse the enemy.

Their enemy could not actually be seen just yet, but it was a long bridge after all. In the distance, Walter could see smoke rising from the guard stations. Oddly enough, for as awful as the guards had treated him and the other humans, he found himself hoping they'd made it out. But maybe not. Maybe their only job was to alert the rest of the city to the danger. Maybe he really was too sentimental.

Looking around, Walter saw that the peacekeepers had already gone. There was no telling where the shell power source was or how long it took to power up, which meant he had to leave immediately, or risk getting trapped on Tacaga for an indeterminate amount of time. That thought was rather unappealing.

He no sooner considered it than there was a flash in the sky and a huge energy wave began descending toward the horizon. Panicking, Walter did his damnedest to open a portal as fast and as strong as he could, but he might as well have been telling a kite not to fly in a windstorm, and his portal sputtered out.

He stumbled back a step, the realization not quite there yet. He hadn't moved fast enough, and now he was stuck. Wasn't this supposed to be like in the movies, where there would be another half an hour of time as the hero force battled setback after setback trying to save the day while the army fought off an advancing enemy that seemed impossible to defeat? Then, just at the last minute, when only one hero remained, he would reach a sweaty, bloody hand and hit the 'On' button, saving the army outside from certain defeat and winning the hand of the pretty girl? Then he, Walter, would slip out through the closing door with only seconds to spare, but still long enough to grab his signature hat? No, wait, that was Indiana Jones. What was this that everything went quickly and according to plan? Worse, how could he be trapped here?

Maybe he could wait it out. The shell was down, which meant that no more Borelians were getting in. Wait until these ones were defeated, then maybe there was a back exit the Governors would tell him to use, on the condition that he got out and stayed out. Or maybe they could lower the shell just long enough for him to leave, then snap it right back up.

No matter the case, there was still the problem of the Borelians continuing to advance on the city. He could see them now, on the bridge. It was impossible to judge their numbers, but given that the bridge itself was probably a six- or eight-lane bridge and the Borelians advanced at a little looser formation than shoulder-to-shoulder, he would place a bet on thirty per row, with an unknown number of rows. The Tacagan army had not advanced, still using some kind of firearm-Time combination maneuvers.

And Walter was just standing there like a rubbernecker. Worse, a moving target. Well, no use waiting for his escort if they thought he'd gone. Time to get back to the laboratory.

His bike was gone, which wasn't entirely unexpected, but it meant that his trip to the train station was going to be that much longer, and the running portion of the fit testing was always his least favorite. He probably looked like a fool as he was the only one still on the streets, Mr. Johnny-Run-Lately. In the distance, the sounds of fighting grew fainter and fainter.

He made it to the train station in decent time and hopped on. Part of him wished the ride was longer so he could catch his breath; the other part of him thought the ride wasn't short enough. When the doors finally opened, he about shot off the train, coming up short as his police senses began tingling again.

Something wasn't right here. He could feel it. How he wished he had his gun. Cautiously, he got on the elevator and punched in the laboratory floor. Even before the doors opened, he knew what awaited him at the bottom.

He ducked, narrowly avoiding a lethal strike from a Borelian wielding a broken glass dagger. He twisted and dodged a second strike. Then he Banded and took off down the corridor until he figured he had some good distance between him and them.

All three of them had broken out of the lab. Looking through the glass, Walter saw the entire laboratory had been trashed. Pieces, parts, things, research, all of it broken and strewn about the room haphazardly, as if a bomb had gone off. Do Chien lay on the floor, his throat slashed open so deep, he could have been beheaded.

Taking half a second to size up his opponents, he saw one was purple, another a more muted silver, indicative of an unknown color. Walter had no way of knowing which was the adjunct and which the disjunct—not that it mattered seeing how they were both deadly—but Tarma he recognized just from the broken horn. Presently, she was two colors, gold with pink beginning to blossom around the oil ports in her skin. Pink, why was it always pink that the *vodraks* defaulted to?

He had little time to dwell on it as he could feel them tearing into his Band. One was not strong enough, but the three of them together made a formidable foe which he was forced to yield to. Again, he dodged and twisted and got out of range of their attacks, Banding again so he could look around for any sort of weapon. The Borelians had only their broken glass, but surely there had to be something in the lab, something that said, "In Case of Zombies, Break Glass."

Walter turned his single Band into a variable one, then began throwing up multiple Bands, rotating them in and out. Essentially, it wasn't just moving the target up and down, but side to side and forward and backward and all different directions to keep the Borelians busy while he inched his way toward the lab. The decon unit and all windows were busted, which made getting into the lab much easier. He picked his way in and looked around. Nothing obvious, but there was one thing he remembered.

Do Chien lay sprawled on the ground, throat slashed. His suit was drenched in blood from collar to waist. Figuring it made little difference since his hands were already covered in blood, Walter peeled back one side of the suit and reached in the doctor's pocket. He found the gun and found it fully loaded.

He stood and turned, startling as he found two of the Borelians just inside the lab, straining against his Bands and slowly inching forward. Tarma was not with them; he saw her heading for the elevator.

Walter raised the gun and fired. Both shots found their target, but between his adrenaline, his police training, and his uncertainty over whether Borelians truly were as physically vulnerable as humans, he did not want to stop. He fired again, choosing the muted silver one and firing again, this time at the hip. This one struck true as well, and blood began to well up from the hole. He did the same to the purple, back and forth between the two, in areas he hoped were fatal, not releasing his moving target Bands until the clip was empty.

Both bitoxics dropped dead, blood flowing in a river toward the drain in the floor. Walter almost counted it a victory until he recalled that there was still one more Borelian to deal with, and she hadn't left the area yet. He threw up another Band and found outstretched claws inches from his throat as Tarma sought to kill him, her Band significantly weaker than his own. For once, the fight seemed to be in Walter's favor.

He stepped back and rummaged through the doctor's suit, but could not locate another clip. He did a quick search of cabinets and drawers, but found nothing. Apparently the gun was meant as a last resort, not for extended combat. No matter. In the carnage and destruction, there were always more weapons to be found, including the Borelians' weapon of choice in this fight, broken glass.

Was there any danger to him if he made contact with Borelian blood? The dead ones on the floor, not likely if the exposed oil was no longer being pushed and had to make contact within seconds of being released. What about the living one, though? Walter considered this as he picked up a long shard of glass and returned to where Tarma stood, frozen in time, gaze still wild with bloodlust.

"She can still kill you."

Walter almost cut himself as a new voice broke the silence. He looked around Tarma to see Rifun picking his way through the remains of the decon unit.

"As soon as you touch her Band, she'll touch you. And she will kill you," Rifun told him. "That would be a bad day for everyone, I think. Would you like me to do it?" He held out his hand.

"What's to keep her from killing you?" Walter surrendered the glass. "Or are you just going to use your revolver?"

"Oh, I could use my gun, true, but when the opportunity arises, I enjoy making my enemies suffer, just a little bit. As for how I'm going to keep her from killing me, well, you seem to have forgotten. I've done this before."

Walter watched, stomach churning, as Rifun embedded thousands of tiny Bands and other inhibitors all along Tarma's arms and head, her entire body, rendering her completely immobile. He set them in her spinal cord, to separate the time between messages firing off and when her body would respond. Then he set a Band in her throat. He couldn't cut off the air, but he could cut off the muscular response, keep her from inhaling and exhaling. Finally, he set a Band in her artery, and Walter watched as Rifun pulled the knife across her throat. In the end, not a drop of blood was spilled as it simply clotted in the artery, nowhere to go. The backup would cause congestive heart failure. Rifun took a step back, released all the Bands at once, and the Borelian dropped dead, with not a defensive wound to show.

"Do I hear a...?" Rifun goaded.

Walter sighed. "Thank you."

"You are most welcome. I look out for my own, after all, and you are one of my body guards. Or perhaps a mind guard. I'm not sure. Either way, it still benefits me to keep you alive."

"Good to know I'm still wanted. How the hell did you get in here? I thought the Tacagans activated their shell or whatever their planetary defenses are."

"They did. The catch is, it only keeps out Time. But even the most powerful shield cannot hold back the Akari. And comparatively speaking, their shell is pretty weak. To that end, I've brought the other leaders. Seeing how it's a bit of a mess down here, they're meeting upstairs. Would you like to join us?"

Reluctantly, Walter agreed, but he wanted to clean up first. There was no way for him to know whose blood was whose on his arms, and he would just as soon wash it all off. The clothes would have to wait, but his arms and hands he could manage. He also found a good amount of dirt and broken glass in his skin, which hurt like hell, but he scrubbed it all away. When he finally got himself dry, he couldn't say he felt immensely relieved, but it was an improvement, anyway.

"So, who really did kill those women, Rifun?" he asked, turning around.

"Cassius always wielded the knife," the man replied, his tone and expression unreadable. "I was simply an observer."

"An accomplice, you mean."

"Perhaps."

It was not the answer Walter was expecting, and the man did not expound. Actually, he seemed much more reserved than normal as Walter followed him out of the destroyed laboratory toward the elevator.

"What's the status of the bridge?" Walter wondered conversationally. "Or any other roads in and out of the city?"

"The army is keeping the Borelians from infiltrating," Rifun answered. "With the shell active, reinforcements can't help them. The Borelians are losing numbers and hope. That's a quick summary of things."

Walter shifted his stance and folded his arms. "That's it? No detailed explanation? No quick wit or sarcastic comments? Not even a smirk? Are you all right?"

"Priorities are a wonderful thing, Walter. Given the circumstances, I prefer to focus my attention on keeping my people safe and not dying."

"And here I thought your charming sense of humor came naturally."

Rifun gave him a look. "Sorry, sweetie, but you know how the pill messes with my hormones."

Had Walter turned any redder, he might have looked like Tommen, sunburned to a crisp. But there was the smirk, just as the elevator came to a stop and the doors opened. On Earth, emergency lighting was often red, but for the Tacagans it was blue. And why not? In a crisis situation, one needed to remain calm. Red induced adrenaline and anxiety; blue calmed it down.

They made for a small conference room where the other planetary leaders, including Milay and Toros, were already gathered. Presently, it seemed as though Milay and Kayla were having an argument over the effectiveness of the shield. Kayla tried to explain that the Akari was different; Milay dismissed it as foolish religion, technology that primitive apes called magic.

"You can't ignore something you've seen with your own eyes," Kayla was saying, giving off the impression of a snarling dog, hackles raised. "The Akari is real. The only good news is that the Borelians don't use it, are untrained in it."

"The ones who were," Rifun interrupted, announcing his entry into the room, "are now dead, thanks to me." He cast her a pointed look and put a mocking hand over his chest wound, accompanied by a small bow. "You're welcome, by the way."

"What news from other worlds?" Mi Chin inquired.

"The Borelians were attacking Ehani when I went to get Xoris and Tambu," Rifun reported. "Xoris was dead, the Xalani dead or enslaved, Tambu and the Etlawa not far behind." He continued before Milay or Toros could speak. "I did not see the Tacagan engineers, nor did I inquire after them. I was simply happy to make it out alive myself. But I think it's safe to say that Ehani is lost to us."

"Attack the strongest and the weakest of us," Sem from Vin Lay stated. "Weaken your strongest enemy while crushing your weakest and foraging on their resources."

"They took one of our worlds just as we took one of theirs," Kayla said, folding her arms. "Ehani is the most plentiful in game and forage, good for farming I bet."

"What is their next most likely move?" Andrew from Aleis wondered. "Where will they go?"

"Brelix has very little water and only one small ocean. They are very inexperienced when it comes to naval warfare. They will not attack Dorigis yet," the Dorigisi woman said.

"Sakaria is a wild card, unpredictable in war," a Sakarian giant said. "We are unlikely."

"Vin Lay is industrializing, which means their mines are open," Walter mused. "But Aleis and Hlohi are still largely primitive and undeveloped. Given the choice, with Aleis having some mining operations, my bet would be on Hlohi, work their way up the chain."

He looked at Kayla and the Wolf brothers.

"I disagree." Mi Chin spoke. "The Borelians have taken Ehani as payment for the world we attacked. But there is nothing to be gained by a prolonged siege on a city, and no country has benefited from prolonged warfare."

"Sun Tzu," Rifun stated.

"Brelix prohibits active drilling and mining, and it takes a long time for the volcanoes to push the metals to the surface, to say nothing of the long excavation and refining process. Operations on their colony worlds is what keeps them breaking even on their needs. Vin Lay is the richest planet in many metals with a very stable crust, and many mines are already open. If they hope to continue the siege on Tacaga and engage in open combat, they will have to manufacture weapons and armor faster and on a larger scale than they already do."

"Why attack Tacaga at all, though?" Toros wondered, and Walter wanted to punch him.

"Psychology and practicality," Kayla answered spitefully. "Psychology, because then all other human worlds are going to be looking to you, to make sure that your defense technology works, that it can save them, too. Practicality, because in launching a simultaneous attack on Ehani or any other world, you can't come to help. If you send troops to reinforce Ehani, you leave yourselves open to attack. If you put up your shield, Ehani falls. I'd be willing to bet that the force that attacked the city today wasn't very big, because they wanted to see what you would do."

"We're doing things reactively," the Sakarian giant lamented. "Three worlds gone, and who else must die or be enslaved before we are able to fight back effectively?"

"We took the fight to them once, and this is what it got us," one Dorigisi said.

"It was coming anyway. That's what war is," Kayla shot back. "Maybe this was their plan all along, and it has nothing to do with the planet we burned."

"Maybe we ought to burn more," Lin from Vin Lay suggested. "Rifun, you have enough men to burn all their worlds, don't you?"

Rifun raised a brow. "If a tactic works, we might as well keep using it. We should, however, consider what we will do if that tactic ceases to be useful. There is also merit in figuring out what the enemy is planning and proactively reciprocate their efforts." He glanced at Walter.

"We shouldn't be forced to depend on him," Kayla growled. "What can we do? If we're fairly certain that Vin Lay will be their next target, how do we protect them? I highly doubt the Borelians are going to wait until the planetary defenses are up."

"Is there any way to create the defenses on a smaller scale?" Sem wondered. "If the Borelians are after our mines, what if we made smaller shields to defend the mines?"

"They would only have to dig new mines," Mi Chin answered. "And unless all your people were under the shield as well, they would slaughter you and destroy the defenses. If you did hide under the shields, they would only have to wait you out, starve you."

There was a pause. Surprisingly, it was Toros who spoke. "There may be a way."

All eyes turned to him, Milay's the most hostile of all.

"Having conquered Ehani, the Borelians will require at least a few days to process the influx of slaves. In that time, small defenses may be installed to protect the larger mines as well as the teams working on the larger defense system. Being so close to finishing, they are not traveling and moving around as much; it's more about coordination and finishing than engineering and building." Toros looked at Rifun. "I don't understand how you got in here through our shield, and we can debate it later. But if the Borelians can't do it, then we have nothing to lose by using it ourselves."

"Except our souls," Kayla muttered.

Toros continued, "We can send supplies and store them in the areas where the small defenses will be erected, but it would be up to you and your men to take them anything else they need, through the shield, especially if it becomes a prolonged event. We anticipate that the defenses will be completed within the month."

"And what about the people outside the shields?" the Dorigisi woman asked. "The larger shield may be protected and it may go up as planned, but if everyone outside has been killed or enslaved, we've accomplished nothing. Even now, the Borelians have access to the defense technology left on Ehani. If they figure it out and figure out how to disable it, get around it, whatever, we're done. None of this matters."

Milay lifted her chin indignantly. "Our engineers had strict orders to destroy the defenses if such a thing ever happened. The Borelians will find nothing."

Walter had his doubts, but he said nothing aloud.

Eventually, it was decided that Vin Lay needed defenses, supplies, and reinforcements. The Tacagans planned and negotiated with the rest of them, though Walter could see that Milay and Toros would be speaking long after the rest of them had gone. He was just happy that they even had a way out, even if it was through Rifun. The man returned everyone to their proper places, saving Walter for last and even bringing a small gift. Literally, it was a gift bag, complete with glitter and tissue paper.

"A gift for Tommen," Rifun said, handing it to Walter. "Payment as promised."

"Is this the cure for Borelian pneumonia?"

"It could be. Only way to find out is by using it. From what I've heard, there is no shortage of test subjects."

"You're not wrong there, but what's with the gift bag and glitter?"

"I thought an unmarked paper bag would be a little too suggestive."

"This isn't much better, I think."

"Well, we can stand here arguing about it, or you can take it to him so he can save his little friends. Which will it be?"

Walter took the bag, then spoke before the man could leave. "You know, I still don't like you."

"That's unfortunate for you, I think. Unforgiveness and poison and all that."

"What's this bullshit mission you've got my son on? You wouldn't send him after some holy artifact if you didn't think you would win in the end."

"I always win, Walter, but we're on a bit of a timeline. Julianna and I have simply decided to tie up some loose ends in the aftermath of the war, though small skirmishes do still happen, I will admit, between the Order and the Akarin. It's a messy, complicated business. The easy things, we're outsourcing."

"If finding your sacred text was that easy, I think you would have already done it. It took the murder of a dozen people before you found the second journal in a damn museum. What is the cost of the third journal, I wonder?"

"Higher to the Borelians than to us, I hope."

"Still not given to monologues, are you?"

"Sadly, no. Now then, if you will excuse me, I have other appointments to keep."

Rifun left.

Walter had no sooner taken the gift bag to Tommen's room than the teenager walked in the door, bundled up and covered in snow from shoveling. He began peeling off his layers and tossing them haphazardly over his desk chair. "Hey. How was Tacaga?"

"Attacked. Ehani, too. It's gone."

"Oh, shit."

"Do Chien is dead. The Tacagans had Borelian prisoners from when Rifun's men burned the Borelian slave world. They escaped in the attack and killed him."

"What about the planetary defenses?"

"The Tacagans are boasting safety. We believe Vin Lay is the Borelians' next target, so they're going to send more resources there to beef up security and hopefully get things up and running a little sooner."

Tommen nodded. "Okay. What's that?"

Walter looked at the glittery gift bag still in his hand. "A gift from Rifun. Says it's your payment for a job well done."

Tommen took the bag and peeked inside. "He actually said that? A job well done?"

"Well, he said it was your payment, anyway."

"Okay." Tommen pulled out a heavy cloth from the bag and unrolled it, laying out five syringes full of green fluid. "Looks like the same stuff he shot me up with." He bundled them back up. "Will isn't doing too great. I need to get one of these to him."

"And the others?"

"I don't know yet, but he's the greatest need that I know about right now."

Walter hesitated but nodded. "All right. Go save your friend. Just don't get caught."

Chapter Sixteen
Toll

It took a week and a half for the medicine to work its magic on Will, who had gone unresponsive by the time Tommen stuck him with the syringe. Once again, another day saved, another friend brought back from the brink of death. If there was any good news to be found, other than Will living, it was that he woke up to a cold nose and wagging tail.

"A dog?" he wondered, his voice hoarse.

"Yeah," his mom said. She looked haggard after days, weeks, of crying and praying. "Someone somewhere got you bumped up on the waiting list. This is Sydney. She's a four year old German Shepherd, mostly black, but she's got tan socks and a tan spot on her belly that she likes scratched."

The dog nosed Will's hand and he found her ears to scratch. "She's mine? Like, she's really mine?"

"Yeah. Mom says I have to get a cat or something in a cage," Eli griped.

"Or you can put him in a cage and have two pets," Tommen told Will, dancing away as Eli tried to punch him in the arm.

So it was that a few days later, once the worst of the sickness had passed and Will was on the mend, that the blind teenager walked out of the hospital, mom and brother on one side, best friend on the other, with Tommen walking beside Sydney who faithfully did her duty to keep Will out of harm's way. Mostly, Tommen's job was balance control on the ice, though he had a hard enough time staying upright himself, never mind helping anyone else.

As for helping others, Tommen chose to help Becky's dad who

had also taken a severe hit from the disease, Mrs. Reisig the English teacher who had saved his sanity on a number of occasions, one total stranger just as an act of kindness, and then he pocketed the last one. He didn't necessarily keep it for himself or because there was a lack of patients, but more as a just in case. If there was some kind of disease resurgence and he needed a dose, he didn't want to go crawling back to Rifun.

Of course, the man was busy doing other things, anyway. While he did take supplies through the Tacagan shields to help the Vin Lay who had come under siege by the Borelians within the last week, his interest lay more in the offensive on the Borelians, taking the fight to them while minimizing the chance of retaliation. Although, to see the man at all lately, one wondered where the smirking hero of the fortress battle had gone. His new, more demure attitude was frightening. Maybe that was what lethal wounds did to a man.

Concerning other things, Tommen still went to see the shrink, and it was getting to be an easier and easier conversation. He still didn't tell anyone he was seeing a shrink, least of all Becky. Since she'd recovered, they'd gotten back into bed, and the sex was better than ever, or it was in his mind. Of course, as far as he was concerned, the sex was always good, and he focused on that as he pumped hard, listening to Becky's ragged gasps beneath him.

"Oh, I missed this," she whispered, pulling him down and close. "I would say I don't know why I waited so long in the first place, but I do, and I think the anticipation was worth it." She gasped again. "And I'm glad I chose you."

Tommen was barely listening as he finished and went limp, sweat making his skin sticky. He lay there on top of her a minute or two longer, then rolled off and blindly reached for his undershirt to wipe his face.

It was Sunday morning, the last Sunday in January. Walter was still at work, Becky's dad was back to work, and her mom was at Mass. Becky had begged off Mass, citing Tommen's essays. He'd gotten most of them submitted, but he still had two more to finish before sending it in before the Saturday deadline.

"You think you can focus a little more now?" Becky wondered, rolling over and kissing him. The farthest he'd gotten was just getting his essays loaded on his computer before getting, ahem, distracted.

"Are you kidding?" he said. "There's a beautiful naked woman in my bed, and you expect me to just focus on something else?"

"Very true. Guess we'll just have to change that."

With that, she got off the bed and grabbed her clothes. Once she was fully dressed, he reluctantly followed suit and plopped down at his computer.

"Okay, okay, where were we?"

Walter got home about ten o'clock. A lot of the guys had returned to work following their illness, but the station wasn't quite back to full force. Although, given the severe staffing shortage, they wouldn't be at full force even with all their guys back. Nevertheless, the shift coverage requirements had eased up just a little.

"Morning, kids," Walter greeted, meeting them in the kitchen. "Up a little early, aren't we? Don't teenagers normally sleep in until noon on weekends?"

"Fear of the alarm gets us up early," Tommen told him, flipping a pancake.

"Well, you're not entirely wrong there. It carries into adulthood, though, so watch out."

"Going straight to bed?"

His dad nodded and yawned. "The shorter shifts are nice, but it only serves to remind me how exhausted I am. And anyway—"

He stopped as his phone rang. Rubbing his eyes, Walter answered. "Morning, Laura. A little early, isn't it?" Pause. "What's wrong?"

Tommen slid the pancake onto a plate and stopped, watching his dad whose expression got grimmer and grimmer.

"I'm sorry to hear that." Walter stepped out into the breezeway and pulled the door closed.

"What's that all about?" Becky wondered, stealing a pancake

from Tommen's plate. "She dumping him?"

He shook his head. "No, her dad's been sick for a while, and then he got hit with the flu-monia. Judging by the conversation, I think he might have died."

"Oh no. That's terrible."

Tommen shrugged. "It is what it is."

"Yeah, well, I don't think that's how you saw it when your dad was dying in a hospital."

That gave him pause, and he elected not to answer. It was easy to forget the emotional trauma and turmoil he'd gone through when his dad was in a coma, the hell he went through to bring him back. It was easier still to dismiss someone else's pain. Was he a callous person for thinking so?

His dad returned a few minutes later.

"Her dad die?" Tommen guessed.

Walter nodded. "Yeah, just this morning. Funeral is Saturday at one."

"Are you going?"

"If I can make it."

He said it mostly just because of present company; Tommen knew his dad would be Banding, driving to Minnesota for the funeral, then Banding and returning home for his shift. It wouldn't be fun, but it was the right thing to do.

"All right, I'm off to bed," Walter announced. "You kids be good. And don't use up all the pancake mix."

Tommen picked up the empty box and shook it. "A little late for that."

His dad scowled but headed to his bedroom.

"If he would have said something earlier, I wouldn't have suggested it," Tommen said.

"Can't go back now," Becky said, taking another bite.

They finished their pancakes and returned to the essays. Tommen managed to get one polished up and submitted before two o'clock, at which time he declared himself done for the day. Becky agreed, and they went out to watch TV. Tommen paused long enough to Band his dad, but continued on to the living room as if nothing had happened. His dad got up about twenty minutes later.

"So when are you guys going back to normal shifts?" Tommen wondered.

"Well, a couple of the guys are set to come back Wednesday. I got Wednesday and Thursday off. After that, in theory, we should be back to normal, or close enough. We're also supposed to be hiring in a couple of guys sometime next month, but it'll be a while before they're on the schedule on their own, off probation. The biggest problem, though, is that you guys used all the pancake mix and all but two eggs."

"Sorry. You never said not to."

"I know, I know. Maybe tomorrow I'll stop at the grocery store on my way home and pick up a few things."

Of course, the payback for Tommen and Becky eating all the pancakes and eggs was Walter eating the last of Tommen's favorite cereal. Well, all's fair in love and war, and food was no exception. Tommen watched in forlorn silence, even as he could feel Becky's smirk from the couch.

"What's on the agenda for today?" his dad wondered, washing his dishes and joining them in the living room for a bit, kicking Tommen out of his recliner.

"Got one of my essays finished and submitted," Tommen answered. "One more to go."

"Good for you. Anything come of them yet?"

"I probably won't hear until February or March."

"You've got enough essays and applications out there; I'm sure you'll get a little something at least. Anything helps when it comes to chipping away at college tuition."

That was certainly true, but at seven in the morning, Tommen's biggest concern was how crowded it was getting in his car, and making sure Sydney's nails didn't poke holes in his seats. He laid down a towel, but he was still paranoid about it as the dog eagerly hopped in the car, as excited as any dog for a car ride. Will climbed in on one side, Becky the other, Eli taking his new spot in the passenger seat.

"So, how was Sydney's first week at school last week?" Becky asked, giving the dog a scratch behind the ears. Sydney lowered her head to give Becky a lick, then nosed her handler to do the same, which Will did lovingly.

"She was a little nervous, a little jumpy. Most of the other students don't understand not to mess with a service dog, and she may have piddled a little on the gym floor because of it, but it was good, anyway. And because I know you're going to ask, Becky, I'm fine, too. Yesterday was the first day in weeks that I woke up feeling normal. No coughs, no sneezes, no aches or pains, none of it. And we're getting to know each other, me and Sydney. Aren't we, girl?"

Sydney was a service dog, but she was a ham, licking Will's face and trying to lay down for a belly rub, but unable due to the confined space and her working harness.

"Get a room," Eli said loudly.

The brothers bantered back and forth the entire ride. While Tommen was glad everyone was back in good health and in chipper spirits, he was glad to get rid of the brothers at the front door of the school. With Sydney loyally by his side, Will no longer really needed Eli to help him, but it seemed to be force of habit, and Tommen circled the parking lot to find a spot, Becky right behind him gathering her things.

"It's starting to smell like wet dog in here," she complained as he parked and turned off the car.

"I know, I need to clean it out. One of these days when I'm home and my dad's still at work. And I don't have essays to work on and I'm not doing anything else."

"Like what?"

Traipsing across the universe on an Easter egg hunt for a madman, meeting foreign diplomats, confronting space pirates, exploring old monasteries, that sort of thing. "Making love to a beautiful woman."

She kissed him on the cheek. "Aw, you're just saying that."

They headed inside, shaking off the snow, and snaking through the halls to their respective lockers. Things seemed to be back to normal, or as much as they could be. The flu-monia was still an epidemic, no doubt about that, but it had worked its way through the school and done what damage it was going to do. There was a notable absence of some students and one teacher at the high school, and counselors had been called in, but otherwise, things were normal. Students came in, bell rang, students went to class or lunch or wherever the bells told them to go.

Only a year left, Tommen told himself. Four months left in this year—well, four and a half, considering all the time they were going to have to make up at the end of the year—and only a couple semesters next year before dual-enrolling. Wouldn't that be nice, to move on to higher education that actually mattered?

He was just heading to meet Becky at her locker when his phone rang.

"Hello?" he wondered, unsure why the number looked familiar.

"Good morning, is this Tommen Forbes?" The voice was male and sounded a little hoarse, just getting over something, probably the flu-monia.

"It could be."

"This is Chris from Rock Construction. We interviewed...a few weeks ago and then pretty much the whole crew, myself included, got hit with this virus that's going around, so I never got a chance to get back with you."

"Oh, yeah. Yeah, hi."

"I just wanted to touch base, see if you were still interested or if maybe you'd found another job somewhere or what was going on."

"No, I've been sick myself and busy trying to play catch up with school and everything. I haven't even really given it a thought."

"Perfectly understandable. Now, to that end, we're playing catch up ourselves with all our jobs that kind of got abandoned for a week or two or three. We could really use some help. If you're interested."

"Oh. Wow. Yeah, I mean, yeah, that sounds great. I'm in, I'm interested."

"Great. Are you available this afternoon? We can get you some tax paperwork and go over where the job is, what's expected, that sort of thing."

"Just at the office?"

"Yup. How does three-thirty sound?"

"Sounds good."

"Great, see you then."

Click.

Tommen shoved his phone in his pocket and raced to tell Becky the news. She was happy for him. When she lamented about never seeing him on weekends, he reminded her that she was usually wrapped up in her sewing anyway. The last three weekends, he hadn't seen her, either for sickness or work. Then she complained about not being able to drag him to Mass or the synagogue. He felt a little relieved until she figured out that she could take him to the evening services instead. Personally, he was banking on her being too wrapped up in her sewing to notice the time and would miss both.

Will and Eli were happy for him, too, though Will complained that once his community service was done and he was home free, he wouldn't have anyone to hang out with on the weekend.

Tommen began to question whether he should have taken the job.

Nevertheless, he walked into the office that afternoon with his head held high, ready to work. Truthfully, he was ready to start getting a paycheck again, but ready to work.

He'd almost forgotten how confusing tax paperwork could be, which was a little strange considering he'd done it less than a year ago for the children's camp. On top of that, he also had to sign a bunch of waivers saying he wouldn't sue the company for his own stupidity, agreeing to get put on the company's insurance, and saying he understood all his rights as a minor worker. He couldn't work more than ten hours a day on the weekend, couldn't work past eight o'clock on the weekends or seven o'clock on weekdays, and so on. According to Chris, his days would be running nine to seven, Saturday and Sunday. Chris didn't see any use in having him work only a few hours during the week because the cost of gas wouldn't be worth it.

It was a wonder the twins had gotten away with working him as much as they had.

But the pay was plenty good, even as an entry-level minor. Twenty hours of construction was easily equal to full-time at the bakery. And hey, he might even learn a thing or two.

"All right, now that your body and soul belongs to us," Chris said, taking the completed paperwork and filing it away, "we'll see you Saturday morning." He scribbled on a notepad and handed it to Tommen, an address. "Be there at nine o'clock. We'll be there at six, so don't worry about finding us. See me, and I'll get you pointed in the right direction. Sound good?"

"Sounds good."

"Okay, let's get you a few things. Follow me."

Tommen followed him into a locker storage area where he pulled out an array of safety equipment. He spoke while he set them out. "You'll need to get some steel-toed shoes at least. We'll provide the hard hat. We also keep gloves, glasses, ear muffs, and masks handy in case you need them, but if you have your own special stuff you want to use, by all means, be comfortable. All safety equipment is mandatory. If I catch you without glasses or what-have-you, you're fired. As soon as you enter the construction zone, whatever equipment we're using, it better be on. Safety is number one. Got it?"

"I understand."

"And I don't care that maybe all you think you have to do is take out your hearing aids. Actually, I do care. I don't want your hearing loss to get worse. You wear muffs right along with the rest of the guys. *Capisce*?"

"Capisce."

"That's *'capisco,'* but it doesn't matter, I suppose. You get it."

Tommen tried on hard hats and gloves until he found a set that worked. Chris gave him a couple of labels to mark them, then went to one of the lockers and put another label on it, right over a faded tag reading, "Mike C."

"This locker is here for your own use, but they are randomly searched. I wouldn't recommend leaving food in here, but I would advise a second change of clothes, first aid kit, things like that.

"Sometimes we'll do some prefab work here in the barn, or smaller restoration projects on the side. If there's going to be some severe weather for a couple of days, rather than send you all home empty-handed, we'll do some precise labeling, measurements, planning, and we'll come here and do some cut work. Then the next day we're out on site, we already have our shit together and can just start laying stuff. That way we're not playing catch up."

"Sounds smart," Tommen commented.

"It won't replace a forty-hour paycheck, but it's better than nothing. Any questions for me?"

"Not that I can think of."

"Well, it's only Monday. Think of anything between now and Saturday, just shoot me a text."

Tommen left the office in a daze. It was official. He was employed. He was going to be doing construction work. He was going to get a paycheck again. He arrived home, found his dad already gone to work, and texted him.

"Just signed the tax paperwork for Rock Construction."

It was a few minutes before his dad replied. "Very good. When is your first day?"

"Saturday. Nine a.m. at some place north of town."

"Good for you. Excited?"

"Excited to get a paycheck again."

"You're not poor."

"No, but I would be if I went too long without working."

"Mind if I quote you to all the welfare recipients out there?"

"No, go ahead. Anonymously, though."

"Afraid of a little angry backlash?"

"I have bigger things to worry about; I don't need to add that to my list."

"Fair enough. All right, good night, kiddo."

"Night."

Tommen headed to his bedroom, momentarily startled but not surprised to find Rifun on his bed, reading one of his Authored Books, thermos in hand.

"Comfortable?" Tommen wondered.

"I am, thank you," Rifun answered, not looking up. "But if you're offering, I would appreciate something to eat. I'm in a mood for pork rice."

"Very funny. Why are you here? Journal study was just Saturday night. And actually, I was getting ready to come see you and tell you that I'm ready to make my way to Psia for the next leg of my little treasure hunt."

"Excellent. Glad to hear it. Unfortunately, that will have to get put on hold for a couple of days." Rifun closed the Book, set it aside, then looked at him. "There have been a couple of developments."

"Has Vin Lay fallen?"

Rifun shook his head, swung his legs over the far side of the bed, and stood. "No, nothing like that." He took a drink from his thermos and faced Tommen. "Vin Lay is holding out quite well, all things considering, though morale is low. Actually, the developments have to do with the Order. On the one hand, the Akarin attempted an uprising this morning. It was quelled quite successfully, though there will be some clean-up that must be done over the next day or two."

"Which is why my mission is delayed."

"Part of the reason. The other reason has to do with your little negotiations concerning the Turitians."

"Hey, I went into that completely unprepared. I tried to play it safe, but that was a bit of a blindside on my part."

"And whose fault is that? And perhaps I misspoke. It has less to do with the negotiations themselves and more with the meeting as a whole. Seems as though the Turitians have been approached by the Hands and the Grandfathers, much like the Elif but with less violence on the part of Tacaga."

"So they rejected the offer, I take it."

"How we're responding is not your concern. My concern is how the Hands found out about it."

"They probably read the mail. I sent a message to the Turitians through the Wheel. I didn't know how else to do it."

"Your knowledge on how to do things has very convenient gaps in it. The good news, though, is that this was planned for."

"Why ask me about it, then? And what other message route can I use?"

Even as he asked it, Tommen knew the answer. He could have gone to Turit directly beforehand and requested an audience, cut out the middleman entirely. He took an even breath. "Okay. I get it."

"Good. The only reason I bring it up is so you know that we are watching. Now then, what are your plans for your next adventure?"

"Go to Psia, find out the whereabouts of Titik, ask him what he knows."

"Why? If Dira didn't have the authentic journal, he wouldn't either."

"If he was desperate enough to attack a royal emissary looking for it, I bet he'd be royally pissed if and when he found out it wasn't the real thing either. And I'd bet he'd try to track down some more information on it, too."

Rifun nodded thoughtfully. "Interesting line of thought. I look forward to seeing where it goes."

He made as if to leave, but Tommen stopped him, saying, "So, if you guys are cleaning up from some uprising and this whole thing with the Turitians, when should I make plans to leave?"

"Saturday. After studies. I'm sure a little knowledge and insight will provide ample motivation for the journey afterwards. In the meantime, I would work on polishing my social niceties and such.

After all, that is why it took so long for you to be prepared this time around, right?"

Tommen reluctantly agreed, and Rifun left.

In truth, he hadn't gotten a ton of studying done on Psia or Titik, though he'd had more than enough time. With little else to do that evening, he found himself in the Archives again.

Oddly enough, Psia was not actually the original Psiaco home world. The home world had been struck by a life-ending meteor, wiping out all Psiaco on the surface like the dinosaurs. The Psiaco who were left—which were those in their small spaceships or in the Wheel—went to a nearby solar system where they found a suitable planet. The planet was not uninhabited; however, the people, the Urid, were quite primitive.

For a time, the Urid worshiped the Psiaco as superior gods and basically handed over all control to them, allowing them to colonize and rule and set up their elite Time Academies. Well, then the Urid got smarter about their superstitions and beliefs, and there were currently some severe race wars going on, the Urid almost always on the losing side as the Psiaco had never seen fit to share their superior technology with their loyal subjects.

Captain Titik, despite being Psiaco, apparently held no prejudice, for his pirate ship was crewed by Psiaco and Urid alike. Or it had been. Digging deeper, Tommen found that a little over a year ago, Titik had been fatally wounded in an attack by a Psiaco policing vessel. His wounds were healed and he lived, but he was permanently disabled. According to the Psiaco Laws of Justice and Mercy, the disabled were not permitted to be held in traditional prisons, so he would remain under house arrest for the rest of his life for his crimes.

Well, at least it made him easier to track down, so they didn't have to go hopping from place to place, actively looking for trouble as if they didn't have enough of it already.

Tommen returned home without incident and went to the bathroom. When he got out, he found Rifun again waiting for him.

"What did I do this time?" Tommen wondered.

"It's not what you've done, it's what you're going to do. The Tacagans are ready to launch the planetary defenses on Vin Lay. Once that's done, you're going to help me evacuate the engineers."

"What about the Borelians already there?"

"The Vin Lay will take care of them. Food and medicine aren't the only things I've been taking them."

Tommen nodded. "Okay."

"I'll get us there, but you'll be opening portals of your own from Vin Lay to Tacaga. It's a little more difficult because you are inexperienced, but it's not much different than the portals from your bedroom to the fortress."

"What about the shields?"

"You'll feel the resistance, but it's cake to break through. The Akari cannot be bound by such feeble means. Let's get moving."

Even just walking through the portal, Tommen could feel the resistance from the smaller shield that had been erected. Rifun was right, it wasn't difficult to break through.

They landed on a hillside looking up into enormous rock formations and cliffs. The sun was well below the horizon, but there was still light in the sky. Looking around, there was little evidence of civilization except for carvings in the stone around the mouth of a cave and steel supports to keep the roof from collapsing. Behind them, in the valley, an enormous war camp with tents as far as the eye could see—which wasn't far considering the expanse of rock formations, but Tommen had little doubt that there was a pretty good force down there. The only thing that separated them was a shield that could only be seen in the right light or with special, filtered glasses.

"I'll take you in to meet this team," Rifun said, starting up the hill, "then I'll go meet the team I'm evacuating in another mine. I have other operatives ready to evacuate the rest of the teams. Once you're done, go straight home."

"What if something happens?"

"Do what you can. I'll check on you. I have a feeling that I'll be done before you."

They approached the cave and were greeted by two sentries. Tommen became acutely aware that he did not have a translator on him, but yelling and waving arms and interpretive dance worked just as well, right? After all, he was just going to open a portal to Tacaga and send them through, right?

Tommen had envisioned the mine as being small, cramped, dark, and scary enough to make one think the roof was going to collapse at any second. Actually, this mine was enormous and well-lit so it might as well have been daytime. Ribbons of green copper split dark black stone the whole length of the tunnel until it opened up into an even bigger cavern the size of a football field. Mining equipment was moved aside to make way for a huge encampment where ordinary Vin Lay civilians made the best of their situation. Women tended to small fires while children ran around and played games or listened to their elders tell ancient tales.

"This way," Rifun said, and Tommen realized he'd moved off several yards.

"How many people are down here?"

"The planet itself hosts a population of just under a billion. This is the smallest of the mines, and there are several open chambers like this one. There are probably a million or more people down here. The largest mine is packed with over ten million."

"Holy shit."

They left the cavern and entered a smaller tunnel, following the twists and turns, making a left at one junction and a right at another, stopping and breaking off into a cave probably three miles or more underground, where a team of Tacagans stood around a huge, well, it looked like a solid silver dome. Tommen flicked through the filters on his glasses until the dome sprang to life in a brilliant display of electricity.

"This is your team," Rifun told him. "They'll tell you when everything is in order and they're ready to go. I'll see you in a bit."

Then he left, and Tommen and the Tacagans were left staring at each other. The Tacagans regarded him with obvious disdain, that they had to be rescued by a Neanderthal, and a teenage Neanderthal at that. For Tommen's part, though, he was glad that this was a lot less pressure than he thought it was going to be. He'd been anticipating a big red countdown clock with red and blue wires, Borelians trying to break down the gates while the engineers worked frantically to finish the last of their work.

In comparison, this was rather dull. After a few more minutes of glowering and glaring, the Tacagans went back to doing whatever it was they had been doing before the intrusion. Tommen could not pretend to understand what they were working on, but he watched with fascination anyway. Just as well that they didn't have translators or they would have annoyed the hell out of each other before anything got done.

He sat there for a good fifteen minutes, watching them work, wondering just how long it took to fire these things up. Maybe because it was a new world and they wanted to make sure everything was done correctly, or it just needed a longer initial boot up. Maybe because they had to get the timing right, pulling the small ones down and getting the planet-wide one up with as little gap in coverage as possible so more Borelians couldn't storm the castle. Maybe—

"Initios," one Tacagan said suddenly.

All but one stood back from the machine while the one who had spoken began tapping. Invisible keys suddenly came to life in an array of colors with Tacagan words scribbled on them. The dome began to hum and glow, and a round port suddenly opened up at the top. Tommen wanted to get closer, but the best he figured he could get away with was an earnest lean from his spot on the wall.

A second Tacagan took a spot on the opposite of the dome and tapped more buttons. A panel opened up, revealing several dim lights. Gradually, they began to light up. One, then two, then five, then all nine, all yellow.

It was like watching NASA, waiting for the counting, waiting for them to say, "Go for launch." Fuel, check. Oxygen, check. Supplies, check. Courage, check. Okay, boys, let's begin the countdown. From one hundred.

The Tacagans did not say much, but worked and reported with the highest level of professionalism. Tommen was pretty sure they were just ordinary dudes on ordinary days when it was just them in the lab, but now that there was a Neanderthal outsider in their midst, they had to turn up the snobbery to an eleven, just to make sure everyone knew who was in charge and who was really going to save the day. Because obviously.

"Domosi ete parati," one engineer reported, looking at all the green lights. *"Esspetos vox sui."*

It was infuriating, really. English stole a lot of Greek and Latin words. Spanish was a Romance language, so it was based on Latin. And yet, the Tacagan language felt just out of reach of understanding. But there were a few words Tommen could make out with little difficulty.

"Pink, quasse, tre...do...eno...jam!"

More buttons were pushed, and suddenly the whole dome lit up green. Switching filters, Tommen could see the shield go up. One by one, the yellow lights on the one side turned green.

Then the Tacagans were moving quickly, speaking hurriedly amongst themselves and filing out of the room. Confused, Tommen followed them back through the tunnels to another small cave. What looked like some sort of TV camera was set carefully in the middle of the cave. One of the Tacagans went to it while the rest stood aside in a group. The one Tacagan looked at Tommen.

"Parato?" he asked.

"Um...I'm ready when you are," Tommen offered lamely.

In too much of a hurry to make any snide remarks, the Tacagan fiddled with the camera-like apparatus and the smaller shield around the mine went down.

"Jam! Jam!" he shouted.

Tommen nodded, suddenly feeling the pressure to escape. He had little trouble thinking about Tacaga and feeling it out; he was even relieved when he found the shield and could push through it. A small portal flickered to life. He seized on it like one might to pry open stuck elevator doors in an action movie. Gradually, the connection established itself and solidified until the portal was stable. Tommen felt dizzy and nauseous, but he motioned for the Tacagans to go through, which they did without a second glance or even a thank you. As soon as they were through, Tommen let the portal snap closed.

He sat with his back against the cool stone wall for a minute or two until the vertigo subsided. He was getting better at opening the portals, but it didn't seem to be getting any easier.

Down here in the tunnels, he didn't hear anything from the chambers, and certainly nothing from the outside. Were the Vin Lay and the Borelians engaged in battle even now? Should he go look? Should he offer some kind of help? He felt like a coward for running, but then, his track record in combat was less than stellar; it wasn't even average. Maybe he really should just go home as Rifun had ordered.

He was less enthusiastic about opening another portal, but this one was more familiar, almost second-nature, comparatively speaking. He stepped through and clambered to his bed, peeping at his clock. A little after nine. So why did it feel as though he'd been up half the night? Sighing, he rolled over onto his back and closed his eyes.

Tommen figured he must have slept somewhat, for his clock read one-thirty the next time he rolled over to check through blurry eyes. Grudgingly, he sat up. He couldn't say quite what woke him; his eyes were still tired, and his body was starting to feel sore, but for the moment, his mind was awake. He fumbled with his hearing aids and leaned over to set them on the charger, but when he swung his legs over to get up, his feet hit something soft. Startled and still half-asleep, Tommen leapt out of bed and hit the lights.

Rifun lay on the floor, unconscious, blood matting his hair on his forehead. A quick glance at his computer desk told Tommen everything he needed to know, as there was blood and hair and splintered wood on one corner.

How long had Rifun been lying there? Should he call 9-1-1? No, he didn't need to invite more trouble. The cops would hail Tommen as a hero, but Rifun would not be contained by a mere jail cell.

He did have one idea, though it was kind of a mean one. Tommen went into the bathroom and opened up the medicine cabinet. Rummaging around, he found the bottle of alcohol. He considered using the small spray bottle, then decided against it. With Rifun still out on the floor, Tommen flipped open the lid, turned the bottle over, and gave it a squeeze.

Rifun writhed, his body contorting in pain, drunkenly rolling over into the side of Tommen's bed, struggling to come back around. The best he managed was getting up on one elbow, head resting against the box spring. He stayed that way for a long minute before getting his whole body around onto his stomach and elbows, rubbing his face. He tried to get up too quickly and went down hard on one knee, one hand covering his eyes. Eventually, he sat back and rested his elbow on one knee, eyes still covered.

Tommen made no sound or movement.

It was another minute or two before Rifun took his hand away from his face, and only then did he notice the blood. He touched the wound and flinched. Then he looked up and saw Tommen.

"What the hell happened?"

"My guess, you came to my room, had a seizure, hit your head on the corner of my desk there." Tommen indicated the corner in question. "You forget to take your meds this morning?"

"The meds and tea only serve to keep the seizures under control; it doesn't stop them completely. And I've been doing a lot of running around today."

Rifun got up from the floor, but only made it as far as sitting on the edge of the bed, resting his head in his hands.

"You okay?" Tommen wondered cautiously. "Like, the seizures aren't getting worse or anything, are they?"

"No, I expect not. Or not that anyone's told me. But a splitting headache is bad enough when it's not compounded by a secondary head wound augmented by a generous amount of alcohol." He gave Tommen a look.

"Would you have rathered I call an ambulance?"

"I suppose not."

"What's the word from Vin Lay?"

Rifun let out a breath. "They're going to be fine. Some areas are going to be under siege for a short time, going back and forth between Borelian and Vin Lay forces, but the shield is in place. No more Borelians can get in. Of course, if any of the Borelians manage to break into the mines and disables one of the shield generators, that could be called into question. From what I understand, though, that's not likely to happen."

"I assume there was another meeting on Tacaga following the activation of the shield?"

"There was. Our gracious Tacagan hosts were humbly grateful for the return of their beloved engineers." He shook his head.

"What about the defenses on the rest of the worlds?"

"Up and running within the next week to ten days."

"Won't NASA or someone detect them?"

Rifun chuckled dryly. "NASA is the one putting it in place. Protects us from meteors, falling satellites and other space debris, and will improve everyone's TV and cell signal by fifteen percent. The details aren't my department."

Tommen studied him. "Let me ask you something. Other than this whole seizure thing, which I think is becoming less and less of a factor seeing how you have meds and seem to be getting used to it—" He ignored Rifun's glare. "—do you really think helping save humanity from the Borelians will absolve you of your crimes against the universe and those you murdered?"

"Does it matter? The Borelians will enslave all of us, regardless, and they'll take particular joy in enslaving me, I think. I'm saving my own skin as much as everyone else's, and as it has been pointed out, I'm the only one crazy, stupid, and brilliant enough to pull off half of what we're doing. And I have an army."

"But you're hoping that, if we succeed, some people out there might be persuaded to look the other way."

"The Elif did. The Turitians do. There are others out there. That's the wonderful thing about morality being subjective throughout the universe."

"And you hope to bring them all under the absolute morality of Richard's journals."

"It's a lofty goal, I admit."

"Yeah, but...what if the Author's morals are different from yours? I admit, I'm only in the first stage of the first book and we have a test coming up, but what if?"

Rifun smiled tiredly. "I like you, Tommen. I really do. Always questioning. Always wanting to know, to understand, to be anchored in something." He sighed and stood deliberately. "But all answers do not come in a single night. Keep studying for your test, and be ready to leave on your mission soon after."

"Are you good to open another portal?"

The man nodded. "One last one, straight into bed."

He left without another word, and Tommen was suddenly alone in his room. Actually, bed did sound pretty good. He still had school in the morning, after all. Problem was, as soon as he climbed in and closed his eyes, he came flying awake in paralyzing fear. His chest was tight, body rigid, mind screaming at him to get away, run away, go anywhere.

Quietly, he sat up and looked around. Everything looked calm, normal, everything exactly where it was supposed to be. It was still dark out and he didn't hear anything unusual outside or elsewhere in the house.

As he ran through his mind everything that looked normal, his muscles relaxed and he could breathe again. If he'd had a nightmare, he couldn't remember what it was, and the only lingering emotion was confusion. Had he been pursued by Shadows again? Had Chandler been there? The White rabbit? Was it a nightmare about the warehouse? The Halloween bombing? Any number of other things his imagination could conjure up at a moment's notice? He didn't know. He wasn't sure he wanted to touch on it and bring it back, either.

He nearly went through the room as his alarm went off, and he stiffly reached to turn it off. School. Just another day of school. Nothing sinister, totally normal.

He did not hear anything else about Vin Lay, save that they finally killed the last of the Borelian forces early Thursday morning and no more had broken through the shield.

Do Chien was dead from the attack on Tacaga, and most of his work had been destroyed, so now they were dead in the water on the toxin research.

Tommen also did not see Rifun again until Saturday when the man came to retrieve him for journal studies. He seemed back to his normal self, albeit his more reserved self. There was no sign of the head injury from Monday night.

"How was your first day on the new job?" Rifun asked, his old sarcasm leaking through.

Tommen shrugged. "Good, I guess."

"Construction, right?"

"Yeah."

"Are you even sore?"

"Not really. It was just kind of an introduction day and I did a little clean-up work is all."

Rifun shook his head somberly. "Kids these days. Well, no matter, you have a busy night tonight. Come on."

He opened a portal and they stepped through without issue.

"How are things with the Turitians?" Tommen asked cautiously. "I didn't totally screw things up, did I?"

"As I said, we anticipated a situation like this, so we were prepared for its possibility." Rifun's tone was dismissive.

"Is there anything I should know about the Order's relations with the Psiaco or Urid before I screw those up, too?"

"The Urid have no involvement in Time. They have not been exposed and the Psiaco have not seen fit to change that, with the race wars as bad as they are. As for the Psiaco themselves, they have numerous elite Time Academies. They're the token puppets of the

Time industry and the Hands. You would do well to avoid explicit mention of the Order or your mission except to those absolutely necessary."

Tommen nodded. "Understood."

"Now then, do well on your test. When you're done, come see me and we'll get you sent off on the next leg of your adventure."

They parted ways, Rifun to some important business or another, Tommen to his journal test.

It was still a strange thing to go to studies, mostly because he was considered the star student, if only for the fact that he was human and he spoke English. He was always called on to read the day's notes, always picked first to recite the homework. It was as if he were the professor of the class, though the instructor was more knowledgeable about the content, even if Tommen did have to correct his pronunciation from time to time. That alone was a strange thing to consider, that he was correcting someone else's English. It made him feel special. Feeling special in this particular class made him feel sick.

He hadn't heard from or seen Chandler or the White rabbit in almost a month. How was he supposed to fight against the Order and their constant propaganda when he only heard from the other side every so often? If he was going to the fortress once a week, he wanted to talk to Chandler twice a week, not once a month. He tried reading and rereading his Authored Books, but he'd lived those stories. The parts that he hadn't been witness to, he was coming to memorize into dull drudgery. He wanted more. He needed more. If proving the Order wrong was so damn important, why did the Author seem to remain silent on the matter?

Class was a little more anxious than normal as Tommen walked in, but the fact that there was a test might have had something to do with it. Students were quizzing each other, some on the knowledge and information itself, others just on the sounds of the English language, trying to make alien vocal chords and appendages conform to foreign sounds.

Tommen resumed his superstar status as soon as he was

recognized, and a number of his classmates flocked to him, asking questions about everything. It was kind of nice to be wanted, to be recognized for genius—or what they perceived as genius—but it was also a little overwhelming. Okay, a lot overwhelming. But it was nice, too.

He was saved by the appearance of the instructor who sharply told them to quiet down and be prepared to be called in any order. And by "any order" that clearly meant Tommen first and everyone else was picked randomly. But Tommen first, because he was special. Maybe Rifun had requested he be tested first so as to get it over with and get on with him mission faster, but Tommen suspected that he was singled out because he was the class superstar. Human, English speaker, Faharoa's favorite.

Testing was done one-on-one, for obvious reasons. The instructor took Tommen to a small room that might have served as a broom closet at one point.

Anything that required simple, rote memorization was easy. Memorizing things word for word and repeating them back was simple. Memorizing names and dates was cake. Remembering the details of those people was a little more difficult. That wasn't to say it was too hard or he had trouble; there was so little really known about the Beloved characters that it was more a matter of remembering which character accomplished which thing, a single sentence as it were, versus a whole biography.

Kalian, orphan girl tasked with finding the owner of a mysterious locket. Rebecca and Thoreau, doomed lovers, like Romeo and Juliet. Faith, a story best forgotten. Tobias, the last of his kind to survive a nuclear holocaust suddenly faced with his own death. Half-Face, prince turned assassin hellbent on revenge and restoring his honor. Strikeslayer, a shapeshifter and general of a vast army of shape-shifters. Shadow-Come-Reaping, a servant under a blood oath and sent to betray and kill her own people. Allison, a story of intrigue and betrayal and forgiveness if there ever was one. Carmen, a woman stripped of everything and given a chance to start over.

There were a few other minor characters that he only had to know the names of, and it all concluded with Richard, considered the final Beloved character, the last the Author would write in an attempt to communicate with her creation.

And that was that. It was ridiculously easy, really, for Tommen, but again, he spoke English. That was half the battle for almost all of the other students.

He was dismissed and told to go on his way, saying nothing of the test until everyone had gone. The next unit was going to be even more in-depth on each of the Beloved characters. The reasoning, he was told, was that the subsequent classes took longer to complete, so they had to make time for them. On that line of thought, going over the material again would ensure they had a solid foundation for future classes.

All Tommen really heard was that they were going to be going over the same damn thing again. And maybe even a third time. Could he just test out and move on? Was that possible? Was there an AP course he could move into, one where everyone already spoke English so he didn't have to wait for these morons?

"You look troubled, my young Apprentice."

Tommen found Rifun in his quarters. He was not scheming or plotting or doing anything more sinister than sitting on his bed and reading a book, his seizure tea in its thermos sitting innocuously on the floor. Even evil rulers needed some down time, Tommen supposed.

"Are there any classes out there where everyone already speaks English?" he blurted.

"Frustrated with your present company?" Rifun did not look up. "I don't blame you. I haven't the patience for them either, which is why I don't teach the lower classes. Or the upper classes, for that matter. I lead, and I lead into battle."

"Yeah? So how's this desk job working out for you?"

"It's a nice vacation from the woes of other human worlds and the thrill of battle with the Borelians."

"Some people go to Europe, or, you know, Africa or someplace for vacation."

"You forget. Africa is my home. What vacation is there in that?" Rifun took a leisurely drink, through his expression betrayed his real thoughts of the tea.

Tommen folded his arms. "Do you ever go back to Madagascar? Do you have any family?"

"I go back frequently, yes. As for family, sorry to say, I have none." He turned a page.

"When are the others supposed to be here?"

"You aren't the only one who had testing today. Suffice to say, later levels have harder tests. They take longer to complete. Be patient. Have a seat if you want."

Tommen did so. "What meds did you say you're on?"

"Midazolam and tarka root tea. Why?"

"Because they are seriously fucking with you. I don't know how else to say it. They are fucking with you."

"We've all undergone some changes in the last few months, I think."

He could not argue with that, nor could he press the matter as Naq walked in the room, but something was going on here. Rifun had been way to placid for way too long. Maybe it was the meds. Maybe it was his brush with certain death. Maybe it was something else entirely which Tommen was unaware of. Whatever the case, something was up.

The other members of his team filtered in slowly, looking exhausted and relieved from whatever testing they'd been involved in, but also ready to get moving on the next phase of their mission. It was a little easier to stand before his group and address them, now that he knew each of them a little better and what was expected, both of him, their group, and the mission at large. Rifun moved politely out of the way, choosing to recline on his bed and not interfere, still reading his book and drinking his tea.

"Today we're going to Psia to speak with Captain Titik,"

Tommen began. "Even if the journal he stole wasn't the original, if it was worth attacking a Turitian emissary for, he may have further knowledge of it and we cannot discount him as a source of information. About a year ago, he was wounded and permanently disabled. Psiaco law prohibits the imprisonment of the disabled, so he is under permanent house arrest. This will make him easy to find.

"The difficulty comes in consideration that the Psiaco are not friendly toward the Order or the Akari in general. If Titik is under house arrest, given his notoriety, there is almost guaranteed to be guards or other corrections officers there to oversee him." Tommen had no way of knowing whether this was true, seeing how he'd neglected to actually research what Psiaco house arrest entailed; one of his many blunders in this leg of the journey, he was sure. "It may be beneficial to attempt to distract the guard or otherwise separate the two. This is entirely dependent on the situation as we find it. Yes, Sisith?"

"In studying the politics and laws of Psia, I came across the information that you have described, Captain Titik being under house arrest. However, recently, within the last few days, the Psiaco courts have heard cases from his overseers describing him as insane. They seek to move him to an asylum. Security has been doubled."

"Thank you for looking into that; I hadn't found anything. Likely that will make it more difficult for us to speak to Titik alone." An idea sparked in his mind. "But maybe not. Again, entirely situational. With any luck, this will be a quick in and out and we can move on to the next part of our journey. Hopefully we can wrap this up pretty quick. Any more questions?"

He paused for a moment, but his team was silent. They understood their jobs; they understood their mission. They only waited for word from their fearless leader.

"Very well, then. Ilit, take us to Psia."

Chapter Seventeen
Captain Titik

The planet Psia boasted a total combined population of one billion. The Psiaco only made up about thirty-five to forty percent of it, less when one considered that about half of them served or resided on a space vessel of some form. In total, only about twenty percent of the ground population on Psia was actually Psiaco.

The Urid were not part of Time. They were not even considered advanced enough to begin to develop methods for space travel, nor imagine the possibilities beyond superstitions that warred with their exposure to the space-going Psiaco. To put it politely, they were a species in transition. It was a roll of the dice as to the response if they ever did see a real, actual alien.

Never mind six. A Human, a Dimica, an Arowa, a Qalik, a Yakik, and a Siboxi.

They'd no sooner touched down than Tommen found the first glaring error in his otherwise brilliant plan. He could easily blame Ilit for dropping them in such an inconvenient location, and for a minute, he debated doing so. Ilit was their travel agent, so to speak. Sisith was the political boni, Rorion the social boni. Between the three of them, someone could have mentioned that the Urid were Scientifically Modest and Unengaged. He might be the leader, but they had their own parts to play, too. They needed to do their own research, too, and in the course of a month, they could have done a lot of research.

That line of thought felt childish and hypocritical, if only for the fact that he should have remembered to mention all that, too, among other points of research he missed that were sure to make themselves known throughout the day.

Truth be told, the Urid and Psiaco were a lot alike, physically. If the Psiaco were modern man, the Urid were like the knuckle-dragging cavemen everyone envisioned on TV. Both had two sets of arms and human-like skin, but the Urid were bulky, top-heavy, and got around like chimpanzees. They also had only two eyes and more pug-like faces. The Psiaco, however, were humanoid and walked upright, balanced in their weight distribution, though they also had spider-like qualities about them, or so Tommen had read though he did not quite understand what that meant. Further, they had four eyes and a longer, more muzzle-like face.

It was strange, the things one thought about while hiding in a small crevasse. The sight of six monster aliens suddenly appearing had roused the Urid to a primal curiosity that quickly turned into primal anger, and Tommen and his ekipa had fled into a forest where they now hid in various places, most of them in small caves and other cloven rocks. It was thrilling, but also embarrassing. No doubt Rifun would have something to say about it when they got back.

Tommen was just about ready to step from his hiding spot when the stillness was broken by some kind of grunting and snuffling just overhead. He remained very still and quieted his breathing, though he could do little to calm his racing heart. Small pebbles and dust bounced off the rock on either side of his hiding spot and he resisted the urge to sneeze. Something sniffed on the ledge, sending more dust into the crevasse.

Something huge suddenly slid to the ground in front of Tommen. His chest seized, but he refused to make a sound. The thing looked something like a panther crossed with a bear crossed with a wild boar. It faced away from Tommen, its nose in the air. Finally, it turned south and carried on.

Still, Tommen waited a good three minutes before daring to poke his head out of the cave. All seemed clear, but he switched to his infrared filter and looked around, just to be sure. He saw all manner of birds and small mammals, but no sign of any Urid or the larger predator. Feeling a little more secure, he allowed himself a sneeze as he brushed the dust from his clothes. He jumped at a sound, but it was only Sisith and Ilit.

"Never a dull moment," Tommen commented. He glanced at Ilit. "Maybe next time, if you can help it, don't drop us in the middle of a primitive, Unengaged society."

"My apologies," the Qalik said humbly.

"Where did the others get off to?"

They found Naq hiding in the burrow of something about the size of a fox. Emet was stuck in the cave he'd found, and it took the four of them to get him out. Rorion had the best camouflage of all, seeming to melt into a nearby riverbed with her watery skin. Other than Emet who was a little flustered about getting stuck, no one seemed too worse for wear given the chase.

"What do we do now?" Rorion wondered, looking at Tommen.

"Well," Tommen sighed, "we need to figure out where we are and where Titik's staying currently. And we need to do it without tipping off the local pitchfork mob."

He actually had a rough idea of where Titik was being held. His hometown was located in a south central country on the northern continent. When given the choice of where one wanted to spend the rest of one's days, Tommen bet few strayed too far from home.

"The Urid village was called Ch'tak," Rorion stated. "They are located in the northwestern prefect of the northwestern country on the northern continent."

"How far to the south central country?"

"Five thousand Earth miles."

"Shit. Ilit, you think you can get us there? Closer, anyway?"

"I will try my best."

They got to the south central country at least, though the northwestern prefect. The good news was they landed only a couple miles from a Psiaco village. When they entered the city, they were not run out by an angry, primal mob, but regarded civilly and approached by only a couple.

"Welcome, strangers," one Psiaco greeted. "You are evidently guests from other parts of the universe through the Wheel of Time."

"That is correct. I am Tommen Forbes, Timekeeper from Earth, Quadrant One, Parsec Eleven, Sector Five, System Four, Planet Thirty-Eight, Region Four, District Four. These are my associates. We're here looking for Captain Titik."

The Psiaco grunted. "I see. So, they have come for him. Very well." He shifted position. "You will need to speak with Keeper Lehr to take custody of him."

"We're not interested in custody," Tommen said quickly. "If he is truly insane, as the rumors have been, there is nothing to be done for him, and justice will be empty. He will only take up space in the Judgment Wing. We would rather leave him to you to dispense justice as you see fit, as he will understand."

"Fair enough. You will still have to speak to Keeper Lehr to get directions."

"Where can we find this Keeper Lehr?"

They were directed to a building that Tommen could have sworn came straight from an old Western movie, the saloon with the swinging doors, where cowboys would tie up their horses and rustle up an ale at the bar, where the sheriff and the bank robbers would have a good old-fashioned shootout at high noon. Walking inside, there was even a bar along one wall, though it did not appear to serve any kind of alcohol that Tommen could see.

"Can I help you, travelers?"

Again, Tommen expected to see the sheriff sitting behind a desk, shiny sheriff badge on his vest, revolver at his hip, pipe in his mouth, ten gallon hat on his head, absently fiddling with a wood carving or harmonica. Instead, this Psiaco stood behind the bar and wore a gray or faded black short-sleeve shirt over a cream long-sleeve shirt and simple blue pants. Several badges were attached to his shirt on the left side, one on top of another like the beginning of a Boy Scout sash.

"We are here to interview Captain Titik," Tommen replied, throwing in a dash of self-importance, "to see if he is worth our time or if we can leave him merely in your custody."

"From the Wheel, then." The Psiaco moved out from behind the bar. "Fair enough, I suppose, though we would like to soon be rid of him." He paused. "He still lives in the southeast prefect. He is scheduled to be moved to Esra asylum in three days."

"Would it be smarter to go to him or have you bring him to us? We'll wait."

"Safer to have you go to him. Insanity gives a man unusual strength. We want to move him as little as possible in order to minimize chances for his escape before he reaches the asylum."

"Very well. Where can we find him?"

"He is kept in a country cabin, one of many once owned by merchants who would sell or rent them to new couples or ill-advised lovers. It is three hundred eighty-four ri to the southeast, at the edge of the Cistern Forest, in the valley between the forest and the foothills of the Amethyst Mountains, the last great plain before the Southern Sea."

Tommen had a hard time deciding whether the man was just displaying his national pride by describing the territory, or showing off and waiting for his idiot audience to beg for more details and better directions. Whatever the case, Tommen had work he needed to get done. He had to be up early to be on the construction site, after all.

"Rorion, how far is a ri?"

"One ri is equal to one-point-three-six Earth miles or two-point-one-eight Earth kilometers," the Dimica recited flawlessly. "Therefore, it is five hundred twenty-two miles or eight hundred thirty-seven kilometers." She looked at Ilit. "A Qalik ken is zero-point-seven ri, therefore, two hundred sixty-eight ken."

Keeper Lehr, while he had not moved, did not seem at all pleased that he had been undermined. Tommen made sure to meet his annoyed glare with a smirk. Fucking hell, he really was turning into Rifun, wasn't he?

"Ilit, you think you can get us there?" Tommen wondered, not breaking eye contact with Keeper Lehr.

"With such specific directions, I think it can be done," the Qalik confirmed.

"Excellent. Thank you for your help, Keeper Lehr. Is there anything else we ought to know before we depart and speak to Captain Titik?"

"No," Lehr said stiffly. "Nothing at all."

Tommen had his doubts. No doubt there would be all manner of angry bears, barbed wire, booby traps, gate guards, and other tests of strength, skill, and teamwork before they could speak to a raving lunatic. It's just how it was, after all. A whole Book had been written about his one week adventure to Sifura's world. Would this little adventure to find the third journal spawn its own novel? Did he really want to read about it afterwards?

They left the saloon, Lehr's glare following them the whole way out. No one on the street paid them much mind except to glance at the alien strangers in their midst. Seeing there was no immediate threat, life went on as normal.

"All right, Ilit, you really think you can get us there?"

"I can."

He opened a portal, revealing the edge of a forest looking down into a valley, foothills rising on the opposite side, the faintest glimmer of an ocean twinkling at the end of the valley, almost invisible as low clouds were beginning to roll through, promising weather of some kind later in the day. Tommen stepped through with little trouble, followed by his team, Ilit the last to come through.

It was a very pleasant scene, in actuality. The trees were a little different, and the mountains were unfamiliar, but otherwise, it was almost like being back home. There was no orange grass or purple moon or anything to really throw it off-kilter, just a scenic mountain valley, like one might find on a postcard. Tommen breathed in the fresh air and looked around from his vantage point.

With his glasses adjusting to the light and climate, Tommen could more clearly see the gleam of an ocean in the distance, as well as the town that had sprung up haphazardly around it, buildings sprawling here and there up one hillside or another. He did not see any real evidence of farming in the valley; he did not see long fields of crops or even tilled soil, just grasses and wildflowers, pristine and untouched, waving in the breeze.

This soft carpeting was interrupted by one small building, squatting low. Had it been Earth, Tommen might have said it was an abandoned homestead, late nineteenth or early twentieth century construction. Going down there, he might have expected to find a museum's worth of artifacts, crumbling remains of an old foundation, maybe a fallen barn.

But from his view, Tommen could see that it was not dilapidated, nor was it abandoned. There was movement in and around the cottage.

"That's got to be the place," he said, hopping off his rock. "Or at the very least, it's a good place to start. Let's go."

He hoped he sounded confident and not arrogant. Just down the slope, a well-traveled road followed the tree line toward the ocean, but there was no evidence of a road or even a path leading to the little cottage. Time to make a path, then, Tommen figured, pushing into the tall grass, his group following.

That was when another glaring error in his plan became evident, not doing research on the local vegetation. He was still clothed in his heavier winter gear, but his hands and face were still exposed. He didn't have any known allergies beyond the common seasonal ones, but he had a good idea of what an allergic reaction looked like. The first problem came as the soft carpeting of the grasses and wildflowers turned into razor weeds that sliced his hands bloody and tugged and tore at his clothes. The second problem came when his arms began itching and he pushed up his sleeves to reveal red bumps covering him probably to the shoulder; his hands and wrists looked positively purple. Given that his left arm remained twisted gray-white scar tissue, he figured it wasn't a good thing for there to be that kind of sudden blood rush because of an allergic reaction. Was that swelling and edema? That looked like swelling and edema. Shit.

The wild vegetation ended abruptly, and the six of them were deposited onto a freshly-manicured lawn stretching about sixty feet in all directions from the cabin. They were immediately swarmed by Psiaco guards in tactical gear.

"State your name and business!" one demanded harshly.

"Tommen Forbes, Timekeeper from Earth, Quadrant One—"

"Are you here to take custody of Morain leRou Titik?"

"No, we're here to assess him to see if he is worth our time and resources. We've already spoken to Keeper Lehr. If Titik is as insane as you believe him to be, then we don't want him. But first we have to interview him to make that determination, to make sure he isn't getting off easy."

For a long moment, the Psiaco regarded them, and Tommen was certain they would turn them away. Finally, the circle around them loosened.

"Very well. See that you interview him well."

Tommen was not certain how to take that statement, but he gave them a curt "thank you" and moved past them.

The cabin itself was not large, certainly not larger than the cabin he'd grown up in as a child. Tommen counted probably ten to fifteen guards in total, and he couldn't imagine more than one or two living there, three to five if they really wanted to cram in there with no personal space. Maybe it was a matter of rotation, that half of them were always on watch. But still, where would they get the food and water to sustain fifteen men? Where would they store it? Did they get daily deliveries from the town just down the valley? And where did they go to the bathroom? The Psiaco had to have invented indoor plumbing by now, but this cabin looked like it predated modern amenities, and even so, this had been originally built for new couples and ill-advised lovers, not as a hotel where hundreds of people used the toilet every day.

Construction appeared crude, but it was sound, Tommen saw. Stone and mortar on the outside gave the cottage a charming, rustic feel, while smooth, polished wood on the inside made it look more like a luxury log cabin for rich snobs who didn't understand true country living. The roof outside was thatched, but the inside was heavy rough-hewn beams and long, thin planks. The same rough-hewn beams were exposed in the doorframes and smaller beams used for the windows.

There were only three rooms in the cottage. The largest room appeared to be living quarters and a kitchen. On one end, a massive stone fireplace that would make *Better Homes and Gardens* jealous dominated the space, making oversized furniture look like it belonged in a dollhouse. Just outside, wood was stacked along one wall, covering the window. On the other side of the room, a single wash basin sat between two huge cabinets that may have been small closets. The door to one of the other rooms was closed, but the second was wide open.

Another, smaller fireplace took up most of one wall in the smaller room, but it was the only thing of note, really. In one corner, an ornate chest with a massive lock sat, unobtrusive and almost unnoticeable. In another corner, an old wooden chest of drawers with a number of scuffs and blemishes, like one might expect to find at a garage sale, or at the end of someone's driveway with a "Free" sign taped to it. There was no bed, only a huge wingback-style chair, positioned so it looked toward the fireplace and the window, but did not directly face either one. Perhaps the most noticeable thing were the chains draped down either side of the chair and attached to the floor. By Tommen's estimate, there had to be some kind of underlying stone or brick for the chains to be shackled to, because the floor alone was far too weak to hold if enough force was exerted.

It was evident that a Psiaco sat in the chair, but it could have been as much a statue as a living being for as much as it moved. Gingerly, Tommen moved around to face the figure.

Everything Tommen had read about Titik said he was a grand, brutish figure, much like a space version of Blackbeard who had been a giant of a man. Titik was supposed to be huge, imposing, extremely muscular compared to most Psiaco, lips pulled back in a fearsome snarl, a weapon in each of his four hands, insane in his own right, but with a certain cunning that made men tremble when they spotted his ship coming toward them.

The one who sat in the chair now was nothing like that. To describe him as ever having been fearsome and imposing would have elicited laughter. Psiaco by themselves were tall and spindly, not exactly muscular; their domination of the Urid had been gained and held through primitive worship and superior technology. Here, now, Titik was even less than that, rubbery skin stretched over thin bones, no muscle tone to speak of, plain gray clothes hung loosely about him like a blanket. Both right arms were missing, one at the shoulder, another partway down the upper arm. His upper left hand was missing, leaving only his lower right arm and hand completely normal. His head was lolled to one side, one eye lazily drooping, the other three staring at something only he could see. An old, dusty hat sat on the other side of his head, about ready to fall off; even so, the hole in his head was evident, likely the source of his insanity. His muzzle was torn and scarred so that his lips did not come together on the right side, but remained twisted open, revealing the last of his fury—sharp, snarling teeth that no longer held any malice. Indeed, he seemed to be gnashing his teeth or muttering silently to himself, but Tommen could not make out the words. He did not give any indication that he even knew anyone else was in the room. And the guards outside were worried about him trying to escape? Tommen had never worked in a nursing home, never even been to one, but Laura had a few stories about little old men and little old ladies who were apparently more crafty and clever than this lump of flesh sitting here now. Could it really all be a ruse?

"Morain leRou Titik?" Tommen questioned, willing his voice to be strong and not break. It wasn't fair to treat people differently because they were old or disabled or both, but he just didn't know how to interact with them, especially on an alien scale. Thoughts of Julie, his special needs lab partner in Chemistry, came to mind.

The man did not respond, just kept muttering to himself.

How were they supposed to get information out of him? Maybe this was a bad idea.

"Morain leRou Titik, my name is Tommen Forbes. I am a Timekeeper from Earth, Quadrant One—"

Now Titik's muttering turned into something that might have been a laugh, a quiet one, but a laugh. He choffed at the end, then said, "You're a liar. All of you. Liars, all." He laughed and choffed and gnashed his teeth. "You lie. You didn't state your rank. Timekeepers love to state their rank. Makes them feel important."

Suddenly he was coming up out of the chair with more speed and strength than Tommen would have thought possible from such a twig. He snarled, "Liar! Liars! Guard, liars!"

Four guards were in the room at a moment's notice, wrestling him back into the chair and removing a link from the chains that held him, holding him down even tighter. Titik hissed, but his three good eyes were fixed on Tommen and his group. The guards offered to stay, but after some assurances from Tommen, they left the room, saying they would be right outside the door if needed.

Titik hissed again as Tommen put up an Akari Band. "Liars..."

"We don't have time for this," Tommen said, putting up his best wall. "We need some information, and you have it. So you're going to start talking."

"Talking, talking," Titik echoed. "Words are like weeds. They spread where they are not wanted and cut all who come in contact with them."

The stinging and itching and discomfort in Tommen's arms quickly came to the forefront of his mind. He beat it down. "You were once invited to train at one of your people's Time Academies, yes? So you are gifted."

"Gifted...some like to call me special. Some did, some did. I was special to them. They wanted to train me, groom me, put me in charge, put me in command. Lead the way."

"Lead where?"

"Lead, lead, lead, rhymes with Hand, yes? It only makes sense."

Tommen glanced at Naq, who clarified, "It does rhyme, in the

Psiaco tongue."

"Lead, lead, but I did not want to lead, not along their path. They said my ideas were the same as theirs, but they were wrong. They wanted blood for power. I simply wanted money. It's the only real pleasure of the world."

"You're talking about killing Urid."

Titik shook his massive, slender head. "Not the Urid. The Reaping. Done so many years ago. So many Hands, so many leads." The captain repeated his dull rhyme several times, choffing and hissing. "Pull too many threads and the cloth comes undone, the secret is revealed."

"You're talking about the Dispersal."

"Scatter, scatter, and scatter they did. They thought they reaped blood and vengeance, but they only scattered the puppeteers. But puppets cannot hold their own strings. With no one to hold their strings, the puppets collapsed, until the time came for the puppeteers to return. And so they have, along with the puppet master."

The strange thing was, Tommen found he understood some of what Titik was saying, or he thought he did. "What was your part in the Dispersal?"

Titik lurched again against his chains, but did not attempt to attack. Whether it was his own will of restraint or had something to do with Emet stepping forward, was unclear. Rather, he merely got in Tommen's face. "Money. Gather the money, save the money, protect it. Hoard it. Spend it. Do what I want, but always save a little part for the puppeteers. They would need it."

"Why?"

"Insurance."

"Against what?"

"The future. They would go to the future. I would stay behind. You might say I was a puppet, too, but I was free for a time. No strings attached to Titik." He choffed. "And protect. I had to protect them. It wasn't much, but others stayed behind. Keep them busy, keep them occupied. Keep them away from the puppeteers. Build the future the puppeteers wanted."

"Why could the puppeteers not protect themselves? Why could you?"

"I am Captain Titik!" the man roared boastfully. "I outmaneuvered six fleets of Riduri war vessels and four more Sikal speed cruisers! I alone navigated the Widurian Asteroid Belt and I held the Prince of Turit hostage!"

Tommen nodded. "That's what we want to talk to you about. You didn't attack the Turitian emissary to hold their prince hostage. You attacked them because you were after something High Commander Dira had in her possession. What was it?"

"Keeping..." Titik repeated the word several times in several different ways. "Keeping, keeping, yes. She kept it, but she didn't have it, not at all. A book not full of lies, but lies itself. Not to be trusted. Not for the power, but for the money, yes. Hold the prince, get the money."

"Did you take the book?"

"Take the book to the puppeteers, that's what they said. But it was a book of lies, the book a lie itself. You are all liars. But money is real. The money was good. Hold the prince, get the money. Why need the book? Money is the only pleasure in the world. Powerful men, weak men, all that matters is money, for we all die in the end, do we not?"

"What happened to the book?"

"The lie died, but the truth survived. Hidden among words. Weedy words. In the heart of a deep, dark hole. The puppets protect it. But they don't know it. Their greatest enemy hidden in their own home, placed there by the enemy of mine enemy."

"The enemy of my enemy is my friend," Tommen recited. "What did you do with the book, though? Did you lose it, destroy it, give it away?"

"Gone now. The lie died, but the truth survived. Protected by the enemy." More choffing. "Pull the strings, pull the threads, make the puppets dance. Money is the only pleasure in the world."

"If the truth survived, where is it?"

"In the home of the enemy. The truth, covered by a lie. Put there by another enemy. Enemies all around. Enemies of enemies, betraying more enemies and becoming friends. Enemies everywhere. They surround you, Tommen Forbes. But to find the light, first you must travel to the heart of a black hole. And come back."

"I hope you're speaking metaphorically, because no one has survived a trip into a black hole."

"They survive every day. Every day, people dance around a black hole, dance in it. The difference is, most simply choose not to come back. It eats them. Consumes them. Money is the only pleasure in the world, after all."

Tommen rubbed his eyes. He'd expected Titik to have little information because the journal he'd taken from Dira had been fake. He'd expected to find less information if the man was supposed to be committed to an asylum. What he'd found was either profoundly mad or profoundly genius, and he couldn't decide which. Was the man truly insane, or was this just a cover up? He looked around at the others in his group. "Leave us."

"I advise against it—" Sisith began, but Tommen cut him off.

"Leave us. It'll only be for a few minutes."

The others glanced uncertainly at each other, but assented. Tommen dropped the Band and let them file out of the room. The guards outside stopped them briefly, but soon enough, only Tommen and Titik were left. Titik had gone back to his nonsensical muttering. Tommen got down on a knee to better look at the man.

"How did you get that hole in your head?" he asked.

Titik stopped muttering, but did not answer immediately. Finally, "The puppeteer controls the puppet, but the puppet master determines the story and the movements."

"Who is the puppeteer?"

"But who inspires the puppet master's story?"

"Who is the puppet master?"

The captain tilted his head. "And when there are two puppet masters with different stories, how do you know which to watch? Who is right and who is wrong?"

"Who are the puppet masters?"

"One has shown his face. The other...remains a mystery."

"Who is the one who is known?"

"I have not seen him. But his face is known."

Tommen shifted position. "Titik, who put this hole in your head? Were you shot?"

The captain choffed again, breaking into uneasy laughter. "I have been shot at, shot through, shot by, shot into, shot over, shot under —"

"Who did this?"

Tommen tapped the flesh just around the hole and pulled back just in time as Titik lurched against his chains, swinging his massive muzzle around and nearly taking off Tommen's hand. The Psiaco captain hissed like a king cobra.

"Who did that?" Tommen asked sharply before Titik could speak. He stood with only an inch or two between his nose and the captain's fangs. "Who put the hole in your head?"

The captain merely hissed at him and settled back in his chair, muttering angrily. Tommen regarded him silently for a moment longer before dropping the Band and leaving the room. He looked at one of the guards.

"How does Psiaco puppet theater work?"

The guard was taken aback, probably by the off-handed nature of the question. "Puppet theater?"

"Just as a hypothetical."

A couple of the guards looked at each other before the one being addressed answered, "The puppet master directs the theater, writing the stories and determining which puppets ought to be used in a given show. The puppeteers are the ones who actually control the puppets."

"So the puppet master is only the choreographer and doesn't necessarily control any puppets himself."

"Sometimes he may, but mostly he watches only the

puppeteers. Why?"

"Oh, just something he said that caught my interest."

"Titik has been insane for some time now," another guard said. "He says many strange things."

"But if you are interested, there is a puppet theater in the town of Forlan, just down here in the valley," the first guard continued.

"Thank you," Tommen replied, "but not today. You may resume your work as you were."

He walked away and met his group outside the cottage where the first Psiaco guard to question them was again questioning them. As soon as he saw Tommen, he directed his questions thusly.

"And what of Titik? Are you taking him?" he demanded gruffly.

"Not today," Tommen informed the guard. "But we may have need of him in the future; his ramblings may not be entirely crazy. For now, though, you may take him to your asylum. I assume he won't be going anywhere else once he is there. If we need him, we know where to find him." He went on before the guard could speak. "I trust you will inform Keeper Lehr of our decision. We have a lot of other work today that needs to be done, after all." He continued, "Ilit, if you could, we need to make a detour down the valley."

The Qalik looked uncertain only for a moment, but complied, and the six of them left the cottage without so much as a "thank you" or a "goodbye." Everything within Tommen screamed that it was bad manners and he ought to be ashamed of himself, but it was the part he had to play.

They ended up only a stone's throw from the edge of town. Here, the buildings were enormous, and while the ocean could not be seen, its thunder could be heard and even felt. Nevertheless, Tommen requested another portal back up to the side of the mountain overlooking the valley, where they'd first come through before walking through the razor weeds.

In retrospect, he probably should have taken a quick trip into town, to see if there was a doctor who had ointment for the wounds on his arms which were purple, swollen, bleeding, and itching like mad. But hindsight and all that, he supposed. He had some thinking to do. He found a quiet spot a short distance into the trees, sitting on a rock that afforded him a decent view of the valley. He sent the rest of his group back to the fortress, instructing them not to tell Rifun or Julianna anything until he'd returned.

Rifun had already made pacts with the Turitians during his revolution. He could have asked them about the journal at any time, but chose not to, instead sending Tommen to make sudden intergalactic negotiations.

If Tommen was reading Titik's story correctly, he'd had some dealings with Rifun in the past, before the Dispersal. Granted, Rifun had taken a pretty good leap into the future through the salt cave, but at any point, he could have gone back to meet up with Titik.

Unless, that was the point. Rifun knew Titik had one of the journals and assumed he'd kept it safe. He goes back, finds out Titik had abandoned the mission, so he shoots him with his shiny revolver. Titik is rendered half an idiot, now Rifun sends Tommen to him, not for information, but to see if he's blabbing.

But that didn't make sense either. They'd already discovered that the journal was fake; they'd learned that last time, under Dira. There had been no real reason to seek Titik after that, and Rifun hadn't stopped them, nor offered any advice. More to the point, Julianna had given the journal to another man, with no guarantees that it would end up in Titik's hands.

Something was missing from the puzzle, and Tommen was torn between continuing his mission as planned and backtracking to the monastery on Kath, or seeking out the men Julianna believed betrayed her, who were apparently as invisible as the journal.

The lie died, but the truth survived, protected by the enemy, placed there by another enemy, unknown to all. Pull the threads and make the puppets dance. The question then became, who were the puppets? Who were the puppeteers? And finally, who was the puppet master? Or masters. Two puppet masters, pulling different strings on different puppets, telling two different stories. Which one to watch, which one to believe?

Or could it be that Titik really was crazy, and Tommen shouldn't put any stock in any of his words? What then? He was left sounding like a loon himself with all his talk of puppets, but with no further information that might lead to the discovery of the third journal.

Looking down the valley, the cabin sat, unassuming amid the razor weeds. Tommen glanced at his arms. Swollen against his shirt sleeves, he might have thought himself muscular, but he knew better. He needed to get something done before there was permanent damage. He couldn't afford any more permanent damage to his left arm, and he didn't need to start on his right, either.

His first stop, then, was home. He only had seasonal allergies, and they were mild, but his dad got them pretty bad and usually kept some over the counter allergy meds somewhere in the bathroom. He found the package from last spring with only a couple tablets left. He popped them out of the packaging and took them out to the kitchen to crush up. Homeopathy wasn't his strongest suit, but he used honey to make a crude, sticky resin which he lathered on his arms as best he could. Within sixty seconds, the swelling started going down, and his color returned to almost normal. He figured he probably should have washed his arms of the blood first because it was also involved in the sticky mess and made it look like he'd just gutted a deer.

He let the resin harden on his arms, then waited about ten minutes before peeling it off, much like he would peel off rubber gloves, though it was a little difficult considering both arms and hands were covered and he still only had limited use of his left fingers. Pollen and slivers from the razor weeds were stuck to the bloody resin, but his arms felt a lot better. They were no longer purple, the swelling had gone down, and, while he hadn't realized it until now, the hot fever was greatly diminished as well. He used a light Band to give himself a few more hours of healing, then used his Funnel Band to siphon the resulting pain away from his left arm.

Briefly, Tommen considered making up another resin and trying again, but he was out of the allergy medicine and didn't have the time. He still had to report back to Rifun and, somehow, get enough sleep before getting up for work. Paychecks were nice, and the later starting time wasn't bad, but there had been something pretty darn nice about being able to sleep in on the weekends. Maybe it was just him.

Glancing longingly toward his bedroom, Tommen opened a portal to the fortress. He considered trying to tap into the supposed emergency exit portal room on the eighth floor, in a hidden back room off of Rifun's chambers, then decided against it. For one, Rifun probably wouldn't take kindly to the sudden interruption or invasion of privacy, and two, Tommen had little desire to get sucked into a black hole if he failed. Best just to play it safe, go to the portal room he knew...and climb thirty-two flights of stairs. At some point, his endurance should increase, right? Or was that just a fantasy he was fooling himself with?

Maybe next year he should join the cross country team; then he could train by running up and down these infernal stairs. No cross country course was worse than this; of that much, he was convinced. He paused when he got to the top, bent over, hands on his knees, breathing heavily. Fucking hell. Finally, he knocked.

"Hiditra."

Walking into the room, Tommen was forced to wonder whether Rifun slept at all, or if he just had Julianna or someone else Band him. Even if the days worked differently here, when they'd left, Rifun had been reading a book and having some downtime, which Tommen might have expected to precede sleep. They hadn't been gone that long, a couple hours maximum. Now, returning, Rifun was back to work in his office getup, no thermos in sight.

On the other hand, some teas contained caffeine. Maybe Tommen had it backwards. Maybe Rifun read his book and had his tea to wake himself up, as ordinary as reading the morning paper and having a cup of coffee before beginning his day.

On the other hand, did it really matter that much?

"My God, man, what happened to you?" Rifun asked at first glance.

Tommen looked at his arms. "Um...razor weeds happened. And allergies. I already got medicine for it, though, so I'm good."

"I should hope so. And be grateful it wasn't worse. Researching a world isn't limited to politics and people. Vegetation is equally as important. But then, for a well-traveled adventurer such as yourself, this should be second nature."

He was needling him, and Tommen knew it. He elected not to respond.

"Now then," Rifun said, turning back to his work, "tell me all about your stunning, heroic adventure."

If by "stunning," he meant "stumbling," and "heroic," he meant "horrific," then yes, Tommen certainly had a tale to tell. He might have omitted the part about being dropped in the middle of a primitive pitchfork mob, but decided to include it, if only to get the humiliation over with now and avoid punishment in case that bit came out later. Tommen had little doubt Rifun was interviewing each of them after the adventure, just to make sure all the stories lined up and no pertinent information was being left out. But being dropped off in an inconvenient location wasn't entirely his fault, right?

"I will admit, Tommen, I was having a bit of a down morning, but your antics always bring such joy to my day," Rifun said, grinning.

"Glad to be of amusement," Tommen muttered.

"Please, continue."

So he did, telling of their trip to the Psiaco city, meeting with Keeper Lehr, and the pretense they used to speak to Captain Titik.

"Was this one better than the last one with the Turitians?" Tommen wondered.

Rifun nodded. "Much better. And completely believable. The Psiaco were trying to pawn off Titik just as soon as he was confirmed insane, but the Grandfathers wouldn't take him. True, he was a Time

Agent and used Time for illicit gain, but he was no danger to the Time industry itself because he did not steal or otherwise illegally deal in Time or Time Capsules. He was a greater threat to the Turitians, really. Did you manage to speak with him?"

"Yes...somewhat."

"He is insane, then?"

Tommen shifted his stance and folded his arms. "I can't decide. I mean, he muttered to himself and rambled on and had some wild theories and analogies, but I don't think they were as crazy as his fellows might think. But to that end, I have to ask, what part did he play in the Dispersal?"

Rifun chuckled and shook his head, almost back to his old self, but still muted. "Ah, Morain leRou Titik. Son of a wealthy Psiaco businessman. He entered the Time Academy when he was, what we would consider to be a young man. The Psiaco are hard-nosed sons of bitches, fiercely loyal to Time, almost as bad as the Tacagans, some would argue. When the Dispersal erupted, the Psiaco sought to seize most of the power for themselves, or at least give themselves a rather unfair advantage in everything. Titik had little love for it. He saw no need to fight. Just cause or not, it brought no glory or pleasure in his eyes."

"Money is the only pleasure in the world. He repeated that a lot."

"Indeed. So he became a space pirate instead, taking advantage of the chaos to build up his own stores."

"And where do you come in?"

"Not me. Cassius. Before we returned to the salt cave, preparing for a jump into the future for an unknown length of time, Cassius bargained with Titik. Gain as much money as possible—which, for a pirate, is pretty much half the point of life—spend most of it how he wanted, but save some for us when we returned. Inflation is terrible and wars are expensive; we would need the funds so we could hit the ground running. In exchange, Titik would become a prominent member of the Order."

"But somehow, he didn't come through, so you shot him," Tommen stated. "That's the hole in his head, and why he's insane. A little over a year ago would put it around the time of the warehouse, just before the coup."

"You're clever, aren't you?"

"Here's what I don't understand, though. You had agreements with Titik. You had arrangements with the Turitians. I'm half-expecting to find some kind of connection between you and the Kolkath when we go there. Why not investigate the third journal yourself? You obviously have the means. Sorry to be blunt and sound like a lazy, selfish teenager, but a few simple questions to people you're already dealing with could have saved me a lot of time and bullshit. Or, even better, send Julianna. She's got the power and the knowledge."

"The means, yes, but not the time," Rifun told him calmly. "And tell me something else, from whom did you get more information? The Turitians or Titik? Think carefully about this." He paused for just a second. "Dira told you what happened, something you already knew or could easily find out from historical records. Titik gave you enough information to tell you his involvement in the Dispersal and his dealings with the Order. What was the difference?"

"Dira is a military commander and Titik is insane?"

"Insane, perhaps, but he has a strategic mind all the same, else he could not have bested the royal emissary. The difference was the pretext. Dira and the royal family Jalar knew they were dealing with the Order, something they know is a dangerous business. They have to keep as much to themselves as possible so as to protect themselves from the Hands. Titik believed you were from the Hands. He's either going to an asylum or an asylum; the only thing that changes are his guards. He has nothing to lose by telling everything he knows, or everything he thinks he knows. Tell him you're from the Order, not only do the Psiaco come after you, but he clams up for fear of another debilitating injury.

"My face is too well-known. Even if I were to use a Disguise, it's a matter of finding the time amid all my other duties. Julianna does have the power and knowledge, but she's also very...passionate. I'm afraid things may not go so smoothly if she were out and about doing the investigation. It's easier to plan against the mistakes of a rookie investigator than try to patch up failed relations between heads of state. And as I said way back when we first told you about your little mission, you're not our only hope. You're not even our best hope. I'm trying to find you a meaningful job here, something more than scrubbing pans and toilets. I'm trying to help you, Tommen, I really am. You don't know how far I'm sticking my neck out for you."

Tommen sighed and shrugged helplessly. "Fine. But I would appreciate a little disclosure so I don't feel like I'm being yo-yo'ed around, doing your dirty work and fucking up on the simplest of errands, much to your amusement. My next goal is Kath, to investigate the monastery where the 'religious text' supposedly came from and the scholars who studied it. Do you or Julianna or the Order at large have any dealings there? Dealings, agreements, anything at all?"

Rifun shook his head. "No. Kath is a newcomer to the larger Time industry, becoming Openly Engaged only recently, after the Dispersal, but still not having a solid foothold. The Kolkath are still investigating Time and their confidence was shaken with the coup. Their interest in the Akari and all factions thereof has increased dramatically over the last year, but was basically non-existent beforehand. I myself have never been to Kath; I don't know about Julianna."

"Okay. That's all I want to know. I really would have been nice to know about the Turitians and Titik beforehand."

"Would it really have made that much of a difference?"

Tommen opened his mouth, but paused. Finally, "Maybe not."

"Exactly. When do you want to leave for Kath?"

"I suppose tomorrow night is too soon, right?"

"Why don't we shoot for Monday night? It will give you a chance to rest after a long night and a hard day's work, hm?"

After a moment, Tommen agreed. One night was the same as

any other, he supposed. Either way, it was going to be a long adventure, a late night, then up for school or work in the morning. How long until spring break again? He needed to find this journal and fast.

He was just heading down the stairs, passing the sixth landing, when Julianna came alongside him.

"Good morning, Tommen," she greeted amiably. "I trust your adventure was productive?"

"Haven't decided yet, but it would be nice to know why I'm being sent to places you can't go yourselves seeing how everyone already knows you there," he replied shortly.

"We aren't sending you anywhere, Tommen. You choose where you think you need to go. Rifun probably told you about having the means but not the time? Well, it is true. Merely gathering the rumors took considerable time, never mind having to figure out which ones to pursue. I'm behind on my work, and he is behind on his, whatever his work is these days."

Don't take the bait. "What do you mean?"

Julianna sighed and lowered her voice. "The seizures have taken a toll on him, not necessarily the convulsions themselves, though that takes a considerable physical toll when they do happen, but the psychology of it. Likely they will be with him the rest of his life."

"Hm...can't imagine what that's like." Tommen intentionally scratched around his ears.

"That's another reason why we want you to do this. You are known as the Faharoa's favorite. As long as you are out there and active and pursuing this, it makes him look busy and involved as well. He's a field general, meant for war. Between the seizures and the desk job, I think he's lost heart."

"It's called depression. He'll get over it."

"This war with the Borelians seems to be the highlight of his life right now, even more so than the journal."

"Then why doesn't he track it down himself? Purpose, meaning, hooray. Seemed to help him when he went blind."

"All faith goes stagnant at one point or another, no matter how zealous the follower."

Tommen shrugged. "Once again, he'll get over it. Either the war with the Borelians will enslave or save us all, or I'll find the journal, one or the other. Then he'll be back to his usual self."

She seemed uncertain, the precise cuts on her face twisting into a caricature of concern, but she nodded. "I hope you're right. If the men ever got wind that their fearless leader was depressed—to say nothing of the seizures themselves—it could cause them to question him, me, our cause. The Akarin would see the weakness and they may try another uprising."

"Shouldn't they have faith in the Akari, not Rifun?" Tommen wondered innocently.

"True, but with exception of the core group who has been with us through the revolution and many years prior, most here are in just the earliest stages of personal faith. Rifun is still the face of victory. He led them against the Akarin and survived Borelian poison. He is practically a god to them."

What happens when they see that their god is but a man, I wonder?

"Find the journal," Julianna continued. "It may bring Rifun back around, help get him back where he needs to be, and it will strengthen the men. Then we can go after the Borelians whole-heartedly."

Tommen still had his doubts, but he promised to do his best and left it at that, hurrying down the staircase before she could say more. For one, he was exhausted, and time was ticking for what little sleep he would get before work. Falling asleep at a bakery was one thing; falling asleep on a construction site was quite different with a little more danger involved.

And for two, there was still the stench of fish in the air when it came to this whole thing. Some piece of the puzzle. What was worse, he suspected either Rifun or Julianna was withholding it from him. What could be so important? He was just a grunt, hardly a match in strength or intellect. The Order was probably the strongest force in the universe right now, matched only by the Borelians. Other than Rifun's seizures, Tommen couldn't come up with anything so damning that no one could know about it, that wouldn't top all of the heinous crimes already committed.

He arrived home to a dark house, everything exactly as it should be. No one was waiting for him, no cryptic messages scrawled on the wall in blood, no candles burning like a huge stone hearth ready to burn the house down. All was quiet, all was well. Tommen jumped in the shower to rinse off any allergy-inducing alien pollen or plant venom still embedded in his skin, and to inspect his wounds. The swelling was gone, his color almost back to normal. The cuts weren't deep, nor were they immune to Time, and he watched as the skin knitted itself back to rights and all evidence that he'd been sliced to ribbons by razor weeds disappeared. The pain and tingling that shot through his left arm once he released the Band drove him to a knee, but the cool water from the shower numbed it quickly.

What the hell was he doing? Running off like a loyal hound to flush out the prey smart enough to hide from Rifun. Maybe he should have said no, let the mission be assigned to someone else. But he couldn't do that, because that someone else would be loyal only to the Order. Tommen was smarter than that.

He went to bed, letting his muscles melt into the cold sheets to calm his aches and pains before warming up under the blankets at relaxing away the knots. And to think he was going to work construction the next day. Or later today. Whatever it was.

He needed to talk to Chandler, get this mess sorted out.

But the man did not come.

Chapter Eighteen
The Vault

If one were to describe the planet Kath in a single word, Tommen might have chosen "orange." It wasn't that it seemed to be a preferred color, a fashion statement or a fad, but everything was just...orange. Something in the atmosphere made it so that all the light from their sun filtered through orange. Therefore, every other light and color on the surface went through a natural orange filter. So his red coat turned a slightly darker orange; his blue shirt became some sort of sickly, nasty, brownish-green; his jeans went from light blue to orange-gray; and his brown shoes turned an even darker brown. But for the first time, his skin had some color to it, though he wasn't sure how much he liked the Donald Trump look, that ugly spray tan orange that wannabe rich girls got when trying to convince their friends they went on an exotic vacation to South America.

Tommen had managed to find time to research Kath and, through some clever research and deduction, found the monastery the journal supposedly came from. It was located about forty miles outside a city in the westernmost country of the western continent. Kath, being new to Time and all the social, religious, and political upheaval that happens following entry into the larger universe, was, even now, forty-plus years later, in the middle of a crisis state, and wars and skirmishes littered even the most remote countrysides. Stable countries and governments had broken down into over five hundred small territories, some controlled by fair and honest governments, others by unruly dictators, others by crime lords and law of the jungle. These days, those five hundred countries, through much war and other back-and-forth, had consolidated into about fifty countries, all with a lawful government of some form, though the spectrum ranged from North Korea to United States.

Irdo, the city they landed in, where the monastery was located, was an ancient city, walled, built to accommodate twenty-five thousand full-time residents, with one hundred thousand residents in times of crisis, and it seemed the Kolkath were in crisis mode. While its use as a strategic point on the western ocean had fallen to the wayside over many decades of peace, the resurgence of war and uncertainty of Time certainly put a fire under the residents to restore the near-ruins to their ancient glory. All around, the alien visitors saw new red-orange stone, freshly quarried, next to whitewashed stone hauled up thousands of years ago.

The six of them kept their heads down and did their best not to cause a scene. They did not need Disguises, nor were they the only alien visitors to be found, but outsiders were regarded with heavy scrutiny and randomly approached by the local police. As long as the six of them minded their own business, made no scene, and did only what they came to do, Tommen hoped they could get in and out without incident.

At first, Tommen had thought to simply go straight to the monastery and bypass the social and political uncertainty. Problem was, the monastery itself was said to be deserted, more of a crumbling tourist attraction than place of worship and holiness. Even if there were clues to be found, having an idea of the historical, religious, and political significance would do them well to figure out what was relevant and what was hearsay and embellishment. Although, with exception of the obvious answer, Tommen wasn't even sure what he was looking for, or hoped to find. A detailed description of what happened to the journal and signed and sworn statements from everyone who touched it after Julianna would have been nice, but he didn't think that was waiting for him at the end of the rainbow.

Instead, their first stop would be the Irdo Historical Society, or its equivalent anyway. Up until a century ago, Irdo had been a city-state, entirely self-sufficient. Its walls protected it from enemies from the sea to the west, and its location in the scrub desert protected it from enemies from the land. Its people were skilled in the art of irrigation and desert cultivation, as well as desert hunting and foraging. If that didn't work, there was always the sea to provide its delicacies. Even now, Irdo was part of the country of Nevis only in name and official documents; the residents still seemed to carry a certain independent spirit, that they survived where no one else could and needed no help to do so.

That said, the residents were extremely protective of their heritage, and all historical records were kept in a vault deep within the earth, said to be impervious to fire, water, and raids. It was guarded day and night by trained soldiers, and only trained librarians and recordkeepers were permitted to go in and retrieve the information within, and even then, the one requesting the information was supervised in order to ensure the ancient texts were not damaged, or even copied. Only trained and designated copywriters were permitted to copy old texts onto new paper to preserve them. Working in the Vault was considered one of the highest honors, and employees were scrutinized even by the mayor himself, and selected with care.

It was hard enough for an Irdoan to get into the Vault, and Tommen had no illusions on how much harder it would be for a group of off-world strangers. As it was, they were still a good half mile or so from the governmental building. In ages past, it was the palace for the ruling family, but these days, it was a more public-friendly governmental building where the mayor ruled the city with his advisers and councilors, where office workers did the nine to five dealing with business licenses, property lines, and alcohol permits, or whatever the equivalent here was. Maybe they had to file for water rights for cattle in the desert, Tommen didn't know.

The Kolkath themselves did not look particularly suited for the weather, either. Humanoid and about the size of a man, the Kolkath had cat-like faces with small eyes and enormous ears. If Tommen read correctly, they were born hairless, but their hair, or fur, never stopped growing. It grew at a snail's pace, but the elders of the people had long hair that dragged in the dusty streets, and it was worn as a sign of pride and wisdom. Reading further, the hair was layered in such a way so as to catch air currents and trap cool air, and the hair follicle structure somehow whisked hot air away from the body. He didn't understand, but whatever the case, it worked for them. In places like Irdo, most Kolkath wore simple tunics just to keep the dust off. Some in Irdo and in other places where the weather was more favorable, Kolkath might not wear anything at all. Only in the colder regions did they clothe themselves similarly to humans.

Tommen regretted not changing into something more suitable; he'd regretted it three seconds into the city. Sweat poured down his body and made his clothes sticky and smelly. His hair was plastered to his skull, and his arm screamed at him. It wasn't as bad as Turit where he fried to a crisp in only a few seconds; this was more like taking a trip to Louisiana in the height of summer while wearing winter clothing. Looking at his companions, only Rorion seemed as uncomfortable; the rest he could not tell or else weathered it better than he did.

The good news, if any could be found, was that as they got closer to the heart of the city and the governmental building, the buildings got taller and blocked more of the sun. The heat still hung in the air and the breeze was cut off as much as the sun, but just being in shade was an improvement.

As he'd sat in the Archives and did his research, a thought had occurred to him, though he wasn't sure how he wanted to approach the Kolkath about it. If they guarded their history this fiercely, there was no way they would have just given something away to Commander Dira, no matter how grateful the Kolkath were to the Turitians for getting them into space, into the Time industry. And even if they had given away the journal in good faith to the ruling family, perhaps expecting them to keep it safe just as they themselves had, the Kolkath would not have been so chill about it being stolen by a space pirate.

Tommen thought about Saul. He had been just as fierce when

it came to guarding the traditions and customs of his people; he wouldn't have just given something away to someone. If he had three good words to say about anyone, it was a compliment. It was next to impossible for a white man to possess a real, original Native American artifact, but that didn't mean he couldn't have some piece of Native American art. The difference was, the white man's art would use cotton thread instead of sinew, glass beads instead of bone, store-bought strips of wood instead of hand-hewn birchbark or ash. Both true to Native American style, but only one was an original.

What if the Kolkath had made a copy of the journal and kept the original stored in their Vault? It would be true to form for them, and it was the safest place to store the original, keep it out of the hands of those like Titik. At the time, Kath would have been Unengaged, unimportant, oblivious to the artifact they possessed. At the same time, in order to copy it, someone had to wield the Akari in order to unlock the Imprint, which meant one of these things was not like the other, and someone was not exactly who they said they were. They just had to figure out where this person was hiding. With any luck, now that the secrets were out and Kath was Engaged, this person was also able to come out of hiding.

It was a tenuous hope at best, but Tommen clung to it. Nothing was ever that easy, not for him. If the Authored Books he possessed so far were any indication, they were getting longer. If there were more Books about his life to be had, the Author had to invent some kind of bullshit obstacle to hinder his progress and pad her page count. What other purpose could there be? On the other hand, did he really expect his life to be as simple as a children's chapter book, where everything was obvious to even a slightly skilled reader, where good and evil were easily defined and more easily spotted, where everything was easy, mysteries so simple even children could solve them? This was real life, and real life was complicated and had twists and turns, and there were very real hindrances to very real missions. But still, did she really have to waste his time? Or was Rifun wasting his time? What was the nature of free will in a novel? Dammit, this was more philosophical than he'd hoped. He needed to focus. He only knew what he knew, and there was nothing to be gained by entertaining this idea or that philosophy. Regardless if there was an Author out there, he had to get to the governmental building and find out more about this journal.

"How is everyone holding up?" he wondered, pausing to look around at his group.

Rorion did not tolerate dry heat well, but she politely claimed to be doing as well as could be expected and would let him know if there was any trouble. The others gave similar affirmations. He regarded them a moment longer and continued on.

The governmental building was the tallest and grandest, as befitted a former palace. The construction was remarkably simple, at least from the outside. Three tall, square buildings with elaborate rooftops, the middle building being the tallest by three stories, connected by walkways in the sky on the first, fourth, and seventh floors, or what Tommen approximated as such. On the north side was a squat building, no more than two stories tall with a simple domed roof, but easily three times the width. Like every other building in the city, the primary construction was the red-orange stone, and though it was yet the original construction, efforts had been made to repaint or recondition the stone so it no longer looked whitewashed, but as glorious as the day it was first hefted into place. The building could not be restored in any other way, as relief carvings adorned every square inch of every wall. They looked purely ornamental rather than fictional or historical, but grand nonetheless. As they neared, Tommen saw that silver metal had also been inlaid with the stone, whether as leaf, overlay, or solid block he could not tell. They gave the building depth and character, its own sort of contrast as color was in limited supply.

The front doors were also made of the same silver metal, plain save for an enormous, circular design that spanned both doors. There appeared to be no real ceremony when it came to getting into the governmental building itself, but they were stopped by a couple of guards when they got into a small lobby-like entryway.

"State your business, foreigner," one said.

"With your kind permission, we need to speak to one of your Vault workers in regards to the monastery north of your fine city," Tommen replied politely.

"The monastery?" The Kolkath's tone said far more than just those two words. It told Tommen that the monastery was not often visited, and not highly regarded. It would be like going to Arizona where everyone expected the tourists to want to visit the Grand Canyon, but were stunned when one tourist wanted to visit somewhere else, somewhere the locals considered insignificant, even laughable that someone traveled so far to see something so small.

"Yes, the monastery. We are conducting a historical study and our work has led us here. We don't know why, and it may prove insignificant or inconsequential, but we would like to make that determination for ourselves."

The guards glanced at one another. Then, "Wait here."

Tommen wondered who would have made them wait, as no guards were posted to keep watch, or none that he saw. They were simply left alone in the room.

The Turitian governmental building had been large and lavish, displaying their history and heroes for all to see and marvel at. The Kolkath governmental building, or at least this lobby waiting area, was like a doctor's office by comparison, and Tommen wondered where the plants in the corner were. The room itself was probably thirty by thirty, the walls bare save for one which had a quote engraved in metal. Highly inspirational, he was sure, even if the language was lost on him. The floor was whitewashed stone. Other than that, it was as dull and boring as could be imagined, certainly not what one would expect from a former palace.

"Rorion, what is this place? Why is it so boring? I thought palaces were supposed to be grand, opulent, obnoxious displays of wealth."

The Dimica frowned. "In ancient times, Irdo prided itself on being a war fortress. It had a strong navy and, during peacetime, would send its warships to protect fishermen along the coast as well as escort merchants to foreign lands. During war, the warships would block off entrance to the bay, preventing any attack from the sea. While self-sufficient, Irdo knew the value in good trade relations with other countries and city-states. They would take the wealth they had gained during peacetime—often the prices charged to the fishermen and merchants—and send it to their allies for food and supplies. Irdo knew its position was tenuous, between the desert and threats from the sea, and so it maintained a practice of practicality rather than lavish opulence."

Smart rulers, Tommen thought.

"That is not to say that there isn't some display of wealth in the interior," Rorion continued, "but one must be invited to see it."

So the rulers of Irdo didn't flaunt their wealth as a neon sign saying, "Rob me!" but kept it on the down low, revealing it only to certain people, just enough to let them know that the city wasn't as destitute and helpless as they might appear.

"Naq, do you know the language well enough to say what this quote is?" Tommen asked, folding his arms and studying the metal sign.

The Yakik looked at it for a moment. Then, " 'The might of a man is not found in a single swing of the sword, but in his enduring will and determination, like the breeze sweeping from the ocean and the heat rolling off the desert. So, too, should the will of the people be as vast as the waters and as merciless as the sands.' -King Turin vur alJoth III "

"Democratic monarchy. I like it."

"The alJoth clan led the uprising that deposed the former King Urith, who wanted to forsake city-state independence and instead join the larger country. The alJoths ruled Irdo for six hundred years," Rorion threw in.

Tommen nodded slowly. Earth history was boring. Maybe because he'd studied it for so long, it felt like old news. The history of other worlds seemed much more exciting, or maybe it was just him. Either way, it wasn't getting them any closer to the Vault to continue their work. And what if they were denied entry? Could they just Band and walk in anyway? Now where had those guards gotten off to? What was this, their lunch break?

He'd no sooner thought it than the door opened and the guards returned.

"We will take you to speak with the Vault administrator," the first one said. "He will decide whether to honor your request."

"Thank you," Tommen told them graciously. "Lead the way."

They stepped through the door, and Rorion's words quickly rang true. The walls weren't covered in diamonds or splashed with breathtaking murals, but there was a quiet air of power in the room. Like the outside of the building, the inside walls were also inundated with relief carvings, these of heroes and ancient tales, but the wealth showed itself to those who knew how to look. The eyes of a ferocious beast were inset with sapphire. The necklace—or maybe it was a chalice or some such thing—was studded with onyx. Little glitters here and there, sparkling for just a moment in just the right light as they passed by.

Overall, the building had the feel of an ancient monument being painstakingly brought into the modern world while still trying to preserve its historical value. No one dared drill holes to run wires for electric lights, but to leave the wires exposed would look extremely tacky, so modern sculptors had to get creative in hiding them, being discreet about the things they were trying to hide without crowding or taking away from all the ancient splendor. While the Kolkath as a whole had achieved sustained space travel, it was difficult to see amid the stone, if it was there at all.

The layout seemed pretty straightforward. From the lobby, a corridor branched off either to the left or straight. The guards had brought them down the straight path, through the relief carvings with the glittering eyes. Every so often, there would be a doorway. The doors were all metal, most of them open, but some closed, some tightly. Once, the corridor branched off to the left and right, but the guard continued straight ahead.

Few people could be found in the corridors. Whenever they passed by a room with an open door, Tommen glanced in and saw even fewer. Well, what did he expect from a governmental building? Didn't seem much different than the one back home, though there was a distinct lack of group tours and school groups in Irdo. Besides, if the complex was as big as it looked, all the real action was happening on a higher floor, not down here with the County Clerk and the Register of Deeds and the Building Commission.

"So, what can you tell us about the monastery?" Tommen inquired of the guards.

"It's old," one replied. "Some say it predates even Irdo, though that is impossible."

"Why do you say that?"

"Irdo was the first city on Kath," the other guard answered. "The old palace in the northeast neighborhood was the first building erected in the city, the first building on Kath. Nothing came before it."

Well, there's your independent, self-sufficient, city-state mindset, Tommen figured. Don't mess with Texas and all that.

"What about now?"

"Long-abandoned."

"Why?"

"The monks who lived there died out, and their religion with them. The structure was kept up for a time, but it has fallen into disrepair."

"But if Irdo is so proud of its history and heritage, why let it go to ruin?"

"It is not worth restoring. Too costly, when restoration is already being done to the city itself. Also, it can no longer function on its own; the irrigation has been left to rot. Since the walls have crumbled, it is unprotected. Eventually, the desert will reclaim it."

Tommen enjoyed history, even if he wasn't a history buff like Varad, but even he hated to see an ancient monument go to ruin like that. Restore it, repurpose it, give it new life. It didn't have to stay the way it was, as a monastery, but give it a chance. Obviously, if the structure lasted this long, its sturdiness and longevity had to count for something. Rebuild and restore, make it last another thousand years or better. But it wasn't his call, and he wasn't going to convince them otherwise.

Eventually, they reached the north end of the building, a set of slightly smaller metal doors similar to the ones at the south end of the building looming over them. The guards opened it with no hesitation or trouble, no secret knock or special password. Not told to wait or stay behind, Tommen and his group followed them inside.

The north building immediately put Tommen in mind of a library. Everything from ancient scrolls to modern tablets lay scattered about in some invisible, precise order across hundreds of tables on two floors, the second floor little more than a landing with what looked like private offices or studies. The decor was slightly more modern, not as much care had to be taken in disguising new lights against old stone. Only the ceiling held any trace of the grandeur found in the main building, jewels glittering here and there, but the rest looked like any normal construction, or what Tommen considered normal. He would have been surprised to find the walls made of two-by-fours, fiberglass insulation, and gypsum covered in paint, but that was how it looked.

They were greeted by a Kolkath dressed in long robes, and there was more obvious wealth contained in them than the whole of the building so far. Tommen might have thought he was meeting the Kolkath Pope from the Renaissance, all the way down to the funny hat and the luxurious slippers. He left nothing to the imagination with his glittery robes embedded with small jewels, nor the necklaces, bracelets, and rings adorned with larger jewels. The man was a walking display of a dozen different precious stones, a target for thieves if there ever was one. He didn't even bother trying to hide behind some mask of false piety, but his demeanor boasted of his wealth and power as much as his robes did. So much for keeping wealth on the down low.

"So, these are my foreign visitors, here to study the history of the monastery," he said. He glanced at the guards. "Thank you for seeing them safely to me. I'm sure I'll be fine."

It was a snobbish dismissal, and the guards left without a word.

"My name is Suri," the Kolkath introduced boldly. "I am the Vault administrator. Come, let us speak in private and see what I can do for you."

They followed him to a corner office. Emet was the last one in, shutting the door behind him with only a soft click.

"All right, what interest do you have in the monastery?"

The change in Suri's attitude was night and day. From proud and boastful and being heard halfway across the room, to bored, disinterested, even routine. He did not like visitors, especially foreign ones.

"The monastery itself, very little," Tommen told him. "Actually, we're here about an artifact uncovered there. A book."

"A book." The Kolkath seemed unimpressed. "Many books were taken from the monastery."

"Yes, but this particular one, you—or perhaps whoever was in your position at the time—gave it to High Commander Dira of the Turitians during Kath's first sustained voyage into space. It was said to be a religious text or perhaps the religious text of the monks."

Now the man seemed to come back around to being interested, if only slightly. "I remember it. I was administrator at that time, yes. I wouldn't still be here today if not for Time, extending my life, praise to Yarsi the Great One."

"Were you there when the book was brought here?"

"I don't understand."

"All this trouble for us to get into a library, the Vault of Irdo, more protected than the mayor himself. I'd be willing to bet that in matters of history and whatever you have down there, you have more power than the mayor, and you say what can and cannot leave. You're not going to just give up something from there. Even if the monastery is dilapidated and the religion dead, you're not going to give up an original text. That's sacrilege for any historian worth his salt.

"The book you gave away was not an original, but only a few select scholars could read the language within and copy it down. I'm speaking that language now, which means the book did not originate on Kath. We want to know, where did it come from? Who gave it to you?"

The administrator gave each of them a hard regard, not speaking for several minutes. Finally, "Wait here. I might know someone who can help."

He left the room, Emet eying him darkly. It was easily twenty minutes or so before he returned, another librarian in far more modest robes in tow. Where Suri was clearly younger, with short to medium-length hair, the new librarian was much older, his fur brushing the ground, just past his robes.

"This is Raba," Suri introduced, without much formality. "He may know more about the book you speak of; he was one of the scholars who studied it."

Tommen encased himself and the librarian Raba in an Akari Band. "Then you understand this?"

The old Kolkath nodded. "The Akari, yes. It has been many years since I last felt it, last used it, but I would know it anywhere."

"Then you can tell us more about the journal."

"Release the Band, please."

Tommen did so, and Raba turned to Suri. "With your permission administrator, I would like to take them into the Vault and show them our old work."

"Just like that?" Suri asked incredulously.

Raba nodded slowly. "Yes."

The administrator was obviously displeased. "Do you think they can be trusted?"

"No more and no less than anyone else."

For a long moment, the two Kolkath faced off: Suri, an angry young tom, debating whether to initiate the fight; Raba, an old tomcat who couldn't be bothered with anger anymore. It was Suri who broke the silence with, "Only one of them may go. The rest must wait here."

Raba simply dipped his head in agreement, though it was not for lack of argument. Rather, Tommen saw a glint in his eyes that said they would be having words later, words that had been had many times over. Nevertheless, he left the room, and Tommen followed. They crossed the open floor of the library to a set of unassuming stairs, polished but unadorned, leading belowground.

"Let me tell you about the monastery," Raba was saying. "Whatever the common folk would have you think, the monastery was not built before Irdo, though, Irdo was little more than a humble fishing village when it was. The monks there were warriors who protected the village if it ever came under fire from pirates, and brought food if the people were suffering. Over time, as Irdo grew and built its buildings and walls, they maintained good relations with the monks. That is, until King Urith came to power. With his declaration of intent to join the larger country, he denounced the monks and shrugged off everything they had ever done for his people. The monks were the ones who raised up alJoth and got him into power. And while the alJoths maintained good ties, the favor of the people fell away, that the monks were so powerful as to destroy and raise whichever leaders they wished. Boys stopped going to the monastery, and the warrior monks died out. Such a tragic tale, really."

The story was fascinating, but it was also a cover for the listening ears as they descended two flights of stairs guarded by armed soldiers before coming to yet another set of metal doors, these ones bound by lock and key. Raba produced a keyring and let them inside, easing the giant doors shut behind them and flicking a switch.

This was the truly modern part of Kath, Tommen thought. This was the stainless steel, pin code entry, retinal scan, fingerprint activated sort of modern he'd expected from the get-go from an Advancing society. It was a warehouse museum, scrolls and texts under strict, climate-controlled, restricted access, lock and key. Tommen followed Raba down one corridor, over a catwalk overlooking several floors, then down more stairs until they reached the ground. Everywhere he looked, Tommen saw rows of shelving and cabinetry, most of them dark.

"The lights in the rows are motion-activated," Raba explained. "Saves on electricity. And it will let us know if someone is coming."

It was a strange thing to hear coming from a cat man in the middle of an ancient stone city.

"What do you know about the book from the monastery?" Tommen began.

"Hm...I think I should explain a little beforehand so you understand why certain things happened. See, Kath was Unengaged at the time. We were only Scientifically Advancing, just breaking into space. With our tenuous connection to the Turitians, everything was brand new for us. There was no good or bad, no sides to choose; everything simply was. As per usual in Unengaged societies, there are still those who are exposed to Time, who still function as Time Agents."

"My people are that way."

"So you can appreciate it. Well, through a series of events that I won't go into, I became exposed to Time, the first Kolkath Time Agent west of the Mighty Whiteclaw; my mentor had to travel long distances to train me. Because of that, my progress was slow. While I was yet an Apprentice Timekeeper, I was approached by an alien—it's been so long, I couldn't tell you what kind or even his name—who was a member of the Cult of the Akari, or so he claimed. Long story short, he trained me in the Akari. With that training, I was able to better understand my Time training, and I advanced quickly, to my mentor's delight. He never knew of my Akari training.

"Now, as I said, Kath was Unengaged, my Time progress was slow, and my Akari training was always done on Kath, so I had very little vested interest in the politics of the Wheel. I couldn't even name all the Hands—I still can't, to be honest. So when the Zero Hour went missing, it caused quite a stir, and it ended in the Fifth Rebuild. You've heard of Rebuilds, yes?"

"I have, but I don't fully understand them. It's when the Wheel changes shape, changes its look."

"The Wheel itself breaks, and it can be reformed by one skilled enough to mold it. There was much chaos and confusion at the time, but I remained largely unaffected. Kath was Unengaged, I was unimportant. My mentor told me to lay low and wait for it all to blow over."

"Sounds familiar."

"Some time after the initial news of the commotion, my Akari mentor returned to me and handed me a book. He said it was immensely important that I take it and keep it safe in the Vault. He specifically requested that a copy be made, that I make it—"

"Because the text was Imprinted."

Raba nodded. "Because the text was Imprinted, yes."

Tommen shifted eagerly in his seat. "What else did he tell you? Do you still have the book?"

"He told me to make a copy and not tell a soul in the universe, not for a long time. He told me to wait, then to one day make a grand spectacle about having it or some news about it. I didn't understand what he meant, but when the opportunity with the Turitians came, I thought that was as good as I was going to get. So I made up the story about finding it in the old monastery. Figured a hundred years was a long time to wait, and if he wanted news about it, that would be news. He forgot to mention that someone was going to come looking for it afterwards, though I suppose that would be expected."

"What about the original? Do you still have it?"

The Kolkath shook his shaggy head. "I don't. When the Dispersal came around and the Sixth Rebuild, another alien claiming to be part of some Akari faction came back, said he needed the original back. Someone knew where it was and it had to be moved. Like I said, a hundred years and I still had the copy, figured I'd lend a hand at throwing off the hounds and make a big deal about giving it to the Turitians. Since then, I haven't hardly given it a thought until you came."

"And you don't remember which alien came to get it?"

"I'm sorry, I don't. I stopped using Time and the Akari long ago, and my memory isn't what it used to be."

"Do you remember if he said where he was going to take it, give any clue?"

"He didn't say. I figure it was for the best. If you don't know anything, it can't be held against you. Well, I suppose it could, but I swear to you, I don't remember anything more. Yes, I had it. Yes, I made a copy. Yes, I let it go. It was not mine in the first place, and I had no good, reliable means of testing whether one was being truthful in his intentions."

Tommen sighed heavily, but nodded. "I understand, and I don't blame you for it."

"But I figure that in doing so, I lived by the words in it. It was a good read, very insightful."

"Do you know who wrote it? Who it belongs to?"

"I believe the author's name was Rishar."

"Close enough, it's Richard."

"As to whom it belongs, I thought it belonged to the Cult, but I don't remember any mention of it in the Zero Hour Revolution." Raba waved a hand and stood. "Well, like I said, my memory isn't what it used to be. I'm just an old tomcat anymore. I'm too old for adventure and intrigue. Maybe my little bit of knowledge will help you in your daring quest, maybe not. But we better get upstairs before Suri starts to worry." He snorted a laugh. "Ah, Suri..."

Tommen did not ask what he meant, simply stood and followed. Their footsteps echoed in the Vault as they ascended the stairs and made for the ground floor. Raba told him some other story from some other part of Irdo history, as much to entertain as to throw off the eavesdroppers, but Tommen was not listening.

So the journal had come here. The original journal had definitively passed through Raba's hands. Problem was, the original had disappeared while everyone else got distracted by the copy, because the Irdo Kolkath could be trusted to keep such an artifact safe and copy it well. Where did the original go, then? Obviously it couldn't have been a Cult member who took it, else the Cult would have possession of it now, or at least have better leads. Could it have been a member of the Akarin? Some other faction? How did he find out?

The administrator seemed to have found some amusement when they returned as he was in the middle of an exuberant tale of survival and self-discovery in the desert, with himself as the main character, when Tommen and Raba walked in the office.

"Did you find what you were looking for?" Suri inquired. His tone was polite, but his body language and posture, assuming they were similar enough to a human's, told them all to get the hell out and stop bothering him.

"We came only for information, and information I have found," Tommen replied. "Raba was most helpful, and I thank you for allowing me the opportunity to look and discover for myself."

Suri glanced at Raba who merely nodded.

"Very well. Then if you require nothing more, I will send for the guards to see you on your way."

Now that he didn't have to play host, Suri dropped the pretense and scowled as he left the room, looking for the guards.

"Ah, Suri," Raba chuckled. "He worked so hard to be noticed to get appointed to the administrator's position, but it is not as grand or rewarding as I think he thought it would be. But like all work in the Vault, it is an esteemed position; one does not simply quit and walk away."

No one responded, and just as well for Suri returned with the two guards who looked both passive and bad-tempered. Farewells were brief, and far warmer toward Raba than Suri; Tommen hoped the difference was not lost on the administrator. Catch more flies with honey than vinegar, he thought.

The guards did not inquire after their well-being or their request. The trip was so short, perhaps they figured Suri had listened to them and turned them away. Regardless, the foreign visitors would probably be the talk around the watercooler for a couple days at least. The others in the group did not say a word, reserving their questions for the safety of the fortress, no doubt.

They were left at the front door of the building without so much as a "Thank you for coming and have a nice day. Don't forget to check out our gift shop."

The interior of the building had been cool, if not air conditioned, and now they were thrown back out into sweltering desert heat. Where they were standing was presently all in shadow, but it was still a good thirty or forty degrees warmer than it had been inside. Looking down the street where the sun was just coming around, he could see heat waves just as clearly as he could look at the ocean and see water.

"We're getting into solar noon," Rorion said, as if reading his thoughts. "The hottest part of the day will last several hours."

"Well, we won't be here for several hours," Tommen replied.

"Are we visiting the monastery?" Ilit inquired.

"No. No, the monastery was a front, a convenient story to explain away the journal. We won't find anything there."

"Then the journal is not here."

"No, it's not. Let's get out of here. I need to make my report to Rifun, then do some more thinking on this."

"What did Raba tell you?" Naq asked.

"He did have the journal. The original journal. After the Dispersal, he was told to make a big show about it and send out the copy, which was the one that went to Commander Dira. But whoever gave it to him in the first place came back for the original and whisked it away somewhere else. No, I don't know who that was. He didn't remember. Like I said, I need to think on this a little more, do some more research, some backtracking, some asking around." Tommen heaved a sigh, trying to breathe in the sweltering heat. "Ilit, get us the hell out of here; I'm dying."

They returned to the fortress without incident, and the first stop they all made was the mess hall so they could get food and water. Or that's what Tommen got, anyway. Most of the others got water as well, but whether or not that was food on their plates, well, it was all about individual preference, he supposed. Still, at least it was real food and not the weird nutritional cubes the Akarin had. It wasn't quite up to par with the Food Court in the Wheel, but it was a homecooked meal, anyway.

"Did Suri tell you guys anything of value while I was down with Raba?" he asked.

Their expressions said everything, but it was Sisith who answered, "Hardly, unless you count his wild and improbable tales of grandeur as educational listening."

Tommen nodded. "Okay. Hey, you never know."

They ate in silence after that. Rorion was the first one done, standing, thanking them for another successful venture, then departing, saying something about getting some sleep. Tommen could relate, but he didn't get that luxury right now. Naq was the next to leave, scampering off to do some other work she was assigned to do when not adventuring with the rest of them. Finally, Tommen finished his food, then excused himself so he could make his report to Rifun.

Rifun was not in his quarters when Tommen finally hauled himself over the last step to the eighth floor landing, nor had he left a note stating where he'd gone or when he would be back. Tommen stood and waited around for a minute or two, just in case it was a quick trip out to grab a snack or hit the head or something similar, and to catch his breath from the climb. But after five minutes or so, Tommen figured he was going to have to do some kind of methodical search from the top down.

He found Rifun on the fifth floor, or what remained of it. With construction going as smoothly as it was, the builders were faced with their final major project, separating the fourth, fifth, and sixth floors, and stabilizing them all so they were solid and functional once more. Rifun was speaking to the foreman who pointed here and there, gesturing and so forth. Well, when rebuilding, why not throw some remodeling in there, too? Tommen stood back and tried not to think of the time ticking by that he wasn't in bed sleeping before another long day of school.

He followed Rifun and the foreman at a distance as they walked around what little was sturdy enough to traverse, all the while thinking that they should at least have hard hats on. Maybe work was already starting to rub off on him. Maybe the memory of this place crashing down around him was still too vivid.

Regardless, he was just starting to consider saving his report for another time when the conversation ended and Rifun began walking away, motioning for Tommen but not speaking until they hit the staircase and started going down.

"All right, my little shadow, how was your trip to Kath, besides short? Is that a good thing or a bad thing?"

"One of the Vault workers confirmed he had the original journal and was asked to make a copy of it in order to throw off the hounds during the Dispersal. But then someone came back, claiming to be part of the Cult, and said they needed it back. He claimed he had no reason not to give it to him. He doesn't remember the name of the person or what species he was." Tommen added quickly, "He's an old man now, says his memory isn't what it used to be since he stopped using Time and the Akari."

"The pitfalls of old age. But it obviously was not a member of the Cult at the time, else we would have the journal here and now, or at least a better idea of where it could be."

"That's what I was thinking."

"What's your next move, then?"

"I don't know; I'll have to think about it a little bit, maybe go back through some of the leads Julianna gave me. But I really can't do much right now when I'm as tired as I am."

"Yes, you've been awake for quite a while, haven't you? All right, then, go on. Let me know when you have something."

Rather than argue, Tommen just did as he was told, slipping down the staircase ahead of Rifun with ease and opening a portal when he was hardly two steps into the portal room. Getting to the fortress was easy; getting back to his room was even easier, hardly requiring a thought. Funny how that happened, difficult things becoming easier with practice. What else was there to learn?

He stepped into his room and let the portal die. The light was on in the living room and he went out to find his dad in his recliner, reading a book.

"Well, hello, stranger," his dad greeted, placing his bookmark and setting the novel aside. "Haven't seen you in a few days."

Tommen shrugged. "Between school and work, I guess not. How was the funeral?"

"A funeral."

"How's Laura?"

"Taking it better than I would have expected, but I think they're all pretty much just relieved that it's finally over; he's not suffering anymore and they can all move on."

"That's good. When is she coming back?"

His dad faltered. "She didn't give a specific date. Right now, they're all rallying around their mother, which I totally understand. They'll be sorting through things, dividing up some of the possessions, figuring out what to do and how to help. Laura doesn't want to leave right away, not until she's satisfied everything is as good as it's going to be, mostly because she's the only one who's out of state."

Tommen studied his dad. "What if she doesn't want to come back? What if she decides to stay?"

"Then she decides to stay." His dad's tone was carefully neutral. "She said it will be a few weeks at least, maybe a month. I told her she still owed me a spring break vacation up there."

"What did she say to that?"

"I believe her exact words were something along the lines of, 'It's Minne-f-ing-sota. No one comes here on vacation, especially during spring break.' " His dad grinned and shook his head sadly. "Mostly, I was just trying to get her to smile again. We'll see what happens."

"Okay."

"Where did your adventures take you tonight?"

"Kath, city called Irdo, to their super secret Vault."

"Ooh, *Mission Impossible* bank job?"

"Not quite. More like the Library of Congress. Actually, I don't even think it was that big. Maybe more like the library downtown. Either way, nothing much came from it. The journal was there—the original journal—but then it was taken away. No one knows who or where."

Walter nodded slowly. "Maybe it's for the best. Are you still going to pursue it?"

"I have to try, or pretend to." Tommen broke into a yawn. "But it won't be any time soon. I've had too many late nights, I can hardly think straight. And with Rifun acting weird..."

"You've seen it, too, then."

"Oh, absolutely. Julianna says it's just depression, between the seizures and everything going on in the fortress."

"It certainly could be, but nothing is ever so simple when it comes to those two."

"Well, she thinks that me finding the journal will bring him back around. I don't know. I haven't even decided what I'm going to do if I do manage to find the stupid thing." He shook his head. "Whatever. I'm exhausted."

"Well, get ready for bed and I'll Band you at least. Tomorrow is only Tuesday; you have a long week of school yet, plus work."

Because he'd totally forgotten. Tommen rubbed his face and headed to the bathroom to get ready for bed. He still needed—wanted to talk to Chandler, but the man seemed to come and go on his own terms. Sometimes, Tommen wondered if he hadn't imagined the whole thing, except there was still the part where he'd met the man in person. So why didn't he come more often to talk to him, guide him, teach him, tell him what to do? Had he been compromised in some way, by the Shadows? Would he give any explanation if and when they did speak again? When would that be?

Tommen got in bed, glancing at the little pot of herbs. He'd used them a few times, and it always proved to be helpful in driving away the nightmares. Was it nondiscriminatory? Did it drive Chandler away as well? That wouldn't make sense. If he used them on a night when he didn't have nightmares, could it call Chandler, like some kind of beacon saying, "Hey, we need to talk"?

He didn't know, and he didn't get a chance to test his theory, because as soon as he rolled over, he was out.

Chapter Nineteen
War on Two Fronts

At journal studies that week was the first time Tommen heard any questionable mention about Rifun. He didn't stick around long enough to eavesdrop on the whole conversation, but heard enough to know that the men in the field were beginning to smell weakness, or if not weakness, that something wasn't quite right. Faharoa's plans were stalled because the man himself did not appear too involved. He sent out his special team to find the third journal, but he himself watched from the sidelines. His men put down the Akarin uprising, but their fearless general was nowhere to be seen. He talked about going against the Borelians, but he hadn't gone and nothing had come of it after the burning of the slave world. He was overwhelmed. He was disinterested. He was bathing in his own superiority. He'd been wounded more severely than he let on and could no longer lead except by name and reputation.

The rumors were endless, or they would be if they were allowed to circulate. And it wasn't as though Rifun didn't have his defenders, those who pointed out that the Order was in a time of transition, and it was a lot of work; he could very well be overwhelmed and couldn't be bothered with every minor detail that came up. When something needed to be done that he couldn't do himself, he called on those he trusted. He trusted his men, appreciated their work and loyalty; he wasn't going to swoop in and save them as if they were incapable, as if they needed a babysitter. Going against the Borelians was not something one did lightly; it needed careful planning and consideration, both the execution and the fallout in the event of success, the likes of which no one could even begin to imagine.

Furthermore, with Julianna's return, they had to figure out their vision for the Order together.

Of course, that called into question of whom to listen to. Most agreed that Rifun and Julianna were on the same page for the moment, but in times of disagreement, who took precedence? Julianna was in charge of the studies and education, so it made sense that she held all authority there. Rifun was easily the military mind, so he should be heeded in those matters. But who was the final, end-all authority? Julianna was Richard's wife; she'd been there for the writing of the journals, she understood the history and the nuance, and in many cultures, she would have familial rights of succession. But while she'd been gone for over a century, Rifun was the general who brought the Cult from a fringe group consisting of refugees and zealots into a full, strong, mighty, forcefully accepted culture, a way of life that was growing stronger every day.

The conversations were quiet, and Tommen told himself they were just genuinely curious mutterings of those who were new to the Order and still trying to figure things out. They didn't want to cause trouble or start any heated political debates, just vent a little and try to sort things out in their own minds. At the same time, he felt caught up in the conversation, in the debate. His first thought was that, of course Rifun was in charge. He always had been, as far as Tommen was concerned. But was that right? After all, he, Tommen, wasn't a soldier anymore, and if he was one of the Artists, his chain of command took him to Julianna, not Rifun. So then why was Rifun overseeing the recovery of the journal? Or was it one of those times when the uncertainty and nebulous circumstances meant either one could be called upon for the actual retrieval of the journal?

Tommen was also forced to wonder whether he should tell Rifun about the conversation, the mutterings. On the one hand, he could be stemming the rumor mill and preventing larger problems later on. On the other hand, why did he care? Why did he feel any loyalty at all? Wouldn't a mutiny be a good thing, give the Akarin a chance to rise up against their captors, weaken the First Order so they couldn't be such a threat? Under normal circumstances, maybe.

The only kink came with the war on the Borelians. Now that the shields had gone up over all the worlds, the Akari-bearers were the only ones who could move from planet to planet. This presented many challenges, naturally. Some said to call it good, don't worry about the Borelians anymore, maybe form a tentative alliance with the Order, in that, Akari-bearers could be called upon as a taxi service for Time Agents to get to the Wheel and back. Otherwise, life could continue as normal. Others suggested forming a full alliance with the Order, training up all human Time Agents in this Akari business, and forming a real plan of attack with anyone who wanted to help bring down the Borelians. Tommen hadn't heard the response from the Turitians or anyone else Rifun claimed to be negotiating with, but while everyone claimed to want to destroy the Borelians, few wanted to try, and even fewer wanted to ask for Rifun's help.

In the end, Tommen elected not to say anything, the biggest reason being that he only heard one conversation, and it came from a bunch of new vaovao. It was normal for new recruits to question their leaders, hate them, curse them, all the way up until the aha! moment when everything became clear and things started falling together. It was true of every military and most decent, worthwhile higher education. Then, at graduation, they would shake hands and exchange nods of respect. The recruit came to appreciate and respect his commanding officer who had pushed him out of his comfort zone in order to prepare him for whatever may come, and the commanding officer came to respect the new recruit who had broken out of his comfort zone and was finally ready to give his all for his country.

These recruits here hadn't quite reached that stage yet. Tommen wasn't sure he'd reached that stage, either, but it didn't matter. It was a phase. It would pass.

And anyway, he had bigger concerns, such as just making it through his journal studies class. He'd kind of hoped Rifun would get the hint and move him out of the idiot class into something more intellectually challenging, at least a class where everyone already spoke English. Fucking hell, it felt as though half his time was spent listening to a bunch of babies drawl out their first baby babble sounds for the first time. He just wanted to scream and run out the door.

He could hardly pretend to care about the stories anymore, either. Going over what little was known about Kalian, the orphan girl with the locket. Hooray. Fucking hell, but if the full story was anything like the small excerpt the Order was teaching, the Author had started out as such a sap. Overall, going through the lessons, it was like listening to a Sunday school teacher go over the story of Adam and Eve. Kids got one version, adults maybe got a little more in-depth, but there was only so much one could study about them. Half the time, it was imagination and embellishment anyway, while the recorded story itself was relatively simple. This was just as bad.

Class could not end soon enough, and this time, Gillingham wasn't around to ask if he wanted to take a test and try to get bumped up. This time, he had to plod along with every other moron.

Leaving the curtained off classroom, Tommen again heard whispers of conversation. This was not unusual, obviously, as students enjoy talking after classes, but the mutterings were again about Rifun. It might not have concerned him, except now the vaovao were taking it to more mature ambany students, those in the fifth and sixth level classes, like middle schoolers or freshmen talking to seniors. The ambany listened patiently and were more likely to defend Rifun, but Tommen knew the rumor mill too well. Something was going to be heard, misheard, misconstrued, misspoken, and it would spread like wildfire.

He glanced longingly toward the portal room, ground his teeth, then turned and headed up the staircase, all the while shaking his head and telling himself it was a bad idea. He didn't need to go. He had no obligation to tell Rifun that the girls on the playground were saying mean things about him. It sounded childish, pathetic. There were a number of people out to kill him, and why should he be concerned with a few vaovao who didn't like him very much, or who, God forbid, questioned some of the things he did or didn't do? They were only vaovao; they didn't understand what he went through on a daily basis, the stress and the workload, not to mention that whole bit about keeping up appearances and not letting on about his seizures.

And why was he, Tommen, so worried about it? Why was he so concerned that he would willingly climb this godawful staircase to deliver a pithy message, like the mailman bringing everyone their daily supply of junk mail?

His knuckles rapped on the door before he could stop them, and Rifun bid him enter.

"Back so soon? Have you a lead on our missing journal?" Rifun inquired. He sat at one of his tables, huge papers rolled out over the tops, sprawling onto the floor. Some looked like maps, others graphs and charts, others Tommen couldn't tell what they were supposed to be.

"No, I don't, sorry. Actually, I came here with a concern."

"I hope it's a big concern. While you are under my direct command concerning the location and retrieval of the journal, all other concerns, you do have a more direct supervisor to take them to."

"Well, yes, I know—" Truthfully, he'd completely forgotten. Who was his supervisor again? An Arowa, yes, but what was the name? Gideon? Gamorah? Something like that? "—but it's directly relating to you."

Now Rifun looked up, his expression unamused. "Oh? More concerns over my personality?"

"Mm...yes and no. I have my concerns about it, true, but others have concerns, too. I think they're starting to notice."

"Notice...?"

"They seem to think you're disinterested and uninvolved."

"Who is they?"

"Other students. I mean, at first, I was going to ignore it as idle gossip, you know, vaovao talk. But then some of the ambany got in on it. They question you, think you did or are kind of wasting the momentum you gained from the Akarin victory. They wonder why, if you plan to go after the Borelians, you haven't done so or announced any plans or—"

"They're mad that they're not included in the war tent," Rifun interrupted.

"Well...yes? I mean, I suppose so."

"Once upon a time, the Cult forces were small enough that it was practical to have all or as many involved as possible. It brought everyone in on the same page, left no one out, and it made everyone feel important, feel wanted. That's great and all, but now we're a large enough operation that it is no longer practical. Too many cooks in the kitchen as it were. I have my plans and my advisors. Not everyone gets a say or else we'd become a Congress. Bicker, bicker, bicker, and nothing gets done. The underlings are here to study, to train, to serve, and to not ask questions. Not of me. They can ask their supervisors or commanders. Yes, we are in a time of transition, rebuilding the fortress, trying to assimilate the Akarin, moving the Order away from purely military into a full way of life and culture, and still figuring out how to hurt the Borelians. It's a big task. Rome wasn't built in a day, as they say."

"Those are the defending arguments, yes, but the rumors are still out there, that you don't care anymore or you were wounded in such a way that you can no longer use the Akari, stuff like that."

"And you would like me to...what? Send them to time out? Make a show of force?" He stood and continued before Tommen could speak. "Quite frankly, I don't think these rumors started at the vaovao level. I think they started at the Akarin level. They can't overthrow us by force, so divide and conquer, just as we did to them. Now then, seeing how you have taken a particular interest in my reputation and well-being, maybe you can help me root out the source. Maybe go down there and start another rumor. We're moving. The First Order machine is going to be turning again. Something big is coming. Don't give any specifics, but as Faharoa's favorite, you've noticed things and heard things, and something has got to be coming down the line."

Tommen shifted uncomfortably. "Is something coming down the line?"

"I expect so. Soon enough." He paused. "Go on then, if there is nothing else you wanted to talk to me about. And start spreading rumors. You're a high schooler; you know how this works."

He did, and he hated it. He hated himself more for opening his big mouth. He wasn't sure what he'd expected Rifun to do, but this assignment was not part of the plan. And he still had to get back home to bed. Dammit.

Nevertheless, he did as he was told, going down to the sub-levels the Akarin now called home. Only the biggest, strongest, most powerful, and most threatening were actually kept prisoner. In the month or so since the battle, many had been allowed to at least visit home, if not return completely. Some were too small or too weak to constitute much of a threat. Some were acts of good faith. Those Akarin who helped with the reconstruction and other duties around the fortress were permitted privileges. But whatever their status, those who were in the fortress at the end of the day slept somewhere in the sub-levels.

"What is your business here?" one Order guard asked.

Common Order members were not permitted to just waltz in and out of the prison, after all. Lessened the likelihood of a hostage situation, Tommen supposed.

"Faharoa has sent me to conduct a general survey," Tommen replied. "He needs to know if any of the Akarin have ever been to Kath. Or if any are Kolkath."

It was an unusual request. A few of the Akarin who were near the gates were listening and began murmuring among themselves.

"Why does he need to know that?" the guard wondered.

"I don't know. He's got something big planned. He's in the middle of a huge productive...I don't know. But he's busy and getting things mapped out; he just needs to know if any Akarin have been to Kath. I'm not a soldier or strategist, just a lackey."

The guard did not disagree. Finally he stepped aside and unlocked the door. "You may stand here in the front and ask your question. Akarin talk. I am sure it will spread. Whether they answer or answer honestly is on them."

"All I can ask."

As soon as Tommen stepped inside, he was greeted with a chorus of hisses, growls, and other noises of disapproval. Clearly, he was remembered as the one who saved Rifun's life. So there was no need to bore anyone with introductions and formalities.

"Is any Akarin here Kolkath? Or has anyone ever been to Kath?"

He expected there to be shouts of rage, telling him to shut the hell up and go the fuck home, but he saw that the news and questions were spreading through the crowd. He waited a good ten minutes for the questions to circulate through and for anyone to come forward, but none did. He was not offended. Kath was only recently Engaged, and there was little reason to go there besides. Despite the naysayers, Tommen thanked them for their time and departed, making sure to thank the guard as well. He was prepared to turn to go to the portal room, then thought better of it. If he was on an urgent mission for the Faharoa who was busily scribbling away at some big plan, then he'd better get up there to report on his little assignment.

In actuality, Tommen just went up a few floors and waited around a bit, trying to count off how long it would take him to get to the eighth floor, get an audience, report his findings, and get back down. He gave himself a little extra time, just in case, then jogged casually back to the main floor. He glanced toward the sub-levels. Hopefully the rumor got started and would keep going. Fight fire with fire. One rumor got started saying Rifun was passive and disinterested, another said something huge was coming. War of the words. Maybe by the time the rumor mill fought it out, they might actually have something concrete to go on. Judging by the maps Rifun had open, there was every chance that something big really was coming down the line.

He wasn't more than five feet from the portal room when someone called out behind him.

"Tommen Forbes!"

Crying a little on the inside and longing only for his bed, Tommen turned. He did not recognize the alien species offhand, though he knew there was one in his study class. It was a bit like an anorexic centaur, small, skinny, body of a four-legged animal while also sporting the upper half of a...not necessarily a man, but a humanoid, anyway, with rubbery, silver-blue skin, huge black eyes, and short, stubby antennae.

"Can I help you?" Tommen wondered.

"You are asking about Akarin who have been to Kath."

"Yes...? Have you been to Kath?"

"I have not, but I know one who has. He is dead now."

"Great. What good does that do me today?"

The centaur alien shifted its...hooves? Paws? Tommen wasn't sure. It lowered its voice. "You seek the third journal."

"That's right."

"His name was Abbal Duma T'Akhar Mureel Sibon."

"Bet that was a fun name to recite in school."

"He was Ururian, from Lipol, Quadrant One, Parsec Eight, Sector Four, System Six, Planet Eleven. He was sent to Kath to take the journal far away during the Dispersal."

"Cool. Where'd he hide it?"

"No one knows. Abbal was a known thief and trickster. After he went to Kath, he disappeared, with only brief mentions of him for several years afterwards." The centaur continued before Tommen could speak. "All the records you have been following describe the path of the fake copy that was intentionally distributed. No mention was ever made of the original, but if you follow Abbal's trail, you may have better luck."

Tommen studied him. "Thanks for the information. Next question, why give it? Most Akarin in there are ready to tear my head off."

"They are," the centaur agreed. "But I am not Akarin. Not anymore. Believe me, I have no desire to see harm come to them; they were always good to me. The First Order is good to me as well.

Perhaps if the Order has its journals and the Akarin have their Authored Books, and we can freely study and discuss, we may come to an understanding. I wish only for peace."

Tommen let out a breath. "You and me both. Thanks for the info. I'll be sure to check into it."

Walking away, Tommen actually found himself disheartened and a little disgusted, mostly at the thought that someone would betray their own so freely. Sure, the alien may have good intentions and a true desire to foster peace, but Tommen had every reason to believe that finding the third journal would bring everything but peace.

He needed to talk to Chandler.

He returned home.

Overnight, the first ferocious storm of February blew into Charleston, coating everything in a glossy sheen of ice. Tommen texted Chris to ask if he was still wanted at the job site since school was canceled. Chris texted back saying that it didn't matter anyway since the ice was snapping power lines. Those that remained in tact came down when out of control vehicles slammed into the poles. No power to the site, no power at the office, and probably too dangerous to be out anyway.

So instead, Tommen headed over to Becky's house where they made love, made breakfast, then watched a movie before her mom arrived home from work, slowly puttering along in her little car, trying to make it all the way home before anything bad happened. She greeted them, offered to make lunch, went to bed when they refused. Becky stretched and made some comment about getting back to work before seeing Tommen off.

He slipped and fell several times on the icy sidewalks, knocking the wind from his lungs at least once. It took twenty minutes to make the three minute walk, and he walked in the door just as his dad pulled in the driveway. Muttering under his breath, Tommen dutifully pulled his car out of the garage so his dad could pull in.

"No work today?" Walter asked.

Tommen shook his head. "No. Not safe, no power."

"I get it. We lost power at the station for a bit before turning on the generators. Power just came back on as I was leaving. Would have been home sooner, but it was a chore getting the car started. That and the roads."

"Well, we still have power here."

"That's always good. Do we still have the news?"

His dad flipped on the TV. Reception was fairly decent, all things considering, and the midday news was just coming on.

"NASA announces a major project designed to keep us safe and better connected," the anchor reported. "Today, NASA announced the launch of the Safe Earth Defense Shield, an energy shield they say will protect the planet from larger meteors and space debris that presently do not burn up in the Earth's atmosphere as it is. They also report that it will filter out more harmful UV rays, meaning you can go out and enjoy the sunshine longer with less worry. Other side effects include improved TV, phone, and Internet reception. While proponents hail the shield as a stunning leap in technology and protecting the planet, critics worry about the cost of operation, whether it could be used for crime and terrorism purposes if it fell into the wrong hands, and what impact it will have on climate change."

Walter waved a hand dismissively. "If only they knew why it was really in place."

"How are the other Time Agents taking it?" Tommen wondered.

"Oh, they're not happy. They have business to conduct, which means going to and from the Wheel. Now they have to rideshare with the likes of Rifun and his cronies. Runner activity has increased, as expected. But In Jezik's global operations seem to have been stemmed, confined to the Middle East and some parts of Asia. Since they can no longer open portals anywhere they want on a whim, they have to travel the old-fashioned way. But, it will make them easier to find and fight."

"Are we fighting?"

"Not us. Not likely. But there are Time Agents in the military who are sketching out plans, I'm sure."

Tommen followed his dad down to his bedroom. "There are, or you hope?"

"Both."

"And the other worlds?"

His dad began methodically removing and storing all the goodies on his belt. "Right now, we're all just sitting tight. The shields are in place, and our first goal is to eliminate any and all Borelians that are already here before going after the ones that aren't. Fighting them here will give us a better idea of what it's going to be like out there."

Tommen nodded. "Makes sense, I guess. So what's the plan, then?"

"I don't know, but from what I understand, the Borelians aren't too happy that we got one up on them. At the same time, however, they're holding their peace, which I find suspicious. My guess is, they're waiting for something."

"Is the Wheel still safe?"

"For now. There haven't been any reports of attacks or kidnappings. Actually, from what I've heard, the Borelians are conspicuously absent from the Wheel."

"That's odd."

"It is, and we should keep an eye on things, but for now, all appears well. How are things in the fortress?"

"I don't know. I mean, there are rumors and conversations, disgruntled grumblings from the underlings, dissatisfaction with Rifun. I figured they were just grumpy grunts, and when I brought it up to him, he agreed. I don't know, but he seems to have some kind of plan in the works. He had maps and charts and graphs all scattered around on one of his tables; I didn't look close enough to really say what they were."

"And the journal?"

"One little sliver of information I should look into, but I don't hold out a lot of hope. I guess I could look into it today, with school being canceled, but taking a day off from everything else sounds pretty nice, too."

"Yes, it does," his dad agreed. "Now shoo."

Tommen left the room so his dad could change and headed out to the living room where the news had switched to continuing coverage of the flu epidemic. The initial scare was over, they said, but that didn't mean it was going away any time soon. Everyone was still advised to wash hands or use sanitizer, get checked out at the first sign of sickness, avoid contact with those who were sick, and, as always, get a flu shot...even though it was estimated to be only fifteen percent effective.

"I'm guessing you're going to stay up for a bit and want me to Band you later," Tommen said, not looking at his dad.

"That would be the idea, yes. Are you hungry?"

Walter cooked up a pizza and they split it, Tommen eating three-quarters, his dad only one-quarter.

"So, what exciting things are going on in Tommen's life?" his dad wondered as they meandered back into the living room. "I hardly see you anymore, it seems, and when I do, it's usually bad news. So let's hear something that isn't about Borelians or Rifun or gallivanting across the universe. How is school?"

Tommen shrugged. "School. Got finals coming up quick, then move to a new semester."

"What are your classes?"

"Spanish, Algebra, English, History, Creative Writing."

"Creative Writing? I thought you hated English."

"I do."

"I thought you would have switched out at first chance."

He squirmed a little. "I was going to, but the shrink kind of talked me out of it. For one, Reisig is teaching it, and I like her. And...shrink says that getting some of my stories out there might be productive."

His dad nodded slowly and finished off his last slice of pizza. "Well, it's good to know you're actually listening to him and taking some of his suggestions."

"Yeah, he's not a bad guy. I've even managed to get him to talk about himself a little bit, you know, when we're talking about our lives before Time."

"Trust and openness is a good thing. Have you told Becky?"

"About seeing a shrink? No, never." He went on before his dad could comment. "It's not her, it's who will hear her if she lets something slip."

"And who's going to hear?"

"Ricky Freeman. Tyler Freeman's younger brother. And any of Tyler's gangbangers who are still in school. I don't want them harassing me, I don't want them harassing Becky or Will or any of them. Better to wait, at least until she's graduated and away from that crowd. Then maybe I'll tell her."

He could see his dad wasn't convinced, but he didn't press the matter, instead asking, "And how are you and Becky doing?"

"Good. I mean, I went over this morning and we hung out for a little while. I managed to pry her fingers off her sewing machine for a few hours." Tommen grinned. "She's counting down the days until she's done sewing."

"She has an end date? I thought her sewing was putting her through college?"

"She says she's got enough in scholarships for the first year, or most of the first year. She has enough saved on her own to get her through her second year. Apparently, she's been in talks with some lab somewhere to do an internship once she gets her Associate's. The work experience will count toward her further schooling in credits and cash, and I guess they're...super eager to do medical research and DNA testing on dwarfs? Like, they're really excited to have willing participants for whatever they're doing and even more psyched that she wants to go into genetics. She's their dream come true, I guess."

His dad frowned and nodded. "Good for her. And where do you fall in these plans?"

"I'm not entirely sure."

"Still planning on going to the same college?"

"Oh, yeah, absolutely. I mean, that hasn't changed or anything. Even if something happened between us, I mean, that's still where I'm going to school. I have to look out for me no matter what. Degrees are nice, but I still need the smarts to back it up; isn't that what you like to say?"

"Yes," his dad sighed. "You two are still being good, right?"

"Yes, Dad. We're being good." He'd told the lie so many times now, he could almost make himself believe it, except for the part where they'd just had sex earlier that morning. "No worries."

"I always worry about you. For one thing or another, I always worry."

"You sound like a mother hen."

"Well...you don't have a mom. I've been having to do both for almost ten years. I have to worry. Cut me a break."

"I'm seventeen, Dad. Not seven. I'm almost eighteen, actually."

"In six months."

"Almost eighteen."

"And what happens when you turn eighteen, I wonder? Other than I can no longer claim you on my taxes?"

Tommen opened his mouth, but couldn't come up with anything clever. Vote? Okay, so what? Get charged as an adult for any crimes he might commit? That didn't sound too appealing. Receive a little card that said he was the property of the U.S. Government and could be forcibly drafted into military service at any time? Happy birthday, Love, Uncle Sam. Smoke legally? He'd never been one for the smoking, and drinking was still three years away. He thought a moment longer. Nope, couldn't come up with anything.

His dad raised a brow. "That's what I thought."

Tommen shifted in his seat. "So what about you, then? What sort of crazy antics are you guys up to in county?"

"Crazy antics, yeah, right. I'm more unpopular than ever."

"Why, what happened?"

"Well, you know that over New Year's I confronted Vin about

being a lazy, duty-dodging T-shirt seeker, right? Well, apparently his wife recently accused him of the same thing. She kicked him out of the house for a few days and now she wants a divorce."

"Okay...? I mean, that's terrible, but—"

"Somehow it's my fault, or so the others in the department seem to think, as if pointing out someone's flaws is a bad thing. Granted, maybe I didn't do it with the best tact and used zero diplomacy, but the man was completely oblivious. I just didn't want someone getting hurt or killed because of his incompetence. And if something did happen, rest assured Kate or Dean would have ripped into him ten times harder for it."

"Ouch. But, what can you do?"

His dad let out a breath and itched his mustache. "Keep my head low, try not to make a scene, do my job the best I can."

"Still thinking you should have retired?"

"Every day."

The midday news ended and the soap opera marathon began. Tommen and Walter both dove for the remote, Walter winning only because he cheated and Banded at the last second. They argued a bit over what to watch, Tommen winning only because his dad admitted his need for sleep at some point. To think he'd gotten home only an hour or so ago and would be leaving for work in only a few more hours. Part of it was the snow, Tommen understood, but it still sounded pretty miserable.

So he spent the afternoon puttering around the house, raiding the fridge, watching TV, occasionally working on his homework, constantly checking his email to see if he'd gotten any of the scholarships he'd so painstakingly fought for with his terrible essays. When the grim clouds blew away and the sun began peeping through, he took the shovel and went to dig out some of the elderly neighbors who paid him generously in hugs, kisses, cookies, cake, and an old two-dollar bill. When he got done and returned home, he Banded his dad through a full night's sleep, then went to the kitchen to start something for dinner.

"If today is your lazy day, what happens if school is canceled again tomorrow?" his dad asked, walking out in full blues and helping himself to a small serving of friend chicken and mashed potatoes.

"Then I guess I'll either be working or...working. One way or another, I have to get stuff done. Lazy day was just for my sanity."

"Oh, I understand, believe me. I don't fault you for it."

They ate dinner together before Walter left for work; Tommen watched him creep down the road at well below the posted thirty-five speed limit. He thought about going back down to Becky's house, decided against it. He thought about inviting her over, decided against it. The biggest reason, she had work to get done, and life wasn't all fun and games; sometimes, work had to take priority. Secondly, her dad would be home soon, if he wasn't already. Tommen didn't expect to get sex again so soon (though it would be nice), but he really didn't want to face her dad's scrutiny. He wasn't mean or anything; actually, he was very polite, even charming, which was much scarier.

He ended up calling Will to see what he was up to, which wasn't much. Couldn't go anywhere or chip away at his community service, so he was just hanging out at home. His mom and brother were at the animal shelter looking for a cat or small dog as a pet for Eli, who had become unbearable in his complaints about Will getting a dog and how unfair it was. Will said he offered to blind his younger brother so he could get a big dog, too, but was quickly shot down.

Tommen ended up driving over there, if for no other reason than to have something to do. Eli had shoveled the driveway that morning, so Tommen had a clear path and parking spot. He could see Sydney standing at the door, peeking through the little window at the top, but the dog did not bark. She got down, then back up. And down, and back up. Even when Tommen opened the door, she did not bark or jump on him, just stared at him intently, huge smile on her face as she panted, tongue lolling, occasionally nudging his hand for a scratch. Tommen had a sudden flashback of his interaction with Yawi outside the cabin shortly after Saul's death.

"Sydney, come."

The dog wasted no time in obeying her master's command and was at his side in an instant, standing attentively, even though her harness wasn't on.

"Well, I can't see it, but my mom says it looks like icy shit out there," Will said, walking into the kitchen. "What possessed you to come over?"

"I had to break my cabin fever somehow," Tommen told him.

"Boss ain't working you today?"

"No power."

"Oh. You got power? We do. You can shower and stay here if you need to."

"No, no, we got power. Just bored."

"I hear you. Shirking homework is exhausting. Your dad working?"

"Always."

They'd no sooner opened the fridge than Mrs. Shaw's car pulled in the driveway. In the front seat, Eli looked utterly thrilled. Mrs. Shaw, less so.

"Call it a hunch, I think your brother got his pet," Tommen observed.

"Oh boy, here we go," Will muttered. "Sydney, settle."

The dog, already sitting, cocked her head at him, then swung around to look as the door opened. Eli walked in first, carrying a crate, and Mrs. Shaw was a step behind.

"Oh, Tommen, I thought that was your car," she said absently, as if Tommen didn't pick up her boys for school every morning.

"All right, idiot, what'd you get?" Will asked, following Eli into the living room. "I'm not hearing any hissing, so it's obviously not a cat."

"Nope. Better."

Tommen stayed back a step or two, unsure what was going to come barreling out of the crate as Eli undid the latch. Beside Will, Sydney lay down and stretched out her neck as far as possible, nose twitching, tail wagging occasionally, if uncertainly. Then the door was open and a small puppy came tumbling out.

Sydney just about went sky high, knocking over an end table that, thankfully, only had a few books and magazines on it (though Mrs. Shaw's reading glasses did not fare so well). The puppy, startled by her reaction, came skidding to a stop. Sydney, obviously embarrassed, quickly returned to her master's side and sat down as if nothing had happened, though she lowered her head to sniff the thing.

"You got a wiener dog?" Tommen asked.

"A wiener dog?" Will went to one knee and held out a hand. The puppy, completely forgetting the scary initial reaction and totally unafraid of the massive German Shepherd, went to sniff and lick his fingers. Will petted the puppy and felt over its long body. "What the fuck, Eli? Are you gay or what?"

"William!" Mrs. Shaw barked, pausing in her cleaning up of the end table.

"Dudes with cats are cool. Lots of famous dudes have cats. Lots of dudes have big dogs, or if not big, tough at least. Wiener dog ain't big or tough. It's a purse pet for women. Dude, if word gets out, you are going to be hit on by every gay guy in school."

"His name is Graham Cracker, and he's mine. You don't have to like him," Eli defended. It was an apt name for the dog who was, indeed, the tan-brown color of a graham cracker.

"I don't have to housebreak him, either. Good luck on that one."

By now, Graham Cracker had tired of Will's attention and was now investigating Sydney. The big dog did not move except to lower her nose for a more thorough sniff, at least until the puppy found a dry teat under all her shaggy fur and decided to try and nurse. Then the big dog stood and moved to Will's other side. The puppy, obviously having gotten an idea in its head, followed, and they played ring around the rosie around Will until Mrs. Shaw told the boys to take their dogs and go to their respective rooms.

Tommen followed Will to his room. Sydney obediently went to her rather lavish bed in one corner and lay down, picking out a chew toy and going to work on it.

"A wiener dog," Will sighed, shaking his head. "Great, my little brother is officially gay. I don't know, maybe if this hadn't happened—" He indicated his eyes. "—then we could have had a little more bro time, a little better relationship, more open, so we could talk, that way he could talk to me first, come out to me first, know he had some support behind him before—"

"Eli isn't gay," Tommen cut in. "And the dog isn't that bad. It's only a puppy right now."

"Wiener dogs don't get that big."

"Maybe not, but it's the one he wanted. The one he could get for the situation. Besides, I highly doubt he'll take Graham Cracker with him to college, which means he'll get left with your mom. You think your mom could or would want to handle a huge dog in the house?"

Will frowned. "No, I guess not. But still...a cat, dude. Cat would have been better. Sydney's great around cats. Aren't you, girl?" The dog paused in her gnawing and looked at him. "I don't know why she freaked out like that."

"She smelled a dog in the crate. Suddenly that thing is rushing toward her. She doesn't know if it's vicious or not."

"Maybe. Oh well, nothing was broken, and everything seems okay now. Of course, we're stuck in my room for a little while."

"Boring as hell at my house, too."

They couldn't play video games, and the two of them watching a movie together would have been just too weird. Tommen suggested bringing in Eli, but Will shot it down. He didn't want the puppy in his room, and having three dudes watching a movie together, considering that one was gay, would not help the situation. Tommen couldn't decide if Will was just picking on his little brother, or if he actually thought that little dogs made men gay. Personally, Tommen liked puppies, and he didn't see any problem with wiener dogs, but he decided to keep his mouth shut.

Mrs. Shaw made dinner, and Tommen left shortly afterwards,

citing already bad roads and more impending weather. If there was school tomorrow, or whenever they next had school, he was not looking forward to seeing what would happen to Eli. Would his brother really start a rumor saying Eli was gay? Or was that just a given, if he ever admitted he got a little Dachshund for a pet? Tommen never had a dog or anything growing up, so maybe that was one vicious rumor he'd been mercifully spared, at least in that way; he'd been accused of being gay numerous times, always by Tyler Freeman or one of his buddies.

He arrived home to a quiet house. The power was still on, Rifun was not waiting for him, and there appeared to be no other catastrophes to speak of. He had little desire to rummage through the fridge and cupboards, and when he did out of sheer boredom, nothing really appealed to him, and the most he ate was a bag of chips.

Afterwards, he went to his room and sat down at his desk to do his homework, turning on his stereo and otherwise working quietly. And for a couple hours, there was little else on his mind other than finishing up the last few assignments before getting into final exams. He did not think about Borelians or Tacagans or sickness or war or Rifun or the fortress or rumors or leads or missions or the journal. He thought about Spanish verb conjugation, math formulas, something significant that was supposed to have happened in the assigned reading novel, the major psychological developments in each stage of life and the conspiracy theories that went with each, and balancing chemical equations. And for a few hours, life was totally normal.

The illusion ended around the time that Tommen went to bed, when he finally closed his notebook, rubbed his eyes, and glanced at his clock. Almost ten. He got online to check school closings for the next day, but as far as he could tell, South Charleston High would be open for business. Fuck.

Grudgingly, he shut everything down, turned everything off, put everything away, and dragged himself to the bathroom. Routines were good things, occasionally, and his methodical movements told his body it was time to prepare for bed and go to sleep, so that by the time he got back to his bedroom and set his hearing aids on the charger, he was ten times more tired than he had been sitting at his desk. He flipped off the lights, then crawled under the blanket.

It was there, right on the cusp of sleep, that normal ended, and reality came swarming back to him like a wave of sticky, black tar. Shadows flooded his mind, each with a different name: Disease, War, Discouragement, Despair, Paranoia, Lust, Greed, Power, Depression, Confusion. They clawed at his mind, some finding more purchase than others to try to climb over his defenses. He opened his mouth to suck in air—whether in real life or in a dream, he could not tell—but his chest tightened, no air could come in and no cry could go out. He looked around for Chandler, for any of the White animals, but all he saw were Shadows. If he focused on one, it took a shape as a wolf or a bear or some creature for which he had no name, but just seeing in his peripheral vision, even when he tried to look with his peripheral vision as he had learned so long ago, the Shadows had no definitive form. They could not be touched, could not be caught and wrestled, could not be caged, could not be distinguished; one flowed into another as surely as water flowed from one ocean to another.

He felt the footsteps even before the great beast appeared. Tommen fully expected to see the cerberus shouldering its way through the crowd of Shadows that had encircled him, but it was not. Rather, it was a dog-like creature, not quite a dog, not quite a wolf, but easily twice the size, with ragged, mangy fur that hung in almost indistinguishable patches, and eyes that were at once red, then purple, then glimmering black.

"Why am I here?" Tommen asked hoarsely. "I walked away."

The wolf-dog creature lowered its muzzle to meet him eye to eye. "You walked away, but we did not let you go. We went with you. And you came back. You always do."

"But I know how to defeat you now, or at least get you off my back."

As if he knew it would be there, he reached in his coat and brought out a candle. Some of the smaller Shadows shrank back, but the wolf-dog was unmoved.

"Having a weapon is not the same as knowing how to use it, small one."

Suddenly, the wolf-dog's paw lashed out, catching Tommen fully in the side and tossing him like a ragdoll. He landed twenty feet away, the candle bouncing from his grasp. He lay on the ground, gasping for air even as he pushed himself up on his elbows and tried to stand, pausing as a huge black paw stepped in front of him, inches from his face.

"You are alone here, small one," the wolf-dog said. A Shadow no bigger than a mouse leaped onto his back, but it carried the weight of a cinderblock and made him stumble, though he did not go down. "You have always been alone."

"Chandler!" Tommen cried.

Now more Shadows began leaping, crawling, slithering onto his body, each one ten times heavier than what they looked. He went down to all fours, then flat on the ground, his face pressed in tarry mud. He couldn't see except through a small hole where the wolf-dog sat, watching the whole event. He couldn't breathe, could barely open his mouth to whisper as dirt filled his sinuses.

"Help," he gasped.

In a sudden surge of strength and determination, Tommen heaved himself up, but did not get farther than his hands and knees. Still, he took in air for all he was worth before the Shadows redoubled their efforts and got him back down again.

"Help. Chandler." He took several breaths while he had the chance. "I can't do it. I don't have a candle." He wheezed in a breath, the weight of the Shadows driving him ever more into the mud. "I don't have any light. Help me, please. If there's an Author out there, I beg of you...help me!"

Tommen came awake, his body rigid, poised to run an entire triathlon on a single granola bar and bottle of water, but unresponsive to his brain's commands. His sinuses were beginning to drain, but his throat would not release to allow the intake of air. His body began to panic, but still would not move. He became dizzy and nauseous, his head feeling as if it were stuffed with cotton.

His foot twitched, and it was like the snapping of a rubber band. His muscles began spasming, and Tommen was convinced he was having a seizure. He curled up onto one side, gasping for air and trying to bring his body under control. Even now, the nightmare was fading, though the wolf-dog's eyes still bored into his mind, brought to the forefront by only a passing thought.

Why had he been back in the forest? Why had he been left alone? Why had no one answered his calls? Why had he envisioned a candle in his pocket, but not a lit one, or at least a lighter to go with it? Had Chandler abandoned him? Had the Author abandoned him? Or had her idea of rescue been to simply wake him up? What did all of this mean? How did he make it go away?

Eventually, he sat up on the side of the bed, feeling as though he hadn't slept a wink. Then he did something he hadn't done since he was nine years old. He prayed. It wasn't a big formal prayer with the hands folded, head bowed, nor was he prostrate before the Holy Spirit. He just sat on the edge of the bed and talked to the air.

"God. Author. I don't know who's out there, but if there's a point to this, I'd really like to know it. A little understanding goes a long way. And if there isn't a point to it, you must not have much going on up there if you get a kick out of fucking with a common man's dreams. If you want, I can turn your attention to some wars going on that need your help. Otherwise, I'd just like to get some sleep. Thanks. Or, you know, Amen. Whatever."

Then his alarm went off.

Chapter Twenty
Dead Ends

With the installation of the planetary defenses, the larger war with the Borelians ground to a halt. Underneath the shield, militaries around the world declared decisive victories against the terrorist organization In Jezik, while Time Agents in those militaries were quick to dispatch the Borelian operatives and dispose of them so as not to let on about aliens being in the midst of humanity. Otherwise, no more Borelians landed on the human worlds, and there was even very little trouble in the Wheel. According to the humans who still traveled to the Wheel via Akari-bearer of any number of factions, the Borelians were noticeably absent from the Wheel and other Time goings-on. While suspicious, no one was arguing, though trips to the Wheel were advised to be made quickly and only for real needs. This meant more leniency for lesser Runner crimes, which had markedly risen.

Tommen was one of those who still frequented the Wheel, as much for ridesharing as anything. Having learned basic portals, he was available to take other Time Agents to the Wheel. Recently, he'd also begun learning basic blind portals, "basic" referring to staying on the same planet. Supposedly, there were changes that had to be made and accounted for as one opened a portal through space, but going from one place to another on a single planet was something he could begin to learn, therefore expanding his range of availability.

At first, it had been a little uncertain and a lot scary. Time Agents regarded him suspiciously, as if he might suddenly kill them, or worse, proselytize to them about the Akari and the wonders of the First Order and how great Rifun was as Supreme Leader. Once they realized he was little more than a taxi driver, they stopped watching him warily. A few even tipped. Only one asked for more information about the Akari; after the planned trip to the Wheel, Tommen had taken him to the fortress and set him free. Either he would find his way back or he wouldn't.

But, being a taxi driver to and from the Wheel gave him ample time and no excuses why he couldn't do some more research in pursuit of the third journal, which continued with what little he found on Abbal Duma T'Akhar Mureel Sibon, the Ururian from Lipol, Quadrant One, Parsec Eight, Sector Four, System Six, Planet Eleven. Pretty much the only information he found on the guy was his Timekeeping record, a short one as he was declared a Runner while he was still a Journeyman. He was, as the centaur alien had described, a thief and a trickster, giving Timekeepers the slip in situations where escape really should have been impossible, like an intergalactic Jack Sparrow.

It quickly became apparent that the Wheel would not have the information he needed, or else he was still too low on the totem pole to have access to it. His dad might, as a Captain, but not him. He did find, however, that Lipol kept extensive records on their Time Agents. Seeing how that might prove more helpful, Tommen had gathered his team and set off for Lipol. He might not have taken his crew—it was only a research mission after all—but they were all still listed as higher-ranking Time Agents than him, and it was actually Emet who got them to hand over the information.

Thief and trickster, thief and trickster, thief and trickster. Everyone who had ever been conned by the guy had the same thing to say about him, and it wasn't good. He was a little more discreet while still an honestly operating Timekeeper. Once he got found out, however, his antics were put on display for all to see and marvel at. Had he wanted an honest living, he might have done well as a magician. Except it wasn't an honest wage he was looking for, but the thrill of the theft and the ensuing chase.

At some point, his antics stopped for a time, and there were handwritten notes in his file that Naq translated as suspicion of involvement in the Cult of the Akari. Tommen internally debated the likelihood of that, or whether he could have been an Akarin. On the one hand, if Cult, they probably would have welcomed his cunning little mind and his antics, getting them into places they weren't before. Maybe he was the one who'd taken the journal to Kath, and Raba simply forgot about it. Maybe Abbal was part of the Cult and that was how he knew the location of the journal, but decided to go back to his old ways, pulling off a huge con on the Cult and running away laughing with their greatest treasure.

On the other hand, if Akarin, it might explain why his antics had seemed to stop for a time, that maybe he'd changed his ways. When the Akarin decided he was reformed and could be trusted, they asked him to use his cunning talents for good and retrieve the journal from Kath. Abbal goes to Kath, gets the journal, then decides he misses the thrill of the con and takes off. It would certainly explain how an Akarin—or former Akarin, as it seemed to be—knew about him and what he'd done, and why the Cult did not.

Or maybe he'd just been an outsider to both parties, keeping up with the news, taking advantage of the chaos of the Dispersal, and decides to take on some high-profile jobs.

Whatever the case, it really didn't matter. He'd had the journal. The unfortunate thing was that he was confirmed dead decades ago. Between Kath and his death, there were only passing mentions of him in this place or that place, who he conned, what he stole. There was one brief article about the items found in his place of residence when he was confirmed dead and the state took over custody of his possessions, returning as many stolen articles as possible to their rightful owners. No journal, or books of any kind, were mentioned.

Tommen made a list of all the places Abbal had visited after Kath and taken that back to the Archives later on, to see if there could be anything of significance to follow. Some places listed were as broad as a planet, where the journal could have gone anywhere. Other places were as unhelpful as a common market where wares passed through dozens of hands every day, and who was going to remember a single book from fifty years ago?

Only one lead seemed promising, and that was a detailed account of the heist of the Duchess' Sapphire on Dimar. It was like something out of a Sherlock Holmes or Agatha Christie novel. The duchess hosted a party on a dark and stormy night, and Abbal invited himself as an entertainer. Thirty-seven people total in the mansion at the time the jewel was stolen, one guest dead, and Abbal the "entertainer" nowhere to be found. True, the one guest died of some health complications unique to his species, but still. Classic Victorian mystery novel.

Anyway, the duchess was long dead now, though her mansion had been tidied up and was now open as a tourist attraction and shrine, the major feature being her extensive library. Seizing the clue, Tommen went alone to the mansion, getting the full, guided tour, learning the history, and casually looking about during the stop in the library. The general rule was looking was permitted, but touching was not. Banding was prohibited as well. But, Tommen figured that what they couldn't see wouldn't hurt them, and he used an invisible Akari Band.

He just about tore that library apart looking for the journal, taking every book off the shelf, opening up some of the larger books to see if they had hidden compartments or books inside books. He even went after the bookshelves, hoping against all hope that maybe the duchess had a secret room that required a secret lever to be tripped or something else cool. Hey, the rest of the story was all Sherlock Holmes, why not take it all the way?

But his search yielded nothing. He tried to ask a few pointed questions from the tour guide, but got nothing. The most he ended up getting out of the tour was a lengthy history lesson and a sticker from the gift shop. No, he wasn't joking.

"Sounds like an interesting day," his dad commented, shrugging on his winter jacket as he prepared to leave for work. "What are you doing tonight, slaying dragons?"

Tommen let out a breath. "I don't know. I mean, I've gone

back over some of the less credible rumors that Julianna had for me, but they're so vague or so old that I might as well throw a dart at a map. I've got...nothing. Nothing to go on."

"Well, it sounds like word of your search has gotten around a little, at least. If someone knows something, they may come forward."

"Yeah, or whoever has it and has been keeping it hidden could take and run away with it again. I can't win."

"Be patient, Tommen. Treasure hunting isn't without its share of setbacks, or else that treasure would have been found a long time ago. Now then, I have to get going to work. Have a good day at school tomorrow. First day of the last semester."

"For this year," Tommen grumbled. "Still have next year."

"Dual-enrollment," his dad said, closing the door behind him.

Yeah, yeah, there was that, too.

Tommen watched his dad roll out, a little more confident now that winter seemed to be coming to an end. It was false springtime in West Virginia, that time at the end of February and beginning of March when the endless cold finally broke. Now it was no longer an endless stretch of misery, but more like pack ice, shining glimpses of the sun peeking through and giving people hope once more. But whether winter moved through like sheet ice or pack ice, it moved slowly nonetheless, and there would be a resurgence about the middle to end of the month that would remind everyone why they all looked at Florida and sighed longingly.

For as much as he complained along with everyone else about the cold, Tommen really did enjoy winter. He'd finally gotten new ski gear and had been out skiing a couple times, even taking Becky with him once. She was good on the bunny hill, and he even managed to train her up on the green runs, but that was where she'd drawn the line for the day. She would putter around back and forth on the gentle slopes, and he could go tear it up and down black diamonds, through trees, and in the terrain park. Tommen avoided the terrain park that day, but he did make sure to stop at Ski Patrol, remind them who he was, and thank them for helping him. He'd been in their office multiple times through the years for one reason or another, but only now did he really appreciate them and want to say thank you. Was that part of growing up and becoming more mature? Whatever the case, Ski Patrol was gracious about it and wished him happy skiing.

Even now, he looked at his gear in the garage, broken in, but still brand new. Spring skiing was always fun. Warm enough that he wasn't ducking inside every half hour, bright and sunny and hopeful, and there was something to be said for doing a little water-sliding on slush. Then, when most people declared the season done and started hanging up their gear, wham! Sudden end of season snowstorm! Then he could go back out in perfect conditions with almost no people to clog up the runs. Ah, heaven...

Sadly, though, there was unlikely to be any spring skiing for him. The hill closed too early in the day, so he'd never make it after school—well, he could, but one hour wasn't much of a trip—and with the weather starting to clear, construction was gearing up for a busy summer, trying to get caught up on everything they'd fallen behind on because of weather and sickness before taking on new projects. Maybe he could ask for a day off, especially if there was a snowstorm in the forecast. He'd been going to school five days a week and work on the weekends for almost a straight month. It was exhausting. Given his other exploits, it was unhealthy. He couldn't just shirk school, but his boss would understand, right?

Chris might, and even Rifun might understand the need for a break, which was the strange thing. Yes, Tommen had been pursuing leads and giving regular reports on the few, unproductive exploits he encountered—he'd have to give one on the failed search in the duchess' library here pretty soon—but Rifun was no longer constantly on him about it. Julianna made a comment here and there, but it was almost as if Rifun had given up. He still had some huge thing he was planning, and his office reflected that, but he no longer seemed interested in the journal. If his demeanor was any indication, he wasn't too big into his big plan, either. Nor did he seem concerned about the rumors and whispers that floated around the fortress. On occasion, he would be back to his old self, smirking, sarcastic, with a thousands things going through his head at once, but mostly he was...dead on his feet.

Julianna said it was just depression. He either needed to retrieve the journal or move forward on his big plans, and that would set him back to rights. Tommen hoped so. He knew what depression looked like; he'd been there. He'd seen Will go through it. He didn't like watching Rifun go through it, if only because the personality changes frightened him, to say nothing of what the man might do if he actually got his mind set to something. But then, watching him seize on the floor, Tommen could only conjure up one emotion: pity.

He got Rifun into his bed, then went snooping around the office. He'd had a plan in his head for a couple weeks, though it felt dishonest, even if it was what he was supposed to have been doing for a while now. Well, he was supposed to have been snooping for a while; the plan in his head was only recent.

He did a brief scan and flip through of Rifun's papers and documents, but could read nothing. It would probably be in his best interest to actually try to learn Malagasy, but laziness usually got the better of him. A huge map was still spilled out over one table, though he couldn't say where it was supposed to be. One of the colony planets, maybe. There were notes and lines and circles and everything else, like the little X's and O's on the chalkboard at football practice. The labels, entirely foreign.

Then Tommen moved to what he was really after. Or a couple things he was really after. He opened up the cupboard where he knew the Authored Books were. No new ones seemed to have appeared, and the ones that were there looked as pristine as ever. That was fine. He'd only wanted to reassure himself that they were there and unharmed. Then he moved over to the more homey side of the room, the one Rifun had sectioned off as his studio apartment, as it were. The man was still out like a light on his bed, hadn't even moved to roll over yet.

Carefully, Tommen began sifting through the drawers, cupboards, chests, looking for anything and everything. False backs, false bottoms, lockboxes, safes. He rummaged carefully through sock drawers and made sure to return everything back the way he found it. He found several safes and lockboxes, then was faced with the daunting task of getting the keys off Rifun's belt.

This was also the day Tommen forced himself to really master Double Banding, creating a Band within a Band so he could maintain Rifun's safety Band and keep his seizures away from prying eyes, but also Band himself so he could take the keys without waking him up.

Tommen discovered a lot of cash in multiple currencies, multiple passports and other government documents, and a number of flash drives. Sifting through, there was one paper he almost passed up until a date caught his eye and he realized Rifun still had his original birth certificate, issued by Madagaskar Française. Rifun Felix Ndolo, born March 13, 1897. Mother: Lalao Andilan. Father: Unknown. It seemed a strange thing to keep until Tommen considered that it might be the only thing he had left of his mother, just her name on his birth certificate. On the top of the certificate, in very feminine handwriting, was another name: Rivotra Felix Andilan.

Maybe he was just being sentimental. Either way, he carefully replaced the papers in the lockbox and set it back in the drawer. It wasn't until the third box that he actually found what he was looking for. One sealed and taped bag held a coarse powder that almost looked like old gunpowder. Holding it up to his nose, Tommen's eyes began to water at how bitter it even smelled. Tarka root, he guessed, the powdered form of the shapeless tuber in another bag next to it, right beside a prescription bottle.

Oddly enough, it looked like any regular script from Walgreens. Tommen set down the powder and picked up the bottle. The name on it was Rivotra Andilan, probably so no normal people connected it to one of America's Most Wanted. Versed (Midazolam), 0.5mg. Take one tablet in the morning with light food or drink. Simple, easy to remember. Just part of the routine. Tommen popped the lid and shook a couple into his palm. Small white capsules with some pertinent pharmacology shorthand etched into the plastic.

This wasn't Midazolam.

Tommen put the pills back in the bottle and replaced it in the box. Carefully, he undid the tape and twist-tie on the bag and took out just a pinch of the powder, putting it in a leftover container he'd taken from the kitchen. Then he tied everything back up, locked the box, returned Rifun's keys, released his secondary Band, grabbed a Book and waited.

Rifun started to come around about ten minutes after Tommen got him into bed, but he remained in an absent, unresponsive, semi-conscious state, staring at the ceiling, for another two minutes or so.

Tommen had the Book open, but he did not read. Someone was poisoning Rifun. The pills in the bottle were not what they said they were. Was the tuber even a tarka root? But if Rifun wasn't going out and getting his own meds, that meant they were being delivered, and Tommen knew of only one person the man might trust enough to bring him the medication he needed.

He looked up as Rifun stirred and stumbled out of bed. Tommen stood as if to help, but Rifun put his hand up and disappeared into a fully-sectioned off part of the room for several minutes. When he returned, he looked pale, but almost normal. He was still silent as he removed his hair tie and quickly brushed his long hair back into something neater, something that didn't look like it had been rubbed around on the floor.

"Ready?" Tommen asked.

Rifun glanced at the messenger halfway in the door, then back at Tommen. "He can wait a minute. What did you want again?"

"I was just about to give you my latest update on the journal search."

"All right, then, go ahead."

So Tommen relayed his adventures on Dimar, from how the lead came about, to the tour, to tearing apart the library searching for the journal, to his failure to find anything of use. Rifun came around a little better and seemed almost interested.

"I don't have anything to go on anymore," Tommen concluded.

"I've looked over all the rumors Julianna told me about, her sheet, her list of leads, but it's just not enough. It's like saying that the journal is out there in the universe somewhere. Great, am I supposed to scour the universe? I will literally die before I find it."

"Has anyone told you that you are very talented at drama and theatrics?" Rifun wondered. "Why didn't you sign up for the school play this year?"

Tommen sighed. "I don't know where to go from here. I mean, word is getting out that we're looking, and I told my groupies to keep their eyes and ears peeled for anything useful, but we're at a dead end. Do you or Julianna know anything more?"

"Nothing useful, I'm afraid. Nothing that will make it magically appear out of whatever cave it's hiding in."

"But do you know anything?"

Rifun shook his head. "Afraid not. Or else I would have gone after it a long time ago, maybe even before I came after the journal you found in your cave. Was there anything else you needed?"

"No."

Tommen dropped the Band and the messenger strode purposefully into the room. "Honorable Faharoa."

"Speak," Rifun commanded. His color had returned, and his voice was firm.

"A message, sir." The alien handed over what looked like folded parchment sealed with wax, like one might expect from medieval kings and lords. "From Quadrant Four, Parsec One, Sector Eleven, System Eighty-Four, Planet Thirty-Six. A planet called—"

"Hlohi," Rifun finished, breaking the seal and unfolding the parchment. Without looking at the messenger, he said, "You may go."

The messenger left, but Tommen hardly noticed. He was more intent on watching Rifun. And for a long minute, it looked as if the old Rifun was starting to break through the shell the drugs had encased him in. He came alive, interested, curious, a thousand things going through his mind all at once as he calculated and recalculated. He hadn't said a word.

"What does Hlohi want?" Tommen inquired innocently. "Have they been attacked?"

Rifun looked at him, as though he'd forgotten he was there. He folded the paper and shoved it in a pocket, crossing the room in long, purposeful strides. "No. But that doesn't mean they're not going to be, very soon."

Tommen hurried after him, out of the room and down the stairs. "I don't understand, what's happening?"

"Hlohi is going rogue."

"I don't—"

"They plan on attacking the Borelians themselves. That plan is bad enough, but theirs is even worse; it will only get them all killed. Or enslaved."

"But I don't understand. How do they plan on attacking at all?"

"Wolf Clan all wield Time, most of them wield the Akari as well."

"Yes, but that's only Wolf Clan. Are they planning on bringing the other clans into this or going it alone?"

"Now you see why it's a stupid plan. Keep up."

Tommen lengthened his stride and increased his speed, which only worked until one foot got tangled up in the other and he fell thirty feet down the staircase. He coughed as the dust cleared and found Rifun standing over him.

"It's not a race," he said with a familiar sarcastic smirk. He held out a hand and helped Tommen back to his feet. "It's a wonder you got as far as you did in your adventures."

"I'm not exactly athletic," Tommen defended.

"That much is for sure."

"Where are we going? What do you want from me?"

"I want either you or your dad or both to go to Hlohi. Find Kayla and talk some sense into her. Barring that, at least get them to Tacaga so they can explain exactly what their grand plan is so they don't get enslaved or blasted into oblivion. Going rogue is one of the dumbest things they can do right now, especially with a small, primitive force like theirs."

"What if they won't come?"

"Well then, I'm pretty sure we'll still have to meet on Tacaga in order to figure out how to respond and protect ourselves."

"What about your big plans you've got laid out up there?"

"I will see about incorporating those, but we need to figure out what just happened on Hlohi." Rifun paused on the landing to the third floor. "You keep going, get yourself and your dad to Hlohi. I'll see you on Tacaga later."

Tommen nodded and took off down the stairs, making it to the first floor in one piece. It wasn't until he was just about to open a portal that he considered that his dad was at work. Checking his watch, Tommen saw his dad would be at work for six or seven hours or more. Unless there was literally a Borelian invasion going on where safety of the entire planet was at stake and so rendered speeding tickets laughable, he wasn't about to go running off across the universe. Even more to the point, he would cite the fact that he was not a leader or ambassador of Earth, like Mi Chin, so he couldn't go around barking orders. Further, Kayla was on Hlohi now, helping the Krydik with their plans and defenses, and Hlohi wasn't about to take direction from a white man. He would also say that Kayla was a grown woman and bull-headed besides; Micaiah had had a hard enough time trying to get her to see reason at times, so what hope did the rest of them have?

Tommen had never been to Hlohi, only knew its universal coordinates, and had never tried a brand new blind portal before, not on his own with no supervision. Did he dare try it now? Did he hope to bypass black holes and all manner of space stuff that could easily kill him? Did he dare hope the Author took pity on his worthless attempts at opening a blind portal and help him along some? Well, only one way to find out, and he prayed it wouldn't be the last thing he did in his life.

Trying to open a blind portal was like jumping into rushing rapids, where the river moved both upstream and downstream and trying to pick out a single marked pebble on the bottom of the riverbed. The first attempt knocked Tommen on his ass, but he was no worse for wear. The second time he dived in, he steeled himself for the sudden pull of the rapids. Even preparing himself did little to soften the jolt.

He wasn't even sure how he was supposed to tell which quadrant was which or which planet. Was he anywhere close? Was it a matter of will? It was hard enough with Time. With the Akari, factoring in Matter and Energy, he might have expected it to be easier, but if this was easier, he hated to think was harder felt like. Could he maybe lock onto Kayla's signal and beam her back—no, wait, that was Star Trek. Here in the real world, he had to go to her.

He found Earth easily enough, and tried to use that as a fixed reference point. First, he had to go from Quadrant One to Quadrant Three. Given that the majority of space was space, that part wasn't actually too difficult. From there, it was just narrowing it down into Sector, Parsec, and so on. But then, once he found what he thought was Hlohi, the rushing rapids all came together in a single current, trying to drag him away. Still, he hung on, and a portal sputtered to life.

Glancing briefly at the landscape on the other side, Tommen decided it looked promising, said another quick prayer, then jumped through.

The air was breathable and the ground was soft. For the first fifteen seconds, that was all that mattered. Tommen rolled over on his back, looking up at blue sky, white clouds, and green leaves. The air was warm, a pleasant summer day. And he was alive.

No sooner had he thought this than arrows, spears, and other sharp objects were suddenly pointed at him, and a troupe of Natives surrounded him.

"Well, fuck."

He did not resist as they forced him to his feet and bound his wrists in scratchy, primitive, unusually strong rope. From there, it was a walk down the crest of a ridge, through a valley, over another hill, up another ridge, and toward a mountain. The party members did not speak to him, though they spoke easily enough to each other, quieting when their forest trail turned rocky and they began climbing a narrow mountain path. Eventually the path narrowed between two large boulders, guarded by two more tribe members. Beyond, part of the mountain looked to have fallen away in ancient times, creating a large, grassy bowl. A stone village had been erected there, extending all the way up to a much older village carved directly into a cave in the side of the mountain, protecting it from the wind and weather.

The Native party that had captured Tommen spoke to the guards at length before being allowed through. His wrists were not untied, and he was paraded through the village like a captured enemy. He got plenty of stares from children who paused in their games or chores to watch the white-skinned man walk through town, but the adults ignored him for the most part.

He was taken to a large community building of some form, high up in the carved village. With the shade and protection from the wind, it was easily twenty to thirty degrees cooler here, and Tommen was thankful to still have his long shirt and pants on. He was made to sit, guarded by one man while the rest of the party went off to...do something? Tell someone he was here?

In one corner of the building, a group of women sat in a circle, making or mending clothes, weaving cloth, trading gossip. One rocked a baby. In another corner, a group of elders entertained young children with tales of old.

"Tommen!"

He jumped at his name and looked to see Kayla walking toward him. He'd only ever seen her in modern, Earth clothing, but she seemed to have reverted to full Native, wearing light leathers and true moccasins, her hair pulled back in a couple of simple, unadorned braids. Tommen opened his mouth to speak, but she beat him to it.

"What are you doing here?" Her tone sounded irritated, even angry.

"You say that as if you don't know," Tommen replied uncertainly.

"I can take a guess."

"Then why ask?" He went on before she could say anything. "I'm just the messenger here. Rifun wants a meeting on Tacaga to figure out what you guys think you're doing. My dad would have come instead, but he's at work and I'm the only one who can get through the shield, so..." He shrugged.

Kayla gave him a look he dared not interpret. She said something to the man who had been guarding him. The man looked uncertain but did as she said, untying Tommen's wrists before leaving.

"You're lucky a Wolf Clan party found you," she told him. "The other clans are well and almost permanently removed from Earth, but that doesn't mean they've forgotten the hardships of the past. God knows what they'd do to a white man these days."

"You guys really think you're going to attack the Borelians?" Tommen hissed, fully aware that the gossip circle in the corner was probably listening more than they were letting on, even if they didn't stare. "You're one clan."

"With allies. Rifun isn't the only one who's been busy lately."

Well, at least someone thought so. "Kayla, don't do this. Not without talking to the other leaders first, at least. Listen, you could have taken your clan and allies and done whatever it is you wanted to do, but you didn't. You sent out advanced notice, knowing that one or all of us were going to come and try to stop you, or at least talk to you. Chances are, you have something to say, and you want someone to shut up and listen. Fine. Go to Tacaga and speak."

"I intend to. And Tacaga be damned, I'm bringing my allies as well. We are not going to let our fate rest in the hands of a maniac."

"Great. Tell them, not me. Once again, just the messenger."

"Whose messenger? I didn't send a letter to your dad." Kayla turned and started walking away. "We're still preparing. Take a message back to your master that we'll be there on Tacaga, but it will be our timing. It may be a few hours."

Tommen visibly flinched when she referred to Rifun as his master, but part of him also knew he couldn't defend against it. Three times the man had lain helplessly at his feet, body twisted in seizure or its aftermath. Three times, Tommen had let him live, even helped him. Nevertheless, Kayla was done talking to him, and he gained nothing by sitting here as an unwanted guest.

He stood and walked just outside the longhouse. Obviously, if Kayla was here, this was Wolf Clan. She'd even said as much. Wolf Clan operated partly here on Hlohi, partly on Earth, so portals and Time and all that was nothing new, but he was still left wondering if he should open a portal right there, or at least go politely outside the village first. Well, they'd already paraded him through town, so it wasn't as if his presence was top secret. And if someone stopped him and asked, he'd just open a portal right there and leave.

More stares followed him on his way out of the village, most of them from children. No one stopped and asked him his business, but he didn't miss the waves of hostility coming off the villagers. Seeing the plight of Earth and Native North America, few in Wolf Clan had any love for white men.

The guards did not stop him from leaving, and he tried to be as polite as possible, thanking them and telling them to have a nice day. They simply stared at him, perhaps the least hostile but easily made up for in confusion. He took a sharp turn around the corner, waited until he was fairly certain he was out of sight, then opened a portal back into his bedroom.

He swore as he looked at his clock. His alarm would have already gone off, but not by much. He could Band and still make it out the door on time, but looking at his bed only reminded him that he hadn't slept at all last night. He might have, if he'd been better about getting to Hlohi and getting closer to the Wolf Clan village. Landing on their border, being captured, and going on a six-hour hike was a bit of a setback.

"Tommen?" His dad was just outside his room. He pushed open the door and flipped on the lights. "Oh, good, you're up."

"Barely," Tommen sighed, yawning. "I actually haven't slept at all. Literally, at all tonight."

"Want me to Band you for a bit?"

"Can try."

He'd no sooner laid down than he was asleep. He'd no sooner fallen asleep than he came roaring awake, blind and confused, fists finding flesh until he was face-down on the ground in a submissive position, his dad over him, just about to break out the handcuffs still on his belt. Tommen relaxed and sucked in a breath, not an easy thing to do with his dad's knee between his shoulder blades, calf pushing his head to one side, one of his arms set firmly against his back, the other still in an iron wrist lock and throbbing painfully.

"You awake now?" his dad wondered cautiously.

"Nice iron wrist," Tommen mumbled into the floor. "That was three to five seconds, wasn't it? New record for you."

"I've had lots of practice. Can I let you up?"

"Your call."

His arm was released, and it flopped uselessly to the ground. He did not move for a long second after his dad got off him, finally pushing himself up and crawling back onto his bed.

"Nightmares again?" his dad asked.

Tommen sat up on the edge of the bed and shook his head. "I don't remember."

"Must have been. I guess next time I'll let sleeping Tommens lie."

He rubbed his face. "Yeah, I guess so. I didn't hurt you, did I?"

"I had you on the ground in three seconds. I should be asking you that."

"Yeah, I'm fine."

"All right, if you're sure." He paused. "You are still going to see the shrink, right?"

"Yes, I am. Every Thursday. You can call him and ask." Tommen sighed and rubbed his eyes. "Guess you have to dump everything out before it can get put away properly, huh?"

"I suppose so." His dad folded his arms and leaned against the wall. "So what have you been doing all night?"

"Playing cowboys and Indians, except I'm the one who got captured."

"Okay, I'll bite. What happened?"

"Kayla sent a message to all the worlds saying Hlohi—and her allies, whoever they are—are going to attack the Borelians. Didn't say how or who or when or anything, or not that I know of. I was giving my report to Rifun at the time when he got the message, and he didn't exactly share its contents with me. Anyway, he said he was going to do some things and round up the other leaders; he wanted me and you to go to Hlohi and try to figure it out, maybe talk some sense into her before going to a meeting on Tacaga. Well, I made it to Hlohi and kind of got captured by...I don't know if it was a hunting party, war party, border patrol or what. Either way, they took me back to their village."

"Did you speak to Kayla?"

"More accurately, she spoke to me. She said that Wolf Clan and her allies will go to Tacaga, but it's going to be in their timing. Sounds more like she's just telling everyone else what's going on rather than looking for input."

His dad sighed and shook his head. "Death ground takes many forms, it seems. All right. Did she give any estimation on when they'll be going to Tacaga?"

"Not really. She just said it could be a few hours."

"Okay. Well, you're going to be at school, so I guess I'll go, try to talk her out of whatever foolhardy plan she's got going in her mind. How are things in the fortress?"

"I'd say same-old, same-old except this whole message from Kayla thing. Otherwise, same-old, same-old."

"Okay. Time for school."

Tommen reluctantly nodded, throwing his hearing aids on the charger for a few seconds before hurrying along his morning routine, Banding here and there so he could have a decent breakfast and still make it out the door on time. He stopped in front of Becky's house where she was waiting on the sidewalk, probably about ready to march down to his house and figure out why he was running behind. After that, it was the Shaw residence, where Sydney was most ungracefully pooping in the front yard, doing her business before heading off to school. Graham Cracker was also out doing his business, but he had to go back in the house afterwards.

"I keep telling him," Will said. "If he goes to a specialist and gets certified an idiot, he can claim it as a disability and bring Graham Cracker with him as a service dog. But no, he won't do it. I told him that since being gay is no longer considered a mental disorder, he can't use that."

"Because I'm not fucking gay!" Eli protested. "You saw—okay, you knew I went with Erin to the Snowcoming dance a couple weeks ago. That is not gay. And anyway, Graham Cracker is my dog. I'm not going to take him back to the pound. He's a puppy. He needs love and care and attention."

"Would you two please shut up," Becky said, finally having had enough of the argument that had graced the car every day for at least a week. "You're going to be arguing about this until the day you die. Or at least until Will goes off to college."

The brothers shut up, if only because they were stunned by her outburst, but they still exchanged small, one-word aggressions the entire ride in.

"Some days, I wish you'd kick them out," Becky grumbled after the brothers got out at the front door.

"It's all right. I'm used to being a taxi."

"Doesn't mean you have to take abuse from your clients."

"Becky, it's fine." He turned off the engine and turned around, cheeky grin on his face. "Besides, sometimes I like it when my clients abuse me."

She raised a brow. "Oh, really? Found something fun you want to try?"

"Maybe later."

"I'll keep it in mind."

They got out of the car and headed inside, hand-in-hand.

"So who else do you taxi around?" she asked.

Humans who were a lot grumpier than her and more obnoxious than the brothers, that was for sure. Tommen was stunned at how many Americans seemed to think that all the mean and nasty people in the world only lived in the United States, and the rest of the world was more welcoming than a Southern Baptist church having a potluck. There were some pretty shitty people in other countries, too.

But, he just told himself that it gave him a chance to get into the Archives. He'd been fingering the tarka root sample all day, wondering how he could test the chemical composition or do something hands-on versus reading about it. Unfortunately, he couldn't come up with anything. Well, he might have, but he didn't feel like trying to break into Tacaga, into Lip, and then break into Do Chien's old laboratory. He wouldn't even know where to start; he certainly didn't know how to actually test the powder. He needed help. For right now, that help came only in the form of reading quietly in the Archives.

The tarka plant was actually native to Sakaria II and later introduced to Dorigis and several other worlds. It acted as erosion control for lakes and rivers while remaining unobtrusive aboveground, blossoming out from a central root, growing between six inches and four feet in diameter like a delicate net covered in tiny white and yellow flowers. Belowground, the central root was between one and eight inches in diameter at the shoulder and could extend between six and thirty inches deep, almost like a carrot. Dozens of smaller roots came from this central root, propagating the plant further. Any one of them could be harvested with minimal or no harm to the plant overall, but if the central root was severely harmed or destroyed, the plant would die. For medicinal purposes, the central root always contained the highest concentration of the active ingredient, but with the knowledge about the root system, secondary roots were preferred except in dire need.

Historically, tarka root was originally used as a comforter before death before it became more common as a heavy painkiller.

Over the years, better research and more refined uses and experiments determined it was better used as a sedative before surgical procedures (and considering the origins of the plant came from more primitive worlds like Sakaria II and Dorigis, one could safely assume that these surgeries were neither sanitary nor pretty).

Socially, tarka was viewed much the same way marijuana or alcohol was seen in the United States. Go out with the dudes or the chicks, have a little fun, get a little high, have a little drink, go home laughing. Supposedly there might be some medicinal properties that could help some people.

Fast forward a few decades, or maybe a century, and tarka root was divided into two main categories: official medicinal strains from the central root of the plant that acted as a heavy sedative or last painkiller; and illicit social strains from the secondary roots that, depending on the dosage, might be little more than a cigarette after sex to a totally buzzed night on the town where you couldn't tell which way was up or even what universe you might be in.

Reading further into the chemical composition and active ingredient, while the concentration of the active ingredient was different between the central and secondary roots, a secondary root could just as easily be used as a surgical sedative at a higher dose, and a central root could be used for a small high in a smaller dose. The actual sedation didn't occur until it got heated up. Being in the ground, the root was dormant, but it only took the temperature of the human body to activate it. Furthermore, the composition itself, once heated, actually looked like a derivative of alcohol. Alcohol was, fundamentally, a depressant, but it also augmented whatever the drinker was feeling for a short time, until the depressant and the brain-pickling began kicking in.

So, yes, tarka root in small doses, diluted in hot tea, probably worked wonders to calm down Rifun's seizures. But it depressed him in the process.

Okay, one down. And whether or not the tarka root in Rifun's drawer was actually tarka root didn't matter, because Tommen didn't have a good way to test the sample he'd taken. The pills, however, those he could say for damn sure weren't midazolam. But how did he figure out what pills they were without having one in hand? He had little doubt that even if Rifun were down or depressed or out of it, he still kept an eye on his pills. And without knowing even what type of pill it was, the possibilities were literally endless. At the very least, Tommen figured he should have copied down the pharmacology information etched on the capsule. Maybe it would have helped, maybe not.

"Hey, I'm ready."

Tommen looked up. His current rideshare was a bad-tempered Costa Rican who didn't appreciate having to ask "one of Rifun's bitches" for help to get to the Wheel, but he had a particularly crafty Runner, whose antics had been getting bolder and even dangerous, he'd had to deliver to the Grandfathers. This was his fourth and last rideshare of the night, and Tommen was ready to go home, even though he'd only been working for maybe an hour, local time.

"All right, let me return these," Tommen said, gathering up his tablets and setting out to return them. The Costa Rican followed him like a hawk-nosed librarian waiting to shush him at any moment. Tommen almost wanted to ask the man what his problem was. Whatever he'd been doing back home, it would still be waiting for him. Time did not pass normally in the Wheel. It didn't pass at all, actually.

Nevertheless, he got the guy home in good time, or what he thought was good time. The Costa Rican simply walked away without a tip or even a thank you. Tommen sighed, rolled his eyes, and prepared to go home. He'd changed into appropriate attire for the tropical rainforest, and now he was returning to something that wasn't quite winter but not yet spring.

He really wanted to get some end of season skiing in. Spring break was coming up fast. If he got lucky and they did get a late season snowstorm, that would make everything perfect. Not that going on a roadtrip with Becky (and her parents) wasn't awesome, but skiing wasn't something he could just do on a whim.

It was eight in the evening when he got home. The house appeared dark, but he knew his dad was off tonight. With his eyes adjusting to the gloom, Tommen could see the light over the oven was on in the kitchen, just enough to see by without lighting up the whole house. Maybe his dad had gone out and forgotten...? No, this was strange. Cautiously, and running through his mind the location of all known weapons in the house, Tommen headed out to the kitchen.

His dad sat alone at the tiny kitchen table. No food was cooking, nor looked as though it had been cooked. The only thing on the table, in his dad's hand, was a beer bottle. His dad did not notice Tommen or else chose to ignore him as he lifted the bottle and took a small drink, staring at the cupboards across from him.

"Dad?"

His dad looked up at him, then back at the cupboards. "I didn't hear you get back."

"What are you doing?"

"Having a beer."

"I have literally never seen you drink. You've been sober for, what, almost a century?"

"Am I drunk? It's just the one, anyway."

"Once again, I have never seen you drink. Not for anything. What happened at the meeting?"

"Wasn't anything to do with the meeting. It's what came after."

"Dad, you're scaring me. What's going on?"

"Laura called. We chitchatted a little, and I asked her about her spring break plans. Then she told me that she won't be coming back to West Virginia. She took her old job back in Minnesota. She also met up with an old boyfriend from high school."

"She left you."

"Yeah. She left me." Walter took a drink, looked at the bottle in the light, half-empty. Sighing, he stood. "I'm going to bed."

"It's only eight o'clock."

"I'm going to bed. At least to lie down for a little while, even if

I don't sleep. Don't Band me. Just keep doing whatever it was you were doing."

"Oh. Okay."

Tommen got out of his dad's way as he moved past, not a hesitation, hiccup, hobble, or waver. Totally sober. Tommen saw the light go on in his dad's room for just a moment, and then it turned off. Tommen stared at the spot for a long moment, trying to process what just happened.

His dad, who had admitted to being a drunken brawler, who had never touched a drink in the whole time Tommen had known him, who never went out for a social drink with the guys from the precinct, who never even looked at the alcohol in the store, who only went near a bar on official police business, who had given more than one lecture on the lures and pitfalls of alcohol, was drinking. Even if it was just one, it was a drink. His son could go missing, his fellows could die, he could be trapped in a black cell for a year, and he wouldn't touch a drop. His girlfriend dumps him, and he breaks out the bottle.

In a way, Tommen had always admired his dad's steely restraint, and even now, he told himself that one bottle in ninety years really wasn't a bad track record. He glanced back toward the hall, waiting just a moment to see if maybe his dad would come back to either finish it or throw it away. He did not appear. Tommen looked at the bottle and considered it. It was just a bottle of straight up Budweiser. He'd never really cared for beer, and wine was for snobby women; he preferred the hard stuff. Still, would anyone really know if he downed the rest?

Sighing, he picked up the bottle and dumped out the remaining contents into the kitchen sink. Then he tossed the bottle in the trash, right on top of the other five. With another sigh, he turned off the light over the stove, then turned and headed for his own bed.

Chapter Twenty-One
War Tent

Walter waited an hour or so after Tommen left before getting into bed. Unable to go to Tacaga himself because of the shields, he needed to catch a ride, portal ridesharing as his son and the other cool kids had dubbed it. He'd hoped that Kayla might be the one to retrieve him, as she was a friendly face, but maybe not anymore if her mind was this far out of line. But when no one came for him, he could only conclude that he hadn't really been invited to the war tent this time. Apparently, he and his friends had done enough to help and no one wanted his opinion. So he got in bed.

He thought he'd slept pretty good. Later he would reflect that he'd probably been Banded. But when he woke and found Rifun standing in the door to his bedroom, Walter instinctively flung his arm out, grabbing the gun under the unused pillow, and pointing it at the man who simply raised a brow.

"Honestly, Walter, if I meant you harm, you wouldn't have woken up. Not here, anyway." Rifun's tone was utterly bored, completely disinterested. "Now put that away, grab some clothes, and let's get moving."

Sighing, Walter pushed back the blankets and got out of bed, but he kept the gun within arm's reach. Rifun turned away and went meandering through the house; Walter could hear him. He grabbed a simple change of clothes, jeans and a T-shirt, and made for the door. He didn't make it before he stopped, turned, and took a few seconds to undo his belt and slip on his holster. There was no telling what could happen at this meeting, and he wasn't about to hope for broken glass. He left his bedroom.

"You have stunning taste in literature," Rifun commented, standing with his back to Walter at the table by his recliner, thumbing through the novel he was currently reading. "Historical fiction of the ancient kind. *The First Man in Rome*. Sounds intriguing."

"It's boring as hell, but oddly enough, I find it interesting," Walter said levelly. "Maybe not as exciting as reading a novel about your own life, but maybe mine is too graphic to document."

"Even my life has been documented, Walter." Rifun put the book down on the pile and turned to face him. "And there is plenty of graphic detail in that."

"Maybe I'll come to your library next time I'm looking."

"Maybe so. But we're wasting time."

"Lead the way, cabbie."

Rifun opened the portal and the two of them stepped through. Walter might have expected to land in the heart of the city, or in the governmental building itself. Instead, Rifun obeyed the requested protocol of the Governors, landing a short distance from the bridge and walking through the gate which was still under construction after the attack, though it looked to be finishing up. Two new guards were sentried there, and they looked young. First job ever kind of young. Were they even out of school?

"Halt!" one said nervously, blocking their path as they approached. "What is your business here?"

"The same business I've had the last three times I've come through here," Rifun told them irritably. "Now let us in."

"Of course, sir," the second guard said. "We're just doing our jobs."

"And a fine job it is," Walter told them as they passed through the gate onto the bridge.

The bridge itself had cleaned up nicely, and there was little evidence of the battle that had raged only a month or so ago. Rifun set a long stride, but his mind looked even farther ahead, or further gone. Walter did not voice his suspicions out loud, that the man had had a seizure recently, and he found himself wondering how long he felt like keeping the secret to himself. Kayla sounded like she was out for blood, and it sounded like Hlohi was preparing to battle the Borelians on their own, or with these mysterious allies, whoever they were. If they succeeded, and the process could be duplicated with minimal losses, was there any real need for Rifun or his army? Could Walter end the charade then?

Or was it not a matter of ability, but ethics? Should he tell the world about Rifun's seizures? Wait long enough, the man will go down, and the opportunity to off him will be right there. Get rid of a tyrant, throw the Order into chaos. Ha! Order into chaos.

But for as much as Walter hated the man, another part of him said that justice had to be done the proper way. If Walter couldn't get him in a courtroom on Earth, then the Hands would certainly take him and throw him to the Grandfathers. Barring that, offer him up to the Borelians. But due process was put in place for a reason. It wasn't his place to overturn it.

At the same time, while Walter might play his part to disguise Rifun's seizures, he wasn't exactly going to take a bullet—or a knife—for the man. If things got out of hand here in this meeting, it would be every man for himself. Walter habitually felt for the gun at his side. But if something happened to Rifun while they were here, the problem then became, how would they all get home?

"No escort?" Walter wondered when they reached the other side and Rifun grabbed a couple bikes.

"Their priorities have shifted a little," Rifun answered, handing off the second bike. "And the new gate guards aren't exactly at the top of their game."

So it was that Walter got his first real look at Lip that wasn't partially blocked by a rolling roadblock of Tacagan Secret Service or the haze of battle. It didn't look much different, really, but an unobstructed view was a breath of fresh air. The bike Walter sat on was of good size, but Rifun looked like a tall man on a small bike and mightily uncomfortable.

They arrived at the train station without incident. Rifun

unceremoniously dumped his bike, but Walter politely set down the kickstand.

"Even if the gate guards didn't call for an escort, I'm surprised we haven't been mobbed anyway by them," Walter observed as they got on the train, the car much less claustrophobic without a dozen guards packed into a tiny space, trying to shield the reviled outsiders from contaminating the innocent civilians with their Neanderthal ideas.

"I'm not complaining," Rifun said, rolling his right wrist while balling and releasing an awkward, three-fingered fist which Walter couldn't help but stare at. "At the very least, they won't get in the way if the shit hits the fan."

"Do you expect the shit to hit the fan?"

"With Kayla, anything is possible, it seems."

"You hurt your wrist recently?"

"I have to handle things differently. Sometimes my hand gets cramps."

It was a blatant lie; even Walter could see that. Rifun might be wigged out on drugs, but he was still alert enough to not show any kind of weakness or give his enemies a way in if he could help it. Walter and Tommen already knew about the seizures; he didn't need to give them anything else to use against him. A hand cramp might not be much, but a man had to salvage his pride when he could. So if it wasn't a cramp, then a nervous tic? Since when? What kind of drugs was he on?

Walter had once arrested a kid for breaking and entering and attempted larceny. The kid was a runaway from east of Charleston. He'd been combative, fighting and spitting and generally being difficult. The only reason Walter had been able to handle the kid by himself, without needing Time, was because the kid wasn't much bigger than Tommen. Parents were contacted, and when they came to claim their son like a dog at the pound, they brought a small pharmacy's worth of medication with them. Once the kid was forced to take the drugs, he had calmed right down and become the generally good, sweet, almost-straight-A student his parents professed him to be.

On the whole, Walter was neither for nor against modern medicine. He was neither for nor against old mountain remedies. He believed that, ultimately, every man was responsible for his own actions, and go from there. But to watch that kid go from punk ass maniac to perfectly normal, sometimes he questioned whether he could believe his own eyes at times. Was it the meds? Had the kid just been playing everyone to make it seem like the meds were working? Had it been some kind of withdrawal? It was stunning. To this day, Walter wasn't sure what to make of it.

He didn't even get to finish his line of thought before the train stopped at the governmental building and the doors opened wide. Rifun was out the door first, Walter trailing and feeling woefully sluggish, even though they were both moving quickly in Base Time. They headed down the corridor, passing the elevator, to another meeting room.

They were the last to arrive, and by no means were the Neanderthal humans the only visitors. Once again, Walter was forced to wonder if he could trust his own eyes. It felt foolish, given that he saw plenty of aliens in the Wheel all the time. Maybe it was just because this was Tacaga. Neanderthal humans in their midst was an abomination. Non-humans were just...worse than that; Walter couldn't think what was worse than an abomination.

It took several seconds for him to realize that one was Sifura, the Hand of Scientifically Primitive and Unengaged Civilizations, and Tommen's companion when he'd crossed the universe for the hasax flower. Her marbled colors were dazzling, even to Walter, though her tigress body exuded sleek strength and agility.

The others, he couldn't speak for, but there were four of them, all humanoid. One, a...bear, maybe? Crossed with a...lizard of some form? Komodo dragon? A second was more lizard-like, with slitted eyes, scales, long tail, and frills around its neck that probably flared out when it was angry. A third, bird-like, with a nose that curved down like a parrot's beak and feathers and sort of pseudo-feathers layered on its skin in strategic places and on its head and arms, almost like wings. The fourth and final was scaled, but less like a lizard and more like a fish, and Walter was almost put in mind of a fish monster mermaid.

"So," he said. "These are your allies."

"They are," Kayla stated. "And with a combined army of nearly a quarter million."

"With sticks and stones," Rifun said casually. "And no Time abilities to speak of."

"Before we get too far ahead of ourselves, how about a status report from all the worlds?" Walter suggested. "That way we have a platform to work from."

It was a short report. All the Borelians that had been on each of the planets before the shields were activated had been killed, and no new ones had come through. Each world, except Tacaga, had a small force of Akari-bearers who could get through the shields to take the Time Agents where they needed to go, most often to the Wheel. Tacaga still denied the Akari, denounced the Akari-bearers, and demanded to know what new technology or abilities they were using, but were simply told that it could not be taught to hard-headed atheists. The Akari was powered by Faith, something the Tacagans greatly lacked. Well, that spawned a whole new philosophical argument, but the bottom line was, the worlds were safe.

"So why do you want to mess it up?" one of the Sakarians wondered. "If we are safe here, or on our worlds, and have nothing to fear, why would we do this?"

"We made a promise to not stop until the Borelians were destroyed," Kayla said harshly.

"Promise to whom?" Milay asked. "Each other? We promised to deliver the planetary defenses, and we have. Our agreement has been met. Our status as an autonomous race is being debated even now."

"We are spear-heading this effort. I have brought the Xur, the D'Bok, the Gin Jor, the Rupi, and Ouin. I have little doubt that Rifun has been busy securing his alliances, though they are not so selfless, I presume—"

"So you do intend to remain with us?" one of the Aleisi asked. "You are not going to attack the Borelians on your own?"

"We will if we have to. I will not abandon this mission." Kayla turned to Walter and fixed him in a glare. "You've said often enough that people fear the Borelians, yes, but they love to hate them, they admire how untouchable they are." She looked around at those gathered. "And what are you all doing now? Reveling in your own safety? Sleeping now? Have you forgotten the fear you once lived under, that your world could be next? What would have happened to Vin Lay if we could not get the smaller defenses up to shield you? What if the Borelians had taken your world?

"Should we do nothing to avenge Treman and Trebald, lost to us before we even understood the threat? Ehani, who perished maybe or maybe not because we took the fight to the Borelians? Because that's what war is."

She paused to take a breath, continuing before anyone could object. "The Borelians are not going to go away because we've decided to hide under our rocks and pretend the threat no longer exists. They don't give up. Remember when the Wheel was closed off to us because the Borelians were hunting for human portals and entering that way? I don't know why they aren't doing that again now, but it is a hole in the defenses. What happens if they don't send an invasion, but just enough to come in and disable the shields? Who here knows how to repair them? Who can do it in time? What if the Borelians pull off an operation like that, with their armies ready to go as soon as the shields go down?

"We got in a great victory when we burned the Borelian farming world. Hundreds, thousands of species looked upon that monumental task with fear when it was proposed, and awe when it was accomplished. All over the universe, they watched as their greatest foe was wounded. Too big to hurt, or too big to miss? Now that the Borelians have figured out the connection between that attack and the human war, word has spread. There are allies out there, but because of politics in the Wheel, many are too afraid to speak up. Unless we give them reason to hope, reason to think that it wasn't a one-time operation, a one-time victory. We must have more victories. More victories means more allies means more victories."

"And you thought you were going to accomplish this by discarding my army of Akari-bearers and going with primitive spear throwers?" Rifun wondered. "Tell me, Aklaq, how well did that work out among your people facing the Russians, or any Native American—even my people—fighting the Europeans? The Borelians are only Engaged Privilege, true, but one Timekeeper in a thousand soldiers can still do more damage than the nine hundred ninety-nine he fights alongside, if the enemy cannot fight back. One skilled Harvester—a Triage, for instance—can do exceptional damage at just a touch."

"And for that matter, how do you expect your allies to respond?" one of the Dorigisi inquired. "They are not only primitive, they are Unengaged. They have never seen an alien, never seen this kind of technology, never seen Time. It is far beyond their military and psychological capabilities."

"We are many races," Sifura said, stepping forward. "We share one world. You all here, you are but one new tribe to us. The Monkey tribe, as Tommen Forbes once claimed. You are strange, but not so different. And the Borelians, the Ram tribe as he called them, yet another tribe. Many tribes, all unique, but still sharing a common goal. Many days, it is simply survival. Caring for one's family, one's clan, one's community. Food, water, the necessities of life. Defending against this atrocious enemy."

"Great. Now how about where it really matters in this instance?" Toros asked. "On the battlefield. One Timekeeper catches you, you are all dead."

"And that is where you all underestimate me," Kayla said slyly. Walter noticed she had a folder with her, which she now slapped down on the table and opened. "Profiles for every Borelian Time Agent, their activity, base location, current location, rank, training, everything. Including all the Grandfathers, past and present. Even now, I have assassins going out and killing these motherfuckers one by one. Thirty-seven are already dead, and that was just today. By the end of the week, I estimate over a thousand should be dead. The week after, ten thousand. The week after, who knows? Engaged Privilege means only their higher-ranking officers are trained. Kill them, and the army itself will begin to break down. Put the fear of God in them. Get rid of them. Take out their strongest while we still have the advantage to do so. The battlefield will easily balance itself out, if not tip in our favor."

"That's assuming they just stand there and take it," a Sakarian said. "They'll catch on pretty quick, I think. Then we may not be taking the battle to them. They'll be coming after us. Any of us, doesn't matter which. Or, if they catch on too much and figure out the Xur and the D'Bok and all them are now our allies, I'm pretty sure their world doesn't have the same planetary defenses ours do. It took months to get our defenses in place. And we can't just let them into our worlds as a roommate for a couple years while the Borelians pummel us. What would you have them do? Where do you expect them to go if things get bad?"

"Xur do not flee," Sifura hissed, flattening her ears and baring cattish fangs. "We stand our ground and die defending it."

"That's nice when it's your ground," an Aleisi commented. "Would you do the same for someone else's ground?"

"When the Gin Jor declares an ally, we are allies for life," the lizard man hissed, tongue flicking out so that Walter could see it wasn't quite human but neither was it solely reptilian. "We are brothers. We do not flee."

Walter shifted uncomfortably. "But like..." He gestured helplessly at the Sakarian, drawing a blank on his name. "—our Sakarian friend pointed out, we can't protect you if things get ugly, if the Borelians come for you. What about your women and children? Are there other tribes who wish to have no part? What about them? Is it fair to sacrifice them?"

"The offer was made to all tribes," Sifura answered calmly.

"The Da Leio do not wish to leave our world, but they will stay behind to fight and protect if the Borelians come. As for the others, if the threat comes to them, they will fight. Such is the way of war. If the D'Bok and Kalb go to war, and the fighting moves north into Rupi territory, is it fair to them? No. They wanted no part. But if the fight comes to them, they will do what they must."

It still didn't feel right to Walter. He had no doubt that their intentions were pure and their hearts were in the right place, even Kayla, but something about it just felt naive. Sticks and stones against modern warfare. Other than small guerrilla operations, when had such a thing ever worked, in the real world? Movies were great. Movies were scripted. Movies could call upon any ex machina they wanted to save the day, whether it was weather, deity, or some surge of inner strength. Real war was not scripted, and sometimes, the heavens didn't listen to the plights of men below.

"Where do you expect the battlefield to be?" Milay asked slowly. "We're not going to lower our defenses in hopes of enticing them onto a battlefield here. I would hope you people aren't stupid enough to try anything similar. And taking the Borelians to their world —" She mildly gestured toward Sifura and the others. "—would be, as Walter has pointed out, suicide, if not worse."

"Assassinate the Time Agents," Kayla stated. "Burn the farming worlds. Do what has worked. Force the Borelians to react. How they do will determine our next move."

"So you haven't thought about this at all," a Dorigisi said. "Burn their farms, they'll raid someone else's farms."

"The enemy of my enemy is my friend. Burn their worlds, gain victories, gain allies. If the Borelians torch someone else's cornfields, more allies for us. Get closer and closer to home, eventually, we'll be on the steps of Ancrath itself."

"Except in their home system, the Borelians have support from above, and I'm not talking the God kind," Rifun pointed out. "Space ships. War ships. Reinforcements. Slightly less bad than an army full of Timekeepers, but no arrow is going to clear the stratosphere."

"Then we'll have to work together to disable them, or keep them busy. The Krydik, those from Wolf Clan, are trained in the Akari as well."

"Barely. To most, it is simply magic."

Kayla ignored him. "The Tacagans are the most advanced of us. I'm sure you could come up with something. A bomb, perhaps. A computer virus."

"What is this, Independence Day?" The comment came from Mi Chin, but she did not expound.

"Fine," Rifun said, cutting in. "So the Tacagans give the Borelians a space war to worry about, and your little friends here are beating the Borelian ground army to death with clubs, spears, arrows, and a little magic. How exactly do you plan to win? Borelians have a societal structure, true, but every single one of them is trained to defend and die for their people and their world. They don't run and hide with the kids. When the civilians start getting involved, that's a lot more soldiers shooting at you. And they know their home turf better than you. More than just the lay of the land, they know the streets, their buildings, their homes. They know where the guns are stored in closets and under pillows."

"Then that makes it easy to know who the enemy is," Kayla retorted, glaring at him.

"And I've noticed that my army is conspicuously absent from your plan. What are my men doing at this point?"

"Minding their own damn business. And you with them. Or maybe I'll offer you up first, see if they'll just take you and go home, call an end to the war."

"Doubtful," Rifun mused, but he was drowned out by the others, all talking over one another.

"His army brought us our first victory that you want to duplicate!"

"They are talented, gifted in Time and the Akari!"

"Many species bring many talents, many strengths to utilize!"

"His army is powerful, conquering those who conquered them

until I believe they are undefeatable!"

"He is monopolizing the balance of power in the universe!" Kayla cut in. "The Borelians are the only foe they haven't defeated. And we all remember what he did in the Wheel. Who is going to keep him in check then?"

"Who is keeping him in check now?" a Vin Lay asked simply. "For one man to keep another in check, both must have an agreement about it. Each man must allow the other to leverage power over him, to tell him to stop. No one tells a Borelian no, for he shall be enslaved. No one tells the Hands of Time and the Grandfathers no, for he shall have his clock broken. No one tells Rifun and his army no, for he shall die. Each one is constantly trying to dominate the other because he will not be told no, he will not allow power to be leveraged over him. And so each has proven to be true. So in a way, each one has his own monopoly."

"Very philosophical of you. What happens if Rifun's army does defeat the Borelians? We've gone from three powers to two, and one has already conquered the other in the past."

The Vin Lay, Lin, was not fazed. "And was conquered. That foe may have been conquered himself, but was he not viewed as unconquerable at one time? And yet he was. No kingdom lasts forever. Except, perhaps, the Borelians. But we cannot stop them if we do not use all our resources."

"A rabid dog once released will devour his master as surely as his enemies," Andrew from Aleis recited.

"And be devoured himself in time," Lin continued. "The Borelians have ruled for a long time. How did they come to power? Did others fear their rise? Were they once fighting against a great evil in ages long past? Was it a similar situation as now? Who can know? But those who feared their rise, feared they would have eternal power. And we continue to give it to them." He looked at Rifun, his expression oddly calm. "We must use all of our resources." He gestured to Rifun. "Those who have great talent to match our enemies on the field of battle and Time warfare." He gestured to Kayla. "And those who have great talent to match our enemies on the open battlefield. Or in the shadows, as the case may be."

Truthfully, Walter was very moved by Lin's little philosophical lecture, and the man's calm demeanor certainly released some of the tension that had built up in the room. But Kayla would not be swayed. She continued to glare at Rifun even as she addressed the rest of them.

"We have our plans. They may not be perfect, but they are our own. Ally yourselves with this monster if you wish. Sell your souls to him for thirty pieces of silver while you're all gathered here. But we will be carrying out our mission as we see fit. With or without you. And definitely without him or any of his men."

Kayla and her allies turned to leave, but before she walked out the door, Walter asked, "Does that mean you would reject Tommen's help if he offered it?"

He looked at her.

She looked at him, seeming momentarily stunned by the question.

She left without answering.

"Well, this isn't going to end well," Rifun said, stepping away from the wall and moving off. "I better go have a word with her."

Everyone was smart enough to let him go and not get in the middle of the bloodshed that was likely about to occur. Indeed, everyone stayed silent for a moment, waiting to hear the scuffles, grunts, and screams. None came, and after a minute or two of silence from the corridor, it was Toros who spoke first.

"Perhaps we should take a brief recess from this meeting," he suggested. "This meeting was not planned, and I imagine some of you may be hungry or thirsty."

It was a weak attempt at a distraction, but a welcome one anyway. No one wanted to go out of the room and risk getting caught up in whatever fight Rifun and Kayla were having, so Milay ordered out and had food delivered, the finest delicacies Tacaga had to offer in fruits, meats, and cheeses.

Walter took a small helping just to be polite and give himself something to do, to think about besides what had just occurred. It did little to accomplish either, and he blindly picked at the food until it was suddenly gone. He'd eaten it all, and he couldn't remember doing so. He shook his head.

"Shit."

"Yes, this is an unfortunate turn of events, isn't it?" Rifun said, coming up beside him with food of his own.

"Thought for sure she would have finally killed you," Walter commented, not looking at the man.

"Oh, she wanted to. She even made a valiant attempt. Tao Jo the Gin Jor leader stopped her, and Sifura was the one who nearly dragged her back through the portal to Hlohi—which I opened, I may add. And because I know you're concerned, she never laid a hand on me."

"My concern is stretched thin lately. I can't afford to spare too much to any one cause. But it's good to know you seem to be back to normal, or getting there."

Rifun frowned and folded his arms as best he could with his plate of food. "I seem to be hearing similar comments these days, all saying that my personality is different. I prefer to think of myself as more focused and more...appreciative of the small things in life. Life itself, even, is a very precious thing."

"Can't say as I have any idea whatsoever of what in the universe you're talking about."

"Your sarcasm is noted."

"And given your history, assuming Tommen read and relayed it correctly, either you didn't learn enough the first time, or you've forgotten what that kind of 'appreciation' is like."

"Giving myself away, piece by piece, until I have only my life to spare."

"Here I thought death was always an option for you."

Rifun grinned. "Ah, Walter. I love our verbal banter. You and your son bring such joy to my day."

"Glad to be of service."

"Well, now that you have returned, perhaps we can figure out what our response is going to be," Toros said, raising his voice so as to grab everyone's attention and bring the meeting back to order. "The first question becomes, do we want to try and stop her? I don't know how, but do we want to try? Yes or no?"

Half the room said "yes" at the same time the other half said "no." Walter called that a tie.

"We can't afford to lose another world. Two, if the others truly are allied with her," one said.

"We will not lose anything the Borelians won't take by force if we don't try something," another pointed out.

"I say let her try," a third said. "Certainly doing something is better than doing nothing."

"That may have been true while we were yet helpless and without the shields. Now that the shields are in place and we can relax a little, we have to plan on how to do the right thing, the effective thing. Something that will make progress in this war in our favor," a Dorigisi threw in.

"She is making progress," someone unknown mentioned. "She has assassins working to dispatch Borelian Time Agents. Yes, they may figure it out, but as long as our losses are none, we are still making the greater progress. If they have to stop because they are discovered, then they stop. We still have the shields. We have lost nothing by trying."

"But what about her terms?" someone else wondered, maybe one of the Vin Lay. "Rifun has been our best hope, militarily, so far. Do we really want to get rid of our only great general, in favor of a hot-headed widow? Regardless of his past, he has the tactical mind to see a problem, map a plan, and execute it. After the attacks, the Borelians know he and the First Order are in on this. They are as vulnerable as we are when it comes to the Borelians' fury."

"He has the better army and the technology," Mi Chin grudgingly agreed. "While I do not doubt the purity of intention that Kayla and her allies possess, strength and numbers win wars."

"Rifun, what are your thoughts?" Toros inquired stiffly.

Rifun swallowed the last of his food and regarded the rest of them with an unreadable expression. "The quiche is delicious. That's my thought." He swallowed again. "But if you're asking about the plans going forward, I will answer honestly that I am generally unconcerned. As it has been pointed out, the Borelians know the Order is involved. That is not a bad dream, it is a fact. My people know it. To that end, we have our own worries and our own operations which we will be conducting here shortly. Large operations. Whether or not you want to be a part of it is up to all of you, assuming you can get your acts together."

"And what are you planning?" Milay wondered.

"Nothing you would be interested in, I assure you," Rifun replied with a look. "The details are still being worked out, as I believe we will only get one chance at success. If anyone is truly interested, beyond a passing curiosity, and wish to, as Kayla said, sell their souls to me for thirty pieces of silver, then you may contact me. At a later date. I don't want anyone here to feel rushed into a decision."

"Can you tell us anything about this big plan of yours?" John asked.

"I would really rather not. I fear it may conjure up an unfair advantage in my fanbase, and I want to give Kayla an equal chance at garnering support. For now, just consider whether you want to help me or her."

"How did it come to this?" a Dorigisi wondered. "Now that we have the shields, why do we have to split like this? She was more than happy to go along with it until the shields were in place."

"Perhaps the Tacagans ought to decide, then," a Sakarian suggested. "If this is the thanks we're giving them for saving our skins—that we're just going to split into squabbling factions—perhaps they ought to decide whose plan we go with."

"We have been prepared for this for a long time," Milay said haughtily. "And we will remain here long after the rest of you have gone. How you choose to go and whom you choose to follow there are of no concern to us. As for the gratitude concerning the shields, while we appreciate even the acknowledgment of such help—only now is it being brought up—" She sniffed. "—our payment is being decided before the Hands. With luck, we won't even be having this conversation because we will have fully separated ourselves from you."

"You think the Borelians are going to care?" Walter piped up. "Human or not, just like Sifura and the others, you aided us. You aided us in such a way that the Borelians, presently, can't even touch us, or not easily. Whether you decide to call yourselves Tacagans, Better Humans, or Masters of the Universe, the Borelians will still come down on you."

"They can try," was all the dark-skinned woman had to say, and her tone suggested that there were already huge political machines in progress that would protect Tacaga and doom the rest of them.

"Well, if they're not going to decide for us, then perhaps this is going to come down to individual preference," the same Sakarian decided. "Those who follow Kayla, and those who follow Rifun. Maybe more will be accomplished if we are on separate teams. Each one has strengths and weaknesses. Maybe they can't work together, but having them both working at all may prove to be advantageous."

"Following that logic, why not leave it every world for himself?" someone wondered grouchily.

"Because we don't individually have the numbers," Walter answered. "And only a couple of us have technology past the Industrial Revolution. Time is a wonderful thing, but having the firepower to back it up isn't a bad idea either."

So then it came down to, which leader did they want to follow? Rifun had the numbers. He had the tactical mind. He had a track record of victory, less one that had been avenged. His army had abilities once dismissed as merely legend or smoke and mirrors. The only moral problem came with his takeover of the Wheel. His only physical problem was his seizures, but no one in the room beyond Walter knew that.

Kayla, on the other hand, had numbers, though smaller. It was unclear whether she had the mind for war. She had only one known victory with her, and that had been as part of the Akarin who were now defeated. Only she and maybe a few others had the Akari abilities, but most of her army had little more than spears and arrows. Her problems were more obvious.

Why did it feel like such a tough decision? The better option was a genocidal maniac who may have finally taken a bite of that humble pie. The lesser option had only passion fueling her and primitive tribal members backing her. But Walter knew her, and her dead husband had been one of his Lieutenants and his friend for a long time.

"Vin Lay will back Rifun," Sem said after a long minute of silence.

It was the only official decision made. Aleis and Dorigis had to take it to their ruling councils while Sakaria refused to speak on the matter, though Walter suspected they leaned more toward Kayla. For a minute or two, Walter couldn't figure out why Vin Lay seemed so passive about it, why they were so confident about choosing Rifun. It wasn't just practically about the armies or abilities; they seemed to be genuinely okay with having him as their leader.

Then he considered the cultural aspect of it. Vin Lay was populated by those of primarily Oriental descent, including some from surrounding regions like India, Pakistan, Siberia, and so on. Far Eastern religions were not based on absolute good and evil, good always triumphing over evil like John Wayne, but good and evil in balance. For some, it was about the good outweighing the evil in order to achieve a greater reincarnation. For some, it was about achieving a greater good on the whole in the universe, sometimes through what men might consider evil means. For them, Rifun had done some bad things, but his willingness to fight the Borelians and save humanity balanced that out. It was the good counteracting the evil. Perhaps, to them, the coup had brought about greater good on the whole. The ends justify the means.

That didn't mean he had to like the reasoning, or agree with it.

Neither did he have to like the man who brought all of this about. But he did like to have an understanding of the thought process behind it.

"Was there anything else anyone wanted to bring up while we're here?" Toros asked, sounding fatigued.

It was a Dorigisi who spoke. "I assume you are hurrying through your emancipation just as quickly as possible, and no doubt you will send grand, embellished letters to the rest of us once it is complete and you have successfully separated yourselves from your Neanderthal cousins. If that happens before our next meeting, where do we want to meet? Where can we meet?"

"Without Do Chien, there's no real reason to have it here anyway," a Sakarian commented dryly.

"And that's another thing," Walter cut in. "What do we want to do about all the research? Everything was destroyed. Anything we want to do will have to be done from scratch, barring whatever was saved in your computer systems." He looked at the Tacagans.

"I vote for Dorigis, to have our meetings," Rifun said. When they looked at him, most of them confused, he clarified, "It's as you said. Brelix has only one small ocean, and they navigate primarily by space ship anyway. They have no naval experience. It may be our safest bet."

"What about your fortress?" someone asked. "Seems pretty impenetrable."

"Obviously not, seeing how I conquered it. And I am suggesting a human world inasmuch as we can all agree that we are human. The Order fortress will remain for use of the Order and its business. That way we can actually get stuff done here without going down all sorts of religious and political rabbit holes."

Pause.

"I second the motion," a Sakarian said finally. "Dorigis as our new meeting world."

"Aye" seemed to be the prevailing response, though the Dorigisi did not look prepared in the least. Eventually, they simply said that they would bring up that issue with their councils also and get back to them.

As for the research, no one had an answer. They knew enough about the toxins to be able to counteract them, and the lesser illnesses that had been loosed on their worlds were more readily curable. Did they really need such extensive research? Part of Walter said no; the other part said that until the war was over, there was no such thing as too much knowledge.

"Well, we can all give it some more thought and reconvene at a later date," Andrew suggested calmly. "I would ask that the Dorigisi be the ones to call the meeting, if indeed that is where we are moving the meetings to. In the meantime—" He yawned. "—I should like to get some sleep. It's near harvest, and there is much work to be done."

Whether it was the yawn or the mention of having work to do, the meeting came to an end and the leaders dispersed to speak amongst themselves. Group by group, they approached Rifun to be sent home until only Walter and the Tacagans remained.

"I still do not believe in the Faith element," Milay said, looking down her nose at Rifun. "Magic is all it is, until we discover what it really takes to unlock your so-called Akari abilities. But rest assured, we will find it."

"I look forward to hearing your findings," Rifun replied smartly. Walter half-expected him to bow, but he merely opened a portal back to Earth, right into Walter's living room, saying, "I will not be joining you. Give my regards to Tommen and let him know I await his next report on the journal."

Walter did not reply, simply stepped through the portal.

It was eleven o'clock. Normally, he would be in bed by now, happily asleep—or happy to sleep was probably more accurate. And he did feel tired, really, but his mind was too awake to allow him to sleep.

Okay, that was a lie, as his clock proved. The next time he looked at it, it was four-thirty. Grudgingly, he pulled himself out of bed. Nice to have the night off, anyway. He needed to quit doing this split-sleep, going to meetings, and everything. He needed to get his

Circadian rhythm back in some semblance of order. Still, he got up and puttered around the house a little, just enjoying the fact that he didn't have to hurry up and get ready for work. Tommen was not home. He could have been over at Will's, or at Becky's, or on some trip across the universe. Walter didn't know, and he was ashamed he didn't know. How many kids had he hauled back to their homes where their parents didn't know the first thing about their kid, but assumed they were out handing out tracts for salvation on street corners instead of vandalizing those street corners and harassing the people giving out those tracts for salvation?

But as Walter reminded himself constantly: Tommen was a very responsible kid. He almost wasn't a kid anymore. Hell, even if the State of West Virginia still said he was a minor, at some point between the soccer fields and today, his little boy had crossed the threshold into being a man. When had that happened? The warehouse? The coup? The summer camp? Walter thought about it a minute, but couldn't really say. Next thing, he was going to be graduating high school, going off to college, living on his own, getting married...well, that last one was dubious, but moving out on his own was certainly in the realm of possibility.

Walter felt old. He'd felt old when he'd finally decided to really turn his life around and seek out his brother, but this was a whole new kind of old. The former old was the exhaustion and shame of a life long wasted. This new old was the exhaustion of a full life that had gone by too quickly. What was he going to do when he went dark again?

He was jerked from his thoughts as his phone rang.

"Laura, I was just thinking about you," he greeted. Not exactly a lie, actually. He had been thinking about her. Maybe even seriously considering the possibility of retiring from Time. Maybe getting married himself.

"Yeah," was all she said.

"Is everything all right?"

"To an extent. I mean, getting things sorted out and divided up. Finding things Mom once thought were lost forever. Finding things she didn't know Dad had like a couple particularly raunchy *Playboy* magazines from the fifties."

"I guess even fifty years of marriage can't account for everything."

"I guess not. There were some old softball trophies and bowling trophies that we're thinking about donating back to the leagues. They can put them in their museums or halls of fame or whatever. No one really has a use for them. Of course, everyone feels guilty about wanting to get rid of them with no real ceremony."

Walter nodded even though she couldn't see. "I understand. How are you holding up?"

"Okay, I guess. It's good to see everyone again, get everyone back together, share everything together. We're moving on."

"I sense trepidation in your voice."

She sighed evenly. "Well, yes. I'm not going to be coming back to West Virginia...as soon as I thought."

He chuckled. "Good. Then I can stay with you when it comes to that spring break vacation you promised me."

He could almost hear her rolling her eyes. "It's Minne-fucking-sota, Walt. No one comes here on vacation, especially for spring break. No...what I mean to say is...I'm not coming back to West Virginia. At all. I'm staying here to be with family. I already talked to my old boss, and I'm back on the schedule next week."

"Oh." Walter wasn't sure what to say.

"And...you know how people like to come and go and visit the house, talk all about how 'if you need anything' and stuff?"

"Very well, believe me."

"Well, I met up with a friend of mine. An old boyfriend from high school."

"You're going out with him again." Walter stated it simply. There was no other way to say it that didn't involve an overreaction that would only cause more problems.

Laura was silent for a long minute. Then, "Yes. We are. I mean, at first, I told myself that it was just catching up with an old friend from high school, you know? Nothing sinister about that. But the more we talked, the more we went out together...I tried to reconcile it in my mind, reminded myself that you were waiting for me...I couldn't do it. Walt, I have home and family and friends here, and it goes back a long time. I don't really know why I left Minnesota, but now that I'm back, I don't want to leave. It's nothing against you, Walter, it's just..."

"I know," he said quietly. "Believe me when I say I understand."

"I don't want us to end on bad terms. It might sound super corny, but I do hope we can still be friends. You know, you can call me any time if you need a listening ear. Or if you find yourself in a medical emergency and need advice." She laughed nervously and choked it down; she was probably crying. "I love you, Walter. But it's just not going to work."

"I know. If you ever find yourself pulled over or being arrested, give me a call. Maybe I'll walk you through it."

She laughed again, quieter, still more nervous.

The call ended as awkwardly as could be expected, and Walter found that he sat in his recliner for an hour afterwards before moving. Thinking about it, he didn't really feel anything. He wasn't even sure what he should feel. His experience with women was limited to prostitutes, a wretchedly failed marriage, and Laura. How was he supposed to deal with this?

Probably not in the way he did, he later reflected. He couldn't say why he grabbed a six-pack of beer, but he knew why he chose the liquor store he did: it was on the other side of the city, out of the jurisdiction of his old precinct. The shop owner didn't know him. He didn't visit this side of town often, so there were fewer people around who might know him. He knew this game. It was called Anonymity.

All the way home, he told himself it was a bad idea. He told himself to turn around and take it back, even though he knew alcohol was non-returnable under normal circumstances. This was a bad way to cope with anything, and with his history, it was an even worse idea. Yet a small part of him said that after a century of being dry, one drink was not going to send him to his grave.

What would Tommen think?

He'll be fine. He can drive. He works, goes to school.

Yes, but what will he think of you?

He'll see that I'm having a beer.

And you, admitted to being a drunkard who beat his wife and child and spent years in jail or prison?

One drink in a century isn't going to harm anyone.

You bought six.

I'll be fine.

A voice in his head—that was growing quieter and quieter the closer he got to home—said that this was only coming back around because of his addiction to opioids, an addiction he'd broken. But now that one addiction had been broken, something had to replace it. Aggravate the nerves and go right back to where he'd been, something familiar from so long ago. He needed to stop and get clean from everything and stay that way. For Tommen's sake, if not his own.

That voice eventually disappeared once he got home and it did not return until much later when Tommen walked in the kitchen where Walter sat, half-way through the sixth bottle.

"Dad?"

Walter looked up at him, then back at the cupboards. "I didn't hear you get back."

It was a lie. He wasn't sure whether it was the alcohol or the shame that upset his stomach suddenly.

"What are you doing?" Tommen wondered.

"Having a beer."

"I have literally never seen you drink. You've been sober for, what, almost a century?"

"Am I drunk? It's just the one, anyway."

Another lie. A lie to cover up his shame. A flimsy cover. Sooner throw a bedsheet over his head and call himself a ghost. The voice came back, telling him of his past wrongs, reminding him that he had a son right here. And, worst of all, that son was both shocked and disappointed in him.

They exchanged some more words. Eventually, Walter took a drink, looked at the bottle in the light, half-empty. His stomach was roiling. Sighing, he stood. "I'm going to bed."

"It's only eight o'clock."

"I'm going to bed. At least to lie down for a little while, even if I don't sleep. Don't Band me. Just keep doing whatever it was you were doing."

"Oh. Okay."

Tommen moved to the side and Walter headed down to his bedroom. Turned on the light, too bright. Turned off the light, saved only by the night light. But then, lying there in the darkness, the shadows cast by the little light seemed to move and take on a life of their own. They writhed, hissed, pointed and laughed.

"Shame," they whispered. "Shame...shame...shame...what's the alcoholic's name?"

"Owain Fforidd," he whispered back.

The shadows hissed with laughter, moving across the walls and ceiling like serpents slithering here and there. He'd been tempted by the devil. And lost.

Chapter Twenty-Two
Friends and Renegades

Tommen woke to dim firelight and a stone ceiling. It took less than a second for him to seize hold of the dream and leap up from the woven mat where he lay, looking and feeling just the same as if he'd risen from his own bed.

Chandler was nowhere to be seen. Judging by the fire which had burned down to almost coals, he'd been gone for some time. Frustration worked its way into Tommen's mind. Finally, he'd gotten back to the cave to talk to the man whom he hadn't seen in probably two months, and the man wasn't even home.

Shame at his frustration gradually seeped its way in until the frustration itself was dissolved. In all the times Tommen had been coming here, all the time he'd spent in the in-between dimension, Chandler was the only one he'd seen besides the White animals. The man had a lot on his plate and he probably got busy. With the Shadows acting up the way they were, the man was probably run ragged. But still...he couldn't take ten seconds to dispense an infuriating riddle here and there, or just answer a question? Were there others Chandler brought into this cave to speak to one-on-one? Now there was an idea.

Tommen added some wood to the fire and had just coaxed some life and light back into the cave when the door to the balcony opened and Chandler walked in.

"Ah, you are here," he observed.

Chandler did not move hurriedly; he did not allow himself to be rushed. But there was a way he moved that suggested he was busy and preoccupied with something, even as he set down his basket of fresh spring pickings and asked, "Are you hungry?"

Tommen shrugged. "I could eat."

He was about to say more and start unloading, but the man held up a hand. "I know. Trust me, we have more than enough time together this evening to speak. Calm down. Clear your mind. Consider your thoughts. Eat first."

It was the hardest thing Tommen had done all day, and he'd done a lot. He watched Chandler strip leaves from stems, chop up carrots and potatoes freshly dug from earth that was just thawed enough to give up its treasures, and add in small chunks of meat taken from a couple squirrels. While the stew was cooking, he expertly fleshed the tiny furs, doused them in brains, and hung them high above the fire to smoke lightly. Any remaining fat—and there were only the smallest squishy portions stuck to the edges of the skins—sizzled and dripped down into the stew.

"Is that healthy?" Tommen wondered. "Fat by itself, fine, but there's brain matter on that."

"Not much, and you'll be fine," Chandler answered, stirring the stew.

Tommen had his doubts, but decided not to push the matter. If he got an upset stomach in a dream, would that carry over into the real world? What did he do if it did? He ran his tongue over his teeth and decided not to dwell on such things.

"So, how is Chandler today?" he asked conversationally.

"I am well, thank you," Chandler replied. "I would ask how you are, but I've seen the parts of your day that I could and heard the recollections of the parts I could not, so I can take a fair guess."

He stood and went to one of the stone shelves to retrieve bowls and utensils. Had that much time already passed? Those potatoes had been stone cold when Chandler brought them in; he'd had to hold them close to the fire to get them to thaw enough to chop. There was no way they could be cooked through already. The carrots, too.

But as Tommen stirred the stew himself and smelled the dazzling aroma, he found the potatoes and carrots were soft and cooked thoroughly. Was this dream-time, where dreams passed faster than normal but details themselves could not be recalled? Or had he succeeded in calming his mind to such a point where only the moment mattered, and all the boring ones just melted away? Sounded hokey, but it was a real thing. In old days, that would be called mountain time. For Chandler, it was probably called Indian time. He smiled to himself.

"Here you are," Chandler said, handing him a bowl. "Help yourself."

Tommen did so, taking just a small portion at first, telling himself not to be greedy even as he knew he was still worried about squirrels brains in his stew.

Truth was, he couldn't taste them, if indeed they had been in there and not simply boiled off. Only a couple drips could have gotten into the stew anyway. He would be fine. Tommen finished his first bowl, then went for a second. Chandler ate politely, silently, watching him with laughing eyes.

"Do you spy on me?" Tommen asked, halfway through his third bowl.

"I check in frequently, when I know I cannot visit," Chandler replied, having stopped after two bowls.

"Does this mean we can, like, talk, discuss, whatever, now?"

The man nodded sagely. "What's on your mind?"

"What the fuck is going on? It's like everything just exploded and took off in a thousand different directions. Why don't we start off with, how do I call you when I need you? I've been wanting to talk to you for over a month, but you're never here. How does that work?"

"Sometimes, I am busy. The Shadows are moving, and we must prepare. You do not see everything that goes on behind the scenes."

"Why are the Shadows moving? What's going on? Have you seen anything? Like, I remember sometimes you said you can see into the future."

"Only when the Author permits it," Chandler said severely.

"And even then, she tells me when I may and may not tell others what I see. Some things, I can see, but then I must only work quietly in order to stop or change a thing, or alter the actions and reactions following that thing."

"You have seen something, then," Tommen stated. "Is there anything you can tell me? Do you know the location of the third journal?"

"It has been shown to me. Before you ask, I will not tell. You will get there in your own time, if I do not tell. If I do, it would not matter. There are events in between that must happen that cannot if I tell you."

Tommen rubbed his face. How could he have forgotten? The man was a prophet. That was almost synonymous with infuriating, right up there next to women. He sighed. "Fine. What can you tell me?"

"What I can tell you," Chandler said as he shifted position, "is that you will be freed from the Shadows, but that does not mean that the fight is over."

It was as close to good news as Tommen was going to get, and he would take it. But first, there was the ever-present, "What do I have to go through to be freed?"

"Divided loyalties, conflict of morality, war of mind, body, and soul."

The man said it as if reciting a grocery list. Divided loyalty? Check. Conflict of morality, check? War of mind, body, and soul? Aisle five, middle shelf, nestled between chronic depression and lifelong therapy.

"Has anyone ever told you that you are absolutely infuriating?"

"You, on many occasions. You also like to call me a preacher, a prophet, a wise guy, the world's best riddle master—"

"I don't remember calling you that," Tommen cut in.

"Hm. Must have heard it somewhere else," Chandler said, though his grin and expression said he'd just made it up.

"Okay, wise guy..."

"There you go again with the name-calling."

Tommen waved a hand at him dismissively. Chandler laughed and reached out to him. "Are you done, then?"

He surrendered his bowl and watched Chandler take them to the wash basin that sat along one wall between a couple sets of cabinets. He had several pitchers of water set off to one side. He grabbed one of these, poured it into the basin, and did a quick wash of the bowls and utensils. Tommen felt guilty, as if he should get up and help, but he remained where he was.

"Are you thirsty?" Chandler wondered, reaching for a couple small cups, then stopping.

"No, I'm okay, thank you," Tommen answered.

The man poured some water into a small kettle and set it over the fire next to the cauldron of stew that was still boiling steadily. Before he sat down, he took the cauldron off the heat and set it in a circle of rocks about twenty feet away to cool. By then, the kettle had begun whistling. Chandler grabbed a cup and a small jar, then poured some water into the cup. He opened the jar, stuffed some herbs into a tea holder, and set it gently in the hot water. Then he returned to the fire, getting comfortable, as if expecting a flock of grandkids to sit at his feet and await his ancient stories.

"Now then," he said swirling his tea around a little, "why don't we go through this categorically? Maybe it will help you keep your thoughts straight. What's on your mind?"

"Okay," Tommen said, dipping his head in agreement. "Let's start with the Borelian war."

"Big picture, then. Go ahead."

"What's going on? Okay, fine, so people weren't happy about having to ask for Rifun's help, but what does Kayla have to offer? I wasn't at the meeting on Tacaga, maybe they already went over this, but I want to understand."

Chandler frowned. "Sorry to say, but I wasn't at the meeting on Tacaga either."

"No, but I don't think you're as ignorant as you're claiming."

The man was silent for a long moment, though he opened his mouth several times as if to start, as if he was searching for the right words. Finally, "The drive to best one's enemies can sometimes be blinding. And it may seem as though building a comparable force without Rifun at the lead would be the obvious thing to do—it may even be the right thing to do—but that doesn't mean it's the smart thing to do."

"So she shouldn't break from the larger group?" Tommen shifted. "If Kayla managed to rack up a few victories, she would gain allies. She may even inspire the Akarin to rebel against the Order. Maybe she could help them throw off their oppressors. Set them free. Holy Moses, part the Red Sea, Promised Land, all of that. Then she would have that comparable force because the Akarin have the Akari. They can do what Rifun and the Order can do. Boom. Rifun is no longer needed. Problem solved."

"Is it? Would it be wise for her to fight the Borelians and the Order at the same time? Would it be wise for Rifun to fight the Akarin and Kayla and the Borelians at the same time? Would it be wise for those watching from the sidelines to choose one side or another, or merely sit idly by and hope for the best? Even the best shields do not hold forever, and many walled cities have fallen simply through patience on the part of the enemy besieging the wall."

"So...deal with the Borelians now, then resume our petty fights later? Is that what you're saying? What's the best course of action here?"

"Even if I told you, how would you put the plan into action?" Chandler wondered, taking a small drink of tea. "What should be, what is, and what is going to be, are all very different things. Wishing to change the past creates nothing but worry. The die is cast and the players are moving."

"Why not come to me earlier, then?" Tommen pleaded. "Tell me Kayla was planning to break so maybe I could warn Rifun, my dad, whoever else, have a better plan in place."

"Because I was busy trying to prevent an even worse future from happening. I—you—we can't always effect the ideal change or the optimal plan or the greatest results. Sometimes, the best we can hope for, in the moment, is as much damage control as possible. You can't wrangle in free will. As I said, the die is cast, the players are moving. I don't understand why the Author has pushed everyone down this road to effect this particular ending—or this divergence is what I maybe should say—but I know that it is good. Because it is her plan. From it, you will be freed. Others will be cast out, cast about. I don't understand it in perfect detail, but I know that it is good. But to get there, there will be more bloodshed. You must tear through the thornbushes to reach the Promised Land on the other side."

Tommen rubbed his face and looked down the cave into the darkness, feeling the faintest breeze whispering through, taking away the smoke from the fire. "Are any more of my friends going to die?"

"Your friends? No. Friendships? Very possible."

He didn't know which was worse, honestly. He tapped his fingers on his knee. "What is the nature of free will in a novel? Do we even have free will, or are we just preordained words on a page? Nothing we do can change this or that?"

"Do the novels appear before or after a thing has happened?"

"After."

"If the Author's act of writing is the present, then what is written must be in the past. Even nonfiction authors must concede that their works are rooted only in the present and past. They may speculate about the future, but they themselves have only the power of the present. The difference is, the Author knows what is going to happen. And she may be present at any time within a novel, simply by opening it up. Try it sometime. Past, present, future. She's all there."

"But that doesn't answer the question." Tommen looked back at Chandler. "If she's just writing—if I go home and start writing in my notebook, my characters don't have free will. They are products of my imagination that do what I tell them to do."

"Now imagine you're writing a story like this one. Why not

simply write that there was suddenly world peace? Why not write that Rifun was struck by lightning and died? Why not write in a million other things that people wish and pray for, that they wonder why God doesn't care enough?" Chandler paused. "Characters have life. We may not understand it because we are only characters ourselves, only human. But we don't have to understand. We simply move on, word by word, to the end of the story."

"And what does fictional-character-heaven look like? Do I get to be a real boy?"

"I don't know what happens. I haven't gotten to that point yet."

Tommen sighed and looked back down the cave, acutely aware of Chandler's gaze boring into him. After a long moment of sullen silence, Chandler asked, "What's really on your mind?"

He looked back at the fire, burning low again, glanced at Chandler and looked away. "Why is my dad drinking again? Okay, once a century isn't a bad track record, but...he lied about having only one, and...it just seemed like it was a stupid reason. I mean, I get that Laura dumped him, and I'm really sorry, but he'll drink for that? And not for any of the hell I went through—or that he went through? What gives? Why would the Author do that?"

Chandler sighed and frowned. "The Shadows are moving, Tommen, more active than I have seen in a long time. Some people are more vulnerable than others. Your dad's history, coupled with his drug addiction, no matter how brief, makes him susceptible to influence."

"Is it going to get worse? How do I stop it?"

"Lucky for you, the Author has better plans for him, though he may not see them just yet. I do believe that this will pass and he will get better. But not all will be rescued so swiftly. And if you want my opinion, the drinking wasn't about the Shadows sinking their claws into your dad—although they certainly did some damage—but about toying with you."

"If they have to threaten my friends and family, it's because they can't threaten me."

"Exactly."

Tommen shifted uncomfortably. "I know you've accused me of it, and I expect nothing less than a blunt, sarcastic answer, but, why do I care so much about what happens to Rifun? Is it just Stockholm Syndrome? I feel like I should hate him more, that I should be doing more to undermine him, ruin his empire. But between the fact that we still need him and his army to fight the Borelians, and watching him seize on the floor...I can't quite muster it up."

Chandler nodded slowly, thoughtfully. "You aren't the tough guy you make yourself out to be, though you are very strong in mind and spirit—and will need to become even stronger still before this is over. You are a very caring, very merciful person, in actuality. Given to bouts of passion and emotional overreactions—even if they are completely justifiable—but more merciful than I think even you realize. And that's not a bad thing.

"It is said that forgiveness is complete when the other person is permitted to freely walk through your mind without the threat of firing squad. In a way, I think you have forgiven Rifun for what he's done. That doesn't mean you don't seek justice for his crimes, but blind, passionate rage does not consume your every thought. Revenge is a very selfish thing. Forgiveness means taking yourself out of the equation and letting the Author do her work. Maybe Rifun will get what he deserves and die in screaming agony, or maybe he won't. Whatever the case, the Author is still using him, and you aren't going to interfere in that.

"To that end, it does not make his actions going forward automatically right or wrong, and his actions will be hotly contested, but between you and him, that personal struggle, it's over."

"But, you've always said that the First Order and the journals will be catastrophe, wolf in sheep's clothing, Armageddon, the universe will crumble. All this really bad stuff."

"It is," Chandler confirmed. "And it will be. Unspeakable things will come to pass from the Order, especially from the third journal. You must be prepared, to defend yourself, to defend others, to speak against the tide of darkness that will overshadow the land. But that's not what we're talking about right now. Right now, we're talking about you. We could spend all night speculating on the big picture things. Fact is, you have almost no influence over any of it. Why worry yourself over it? I understand that you are worried, but active worry will get you nowhere. Right now, you must focus on what you can do, what you can influence."

Tommen sighed and thought a moment. "I can influence Rifun. What's happening to him? What are those pills? How does him taking or not taking them affect his decisions and the outcome of this war?" He put up a hand. "I know, I can't worry over every little detail, but I have to ask. Is there anything I can do? I know someone is poisoning him. Is this the Author's justice, or should I say something?"

The man frowned and did not answer right away. Then, "Honestly, I was trying to think of a clever and infuriating way to say this, but nothing came to mind that would work. The poisoning will right itself. It will cause the foundation of the fortress to shake and many will tremble; the ground itself will split open and the Shadows will come forth to spread over the universe. But the poisoning will right itself. Best not to say anything."

"Best not to say anything?" Tommen's brows went sky high. "What could be worse than the ground splitting and Shadows spilling out? What happens if I do say something?"

"Then the same thing happens, except with the added bonus of being sold into Borelian slavery and having no good way to end the tyranny quickly. As I said, we don't always get the answer we'd like—that it will end the war, the Borelians are vanquished, and we all live happily ever after—but it is the better of the two options."

"Well, you're not wrong there. I don't like the Shadows, but I don't need to sprinkle my misery with slavery." Tommen frowned. "Does that mean that we pretty much have to back Rifun in this Borelian war?"

"Wait," Chandler stated. "Wait a while and your question will answer itself."

"In the same way that I am definitely going to find the third journal?" Tommen shifted position. "Tell me more about that. You said you can't tell me where it is because something-something-something has to happen and if you tell me the ending, it won't happen and something-something-something bad stuff."

"Interesting way to phrase it."

"What can you tell me? Okay, if I'm definitely going to find it, how can I make it not a catastrophe? What should I do with it once I get my hands on it? Should I hand it over to the Tacagans? They hate religion, probably stuff it in a secret vault so it doesn't contaminate their people. Should I burn it myself? Should I hide it away for another century, like the Kolkath? Should I hide it in my closet indefinitely and just claim I never found it?"

"When you find it, all will know, not just you, not just your adventuring team. They will know even before you touch it that you have found it. Hiding is not an option."

"Fire, then. The museum journal proved that they're waterproof. They can't be fireproof." He paused and eyed Chandler suspiciously. "Can they?"

"In this matter, you will be faced with two choices, whether to keep it or surrender it to the Shadows."

"Keep it," Tommen answered quickly. "I don't like the Order, don't particularly like the idea of them having it, but it can't be worse than the Shadows having it."

Chandler put up a hand and he fell silent. "Your next choice, then, will be whether to surrender it to the Shadows or the Shadowmaster."

"Sh-shadowmaster? Are you talking about the cerberus?"

"I am speaking of the one who dines with the cerberus. And do not be fooled. The Shadowmaster has no real control over the Shadows, as puppets cannot pull their own strings, after all."

Memories of the interview with Titik swarmed through Tommen's brain. "Then you know who the puppets and the puppeteers and the puppet masters are."

"I do."

"But you're not going to tell me."

"No. To do so would be to invite trouble. Far more trouble than either of us can handle."

"Except with the Author's help, am I right?"

"Tommen, there is Faith, and then there is stupidity. Faith is trusting the Author to work everything out for good in the end, regardless of your circumstances or ending, be it happy or sad. Stupidity is walking in front of a firing squad and thinking the bullets won't kill you. I am strong by the words of the Author, and I and the Whites do well to keep the Shadows at bay. But any one of us can be overwhelmed by a Shadow, be it strong enough." Chandler shifted position. "But that is not for your concern. Right now, we are working through the things that ought to be your concern, and how to best handle them. So then, what else in on your mind?"

Tommen hesitated. Then, "When I do get the journal, and the shit hits the fan and everything else, whatever happens, how am I going to find the truth about the Author? About who's right? I'm having a hard enough time as it is."

"Are you?"

"Yes, I am. I go to journal studies once a week or so, but this is the first I've seen you in months."

Chandler frowned. "While it is true that guidance is necessary in forming correct ideas about faith, being overbearing often has a paradoxical effect. You have four Authored Books. Four. The only person who has more Books at this time is Micah and Micaiah, and even their Books testify that your story isn't over yet."

Tommen shrugged. "Great. It's the same four Books. I've read them, reread them. I practically have them memorized. Not saying that I'm eager to read more of my own fuck ups, but I need more."

"I disagree. I think that these four are exactly what you need right now, at least until you are freed from the Shadows and can process more."

"Why do you say that? Did the Author tell you that? Am I getting more after I'm...freed from the Shadows?"

"Without understanding the details of the discovery of the journal or being freed or any of that, I cannot give you a definitive answer. I don't even know what timeframe the Books would cover, how they begin or end. Until that is made known, it is all speculation. While speculation can be fun and even productive at times, we mustn't carry it too far, lest we become disappointed by our own assumptions."

Tommen rubbed his face. "Okay. Okay, okay, okay."

A long silence stretched between them as Tommen tried to process everything. So, he was definitely going to find the third journal; that much was a given at this point. But between now and then, something major had to happen. Then, once he got the journal—which would apparently be met with parades and fanfare—he had to make two choices, whether to keep it or give it to the Shadows, and whether to give it to the Shadows or the Shadowmaster. Couldn't he just burn the damn thing? Why did the earth have to split open and all that?

"What would happen if I just told Rifun that I wasn't going to search for the journal anymore? Or if I told him that it's just lost? What if he sent someone else?"

Chandler refilled his cup. "I'm afraid that, due to certain events upcoming, even that is no longer an option."

So, he was definitely going to find the third journal; that much was a given at this point.

Socially, he'd apparently forgiven Rifun without ever really realizing it. He supposed it made sense, in a way. He no longer passionately hated the man, but neither did he blindly support him. It was simply a matter of doing what he asked and waiting for justice to find him, without being a passionate revenge-seeker in that regard. Everything about it simply was.

To that end, Tommen was less thrilled about having to stay silent on the whole poisoning thing, but he was less keen on being sold into Borelian slavery. If the earth must split and Shadows come crawling out of the depths, let there be no Borelians involved. But if that was going to happen when the poisoning righted itself, and he had these huge, impossible choices to make when he found the journal, that meant—probably—that this was all going to hit at once. This was going to be another battle, or something just as big. Tommen felt his stomach twist and his chest tighten.

"Worry does you no good," Chandler said, as if reading his thoughts. "Focus on what you can control, what you can do."

Tommen took a tight breath and let it out again, but his fear would not release. He did this several times until he could find the breath to answer, "I can continue my search for the third journal. If the ending is inevitable, the sooner I take control, the more I can control, maybe make the fallout a little smoother."

To his dismay, Chandler shook his head. "It's a nice sentiment, but I want you to have no illusions. This will get messy. And violent. But the sooner you take control, the easier it will be to control yourself, your reaction to the fallout. See the difference?"

He nodded solemnly. "Yes."

"Keep going."

It was another long minute of silence. What else could he control? If he was definitely going to find the journal and there was definitely going to be some kind of explosive fallout, suddenly he was just a pawn in the Author's hand. Die is cast, players are moving. Pawn moves forward one or two, diagonal to capture.

"I can control the flow of information," he said suddenly. "Walking in two worlds, I can communicate between the two, or one to the other, anyway. Should I spread word about the journal? I don't know what, but some kind of word or rumor? Should I help spread the rumors about Rifun being disinterested? Should I fight them? Should I start an anonymous rumor about his seizures?"

Chandler nodded thoughtfully. "Information is a heady thing. Men have killed for less. But the only information that remains to be gathered for the completion of this particular epic is the information you need to find the journal. All else is moot, and may actually serve to make things worse."

"Why is it a notable day when you give straight answers?" Tommen asked. "Why can't that just be every day?"

"We've already gone over this, Tommen, and I am no longer in a mood or position to indulge your childish frustrations."

It was a sharp rebuke, and Tommen visibly flinched. But Chandler was right. They'd come too far and the stakes were too high to sit and whine about how life wasn't fair. Chandler was giving him everything he knew, everything he was permitted to give. He wasn't a Magic 8 ball, and sometimes the best he could do was speak in vagueries and riddles. Tommen might have likened it to describing a dream that, while sleeping, had been so clear, but slips away quickly at the return to consciousness. Ideas and feelings are remembered, maybe a brief flash of action or a still on a person, maybe a few words of dialogue, but the whole picture and its meaning had gone.

Tommen took several deliberate breaths. "Is there anything you are able to tell me, about what I should do next, where to go, who to talk to, how to discern one answer versus another being correct, anything like that? Can you give me a hint about what I'm looking for? Can you explain any more of Titik's words, seeing how you brought up the puppet analogy?"

"Everything is exactly as he said."

"Did Rifun shoot him in the head? Is that why he's crazy?"

"Do you believe he's crazy? If everything he says turns out to be true, even if he did not explain it explicitly, does that make a man crazy? What about men who hallucinate and proclaim diamonds and emeralds raining from the sky and cats driving cars?"

Tommen frowned. "So he isn't crazy?"

"It's not my place to say one way or the other. All I know is that he helped you and you should pay attention to what he says. You may have figured this out, but don't take his words literally. You have to think abstractly." Chandler put up a hand before Tommen could speak. "Not here. Don't speak of it or overthink it. When the time comes, you will understand."

"That's what I'm afraid of."

Chandler emptied the last of the kettle's contents into his cup, finished off the cup, then took both to the washbasin where he slowly, methodically washed them and set them aside to dry. His calm, unhurried movements finally got the tightness in Tommen's chest to release and he took a huge, quiet gulp of air, settling down before the man returned, now empty-handed.

"Question," Tommen said, studying his feet.

"Listening," Chandler replied.

"I know you said that the poisoning will right itself. And that I should just not say anything about it or Rifun's seizures or anything. Fine. I'll just take your word for it. But do you know what the pills are? Or even what that root or powder stuff is? There are a lot of variations with poison, and if something happens while I'm there—thinking maybe I'm just covering for a seizure when it could be worse—I want to know what to do. I may not be Laura, but I know the last thing you want to do to someone who's not breathing is give them a depressant, and if someone's wigging out, you don't want to give them uppers and get them even more excited. Furthermore, if someone is poisoning Rifun, there's every chance that more people are or could be poisoned. I just want to have an idea of what I could be up against."

The Native man shook his head. "No one else is being poisoned, and you will not be put in such a position. As for what the pills actually are, you will find out soon enough." He went on before Tommen could speak. "That road is closed to you. You have no business going down it. It will resolve itself. Focus on what you are meant to do, what you can do, what you should do. Do you understand?"

Tommen sighed. "Yes."

"I know it's tempting. You want to feel in control. It's not going to happen. The hardest thing for a merciful person to do is let go and stand back."

He shrugged and nodded. "I guess. What about my dad? You

said that the beer was a one-time thing? What about pills? He was addicted once; I don't want to see him go back."

Chandler shook his head. "That I can say with confidence, he is done. For the foreseeable future. For the moment, until whatever happens with the journal and Rifun and everything else, you don't need to worry about your dad."

Tommen breathed a sigh of relief and visibly relaxed. He frowned again. "What about Kayla? I know you said that I don't lose any friends, but I will lose friendships. Is she one of them?"

For a minute or two, Chandler was silent, his expression unreadable. Finally, "I know it's useless to tell you so, but don't worry about Kayla. Her road is closed to you also, and what you think you see and what actually is, are two very different things. But to shatter the mirror now would all but guarantee loss in the war against the Borelians, and the effects would ripple out until whole empires collapsed."

"What secret is she hiding? Yeesh." Tommen shook his head. "Sorry I asked."

"Don't be sorry. Caring for friends is nothing to be ashamed of."

"And Becky and Will and everyone? They're all going to be safe, too?"

Chandler nodded. "They will be safe."

Another silence settled between them. After a short time, Chandler stood and added some logs to the fire, gradually bringing tongues of fire out into the open, illuminating more of the cave, casting shadows over the contents of the stone shelves.

"Where are the White animals?" Tommen asked. "I haven't seen the rabbit in quite a while."

"The burrowers are most useful for spying and reconnaissance, which has been the primary goal lately."

"I thought the rabbit hated reconnaissance?"

"He does. But as he is a burrower, if he does not burrow, he is not doing his job, he is useless. He rescued you, true, but open combat is not what he is meant for."

"That would be Yawi, right?"

Surprisingly, Chandler shook his head. "Yes and no. Yawi can and does fight, but wolves are communication, coordination. Most often, it is the bears who will fight."

"Oh. Well, I guess that makes sense."

"Do not concern yourself with it. You will not be present in our battles. You would not survive. Focus on your world, your mission, your battles."

"That's harder than it looks."

The man smiled warmly. "I know."

Tommen looked away down the cave and back again. "I know I've asked before, but is there anything else you can tell me about anything? Anything concrete, something I should or shouldn't do? When is all this going to happen, anyway? Next week, next month, six months from now?"

"It will happen in its own time, though I will fair warn you that your next actions are the tipping point, the catalyst to start it going."

"What if I put them off indefinitely? Then it will never happen, right?" He knew it sounded childish even as he said it.

Chandler did not rebuke him, but instead laughed. "Your curiosity won't allow for that."

"My curiosity?"

"Oh yes. It is only human nature to be curious, is it not? To solve a mystery once opened?"

"I guess so." Tommen shrugged. "That means that this is all going to happen pretty soon, then?"

"Does it matter? Take it in stride."

Chandler was right, and that was probably the worst part.

They sat by the fire for a while, enjoying the light and warmth. Eventually, Tommen lay down on the woven mat.

"Chandler?"

"Hm?"

"Should I tell my shrink about our meetings? Do you think he would get mad?"

"Why would he get mad?"

"He'd either see you as competition, or he'd get pissed about how anxious you and your weird little prophetic riddles make me." He shifted position. "Maybe I won't tell him."

"Maybe not."

Tommen yawned, then asked, "What does it look like, on your end here, when I fall asleep and then suddenly wake up in my own bed? Do I just disappear, fade away, or what? Or is there like an Imprint of me sleeping here?"

He could feel Chandler's smile even if he couldn't see it. "No, it's more of a fade, as your mind climbs back out of REM sleep."

"So I am dreaming. But then how come, if I eat here, I wake up feeling full? Or like the herbs or the candles or whatever? That seems a lot more real than just simple dreams. But at the same time, if it's more than a dream, I should wake up feeling exhausted, especially since we've spent pretty much the entire night talking. But I know I'm going to wake up well-rested, just like a good night's sleep."

"The Author moves in mysterious ways, and so do I. Don't worry about it."

"How can I not?"

"By focusing on what you need to focus on, what you can do and change."

Tommen sighed and nodded. "I need to find the third journal. Everything else will happen as it will."

"Exactly."

"Okay, fine. Guess I'll just keep plodding along like I am."

He closed his eyes, but fought to keep himself awake—er, asleep?—just long enough to say, "Chandler?"

"Yes?"

"Thank you. For talking to me and explaining things and stuff. You're infuriating as hell and don't always explain things like I want, but it's okay. In the end."

"You are most welcome. And don't let yourself become

paralyzed with fear at every step. The Author has things under control. For incidental things, you can always go back. For doors that can only be passed through one way, you can't accidentally go through them. It will work out in the end."

"Faith, not stupidity."

"Faith, not stupidity."

"Mercy, not revenge."

"Mercy. Not revenge."

Tommen took a breath and let it out, knowing it was the last time that night that he would breathe in the smoke from the campfire and the tepid air of the cave. The next time he was conscious of inhaling, it was stuffy and warm. His room. He rolled over and punched off his alarm right as it went off.

He sat up and rubbed his face. He'd been up probably half the night, if not longer, but he felt refreshed and well-rested, just as he knew he would. He knew he had to get up and around for school, and he did, but he did not rush. He did not feel hurried. Everything moved in its own time.

Except the part where the bathroom was occupied and he wasn't aware of his urgent need to pee until he couldn't go. Then he may have Slow Banded until the door finally opened.

"Morning," his dad mumbled.

Tommen may have returned the greeting, he didn't know, but he got in the bathroom just as quick as he could. By the time he emerged, his Chandler-induced sense of calm had disappeared, and he was back to his normal, harried morning routine. He went to his bedroom to change clothes, grab his hearing aids and glasses, pack his bag, and try to remember what day it was and what he was supposed to be doing. Then it was out to the kitchen for breakfast. As he went out, he passed by his dad who almost appeared asleep in his recliner, at least until Tommen stopped to look and one eye popped open.

"Yes?" Walter wondered.

"Oh, I just thought maybe you were asleep," Tommen said uncertainly.

His dad closed his eyes and sighed. "I'm hungover. I haven't been hungover in a century. Give me a break."

"Oh." In a way, it was kind of amusing, and Tommen wondered if that made him a bad person. "Want me to make you some coffee?"

"No, thank you. Caffeine is the last thing I need right now." Walter sighed again. "Dammit. I forgot how awful this felt. Makes me wonder how I ever pulled off being a drunk."

Tommen frowned and said, "Drunks don't stop drinking long enough to get hungover, or if they do, they drink more to make it go away."

"I was a damn fool. Back then and last night."

"Maybe it was just something you needed to do. Remind yourself why you could never go back."

For a long moment, his dad was silent. Then, "You're a good son, Tommen. Yeah, I guess I'll take that coffee."

So in the middle of making French toast, Tommen got the coffee going and took a mug out to his dad who managed to sit up. After a minute, he brought a couple slices of peanut butter toast out to him as well. His dad took the toast and stared at it for a second.

"You shame me, kid. But it's my own fault, I suppose. For my own damn good."

"I do it because I care," Tommen told him. "What's on your agenda for today?"

"Well, I figure that once you leave, I'll go to bed, try to get some sleep and maybe take the edge off the pain before work."

"Yeah, hungover cops are bad for PR."

"Please, it wouldn't be the first time. Charlie is famous for it. Mike on first shift is just as bad." His dad took a bite of the toast and waved him off. "Go get your breakfast. I'll be fine."

Tommen nodded and returned to the kitchen where one side of his French toast was a perfectly inedible black, but the other side was fluffy, eggy, goodness. Carefully, he peeled off the blackened remains, tossed those in the trash, and started a second piece while he dressed the first in syrup and sugar before tearing into it. By the time the second piece was done, his dad had come out to the kitchen to rinse his coffee mug and the saucer the toast had been on.

"Want to borrow my glasses?" Tommen asked, holding them out. "They double as sunglasses."

"Very funny," his dad said, not looking at him. "No, thank you, I will be fine." He turned off the water. "I'm going to bed."

He started out of the kitchen into the living room, but Tommen called after him. "Dad."

He turned.

Tommen faltered for half a second. "Don't scare me like that again. Please. I saw the other bottles."

His dad took an even breath. "I know."

And he disappeared down the hall.

Tommen stared after him, wondering if there was a chance Chandler could be wrong. What if his dad wasn't done? What if this was the beginning of another addiction cycle? The last time, he'd gotten lucky because of the attack by the blue Borelian. How did this one get resolved, if not the hard way?

He shook his head. *It's not about your dad. The Shadows are using him to get to you. If they threaten friends and family, it's because they can't threaten you. But how does that work, because they have threatened you? They have circled you and tried to kill you. Tried. But they couldn't. Last time, you had a candle. Maybe next time, it will be a lit candle. Chandler said you're going to be freed from the Shadows. If he knows it, that means they might know it, too. And they don't easily give up what's theirs.*

Be on guard, Tommen, Chandler's voice whispered in his head. *The war doesn't truly begin until you're free. Then everything is fair game.*

Such happy thoughts he had right before heading off to school, he mused, finishing off his breakfast, washing the dishes, then grabbing his bag and his keys and hurrying out the door. And if everything was tumbling toward this huge, earth-splitting climactic event, it wasn't likely that his thoughts were going to improve over the next God-knew-how-long.

As always, he picked up Becky first. She climbed in back and immediately started talking. Mostly it was about finals. Swinging around to pick up the Shaw brothers, their morning chatter was pretty much the same thing. It only got heated when Becky mentioned that these finals were going to be her last ones ever, at least for high school. Seniors who'd kept up their grades consistently over their junior and senior year and were in compliance with the absence policy did not have to take the finals at the end of the third semester. She fit that model perfectly. Will, on the other hand, did not. Mostly it was him telling her to stop bragging, and her saying that she wasn't bragging, just stating facts. Sydney sat between the two, looking back and forth as each spoke, almost acting as a sort of referee, though her opinion was decidedly biased.

It made Tommen glad that he'd decided to give a damn about school this year, enough to keep his grades up over that threshold. As long as he kept them up for the first two semesters next year and wasn't absent too much, he wouldn't have to take his second semester exams, just skip right to college in the spring.

As per usual, he dropped off the brothers at the front door, then circled for a spot.

"I know I'm not really excited about exams starting," he said, pulling into a spot, "but I'm finding myself more and more excited for an upcoming anatomy exam." He looked behind his seat to watch her reaction.

Becky raised a brow. "Oh? Didn't know you were taking anatomy. Again. Did you fail last time?"

"No, this is the advanced course."

"I see. And when is this exam?"

"I don't know. It's a partner exam, and my partner hasn't told me when."

She smiled and sat forward to kiss him. "I wasn't aware that it was my decision."

"It's always been your decision, I think."

"Right about that. I guess I'll just have to get back to you."

With that, she opened her door. He followed suit and they walked into school together. It was still cold outside, but more at the level of an uncomfortable chill, versus the bone-biting icy grip of death that had sat over Charleston for weeks now. Of course, that meant that the snow would start melting, which meant slush. Looking at his shoes once they were inside, he wasn't prepared for slush, for wet feet. He'd gotten his steel-toed boots for work, but now he needed regular sneakers. He'd just started getting a paycheck again. Good paychecks. He didn't want to spend money on shoes. Or clothes. Or anything else, really. Right now, he just wanted to bank.

Well, it was a dilemma for another day, he figured. And if he couldn't make up his mind, no doubt the slush would do it for him. Oh well. Off to exams.

Chapter Twenty-Three
The History of Forever

Exams passed without incident. Because of the structure of the exams, Thursday and Friday were both half-days. Thursday, while Will went to finish up his community service and Eli took the bus home, Tommen took Becky home where they both "studied for an anatomy exam" before watching a little TV, making food, and waiting for her dad to get home, by which time Walter would be gone to work. Tommen arrived home to an empty house where he raided the fridge again before slumping into the couch. Exams meant no homework. Exams meant he felt justified in not doing jack shit for the third journal or anything relating to the Order. And Rifun did not come calling.

Friday after exams, it was basically the same routine, except instead of taking Becky home, they went skiing. Once again, he spent about an hour or so giving her instructions and pointers. Then she shooed him away so she could safely ride the green runs—testing out his instructions and pointers, don't worry—and he could go zipping here and there and everywhere he was and was not supposed to be. He earned a tongue-lashing from a Ski Patroller, but that was the worst of it, and they left at the end of the day no worse for wear.

"Maybe next year, if we can go out more, maybe I'll get you up to blue or even black runs by the end of the season," he commented as they headed home. Technically, he wasn't allowed to be driving with passengers without an adult because this wasn't a work or school event. He figured that as long as he didn't get pulled over, what the cops didn't know wouldn't hurt them.

"I highly doubt that," Becky said. "We don't go skiing that often, and I don't think I'll ever quite get there."

"Why not?"

"Because I see the injuries and it makes my stomach flip. Like, there was this one guy on this one run I was on, so it was an easy run, and he was screaming like a baby because he'd blown out his knee. Or maybe it was his ankle, I don't know. Ski Patrol looked like they wanted to shove a gag in the guy's mouth. But I just about threw up my hands and went inside."

"Yes, but you probably thought the same thing from the bunny hill. You probably thought you would never make it to the big hill; maybe you said you didn't want to. But now you're on the big hill. Tell me you're not having fun. Come on, tell me, 'The big hill sucks and I want to go back to the bunny hill.' "

She squirmed a little. "It is kind of nice to have more than two runs that last longer than five seconds. And it is kind of nice to have a little more mature, polite patronage rather than a bunch of snotty kids."

"So there you go. It's not all bad."

"No, it's not. But I still don't think I'm going to be running black diamonds any time soon. Certainly not this year."

"Maybe next year. And after that is glades."

"Don't even say that. I don't want anything to do with trees." She added quickly, "Or the terrain park, since I know that's next out of your mouth."

Tommen grinned and gave a snap and an "Aw, shucks."

They arrived at Becky's house about six-thirty. Being that it was Friday, Dr. Polski was busy making up his food for Sabbath and he offered to make them dinner while he was at it. Whatever he made, Tommen couldn't pronounce the name of, but he enjoyed it well enough and even had a second serving.

"How is the construction business going?" Dr. Polski asked conversationally, putting a pan in the oven. "I imagine it's a big change from the bakery."

"Yeah, no kidding. But I like it. I mean, I enjoy the physical work," Tommen answered.

"What do they have you doing? You're not eighteen yet, are you?"

"No, not yet. Right now it's mostly gopher work, grabbing this and that, tools, materials, handing them to the guys so they don't have constantly run up and down ladders. Holding ladders. Safety spotting. I'm not allowed to use the big power tools, but the foreman lets me use drills and some air tools. Says that once I'm out of school and working the real deal, even though I'm still a minor until August, he'll let me start on a few of the power tools, ones he says I probably already know. Sawsall, chop saw, things like that."

"And do you know how to use those already?"

"I get the gist. I'm not an expert, though."

"Time and practice. Who knows, maybe you'll find a career in the trades."

"I'm sure there are careers out there in the trades, but I'm still thinking I should go to college."

"Still interested in physics?"

"Absolutely."

While he kept up the good face, truth was, Tommen wasn't sure how he felt about going to college for physics anymore. He still enjoyed science; don't get him wrong, he loved it. But he seemed to be stuck in a swirling conundrum. The science he would learn was different from the science he knew. How would a physics professor feel if Tommen could demonstrate the ability to literally alter the physics of the universe? True, taking physics classes and having an understanding of the basics might be helpful, but at this point, it just felt useless. It would be like telling an old man who had been building houses and barns his whole life that he didn't know anything about building because he'd never gone to school, because he'd never learned "the basics." Or a boatbuilder who'd built his first boat before he was a teenager. Or any number of things. Tommen could manipulate the fabric of the universe, tear holes in it to go wherever he needed to go, could feel how it moved and changed, and he wanted to pay someone to give him a one-dimensional explanation? Sorry to say, but when it came to practical use, Rifun was the better instructor.

On the other end of this conundrum was the fact that he really, honestly enjoyed his work. It wasn't necessarily the construction per se, but the physical aspect of it. He could look back at the end of the day and see where a skeleton of a house had finally gotten OSB, insulation, starting on the siding on the outside and drywall on the inside. And he could say he helped do that. His dad lamented that the physical work increased his food intake by about a thousand percent, but it felt good to use that energy instead of letting it stew in his mind unproductively. He felt like he meant something, as if he could accomplish anything. Put bluntly, he felt like a man.

He left the Polski house after dinner and headed home, watching thick gray clouds roll in, almost certain that it would snow overnight. He flipped on the news when he got home and watched the weather. Sure enough, there was snow coming. He felt a brief moment of regret that he couldn't go skiing, then decided it wouldn't have been so great anyway. While he was adept at powder skiing, it really was a snowboarder thing. Let them have their fluff. He'd be busy...working...getting a paycheck...

Tommen had developed a habit of looking around the house, just to make sure nothing had been disturbed. He didn't see any evidence of mischief, whether of the breaking and entering kind or of the Rifun leaving a present for him kind. Actually, other than the flu-monia medicine, Rifun hadn't left anything for him. Maybe it was just as well; it had been freaky weird to get sex presents from another dude. There was just something wrong about that. Very, very wrong.

Satisfied that all was well, he returned to the living room and casually watched the news while surfing the Internet on his phone, occasionally looking up as the big story centered around the ongoing flu epidemic. The worst of it was over, at least in first world nations like the United States and most of Europe. Now the problem was getting medicine to developing nations and rural areas in Africa, India, and China. Personally, Tommen wondered how bad the problem could actually be in those rural areas. If no one went there, the disease couldn't spread. Therefore, there was no need to get medicine to them. Problem was, if the disease did make it to a rural community, it would spread and kill ten times as fast.

Oh well, it wasn't anything he could control. The major problem had been taken care of; the Borelians couldn't unleash any other diseases on the human race, so once this was over, it was on to the next major health catastrophe. And then the next and the next and the next, until the end of time.

He grabbed the remote and started flipping through the channels, eventually settling on a documentary about black holes that was just coming on. Was he trying to convince himself that he still loved physics and that was what he wanted to do with his life? Maybe.

"Billions and billions of years ago..." the narrator began.

Tommen mentally paused. Billions of years ago. Billions, with a B. He leaned back on the couch and looked down the hall toward his bedroom where the Authored Books sat quietly. If the universe began billions of years ago, did that mean the Author was billions of years old? Or had she retroactively added billions of years? Considering the picture in the back, she couldn't have been older than thirty—and that was an insult. Did that mean the universe was only thirty years old? No, because his dad had been a century sober. Did that mean that the universe was however old the Author said it was? She controlled the writing, she controlled how everything came into being. Maybe "One day" was really all it took. Sort of like, "Let there be light"? Was this part of that day like a thousand years and a thousand years like a day? But then, if the Author wasn't infinite, if she was just some woman from Michigan with too many cats, maybe there was a God out there who was infinite. And what God said, went, right? Was that still part of a multi-verse theory? Fucking hell, half a sentence into the documentary and he was already screwed.

The documentary, while fascinating, basically boiled down to two key concepts: First, black holes were massive and massively powerful. It's a really bad idea to get sucked into one. And second, no one knew what lay inside a black hole. Part of the reason for this was that, in theory, time itself bent differently around black holes so that if one got close enough, time would slow down so that person could watch the entire rest of the universe pass by, even die.

Tommen's thoughts went to the inverter in the fortress. Its whole job was to keep the fortress and the planet it sat on from falling into a black hole. If anyone pressed that big red button, the shields would go down and they would get sucked up in the vacuum cleaner of the universe with no time to escape, assuming the planet didn't explode first.

Naturally, upon the stunning revelation that black holes were big, powerful cosmic vacuum cleaners that no one knew what was inside, the documentary then took the time to speculate on what could be inside a black hole, citing vital information sent back by NASA probes—from a safe distance of a couple million light years. They didn't actually know what was in a black hole, either.

He thought about Titik's words. "To find the light, first you must travel to the heart of a black hole. And come back."

Well, if NASA couldn't do it with all their fancy machinery, he couldn't do it by himself. But, yay, metaphors. He stood and went out to the kitchen, rummaged around for a soda or something, more out of habit that needing anything.

They survive every day. Every day, people dance around a black hole, dance in it. The difference is, most simply choose not to come back. It eats them. Consumes them. Money is the only pleasure in the world, after all.

Tommen stood, nearly smacking his head on the inside of the fridge.

Money is the only pleasure in the world.

In that instant, Tommen wished he'd had a tape recorder so he could replay the whole interview. But he also knew that the old captain hadn't been as nutty as his guards assumed. Titik knew. He knew too much. That was why he'd been shot. But that didn't make sense. He'd been shot because he had failed to retain enough money for Rifun and Cassius to fund their terrorism, right? So how could he know...?

Tommen's phone went off and he was almost happy to find it

was a Time Agent asking for a ride to the Wheel. He agreed and made a quick jump to Canada to pick the woman up and take her to the Wheel. She apologized, saying it might be a while as she had business all over the place, but she only wanted to make one full trip rather than a bunch of little ones. Tommen said it was fine; he wasn't needed right away back home. She thanked him, apologized again, then took off to wherever she had to be. He made his way to the Archives.

The secretaries were beginning to learn his face and they let him right on through, not that they gave him much hassle any other day of the week. Still, he greeted them politely and stepped into the dizzying tessellation that was the largest library in the universe.

He thought about asking for directions to the section detailing the events of the Dispersal, then decided against it. He had time. He could look for himself and maybe come across something by chance. But for as huge an event as the Dispersal was, how he did he begin to research it? It was like saying one wanted to research World War II. Great. It was a huge event that took place, as the name suggested, all over the world. There were battles and leaders and ideology and weapons and heroics and atrocities. How did one just "research" World War II?

Well, the most popular or most logical thing to research first when it came to events like World War II was prominent, decisive, or unusual battles. During the Dispersal, there had been few "battles" to speak of, at least as it directly related to the Wheel or the Hands. Assassinations were carried out in secret, many of them by Cassius, aka Calis Cutthroat. There were skirmishes here and there, but nothing huge or game changing until the very end of the Dispersal, when the next elections came around. Details were scarce, but it prompted another Rebuild. After that, everything settled down until the Zero Hour Revolution.

Tommen rubbed his face and briefly wished that he had brought a notebook or something with him to better organize his thoughts. He racked his brain, trying to remember if Titik had said anything else insanely inspirational, but came up with nothing. Well, not quite. The man had repeated the concept of puppets numerous times. He said that he had been charged to keep a portion of his stolen gains for the puppeteers. That would be Rifun and Cassius. Rifun and Cassius, then, would be manipulating puppets. Was it too far-fetched to think the Hands were those puppets? They had everyone all strung out at the last elections, at the coup. Puppets cannot pull their own strings, and the Hands were powerless to stop Rifun and Cassius when they took over.

Money is the only pleasure in the world.

Yes, it would make sense that as much as Titik referred to his own greed and pirating activity, he would also use it as a reference to the Hands, the Time industry that made them so wealthy, so powerful.

Tommen stood and walked down one row and up another, running a hand through his hair. Titik had only had the fake book, not the real one.

But it was a book of lies, the book a lie itself. The lie died, but the truth survived.

A book of lies. So, obviously, Titik never bought into the ideology of the Cult; he was just in it for the money and whatever position of power they gave him afterwards. The book itself being a lie was referencing that it was just a copy, not the original.

The lie died, but the truth survived.

Was it possible that he had, at some point, possessed the original journal? Maybe before being approached to store up money? He could have had it, discarded it, been approached, realized the worth of the book, tried to get it back. But that wouldn't make sense either. He'd attacked a Turitian royal emissary for a fake.

Maybe Titik was two-timing the Cult, and that was why he'd been shot. He did have the original, but made a grand show of attacking the Turitians for a fake in order to throw them off. Rifun finds out, shoots him in the head. But again, if that were the case, why not have better leads on the original? So far, the only concrete lead rested on Kath, in the Irdo Vault.

Someone knew something but wasn't saying anything.

Tommen stood and made another lap around the rows. Titik knew more than he was telling, or saying explicitly. Was that because he was trying to hoodwink his guards, or because he really was insane and could only form coherent thoughts through weird, insane analogies, like trying to describe a dream?

He made several more laps, coming to a stop when he almost ran smack into his rideshare.

In normal times, when opening portals to the Wheel, the portal stayed open until the one who had opened it returned home. They could be forced closed, but generally speaking, they stayed open. The lady could have returned home at any time. These days, with fears of the Borelians lurking about, it was decided that the safest course of action, if possible, would be to force close the portals, so the Borelians couldn't travel back through. That also meant forcing them open from the Wheel back home, an infinitely more difficult thing to do as the technology in the Wheel did not like it.

But for as difficult as it was, Tommen got it done, sending the woman home and letting the portal dissipate. Once that was accomplished and he regained his senses, he started back through the Wheel. His initial thought was to head straight for the Archives and begin again, come at his research with a fresh perspective, a new angle. Unfortunately, he couldn't conjure up anything like that, so he instead made a detour to the Food Court. Maybe having something in his stomach would inspire something, or at least quiet the growling and grumbling.

With everything that was going on between the humans and Borelians and with the Order, the Wheel and Time industry was a surprising breath of fresh air. It was unshaken by the Borelian war with humans, just a normal, neutral marketplace where, as long as sales didn't get interrupted, they didn't give two shits about the personal affairs of its members. While cold, it was oddly comforting. And as long as Tommen kept his mouth shut about the Akari, and any and all related activities and people, he wouldn't be scooped up by the Grandfathers and deposited in a cell in the Judgment Wing. But did that include searches in the Archives? Surely he couldn't be penalized for looking at something they provided freely as static information. Right?

Well, he still needed to get some research done. If the Grandfathers did come after him, at least he'd learned enough about portals to know how to escape. He could probably never come back, or at least not for a long time, but he wasn't going to be helplessly hauled away.

As he methodically made his pizza disappear, Tommen's mind was split into two lines of thought. The first line was wondering when the Akarin Archives were going to be excavated and restored. It looked as though work had begun in earnest, but how long would it take? Assuming they did get the structure rebuilt and stabilized properly, what would be salvageable? Literal tons of rock had crushed everything, ceiling to floor. Would there be anything to save? Had original copies of ancient texts perished forever? Tommen wasn't a historian and even he felt a little queasy at the thought of so much authentic history going to waste. He made a silent wish or hope or prayer that something could be found. Half of the stuff. A quarter. Not everything could be lost.

Then he considered that maybe the Akarin Archives would have more information on where Richard's third journal was. If they had anything to do with its disappearance, they had to have some kind of map to it, or a chain of accountability, in the event that the Cult went looking and the Akarin needed to re-find it so they could re-hide it. Tommen also found himself wishing for someone to talk to about it. But Micaiah was dead, Micah gone, and Kayla...somewhere out in left field, to hear his dad tell it. Either way, she wasn't such a friendly face right now, would probably tear his head off before telling him anything useful.

His second line of thought came from his amazing powers of perception and people-watching. He couldn't put an exact word to it, the mood of the crowd, but it was located somewhere between anxiety and fear. The movements of the people were off. Something wasn't right. Had they heard about the attacks on the Borelians? Did they fear retaliation in the Wheel? The Borelians were noticeably absent here; what did that mean? Did they expect Rifun and the First Order to try something, another coup? Did they expect humans—a species once ignored, now regarded as fearfully as the Borelians—to try something on a larger scale?

His pizza finished, he cleaned up the best he could and headed out, feeling rather important for being only an Apprentice Timekeeper. Ah, Timekeeping. It felt like so long ago that Timekeeping was his whole world, his whole business. Learn Time, master the arts, get promoted. Since learning to use the Akari, Timekeeping felt...hollow. Meaningless. Childish. Like playing with toy cars again after being given the keys to a Mustang or Camero. One, you had to pretend to have power. The other, you actually had it.

Tommen returned to the Archives, a new thought in his head. Kath was only recently Engaged, which meant that any unusual activity—such as alien sightings and visits—would likely be more well-documented. Captain Picard talking to a Vulcan in 2495 wouldn't even register as a footnote of any text. Talking to a Vulcan in the 1970's, however, that would be something worth noting. By someone. Maybe a marine biologist. Ha ha ha. Maybe he should peruse Kolkath dissertations on whales. Ha ha ha.

Jokes aside, he looked through the Archives for any mention of strange visitors to Kath during the Dispersal, or that time period. Part of him said he should cut the crap and go back to Kath and look through the Vault, or get Raba to look through the Vault. The other part of him said it would be a waste of time anyway.

After some fruitless searches, he returned to Captain Titik. The man was crazy, but what about a time when he wasn't crazy? Did anyone keep a record of his logs? Ask and ye shall receive, for Tommen found a tablet containing the transcripts of the logs of Titik's ship, turned over to the Grandfathers a year or so ago when the Psiaco originally wanted to have him prosecuted in the Wheel and taken off their hands. It didn't just contain the captain's logs, either, but all records of the vessel, right down to all the unpaid repair bills over the years. Did Titik have any overdue library books, too?

Tommen scanned the easy stuff first, things that were only a single page, easy lists, documents he could scan and find without having to go too in-depth. The first thing that caught his eye was the crew compliment, dated Earth date: 1975. While a majority of Titik's crew was Psiaco, with the largest minority of Urid, he did employ other species as well as he raided and pillaged across the galaxy. Listed there, under Miscellaneous Crew As Yet Untested, was Abbal Duma T'Akhar Mureel Sibon, Ururian.

Now what was he doing, running around with Titik? Maybe, in his exploits, conning people left and right, he'd been captured by Titik, pressganged into service.

Technology was a wonderful thing, and it didn't take sixty seconds for Tommen to cross-reference Abbal Duma Whatshisface and bring up every entry where he was listed or mentioned. There weren't many, but just enough. Tommen brought up the Captain's Log and hit Play.

"Captain's Log, the first day of Murath, 4312. We raided a Miloriuan spice Trader..."

Blah, blah, blah, business as usual. But to his credit, Titik was, at one time, a real force to be reckoned with, or so he looked and sounded. To see him chained to a chair, rambling on about this and that now seemed...cruel. Pathetic.

"There was a stowaway onboard, an Ururian named Abbal Duma T'Akhar Mureel Sibon," he said. "Gods know why Ururians insist on such long names, and why they insist on being addressed by them fully. According to the Miloruians, he is as much con artist as entertainer, ready to rob a man of any possessions he has. And if a man has no possessions, he'll steal the skin off your back. He is currently sitting with the rest of the useless prisoners until I decide what to do with him."

He went on about more stuff after that, but Tommen hit the Next button, passively listening through the daily musings until Titik got to the point.

"Today I discovered Abbal Duma T'Akhar Mureel Sibon using the Akari to try and cheat at cards with some of the senior crew during their recreational time. I knew it only because of my exposure to it thanks to Rifun Ndolo and Cassius Hand. When confronted about it, he denied it publicly. Later, when I spoke to him privately—" Tommen highly doubted they had a pleasant chat over Starbucks lattes. "—he claimed to be a member of the Akarin. When pressed, he admitted to being a former member of the Akarin, but he was dismissed because of his dishonest antics. I inquired as to his knowledge of the Cult of the Akari. He claimed to know only rumors. When I asked if he had any interest in learning more about them...he readily agreed."

Because that wasn't ominous. Tommen went to the next log, dated roughly eight months later, and waited.

"Abbal Duma T'Akhar Mureel Sibon has proven useful to my crew and my secondary mission. His con games have brought us great fortune and even turned the tides of battle in our favor with his sleight of hand. But as easily as he will do this for us, I have little doubt that, given the chance, he will use it against us as well."

The next log was nearly a year later.

"The Ururian, Abbal Duma T'Akhar Mureel Sibon, has formally requested to disembark. As part of the crew, it is his right after two years of service, which he has given. I mistrust him. Perhaps it was an error on my part to bring him into the Cult of the Akari and expect him to feel any loyalty. His loyalty is only to money, with no sense of brotherhood. But he knows too much, I fear. We are three weeks from docking at Emithen Station for routine maintenance, shore leave, and supplies. In that time, I must make a decision whether to let him go, or kill him instead."

One week later...

"The con artist has truly perfected his craft, able to slip attempts by assassins and hide, even from the heat sensors. Being Ururian, he does not give off a heat signature significant enough to be detected. We are still two weeks from Emithen Station. In that time, he must come out for food and water. We will find him."

Two weeks later...

"The Ururian is gone. No doubt he has had dogs on his trail before, and he knows how to run. From witnesses at Emithen Station, he jumped on a vessel bound for Kath, an insignificant world only just stepping into Time. No doubt he will make great profits there to further his con games. While I have made it known that Captain Titik searches for him, our pursuit will not be active. But if I see him again, he will be dead on sight."

And that was the last mention Titik gave of Abbal Duma T'Akhar Mureel Sibon, the Ururian con artist.

Tommen leaned back in his seat and stretched, formulating a timeline in his mind, but coming up with little. Even if Abbal Duma etc. etc. had been the one to take the journal away from Kath, Tommen was still stuck with a dead end trail. Personally, he had kind of hoped that there would have been one last log, many years later, where Titik finally catches up to him and gives him his due. No such luck. The story just ended right there. And he was right back to where he had started. Nothing new or useful had been gained except for an interesting story.

At last, Tommen stood, replaced all of his tablets, and left the Archives, heading for home.

It wasn't until Monday after school that Tommen headed back to the fortress with the intent of asking about those Archives. But, as he discovered, he didn't need to. True, it wasn't exactly back up to code, and everyone who wasn't a construction worker was barred from entry, but great progress had certainly been made. There were three distinct floors again, fourth, fifth, and sixth. Most of the heavy rubble had been cleared as workers labored away to finish their last huge project.

To that end, most of the books and artifacts had been cleared away as well. A huge group of scholars—ahem, Philosophers—had gathered in one of the recreational halls on the first floor to sort through things. Much of the library had been brutally crushed and utterly destroyed, but not all was lost. Tommen jumped in and offered to help, figuring that was more polite than barging in and asking what they had available. They would probably have him escorted out by security. And maybe he would find something by chance.

The Philosophers were skeptical—they had a system going, and they didn't want him to mess it up—but they put him to work as a gopher. He didn't sort the books, but they gave him the sorted books and told him which pile to toss them in. Looking at the mess and thinking about what the Archives had looked like beforehand, he estimated that a tenth to a quarter of the material had survived in relatively decent condition, another tenth or so in workable condition, and the rest totally obliterated. Books were ripped in half or burned, scrolls as ancient as desert sands were nothing but dust. Parchment text had come unwoven as easily as an ugly Christmas sweater. What if the answers he needed had been destroyed?

After a few hours, the Philosophers told him to take a break. He did so, from their work, but he pawed through the piles—always gently, lest they yell at him. He started in reference, looking through logbooks, record books, easy things he could scan through. He found a book called Book of Whispers. Vaguely, he remembered Whispers were Akarin members who were inactive or "former." Only about half the book was in tact, but he carefully opened the cover and turned the pages.

It wasn't just a list of people who were inactive, but the reason why they'd been listed. For some, it was simply that they hadn't been seen in a long, long time. For others, they'd publicly denounced their involvement with the Akarin. Then he came across that little diamond among the coal.

"Abbal Duma T'Akhar Mureel Sibon, Ururian. Listed as Whisper on [local time: January 14, 1965]. Reason: Failure to deliver package."

Failure to deliver package? Damn, mailmen just couldn't catch a break, could they? But then, the only package Tommen could think of that would be so high-profile would be the journal.

Abbal was a former Akarin, as confirmed by Titik. According to the centaur alien, he'd been sent to Kath to hide the journal from the Cult. If that was the case, why the failure to deliver? Was there another high-profile package out there? No, couldn't be. If Julianna gave the journal to one man who gave it to another man who gave it to Abbal to take to Kath, unless they did all of that in a matter of days, a slow, careful, drawn-out timeline would make sense.

But what if he hadn't been told to take it to Kath? That was what he did, but was it what he was supposed to do? Abbal was a con artist; the whole universe said so. Knowing the Kath were excellent recordkeepers and could make perfect copies of anything, what if he decided to pull the biggest con of all? Make a copy, tell the Kolkath to copy it and make a show of it, make a show of having something the whole universe feared and one mad cult was desperate for, then return later to take the original for himself.

Before he can do that, he's captured by Titik who proclaims himself part of the Cult and threatens Abbal. The details may or may not have been important—regardless, they were lost in history now—but he scares Abbal. Abbal thinks Titik is going to find him out, so he jumps ship, heads back to Kath to take back the journal.

Tommen rubbed his face. All fine and dandy, but that was still all beforehand. Nothing to tell where he took it afterwards. Except, perhaps, the one place where he was supposed to have taken it that he didn't.

Something pricked the back of Tommen's brain, something that he ought to consider but couldn't figure out why. All of these things occurred around major events in the Wheel. Cassius was Zero Hour in the 1860's. His disappearance triggered a frenzy in the Wheel, especially among the Hands. 1960's, there was the Dispersal. Each time, though, both events resulted in a Rebuild. The Wheel now was in its Seventh Rebuild (there was debate over seventh versus eighth, given Rifun's redecorating and the slight modifications made afterwards, but the general consensus was that it was the seventh). The

Dispersal resulted in the Sixth Rebuild. The Missing Zero Hour resulted in the Fifth Rebuild. He remembered Sifura telling him a story about the Third Rebuild.

What the hell were these Rebuilds and, other than changing the desktop theme of the Wheel, why were they such major events? More to the point, how did they happen? If only a few knew how to Rebuild the Wheel, what was that knowledge rooted in? Was it just chaos that Abbal might have been taking advantage of? There was something important about it, Tommen knew that much.

Tommen got called again to help sort books. He rubbed his eyes but complied. He had to get home and get to bed at some point, but the mystery, that break, he could see it right on the other side of his mental fog. It was there. The answer. He brooded over it heavily as he helped the Philosophers sort through more books and texts. When they released him for another break, he returned to the reference pile. Dammit he wished these things were as easily cross-referenced as the tablets in the Wheel. It was almost an hour before he found another book that caught his attention.

Book of Builders, was the title. He picked it up and took it aside to sit and read, carefully turning the old pages, pausing whenever he heard them creak or, God forbid, crack. Maybe he could touch the pages with Matter, get them to repair themselves...

Andrew O'Dell and Nathan Wilde were both listed. Highly gifted, rank of Admiral among the Akarin, but in hiding. Doing undercover work.

So they had been Akarin who had gotten the one up on Julianna, perhaps pretending to be converts when really they were undercover. She had turned over Richard's third journal to the Akarin without even realizing it. In a way, it was almost comical. Tommen nearly laughed out loud and gave the finger at no one in particular, but mentally sending it to Julianna. But he refrained, instead settling for a snicker that he tried, badly, to cover with a cough. When he searched for their last-known location, the only reference he found was "in hiding."

Master Builders, two men who were capable of changing the Wheel itself. How did one do that? Where did someone learn? Was it just high-level, super-secret Akarin stuff? Was there anyone sitting down in the sub-levels who could do such a thing? If so, why didn't they just rearrange the molecules in their cells—or their guards for that matter—and set themselves free? Why didn't—?

Tommen knew the answer even before he finished the question.

Suddenly, he understood.

He understood everything.

Carefully, he closed the book and returned it to the pile. He thanked the Philosophers for letting him help, and explained that he had to be going. They thanked him for his help and let him go. But rather than going to the portal room and going home, he started up the stairs, making for the eighth floor. His intent of being a badass John McClane-type action hero—cresting the final flight of stairs, dusty, dirty, and bloody, but hardly breaking a sweat and ready for more—dissolved by the third floor, and he was again Tommen Forbes, the skinny little white kid who could never hope to outrun a rooster, never mind a bear, a dinosaur, or an avalanche. Well, the avalanche he might have a shot, assuming he had his skis.

He reached the top, telling himself to stop being a baby and start being a badass, but it hurt to breathe, man. Maybe he should get tested for asthma one of these days because he should be used to this by now. After taking a few seconds to recuperate, he straightened and knocked on the door. No answer.

Carefully, he pushed the door open, Banding as soon as he could look around. Rifun was nowhere to be seen. He dropped the Band, waited another minute, called out a tentative, "Hello?" and waited, heart pounding. Still no answer. Looking behind him down the stairs to make sure they were clear, Tommen Banded, pulled it tight around himself, and stepped inside, dragging the door shut behind him.

His first mission, while he was thinking about it, was raiding

Rifun's dresser for those pills. If he counted them and found one missing, well, pharmacists were held to a higher accountability standard but couldn't be perfect all the time, right? It was a lame excuse, he knew. He could also hear Chandler's voice echoing in his mind, telling him not to get involved. Tommen promised the voice, or maybe himself, that he wasn't going to actually say anything; he was just curious to know what it was, really.

Minor mission accomplished, he crossed the room to the inverter. It was small, efficient, barely even made a hum in a quiet room. Or was that because he was still in a Band? No, no, he didn't remember ever hearing it before.

Whatever. Didn't matter. The inverter prevented the planet from falling into a black hole. In theory, under normal circumstances, when one got close enough to a black hole, where all the matter in the universe was getting sucked in, time slowed down so that a person—assuming he was still alive and not stretched out like a noodle—could see the universe pass before his very eyes, all of time in only a few seconds.

The Wheel was the opposite. When a man went to the Wheel, time at home stopped. When he stepped through the portal, sickness was very common, as if his insides had been compressed and then allowed to spring back out again, sucking the air from his lungs and the strength from his limbs. When a man went to the Wheel, it was impossible to map it because it was dimension upon dimension, layered, stacked on top of one another until it formed a single, incoherent mass, all of it converging into a huge ball of fuck you. Endless time. Endless energy to power it continuously through the centuries.

The Wheel of Time was what lay on the other side of a black hole. All black holes in the universe, converging on this one spot. That was the reason it was so hard to bypass the portal stream to the Wheel, because it used the power of the black holes to sustain it. That was why the Rebuilds were so significant, and why so few could become Builders, because it was reshaping a huge part of the universe, bending the truly raw elements of creation itself. And at some point in the distant past, maybe even the First Rebuild, the Akarin—or whoever they had been way back when—had been kicked out of their own home, sent back through a black hole and landing on Iurinta where they evicted the Iuri, Shatai and Kitir, and built their fortress and the power inverter in this room. And if there were any Builders in the sub-levels, they couldn't Build because to do so was to destabilize the inverter and send them tumbling into the black hole. Maybe attempting to Build anywhere outside the Wheel was to invite trouble.

That was why Rifun had been so obsessed with setting up his kingdom in the Wheel of Time.

And that was where Richard's third journal was hidden.

"The lie died, but the truth survived," Titik had said. "Hidden among words. Weedy words. In the heart of a deep, dark hole. The puppets protect it. But they don't know it. Their greatest enemy hidden in their own home, placed there by the enemy of mine enemy."

The lie died, but the truth survived. The fake journal was gone, but the original one was still out there.

Hidden among words. Somewhere in the hell that was the Archives.

In the heart of a deep, dark hole. A black hole.

The puppets protect it, but they don't know it. The Hands were oblivious to what lay behind their walls.

Their greatest enemy hidden in their own home, placed there by the enemy of mine enemy. Placed there, by the Akarin.

"To find the light, first you must travel to the heart of a black hole. And come back. Pull the strings, pull the threads, make the puppets dance."

Titik had known all along where the third journal lay. Likely, he had told Rifun. Something about where the journal was specifically buried required a Builder to undo. But neither of them were Builders. That had been Rifun's obsession with the museum journal, the Book of Abilities. Maybe Richard had unlocked the secrets of Building. Unlock that, get the third journal, possess all three journals and the ability to bend creation, even reality itself.

But Richard hadn't figured out Building, or not quite as it was. The difference between Cult abilities and Akarin abilities. Subtle. Mirrored. But not the same. That was why Rifun and Julianna sent Tommen to do the dirty work now. The faith of a skeptic. They didn't need loyal lackeys who believed and did exactly as they did; they couldn't use them. And the Akarin certainly wouldn't help. But the faith of a skeptic who had power and Faith that he didn't even realize yet...that might be the key. Threaten him, befriend him, do whatever they had to do to make him cooperate.

And if it took Builders to free the journal, everyone would know about it, just as Chandler had promised. There was no way he could do this in secret. But he wouldn't be able to do it at all without finding some Builders. Maybe now it was a matter of finding Andrew O'Dell and Nathan Wilde. Maybe that was the thing in between that had to happen.

Tommen left the room and dropped the Band. He made it about ten steps down the stairs before spotting Rifun, heading back up. Well, at least he didn't look exhausted, as if he'd just run twenty marathons.

"Ah, my young Apprentice," he greeted amiably, if distractedly. "Were you looking for me?"

"Um, no. I mean, yeah. I mean, it's not really important. Just...I think I may have found a lead on the journal."

"Very good. Do you need your team assembled?"

"Not yet. It's just a planet right now; I want to narrow it down a little more first."

"A good idea. Don't waste time unnecessarily. Very well then, on your way."

So Rifun was back to passive and disinterested. Tommen felt the pill in the itty bitty pocket in his front jean pocket. What the hell was this thing? No time to debate it now. He hurried down the stairs, slowing only when he got to the construction crew on the sixth floor. No running—ever!—in a construction zone, unless you're running away from something. That was a rule. A very good rule, Tommen thought.

He couldn't say why he felt so rushed all of a sudden. There was no time limit. But at the same time, it felt that even as he discovered the location of the journal, even if the information had all been quiet and internal and he mentioned nothing of it, that something out there still knew. As if the Shadows themselves watched him, invisibly, from dark corridors and half-glimpsed images in his peripheral vision. They were watching him. Waiting to see what he would do, who he would tell. Then they would report back to their Shadowmaster. Then all shit would hit the fan.

It was like a waking nightmare, and going through a portal—even a familiar one—did nothing to help matters. He clawed his way into bed, almost unable to breathe, gasping for air as though he'd been waterboarded. With shaking hands, he brought out his phone and opened his messenger. After a minute or consideration, he put it away and rubbed his face.

Fucking hell. It was almost as if his brain exploded, the information overload, between the straight facts and philosophical implications. This was absolutely unreal. Impossible, even. There was no way he'd just accidentally stumbled onto this. Except maybe by some preordination from the Author. But if it took divine intervention for a stupid teenager to discover this, how had Rifun figured it out? Did anyone else out there know about it?

Or had someone else figured it out? Had someone figured out that the journal was in the Wheel and taken it, and that was where Rifun had lost it? No, that wouldn't make sense. If that were the case, that was probably where he would have started in the introduction to this little investigation. So then, the journal was still there in the Wheel, somewhere in the Archives, locked in some trap that only a Builder could decode.

There was probably a tidy list of Builders out there somewhere. Hell, Tommen had just been reading through a book of Builders. But he wanted to ask the ones who had been involved, who had started this whole thing. Starting tomorrow, he was going to have to start a search for Andrew O'Dell or Nathan Wilde, and hope that one or both was still alive. If he got lucky, maybe he would see Chandler tonight and could ask him. But when had he ever gotten that lucky?

Tommen glanced at his clock. A little past ten. Yes, now was a good time to go to bed and sleep it off. Maybe in the morning, he could convince himself that this had all been just a bad dream.

Chapter Twenty-Four
Manhunt

Andrew O'Dell. Born in Ireland in 1643, he led a quiet life as a fisherman until 1671 when he was exposed to Time. The story went that he'd been out fishing, as per usual, when a squall swept in. He was unable to get back to shore and his boat began breaking apart when suddenly it all stopped, or so it seemed. The storm still raged on around him, but his boat had been tossed into the air and that was where it stopped. No crash, which would have surely busted his boat to smithereens and condemned him to death.

As he's sitting there wondering what's going on, a man climbs into his boat. Being a good Catholic, Andrew went to Mass regularly and he knew very well the depictions of the Christ and all the saints. This man didn't look like any of them, yet Andrew was loathe to call this demonic work. The man introduced himself as a Time Agent, a Timekeeper to be precise.

Long story short, the man, by the name of Matthew, got Andrew into Time and training as a Timekeeper. While Andrew was happy to be a constable, he was interested in more familiar, more honest work (because controlling Time itself was the devil). He left Timekeeping to become a Merchant, one of the few honest ones out there, or so it was claimed. In 1717, he was outed as an Akari-bearer. In an effort to save himself and his family from harm, he went into hiding. In 1917, two centuries later, his presence and disappearance was recorded, little more than a passing mention. Since then, nothing.

Those were the records found in the Wheel Archives. Tommen found little in the remains of the Akarin Archives except that he had been formally accepted in 1715. He had done some work with the old

Cherokee, had a somewhat indirect hand in establishing the Krydik on Hlohi, though his effort was comparatively minimal in that regard. Then he did some work for the Akarin, somehow reached the rank of Master Builder, and vanished in 1979, or that was the last recorded entry that Tommen found.

The good news was that with such a recent record and him in good standing, there was a chance that one of the Akarin remembered him. Now if only they would talk to Tommen.

Next up was Nathan Wilde, born in 1588 in Liverpool. His mother had died in childbirth, and his brother from scarlet fever when he was two, leaving only him and his father who was, as it turned out, a Harvester himself. He took the years of his wife and dead son and later gave them to his living child to bring him into Time. (Tommen couldn't decide if it was a romantic or sick notion.) Then, in 1620, they crossed the Atlantic to try their hand at taming the New World.

While Nathan's father trained him up to be a good Harvester in trade, the man could never instill the self-righteous, indignant attitude common among Harvesters. The elder Wilde was indifferent toward people in general, and openly disdainful of the "savages" known as the Native Americans. Nathan, however, took pity on the Natives. According to the Wheel Archives, with the help of another Merchant and a couple Timekeepers, they brought Time to the Native Americans. When it became apparent that even Time could not save the Natives, Nathan and the others went in search of a habitable world and found the one that would become Hlohi.

The Natives were not thrilled about the prospect of moving—again—but going to a place where there were no white demons held a certain appeal. Nathan and the other Time Agents helped orchestrate the Migration, which would eventually lead to the events surrounding Anagalisgi's capture, near-hanging, and subsequent imprisonment in the in-between dimension.

As it might be expected, the British colonists and soldiers were not pleased that their own had conspired to spirit away the savages. Court was held. Nathan and the others were sentenced to hang. But before the rope could touch their skin, there was a flash of lightning and suddenly they disappeared. In actuality, they just opened up portals and got the hell out of there. But they were forever labeled as sorcerers and conspirators of the devil. Not that it mattered since they never returned to that place.

As for Nathan, he remained on the down low. His record was nearly empty until 1810 when he was accused and apprehended for being a Runner. The details were unclear, but all that was known was that he somehow escaped custody and vanished. Simply vanished.

Akarin records, what remained of them, were not much more helpful except to clarify that it was Nathan and Andrew using the Akari to help the Natives. Otherwise, the most Tommen could find was that he and Andrew O'Dell had studied together to become Master Builders. Whether they were good friends, mere colleagues, or familiar strangers was unclear. Other than that, the man was a ghost. Or maybe he'd been a prominent member of the Akarin community and the destruction of the Archives simply erased him.

Tommen sat back and yawned. Another day of helping the Philosophers sort books. They'd barely made a dent, or that was how it felt. In reality, they were just being slow and methodical about it. The construction would take a little time yet, so even if they did get everything done, they would still be waiting.

He stood and stretched. Everything in him said to race down to the sub-levels and interview as many Akarin as possible. He also knew that wasn't going to happen today. He had to get home, do some homework, cook some dinner. Sex was out of the question since all parents were home tonight, but that was okay. And anyway, Becky was still sewing, sewing, sewing away, declaring that if she hit her goal of production and money, she was going to close up shop at the end of the school year and take the summer to do whatever she wanted to do. When Tommen asked her what she wanted to do, she promptly declared, "I don't know."

And that was that. Tommen returned home where he'd dragged his suitcase out of his closet, but that was about it. Spring break was three weeks away. He was going with Becky and her parents on a vacation to South Carolina and Florida, with maybe a one day mini-vacation in Georgia somewhere in there. Now was the time to start thinking about what he was going to take with him. Swim trunks, definitely. Sandals, check. Shorts, check. These things he could pack now seeing how it was still too cold here in West Virginia to sensibly wear them.

"Running away on me?" his dad asked, pushing open the door.

Tommen looked up. "Huh? Oh, no." He explained what he was doing.

"Little early, isn't it? No, wait, it might take you three weeks to figure out how to impress a girl."

"Dad..."

His dad was still in a bit of a down mood, but he'd come back around since Laura left him. They didn't talk about her much except in passing, when stating facts. Tommen didn't ask what his dad was going to do over spring break since his plans had been canceled. Probably go back to work, like everyone else.

He also hadn't told him anything about his discoveries about the Wheel, the Akarin, the journal, or any of that. He couldn't find a way to say it that didn't make him sound like a nutty conspiracy theorist. He did, however, inquire as to missing person search methods, especially when those cases appeared to have been cold for decades. The police did not usually get involved in missing persons cases except on an administrative level without reasonable suspicion, but with his many years of experience in the department with the city police, Tommen figured his dad knew a thing or two.

"Well, seeing how I suspect you are referring to a Time Agent, or variant thereof, I think a few search methods may have to be modified slightly," his dad mused. "Some Time Agents will change their names as they go dark and resurface, but their registered name in the database stays the same. Sometimes they will record their name changes, and sometimes they won't. It's not a mandatory thing.

"You'll want to interview other Time Agents who knew them, served with them in some capacity, or something of that nature; we Time Agents like to keep in touch over the years. Helps us stay sane. And don't discount known friends and associates from past lives. It's rare that a Time Agent will change himself so completely from one life to another. There's usually great similarity and overlap. Sometimes, something mentioned or referenced over and over again can give clues to future pursuits."

Tommen nodded. He'd figured as much and had planned to do all of that, but it was nice to have the reassurance, especially coming from a former Missing Persons investigator.

So it was that the following day after school, Tommen found himself in the Archives again, looking for any known associates of either man. Problem was, O'Dell had a century gap in his record. Wilde, even longer. The Akarin Archives weren't much help either. Their records were more practical, and most of them were missing anyway. After several hours of searches that turned up little and less, he finally gathered his nerves and went to the sub-level gate.

"What do you want now?" one guard asked.

"I need to speak with any Akarin associates of Andrew O'Dell or Nathan Wilde," Tommen explained. He added, "It is relating to a mission that Faharoa himself has tasked me with, and that will directly impact the bigger plan he's bringing together. I need the information. Today."

The second guard chuckled. "We will let you in today. Whether or not they give you the information today is another matter."

Apparently, the best way to get by these guards was by amusing them with something they perceived as impossible or childish fantasy. Nevertheless, in his peripheral vision, Tommen could see the word was circulating, both about the question and the big plans Rifun had going. The guards opened the gate and he stepped inside.

"I am looking for anyone who knows or used to know Andrew O'Dell or Nathan Wilde!" Tommen announced. "You will not be punished for association!" He couldn't guarantee it, but he figured it was helpful to throw that in there. "They are human. Male. They were or have been Akarin for decades, even centuries. They were Master Builders who studied together..."

He trailed off as the din of conversation picked up and began to swirl around the room at the mention of Master Builders. From the back of the room, somewhere in the darkness where the stairs led to the next sub-level, there was a commotion. Peering into the gloom, he saw someone making their way forward, and plenty of hands reaching out to try and hold them back. The figure shook, peeled, and slapped them away, coming ever closer. Uncertain of its intentions, Tommen glanced at the gate, tried to judge distances, reaction time, what to do if something went wrong.

Then the figure got close enough to speak to comfortably. It was a Grunjor, or a close relative, anyway, it seemed. Maybe closer on the relative side. Where all Grunjor were the same—built from some special rock, given a name and a task with no specification as to gender or personality—this one appeared almost feminine, and perhaps unable to do the same physical or metaphysical manipulation of her body. But maybe she could... No! Snap out of it! He had an interview to conduct.

"My name is Jali," she said. "I knew Andrew O'Dell and Nathan Wilde. We studied the Building arts together."

"Great. Are you willing to talk?" Tommen wondered.

"As much as I can, on one condition."

"Name it. We can discuss it."

"I wish to go home. I have a daughter. She hasn't seen me since the attack. I fear what she believes has happened to me."

Tommen nodded. "I'll see what I can do." He looked past her to the seething mass of Akarin. "Why don't we go out, take a walk, get something to eat?"

She did not disagree. The guards grunted disapprovingly but did not stop them as they left the little prison gate and made for the mess hall. Tommen did not speak until they got their food and did not launch into the interview while they ate.

"What's your daughter's name?" he inquired.

"Baja. She is four years old," Jali answered politely. "For my people, she is halfway through her childhood."

Tommen nodded. "I'm seventeen years old. Less than a year and I'll be a full adult."

"So young yet. How did you get mixed up in this?"

"Ah, it's a long story. I've got Authored Books about it, though. Maybe you can read about it someday."

Her expression turned unreadable and she remained silent, watching him. They finished their food, then got down to business.

"By now, you've probably guessed why I'm here, what I'm doing," Tommen began.

"You're searching for the third of Richard's journals," Jali stated. "And, in doing so, bolstering the army for an attack on the Borelians."

"Something like that, yes. I know where the journal is, but the trap it's set in can only be safely released by a Builder. I believe Andrew and Nathan were the Builders responsible for putting it in the trap in the first place. Now I need to find them. Do you know where they are, or what happened to them? The last record I can find for Andrew was over thirty years ago. But that was in the Akarin Archives, which, you may know, kind of got destroyed. They were Master Builders, and if you studied together, that means you've been around long enough to have known them a while. Do you know what happened to at least Andrew?"

"Andrew liked to tell stories of what he called the Old World," Jali began. "He was a fisherman, a farmer, a Merchant in Time. He preferred hard labor, honest work as he called it. He lamented the Great War on his world, even wept over how his people tore themselves apart. The Time industry and the Wheel was not so different, which was why he preferred to stay in the Akarin fortress as much as possible."

"What about the journals? That was before the Great War."

Jali nodded. "Yes. I think that was why he lamented the Great

War. When he became a Builder was about the time Richard began his heretical revival. Andrew was an exceptional student with great skill in all areas of the Akari. He easily got into the Cult with intent to feed the Akarin information. When Julianna's plans became known—to flee across this ocean of the Atlantic people and take the journals with her into the future—he was sent to intercept them. One journal was left with the Cult at the time. Another disappeared and was later recovered on his world. The third she entrusted to him, Julianna believing he was a true supporter."

Tommen stopped her and paused, searching for the words to the question he'd been thinking all along but had no one to ask. "Why not destroy the journal immediately? Why hide it and draw this out as long as it is?"

"That I do not know for sure, but I have a speculation. In your quest, have you come across the name Abbal Duma—?"

"Yes, I have."

"He was also Akarin, or so he claimed. He was a con artist, always had been. For a while, he changed his ways, but when he heard of the journal being captured, I think he saw only profit. Andrew took the journal first. He was good friends with Nathan Wilde, so it was not unusual to think they should both have it. But where Andrew was more rigid and decisive, Nathan was more emotional and easily fooled. I believe Abbal somehow conned Nathan into giving him the journal, or else stole it outright. Then he took it to Kath where a copy was made. That may have been a smart thing to do, really, but then the original journal disappeared." She studied him. "And you say you know where it is?"

"Maybe. I have a pretty good idea. But without being a Builder and being able to get into the trap, I don't know a hundred percent that it is where I think it is."

"I am a Builder. Take me."

Tommen shook his head. "Not yet. The fewer people involved, the safer it is. Trust me, I'm doing it for your daughter. If, for some reason, I can't find Andrew or Nathan, I'll come back to you. But for now, just go with me on this."

"How can I go with you if—?"

"It's an expression. Means roll with it. Go with the flow. Trust me. Can you do that?"

"It seems I have no choice."

"Your frustration is noted. Any idea what happened to either of them, though? I mean, are they down in the sub-levels somewhere? Did they die by some other means?"

Jali made a gesture that Tommen took to be a kind of shrug. "I do not know. Andrew, I think, grew weary of the fighting, both within and without. He may have retired. Nathan, I believe he said he went on some kind of pilgrimage or quest. He did not weather the Dispersal so well. I think he wanted to find and help others who were struggling. I do not know their exact locations. I am sorry."

Tommen nodded. "That's all right. I think I have an idea of where they might be, or at least one of them." He stood. "You have been very helpful. Now then, let's see about getting you home to your daughter, shall we?"

Of course, it would be his luck that she was lying. Or, not technically lying, but not disclosing the entire truth. Jali did have a daughter. She also had a son. A very large son who was Tommen's approximate age, as far as that species went. Who was not half as kind as Tyler Freeman had ever been. When Jali mentioned that Tommen was working for Rifun to find the third journal, well, he crawled into bed that night with every ice pack in the house draped somewhere on his body. Building was apparently the pinnacle of Akarin teaching, which meant Jali knew a trick or two, including how to make injuries immune to Time. He would be feeling these for a while.

He overslept his alarm, but his dad got home soon enough to wake him up. Tommen groaned and lazily threw his arms over his eyes as the lights flipped on.

"Sorry to say, kiddo, but there is school today," his dad told him. His brows went sky high as Tommen pulled himself upright. "What happened? Another battle? Are you okay?"

"No, I got in a fight with a close relative of a Grunjor. And his mom knew enough tricks to anchor the injuries in Base Time." Tommen took a shallow breath, the best he could manage. "I already did some Feeling. Nothing's broken, but there is some pretty deep internal bruising. I didn't piss blood last night, though, so I think I'm generally okay."

"All the same, do you want to go to the hospital?"

"Urgh. Not really."

"I really think you should. See how you do getting ready for school. Start by picking up all the ice packs you seem to have flung around last night."

It was a chore, and Tommen could feel his dad's scrutinizing gaze, fully dad, fully cop, but nothing he could do. Tommen handed off the ice packs and went to the bathroom.

Holy shit. If the colors on his face were a Michaelangelo painting, Tyler Freeman was a fingerpainting kindergartener. There was almost nowhere on his face where his pasty white skin could shine through; it was all black and blue and purple, though the actual swelling was minimal, save for a lump on his left cheek. He had a pretty good hematoma just below his left shoulder, over his collarbone, and another on his right hip. His whole body looked covered in flowering purple moss, and his left arm was swollen, though the edema hadn't started yet, and he could barely move any of the fingers on his left hand. He found another small lump on the back of his right calf. As for pain, he bore so much of it that it no longer registered as anything more than having eaten too much or maybe a stomach bug, the way his abdomen twisted and tightened and slogged around. But he still didn't piss blood, and that was what counted.

"You're going to the hospital," his dad stated when he emerged from the bathroom.

"I'll be fine. Honestly, I will. I'll just be moving a little slower." Tommen shuffled back toward his bedroom.

"I don't want to take the chance. Honestly, you look worse than you ever did after a fight with Tyler Freeman, and I don't want to send you off when there could be something going on internally."

"I slept through the night."

"You passed out. There's a difference. Get dressed. Call your friends. I'm taking you to the hospital."

He had little choice it seemed. He called Will and Eli first, who had to suddenly scarf down their breakfast and hurry up before the bus rolled by in about ten minutes. Then he called Becky who immediately started nosing into his business. He simply told her that he wasn't feeling good, he was going to the hospital, and left it at that. Let her draw her own conclusions until he got back to school and could see the damage.

"Do I get breakfast first, at least?" he whined as his dad all but pushed him out the door.

"No, not until the doctors clear you," his dad said firmly, shooing him along.

The ride to the hospital was long, and the weather didn't even seem that bad. Maybe it was just him. Maybe something really was wrong. At the very least, he was allowed to walk into the ER under his own power. The expression on the receptionist's face was pure disbelief, and she looked to Walter for answers. *You actually let him walk in here? Why didn't you call an ambulance?* It only then occurred to Tommen that his dad hadn't changed out of his blues; he was still in full cop mode.

"He needs to be checked out," Walter stated.

"I'd say he does," the receptionist agreed. "Is any one thing hurting more than another? Any major complaints?"

"Um...my stomach—I mean, my abdomen hurts a little, but that's about it. I don't really feel the pain anymore at this point," Tommen answered dully.

At six in the morning, the ER wasn't overly busy, and he was shown to a room within five minutes, though it took another twenty before the doctor arrived. In that time, his dad called the school to say he would be late or maybe absent, and then Tommen relayed the story of the interview—omitting the part about knowing where the journal was—including taking the woman home on good faith, only to be assaulted by her son.

"She said to take it back as a warning to all other traitors," he finished. "Apparently the Akarin don't like me too much."

His dad took a breath as if to speak, but then the door opened and the doctor walked in.

"My goodness, looks like we had a rough night," he observed. His tag read O. Thomas. He looked at Walter. "Is this a matter of an investigation?"

"Not officially," Walter replied. "I'm his dad. I work third shift, came home and found him lying in bed covered in warm ice packs. He overslept his alarm. He tells me he got into a fight last night. Didn't want to pursue, didn't want to come in, but I made him."

"Okay. Well, I see your chief complaint is abdominal pain. I'll check that out in just a second. Does anything else hurt, stand out in any way?"

"Just my arm." Tommen painstakingly rolled up his sleeve to show off his left arm.

"All right, then. Looks like we can start anywhere we want."

So began a several hours long series of interviews, tests, labs, and a hell of a lot of waiting around. Because of the hematomas—the doctor said a lump the size of his fist was equal to about ten percent blood loss, and he had two large ones and two small ones—he was given two units of blood, plenty of fluids and oxygen, and treated for generalized shock.

"You'd think I was dying," he said, grinning. "I've come in way worse."

"Exactly," his dad said seriously.

It was ten or eleven o'clock when his dad called the school again to just say he would be absent for the day. Oddly enough, Tommen was relieved. Well, it wasn't unusual for him to not want to go to school, but at least he no longer felt anxious about being late, and maybe it was a smart idea to take the day off to rest and recuperate.

In the meantime, Tommen had plenty of time to think. And he

reflected that in all of the Authored Books he'd gotten so far, he, or someone he was close to, always wound up in the hospital. There was always some kind of hospital scene. Why was that? Oh yeah. The Books said the Author was an EMT who enjoyed poking wounds a little more than she should. She was a sadist, and she enjoyed tossing her little voodoo dolls into the fire. Her little Tommen voodoo doll especially, it seemed. Just couldn't go too long without getting injured. And this time, it hadn't even been battle or provocation or anything like that. It had been in his genuine attempt to help someone. No good deed goes unpunished, he supposed.

But then, that called into question whether Jali had been speaking the truth, or just leading him along so she could get what she wanted. But if she wanted to do that, there were any number of things she could have said. She could have said Andrew and Nathan were living on Mars. Maybe she hadn't expected to really get taken home until her story checked out. He'd taken a big chance on her, and her son's wrath would be nothing compared to whatever Rifun or Julianna would do if they found out he let a Builder escape. Builders were few and far between, a hot commodity when it came to valuable prisoners. Well, with any luck, they wouldn't have to find out before he found the journal and all the earth-splitting, fortress-shaking shit hit the fan.

"Oh, hey, I have a question," Tommen said the next time the doctor came in. Forcing his arm and hand to cooperate, he dug in his coat pocket where he kept the pocketed pill safely stowed away at all times, waiting for a chance to ask a professional what it was. He held it up. "I found this in school the other day. I was wondering what it was. I mean, I wasn't going to take it or anything, but I was just curious."

The doctor took the pill. "Well, I can't say right offhand, but I can run the information etched in here, or just run a general lab."

"Please do," Walter said. "If there's a pusher in school, I want to know what he's pushing."

"Absolutely. In the meantime, I have the results of all the tests and labs."

In a nutshell, he was going to hurt like hell for a week, but he would be fine. He had bruising to his stomach and liver, but nothing serious. He probably wouldn't feel like eating much for a few days, and if he was in construction work, maybe talk to the foreman, see if he could get the weekend off.

"If you don't have any questions for me, I'll see if I can't do a quick test on this pill," the doctor finished, glanced at them for a second before leaving the room.

"Where'd you find the pill?" his dad asked.

"Outside someone's locker," Tommen answered smoothly. He didn't want to tell about going snooping through Rifun's things, mostly because he was undecided on this whole forgiveness-versus-Stockholm-Syndrome battle he'd been toying with in his mind. He knew very well what Stockholm Syndrome was. It was submitting to and agreeing with a captor after a period of time, when mental barriers had been broken down until actions once regarded as evil suddenly no longer seemed evil, or they were at least greatly justifiable.

Tommen didn't know what forgiveness looked like. As far as he knew, it was reserved for religious people who'd been saved by the Lawd and hallelujah, praise be, glory, glory, amen! Or maybe hugs and smiles and "Sorry / I forgive you" exchanged for petty things like spilling coffee on someone's car seat or cheating off of someone else's test.

He'd never really heard of forgiveness on the scale of kidnapping, attempted murder, another attempted murder, genocide, actual murder, murder again, and murder in the form of a siege.

Forgiveness is letting someone walk freely through your mind without fear of a firing squad, Chandler had said. It's taking yourself out of the equation and letting the Author do her work.

Tommen could never forget being held hostage with a gun to his head. The memory remained a vivid nightmare. And yet, he found that he really couldn't conjure up the rage, the drive to hurt Rifun in any way possible to get back at him, to go to battle to overthrow his empire. But neither could he conjure up flimsy justification for it. It had been an evil act. Tommen couldn't even say that he felt satisfaction over Rifun's seizures, as if they were some just dues. Maybe they were. But it was the Author's work. Tommen was merely a bystander, tool of the Order, servant of the Author. Had he really thought that?

Oh, if he really wanted to, he could nurse the emotions that still tainted those awful memories, bring the two-dimensional picture memory to a living, frothing monster, and yet he didn't. Because that monster was a Shadow. Maybe many Shadows. Rage, Anger, Hurt, Betrayal, Fear, Revenge, Bitterness, Lifelong Therapy, Unforgiveness, all possible names. But the Shadows would not be controlled. They would attack and hold him down, feeding on him. Because he always returned. Except this time, he refused.

Was this was forgiveness looked like? Could he forgive? Three times, Rifun had lain helplessly at his feet in convulsions. Three times, Tommen had let him live. Not because he enjoyed some kind of power rush, not because he enjoyed some convoluted version of revenge for his wrongs. But because he had mercy. Mercy with no explanation whatsoever.

So it was that he was pleased to crawl into bed that night and find Chandler waiting for him on the other side. The man had the look of exhaustion after a day of honest labor.

"I think we've both made a lot of progress today," he observed as Tommen adjusted his seat by the fire, even more pleased that his injuries did not carry over and he could get comfortable here. "What's on your mind?"

"I think I understand the forgiveness thing," Tommen said, staring into the coals. "But what do I do with it? Should I keep serving Rifun, working for him, doing what he says? His actions are evil, and I can't imagine they are going to get better with the third journal. Good enough to forgive, not dumb enough to go back, as my dad likes to say in domestic violence cases. How do I stop enabling him?"

"At this point, there is only one path you can follow, and you must follow it to the end," Chandler told him. "Everything that happens...I do not understand it, but it is still the Author's work. It may seem as though everything spirals out of control, but she is still in charge. Never forget that."

"But if this is me walking away, being freed from the Shadows —"

"It is not. This is freeing you from many Shadows, true, but the true walking away has yet to come."

Tommen paused. "All right then..."

"What else is on your mind?"

"Did you know? About the Wheel?"

"That's a vague statement."

He was pretty sure Chandler knew exactly what he was talking about, but explaining it to someone helped get his thoughts a little more organized. He shared his findings about the Wheel, why it was the way it was, how it operated, how the Rebuilds worked, how the Builders fit in, all of it.

"The only thing I really don't know is a definitive timeline of events surrounding each Rebuild," he concluded. "The Wheel Archives are going to have far-fetched myths, the Akarin Archives, assuming the texts even survived, are going to be incredibly one-sided. Or I would think so. Do you know what happened?"

Chandler nodded. "I do." He shifted position, ready for storytelling.

"The Author made the Wheel of Time for the enjoyment of her creation, her characters. The ability to mold the fabric of the universe. Time, Matter, Energy, all at their fingertips. Tiny creators themselves, of a sort. But some...began to see themselves as Creators—big C—Authors of themselves, even others. There was a war. Akarin and Cult, Whites and Shadows. It was a bloodbath. But the Akarin prevailed. They Rebuilt the Wheel, intending to mold it just so in order to keep out the Cult. For a time, the Cult disappeared, vanished into the greater universe.

"The Akarin who were left celebrated their victory, but then...turned out to be little better—understand that this is over a period of decades, even centuries. And soon, it wasn't half of them who thought they were capital-C-Creators or capital-A-Authors, but all of them. It is said that the Author herself destroyed the Wheel then, initiating the Second Rebuild—it is said that the shockwaves from this destruction reverberated across the entire universe, changing entire planets, entire species. Then, rather than give the Wheel back to the Akarin, the Author turned it over to the first Council of Hands. The Akarin were banished to Iurinta, just on the outskirts of the Wheel—the black hole, as you know. It was also then that the first fragments began to appear, educating the small group of refugees who had remained loyal and survived.

"The Cult, seeing the Wheel's weakened state, attempted a hostile takeover, which ended in the Third Rebuild. After the Third Rebuild was the longest recovery time the Wheel had ever seen, and there was a great span of peace. Or, rather, not-war. There is a difference. Both the Cult and the Akarin were incredibly weak, mere shadows of the power and greatness they had once been, though there was still undisguised animosity between them.

"Incredibly, the Fourth Rebuild had nothing to do with them, but the Hands who had heard of this great Akari power and wanted to try and use it for themselves. Obviously, if it ended in a Rebuild, it didn't go well."

"The Missing Zero Hour triggered the Fifth Rebuild," Tommen stated. "The Dispersal the Sixth. The Zero Hour Revolution the Seventh."

"Correct."

"Rifun was hoping the museum journal, the Book of Abilities, would make him a Builder, so he could take the third journal, establish his kingdom, and make him emperor for life. Basically."

"Basically, yes. Becoming a Builder is no small feat. Builders are chosen by the Author herself. Anyone can study the arts in a textbook, but if the Author does not grant you the ability, you have nothing, no power."

"Why give the ability to Nathan Wilde? If he was so emotional as to be conned by the universe's most notorious con artist...?"

"We are only human, are we not? Can we not make mistakes?"

"This seems like a pretty big mistake."

"But was it a mistake?"

Tommen opened his mouth, closed it, opened it again, closed it. Finally, "But you just said..."

"I only asked if you expected him to be perfect. I did not say that his mistakes could not be used for other purposes. The Author can take any mistake and make it good."

"So...even though he fucked up by getting conned, the Author made it good by having a copy made and that whole fiasco so the Cult would go one way and the Akarin could take it another way and everything turns out okay."

Chandler nodded. "And there is one more thing yet that must happen before this all pans out and you see the Author's work."

The kettle over the fire began to whistle. Chandler took a cup and filled it. He offered it to Tommen who was set to refuse, then thought better of it. Stupidly, he tried to drink right away, but the tea was too hot yet. Thankfully, Chandler did not notice as he had gotten up to retrieve a second cup for himself. He gathered his little herbal tea mixture and returned to pour himself some hot water.

For a good five minutes, they sat in silence, contemplating the fire as it mesmerized and dazzled all who looked upon it. As much as it fascinated Tommen, there was still the lingering fear, set in motion from the camp, forever embodied in his left arm, twisted flesh that would never recover. He took a drink of his tea.

"What's on your mind, Tommen Forbes?" Chandler asked finally.

He took another drink and set the cup off to the side. "Where are Andrew O'Dell and Nathan Wilde?"

"You know where they are. And who they are. You've met them."

"So they are who I think they are?"

The old man nodded sagely.

"Are they are going to help me?"

"They will."

"And after that is when it all hits the fan."

"Yes."

Tommen shifted position and looked around the cave. He ran his tongue over his teeth. "Would anything catastrophic happened if I chose to wait until after spring break before doing this? Believe me, a vacation would do me some serious good."

"Before or after the shit hits the fan?"

He paused. "You're right, better to do this before spring break, get it over with." He picked up the cup and took another drink. The cup was not very big, and soon it was empty. "Am I at least going to make it to summer vacation before anything else exciting happens?"

Chandler sighed dramatically and shook his head. "I'm not a fortune-teller, Tommen. I only see what the Author shows me."

"What are you talking about being a fortune-teller?" Tommen asked as Chandler refilled his cup with water and herbs. "Everything you tell me is bad news, doom and gloom, Armageddon type shit. I'm not coming to you for stock tips, say it that way."

"You wound me with your words."

Tommen nearly spit out his drink. "Your words almost get me killed. What are you complaining about?"

The man laughed, and Tommen with him.

"Is there anything else on your mind tonight?" Chandler wondered, reining himself in.

"I don't think so," Tommen admitted. He took a slow drink, thoughtful, contemplative. "I think I really just need to gather my nerve and take the plunge. Hooray, another epic climax to another Authored Book. I hope she tops the New York Times bestseller list for this one. The last one was good, but this one's got to be ten times better, or so say the critics." He grinned and shook his head. "I don't know."

"Get some sleep," the man said gently. "Up for school tomorrow."

Tommen did not fight the fatigue that suddenly washed over

him like a warm summer breeze, though he did wake up, initially confused. His alarm was going off, and it was the correct time for the correct day. Then, as he rolled over to punch it off, he realized he wasn't in gut-wrenching pain. Sitting up felt totally normal. Getting up and heading to the bathroom, he flipped on the light and found all his bruises had gone. The only indication left that he'd been in a fight were small yellow bruises where the hematomas had been, and they didn't hurt no matter how much he pressed his thumb into them. When he released the pressure and everything returned to normal, the bruises might have even gotten a little smaller, slowly fading away. Even his left arm was normal again, save for the permanent burn flesh.

He got ready for school like any average morning, changing clothes, grabbing his backpack and rummaging around for his homework, heading out to the kitchen for breakfast where he met his dad just as he walked in the door.

"Holy cats," his dad said, stopping in the doorway. "Thought you got beat to hell yesterday?"

"I did," Tommen replied simply, cracking a few eggs into a frying pan and hitting the lever on the toaster.

"Thought you said they were immune to Time? Actually I know they were, because I tried to Band them and couldn't."

"They were. I think Chandler did this."

"Chandler?" It took a second for the recognition to dawn on Walter's face. "Ah. Well, good for him. Good for you, really."

"Guess it's a good thing I didn't take any pictures yesterday. People might be suspicious." Tommen grabbed a plate just as the toast popped. He got that out and buttered them, just in time for the eggs to get done.

"Yes, they would. Going to school like normal, then." Walter dragged the chair over to sit in it and untie his laces, leaving Tommen to stand and eat his breakfast.

"And the shrink this evening," Tommen reminded him.

"You sound eager to go."

"I'm just glad I'm not limping along like a sack of bones.

Makes me ready for anything."

"At least until tomorrow when you have to get up early for school. Or the next day—" Walter grunted as he slipped off the first boot. "—when you have to be to work."

"All right, all right, kill my mood, why don't you?" Tommen finished off his food except for one piece of toast and tossed the plate in the sink. "Bad night at work?"

His dad shook his head, slipped off the second boot, and stood, pushing the chair back in its place. "No, it was a pretty quiet night, actually. I'm no longer the most unpopular guy in the precinct. That honor went to Vin."

"What'd he do?"

"I told you his wife is filing for divorce, or she wants to? Well, being a quiet night, he decided to cruise by home and have a screaming match with her. I don't think he intended to argue with her, but that's how it turned out. They ended up waking up the neighbors...who called the cops. Kate went out to it. She reamed him a new one. So he's her new least favorite officer right now."

"Oh. Lovely. And you?"

"Still on the shit list, but no longer at the top." He put up his hand and headed for the living room. "And I am staying out of this whole debacle as much as I can."

"Sounds smart." Tommen finished off his toast and grabbed his keys. "I'll see you later."

He headed out to his car and zipped toward Becky's house where she awaited her chariot.

"What happened to you yesterday?" she wondered, clicking the seatbelt. "Flu-monia finally catch you?"

"No, I don't think so. I guess it was just some small twenty-four hour stomach bug," he replied, glad she couldn't see his face. "Either way, I'm good."

"Well, I don't need to be sick again, so I am staying as far away from you as possible."

"Shall I make sick little handprints all over your locker?"

"Nyah!"

He laughed. She couldn't hold her superficial anger longer than three seconds, and soon she was laughing, too. Then she launched into a short story about her terrible, awful, no good, really bad ride on the bus the previous morning.

Will and Eli got the same story, and he got almost the same reaction, and almost a similar terrible story about them having to ride the bus. Tommen also reminded them about how much they coughed and sneezed all over his car when they got sick, and they just waved him off dismissively. All in good fun. Watching the brothers walk into the school, Sydney faithfully by Will's side, and Becky still in the backseat, Tommen found himself longing for a normal life, where fun and friendship wasn't in constant danger of being taken away from him.

Chapter Twenty-Five
Plain Sight

It was only the beginning of the new semester, so it wasn't as if Tommen had missed a whole lot. Missing only one day cost him, what? A couple section reviews and a pop quiz? Easy to make up. It was hilarious and yet almost disheartening that school was this easy. As it was, he took his seat in each class, like usual, and scribbled in his notebook. The teacher would think he was taking notes, when in actuality, he was making up the section reviews and whatever else he had missed. It was only, what, the second week of the semester? They didn't have their first tests until tomorrow. Easy peasy.

Spanish he normally hated, but this time around, he might enjoy it, and maybe even surprise Mrs. Perez a little by doing well, or making a darn good effort. It was his last Spanish class, after all. Three years of infierno was finally coming to an end. When he turned in his homework, her eyebrows went sky-high and her jaw dropped a little.

"¿Qué es esto?" she asked. (What is this?)

"Mi tarea," Tommen answered simply. (My homework.)

"Está hecho correctamente. Y está en español." (It's done correctly. And it's in Spanish.)

"¡Sorpresa!" (Surprise.)

"Diré. Creo que podría necesitar un poco de aire." (I'll say. I think I might need some air.)

"Creo que deberías ignorar la tarea de esta noche por eso." (I think you should ignore tonight's homework assignment because of it.)

She gave him a look. *"No te hagas inteligente. Siéntate."* (Don't get smart. Sit down.)

He did so, though he continued to stun her by being a model

student for the rest of the period, speaking almost entirely in Spanish—bad Spanish, judging by Mrs. Perez's nails-on-chalkboard expression—taking notes in Spanish, and speaking not a single word in Welsh, Irish, Hungarian, Hebrew, or Polish. He thought she was going to have a heart attack before the end of class.

"Tommen," she called before he could walk out the door. He turned. *"Te estoy vigilando. No compro tu pequeño acto. Algo pasa, y voy a averiguar qué."* (I'm watching you. I don't buy your little act. Something's up, and I'm going to figure out what.)

"¿Y arruinar la diversión?" (And ruin the fun?)

She put two fingers to her eyes and flicked them back and forth between herself and Tommen several times. He laughed and walked out the door. It never got old.

Algebra was pretty standard. Mr. Keller had apparently found something, the beginnings of his groove, and he was a little more relaxed this semester. His teaching was still a little choppy and stunted as he worked to figure out his teaching style compared to his students' learning style. Tommen bet that by the end of next year, he would have found his groove.

It was the only class that he couldn't quite finish the catch-up assignment in time. Well, strictly speaking, he could have, but what would have been the point? Still had tonight's homework stacked on top of it.

English was still a hybrid class for him, half the time spent in the classroom and half the time on the computer. Tuesday through Thursday was spent on the computer, and he headed down to the library, taking a seat next to Will who was loading a course disk into the CD drive of his computer. Sydney, knowing acutely that she was on full duty right now, did not move a muscle from her spot under the table.

"What's up?" Tommen asked quietly, logging in.

"Hey, man," Will greeted. "Got pretty much the same damn classes as last semester, in almost the same damn order. Lucky for me, though, I can change up the order however I feel like."

"I wish I could do that. I don't know if I'd want to have English first just so I can get it out of the way, or last so I could go straight home afterwards."

"Yeah, but right now, you go to lunch right after. Is that really so bad?"

"Hm...you may have a point there."

Food after a terrible class was pretty nice, Tommen figured, loading up his program. And the online portion wasn't all that bad. It let him work at his own pace without the teacher looking down her nose at him or the other students whispering about him. Was it really his fault he'd struggled with English so much for years and was basically playing catch-up now, when it really mattered, when they all got it?

Still, he said nothing out loud, just plodded along on his own, occasionally trading jokes or chatting with Will, at least while the librarian wasn't looking. Despite being told that they were to stay logged into their respective programs until the very end of class, the two were packed up at five minutes til. Then, as soon as the lunch bell rang, they darted out of the library, the closest room to the cafeteria. Not that it mattered since they were both brown-baggers anyway and had to go back to their lockers to retrieve their food, but it was still a neat thing. Some days. Other days, it was torture to sit there with both the cafeteria and library doors open, smelling the food as it cooked. It was cheap, frozen, mass-produced food, but when hungry, it was heaven. Or hell, as the case may be, and Tommen's stomach rumbled.

"Take my lunch, dude," Will said, coming alongside him. "I have to take Sydney out."

So while Will took Sydney out to do her business, Tommen grabbed a table and slapped both lunch bags down for emphasis. As he was pulling out his array of food, Becky sat down next to him, Eli across.

"What's everyone doing this weekend?" Eli asked immediately.

"Probably working, like every weekend," Tommen told him.

"Well, yeah, during the day. What about at night?"

"I don't know. Why?"

"Aiden Cruz, the junior? He's having a party at his house this weekend. Everyone's invited. Literally, everyone."

"Because that doesn't sound dangerous," Becky commented. "I think I'll pass."

"Me too," Tommen agreed.

"You guys are no fun. Where's your sense of adventure and thrill-seeking?"

Sorry, I left that back at the fortress, before I got the shit beaten out of me.

He hadn't even considered how he wanted to bring up the subject of his manhunt. He knew where Andrew and Nathan were hiding—or he had a pretty good idea, anyway—now it was a matter of approaching them.

He pushed the matter aside before his grim train of thought showed on his face. A few minutes later, Will joined them.

"I'm not going to be here for lunch tomorrow," he announced.

"Why not?" Becky wondered.

"Mrs. Ellis from the elementary school came over. She wants me to give some kind of presentation to the kids about service dogs. I said I'd do it, but I don't know why. I have no idea how to talk to little kids."

Becky waved a hand. "It's not hard. Little kids are easily entertained. You walk in, say, 'Hi, my name is Will. And this is Sydney. I can't see, so she has to see for me.' And describe what she does for you throughout the day. You don't have to use big words or anything, and it doesn't have to be a long speech. Kids also have very short attention spans, and they're going to be thinking more about wanting to pet the dog. So you also explain to them that they shouldn't automatically pet a service dog without asking the handler first. Boom. Twenty minute presentation, over in a flash."

Will mulled it over a bit, but did not disagree; he was distracted by having to scarf down his lunch to make up for the time lost in speaking to Mrs. Ellis. He'd no sooner finished than the bell rang and the mass that was the student body groaned and slowly moved to head to fourth period.

For Tommen, that was history. More specifically, 20th Century Pop Culture, focusing on the movies, music, fashion, and all the other exciting stuff about history versus boring important people, war, and political scandals. Every week was dedicated to a different decade. The class had been divided into teams, and that was who they would work with for the entire semester. Last week, Tommen and his team had researched fashion in the 1900's. This week, it was music of the 1910's. If the rotation kept up, next week would be sports of the 1920's. Every Friday, they had to give a presentation. No tests, just the final exam at the end. It wasn't a bad class. Actually, he quite enjoyed it. It was researched history, found on the Internet, not dictated history read in a book.

The only class he was really anxious about was Creative Writing. Right now, they were simply going over elements of a story (but seriously, if you didn't know what plot and characters were by high school, there was just no hope for you as an author). Next week, they would be writing. Tommen had worked out an agreement with Reisig that he would simply translate select stories in his notebook, versus writing something from scratch. It would still undergo some editing, but she would be his editor because she could better appreciate the difference in language. English had the most number of words for a language, with some ridiculous nuances. Welsh didn't have quite that much. It had nuance, yes, but—

Oh, shut up. You could give a whole lecture on Welsh in Welsh. It's a beautiful language that you feel privileged to know as your first language and you could never make anyone else understand. Shut the hell up and just focus on your writing.

So he did. The class was basically divided into two groups: those who could write, and those who could barely hold a pencil and string three words together. Then there was Tommen, once again "that kid" who was going to translate his original Welsh stories because he was special. Teacher's pet.

He was still anxious about revealing his stories to the world. While the shrink had said it would be productive, and Tommen was tentatively agreeing, he made the compromise that he would only show off the true fiction stories. Anything that was nonfiction would stay with him. And so the bargain was struck.

The bell rang, signaling the end of the day.

"Only one more week of community service," Will said, meeting up with Tommen at his locker for a brief minute.

"Congrats, dude," Tommen told him. "You going to work for that audiobook, braille guy?"

"Yeah. Already contacted him. I get my community service done, get all the paperwork and shit taken care of with the judge and the courts, he's going to start training me over spring break, have me training full time, you know? Then he's going to work me part-time until the end of the school year. Full-time over the summer, and then go from there, see what college brings."

"Still going to college, then?"

"Guy's already promised me a raise if I do. Fifty cents as long as I'm in college, going for something. Another four dollars when I complete some kind of English degree, or something related, you know?"

Tommen whistled. "That's a pretty hefty incentive."

"Yeah, it is. Listen, man, I'll talk to you later. Sydney, come. To the bus."

They headed out to the buses and Tommen made for his car where Becky was already waiting.

"Can you come in tonight?" she wondered as they neared her house.

"No, I have some catch-up homework I need to get done," he told her. It wasn't exactly a lie.

"So where do you go every Thursday night?"

He pulled up to the curb and parked. "Huh?"

"Every Thursday, I watch you leave your house at quarter to

seven. You don't get back until, like, nine. Where do you go?" Her tone also asked, Can I come with you? Why are you excluding me? Is there something else going on? Someone else?

"I'd...rather not say..." He ground his teeth. He hated the look that crossed her face. Then, "Fine. But you have to promise not to tell anyone."

"Tell anyone what?"

He hesitated. "I go see a shrink."

She blinked. "That's it?"

"What do you mean that's it? That's social suicide in high school."

"Everything that isn't rich and snobby is social suicide in high school. When we first met, you looked ready to commit real suicide, which is much worse. Even now, you're deaf, Will's blind, I'm short, and Eli's annoying. We are the table of social suicide." She sighed. "I still won't tell anyone, but honestly, it's not that bad." She frowned. "Actually, it's kind of a good thing. You're braver than I am."

"Well, my dad forced me to go the first couple of times, but...it helps. I think it really does. So...that's where I go on Thursdays."

She nodded. "Okay. Guess it won't do me any good to ask if I can come with you, but that's all right. Guess I'll see you tomorrow morning."

And she got out, grabbed her things, and went on her way. She hadn't laughed at him, hadn't buried him under a mountain of nosy questions. She'd called him brave. And she'd left him alone.

Tommen breathed a sigh of relief as he pulled away from the curb and headed down the street to his house where his dad was already awake and puttering around for a few minutes before having to leave for work.

"Aiden Cruz is having a party this weekend," Tommen reported, walking in the door.

"Wonderful," his dad sighed. "All right, I'm sure we'll make it out there at some point. We'll just have to bring a couple dozen extra pairs of cuffs." He paused. "How'd you hear about it?"

"Eli said he wants to go. 'Everyone's invited.' "

"Better hope he isn't there when we show up. Or if he is, he better be cleaner than a new penny."

"I didn't say nothin'. Let him learn his own lessons. I'm not his dad or his brother."

"Well, with any luck, Will has enough sense to stay away himself, and maybe to try and talk his brother out of it. But that's on them."

They chitchatted a bit until Walter had to leave for work. Then Tommen retreated to his room to start on his homework before it was time to go see the shrink.

The drive was the same, maybe a little better since the sun had come out for a short time to melt the snow off the roads, but Tommen was filled with dread. It wasn't that he didn't want to talk to his shrink; it was the subject matter that concerned him. Maybe he should save it until the end. No, he couldn't. It was obvious, even to himself, that he was preoccupied. Pretending to brush it off as school or friends or the fortress or the nightmares or any of the other usual stresses wouldn't work; the shrink knew him too well, damn him.

He pulled into the parking lot of the park and got out. It was the same park that had once been his home, where the trails led to Forbes Cave, or what was left of it. This time of year, they sat in the little building that had bathrooms, vending machines, and maps, but the shrink had said that once summer came around, he wanted to take walks around the trails; maybe Tommen could show him around the old homestead. So to speak.

Tommen glanced warily at the shrink's car as he walked, hesitating for only a moment once he got to the building and opened the door.

"Good evening, Tommen," Harold greeted. "It's looking more and more like spring out there, isn't it?"

"Don't fool yourself," he told him. "We're due for another snowstorm in a week or two. Then we can start thinking about spring. Then we might get another storm around the first week of April. After that is when we can really start planning for spring and summer."

"Of course. You know your weather better than me." The shrink looked at the slushy snow stretched out beyond the door. "I just see snow and..." He shuddered.

"Well, you can plan for snow and hunker down nice and warm. Tornadoes, well, those are a different story."

"You're not wrong there."

"Kansas, right?"

"Yup. We do get tornadoes, but as far as I know, no one has ever actually traveled to Oz from Kansas. At least, not where I live."

"But you said you're from Vermont. Don't you get snow there?"

"We don't choose where we're born."

"Not according to my ma," Tommen laughed. "She always prepared to have me in bed, same as all the others. But no. She said I just had to hold out until she went out to the barn."

"So you really were born in a barn."

"Exactly."

The shrink laughed, and even Tommen got a chuckle, but he wasn't in the same mood he normally was as he said, "We don't choose where we're born. We don't choose real life. But we can build pretty creative lies, can't we?"

Now the man calmed down and got serious again. "We can. As Time Agents, we have a rare opportunity to make our lives whatever we want them to be. Rich, poor. City, country. Educated, uneducated."

"Akari-bearers also have unique opportunities to don Disguises."

"You've told me about it, yes. Manipulation of Matter."

"Except common Akari-bearers can't hold their Disguises while they're asleep, and the average skill level of the Disguise, combined with the replication rate of a species' DNA means most last only a few hours."

"I suppose..."

Now it was Tommen's turn to play shrink, and the man across

the table was looking pretty wary.

"It is possible to manipulate some traits absolutely, but few can or will do this on a large scale. It takes too much time and effort. And besides, once you get to that level of skill, you're eligible for even further training. Do you know what that training is?"

"I think you're about to tell me."

"Building. The changes a Builder makes can be effected permanently, making a Disguise not a Disguise, but a whole new face. You can sleep in it, wash it, wear it, because it basically has become your normal face. It also can't be detected by Test, because it is your base DNA that has been altered. You can become anyone you want to be." Tommen paused. "Isn't that right, Nathan?"

The man sighed heavily and removed his glasses, stuffing them in his breast pocket. "How did you figure me out?"

Tommen shrugged. "It was the only logical conclusion, once I learned a little more about you. You're described as being very emotional, very empathetic. After the Missing Zero Hour and the Dispersal, you wanted to help people, help Time Agents cope with everything that was going on. I think you heard about my dad looking for a shrink for me and jumped on the chance for two reasons. First, you want to help. Second, you knew that I was training under Rifun. You knew Rifun had conquered the Akarin. It was only a matter of time before he went after the third journal. You wanted to use me as a judge of how close he was getting, even better when I told you that I was tasked to find it. I think you didn't expect me to make it this far."

"Quite honestly, I expected you to go after Andrew first. His Disguise is the more obvious one. Hidden in plain sight."

"We'll get there, don't worry. But what I'm curious about is—"

"Why, if I can alter myself so completely as to be resistant to Test, did I stick around to monitor his progress and not run yet again?" Nathan cut in. He nodded. "I always knew this day would come, when the Cult would go sneaking around, searching for the journal. I thought it had come with the Zero Hour Revolution, but I knew that if I got captured and taken to the Archives to unlock it, I would just as soon destroy the Wheel and be done with it. It never happened."

"But Rifun Rebuilt the Wheel."

"No. He did a little remodeling, but it was not a true Rebuild. A Build can only be done by a Builder. He had none on him, else he would have found the truth. Same with the Hands. For as much as they profess hatred for the Akari, they are still forced to call upon us Builders when catastrophe strikes and they need a Rebuild."

"So then what's the truth? What does it take to Rebuild or be a Builder or whatever? What would it take to release the journal?"

Tommen didn't like the grin Nathan got as he stood. "If you want the full answer, take me to Andrew. Or where and who you think he is."

That was a little easier to handle. All it took was a short trip to Aleis.

Stepping through, it was like walking into a children's picturebook split between *A Day at the Farm* and *The Old Puritan Village*. They stood on ground so flat it could be used to make levels. To Tommen's left, farms as far as the eye could see. Old Amish, Puritan, the true Old World, where the men went out in groups of twenty to cut down trees and shave them down into enormous beams. Then they'd all gather round and have a barn-raising, swarming like ants over the roof and walls, half-finished by dinner and pounding on the last forge-fired nail right as the women rang the bell for supper. The unmarried men were still clean-shaven, while old veterans of matrimony had beards halfway down their overalls. Birth control was nonexistent, so kids came by the dozen, which was just as well because someone had to help with all the chores: cooking and washing and building and mending and forging and shoeing and training, and somewhere in there might be a little time for play, the folks gathering inside the brand new barn for some good old country fun. Animals went out to graze on hundreds of acres of lush green grass, occasionally one singled out to be brought back to the barn. For what, the other animals didn't know, because no one ever came back to tell.

To Tommen's right was a town. Take a picture and he could have showed it off as an original photograph of Jamestown, minus the wall. The church was the most obvious, spiraled steeple rising a whole floor above all the other roofs. It was impossible to tell which building was which, but there was probably a blacksmith, a doctor, a few market stalls, maybe a trading post for travelers who came through, maybe some version of the Pony Express. He could see the roads were dirt, though a few farms had what looked like stone or gravel around their homes. Not far from the town, the ground sloped sharply toward a beach, half of which had been constructed into a harbor. Small fishing boats bobbed in gentle water.

"I feel impossibly modern and outlandish," Tommen commented. "They're not going to run us out with pitchforks and torches, are they?"

"Unlikely," Nathan answered. He started toward the town. "Come on. This time of day, the council is probably meeting."

It was a nice day, but it was by no means hot. In fact, it barely registered as modestly warm. Looking around at endless fields of wheat, corn, or whatever the Aleisi equivalents were, Tommen guessed it was autumn (there were no trees as far as the eye could see for him to make a better judgment) which meant it was harvesting time. The council was probably gathered together to figure out whose fields were ready to harvest, who needed help, who would go where to help, and so on.

The town wasn't more than a couple miles, but they were spotted almost as soon as they started moving, Tommen was sure. By the time they arrived, most of the denizens had gathered, though there weren't many. As expected, Tommen spotted the forge, a few market stalls being erected for the impending harvest, and some kind of what looked like a stable with a horse rail out front, though no horses were tethered to it. Nathan strode confidently through the town, making a left and heading for a building that looked about like any other, maybe a little bigger, a community center of sorts. A young man no older than Tommen stood at the door.

"The council is in session," he reported, glancing nervously between Nathan and Tommen. "You can speak to them when they are finished."

"The council is going to be in session all day," Nathan told him. He went on before the young lad could say more. "Just do me a favor. Go in. Go to Andrew. Just tell him that Nathan and his boy are here to speak to him. Then come back out. What he does after that is not on you."

For a minute, it looked as though the young man was going to refuse. He bounced on his toes a time or two, then turned and went inside. He was back within sixty seconds. Before he could find his tongue, the door opened again and Andrew—who had been one of the Aleisi ambassadors to Tacaga for months now, whom Tommen had seen on several occasions—stepped out. He looked at Nathan, looked at Tommen, then, without saying a word, motioned for them to follow him.

They walked around the back of the building where a horse and buggy waited. It needed a little assembly, however, and Andrew's horse was not thrilled about being taken away from the watercooler—er, watering trough with the other horses—but he obeyed. Then the three of them climbed in, Andrew clicked the reins, and they were off.

Before they started talking, Tommen knew a brief moment of total glee. He was seriously riding in a literal, hand-crafted Amish buggy. That was just so fucking cool, man!

"Did he figure us both out, or just you and you led him to me?" Andrew asked.

"He says he figured us both out, but he was seeing me first, anyway," Nathan answered.

"So you really are Andrew O'Dell," Tommen stated.

"I am. If you know that, then you know that I was a humble fisherman when I was exposed to Time. I worked as a Merchant before becoming an Akari-bearer. When the Hands came after me, I left Earth and came to Aleis. Farming, fishing, honest work is righteous living, so says the Lord. I've bounced back and forth a couple of times, and

Nathan and I helped the Cherokee migrate to Hlohi. I continued my Akarin studies, eventually becoming a Builder."

"What happened to the journal?"

"During that time, Richard Brown was beginning his heretical movement. I and several others were chosen to infiltrate, to make him believe we had converted. The man was a moron and believed it. He had little choice. He couldn't scrutinize everyone; his ideas were new. There were no standards of judgment yet. Julianna was skeptical, but even she could not deny that. They had to let some people in or else they would have no followers at all. I won them over easily. They came to trust me with information I would take back to the Akarin.

"After Richard died, Julianna planned to escape across the Atlantic. The idea was to make it look as if Cassius pursued her, making her husband a martyr and her desperate. It would win converts, she said. And it did. She left one journal with Isthim to keep the Cult together. The other she gave to me. Then she left for America."

"How did it get into the hands of Abbal Duma Whatshisface? How did the Kolkath get it?"

"Abbal was part of the Akarin then, also, though I don't believe he was ever truly Akarin. If you know his name, you know his reputation as a trickster and a thief besides. I had the journal, and I showed Nathan. Somehow, Abbal got word. Through a series of events and conversations that I still run through my mind to figure out where we went wrong, he got his paws on the journal. We told him, fine, okay. Maybe his reputation would work in our favor. Abbal Duma did not let anything leave his possession that he did not intentionally let go. In a way, it was safe with him. We made arrangements to have him bring it to the Wheel.

"He didn't like that idea. It wasn't enough fun for him. He thought it would be much better to take it to Kath. The Kolkath could keep it safely in their Vault, and if he had them make a copy and send that out, it would throw the hounds off the scent. In all reality, it was a brilliant plan, and we went along with it.

"The problem came some years later. Abbal came to us again. We'd been keeping tabs on the copied journal, knew that Morain leRou Titik, a Psiaco pirate, had taken the journal. What we didn't realize, and what Abbal told us, was that Titik was part of the Cult. Now he knew that Abbal was involved, and it was only a matter of time before he figured out where the journal was hidden. So we told him to go back and retrieve the journal, meet us in the Wheel so we could do what we should have done the first time."

By now, they had well and cleared the town and were moving along at a good trot across open country. On one side, golden wheat waved to them in a gentle hello. Beyond that, visible only because of its height, corn stalks reaching for the heavens. On the other side, open pasture, horses and cows and sheep and goats, heads down, working busily to mow all the grass down before winter. Dotting the landscape were enormous bales of hay, sitting in the middle of neat rows, freshly cut. Then, spiraling tall and almost out of place, a farmhouse, tiny people with even tinier children moving here and there. And still the road stretched long in front of them and behind them, the town growing ever smaller. Tommen felt both giddy and a little homesick. But these were flatlands, not his mountains, and he swallowed his thoughts.

"We waited in the Wheel for him," Andrew continued. "We waited. And waited. We waited a long time. Finally, we returned to the Akarin fortress and asked after him. No one knew what had become of him. All agreed that he had been there and had full intent of meeting us in the Wheel to give us the journal. Then he vanished.

"Thinking it was a trick, we grumbled about it a bit, but there was nothing we could do except wait for him to come back to us with some other game in his head.

"He did not reappear for five years, and he was nothing like the trickster he had been. He'd been beaten, whipped, poisoned, starved, every atrocity that could be done to a living soul had been unleashed upon him. On his way to deliver the journal to us, he'd been captured by Borelians and sold into slavery. He'd been marketed as an entertainer, but his first attempt at pulling one over on them and escaping had landed him in the fields. He did not speak much about his time as a slave."

Tommen glanced at Nathan, then Andrew. "What about the journal?"

"They had taken everything from him, all of his possessions, which included the journal. When he told them what it was, he said they got a good laugh out of it. Most Borelians are atheistic, but some worship Tujor, the god of death. They took the journal to the temple and locked it away in some tomb or vault, a mocking tribute or offering. Then they sent him away to the auction block.

"When he did manage to escape—and he did not say how he did it, only that he did—he risked himself even more by stealing the temple key, or the key to that particular vault. He did not have the time or means to attempt to recover the journal, but the thing about the temple keys, he said, was that they were so old and worn, there was exactly one key to one lock, and one lock to one key. A new key could not be forged for an old lock, and to replace a lock was to replace an entire door, and the Borelians are loathe to just casually replace such a monumental piece of history, if not religion. So it will simply remain locked."

"Wait a minute," Tommen cut in. "So you're saying..."

"The journal is in a Borelian temple, and the key to the tomb it's in is hidden in the Wheel. Even if Rifun had managed to unlock the secrets of Building and gotten into the Core, he would have found only the key. Once, he may have had a chance at getting into the temple because of his alliance with the Borelians. To do so now, however, would be suicide."

Tommen felt the blood drain from his face, but then he came back to himself. Chandler had said only that he would find the journal. As in, discover its whereabouts. He never said anything about actually possessing it. Right? Or had that been part of deciding who to give it to? Fuck...

Keep it, give it to the Shadows or the Shadowmaster. The

Shadows would be indicative of the Order. The Shadowmaster, the Borelians. Had to be. But he knew he couldn't keep it. If he got his hands on it, his only choice would be to give it to Rifun and Julianna. Fucking hell, he really was backed into a corner, wasn't he?

"We need to get that journal," he stated.

"Agreed," Andrew and Nathan said.

"You're agreeing with me? I was expecting more resistance."

"At this time, it is still an element we can control. With the Borelians at war with humanity and the Cult, it is only a matter of time before someone brings up the journal again. If the Borelians make the announcement, Rifun will follow like a mad dog. Without the key, the Cult would be slaughtered. While it would not be bad to see them gone, such a fate should not befall anyone, and it would leave humanity all but defenseless against the Borelians for any future attacks. Sorry to say, but we hold little faith in Kayla and her army. You may tell Rifun that, in the context of this war, Aleis will side with him."

"If you get the key and tell Rifun all that we have told you, humans can go on the offensive," Nathan continued, "before the Borelians can plan an ambush. The Borelians will never expect an attack on their home world. They are too powerful. It may create enough of a gap to get in, get the journal, and get out. Humanity claims a victory, Rifun gets his journal."

"Wouldn't it be a bad thing for him to get the journal?" Tommen ventured. "Why not tell him, so if the Borelians do make an announcement, he doesn't fall for the bait? You know, leave everything as it is."

Both men shook their heads.

"Too many powerful players and too high in the stakes," Andrew said. "Better to have everything where it belongs, out in the open. Show all the cards, as it were."

Tommen hated to admit it, but he had a point. The sooner they were on an honest battlefield, the sooner the war was likely to end. No more of this back and forth, hit and run away, assassinations, undercover operations, and so on. Two armies, one field, one flag, winner takes all. Loser...ends up in slavery. Or dead. War was a terrible thing. There was no sympathy toward the loser.

"So, why did you have to bring us all the way out here to tell me this?" Tommen inquired, looking around.

Andrew gave a click and a flick of the reins, taking the buggy down a trail to the left, off the main road. A short time later, a little white house appeared in the distance.

"I didn't bring you all the way out here to tell you that. It was nice driving conversation, though. No, I brought you all the way out here to help me with a few things. Most of the men are making the harvest rounds, but there is still work to do. Extra hands make light work, and I need help."

Well, they'd walked into that, hadn't they? Still, there was no reason not to help, and Tommen and Nathan spent the better part of a morning helping Andrew repair his horse-drawn hay baler. One of the hitches had broken, both the shaft and the metal attachments, so if he put his drafts in there, they would only be pulling one side. With modern tools, it was a half-hour project. With only Old World tools, it was two hours or better.

Once he was satisfied it was complete, it was time to meet the boys. Four massive Belgians poked their heads out of their stalls as Andrew pushed aside the big barn doors. Tommen was good around horses. Normal horses. Drafts were not normal horses. These horses looked like they could eat regular horses and still be hungry. Nevertheless, he obediently took the reins as he was given them. He got Jack. Nathan took John. Andrew led Bo and Nathan. The horse's name was Nathan, after his best friend, so there was Nathan the man and Nathan the horse.

The horses knew their job, and they waited patiently as Andrew got them all in their harnesses, one by one. Jack lowered his head and sniffed Tommen, smacking his lips as if trying to eat the hood of his jacket.

"He likes you," Andrew said, grinning as he brought Jack's

harness to him. Hell, the horse practically dressed himself, knowing exactly which hoof to lift and when, where to step, exactly what was expected.

"They're very well-behaved," Tommen observed, almost sad to see Jack led over to the baler and locked in place.

The not-quite-an-Amish-man laughed. "You want to know the secret? Don't tell the other men." He paused and lowered his voice even though they were the only three people for probably two miles in every direction. "I don't have children to spoil them and teach them bad habits."

Tommen grinned and stepped back out of the way as Andrew climbed up on his contraption.

"We'll not get your key today," Andrew said. "Tell Rifun what we have told you. Watch his reaction and discover his plans. We will coordinate around that."

With that, he clicked the reins and gave a shout and the four massive drafts began moving, their smooth muscles rippling under short hair, dragging the baler behind them. Tommen watched them go as best he could for the cloud of dust that kicked up behind them. A minute or two later, he could see them more clearly, dragging the cut hay and rolling it up like a snowball. Soon that little matted knot would be a tasty treat on a cold winter night for a big draft horse. Or four.

"Now that's cool," he said.

"The things modern technology deprives us of," Nathan agreed, sighing. "So then, now that you understand the full story, what do you intend to do? I know what he told you, but what are you actually going to do?"

Tommen frowned. "I'm not going to go running to the fortress right this instant, for one. Today is only Thursday. Well—" He check his watch. "—Friday now, technically. I think I'm going to take a day, think it over, try to explain it to myself first, let it sink in. Saturday, I have journal studies. I'll go to those, maybe see if I can't probe some extra information from the instructors and other students, get a feel for the mood of the Order, see how they would react to an attack on Brelix itself. If that all feels good and right, then I'll take it to Rifun."

Nathan nodded slowly. "Okay. Anything else? What about Julianna?"

"No. Not her."

"Why not?"

Because I trust her even less than I trust Rifun? "She's only in charge of the studies and education. She may be seen as 'in charge' by some of the vaovao, but she doesn't have the tactical mind that Rifun does. If there is to be an attack on Brelix, we're going to need true leadership and strategy, not wishful thinking and hopes pinned on untested maneuvers."

"And what of Kayla and her army?"

"Once Rifun makes the call to go ahead and attack Brelix—or, you know, start making the formal plans and stuff—I'll approach her again, or maybe send my dad next time, I don't know. If we just tell her that it's an attack on Brelix and leave out the bit about the temple and the journal, we may win her support. She can lead her own charge, but we'll be fighting for the same cause on the same battlefield instead of fighting each other."

"What if she doesn't agree?"

Tommen shrugged. "Then she doesn't agree. But she's not going to go running off to the Borelians to tell them our plans."

Nathan shifted his stance. "Why not? If she gives the Borelians advance notice, they prepare an ambush, they take out her second greatest enemy—or maybe she sees the Cult as her greatest enemy, I don't know. Then, while their backs are turned, she comes riding up their ass. Two enemies with one stone."

Tommen opened his mouth but could find no words. Kayla wouldn't do that, would she? Well, why not? She'd already donned a Disguise and stabbed Rifun in the chest. What was a little two for one? Set her two more powerful adversaries against each other, wait until they were good and tired, then take them both out with her smaller army. Even if she didn't decimate the battlefield and leave no enemy alive, she could still do some pretty hefty damage. Finally he sighed and said, "I don't know. I wouldn't even know how to ask in such a way as to ascertain her intentions if I did tell her."

"That's okay," Nathan assured him. "I think I might have a way to persuade her, if not to help, then at least to not tattle on us."

"How is that?"

"Don't worry about it. Leave it to me. Just do what you're going to do about waiting, interviewing your peers, then telling Rifun. By that time, I'll have our answer."

Tommen didn't like blindly trusting someone with such a monumental task. He liked it even less considering he'd been confiding his life to this man for the last two and a half, almost three months, and he said as much.

"I understand your frustration," the man said graciously. "I really do. I can respect that you feel a certain amount of trust has been betrayed. But I assure you, as much as I was listening for keywords for myself and my safety, I really was trying to help you. And I told no one anything you told me. After this is all over, with a war on Brelix itself, you will still need help. If you want, I can refer you to another Time Agent psychologist—"

"Oh, hell no," Tommen interrupted. "If I'm getting into this shit neck-deep, or over my head, you're fucking going with me. Then we can go insane together."

Nathan laughed. "I like it. Come on, let's go home. I think we can call the manual labor here and calming atmosphere progress enough for today."

Tommen readily agreed and took them back to the park.

Their departure was hindered slightly by the absence of their vehicles. In the muddy slush that had hardened, Tommen could see the tracks of a tow truck and its operator.

"Shit," he hissed.

One in the morning, a passing cop could have looked at their cars and had them towed. No overnight parking, so saith the sign. Services provided by Bud's Towing.

Problem was, Bud's Towing was known as the biggest asshole group of tow truck drivers in the county. The company was used for all the "Are you serious?!" tows, like towing out of little roadside parks because a vacant car was "suspicious." Respectable needs like flat tires and accidents called reputable tow companies like Kanawha Towing, Countywide, Mike's, Anytime, or AAA. But nope. Had to be Bud's for this one.

Bud's Towing operated twenty-four hours a day. Their yard was only open from ten until two, and it was tucked back in the shadiest part of town imaginable. There was no guarantee, after the first day, that they didn't part out your car to a junkyard, and they would still charge full price to break the remains out of jail.

"I...can't call my dad about this," Tommen said, running a hand through his hair. "And I have to get to school tomorrow, and I can't just leave to go pick up my car..." He let out a breath. "All right. You know what? We're going to steal a couple of cars tonight."

"How do you plan on doing that?" Nathan wondered. "More to the point, isn't your dad a cop? Has he taught you nothing?"

"All I need is a truck. And I know just where to find one."

"Where's that?"

Podunk Town, Minnesota. Central Time meant that it was an hour behind, but midnight was midnight. Tommen knew Laura left her keys in the visor, and she was out on a run with the ambulance anyway. He threw up a Band so no one in the surrounding houses could hear the engine rev. Then, in the weirdest and probably dumbest use of his abilities thus far, he opened a portal, stretching it until the whole vehicle would fit, and drove through, right into the middle of the street in front of his house. He pulled Nathan into the Band and motioned for him to get in.

"Do I even want to know what you're planning?" the shrink wondered.

"Something that would make even Ryan proud, I'm sure," Tommen replied. "Now then, when I tell you to, there's a strap behind the seat here. Take it and hook it to the car—mine, yours, I don't care which you grab first. Jump in the driver's seat. I'm going to pull it back through and I just need you to maybe steer a little. Then I'll reposition, same thing with the second car."

"This is illegal..."

"So are a lot of things."

"What about the boot?"

Tommen gave him a look. "You're a Builder, capable of rearranging the Wheel, the fabric of creation itself. And you're going to worry about a boot?"

The man still looked uncertain, but if he had any more objections, he kept them to himself, instead motioning for Tommen to continue.

It wasn't terribly difficult to open a blind portal into the yard at Bud's Towing. As Nathan jumped out and was busy looking for a good place to hook to a car, Tommen wondered what would happen if this all got caught on camera. Probably the boss would issue a mandatory drug test for everyone, then call up the security company to ask what the hell they were trying to pull with their cameras.

Nathan jumped in the front seat of his car and gave a shaky thumbs up. Tommen put the truck in reverse and slowly walked the car off the towing lot. For a second, he wasn't sure the man would go back to get his car, but then he moved to the side and waited for Tommen to open the portal again.

Once both cars were rescued, Tommen returned Laura's truck, making sure to replace the keys in the visor, then went home where both his car and Nathan's car were in the driveway.

"One more thing I need to do, just to be sure we're in the clear," Tommen said before Nathan could speak.

He opened a regular man-size portal into the towing office and rummaged through the tickets and files. He found the ones for the cars in question and shredded them. Poof! Gone! Like it never even happened. Then he returned home.

"That was highly questionable," the man told him sternly.

"If it was my own damn fault, fine," Tommen said. "That's one thing. But when we're out on universe-saving missions, I don't feel like getting punished for being a little late getting back. I'd send the tickets to Andrew if I thought it would help."

"If we're off on universe-saving missions, you ought to look at a parking ticket and laugh."

"Aren't you the one who likes to point out all the little micro-stressors that build up throughout the day?"

"I feel like the stress of everything you just did to get the cars back would be more than just paying the ticket."

"You don't know Bud, then. Whatever. Don't thank me. Go back to Kansas or wherever it is you're staying."

The man gave him an unreadable look. Then, "Good night, Tommen. I will see you next week, if not before."

Then he ducked in his car, started the engine, backed out of the driveway, and drove away. Tommen watched him go, then headed inside. Two in the morning. Feeling the warm air inside the house made him sleepy, this compounded by all the portals he had just opened, and he was yawning even before he got his shoes off.

He scribbled a note to his dad, saying that if he got home in time, to Band him so he could get a full night's sleep. Whether or not it would be restful was yet to be seen. After the night he'd had and all the information he'd gotten, he wouldn't have been surprised if the Shadows decided to pay him a visit.

Keys, journals, temples, Shadows, Shadowmasters, Borelians, Cult, Akarin, wars, armies...so much information, all of it swirling around in his brain. Tommen could recall the basic, important information, but the details were starting to blur together. How did all of this work? How had this all come to pass? Who had woven all these threads together here and there, crossing, doubling-back, friends, enemies, traitors, spies...it all seemed so surreal.

He went to the bathroom and squeezed some toothpaste onto his toothbrush. He half-expected to look up into the mirror and see some ghost or demon or other phantom staring back at him, but it was only his reflection. Just Tommen Forbes, seventeen years old, almost the spitting image of his father, missing only the thick beard. Wait a day or two and that would grow in. Brown eyes, brown hair, pale as death, high cheekbones, slightly lopsided casual smile that most girls found charming, teeth that had taken many years and many thousands of dollars to finally correct, including his fake ones. Tall, skinny, his stomach as much a black hole as any black hole leading to the Wheel, but starting to get a little muscle on his bones from the construction work.

And he could manipulate the fabric of the universe—not on the scale of the Builders, but getting there, and certainly more than the average person on the street—and he traveled through black holes on a daily basis.

Tommen got in bed, stretching out under the blankets. He lay there for a second before rolling over and reaching for a lighter. He lit the candle on his stand and threw a pinch of Chandler's herbs on the flame. Just in case.

Chapter Twenty-Six
Head Down

Thanks to the candle and the herbs, Tommen did not have explicit nightmares, and yet he seemed to have worse dreams about the Shadows clawing at the edge of his consciousness, trying to break through whatever shield the herbs had created. He could feel them, almost see them, pacing, hissing, gnashing their teeth, and occasionally throwing themselves against the barrier, trying to break in. While frightened at first, Tommen eventually settled into an uneasy fascination.

Why did they hate him? Because he was looking for the third journal? Because he talked to Chandler? Because they knew of his double-crossing the Order, or his plans to? What had led them to him?

They hate you because you are, a small voice told him.

I am what?

You are. That's all. You are one of the Author's characters, and that is enough. They have always stalked you, sitting in the background, whispering in your ear. Now, though, you know of their existence and actively try to resist. That makes them restless. Try to walk away, they go ballistic. Become freed from them, and their only mission is to kill and destroy.

But the herbs provide a protective barrier.

Only for a short time, and that doesn't mean they can't still slip through, the smaller ones.

Tommen flinched and looked around. Nothing attacked him, but it was like spotting a rat in a kitchen. You stared at it. It stared at you with beady little eyes and grimy little paws. The Shadows stopped in their tracks. Some scurried back to the barrier and slipped through invisible holes. When Tommen took a step toward those that remained, they fled as well.

"How do I get rid of them?" he asked aloud. "How are they defeated?"

With Light, the small voice answered. *And even then, they are never truly defeated, only routed, sent back to lick their wounds and wait for another opportunity to strike. You may have the power to drive them back, but only a White can truly defeat a Shadow.*

But I suppose that means that a Shadow can defeat a White.

Yes, but not easily. The Author routinely favors the Whites, for they are hers.

Then who do the Shadows belong to?

There was no answer.

Tommen walked up to the barrier. The smaller Shadows scampered away, but the larger ones, those about the size of a dog or bigger, they stayed to glare and snarl at him. They made up the majority of the force he could readily see, but behind them in the distance, he could see the malignant eyes of the wolf-dog, the cerberus, and a number of other enormous creatures, even a dragon, if he could read the outline correctly. The small Shadows were the scouts, the ones who breached a hole large enough for the medium-sized Shadows to get through, the bulk of the forces. But the cerberus, the wolf-dog, the dragon, those were the generals, the ones who made the plans and called the shots. Were there even more above them, even greater beasts? Tommen wasn't sure he wanted to find out.

But that meant there had to be bigger, stronger, greater White animals as well. He'd seen the small rabbits, the larger wolves and bears. Where was the White cerberus, the White dragon? Even if not those creatures exactly, where were their equivalents? What did it take to rouse them from their slumber? If the Zero Hour Revolution and defeat of the Akarin wasn't enough, what would be? If it was about the journal, why this journal? Why not the museum journal?

Because it wasn't about the journal. It was about the Borelians. The Borelians were the greatest powerhouse of fear and cruelty in the universe, and Tommen bet that if anyone had the backing of the Shadows, it was them. It was an intertwined empire, and the Shadows weren't about to let it go without one hell of a fight. But if that was the case, why did they seem to also operate in the Order? And the Akarin, for that matter?

The Shadows don't choose sides. They are a side. You choose them.

Tommen stopped a mouse-sized Shadow with just a look as it tried to wiggle through the barrier. Not all Shadows were big and fearsome. Some were small enough to whisper softly in someone's ear. Being so small, they seemed weak, and some just let them go freely, thinking them harmless. But then the barrier weakened.

Tujor was the Shadowmaster, or the Borelian iteration of him. The Borelians had not only chosen the Shadows, they embraced them, at one time worshiped them, built an entire kingdom around them. Were there other so-called Shadowmasters out there? Maybe.

There was going to be a battle, and it was going to take place on Brelix, in a temple dedicated to Tujor. If that wasn't an almost literal trip to Hell, Tommen didn't know what was. Given his track record from the last battle, he would probably be told to sit this one out. And how he desperately wanted to. But he also knew that the Order was a pretty good-sized Shadow stronghold as well. He couldn't just give away the temple key and entrust it to someone else to know what to do. The battle wasn't going to go well; he knew that intuitively already. If he wanted to retrieve the journal, he was going to have to do it himself.

A small thought entered his mind. What would happen if he just gave the Borelians back their key? What would happen if they actually got it back during the battle? If he did as he was told and made all the arrangements with Rifun and whatnot—making sure he understood the consequences, possibly an ambush, et cetera—and the Borelians still got the key, what would happen?

Tommen shooed away the tiny Shadow fly, and it darted back toward the barrier. If the Borelians got the key, and they knew why the Order had come, the Borelians would take the third journal themselves. It wouldn't take a lot to open a back-portal to the fortress and steal the other two, thereby destroying the Order and the Akarin or else wresting control of both. And there was no coming back from that.

What about destroying the key? In the throes of battle, while the armies lay siege to the gates of Mordor, take the key up to the fires of Mount Doom and throw it in, melt it. One key to rule them all and such. It would hold everything in a stalemate.

Until the Borelians decided to change their doors, wondering just what it was that was so important that they would be attacked on their own world. Then they had bait. Or if the Borelians didn't do that, no doubt Rifun would only make plans for a secondary attack, focusing on the temple. Again and again until all was lost. And the Borelians still had the upper hand. There was only one shot at this, one battle, one chance at a diversion, and it wasn't going to be a pretty one.

Tommen stepped away from the barrier, moving back and back until the individual creatures melted into one ocean of shadow, dotted with glittering, malicious eyes. Leave the Shadow battle to Chandler and the Whites. They know what they're doing. Right now, focus on the physical battle with the Borelians and what it's going to take to break into the temple and retrieve the journal.

A lifetime of therapy afterwards, that's what, he thought ruefully. And a whole lot of whiskey before.

He turned his back to the barrier, and the creatures began screaming at him. He walked away. As he did, he knew that this wasn't the freeing Chandler had spoken of; he could feel the thin tendrils still connecting him to them. He also knew that when that time came, it was going to be the hardest thing he'd ever done. And then the war would begin.

Still, he walked away. He did not look back. The light began to fade dramatically until it suddenly went dark and he was yanked forward into wakefulness by his alarm. He jumped, momentarily spooked, then rubbed his eyes and blearily looked around for his clock, punching it off and lying there for just a second before sitting up on the edge of his bed.

Damn school, always getting in the way of my philosophical breakthroughs, he thought with a certain sense of dry humor, and yawned hugely. He knew he'd been given a glimpse into an unseen world. He knew that without Chandler, the stark fear of the Shadows would have consumed him, and who knew where or what he would be? Sometimes he tried to tell himself that they were only bad dreams, but his heart, his soul, knew better. And then, just in his peripheral vision, looking at the shadows in the corner, he would swear he could see beady eyes watching him. When he turned to look straight on, they were gone.

The hairs on his neck prickling uneasily, he got up and made for the bathroom, the unease and fear and philosophical points slowly fading until it truly felt like nothing more than a bad dream. He knew what conclusions he'd come to, and he had little trouble bringing the dream to mind, but for now, the waking world ruled.

Once the dream wore off and real life settled in, fatigue began to slog through his mind, slowing his thoughts and his movements. His note was still on the table in the kitchen. Tommen had no sooner thrown it away than his dad pulled in the driveway. Dammit. Oh well, what was he going to do? Go back to bed?

The thought was appealing.

"Good morning, Sunshine," his dad greeted, walking in the door. "Do you need me to Band you for a little while?"

Tommen was ready to say no, then thought better of it and agreed. He needed to be able to think clearly and consider and process his options for how he wanted to pursue this key and journal and war business.

"What was last night's adventure?" Walter wondered when he lifted the Band and Tommen yawned, recovering from another four hours of sleep. He couldn't say he felt better at the moment, but he would be thankful later on in the day when he needed his brain.

Tommen rubbed his face. "I know where the journal is. And I know what it's going to take to get it."

His dad nodded slowly. "Sounds like a productive evening. Mind if I ask where it is?"

"As long as you promise not to tell anyone yet."

"All right."

"It's on Brelix. Locked in a Borelian temple."

Silence.

"You're serious?" his dad questioned. "You know this for a fact?"

"Andrew, the ambassador from Aleis? Real name is Andrew O'Dell. He was a Merchant Time Agent before becoming an Akarin. My shrink? 'Harold'? Nathan Wilde. Former Harvester, also Akarin. And they're not just any Akarin, but Builders. Capable of changing the Wheel and manipulating the fabric of the universe at a God-like level. They infiltrated the Cult when Richard was still alive and preaching. When Julianna left for America, she entrusted one of the journals to Andrew and Nathan. They lost it to a thief who took it to Kath where a copy was made and sent out. They finally got the thief to bring the journal back to them, but on the way, the thief was captured by Borelians. They took the journal and locked it away, but he managed to steal the key to the vault and escape."

"And he has this key now?"

Tommen shook his head. "No. He gave it to Andrew and Nathan for safekeeping because the Borelians were still after him. They caught him and had him executed."

Walter let out a breath and nodded. "Well, it would explain the conflicting information and the dead ends. What are you going to do now?"

"I have to retrieve the journal. Andrew and Nathan are going to get the key, or help me with getting the key—it's locked away somewhere only Builders can access. Then I'm going to tell Rifun about it. And maybe Kayla. I don't have all the details worked out yet exactly."

"Why? Why not let the Borelians have it?"

So Tommen went through the list of objections, explaining each one and cementing it in his own mind that this was the way things had to be.

In the end, his dad seemed resigned to it, but still had one last objection. "Even if you do get the journal, why turn it over? Why not destroy it? You want to break faith, that's one way to do it."

"Solid faith is never broken, and that's the problem."

"Well, I can't say as you're wrong." His dad made a motion. "Come on. Up for school."

Tommen got off his bed and carried on with his routine, slapping some bacon in a pan and punching on the toaster. His dad appeared a minute later in shorts and an undershirt, ready for bed.

"No meetings on Tacaga this morning, I take it?" Tommen wondered, indicating his attire.

"Well if they're going to accuse me of being a Neanderthal, I figure I should at least act the part once before they disown us forever," Walter told him, stealing a couple strips of bacon.

"If Tacaga leaves, where are the meetings being moved to?"

"Dorigis sounds like the popular option."

"Going pirating then."

"Aye, cap'n."

Walter stole another strip of bacon. Tommen gave him a look, but his dad just smiled and headed back toward his bedroom, crunching on the strip and wishing his son a good day at school, telling him to try to not get into any universe-ending trouble. Tommen could only say that he would try.

Problem was, that really was the only thing he could do at this point was try, but trouble always seemed to find him anyway.

He fried up some more bacon to make up for the strips his dad stole, then scarfed down his breakfast, grabbed his backpack and keys, and headed out. Just another Friday. First Spanish test for the semester, first—no, wait, actually this was the second Algebra test, first English test, presentation day in History, and Creative Writing...well, that was just another day. They didn't really have tests. They would take a short quiz on the elements of a story, probably, then start in on the actual creative writing part of the Creative Writing class (some of the more adept writers had begun to wonder).

Becky climbed in the back, shivering.

"I thought it was supposed to be spring soon?" she complained. "Where did this temperature drop come from?"

"Not until next month," Tommen told her. "Come on, you've lived here for over a year now; you should have an idea how this works."

"Sorry, we can't all be mountain-bred, mountain-raised, mountain men."

"I think the word you're looking for is 'perfect.' We can't all be perfect."

"Yeah, sure, whatever you say. Hey, how was your shrink session?"

Intriguing. That's a good word. "Um...good? I think?"

"Sorry, those things are kind of supposed to be private, aren't they? I don't mean to pry. I just want to be supportive and stuff, you know? I hate it when people are down or upset or anything like that."

"Thanks, I think." He cleared his throat. "But if you really wanted to be supportive, it would be nice if you kind of left it alone."

"Oh. Sorry."

"No, it's all right. I mean, I appreciate the thought. Just...let me have my own time and space here, you know?"

Becky agreed, then went into something about all the tests she had for the day. Tommen listened passively as he made his way to the Shaw residence where the brothers and Sydney were waiting, breath puffing in the cold like a trio of smokers.

"Took you long enough, dude," Will complained, climbing in and shutting the door.

"Same time every morning," Tommen told him.

"You are two minutes late," Eli stated, pointing to the clock on the dash.

"We are obviously all going to be so late for school, we might as well turn around now and go back to bed."

"I second that," Will mumbled, breaking into a yawn. "I swear, the only reason I can stay awake for school is because it's such an ingrained routine. But I guess that, like, if that routine breaks down, then my sleep cycle just goes all to shit."

"That's called your Circadian rhythm," Becky said smartly. "It's dependent on light as much as routine."

"Well, I don't get any of the light part of it, so I need the routine, I guess."

"Work for the braille guy, you'll get plenty of routine with a job," Tommen said.

"Yeah, I know, I know. Still, there are some afternoons where I get home from school and I just want to fall into bed and sleep for days. But I know I can't because otherwise I'll be up all night. It sucks because I can't deviate too much on the weekends or else I just fuck myself up. It kind of sucks, you know?"

"No, not really, but I can imagine."

Actually, he kind of could relate. He'd be getting ready for bed, and Rifun would come calling for studies. Or he would have to run off to this world or that world for an adventure where the day was just getting started. It was like the world's worst case of jet lag. The only reason he was saved was if his dad got home in time to Band him for a full night's rest. Otherwise, he was just as exhausted as the rest of them. At least over the summer, he had a better chance of his dad getting home before he had to go to work, so anything he did could be covered up by a full night's sleep in only a few seconds.

Some days, having the ability to manipulate the universe was pretty cool. And useful.

Per the routine, he dropped the brothers off at the front door, then circled to find a parking spot, and he and Becky walked inside together, talking and laughing until they split to go to their respective lockers. Today, Tommen had no sooner tossed his backpack in his locker than Mrs. Wendell poked her head out of her office and called to him, motioning him inside.

"What's up?" he wondered, stepping in her office.

"Good news," she told him. "I got word today that you have been approved and awarded three grants and three scholarships. The grants are based solely on demographics, scholarships being the ones you sent in essays for. You'll probably get an email about it later, but I also got the news and the paperwork. I'm currently working with Mr. Larson, the guidance counselor at WVSU, to get you all set up for your first semester starting next spring. At this point, it looks like the spring semester and most, if not all, of the following fall semester will be covered."

"Sweet! Which ones did I get, do you know?"

She clicked around a bit on her computer. "Looks like you got the Disability grant, the English as a Second Language grant—which only covers English classes—and the First-Generation Immigrant grant. I also tried to get you set up for grants that normally go to low-income families and children in single-parent households, but no go. And there are a number of smaller pell grants that are regularly tossed in just as an incentive for in-area residents, to keep things local. As for scholarships, you got the Appalachian Historical Society scholarship, the Morganson Memorial Police Families Scholarship, and the New World Immigration scholarship. All in all, you're looking at...thirty thousand dollars in free money to go to school."

Tommen leaned back in his seat and ran a hand through his hair. Thirty thousand dollars. And how much had he planned to save over the summer from his job? Five grand, tops? Maybe another thousand if he cashed in some of his turns? This was five times that. He'd spent months, countless hours, scribbling out essays. Out of the dozen or more that he applied for, he expected maybe one to come through, maybe a thousand dollars just to pay for his textbooks. But thirty thousand? Holy shit.

"This is good news," Mrs. Wendell told him, grinning. "You can take it home to your dad tonight. I'm sure his wallet will feel a little lighter."

He laughed. "His wallet? How about mine? No student loans for the first two semesters? Yes, please!"

"Well, there are plenty more scholarship opportunities out there. Last semester of high school, they start opening up to seniors and juniors with dual-enrollment prospects. Look into them; nothing says you have to stop now. See if you can't rack up some more, get as much paid up in advance as possible."

"I just might, at the rate I'm going. Thirty thousand dollars..." He let out a breath. "That's just...unbelievable. Stuff like this doesn't happen to me." Without something going tragically wrong to render it all moot.

"It does when you work hard and have family and friends to support and guide you." She nodded. "Well, I just thought I would give you the good news. There will be some paperwork coming down the pipe for it, but we'll worry about that in the coming weeks. Sound good?"

"Sounds great. Thank you."

In his stunned daydreaming, trying to figure out exactly what thirty thousand dollars would look like in cash, he apparently forgot how to stand and walk because the first thing he did when he tried to stand and leave Mrs. Wendell's office was get his feet tangled in the chair and nearly fall face-first into a solid steel door. He assured her he was fine, and, skin flushing bright red, got out of there as quick as possible.

He returned to his locker and texted his dad the good news, knowing he wouldn't get a reply for a while, maybe not even before he got home later.

"In trouble already?" Becky wondered, approaching from the direction of the bathrooms.

"Nothing of the sort," he replied, and told her what Mrs. Wendell had just told him. Becky's face lit up.

"See?! I told you! A little hard work and a little elbow grease is all it took."

"And a little English major to critique."

She shrugged. "What can I say? It's a gift."

"And now it's my gift."

"Gosh, now I feel like I have to go submit a whole stack of essays myself to generate some more income."

"You're already two years ahead of me."

"No, I am officially one semester ahead of you, financially speaking. If you include a tenuous internship with the research lab, that makes four. I want to maintain my six. At least three. So tonight, once you drop me off, I will be scouring the Internet looking for scholarships to apply for to try and boost my numbers. I'm sick of essays, but I'm sick of sewing more."

"Hey, don't let me stop you. I've got all sorts of crap I need to deal with the next couple of days, and at some point between that and work, I need to eat and sleep."

Becky waved a hand at him. "Please. You're a guy. You'll always find time to eat and sleep."

He bent down and whispered, "And fuck."

"No, not always. Sometimes you do get preoccupied. Eating and sleeping are definitely higher on the list for you guys, whatever you claim."

He straightened and folded his arms. "And what's at the top of the list for women?"

"Eating. Sleeping. Planning world domination. That sort of thing."

"Uh-huh."

"I don't know; that could just be me."

"Well, considering you're not exactly normal to begin with, I think it might just be you."

"Thanks a lot."

"You're welcome."

She opened her mouth to say more, but the bell rang for class. Tommen grabbed his Spanish book and headed down the hall. He hadn't quite decided how he wanted to approach the test. All the normal work he'd done very well, nearly perfect, much to Mrs. Perez's suspicion. Should he go for the full heart attack and ace the test, or give her what she was expecting, which was just enough to not fail the test, but otherwise mostly Welsh and other non-English, non-Spanish answers?

Even as he walked in the room, he could feel her gaze on him. She was studying him, trying to read him, trying to judge what kind of stunt he was going to try and pull. He sat down and gave her a knowing grin. The last semester of Spanish; they were both going to be playing it up, he was sure.

The late bell rang and a couple stragglers slipped in while the teacher's head was down, busy shuffling papers until she got the stack she needed. Tommen could see a sticky note was attached to the bottom one. The answer key, maybe, but if he read it right through the light, it almost looked like it said, "Tommen."

"All right, class, this is your first test of the semester. It only covers the material we've learned this semester so far. Take one, pass it back. Tommen, don't take one, just pass the stack. Make sure your name and the date is on the test. You can start as soon as you have one. When you are finished, bring it to me, and you can move on to Grammar 3.2.1 in your books. Your homework is only to read it over the weekend. Quiet, please."

Confused, Tommen let the stack pass him by. Mrs. Perez approached him and handed him his test personally, taking off the little sticky note.

"I rounded up a few friends online," she said. "I told them what you've been doing since day one of Spanish I, and they crafted this just for you. It's the same test as everyone else, but...different. I think you'll appreciate it."

Raising a brow, he looked over the test, astonished to find that everything that would have been in English had been translated into Welsh. All the instructions, all the vocabulary and verb structures and sentences, all Welsh, though the instructions did say to translate all the Spanish back into English. He looked up at her, but she was already walking away, probably a little self-satisfied. And hell, why not? She'd gotten one up on him this time, beating him to the punch. Well-played, Mrs. Perez. Well played.

And hey, this would be kind of fun. And weird. He read Welsh novels, and he kept his translator set to Welsh in the Wheel to read the tablets and stuff, but to see official schoolwork in his native language, it was both stunning and exhilarating. It was fun; it was awesome. In a way, it was something he hadn't realized he'd been longing for until he got it.

He decided to go the polite route and ace the test, doing everything exactly as it was supposed to be done. He was not the first one done by any stretch of the imagination, but he was probably the only one who had become excited about the test, had taken the time to do a good job, and wasn't worried about the results. Looking around, his classmates had expressions ranging from mediocre disinterest to dreading failure. When he took it up, Mrs. Perez reattached the sticky note with his name on it and set the test on the top of the stack.

Tommen returned to his seat and even went so far as to actually open up his textbook and read the next grammar section instead of burying himself in his fiction notebook. So far, today had been pretty awesome. Part of him dreaded what sort of awful fate awaited him when he got home—assuming the house hadn't burned down—but another part of him said that this was just a really good day and to enjoy it. Don't worry about what might come later. Live in the moment.

But the worry was there, even if it didn't really manifest itself until Algebra. The little Shadow called Worry had wormed its way into his brain and made a nest. Something about the math, the way the numbers all fit together, it made him think about the key that was hidden in the Core of the Wheel. What did the Core look like? What did the center of Creation look like, that by changing one thing it could affect the whole of the universe? Was it like a raw energy field? Was it a holodeck? Was it like a Run program, typing lines of code? Something entirely different?

He wanted to know. He was scared to find out. He had to see. He wanted to just go and look, not start another battle because of it. What if something went wrong? What if Rifun rejected the notion?

What if Julianna found out and became angry? What if, what if, what if? Tommen tried to push it all down and remind himself of Chandler's words. He was going to find the journal, and he was going to have to make a choice on who to give it to. Yes, there were a thousand other things happening, but that should be his focus. He had no business trying to control anything else; focus only on the road and the task set before him.

Sadly, that road led to Brelix, the last place in the universe he wanted to go. Even jumping in a black hole sounded like a viable alternative. And going into a Borelian temple to their god of death? Please, just kill him now and get it over with.

He headed off to English in a rather grim mood, made worse by the fact that he was going to English and it was classroom day. On top of that, it was test day. And this teacher was not so nice as to translate the test into Welsh. That would sort of defeat the purpose of an English class, he supposed, but wouldn't that just make it a little more interesting? Just once? He smiled to himself. He'd changed the master language on his network account to Welsh—which wasn't supposed to be possible without administrator permission, but what the tech guy didn't know wouldn't hurt him. Whenever he submitted his work online, it apparently got sent as a specially-formatted PDF file to the teacher, which included everything, verbatim, as it showed up on his computer screen. Imagine the teacher's surprise when she opened the first file and saw all the questions had been changed to Welsh. That hadn't gone over well. So Tommen had to remember every day to change everything back over to English before submitting his work. Then he'd just change it back afterwards.

Tommen Banded to give himself enough time to finish the test and not be the last one to turn it in just as the bell rang. The teacher made some passive-aggressive comment about him being in a Creative Writing class and you couldn't be a good author without being a good reader. There was some sense to that, Tommen supposed, but why was he expected to write like a bunch of dead guys from over a century ago? Was every horror writer expected to be the next Stephen

King? Was every dystopian author compared to George Orwell? Go into any bookstore and basically every teen novel was a copy off every other within its own genre. The reason King and Orwell stood out was because they were unique in their own craft. But even on that note, what made their works stand out as worth preserving? Who decided this book was a classic that must be taught in English classes and studied in book clubs forever, while this other book was destined for the resale bin? All books ended up in obscurity eventually, didn't they? Just from changing audiences and tastes?

And to that end, what books did the Author read? Or was it different because her books were, like, the Books? It was like asking where God got the inspiration for a platypus. He didn't just pick up a children's book of animals and pick stuff out; He was the inspiration, He made the platypus. He inspired others. In the Author's world, maybe Stephen King didn't even exist. Maybe she invented Stephen King. But if this was multi-verse theory, maybe she was projecting her world into the world of her Books. After all, her author bio said she lived in Michigan. Well, if her Books so far were set everywhere but Michigan—West Virginia, Ireland, Madagascar, Wales, and so on—then either she picked some obscure state in her Books to lie about because Michigan didn't really exist, or Michigan did exist, she lived there, and she was just taking her world and plastering it into her Books, with a few additions.

But if this was universe theory, then that didn't matter. He didn't matter. Because he was just words on a page. If he went to Michigan and managed to find the small town no one had ever heard of, would he find the Author? Maybe the small town didn't exist, not in this universe. But that brought things back to multi-verse theory, didn't it? Was heaven another universe, a dimension, what? In basic religious concepts, did people operate on a universal or multiversal scale when it came to this life and some kind of afterlife?

Tommen rubbed his face. Fucking hell. Maybe he should major in philosophy and comparative religion in college, make sense of this shit.

The bell rang and it was the lunch stampede. He grabbed his lunch and waited around for Will for a few minutes until he remembered that Will was going over to the elementary school to give a presentation. Tommen started toward the cafeteria, meeting up with Becky in the hall and Eli at the table. Eli wouldn't shut up about the awesome party he planned on going to. Tommen politely warned him not to go, but did not give away his dad's plan to swing by at some point with a few dozen extra pairs of cuffs. Not going to a party because you knew there would be cops was not the same as not going to a party because it was a stupid idea. Sorry to say, but Tommen had a notion that Eli needed to figure out for himself that it was a stupid idea to go to the party. Hopefully Will had already learned his lesson and would stay away himself.

Presentation day in 20th Century Pop Culture went as it always did and would until the end of the year. Start with the Food group, then Music, Fashion, Sports, Toys and Games. The TV and Movies category wouldn't start until the 20's.

For his part of the project, Tommen had been tasked with finding brief samples of the different music from the 1910's. At the time, there was still a lot of symphony and orchestra, but there was also a blossoming of jazz, blues, a whole swath of military marches and dirges owing to World War I, and a hell of a lot of brass bands, also called big band, that wouldn't really take off until the Roaring 20's. In a way, Tommen didn't mind the music, even as his classmates got these looks, wondering how in the world people survived without rap, pop, and rock and roll. He'd grown up on mountain music (yes, the kind where people screamed and ran away when they heard the banjos break out), which was a certain style of country, redneck, blues, all mixed with traditional Welsh folk music. So while he did listen to a bunch of more modern stuff, he always kept a stash of old time music, for the days he was feeling either particularly homesick or particularly nostalgic.

Creative Writing was a good class to have at the end of the day. It was a teacher he liked, and the work wasn't bad either, though his anxiety increased as Reisig announced that after a short quiz, they would begin working on the outlines and first drafts of their first real stories. The criteria for this one was a short story, minimum of 2,000 words, maximum of 5,000, adjusting reasonably for Tommen and his translation, but he was the special case.

On paper, Tommen thought that his assignments would be the easiest. All he was doing was translating his stories, right? Wrong. His first problem came when he got about two sentences into the translation and had to stop. After a few minutes, Reisig caught him staring at his paper and moved to intercept.

"You look perplexed," she observed.

"I'm stuck," he said. "I can't translate this. I mean, I know the word. I know its rough translation. But it doesn't feel right. And if I don't get it right, then it throws the whole thing off later."

Reisig pulled up a chair and sat down beside him, looking at his paper. "Do you think a thesaurus would help?"

"I don't know. Honestly, I'm more stunned by the problem, that I even have one. I mean, I speak Welsh and English fluently, so what's the deal? I never have this problem in Spanish."

"That's because Spanish class deals with very direct, very easy translations. You can go back and forth and there is always a right or wrong answer. Welsh is your first language. It's how you think. You're probably using a whole sack full of idioms, nuances, euphemisms, and don't even realize it, and it just doesn't make sense in English. There is no right or wrong here, necessarily, it's a matter of context and flavor, how you want the story to sound and flow. Writing any story isn't just about stringing words together and making sentences, it's about communicating ideas. Colloquial language and literary language can be very different things. Maybe instead of trying to go at this word-for-word, think about what you want to say. What ideas do you want to express and convey to the reader? If nothing else, get a rough translation of the whole thing, then mark up what you don't like about it. Then you can consider the changes in the context of the story, not just the sentence."

Tommen continued staring at his story, his scrawling, slanted handwriting laughing at him. "I think this is going to be harder than I thought."

"I don't doubt that. Give it some thought over the weekend. I'll grab a thesaurus for you to use."

She did so, but he couldn't say as he made much progress in class. He thought he found the word he was stuck on, but it didn't feel quite as...in-depth as the original word. Then he found himself almost offended at the thought of translating his work, as if doing such a thing would cheapen it. He'd done this once before, but that had been quick and messy. This, here, now, was a work of art. Well, like Reisig said, get a rough translation just so he had something down, then go back and shine it up later.

The bell rang and school was out for the weekend. When Tommen arrived home, his dad was just finishing up some small project or another in the garage.

"Well, there's my rich, young, college-bound son," he commented as Tommen pulled in the garage and got out.

"So you did get my text."

"Well, by the time I got it, you were almost out of school. Figured I'd save us both twenty seconds and wait until you got home."

"Yeah, it's great! Mrs. Wendell turned me onto a few more scholarships that are opening up for the spring and summer. I thought I'd at least try for them, if I could."

"No harm in trying. Might get lucky. Got any big plans for this evening or overnight?"

Tommen shook his head as they headed inside. "No plans that I'm aware of. Why?"

"I don't know. Just seems like every time I turn around, you're dashing off on some heroic adventure. And then this morning, after you told me about the journal and its whereabouts, I figured something big was going to come of it."

"Not yet. Not until at least tomorrow night. I decided I wanted to take one day to myself, try to process it all, come up with a plan of action, all of that, you know?"

"Makes sense, I suppose. Just do me a favor and be careful. Don't get enslaved by the Borelians. Very few causes are worth dying for; I don't consider Rifun's cult to be one of them."

"No argument from me, trust me on that. But it is still something I have to pursue."

He could see his dad was less than thrilled at the thought. Nevertheless, options were few when it came to the Borelian war, and fewer still with the Order involved. Kayla's wild card wasn't helping things either.

"Cruz still having his party this weekend?" Walter asked finally.

"Oh yeah," Tommen sighed. "Eli said he's really excited to go, too. I didn't tell him that you guys planned on showing up."

"Sometimes you only learn the hard way. But, like I said, as long as he's cleaner than a new penny when we get there, he won't get in trouble."

"Do what you gotta do."

His dad got ready for work a little early, taking some extra time to fix himself an egg salad sandwich for lunch. Tommen got back at him for the bacon that morning by stealing the leftover egg salad and making himself a sandwich as well.

"All right, wise guy," his dad said, shielding the remaining salad and eating it quickly.

"You stole my bacon this morning."

His dad waved him off, finished his food, and headed to work, as always telling Tommen to be good and stay safe, which Tommen promised he would as much as he could.

Then he was left alone. It was a Friday night, which meant there was plenty of time to ignore his homework. He didn't have to get up any earlier for work than for school, so he didn't have to jump in bed right away. And even so, his dad would be home early enough—barring some incident at the end of his shift—to Band him if he really needed it.

Problem was, Tommen couldn't say as he had any pressing plans. Everything he was going to do to get the Armageddon ball rolling, he was going to do tomorrow. Tonight was his night of breathing room, to do something other than think about the hell he was about to unleash. Except he couldn't think about anything other than what was about to happen. And he didn't even know what was about to happen. The fear of the unknown was almost paralyzing, even as it was almost hilarious to think about. Not because it was funny, but because it was just so unbelievable.

He went to his room and opened up his assigned reading book from English. He hated it, but it might prove useful in distracting him. And it did. By the time he looked up at the clock after finishing his two chapters, almost an hour had passed. He wasn't a fast reader, and these old novels had ungodly long chapters. Seriously, guys, take a breather every once in a while. Stand up, stretch your legs, get some lunch. Hit the pause button.

He thought about continuing reading, maybe just finishing the book so he didn't have to worry about it. Whatever was going to happen tomorrow night, the last thing he wanted to be thinking about was his reading assignment. And in the chaos of battle, that was probably going to be exactly what he would think about, after saving his own skin, of course.

To that end, he finished all of his homework, just to get it off his mind and to-do list, as well as eat up some more time. The more he slowed down and tried to buy time, the more he thought about not thinking about the weekend, the more he ended up thinking about the weekend. Even when he finally got in bed and double-checked his alarm, he still ended up just staring at the ceiling.

Tomorrow is work, he told himself. *Construction work. Remodeling work. Going out to the same damn house we've been working on for the last two months. Nice house, really, just old, needs some serious fixing up. Plus the owners want to put on an addition, a sun room, with yet another addition of a screened-in back porch, plus a fuck ton of landscaping that is thankfully not our job. Our work ends where the planting begins. We just do the heavy labor construction.*

Tommen yawned and rolled over. It was supposed to be a nice day tomorrow, so it wouldn't be too bad for him to run around being the gopher, certainly better than slipping and sliding in ice-cold chills with a circular saw in hand. Although, he thought he might have preferred that to whatever was coming next.

Chapter Twenty-Seven
Greater Wisdom

There were times when Tommen was completely aware that he was sleeping, which sounded quite a bit like an oxymoron. And yet, this was one of those times. It started when the darkness of sleep itself took on a life of its own. Nothing changed, visually, that he could tell, but the whole atmosphere of the darkness changed, mutated. It took on a life that was cold to the point of being almost wet, slimy, like how one might imagine feeling just before being swept away by the kraken or any sea monster from a 60's B-movie.

Tommen shuddered, and that was the first he felt of his body. Gradually, the darkness broke into blobs of distinct color that sharpened into images that were too dark to make out. Despite this, he knew exactly where he was.

He scrambled to his feet, unsure how or why he'd come to be lying in the dark forest in the first place. Who decided when he woke in the forest and when he woke in Chandler's cave? For a long moment, he stood very still, watching, listening, feeling. It was as if the very air could see him and was reporting back to the Shadows.

In this part of the forest, he could not see the path out, though a gut feeling told him that it was closer than he expected, but the gate was heavily guarded. Gingerly, quietly, he reached inside his pockets. He found two candles in each jacket pocket and a lighter in the front pocket of his jeans. So this time, he was prepared. He wanted to be prepared. He wanted to get the hell out. But the Shadows were here, watching him, waiting for him to make the first move.

They wanted to confront him, to stop him, to scare him. They wanted him at their mercy. If he started running now, put the cart before the horse so to speak, they would overpower him. Because he would be afraid. He didn't want to be afraid, and the only way he knew of to not be afraid was to confront them, confront the Shadows.

Immediately, he began having doubts. He could confront them in some epic duel, maybe, but could they kill him? In a dream? In his dreams with Chandler, he woke feeling refreshed and was always full from whatever food he'd eaten. His wounds had been healed, even. Was it possible to go the other way, take injury in this place? He didn't see why not, even if it didn't make sense to his more rational mind.

Focus on your own battles, Chandler had said. You would never survive our wars.

Did that mean he shouldn't fight the Shadows? How then would he be freed? On the other hand, this was the Shadows' home field. They had every advantage here, and he doubted it would be a fair fight.

Even as he thought it, a hair around his ears twitched and bothered him, and he found himself swatting away a Shadow no larger than a mosquito. Whispering in his ear. Whispering Doubt, for that was its name. Looking at it, he knew its name, its specialty. He kept it in sight and blindly dug out the lighter. It was an easy-lite lighter, and as soon as he whipped it open, flame burst forth.

The mosquito gave a scream like a banshee. Startled, Tommen dropped the lighter and covered his ears, putting one foot over the lighter so it didn't mysteriously disappear. The tiny mosquito spiraled to the ground as little more than a tendril of smoke, flopped around on the ground a bit, then hopped and zipped and buzzed away, wounded, but still not dead. Tommen knew from experience that a lighter and spray bottle of alcohol worked wonders on ants, spiders, and mosquitoes; that had clearly not been an ordinary mosquito. But why had he expected it to be?

Tommen let his hands drop to his sides. Just as he bent to pick up the lighter, the ground began to shake. He quickly snatched up the lighter and shoved it in his pocket as he got in a defensive position—more for his own security seeing how it would do little to actually help in a fight—looking around for whatever was about to come barreling out of the underbrush.

He had just enough time to register claws at least six inches long and teeth sharper than any knife before he hit the deck. He could smell greasy, matted, stinking fur as it passed over him, maybe left a trail of used oil in his hair and down his back—he hoped that didn't transfer back to the real world; he would never get that out of his bedding—and landed with a quaking thud behind him.

Staying low, Tommen turned around to see it was a starved, mangy tiger or some other big cat which had almost shredded him to jerky. It prowled around him but did not go again. All around, moving through the forest like smoke, more Shadows appeared. They encircled him and left him nowhere to run. He flicked open the lighter and made as if to grab a candle when the ground began to tremble in regular intervals, as heavy pawsteps got closer.

"Well, well, well," the cerberus said, stepping into view, "look who decided to return."

"The gray boy," one head hissed.

"The half-wit," the third agreed.

In his peripheral vision, Tommen saw the wolf-dog also approach, about forty feet to the left of the cerberus. Both of them looked twice as big as the last time he saw them.

"If I returned," he said, "it's only because I intend to walk away for good this time. And if I have to fight my way out, I'll do it."

Before any could speak, the dark forest suddenly went pitch black, and a gust of wind swept through the small clearing, blowing out the flame on the lighter and nearly knocking Tommen over. He felt his chest tighten and he prepared to be assaulted by every Shadow in the forest. Then the dim light returned and about fifty or sixty feet behind him, a dragon—an honest-to-God, four-legged, winged dragon with...seven, eight, nine...ten horns, and four glowing, ruby-red eyes—landed. It looked like it could use the Kanawha valley for a bathtub. Just the claws on its front feet were bigger than a freighter. It made the cerberus look like Graham Cracker, and the rest of the Shadows even smaller. But the thing that separated the dragon from the rest of the Shadows was that it was an absolute shape. Still made of darkness and shadow and the stuff that comprised a light-sucking black hole, but a solid shape. The rest of the Shadows could melt and merge and move at will, sly and smooth, but the dragon held its form, as if it were a real, tangible beast. Even the cerberus and the wolf-dog were not so solid. Tommen could see the individual scales over the entirety of the dragon's body, the plates that made up sharp spines, the scythe at the end of its tail. But where some scales glimmered like jewels and reflected the light, these were the opposite, sucking in all light and all hope as the beast moved, entrancing even Tommen for a good minute or two. But most of all, every single Shadow in the vicinity, the cerberus and wolf-dog included, yielded to this great beast. They did not dare look away or make any kind of movement without this thing's permission. Silence hung in the air.

Finally, the great dragon moved its head, and it was like the snapping of a rubber band. Time resumed, and the beast lowered its head to look at Tommen, a whale examining krill before snacking upon it. Its breath smelled of acid and smoke, as if looking into a volcano about to spew magma. Did this thing breathe fire? How would that work if Light destroyed these things? Was it some kind of...Shadow-fire? He didn't want to find out.

"I've heard a lot about you," the beast said, its voice rumbling like an earthquake. "You've been causing...trouble." It hissed a little on the s. "Now what is all this about, hm?"

Tommen had fully expected to be blasted with fire. He would have even taken hot rage straight from the fires of Hell. He had not been prepared for the tone of a dad who was wondering why his young son was so upset lately, crying over spilled milk. It caught him off-guard, but he did not lose his resolve.

"I know who and what you are," Tommen said. "And I'm—"

"Oh?" Now the dragon shifted again. Tommen danced backwards as the dragon slowly lay down, front legs out in front, wings folded neatly, filling the entire clearing and then some. "And who and what am I? Are we?"

"You're the Shadows. You give the Borelians their power, helped them build their empire. But that's not all. That's just the largest physical representation of your power and prowess. But you don't like to put all your eggs in one basket. You are evil. You fill all the little gaps in the universe, sowing discord here and there, raising up some leaders, destroying others, an eternal chess game between you and the Whites." Tommen knew he had misspoken even as he said it, and he added, "No. You don't fill the gaps. You create them. You take the mortar out the bricks and watch things fall. That's what your scales do; they suck all the hope and joy and goodness out of people, making you stronger, and I'd be willing to bet that you are the parent of all these Shadows here."

The dragon snorted through huge nostrils, and large puffs of smoke came from them. "You are wrong, dear child. I am not the parent of the Shadows, as how one begets another. But I did create them. Look around."

Tommen did so, and he saw that the ethereal forms of the Shadows were less pronounced, thin slivers of shadow feeding into the endless, hollow scales of the dragon. Then he knew.

"They were Whites once," he stated. "You took their power and energy to feed your own form, your own strength." He went on before he could stop himself. "That was the First Rebuild. Something happened—"

"That was before the First Rebuild," the dragon interrupted, standing now, its voice growing louder, booming like thunder. "I am the reason the black holes exist. I am the reason the Author saw fit to create the Wheel to protect her creation. But I took away even that from her. And I will take away everything else as well." It lowered its voice now. "Anagalisgi has not stopped me yet, and he has greater Faith than you, small man."

Tommen found himself grinning as he reached and felt in his pocket. He looked at the dragon, straight in the eye. "Faith the size of a mustard seed." He flicked open the lighter once more. "And firepower to back it up."

He brought out the stick of dynamite, lit it, threw it under the dragon's massive body, then took off running. He heard the crackling sound for only a brief minute, reaching the edge of the clearing before it blew, throwing him into the air. It wasn't actually the kaboom that made his ears ring and head spin, it was the shrill shriek of the dragon, and he found himself hoping he'd walloped it a good one. Maybe ripped open its belly and spilled its guts all over the forest floor.

Then came the impact. Bone crunched and organs sloshed as Tommen went head over ass for a good twenty yards, barely slowed down by ferns and undergrowth, but definitely stopped by a sudden tree. He was on his right shoulder, arm crumpled under him, left leg straight up the trunk of the tree, right leg splayed out in another direction, left arm thrown up over his head, over his ear. What little he could see was blurry, and his head felt stuffed with cotton. All around, he could hear unearthly noises—shrieks, trills, roars, and other sounds he had no name for. Pain, surprise, fury, vengeance, murder, all these things he was pretty sure the Shadows would be feeling after that. He was also pretty sure that he should probably move before they found him like this.

Images and memories of Halloween assaulted his brain. He managed to get his hands to his face to cover his eyes, and it took a long second for him to realize that the pathetic groaning noise was coming from him. He forced his vocal cords to shut the hell up and some semblance of order returned to him, enough to force his body to move and get in a better, preferably upright, position.

He managed to get his left leg down, and he flopped on the ground. If there was ever any doubt that he could be wounded here in the forest, it was gone now. He was pretty sure he'd broken more than a few ribs, maybe bruised a lung and several other organs, maybe bruised the rest of his skeleton while he was at it, concussed himself pretty good, and a whole host of other things he couldn't quite register because he just didn't feel quite right.

His stomach turned over and he puked just as he got on all

fours. He didn't have much to give, but throw up he did. Once he was done, he stumbled to his feet and looked around. Something ran by him, hardly brushed him, but it still put him back on all fours. His head was pounding something fierce. Even the dim light felt too bright, and the distant, needling sounds may well have been nails on a chalkboard for all he knew. He felt more than he heard, movements of a large body, but not a single body, many bodies. A stampede, that was the word.

It was an absurd thought, and he found himself grinning stupidly. Well, he was upright, anyway, so that was a good start. Around him, life began to resettle itself, images and sounds realigning with what he knew they ought to be, but that still didn't explain the grunts and growls and snarls he heard in the distance. He pressed himself against a tree and tried to look around from what he hoped was a safe vantage point. He could see nothing, or nothing distinct.

Something flew past his face like a bullet, and he jumped, his heart almost leaping out of his body. It ungracefully zipped through the air near the ground, almost drunkenly, Tommen thought, until he saw what might constitute Shadow blood. Why was it going this way, though? Where it was heading was deeper into the forest, where the dynamite had gone off. Wasn't it? Tommen looked around. He couldn't say for sure, since his sense of direction had been literally tossed into the air. He was all sorts of discombobulated, which did not bode well for him if he found himself in a position where he would have to run for his life. If the dragon made a comeback; it would certainly be gunning for him.

The distant sounds were getting closer, and while he still couldn't see anything, Tommen might have said they sounded like animals, fighting, like how his dad once helped bust a dog-fighting ring in uptown Charleston. That had been a trip, he said, but never elaborated on what he actually meant or saw.

The ground began to shake, and Tommen frantically looked for a bush to hide under in the event that the dragon was out for revenge. He didn't get to look for three seconds before the undergrowth exploded and a huge beast burst into view, skidding to a stop ten feet from him. Its shape was something like a huge, mutated, eight-legged Labrador, its slavering jowls opening up unnaturally large, like one might see in a horror movie, revealing a front row of dog teeth, but a second and third row of shark teeth.

It snarled at Tommen and leaped into the air, almost as if it knew it could afford to make the pounce dramatic because its prey was rooted to the ground in fear. But while it was yet in mid-air and Tommen was blindly reaching for the lighter and a candle—hoping it would be another stick of dynamite, or just as effective—there was a deafening roar, a flash of white, and the Shadow beast was knocked out of the air.

In the blackness of the forest, the white was blinding, almost a light unto itself, and it took Tommen a minute to realize that this White animal was, in fact, a bear, just as Chandler had promised. It was on top of the Shadow, wrestling it down, clawing, biting, roaring but not giving an inch as its dark opponent writhed underneath it, almost getting away but not quite.

A second Shadow appeared then, the flying thing which Tommen now saw was like a crow-mutated bat, if that could be an acceptable description. It was no longer bleeding and broken, as it had been when it flew by only a minute earlier, but its movements were still stiff, like taking care not to break a scab and split open a wound just before it's healed. Its attack from behind surprised the bear which reared up on its hind legs, arms clawing for the flying pest but unable to reach. The dog Shadow wiggled free, then turned on the bear, taking it right in the belly.

Tommen opened his mouth, unsure exactly what he intended to say, when the bear fell back, hard. The flying Shadow, having eagerly sunk its claws into the bear's flesh, was unable to retract its claws in time before it was crushed under the grizzly's weight. Then, with it out of its hair, the bear rolled onto its belly. The dog Shadow saw this coming and got out of the way.

The flying Shadow twitched, solid form melting back into

amorphous shadow, just enough that it could put itself together enough to start crawling away. The bear realized this also. It made a charge for the dog Shadow which leapt away, then took the momentum and threw itself back toward the flying Shadow, landing squarely on its body—assuming it had a body, which it looked as thought it did, in the present moment. Tommen did not know how a shadow or smoke could be ripped to shreds like claws through Jurassic Park sequel posters, but somehow, the bear did it. The flying Shadow gave a gurgled scream and then went still. The form dissipated into fog-like smoke and vanished into the brush.

But the fight was far from over. As the dog Shadow and the white grizzly faced off, Tommen could hear the distant animal cries getting even closer. Peering through the dense forest, Tommen could see more flashes of white interspersed with the slick movements of the Shadows.

"Run, Tommen!"

He jumped and whirled to see the bear had the Shadow down on the ground, massive paw on its throat.

"Get past the line of Whites," the bear commanded in a deep, rumbling, almost comforting voice. "They have cleared a path for your escape. Keep running until you clear the forest. Find Anagalisgi!"

Tommen didn't need to be told twice to start running, but he'd hardly taken two steps before he was knocked to the ground. At first he blamed whatever concussion he'd sustained, until he realized that the whole ground was shaking. A great wind whooshed through the trees, followed by a sound he could not place but knew, and he knew it in a bad way. The twisting skin on his left arm reminded him quickly; it was the sound of a very hungry forest fire. But why would there be—?

The dynamite. Of course! Did dynamite cause fires, though? He supposed it could, in the right circumstances. But then, why the sudden wi—oh, shit.

He got to his feet just in time to see a billowing black column of smoke consuming the forest around him, coming straight for him.

Then he realized, that wasn't smoke, not only. That was black fire. The dragon breathed fire.

"Run, stupid human!"

Tommen half-expected to see the rabbit, but instead found himself picked up by the collar of his shirt and jacket, like a kitten picked up by the scruff by its mother. Except he was being bounced along the front of a grizzly bear. His brain sloshed around and he couldn't make out anything more than colors as they blurred by. Mostly blacks and grays and an assortment of fashionable in-between hues, but occasionally there was a burst of white that he couldn't decide if they came from a White animal or maybe stars as he occasionally whapped his head on a tree or the ground.

"Okay, okay!" he shouted, finally finding himself enough to wiggle and struggle and flail around. "Put me down!"

The bear did not appear to have heard him at first, but finally it skidded to a stop.

"When I tell you to run, you run!" the bear growled.

"Great. Fine. But there's a motherfucking dragon back there who breathes fire! Do you hear me?!"

"I know!" The bear's lips drew back in that iconic grizzly roar. "How do you think I didn't know that?!"

Well, that was the question wasn't it? But the bigger question was, "How do you expect to outrun that?"

"Would you rather stand here and wait to be roasted alive?" The bear shook its head. "The rabbit was right. You are stupid."

Tommen rubbed his eyes, but his annoyance was cut short as he felt the rush of wind again, differently this time. He looked up to see the vaguest outline of a dragon, gliding above the trees, black fire raining down perpendicular to their present position, maybe a half mile or so back the way they had come.

"We have to get you out of here," the bear said. "Once we are safely in our lands, the Shadows cannot easily follow, and the dragon's power is greatly diminished."

Tommen took a step back as the bear advanced. "Please, don't carry me in your mouth again. Let me ride on your back."

"Do I look like a horse to you?"

"No, but I think we'd both be better off for it."

The bear was less enthusiastic about it, but agreed.

Tommen had never trapped a bear in all his exploits, nor had he shot one. His closest encounter to a bear had been on a hunting trip with his pa and Teo, but he hadn't been allowed to get close until the thing was dead. He remembered the feel of its fur, musty, dusty, dirty, oily even. It had taken multiple careful washes during tanning to make it feel soft and smooth. The white bear's pelt felt like that, smooth and clean; Tommen's hands didn't feel sticky or grungy at all.

He kept his head low to avoid branches and brush, and he breathed in a scent of birch bark from the bear's fur, mixed with fresh white pine. It helped to calm his nerves as he bounced along, and soon enough, he spotted the treeline. They burst forth into a blinding field of tall grass, the bear not stopping for a good quarter mile. Then they turned and looked back.

Tommen saw only the briefest glimpse of the dragon over the tops of the trees, but it was heading away from them, deeper into the forest, Air Force One looking to land on a country airstrip. His chest seized as the undergrowth rustled, but it was only a small troupe of White animals. Bears, tigers and other big cats, even monkeys of all shapes and sizes. And a horse. It trotted out, looking rather irritated for an equine. It gave the bear a look. The bear snorted in reply. A whole conversation had transpired. Then the horse moved on.

"He was supposed to be my ride out, wasn't he?" Tommen said.

"Yes," the bear confirmed.

By now, the other Whites had caught up to them. The bear had only to move one shoulder and his unwanted passenger slid most ungracefully to the ground on his ass.

"You're safe now," the bear said before Tommen could speak. "You can walk."

So he did, feeling a little embarrassed but not entirely sure why. Were all the Whites grumpy, or just the ones he talked to? He decided it best to just keep his mouth shut.

They made their way through the field, cresting a ridge overlooking the valley where Charleston lay, asleep, unsuspecting. Even though he knew what he would find, Tommen looked back and found only more mountain range, with no evidence of any fields or forests or Shadows or dragons. A million questions looped through his mind, but he couldn't actually pin down any one to ask, and even then, he figured his better bet would be to save them until he talked to Chandler.

Now that they were out of that weird, secondary layer of the in-between dimension, some of the White animals turned off and went to do their own thing. Tommen startled as a cluster of monkeys jumped into the trees, whooping and hollering and screaming like, well, a bunch of monkeys. A couple of the big cats also detached from their group, as well as a few of the bears. All that was left besides Tommen was the bear who had rescued him, the horse, a couple cougars, and an orangutan.

But then they started to gain traveling companions. White birds twittered overhead, calling brief greetings as they landed on branches overhead. Squirrels, chipmunks, woodchucks, and other burrowers popped up here and there, chittering away to each other before disappearing back underground. And then, that one familiar voice.

"I knew it! I absolutely knew it! Didn't I tell you I knew it? I knew he would try something stupid!"

And there was the rabbit, walking toward them on his hind legs, pointing at Tommen.

"Hi, Rabbit," Tommen sighed.

The slow-moving convoy stopped. The battle-weary bears and cats halted for this little, big-mouthed burrower.

"I told him something like this would happen," the rabbit went on. "Faith without guidance is arrogance. And what's more arrogant than lighting a match under a dragon?"

"You?" the bear grumbled.

"I heard that." The rabbit turned his mouth on the bear. "And I'll tell you something else. Whatever was going to happen before, that Anagalisgi has been talking about, it's about to get ten times worse. For us and them." He looked at Tommen. "Brelix is the dragon's largest stronghold in their dimension. They're heading straight for it, Tommen with them. You think the dragon isn't going to send everything he's got to try and destroy him? Tommen has already caused a lot of damage—maybe even more than Anagalisgi in his time—and that's not going to go unpunished."

"Nothing ever goes unpunished with the dragon," Chandler said.

The man was invisible for a long moment, but the rustling in the undergrowth gave way to the long-haired, dark-skinned man soon enough. Two steps behind him was another White, this time, a white griffin. A magnificent creature, it was easily the size of one of Andrew's draft horses, probably bigger.

"And the dragon needs no reason to punish those who oppose him anyway except for the simple fact that they oppose him." Chandler took a seat on a nearby stump. "The fact that he has noticed Tommen at all means we are making progress, and I hold out hope that the impending battle or war on Brelix will go well for us, or as well as can be expected."

"Nobody knows about any of this," Tommen cut in. "The Shadows, the dragon, even I don't know how much I really believe it sometimes because it just sounds ludicrous. But the guys out there—" He gestured wildly off to one side. "—they think it's just any other battle. They think they're fighting only what they can see. All of this here, it's invisible to them. How can they even understand the forces at work here? Are they even at work? Am I going crazy?"

"Sometimes I wish it were that simple," Chandler said. "If everyone were crazy, nothing would matter and rules would hold no meaning. But we aren't crazy, and we live in a world of rules. And with rules come stakes. With stakes comes this."

"Dragons, griffins, and three-headed dogs?" Tommen

wondered, raising a brow.

"The easiest things to dismiss are often the most powerful," the man replied smoothly. "People will dismiss the Devil, but they can't dismiss evil. People will dismiss God, but they can't dismiss good. But in dismissing the things from which they come, people open up themselves to far greater forces. Like being on a boat and wondering why shore isn't bobbing with them." He stood. "But we have more to discuss, and dinner is almost ready. Follow me."

The Whites followed them for a good distance, breaking off gradually until the only White that stood with them at the entrance to Chandler's cave was the griffin.

"Take the birds and the burrowers," Chandler commanded it. "Keep an eye on the border."

The griffin dipped its head, unfurled massive eagle wings, and lifted into the sky. The wash was powerful, but did not topple Tommen to his seat like the dragon's had. Once it was gone from sight, the men entered the cave.

"So is the griffin your White animal?" Tommen wondered.

"No." Chandler shook his head.

"Do you have a White animal?"

"I did, but he is no longer a guide. The Author is my guide now. As for my White, we still see each other and speak fondly, but we are no longer master and student, but both masters."

"Ah. Graduated to the Jedi Council, did you?"

"You might say that."

"So who or what was your White?"

Chandler gave him a look, and for a moment, he thought the man wouldn't tell. Finally, "The woodpecker."

"Woodpecker?"

He nodded. "The pileated woodpecker."

Tommen blinked. "Why? I mean, why that one?"

"Woodpeckers are believed to tap out the heartbeat of the earth. Why not that one?"

Silence ensued while Chandler built up his fire, bringing his stew pot back up to a boil. Tommen, not wanting to be useless, went over to the cabinetry and carefully started looking around for bowls and spoons, neither of which was difficult to find.

"The rabbit was the first to alert us to activity in the forest," Chandler said, filling his bowl. "Said you might be involved. I got a small force mobilized and sent them after you. They were heading that way, nearly there, when they heard the explosion."

"I had candles and a lighter this time," Tommen said, digging out the three remaining candles from his coat pocket and the lighter from his pants. "When I went to grab one of the candles, it turned into a stick of dynamite."

Chandler frowned. "Fascinating. Well, if such is the case, then it was clearly the Author's doing. And she apparently favors you for greater things."

"What do you mean? Wouldn't it have been her doing anyway?"

"Yes, but consider this. You were ready to fight a dragon with a candle. You grabbed a candle at random, am I right?" Tommen nodded. "If you had known beforehand that you had dynamite, you would have acted and reacted differently."

"I suppose so." Tommen moved to fill his bowl.

"He who is faithful with little will be entrusted with much. The Author entrusted you with enough power to wound the dragon, even at risk to yourself, because you were willing to risk yourself when you had only a candle."

"But I had no way of knowing you guys were coming."

"No, but she did. She could have let you have the candles, drawn out the fight until we got there. But you did that on your own, without us—or not right away. Point is, if there was ever any doubt that you were going to walk away from the Shadows, it is gone now. You have been freed on the spiritual level. Now it is time to take care of things on the physical level. And that will be much harder to do."

Tommen nodded but saved himself from having to verbally answer by taking a spoonful of stew and shoving it in his mouth.

Leftovers from the night before. He looked up; the squirrel pelts were gone.

"Don't worry, no brain matter today," Chandler told him, sitting down on his mat.

Skin flushing red, Tommen also took a seat.

"So," Chandler said. "Let's talk."

"All for it. You start."

"You found who and what you were looking for."

"I found a lot more than that, I think. But I don't understand why you couldn't just tell me all this in the first place. If you knew the Wheel of Time was the center point of all black holes, and if you knew where Andrew and Nathan were hiding, why not tell me? Why make me go through all of this?"

"Why do good teachers let their pupils explore and build models and conduct experiments and touch and feel and manipulate?" Chandler countered. "It is because the experience cements the knowledge and there is tremendous intellectual and spiritual growth that occurs when you are able to do things for yourself. Quite frankly, all you did was take a trip to the library and follow the paper trail."

Tommen sighed and stared at his soup for a moment before looking back at the man. "And you knew where the journal was."

"The Author showed it to me eventually, yes."

"But I had to make the connections for myself. The Wheel, my first thoughts on the journal's location, Andrew and Nathan's identities, the real location, what it was going to take to retrieve the journal, and now this battle with the dragon and the Shadows."

"Precisely. Faith discovered, not dictated."

"What was Rifun hoping for, though? That I would find it all out, get an Akarin Builder to help me, and turn the journal back over to him? If all the Builders are Akarin, and the Akarin hate Rifun's guts, and Builders are also the most powerful force in the universe short of the Whites and the Author herself, I mean, a Builder wouldn't just let me walk away with it, knowing I was going to take it straight to their worst enemy. Unless..."

"Unless...?" Chandler coaxed.

"Unless Rifun already knew the journal wasn't in the Wheel. A Builder wouldn't give up the journal, but he would gladly let Rifun have a key to a Borelian temple. Probably hand it over himself and tell Rifun to go fuck himself with it." Tommen shifted position and nearly dropped his stew. "That's what those maps in Rifun's office were. He knew I was getting close to the truth, so he started planning his attack, started spreading the rumor about something big coming down because there is something big coming down. Then, once I made the official announcement and turned over the key, all his pre-planning would be already done. I'd just give them the green light to move out." He ran a hand through his hair. "Holy shit." He shook his head. "It was a set-up all along. Make me feel useful, get me out of the army and started doing pseudo-Scout work. That's the bait. The faith of a skeptic would take me down the road it did, examining everything, looking for everyone, all the clues, proving everything to myself first before taking it to him, confirming what he already knew. Maybe he hoped I would come over more to his side, I don't know. Once I got to the Builders, I would not only get the key to the temple...but I would hand over everyone who was ever involved, confirm the chain of events, the chain of custody." Tommen looked at Chandler, knowing his eyes were probably as big as saucers. "He's going to go after Andrew and Nathan as soon as I tell him. What about Suri and Raba? The Kolkath?" He shook his head. "My team was as much turning over Rifun's enemies as keeping my ass afloat—"

"Tommen."

Chandler's calm demeanor broke the hysteria which was crawling over Tommen. He sucked in a breath, took a bite of stew, and tried to relax.

"Rifun did shoot Titik, it's true, because Titik failed to deliver on funds," Chandler said calmly. "But he won't be the one to go after the Kolkath or the Builders."

"Then who...?" Tommen knew even before he asked the question. "Julianna. She gave me the list of those who were rumored to have the journal. She just needed confirmation on which ones. She's the one poisoning Rifun. I'd bet my next paycheck that she's responsible for some of the rumors floating around the fortress. And I'd bet every paycheck for the rest of the year that if she has any say in the plans to attack Brelix, she's arranging things just so in order to eliminate her greatest opponents, starting with Rifun, who's too drugged up to care much."

Chandler repositioned himself, straightening one leg. He took a bite of stew. "All right. Let's say everything you've said turns out to be one hundred percent correct—"

"Isn't it? I mean, I like conspiracy theories as much as the next guy, but is it true?"

"I don't know, but I think we're about to find out here pretty soon. Pretending that it is true, however, what are you going to do about it?"

"Well, I tossed a little dynamite under the dragon, gave it a pretty good thump. I don't think she'd come back so easily from it."

"Then you would most assuredly have the Order after you. Once they stripped you to bones like piranhas, there would be a huge political fallout there. I don't expect the Akarin would save you. And there is the matter of the Borelian war."

"I only need to kill Julianna. Rifun can still lead an army. Besides, if she's gone, the poisoning will right itself, right? The Order hates me, the Akarin hate me. I'm home free. Walking away, like you said."

Chandler frowned. "Do you ever watch world news, the kind where they show little kids being rescued from flood waters or caves, pregnant women saved from mud slides, things like that?"

"Sometimes, I guess, if my dad turns it on."

"There is a difference between your personal ending, and the ending overall. For the children saved from rising waters, they have a happy ending, even as their whole village gets washed away. In this instance...the only one getting a happy ending is you. You will be freed from the Shadows. And maybe that's enough. But there is no overall happy ending. Not this time around. Killing Julianna will only make things worse, as much as it pains me to say so. The road that you are following now, this is the road you must follow to the end. Remember what I said about one-way doors?"

"Incidental things can be back-tracked, but you can't accidentally walk through a one-way door?"

"Exactly. Some one-way doors I think need to be welded shut, dead bolted, barricaded, then have armed guards at all times. That is one such decision. Most all the decisions you make from here until the end—wherever the Author sees fit to end this particular epic, which I suspect will be the battle—are going to be one-way doors. Choose your path wisely."

"But if they're all unhappy endings, why does it matter?"

"Because it's not about the happy ending, but effecting the ending that is the least bad." He continued before Tommen could speak. "We all want happy endings. Sometimes, there aren't any, and we have to take what we can get and trust the Author to do the rest. I'm sorry, but it's the best I can give you."

"Pretty poor best," Tommen grumbled, scraping his bowl. "Why can't the Author just write world peace already? Or, you know, Whites triumph over Shadows. Order defeats Borelians, puts aside murderous past, reconciles with Akarin, defeats the greed in the Wheel, happy ending and universal peace for everyone! Hooray. Fine, so if there has to be an epic final battle, then I guess I won't deny the audience that sort of awesome fulfillment; I enjoyed Star Wars, too. But come on...when does it end?"

"It ends when everything the Author has set out to be accomplished has been accomplished," Chandler stated simply, his tone suggesting he was growing weary of his guest's complaining.

Tommen rubbed his eyes. "Do you know anything about what happens after this fabled battle on Brelix? I know you said no one dies and I get a happy ending, but what about after?"

"Merely the calm before another brewing storm, I suppose," Chandler answered. "Such is the way of life."

"So you don't know."

"The Author has not seen fit to show me anything, no. Today has enough worry of its own; we don't need to take on the troubles of tomorrow as well. Focus on the present, the upcoming battle, the road that must be taken now."

Tommen nodded. "Okay." He let out a breath. "So, tomorrow, I need to focus on work while I'm at work—"

"A good idea in any workplace, but especially at a construction site."

"—and then after I go to journal studies, I need to talk to Rifun and tell him...what? Just that the journal is in a Borelian temple, or should I confront him about this whole thing? I know you said to let the poison right itself, but what about Julianna? If she's got some underhanded schemes going on, and if she has any part in the planning to attack the temple, a lot of innocent people could die. Yeah, sure, their theology is a little off, but they shouldn't be sent out into a minefield just because they don't know the difference between her and Rifun. I get it, people die in war, and not everyone gets a happy ending. But I'm trying to make it as least bad as possible."

Chandler dipped his head. "I understand. I appreciate that you are trying to follow my advice. Now have a little more. Do only your part. Do what you are supposed and expected to do. Nothing more, nothing less. Let the Author dispense justice where and how she will; let her show mercy where and how she will. Julianna can make no plan that the Author cannot counteract. But the more you try to control, the less control you have. Does that make sense?"

Reluctantly, Tommen said it did. "Be a dog, get thrown a bone, and be forgotten. Let everything else do what it will."

"That would be one way to say it, I suppose. But at least have a little higher opinion of yourself than just a dog."

"Oh, I do. Sometimes people tell me I have too high an opinion of myself." Tommen waved a hand. "You don't have to agree; I know I can be a little self-centered sometimes."

Chandler raised a brow but did not say anything more, instead helping himself to a little more stew, which he ate in slow, methodical bites.

"Did you ever have a girl?" Tommen asked. "You're a young man. Well, younger man, not quite middle-aged, I think. You ever have a wife and kids?"

Chandler wiped his mouth and set his empty bowl aside. "From a young age, I knew my path was different from anyone else's. As a young man, just starting to really look at girls, I sometimes entertained the notion of having a family. When I was about your age, I even initiated the courting ritual once for a young woman, but the priests proclaimed it unsound and that was that. After that, we had troubles—more troubles, I should say—with the white men and Time and everything else. And I knew in my heart, my inner being, that such a life was not for me. My coming here to the in-between dimension sealed my fate. And before you ask, I have no regrets. Each is called to his own path. Sometimes I would like to have known what my life would have been like, had I not been so different and had I made the Migration with my people, but I am content here."

"Maybe someday the Author will release you from this dimension so you can. Just once."

"I don't know about that." Chandler took his bowl and Tommen's bowl and made for the wash basin. "I am content either way."

Tommen waited patiently for him to wash the dishes and return.

"What's on your mind, Tommen Forbes?" Chandler asked upon returning, sitting on his mat.

Running a hand through his hair, Tommen answered, "I don't know if I can do this. Not again. I'm not a soldier. I failed vaovao bootcamp. I can't do war and battle, not again. Certainly not so soon. Indiana Jones or not, I don't know that I can really make it. And it doesn't help that my shrink is in on it this time, too. I mean, what if he needs therapy afterwards? I'm screwed."

Chandler laughed briefly, then grew serious. "War is a terrible and tragic thing, and its effects can be felt long after the fighting is over."

Tommen studied him. "What memories do you have? I think you once told me you were responsible for leading the war parties to distract the white men while your people got away."

"Well, I did not lead them; that was my brother. But I do have memories of riding into battle on horseback, of gunfire and arrows, shouts of men all around. White men, riddled with arrows, trampled under horses. My own friends and family, killed, if not in battle, then in agony as lead bullets seeped poison into their blood. I have memories of being captured and imprisoned, and sometimes I do wake up, cold and sweating, swearing that the rope is again around my neck. And let me tell you, those battles happened long ago. My nightmares are few and far between anymore, but when they come around, it is as if it all happened only yesterday."

"And the Whites and Shadows? Have you been in any fights there?"

"I have never been in the middle of such a battle, but there is one who has."

"Who's that?"

"You met him once. My nephew, Sabelu."

Tommen blinked. "Saul fought the Shadows?"

Chandler shook his head. "No. The Whites fought the Shadows, buying him time to complete his mission. You can read about it one day when this is over."

"Wow." Tommen shifted position. "But I thought you were the commander or something? Making the plans, leading the charge and all that."

Chandler again shook his head. "The Whites do not answer to me. I have developed enough of an understanding to give small orders, basic directions, but they look to the Author for action. I am here as more of a...wise man, a counselor. My duties lie more in the realm of helping humans navigate the complexities of how the Whites and Shadows overlay goings-on in the real world, as I did with Sabelu."

"Like how Brelix is the Shadow stronghold, the Borelians their...puppets, their physical manifestations."

"Exactly."

"There's no way we can win. If Brelix is Shadow-controlled, and the Order is Shadow-controlled, the Shadows aren't going to turn on each other. They're just going to sit back and watch the bloodshed, then sweep up the pieces. Everything goes back to normal for them."

"Once again, what can you control?"

Tommen let out a breath. "Only my actions and reactions. Do what I'm supposed to do, let the Author work out the rest."

"Precisely."

"Do the Whites control anything? Do they have any strongholds we can call on?"

"Rarely do the Whites ever 'control' anything. Wherever there are Whites, there are Shadows trying to depose them."

"Why isn't it the other way around? Where there are Shadows, there are Whites trying to depose them?"

"Why indeed?"

Tommen frowned and sighed. "I know you're going to chastise me for saying so, but I have to. I don't want to do this."

Chandler nodded. "I know." He made a motion. "Get some sleep. Go to work and focus on work. Be safe on the job. Always. Then focus on the studies. And then focus on your task. One thing at a time."

"One thing at a time," Tommen echoed, moving and repositioning his body until he lay stretched out on the mat.

"And just think, the sooner you get this done and over with, the sooner you'll be going on spring break with Becky."

"Yeah, there is that, I guess. I'll need a vacation after this."

"Good night, Tommen. Sleep well."

He always did after a trip to Chandler's cave, though there was a lingering fear in the back of his mind that once he left the safety of the cave and the protection of the Whites, that the dragon would be waiting for him. He'd delivered a doozy of an injury, or at least a surprise, and gotten away, riding on the back of a motherfucking grizzly. That dragon was not going to be too happy about that. Tommen remembered thinking that he was going to have to use those herbs every night until the battle was over in order to stave it off. But what if that didn't work? He didn't understand how it worked in the first place. Was it just based on sheer belief? If that that was the case, he was screwed.

And while the dragon did not appear to him in the time between him leaving Chandler's cave and his alarm going off, Tommen still woke up that morning with a certain sense of uneasiness, maybe even dread.

Chapter Twenty-Eight
Higher Education

The nice thing about a manual labor job was that it left little time for worrying about other problems, no matter how large they might be. Dragons and Shadows and impending war? Small potatoes compared to the remodel job they were on. It wasn't that the homeowners were high and mighty snobs who wouldn't take no for an answer—according to Chris and a few of the guys, they were comparatively reasonable—but they were pretty darn clueless when it came to actual construction. When they first proposed the idea for a remodel, Chris had explained that one wall they wanted taken out was a primary load-bearing wall and it couldn't be done the way they wanted. Okay, fine. Homeowners go back, talk it over a little, adjust their plans, want to talk again. Their news plans still involved taking out the wall, and the little columns and half-walls they proposed just wouldn't cut it, not how they wanted it. Okay, fine, back to the drawing board.

It took six tries before Chris finally talked them into hiring a real architect who could sit down with them, talk about what they wanted, and come up with a feasible plan of action. So while the wall stayed in place—thus interrupting the otherwise uninterrupted utopia the homeowners had envisioned—now there were two huge rooms that had to be remodeled just so, instead of one. And they were completely different in their styles. It wasn't difficult to do, just time-consuming. The good news was that the crew figured they would be packing up during or just after spring break, just in time to surprise the homeowners when they returned from their vacation in Tahiti.

Tommen enjoyed the work, anyway. He didn't deal with the

homeowners, be they ignorant, snobby, know-it-all, or retired and desperate for someone to talk to; he just got the tools, ran them around, and did some minor work. He liked most of his coworkers, got to know some of the subcontractors, and figured he was liked well enough in return. At the very least, he made a small name for himself as one who was unusually strong for his age and size with lightning-fast reflexes. He tried not to freak anyone out, but he wouldn't say he didn't use Gravity to make things lighter for himself, or Time to give himself a chance to react to falling objects. Hell, on heavy work days when he wasn't allowed to do a whole lot, he'd found himself dabbling in Light and Magnetism: Light, trying to intensify it so as to light up the room better on cloudy days and bend it into small areas, especially for the electricians so they could work safely in tight spaces; Magnetism, so small metal pieces that weren't normally magnetized would get swept up by the magnet at the end of the day. Once, he'd used Magnetism when he saw a hammer fall from a ladder. It was heading straight for another guy who was busy doing something else. Even with a hard hat, a hammer could still daze a guy, or injure another part of the body, like the poor guy's back. Tommen had manipulated the Magnetism of the guy's enormous belt buckle as well as his suspender slides, changing the polarity so that the hammer was thrown away from the guy by a solid five feet. No one had really seen it, and no one could figure out quite what had happened.

So whenever things got a little slow for him around the jobsite and he got put on broom duty, Tommen considered what other properties he could manipulate. Viscosity, paint, for instance. He puttered around a bit, learned how to take the water out of the paint so it dried, but couldn't quite figure out the opposite. Didn't matter, he supposed. The only time paint needed to be wet on the job was when it was still being used. Sound was a big one, too, though he couldn't decide if his trouble with ti came from his own deficiency. He knew how to Imprint it, package it up and set it off later, but he couldn't figure out how to turn down the volume in real time.

There was a lot that went into manipulating the physical

properties of the universe, and it worked up a ferocious appetite, much to his dad's dismay. Tommen could easily scarf down a lunch two or three times the size of the other guys. They ribbed him for it, naturally, lamented how they used to be able to chow down like that and not gain weight, and it was all in good fun. Generally speaking, Tommen liked his job, and he was even kind of looking forward to working over the summer, even if that meant his hours were going to quadruple overnight.

"So, I hear next year you're going to be a senior and then it's off to college," Matt, one of the usual guys on the construction crew, commented that afternoon, flipping open his lunch box and sitting beside Tommen.

Tommen's mouth was presently full of food, so he could only nod.

"Good for you. What's your flavor? Trades? Business?"

"Physics," Tommen answered, his mouth dry. He took a drink of water and continued mauling his sandwich, the first of three.

"Physics? Like...Sheldon Cooper, Big Bang Theory kind of physics?"

Another nod.

Matt gave him a funny look. "What are you going to do with yourself puttering around in a lab all day? Don't get me wrong, science is important and contributes a lot to modern society and invention, but you do good work here. Construction is a growing field, lot of useful skills. For one, I don't have to pay anyone to come fix my house or put on an addition—which I've done twice at my wife's behest." He rolled his eyes.

"I don't know," Tommen answered honestly. "I mean, I like this work, I really do. I applied because I wanted more physical labor, you know? But I like science, too. I just...I used to be so sure."

Matt laughed uproariously. "You're not even eighteen. You're not sure about anything, I don't think. Not really. You'll change your mind a thousand times between now and when you turn thirty, and a million times more between between thirty and your deathbed. I change my mind a lot, and I'm thirty-eight. Don't assume that your first love is your last love. Keep at it, do good work, construction is probably going to pay your way through college. And you never know, it may even grow on you and you might return."

"And be the only construction worker ever with a PhD in Theoretical Astrophysics." Tommen grinned.

Matt pointed to several of the guys still working. "Joe there has a Master's in Business. Owned his own business, shut down because he got tired of dealing with all the bullshit between the government and your average public. Jake, Bachelor's in Theology, of all things. You probably noticed we call him the Chaplain, well it ain't for nothing; talk to him if you got a problem. Pete over there is working on his Bachelor's in Fire Science; he's also on the city fire department, pulls overnight shifts three days a week. Shawn is going into Nursing this fall, probably leave us after the first semester or two, as fast as the hospital snaps up the students. Marie, one of the masonry crew? She's got herself a full-fledged Apprenticeship, working toward her Journeyman even while she's going to school for the same damn thing. I think it's redundant, but it's helping her advance faster, I guess. Going to get her Associate's here this spring."

"So what is your degree in?" Tommen wondered.

"Ha! I don't have a degree. Honestly, I don't even have my high school diploma. Yeah, that's right. I dropped out when I was sixteen to work for Roger, who owned this company before Chris took over. Course, I got real lucky that Roger took a chance on me and I had a good enough work ethic that he didn't care that I was a dropout. But you look like a smart kid, smart enough for astrophysics and smart enough to survive in the real world." Matt chuckled. "Look at me, preaching more than the preacher. Hey, Jake! Maybe I ought to take your job!"

Jake was at the top of a twelve foot ladder. He looked around at his name, saw Matt waving his arm, but did not apparently hear what was said. When it appeared that he wasn't actually needed, he gave an unsure smile, then went back to his lunch with a view.

Tommen and Matt finished their respective lunches and returned to work. Tommen looked around at all the guys, wondering what they were doing here if they had degrees. Those things weren't cheap, and not easy to come by. Tommen paused and considered just how much he wanted to go to school for physics, considering—he threw up a Fast Band and looked around, the world still—he was pretty much already past whatever they had to teach.

And there was no mention of dragons or war or anything of the sort.

It wasn't until he pulled in the garage that evening and tossed his keys on the counter that he actually remembered what he was going to be doing later that night. A rock formed in his stomach like a peach pit, and he headed to the couch and flipped on the TV. Focus on one thing at a time. He didn't have to go to the fortress just yet, and homework was the last thing he felt like doing, whether for his normal government-run daycare or the Order's forced propaganda.

He watched a few episodes of the show he was following, then turned off the TV, mentally preparing himself for whatever may come. On the one hand, the night could end in chaos and pandemonium. On the other hand, nothing of real interest might happen, either. Only in the movies was such information given and a winning plan of attack formulated right then. Real wars demanded some measure of time and strategy. Yes, surprises had to be accounted for, but time was a commodity when it came to war, and if one had the time, use it wisely and plan. As for Tommen, he would simply do his expected task. Report the information and wait.

But first, he had to focus on the task that came before that, which was passing the final exam for stage one and getting cleared to go to stage two in journal studies. Honestly, he could do everything the instructor asked in his sleep. He could be the one teaching the class. He really wasn't worried. And because everything was one-on-one audio-oral, as soon as he finished, he would be dismissed, no waiting for everyone else to turn in their papers, sitting quietly and pretending to care about the next unit. One and done, thank you, have a nice day, congratulations on acing the exam.

The fortress was unusually busy when he arrived. At first, it looked like the average day at the construction site. Chaos, working, stuff going here and there, people going here and there with stuff. Looking more closely, he saw that it was actually closer to opening day on the site, when all the furniture had to get moved, sometimes into other rooms, sometimes into a shed out back, sometimes in a truck so it could taken to an off-site storage unit.

"What's going on?" he asked of no one in particular.

After a bit of probing, he was informed that the upper levels which had been crushed had finally been restored and were ready to move into. The first floor had been designated for non-essential functions: cafeteria, recreation, public meeting areas, social things like that. With the portal room nearby, it was meant to foster a sense of community. The second floor was reserved for the lower soldiers, vaovao and afovoany, who made up the bulk of the forces, ready to protect the first floor if it came under attack, or make for the portal room so they could go and fight wherever it was they were supposed to go and fight.

The third floor was going to the lower ranks of Artists, those who followed the Book of Commands (once it was found) and were responsible for the culture of the First Order, the main face of the group, the average joe on the street. Tommen was one of those, he knew. Something about an Archeology division and an Interculture set. He wasn't entirely sure. Maybe it would be explained later.

The higher ranking soldiers and middle-management officers claimed the fourth floor, as much to offer quick reinforcements to the grunts on the second floor as protect everything on the floors above them, which included the fifth floor, dedicated entirely to the Philosophers, their overseeing Book of Philosophy, and the newly-renovated Archives, as well as the higher-ranking Artists. Apparently, once one advanced high enough in the Artists, the line between Artist and Philosopher started to blur.

The highest ranking soldiers occupied the sixth floor, and

included Rifun's advisors, primarily military, but also other social, political, religious, and linguistic disciplines. Rorion was slated to be one of those advisors, Tommen knew, from conversations they'd had while out and about on their adventures. In a way, he was a little jealous, because of the prestige the title carried. In another way, he was a little intimidated that such a high-ranking official had been tapped as part of his team, and she hadn't tried to take over. But on the other hand, he did not envy her having to climb so many fucking flights of stairs, something like twenty-eight flights of stairs back home. Well, she'd be physically fit, as would the other officers. Physically fit soldiers were important.

In the past, the Akarin had kept their food and weapon stores on the seventh floor. Tactful, yet impractical. Had the Akarin not been kept prisoner in the sub-levels, most of the supplies would probably have been moved there. However, it was a decidedly bad idea to keep one's food and weapon stores in the hands of the enemy. That said, all weapons were kept on the seventh floor, as well as a bulk of the food supplies, most of them with a very long shelf life. But some food stores, especially the perishable ones, were kept in the sub-levels for convenience. Even if the Akarin revolted and took control, the food wouldn't last them very long.

Finally, Rifun's quarters remained at the very top on the eighth floor; that much hadn't changed at least. But would it really have killed him to take an office on the first floor? Even the fifth floor with the Philosopher's would be better. Hell, the seventh floor would cut out four flights of stairs. But no. Had to be at the very top.

Tommen dreaded that climb, but he told himself not to worry about it. First he had to find his class and complete his exam. Just one thing at a time.

With all the floors fully operational now, did that mean he would be studying on the third floor with the other lower Artists from now on?

So many flights of stairs.

Fucking hell.

He found his class assembling in one of the recreational halls, like normal. What wasn't normal was that there were fewer classes on the whole, and a lot of the screens had been taken down. It was like watching the student council take down all the decorations for the dances and stuff, stripping the room bare so it looked ten times bigger than it used to.

All the excitement generated plenty of rumors, and Tommen did his best to listen without listening. Most of the chatter was general excitement over the construction being finished and finally moving into the new accommodations. There were several mentions of Rifun, all in a positive light, from what Tommen could discern. Some were talking about how his vision was finally being realized after perceived stagnation. Others were talking about the fabled "big plans" set to come down the line just as soon as everyone was settled comfortably in their new digs.

But there was some new talk, too, this time mentioning Julianna and how she was going to take over the Philosophers and the Artists, how she could, with the construction finally over, realize her husband's dream of a powerful, unified, culturally relevant First Order. Everything was falling into place just perfectly. All they needed was the third journal, the Book of Commands. Which Rifun was slow to produce, but he had big plans, and after how many decades, what was a little while longer, so long as he didn't lose the momentum of the finished construction excitement. Morale was high right now, best to use it wisely.

The overall mood was positive, but the undercurrent of uncertainty and even threats made Tommen's skin crawl. Julianna was up to something, and while he wasn't in the direct line of fire this time around, that didn't mean he wasn't on the menu for later.

One thing at a time. Focus on your task. Do only what you are expected to do. Don't force yourself into situations you can't control.

He found his class, one of only four still in the recreational hall. It was like walking into a room full of junior high girls, as hyped up as everyone seemed to be. It seemed to be a pretty even split, between excitement over the moving, and terror over the exam. Those who were confident in the exam weren't talking about it, and those who weren't confident were envisioning terrible things befalling them if they didn't pass. Most were quizzing each other.

Tommen had become as popular as the instructor as far as being a well of information. It wasn't that he knew everything in the book they were studying; he had pretty much just memorized everything they were presently learning. And God Almighty, it was boring. After what was basically a full semester of learning the same names and the same one- or two-sentence descriptions of the same people, learning the same two glorious words, he was ready to tear his eyes out.

The instructor walked in an immediately began speaking.

"Welcome, students. No doubt you have noticed some of the excitement going on. I realize it may be a little distracting, but we will work through it. Today is exam day. Same as the tests, but I will be giving you no starters or suggestions if you falter. You may skip any question and so forfeit it.

"When you are done with your exam, you will be dismissed with specific instructions, relating to the move. I will save you some time, you are going to the third floor. Go there for your next assignment. Once that it complete, if possible, it would be appreciated if you could help in some of the moving activity; however, if you have things to do at home, you are free to leave."

Tommen fully expected to be called first; he always was. The instructor knew he was the best and tried to get him out the door as quickly as possible so he could do other things, usually adventuring things, as requested by the Faharoa.

Today, he was not called first. Nor was he called second. Or third. Or anywhere in the top ten. Confusion, then fear, wormed their way into his brain. Why was this happening? Had he done something wrong? He hoped to God or the Author or whomever that he wasn't being held back. He couldn't think why he would be, seeing how he knew everything they'd been taught. Or maybe that was just it. The instructor was punishing him for showing him up. After his exam was done, the instructor was going to make some weird threat or at least have a hard lecture about being better than one's teachers. Could he really help himself? He was past this baby crap.

The instructor returned and called the next student. Still not Tommen. Didn't even look at him.

Or, maybe, God help him, the instructor was going to ask if he wanted to teach the next class, seeing how he was so bored with it. It should be no problem, right? After all, if he was so smart and knew everything, he should also know very well how to impart the knowledge to others. Then the instructor could move up the ladder himself and get away from all these imbeciles. Maybe that was just how it worked; he who was the best student became the next teacher. Wouldn't that be something? Not telling the students beforehand helped to figure out who was actually learning and knew the most.

The students dwindled down, from thirty to twenty to ten, finally to five. Tommen was bored. An hour had to have passed, at a minimum, maybe even two. And of course they couldn't leave in the event they ran into one of the other students and got an in on what the questions were going to be and how to answer.

"It'd be nice if time here was like the Wheel," he sighed, speaking mostly to himself. "At least then I wouldn't be losing a ton of sleep right now."

One of his remaining classmates, an Elif, grunted an agreement, apparently as disgruntled as he was about being left behind for so long. Where did this Elif normally come in? Was he the first one after Tommen normally? In the top ten? Was there really a set order and the instructor was just going backwards today?

"Where do you think the Wheel comes from?" Tommen asked absently. "How does it operate the way it does, you think?"

"I have heard that those in the third level begin to learn of it, and the fourth and fifth levels make special studies of it," the Elif said.

"What do you think, though? What did your Time Master ever tell you about it?"

"I was an Apprentice for only three kipa before I joined the Order. The Time industry means little to me, and the Wheel remains a mystery."

Tommen nodded solemnly. "Oh." He shifted his stance thoughtfully and folded his arms. "I heard it was in the middle of a black hole."

"That's stupid. No one could survive a black hole. Even this fortress needs special shielding. And anyway, a black hole makes time go faster. The Wheel stops time."

"Right, right." He shrugged. "Guess we won't know until we get to the third level, maybe the fourth."

The Elif did not reply, and there was no further conversation as one student was taken, then another, then another, until only Tommen and the Elif were left. The instructor returned and took the Elif.

"Oh, for crying out loud," Tommen hissed under his breath.

He made several laps of the screened area, wondering if he was going to be the last one left in the entire hall by the time he got out. Later he would consider that he should have spent his time thinking about how he was going to approach Rifun regarding the information about the journal, but in the moment, he was a selfish teenager wondering why he, the favorite, hadn't been called on first by the teacher. The screen only wiggled and he was making long strides across the sectioned-off room, nearly plowing into the instructor.

"I suppose you would be ready," the instructor observed. "Follow me."

Well, he wasn't the last one in the recreational hall, but pretty damn close. Only two sectioned off areas remained, and one of them was now empty. Busybody workers, once the instructor gave them the all clear, descended upon the screens like hungry piranhas, tearing them down and whisking them away to parts unknown. Looking around, the hall seemed to have expanded from the size of the gym at school to a professional football stadium. Maybe it was just him. He bet if he yelled something, it would echo, but he didn't dare.

Despite all the moving and the changes, the broom closet they used for testing remained unmolested. The two of them ducked inside, the stone door sealing out all the chatter and noise from outside. Tommen could never decide if he was about the receive an impossible mission, should he accept, or get raped. So far, it was just testing, but he was never one hundred percent confident.

"All right, now then," the instructor began, then paused. "I'm not going to test you."

Tommen couldn't decide whether to jump for joy or shrink back for fear of what else could be coming. "You're not?"

"You've already demonstrated beyond any reasonable or unreasonable doubt that you know what's going on, what's been taught. You're bored; I can see that. Quite frankly, everyone can see that. So, no, I'm not going to test you. Nor am I going to send you to level two."

Oh, shit, he was going to be assigned as a teacher. Worse, he was going to get kicked out of class entirely.

"Instead," the instructor went on, "by personal request of the Faharoa, you are jumping straight to level three of the Book of Philosophy with instructor Tayen Du'ul, classes to begin in twenty-one days. Hopefully it proves a bit more challenging with more depth of study and more students who speak English well enough to use it effectively. Also by request, you are taking on a second class, level one of the Book of Commands, Julianna Brown herself instructing, classes to begin twenty-five days hence."

Tommen knew that Julianna had been teaching some of her more promising and loyal pupils about the Book of Commands just from sheer memory, but the fact that there were now levels and it was being opened up to some of those who were less than blindly loyal, they really expected to have the third journal within the month. Chandler was right; there was no way that he was going to be able to "sneak" the third book past anyone. Everyone would know as soon as he had it.

"This is...unexpected," he said, knowing it was the truth as soon as he spoke. "I don't know what to say. Thank you, I suppose.

Thank you for moving me up."

"Personally, I would have moved you up a long time ago, or even had you teach the class." The instructor's tone did not convey the sort of warmth that comes from a teacher recognizing budding talent in a student; rather it was more leering, as if it was Tommen's fault that he'd been stuck in a boring class that he'd basically mastered after two days. "But we don't always get what we want." The instructor shifted his stance. "As I said, report to the third floor for your next assignment, whatever it is. It looks like most of the moving and clean-up has been done and they're finishing up, but regardless, if you can stay to help, please do so. Otherwise, congratulations on passing the class. I hope you do well in future classes and other endeavors."

The words were mechanical, drawn out through rote memorization and habit, with little enthusiasm and less hope. The instructor didn't care as he opened the door and stepped out of the closet, not even a goodbye or a handshake.

And that was that. Tommen had been kept waiting for two hours or better just so he could be told that he passed his exam by default, was skipping a level, and he was adding a class. That part he didn't fully understand yet, but figured it was probably part of his "next assignment" which he would receive on the third floor, which he made his next destination.

A bee-like alien was waiting at the entrance to the third level, where it looked like moving day in a college dorm, everyone moving to and fro, looking for assigned rooms, moving furniture, looking for friends, the whole nine yards. While all the noise got pushed into Tommen's ears anyway, the hum of the bee alien's wings was a bass drone that beat against his hearing aids, like listening for the ocean in a conch. Though he was more than accustomed to his hearing aids by now, the hum was unusually and divisively uncomfortable.

"Name and universal coordinates," the bee inquired, looking at a stack of papers like any other official checking in campers and college students.

Tommen gave them without thinking, putting hands to his

ears to cover them and try to block out the drone. The bee spoke, but he just stared at it. Finally, he asked, "Can you stop hovering, please? It's really...I just...I can't hear you."

For a moment, the bee did not move, but studied him closely. Finally, it complied, landing on the ground with the papers. The sudden absence of the drone was just as painful as its continuation, but the discomfort subsided and Tommen let his hands drop. "Thank you. What were you saying?"

"You are listed as being from an Unengaged species; therefore, you will not have a permanent bunk. You will, however, be permitted to use the temporary beds, and may apply for extended stay beds."

"What's the difference?"

"A temporary bed you may use for not more than three nights. An extended stay is limited to not more than eighty-one nights, and no more than twice in one year."

"Right, got it. Can I at least see them so I know where they are?"

"You may. This is the lower Artist level."

Basically, even though he didn't have a permanent room, this was still his level. He could come here, hang with his friends, get into a little mischief, and not have to ask permission.

The Akarin had used the third floor for offices and meeting rooms, so there was little to be done structurally; most of the work here had just been to get in beds and storage units for personal items. Homier than what he expected the soldier barracks to look like, he supposed, very much like a college dorm. Informal, upbeat, strange smells and even stranger conversations that he only caught bits and pieces of.

The temporary beds were located very close to the staircase for easy access. These were the empty dorm rooms. Cold, drab, practically neon invitations for midnight romps and other illicit activity. The extended stay beds were more like hotel rooms. Not personalized like the dorm rooms, but clean, welcoming, with appropriate storage for a little longer stay.

A sudden wash of fatigue reminded him that he still had to get to bed at some point, but he couldn't leave until he'd reported to Rifun. Taking a breath, Tommen made for the staircase. The die is cast, the players are moving. Time to see how the cards fall.

Rifun was not immune to the excitement of moving and remodeling, and his quarters had been rearranged as well. Now, rather than a haphazard dorm-room-slash-studio-apartment thrown together using mismatched second-hand furniture, it almost looked like two or three distinct rooms. The separation was still done via furniture, but less of a four-foot dresser and more of a seven-foot-plus monster desk-slash-bookcase-slash-entertainment-center made of solid cherry. All the furniture in the room either matched, as if part of a set, or was tastefully different, an accent rather than a distraction. Small coffee tables had been replaced by a proper meeting table. A huge ream of maps was held on the wall by something that Tommen thought looked like a projector screen; maybe it was just a fancy map holder. On one side, corkboards with a ton of notes pinned in some semblance of order. On the other side, whiteboards with notes here and there. Stylish cabinetry and chests of drawers made the office space look as though it belonged to a fancy New York lawyer.

With the new setup, the private bedroom area was not as visible except for a couple of dressers marking the informal entry. The bed, the chest, and all personal effects were now rendered invisible to the casual observer. The bathroom, assuming there was one up here, was now completely invisible. Tommen found himself wondering, with a dash of dry humor, whether that had been a problem for Rifun, people wondering if he had a public restroom up here.

The man himself was nowhere to be seen at first, but as Tommen turned to go, he just caught a glimpse of him in his peripheral vision, entering the office by a different direction.

"My young Apprentice returns," Rifun commented, almost disinterested as he moved about his office. "I trust you got my gift?"

"Getting moved up to level three? I did. Thank you." Tommen kept his tone carefully neutral. "What about the second class, though?"

"Second class?" Rifun was out of it, but he appeared genuinely surprised, pausing for only a moment to look at Tommen before going to the whiteboard and scribbling some notes, occasionally referencing the front map.

"Apparently I'm taking on a second class, level one in the Book of Commands."

"News to me. Certainly wasn't my doing. But I suppose it will do you some good. It will keep you occupied, anyway, if level three of Philosophy bores you as much as level one."

"I don't expect it will bore me, but the Book of Commands class ought to be interesting. Especially if the journal itself were to be part of it."

"Found it, did you?"

It took everything within Tommen to simply answer as calmly as possible, "I did."

"Do you have it?"

"Unfortunately, no. Turns out, it is held in a Borelian temple. On Brelix."

"Yes, that's where most Borelian temples are located. Do you know which one?"

"Uh..." Fuck. Forgot about that part.

"I'm only kidding. A prize that valuable, there is only one temple they would hide it in. The Temple of Tujor in Ancrath."

"Are you sure?"

"Of course." Rifun finished his notes and capped the marker. "They would offer it up to their death god in hopes of gaining the power within it. Cosmic osmosis, I suppose. The Temple of Tujor is where they'd hide it."

"They have other temples?"

Rifun faced him. "The Temple of Power, the Temple of Victory, the Temple of Money, the Temple of Labor, the Temple of Pleasure, the Temple of Despair, the Six Facets of death, or so they somehow believe. Tujor rules over all of them, of course. The Borelians, those who are religious, may make specific requests at any of the smaller temples, or petition the god of death himself, hoping for a larger reward."

Tommen frowned. "Guess Isthim forgot to go to Black Mass the day she died, huh?"

"The Borelians do not fear death. They welcome it. In battle is the only good way to die, as much their salvation as the crucifix is Catholic salvation."

Tommen shifted his stance. "So what do you want me to do? Going on adventures with my little team is one thing. There is no way we'll be able to pull off going to Brelix and getting inside one of their death temples and stealing a prized commodity and getting out. I'm sorry, but it's impossible. And I'm not willing to risk myself for a suicide mission."

"There won't be a suicide mission." Rifun moved around the huge meeting table. "At this point, with the location of the journal confirmed—and you are absolutely certain this is where the journal is?"

Tommen nodded. "The ones who hid it there told me themselves, told me exactly where to find it and how to get to it."

"With the location confirmed, there is now only the big plan."

"The one you've been working on for a while now."

"That's correct. Only the final preparations need to be made. Then, once everyone is comfortably moved into their new beds, well, we'll see who gets to actually sleep in them."

It was a terrible thought to consider. All the excitement in the Artist dorms. If any of them were tapped to march into battle, some of them wouldn't be returning. They wouldn't be going back to classes, to learn and study. They wouldn't be staying up late with their friends, chatting like a bunch of high school girls and ordering pizza in order to sustain them through a cram session. All the effort of moving in...only to die.

"And what is my part in this?" Tommen inquired, forcing his voice to remain even.

"You've done your part," Rifun told him. "You located the journal, using your team and superb sleuthing skills. That is what I asked of you, and you have delivered. Not exactly post office material, if you catch my meaning, but you'll do. And you're done."

It was what he'd always wanted to hear. He was done. Rifun wasn't asking him to fight. And yet, Tommen knew there couldn't be any other way. He sighed internally and shook his head. "No. I'm not done. I need to get the journal."

"It's in the Temple of Tujor. We'll send in a special force."

"You can't do that; it won't work."

"Why not?"

Shit, why wouldn't it work? "The faith of a skeptic. Finesse, not force. Your men will storm the temple, ready to die for the cause. It's a temple of death. That's what the Borelians are expecting; that's what they want. You have to send someone afraid to die, but more than that, you have to send a coward. 'In looking for a way out, a coward only hastens to his death.' It's a Borelian saying, but it's also very applicable. Force a coward into the temple. He will be able to follow a string of clues that will lead him deeper and deeper into the temple, into its vaults, to the heart of Tujor himself. It's just the way the temples are built. That's where the journal is being kept."

It was a string of total bullshit, but Tommen desperately hoped he looked and sounded sincere.

"And you're hoping I choose you to be my coward," Rifun stated slowly. "While I admire your sudden courage to go that far, I have no shortage of loyal cowards who would do the same. What does the faith of a skeptic have to do with anything now?"

"Because as a skeptic, I will be looking for every way to betray you and the Order. The Borelians have the highest standards of loyalty among their own, and to an extent, they expect it from their adversaries as well. Mutiny is not well-received by the god of death, and it will only lead to Tujor's wrath. In the heart of the temple."

Rifun studied him for a long moment. Tommen forced himself not to cow under the stare. Finally Rifun said, "I admire your cunning. Your reasoning puts me in such a position that I cannot tell you no, though I suspect most if not all of what you just said is total bullshit. I suspect there is more to the story, more to your reasoning, why a failed soldier and traitor to all wants to venture into the heart of a Borelian temple. I think there is more down there than you let on, and whatever your source told you is very compelling to you. I'm curious to know what it is. Therefore, I accept your request to be to the one to retrieve the journal. I will bring in my advisors, finish up the plans we have, and then let you know what we expect of you."

"Fair enough."

"Good. Now then, why don't you go home before this gets any more interesting, hm? I will send for you when I am ready."

Tommen was too glad to get out of there in one piece, and he practically sprinted back down the stairs. Had he really just done that? Had he honestly gone from trying everything to get out of battle to trying and lying his way back in? What was wrong with him? Chandler had called him loyal and he himself suspected some kind of Stockholm Syndrome. Even with Chandler pronouncing him nearly free, Tommen was sill forced to wonder whether he wasn't still under some sort of psychological influence. There was no other way to explain it.

Except, this was what had to be done. No one else would have the choices he would have to make. No one else understood the choices; they would do as the Shadows bid them. But he saw. He knew. He understood the choices, what was at stake. He understood that it wasn't about the ideal ending, but simply the least bad. There was no easy, straight answer, no way to weasel his way out and still be okay. He had to do this. This was a one-way door, and he was walking through it deliberately.

When he got home, the first thing he did was go to the bathroom and throw up. It was the only thing he could think to do. He couldn't even say why, except that in the cool stillness of the house, he could hear echoes of the last battle roaring through his mind. Death and destruction everywhere, augmented grossly by Time and the Akari. Now they were going up against a race that was death itself and worshiped their god of death, the dragon by the name of Tujor.

Tommen remembered the heart-pounding fear. Fear of battle as it raged in front of him. Fear of battle and the microportals, picking people off at random from yards away, trying to make himself small so he wouldn't be spotted and killed without ever having a chance to defend himself or confront his attacker. Fear of death as he blindly tried and failed to save lives, no matter whose side they were on. Fear of being killed, his dad never knowing what had happened to him. Fear of going to sleep and not waking up. He could smell the blood and guts, feel the crunchiness of the air as physics were manipulated back and forth in all manner of grotesque ways until he wasn't sure how the planet didn't go tumbling into the black hole.

He threw up again, his heart racing, pounding in his chest, the blood roaring in his ears so he might have expected the bee alien to be hovering right behind him. He stumbled back to his room and put his hearing aids on their charger, as if it could block out the noise in his head. He sat down on his bed.

And he had literally volunteered to go back into that. Didn't matter that his mission was different, that he would not be expected to fight or render aid; he was going back onto the battlefield, into the chaos and the fear and the death, hoping and praying to make it just ten more feet. And then there was the temple itself. Would it be nice and quiet, as a temple ought to be, or would it become an enclosed battleground, bullets burying themselves in ancient stone? Would he be solving ancient riddles and puzzles, or cutting down ninja warrior monks?

"Fucking hell," he whispered. "God, I don't know what I'm doing, and I really don't know what the Author has planned for me here, but if it's all the same to You—either of you, I suppose, I still don't quite know how this all works—if there's any way I can get out of this, show it to me. Actually, why don't you just go ahead and break my leg? Like, a couple days before You know they're going to leave, just break my leg. Car crash, skiing accident, workplace injury, I don't care. Do that, I'll probably start screaming in pain and maybe utter a curse word or five, but I'll remember this. And we'll be cool. I'd rather break my leg than do what I just said I'd do. Is that kind of promise still binding if I said it to a genocidal maniac?" He sighed and shook his head. Half to himself, he asked, "God, what have I done? What's going to happen now? Is there any other way?"

Reluctantly, he got up, returned to the bathroom to rinse his mouth out, brush his teeth, and carry on with his normal nightly routine. He wasn't going to get much sleep tonight, but he found himself oddly okay with that.

He half-hoped to speak to Chandler again, but two nights in a row was already unusual. Three in a row was bordering on the impossible. Besides, now that he'd done what he did, Tommen was sure the Shadows were gearing up for whatever battle they would be fighting against the Whites. Would there be Whites involved at all, if both sides were Shadow-controlled? He let out a breath. Didn't matter. It wasn't something he would be involved in, nor could he worry about it. He had enough worry of his own. He was literally getting sick from it, and he didn't need a shrink to know that wasn't a good thing. Well, it was unlikely Rifun would send for him in the next twenty-four hours. Time was a commodity in war, and when one had the time, take the time and plan. For Tommen, he would have to take the time to calm down and prepare himself for this new mission.

But that was the nice thing about a manual labor job, he supposed. It didn't give much time for worrying about anything but the present task.

Chapter Twenty-Nine
Plans and Perpetrators

It was Wednesday before Tommen received the official note of summons from Rifun, but the actual requested meeting was Thursday at three-fifteen in the afternoon. He'd have to book it home from school. If Becky didn't live on the same street, he might have been able to lie about really having to be somewhere. Problem was, Becky lived on the same street and would rat him out as soon as she got home. It might not have been so bad, except he also had to take Will and Eli home.

In the end, he may have Banded just a little bit, once they were out of the city and on roads that were more or less deserted. He was careful about it, not going so Fast as to stop time completely, but shaving several minutes off the normal route time, pulling in the garage at ten after three.

"You're home early," his dad observed as he walked in, making long strides toward his bedroom.

"Message from Rifun," Tommen said briskly, tossing his backpack on his bed. "There's going to be some kind of meeting in..." He checked his watch. "Five minutes."

"I see." His dad leaned in the doorway and folded his arms, clearly uncomfortable about the whole thing. "Do you need me to do anything from this end? I have tonight off."

"Um...I don't know. I don't know exactly what's going on—I have an idea, but that's all. Maybe just be ready to potentially call a meeting of the other leaders. And Kayla. She's still a wild card."

"That she is. All right. Just be careful."

"I can only try. And believe me, I do try."

His dad dipped his head once. "I know."

Tommen opened a portal to the fortress, surprised at the resistance he felt. Now that he'd gotten more accustomed to opening portals, especially ones this familiar, it was no different than walking through the front door of the house. This time, though, it was as if the door had been barricaded on the other side and he had to push and force his way through, squeaking out just enough of an opening to slip inside. The portal snapped closed.

Something big was going on; that much he knew just in the first ten seconds of being in the fortress. His intuition was solidified partly by the crowds that were backed up all the way to the door in the staircase atrium, and partly by the shouting and general din of the crowd. From his vantage in the back, Tommen could see the overall mood was anxious, though it was on the downslope, as if there had been chaos that was now being brought back into order.

But there was something else in the air, one not easily forgotten, though it didn't reach Tommen until he found a spot where he could climb and look up over the crowd. Then it was like being punched in the face.

Blood. He'd smelled enough of it to know it in an instant, and it made him gag. He got back to the ground and forced himself to think of something else so he didn't throw up. A little blood he was generally still okay with. A paper cut, an accidental slice from a knife while cutting potatoes, that was fine. It was ordinary. Usually it was his own blood and there wasn't much of it. He could Band it, clot it, heal it, carry on. But the blood out there was a little more than a paper cut. It was everywhere, a pungent stench that coated everything, and he wouldn't have been surprised if there was a pool of it in the main atrium itself.

And you think you're going to rush into battle, he thought miserably. *You're going to go to the most hostile planet in the universe, engage in a battle that ends in only death or slavery, break into a temple dedicated to the god of death, and come back out? Why do you think you can do this? Why do you think you have to do this? Why you? What makes it so you are the only one who can do this? What makes you the Chosen One? Why is the Author insisting on breaking you down that far? It's one thing to feel the call of the U.S. Army; it's quite another to be a coward and throw yourself into situations you know you can't handle.*

But if I don't confront those situations, I'll never be able to handle them.

You don't just walk into a gym and load up five hundred pounds on the bar because that's your end goal. You need to work up to it. Some people just aren't cut out for this. Talk to Rifun. Back out of it. Stay on the sidelines.

Tommen, down on one knee and still fighting an upset stomach, shook his head, mostly at himself. *No. I've been tasked to do it. I said I would do it. Now I'm going to do it.*

Wearily, he stood and returned to the crowd, trying to focus on the actions of the crowd and ignore the overwhelming stink of blood.

"What happened?" he asked of no one in particular. "What's going on?"

"The Akarin attempted another uprising," someone answered.

"I assume they were put down."

"Yes, only recently."

"What's all this, then? Cleanup?"

"They're looking for the planners and the instigators."

Tommen let out a breath. "Punishment."

"Of course, as is to be expected."

"Of course. Expected."

"Although, it is made more difficult with the arrival of Aklaq White Bear for negotiations. It is unclear if she had anything to do with the uprising."

Aklaq? Kayla was here? For negotiations? Tommen frowned. Nathan had said that he would speak to Kayla to try and get her to come around. Even if she wouldn't help, he would try to make it so she wouldn't tattle, either. So what was going on, exactly? How was this going to affect the attack on Brelix? Would it be delayed? Altered? How was this going to affect the retrieval of the journal? Kayla wasn't going to like that bit, even less if Rifun told her that he, Tommen, volunteered to be the one to get it.

Oh, today just kept getting better and better.

A passing thought reminded Tommen that he had a session with his shrink later. Was that still on, or was Nathan here somewhere, maybe with Kayla? With no cell reception here at the edge of a black hole, Tommen couldn't exactly just check his text messages or his email. Maybe if this unmoving crowd remained unmoving, he could slip out really quick, jog back home, check the time, send a text to Nathan, figure it out, come back later. Once the blood had been cleaned up.

Still, he waited politely in the back of the crowd. After a short time, it began to thin. Uprisings were thrilling, and the hunt for the ringleaders was also fascinating to watch, but if results didn't come quick, well, people had places to be. There were day-to-day operations that had to be attended to, after all. Tommen managed to step into the large room at the base of the southwest staircase and noted that the worst of the blood smell was gone, though he could see the stains on the staircase, the floor, the railing; he spotted some pretty mean splatter patterns all along the wall of the room as well. Apparently this uprising had gone better than the last, as far as the Akarin were concerned, but they just didn't quite have that edge they really needed to have a chance to win back their home.

Cautiously, as more and more people disbanded from the waiting crowd, Tommen took a look around. Any bodies had been taken away, entrails discarded, blood cleaned up as well as could be expected for the time being. Even the smell was mostly gone except for one spot about twenty feet from the bottom of the stairs, where gray stone was now a sickly brown-black. Tommen moved quickly away from that spot and found himself heading for the sub-level stairs. The guards there blocked his path and did not look in a mood to argue. Rather than push the issue, Tommen backed off and headed for the main stairs. He had been summoned, and he would obey. The meeting was obviously going to be a little later than expected, but until he was told that it was canceled and they needed to reschedule, he would play dumb and just go along with whatever was happening.

But where to go? With all the excitement over moving and everything else, where were the meeting rooms now located? Rifun's quarters seemed as logical choice as any, especially given the more formal, meeting room decor, but what if that wasn't it? With Kayla in the vicinity, especially after an uprising, he might not want her to get so close to the inverter. Who knew what her state of mind was, whether she would be so against pressing the big red button?

Sighing, Tommen started up the staircase. He got to the second floor when he stopped and looked up. Gravity had be strung along on a track; it wasn't just a free will effort, flying here and there like Superman. Because of that, very few used it to get from one floor to another. If two tracks happened to cross, well, bad stuff happened. If other physical forces were used or manipulated in an area where the track was, bad stuff happened. Looking around, though, the stairs did appear to be mostly empty. And he didn't really have to try to go from the second floor to the eighth in one shot (the longer the track, the greater the risk something bad would happen). One floor at a time. That was all he needed.

Other than easing the load on heavy items on the job, Tommen didn't work with Gravity a whole hell of a lot, and he peered over the edge of the staircase nervously. Four times a normal Earth staircase. One floor here meant he was four floors up at home. That was a long way to fall if shit happened. He wasn't dumb enough to just step over the edge and build a track; he would stay on solid ground to start, thank you.

His Gravity was as slow as he was nervous, but he was able to start on solid ground on the second floor, slowly slip up to the third floor, and deposit himself, clumsily, onto the staircase there. His landing was less than graceful, but he was unharmed, if a little shaky. He took a minute to collect himself, looked around to make sure the stairs remained more or less clear, then repeated the process, this time with a little more confidence.

He paused once when he got to the sixth floor, where the

higher officers and advisors were now housed, just to make sure the meeting wasn't taking place somewhere on that particular floor. Given that the floor was largely empty, he assumed it was not.

Still, Tommen gave the whole floor a good sweep before turning away and making for the stairs again where he used Gravity to lift himself to the seventh floor. Was it possible to just set a Gravity track and leave it running, like an invisible elevator? Or, you know, the alien beam from bad sci-fi movies, being taken into the alien ship? Of course, such a thought was wildly impractical, just given the sheer mass and weight of the various alien species; there would need to be dozens of these invisible elevators, the logistics would be a nightmare, and it was just impractical. Nope, nope, not going to work. Stairs it is, with an occasional stroke of luck for a personal elevator.

The only thing he could figure was that the door to Rifun's quarters was soundproof, because there was no way he and Kayla weren't screaming at each other, or that she wasn't screaming at him, anyway. Or Julianna screaming at her. Whatever the case, someone had to be screaming at someone and Tommen couldn't hear it as he approached the large doors and hesitantly knocked. He was bid enter, which he did with not a little trepidation.

It was indeed a war council meeting, and for as well as it was going, Tommen wondered if he shouldn't have brought his winter jacket and some ice skates. He half-expected to see icicles forming on the table where Kayla gripped the edge with white knuckles, gaze murderous but with a certain calm that makes one wonder. She fixed Rifun with this stare, but the man almost did not appear to notice. He was more intent on speaking with one of the others in the room, whom Tommen could only assume were military advisors. From what he could tell, Julianna was not present; he couldn't decide whether that was a good thing or if he shouldn't figure out what she was up to.

Focus on the task at hand, do what is expected of you, consider only what you can control. One road, one ending.

"Ah, you did make it," Rifun said, looking at him. "I thought you might have gotten caught up in the excitement downstairs."

Tommen decided to play dumb. "What happened?"

"Another uprising, and I must say, the timing of it was astounding." Rifun looked back at Kayla.

"I thought the meetings were supposed to take place on Dorigis?" Tommen wondered, deliberately changing subjects. "Neutral territory or something?"

"It was Nathan's idea," Kayla said, her voice a razor. "Come here under a flag of truce and good faith, discuss our intentions for the Borelian war, maybe strike a deal."

"This latest uprising certainly has thrown a wrench into those plans," one of the advisors stated. "She couldn't be trusted before, and she certainly cannot be trusted now. Be glad he is showing you this much mercy, wench, after your attempt on his life."

"I'm sure if I hung around him long enough, I might come to like him." She turned her icy gaze on Tommen who looked at his feet to make sure they didn't freeze to the floor. She looked back at Rifun. "I have only one term, if you want us to fight with you in any capacity. Your only other option is to hope I don't run off back to the Borelians with your little plans here. Tattling, as you put it. And then bite you in the ass while your backs are turned. The Borelians, too. Face both enemies, destroy you both."

"With spears and arrows, I will remind you," Rifun mentioned calmly. "And I may have been open to listening to your proposal except for this little incident we had this morning. Someone must be punished for it."

Kayla studied him for a long moment. "Have you found the ringleaders?"

"Working on it."

She shifted her stance and folded her arms, her eyes never leaving Rifun. "Let me down there. I'll find them. I won't turn them over to you until I have spoken with them. Maybe something can be arranged."

This was hostage negotiation, Tommen realized. The only reason Kayla was here talking and even considering fighting alongside

Rifun was the possibility of freeing the Akarin still held in the sub-levels. On the one hand, simple logic dictated that Rifun would have fewer problems with uprisings if he didn't have any prisoners. Realistic logic determined that if the Akarin were allowed to go free, they would certainly augment Kayla's forces going into battle, but could just as easily turn on the First Order afterwards, try to take back the fortress, this time with a quarter million Xur, Gin Jor, and the like at their backs. And Kayla had one hell of a leverage point, that being the ability to alert the Borelians to Rifun's plans.

Of course, thinking about it, Rifun had the same leverage against her. The difference was, Kayla was less of a threat to the Borelians, and the Borelians were smart enough to know that even if Rifun went to them with such a warning, there was no reason to think he was just going to sit idly by, knowing he was the more wanted criminal. They would be prepared for him as well, if they didn't arrest him on the spot or take the opportunity to bring the fight to him instead. Better to have one or the other or both hit the Borelians completely unawares.

Kayla was permitted to go to the sub-levels and speak to the Akarin. She was under no obligation to turn over the ringleaders at this time, but she would figure out what was going on, what their thoughts were, how they wanted to work things out. Despite the Akarin having a more rigid hierarchy and ruling structure, even in captivity, Kayla still operated on the Native principle of not presuming to tell another man what to do or how to act.

"This could take a while," Rifun mused. "And without knowing her position more certainly, any planning we do could easily prove fruitless."

They were dismissed to stretch their legs, get some food, and reconvene in an hour. Tommen was not given any special instructions, so he decided to simply go along with it. He made his way down to the first floor and got himself some food from the cafeteria. Even when he was finished and heading back up, the sub-levels were still blocked by guards who now seemed to have a permanent sneer plastered on their faces.

Tommen used Gravity when he could, but the stairs were becoming a little busier, and he didn't need to fall to his death from twenty stories up. Still, he didn't feel nearly as bad as he did when he walked up all eight floors, and he arrived in the meeting room no worse for wear. The hour wasn't quite fully up, but most of the advisors had returned already, save one which came in behind him. Another fifteen minutes passed before Kayla arrived.

"And Moses comes before Pharaoh once more," Rifun commented dryly. "What do I get for letting your people go?"

Kayla gave him a sour look. "I found the ringleaders. I congratulated them, in the event you were wondering. And we have come to an agreement on our proposal, even taking into account this morning's 'incident' as you call it."

"Listening."

"You free all the Akarin to fight, understanding that they will be under my direction and the direction of my commanders. Further understanding that we will fight against the Borelians, we will not warn them of your attack, and we will conduct our own operations. We may work in conjunction in an overall attack, but we will not fight alongside you. We will not protect you. We will not come to your aid."

Rifun frowned. "From this side of the table, that doesn't sound advantageous to me at all."

Kayla held up a hand. "Once the battle is over, assuming we aren't all dead or sold into Borelian slavery, the bulk of the Akarin go free. You will not recapture them; you will not pursue them. However, in exchange, you will, at your discretion, be permitted to take myself, all but one member of the Council, and the ringleaders of this uprising, prisoner for yourself to do with as you see fit, be it mercy or punishment, up to and including execution."

"Kayla, no!" Tommen blurted.

Her head snapped his direction so hard he was amazed she didn't get whiplash, but her expression was anything but comforting. "Shut up. You have no say in this. If it were in my power to offer you up as well, I would."

She could have just stabbed him in the chest and it would have been kinder as Tommen physically stumbled back a step or two. She hated him. It wasn't just that she was annoyed or disappointed or frustrated with him; she truly loathed him, considered him a traitor guilty of treason and blasphemy against the Akarin, maybe even the Author herself. He tried to bring up Chandler's words to reassure himself that he was doing the right thing, but they eluded him now in the face of this sense of betrayal. This death of friendship.

"How do I know you will keep your end of the bargain?" Rifun wondered, folding his arms. "The battlefield is a chaotic place and war is exhausting; likely we will be more concerned with simply returning to our own beds at the end of the day and sorting things out later, giving you ample time to escape."

"The Council and some others of my choosing will remain here, in your little dungeons, as leverage. When I return with the ringleaders of this uprising, you will let them go free."

Rifun frowned. "I want the names of the ringleaders, that way I can be sure they're all accounted for at the end of the day, sure that one didn't slip through the line."

"Easily done. Assuming we come to an agreement."

"But I wonder about you. You are more valuable than hostages 'of your choosing' sitting in my 'little dungeons'. How do I know you'll come back to free them and not simply leave them to die?"

Kayla glared at him. "That is something only you would do. But I guess you will just have to trust me."

Rifun raised a brow and undid the buttons on his shirt, pulling the fabric back to reveal the twisted scar tissue. "This is what trust cost me, especially trusting you. You're going to have to do better than that."

Their gazes did not waver from each other as Rifun buttoned his shirt back up.

Finally Kayla said, "Fine. I will fight with you."

Rifun grinned. "No, you won't. You'd stab me in the back just as soon as you got the chance. I have a better idea." Rifun looked at Tommen, and for a moment, he was transported back to the warehouse. More specifically, the van ride before they arrived at the warehouse. Either Rifun's bloodlust was up at the prospect of battle, or else he'd discovered the poisoning and it had indeed righted itself; he was damn near back to his old self.

"You'll be fighting with him," Rifun stated. He motioned Tommen closer to the table. "He's on a special mission to steal Richard's third journal back from the Temple of Tujor. Seeing how he's supposedly uncovered secret knowledge that only a coward can unlock mysterious clues and invisible doors that lead to the journal, he volunteered to go himself. But a coward is not a coward for no reason, and he'll need someone to watch his back. Given your history together, I can think of no one better suited to the task of simply keeping him alive."

The look that crossed Kayla's face was unreadable, but with a certain measure of bewilderment and a touch of a childish, "That's not fair!" She'd ride into battle for the Akarin, grudgingly go along with Rifun, but she did not want to work with Tommen. To an extent, he didn't want to work with her, either, especially since she just admitted to wanting to offer him up for execution as well.

"And to ensure your cooperation in light of your recently-acquired disdain for him," Rifun went on, "if he does not return unharmed, I will pursue the Akarin. I will recapture them. And I will exact brutal punishment, 'up to and including execution' on all of them, starting with you, which I will personally handle."

Kayla looked at Tommen, then back at Rifun. "I do this, my offer still stands, but the ringleaders of today go free."

"You were worth more than all of them combined anyway."

"All right. I'll do it. What's the plan?"

"How many of your forces can we expect? Numbers, strengths, weaknesses, all of it."

Kayla was reluctant to give up her army's strengths and weaknesses, but the bargain had been struck. Her life and her people's lives were on the line, and there was no going back now. Once they set foot on Brelix, it was all or nothing.

"The Gin Jor have the greatest numbers, but the D'Bok are easily the strongest. The Xur are the fastest. The Rupi have crude gliding capabilities and are able to read the atmosphere, predict the weather, and are specially tuned into magnetic and electromagnetic fields. The Ouin are arguably the weakest group in terms of physical strength and their ability to handle Brelix's dense atmosphere, but they are also the hardest to kill. Their skin is incredibly thick and very slippery, difficult to penetrate, impossible to touch and handle."

"How much do we have to worry about clan rivalry?" one of the advisors inquired.

"Little or none. They are fighting a common, powerful foe. They can set aside their petty differences."

"Good to know." Rifun went to the wall where a huge map hung. Or it looked like a map. The whole thing had been washed out so that black soil turned gray, enough that marks and labels could be read. It wasn't a complete planetary map, maybe more of a regional one. To the west was a shoreline, marked, "Ocean." To the north were rugged mountain ranges and volcanoes the size of Oklahoma, or so they seemed, the molten lava clearly visible in the satellite-like photos. The region was labeled, "Land of Tujor." The south and east were simply land; Tommen was unable to make out any prominent, distinguishing features except for a canyon to the southeast that was probably an active fault line. Near the coast was a large, sprawling metropolis, in the midst of land that looked almost green, simply labeled, "Ancrath."

"This is Ancrath," Rifun began, sarcasm tinting his voice. Yup. Wherever he'd been, he was back. "It's the capital city of Brelix with a population of about two million."

"That's all?" Tommen wondered. Even as he spoke up, he knew what the reason would be.

"The Borelians are scattered across three systems and have a lot of slaves to control. With how unstable Brelix is, it makes sense.

However, that does not make it an easy target. Those who do live there are grizzled old warriors who know a thing or two about warfare. And if they need help, they can always call on their trusty space fleet to swoop in and save the day.

"The good news—" Rifun gave Kayla an unreadable, if smirking, look. "—is that the Borelian army is currently in some turmoil, given that a good chunk of their higher officers have mysteriously dropped dead over the last two weeks or so. Two things have happened which we must be prepared for but can take advantage of. First, only five remain on the Council of Ancrath, and only two Great Admirals of the Fleet. When the assassinations became a noticeable threat, it was decided that the best course of action was to scatter them, not have them all in one place. They still meet, via space communications, but they are physically separated and under heavy guard of the Time variety.

"As for the Holy Men of War, they are as numerous and as mysterious as the Secret Police. We have no way of knowing how many there are or how many have been killed, if any at all. Their exact duties and abilities are unknown to us, so we must assume that they are on par with our own, if not exceeding. We take no chances. Educate your men on basic sucker strategies so they don't get killed by preventable stupidity.

"Now the second thing that has happened in response to the assassinations is that they have grounded a good portion of their space ships. They know they can't wage space war on humans, so strutting their feathers in space is useless. They're bringing their soldiers back down to the ground. On the one hand, that's more soldiers on the ground. On the other hand, it's fewer in the air, which is our bigger concern."

He tugged on the map and it sprang up, rolling up and revealing a detailed city map.

"This is Ancrath. This building here is their governmental building." It wasn't quite in the center of the city, instead situated more toward the ocean side of things. "With the Council and the Admirals scattered, the only value in attempting to seize it is symbolic. However, there is likely to be a great deal of information stored there, and I have little doubt that the Holy Men of War will be there to protect it.

"This here—" Maybe five miles east of the governmental building, if Tommen could judge distance accurately. "—is the Temple of Tujor and the surrounding Six Facet temples. Few Borelians are actual worshipers of Tujor—most are superstitious at best—but it represents a great pillar of their culture and history as well as a source of fear to the outside universe. He who topples Tujor topples death itself. For the Borelians, the government and the military is everywhere, but Tujor is here. The temple, I expect, will be more heavily guarded, more likely to earn a response than the empty governmental building.

"Now then, knowing all of that, we are presented with two major problems. Anyone want to take a guess?"

"We're splitting our forces," one advisor stated.

"Excellent. And the second?"

"They will still have space support," another said.

"Okay, so we have three problems. There is something specific that I'm looking for. Anyone? No?" Rifun tugged on the second map and it rolled up to reveal charts and bars and graphs and other fancy jargon. "Even with basic translators providing a small atmospheric shell around each of us, no one can survive on Brelix for very long unassisted. The slaves you will see on the surface will either have external gear or have had some kind of invasive—and likely not painless—surgery to make it so they can survive. As you can see here, in the math, based on mass and biological composition and needs, the longest that anyone can survive on Brelix with only the translator shell, is fourteen Base Hours. The shortest is three Base Hours. After that, you must return to a neutrally tolerable atmosphere for at least the same duration of time before attempting another venture.

"Failure to leave after the appropriate time will lead to permanent damage, and the length of time you can still survive on

Brelix, again, varies by species. For the three-hour species, you have another thirty to forty minutes of increasing pain and permanent damage to your entire body before you die in agony. For the fourteen-hour species, another three to three and a half hours. For humans, such as myself as others in the room, we have six hours in the shell, plus another fifty to sixty minutes. I don't have the math done on every single species, but the computations are available if you wish to do your own or have them done.

"That said, our attacks must be sorted into waves, and for ourselves, we must be very conscientious of the poison air we are fighting in. I would highly recommend everyone find a timer of some form and keep it on your person. Set it for thirty minutes less than your allotted time, giving yourself time to get out. And I expect all of this information to get passed down. Is that understood?"

The advisors nodded gravely. Dying in battle was one thing. It was noble and heroic and brave and would be sung about for centuries. Dying because you weren't smart enough to get out of a toxic environment that you knew about and were fully prepared for, even had a timer with you to let you know when to get out, that was just stupid, and the only mention you would get would be as a footnote, an object lesson to future recruits in what not to do.

"Now then, I know we've discussed some of these things at length, how to address these problems," Rifun said, returning to the table. "But now that we actually know what our goal is and who all the players are, why don't we figure out exactly what we're doing so we can get out there and actually do it, hm?"

In a way, it was comforting to have Rifun back to his old self. Whacked out on drugs, any man could be truly unpredictable. Violent, passive, anything could happen. But when a man was what he was, no matter how hard he tried to be unpredictable, he still maintained his core personality, so that even unpredictability became predictable. Tommen just hoped that the Borelians didn't realize that as well, hadn't figured that out from their time in alliance with Rifun. But if he, Tommen, had been able to figure this out in only a few minutes with zero battle training, the Borelians would have figured it out ages ago.

They were screwed.

"The Borelians aren't too happy about the planetary defenses, and they've been shaken by the recent string of assassinations, but they are still stronger and more numerous. We cannot let them realize that. Our first strike will be two-fold, one on the ground in a place we will not be expected, and another force appearing and disappearing guerrilla-style on the ships. When the commanders on the ground go to the Great Admirals for help, our second strike will be against them, cutting off higher authority and shaking the confidence of the ground forces. Then the initial ground strike will retreat for a short period."

Rifun returned to the maps and pulled down the map of Ancrath. "Once that is done—a short enough time to throw order in chaos in the ranks, but not so long that they can establish new leadership or muster men and resources effectively, I predict about ten to fifteen minutes—we'll deliver a series of attacks here, here, here, here, and here. Ancrath is not a walled city, but these are the major highways in and out and this is the harbor. They are predictable targets.

"The attacks here will be longer affairs, but they are by no means less dangerous. In fact, they will be more dangerous because our forces will be sorely outnumbered. However, the soldiers who do respond will most likely be grunts, a force to send out and belay the threat while the higher-ups still figure out what to do. This means they will have no Time abilities." He looked at Kayla. "If your tribal army has any hope of helping and not being slaughtered before they even see their enemy, this would be the place. Have your Akarin ready to defend against any Time attacks and be prepared to get them out quickly, but I believe this may be their only opportunity."

Kayla looked ready to protest, saying that her armies were under her command, not his. But at the last minute, she appeared to bite her tongue and grunted an agreement. "They will hold their ground."

"You may organize them how you wish, but I expect this

assault to last at least an hour. Long enough to draw the Borelian troops into the fray and get them away from the city center. And then I expect it to continue as long as possible, give us the advantage at the temple and the governmental building."

"Won't there be a force dedicated to protecting the governmental building and the temple?" Tommen asked.

"I expect there will be, but this will divide their forces. War Tactics 101. Remember Sun Tzu? Read it and refresh your memory."

His tone was dismissive and he returned his address to his men, but before he could get two words in, Kayla spoke up.

"The Akarin will also attack the shipyard to the east of the city, where most of the Borelian space ships are docked."

Rifun turned. "Pardon?" His tone and expression conveyed something that said he was amused at some small victory, as if his charm had won her over into willing cooperation.

"Once the Xur and associated forces have the Borelians well occupied at those sites, the Akarin, specifically those of space-traveling variety, will attack the shipyard. The bulk of their forces may be on the ground right now, but if they get any of those ships in the air, it's over for us before you can get to the temple or the governmental building. We attack the shipyard in our own operation, commandeer the ships if we can, start blasting the hell out of the city. Cause chaos. Any ships come down, we attack them. If possible, we take the space fight to them, confuse them, keep them occupied. One of the Council members and one of the Great Admirals are still in the same system, hiding on their own ships at different planets. If we get the opportunity, we'll go after them as well."

Rifun grinned and dipped his head. "I like your line of thought. We'll need a line of communication between us, then, so we can coordinate without getting involved in too much friendly crossfire."

He still didn't trust Kayla not to turn on him, and Tommen didn't blame him. Turning on one's ally on the battlefield was one thing. Turning on one's ally with the fighting power of a spaceship, that was something else entirely given that there wasn't a whole lot to be done against the spaceship.

Tommen got a feeling in his body similar to the one he'd gotten in the Amish buggy. Talking about spaceships and space battle, it was all so cool and geeky and very *Star Trek*. Battle was still scary and made his stomach churn, but just the idea was pretty romantic.

"The Akarin will then attack the shipyard," Rifun went on. "The Borelians, seeing this new threat and possibility of their enemy getting their hands on such firepower, will send more troops there, possibly even pulling from any forces dedicated to the temple or governmental building. Soldiers on the ground can do little against a spaceship after all. This will give us an opening to begin our attack. We may have some advantage, but we will be divided also."

He paused and faced those gathered. "The goal here is not to conquer Ancrath. We are not going to besiege it in hopes of calling it our new home and stronghold. As pointed out already, we would not survive long. The Borelians know this. Whatever fight we give, they have only to wait for us to succumb to their atmosphere. Wait long enough, they may bring the fight back to us, and then we're in trouble. We must bring on a fight severe enough to be feared, to be met in open battle, not a lazy conflict. We must appear as a genuine threat. The shipyard, the temple, the governmental building, all threatening, full force, as much as we dare. But we must also appear as though, had we the time, that we could do even more damage.

"Our goal, at the end of the day, is two-fold. From the temple, we want the third journal. From the governmental building, we want information, as much as can be gained in the time we have. Everything else is purely psychological. Damage, destruction, fear. Ancrath means nothing to us. We cannot have it; therefore, it is no loss to us if things get destroyed. Am I understood?"

Murmurs of assent.

"Good. Now then, let's talk about the temple first, seeing how the journal is the higher priority for us. The Temple of Tujor is located here, in this complex. The interior of the temple itself is about half the size of this fortress, at least above the ground. Belowground, we have little or no information. The smaller temples around it are half the size of that, maybe a little smaller. Our initial assault will simply be to keep any guards or soldiers busy, enough to cover Tommen and Kayla while they look for the journal. Once they have it, then we can start on real destruction. We can't allow ourselves to be cornered in the main temple, so we're going to establish ourselves in all of them, hold down the whole complex if possible. Those in the smaller temples can wreak as much havoc as they want, but the main temple cannot be so damaged until the journal is retrieved. As soon as that is done, all bets are off. Wreak havoc for as long as you can.

"As for the governmental building, information is key. People, places, stratagems, I shouldn't have to tell you what you should be looking for. As much information as possible, as much damage as possible, as fast as possible.

"The journal is our finish line. We cannot take the city; we couldn't hold the city if we did. Our goal is the journal and as much damage as possible. Once the journal is gotten, a signal will be given. Continue to fight as long as you have strength, but if you become overwhelmed, get out. Never let the Borelians take you alive, but I shouldn't need to tell you that, either. If possible, get in and out in your entire unit. Numerous small portals are more dangerous than one large one. We can't let the Borelians cross back here. A small force will stay behind here tasked with that very thing. If too many Borelians come back through, they have the ability and my permission to scramble the Energy in the portal room, effectively stranding everyone left behind unless they can get out on their own. Is that understood?"

Scramble the Energy? There was a way to do that? Was it similar to the Tacagans' planetary defenses? Tommen made a mental note to ask about it later. As for Kayla and the other advisors, there was cold, stoic agreement. It wasn't fun, but this was war, and war was rarely fair, especially for the losers.

More plans and details were hashed out, but Tommen's attention began to wander. He got his assignment, knew what he was supposed to do, now he wanted to go home. Obviously they weren't attacking today, hopefully not tomorrow, and he needed sleep. It was Thursday, he'd probably already missed his session with his shrink, and he had three tests to look forward to in school tomorrow morning. Could this wait until Saturday, maybe Sunday night? Or the Friday before spring break? He got that weekend off work, but Dr. Polski couldn't travel on Saturdays because...God, Tommen supposed, which meant he would have some free time on hand.

Actually, hell, if humans could only be on Brelix for six hours at a time, he could do this overnight any time. Guess there was something to be said for operations on a planet with a dangerous, unstable atmosphere, and an even more dangerous and unstable crust. What if there was an earthquake while they were duking it out? Or what if a volcano erupted? Nature was not something you could really plan for, and even so, you usually just had to go with it.

Eventually, they were dismissed. Tommen only caught the last little tidbit about Rifun and Kayla going to Tacaga for a meeting. Neither had heard anything about the Tacagans being granted their godlike autonomy yet, neither had the Dorigisi gotten back to anyone about hosting the next meeting. Better to go with what they knew. If the Tacagans got all huffy about mere humans intruding upon their own sovereign ground, well, it was their own damn fault that their messaging system failed, seeing how they'd trapped themselves on their own planet because they didn't like Akari-bearers.

But that was neither here nor there; the meeting was dismissed. The advisors left promptly to rally their men and get orders sent down the line. Kayla turned her back and stalked off, her overall disposition unhappy but otherwise difficult to read. Only Rifun remained, cleaning up the meeting room and generally tidying up a bit. Tommen watched him quietly for a minute or two. Once the meeting room was tidied, Rifun headed into his personal apartment area, returning a minute later with his thermos.

"Still on the meds, huh?" Tommen asked.

"Still having seizures," Rifun told him, not looking at him.

"What you said earlier, about...scrambling the Energy in the portal room? What does that mean?"

"Means that those who open portals based solely on the Energy and the feel of this place won't be able to do so anymore. It's difficult to explain. Subtle changes in the Gravity, Light, Heat, the things you reach for when opening a portal, suddenly gone, changed. It would be the same as opening a blind portal for the first time here. You would have to reacclimate yourself to the portal room. The only thing it doesn't change is opening a portal via coordinates, which takes into account the universal coordinates as well as regional GPS. But, seeing how there is no map of this planet and no one is quite sure where the fortress could be because no one can go outside to check, no one travels here by coordinates."

"Oh. And the alternative of falling into a black hole is probably a pretty good deterrent, too."

"Indeed it is. Now then, was there anything you needed? At this point, the ball is rolling and I have stuff to do."

Tommen left Rifun's quarters, pausing on the staircase and looking down, somewhere between the seventh and eighth floors, where Julianna was speaking to two of the advisor generals. There was no telling how long the conversation had been going or what they were talking about, but Tommen made sure to keep moving and stay out of sight as much as possible. Act natural in the event they saw him or he just happened upon them while walking down the stairs.

Whatever it was, when Tommen got within fifty feet of them, Julianna thanked the advisors with a smile, then turned and started up.

"Ah, Tommen," she said, grinning almost warmly. And by "almost warmly" it was more like "not coldly." "Rifun told me about your desire to volunteer to retrieve the journal. Very noble of you. A noble coward."

"If by 'noble' you mean 'foolhardy' then sure, I guess I'll agree."

"Well, regardless, once you get it and Rifun is done parading you around with it, make sure you get it to me before something happens to it. I imagine the celebrations will simply be uproarious, and

I don't want it to get damaged before we have a chance to read and study from it."

Is there anything that can destroy it? "Yeah, I heard you wanted me in your class."

"Of course. I hand-picked my first crop of students, from the beginners to the experts. You've come a long way, Tommen, and I want you to get the full experience once we have all the journals."

"Flattered. Listen, I...have my own appointment I have to make. Doctor's appointment."

She waved her hand. "Of course, of course. The uprising did put a bit of a delay on things, and it's not as though we have a ton of time to waste, not like they do in the Wheel. Yes, go on, go talk to your doctor or dentist or whomever you need to see."

She continued her way up the staircase, and Tommen turned and made his way down. Her demeanor made it impossible to judge what she knew, if anything, but he had to assume she knew everything that was going on. She knew about the journal and the key, knew about Andrew and Nathan, knew everything and was three steps ahead. But even if that were true, what could Tommen do about it?

Nothing. He had to keep going along the road he was on, focus only on his task, and do exactly as he was expected to do. There was only way one this could end.

When he touched down on the first floor, the blood smell was gone, the huge stain on the floor had been cleaned so that it was little more than what might be dismissed as natural age discoloration, and life had returned to normal. He glanced one toward the sub-level stairs. The guards still appeared a bit disgruntled, but no worse for wear. Ignoring them, he made for the portal room and slipped back into his bedroom with ease.

Twenty after seven. He practically dove for his phone and called up Nathan.

"For a few minutes, I was worried you hated me," the man began.

"Sorry, got delayed. Rifun again. If you're still at the usual spot, I'll come meet you. Actually, I'll meet you wherever you are because...shit gonna happen. We need to talk."

"Yes, I thought we might. I'm at the usual spot."

"Cool. I'll be there in a minute."

Tommen hung up and headed out to the living room, pausing when he considered that his dad was supposed to have the night off, yet was nowhere to be found. He went out to the kitchen where a note lay on the table.

Got called into work for a short cover shift. Theoretically should be off around four, but we'll see how it goes. You know how it works. -Dad

Well, it looked like his dad's handwriting, and there did not appear to be anything particularly sinister about it. Besides, aside from the Borelians, anyone who would want to hurt and-or kidnap his dad (and had a chance of pulling it off) had all been in the fortress at the time. Except Julianna. But that wouldn't make sense.

Just to be sure, Tommen texted his dad.

"At work?"

"Hooray," his dad replied.

"Okay, just making sure."

"Interesting things at Book Club?"

"Ha ha ha. Yes. I'll talk to you later."

Feeling a little better about everything now, Tommen got in his car and Banded his way to the park, a treacherous drive in itself without adding in the weather lately. With spring just around the corner, it got above freezing during the day, just enough to make the snow wet, then the temperature dropped at night, turning it all back to ice. As such, Tommen slid into a spot more than parked, and waited just a second before actually getting out of his car. Hopefully, the light on in the pavilion and presence of people would deter any ticket-happy cops tonight.

He shoved his hands in his pockets and headed up the slope to the pavilion where he knew Nathan would be waiting. But when he opened the door, he stopped.

Kayla sat at the table across from Nathan. While she didn't look angry per se, she was a long way from happy, and her gaze was like an iron vice when she looked at Tommen.

"I know it's your shrink night, and I'll be happy to let you guys have a chat, but first, I think there are a few things we three need to discuss. Sit down."

Tommen sat.

Chapter Thirty
Red Wire, Blue Wire

I'm willing to give you the benefit of the doubt," Kayla began, her voice stony. "You found the third journal. You know what it takes to get it. We are now in such a position as to destroy it once we get our hands on it. But this is going to be a coordinated effort."

"Okay." Tommen was reeling, and as such, he felt too slow to keep up with Kayla's fast-moving train of thought, and too weak to try and contradict her. After all, he had choices to make, and who was to say that she wasn't part of it? For now, he would just have to go with the flow; battle changes everything, anyway.

"Rifun didn't say exactly when he wants to march, but I imagine it will be soon. As he mentioned a number of reasons, it is going to have to be a swift operation. First my people on the outskirts of the city to draw them away, then the shipyard, then the main operation. I estimate we'll have approximately half an hour to forty-five minutes between the initial order and when we move in. Nathan here says getting the key shouldn't take more than twenty minutes."

"But time stops while in the Wheel," Tommen interrupted. "Wouldn't it be better to wait until we're right there at this...door, vault, chest, whatever it is? Get there, go to the Wheel, get the key, come back? It would minimize the length of time we actually have the key, minimize the risk of theft or anything else."

Nathan shook his head. "Hiding the key in the Wheel was hard enough the first time around, and it caused what we might liken to a brown-out. I don't know what will happen when we get it back out."

"So let's get it now. If something bad happens, then there isn't an army out there depending on us while we're trapped in the Wheel."

Again, Nathan disagreed. "It's not safe, and if anyone goes snooping, wondering what we were doing, what we were after, especially a Borelian, and it's discovered, it will tip off the Borelians and render our attack useless."

Tommen rubbed his face. "What's the likelihood of someone finding out, though?"

"We hid the key in the Core of the Wheel. The only reason we got away with it was because we were tapped for the Rebuild, so we could do whatever we wanted. This time around, there is likely to be some form of security, and if not, well, as the saying goes, the secretaries know everything."

"So that's that," Kayla stated, her voice softening just a touch. "Now then—"

"But what if the key gets lost or stolen in battle?" Tommen asked.

She gave him a look. "I'll hold onto it. It won't get lost or stolen. Now then, assuming we don't die on the battlefield and make it past whatever guards and booby traps protect this thing, and assuming the key actually works and we get our hands on the journal, how do we want to work it so it gets destroyed?"

"Well, the deal is that I have to come out unharmed and with the journal," Tommen began. "If we're trying to save as many Akarin as possible, we should probably start there."

Kayla reluctantly agreed. "Yes, but no doubt Rifun will want to take it as soon as you bring it out."

"What if we replaced it with another fake?" Nathan suggested. "Keep the original for ourselves, hide it away, and hand over a fake? Just say it was always a fake, or that the Borelians made another fake in order to try and lure in Rifun and the Cult after he betrayed them."

"Yes, but where would we get it? It takes time to make a convincing fake. It took the Kolkath years."

"Skip the fake, then," Tommen said, shrugging. "They don't need to have an actual fake if they're just putting out the rumor. Lure in the Order, try to kill them all. Their only misstep was not anticipating that we would attack first."

Nathan frowned and leaned back. "Maybe, but with the original now confirmed to have been on Brelix...the Borelians don't let things go easily, as their slaves prove. Whether it was a fake or a ruse, Rifun would become infuriated, kill the Akarin, then go back for more. That's fine and dandy, except the part about killing the Akarin."

"What about this?" Tommen began. "Why not give it to them?" He went on before Kayla could protest. "Give it to them. Just to start. Hear me out. Give it to them. Honor the agreement, maybe negotiate some more leniency. Then, later, when they're all partied out and passed out on the floor, steal it back. Steal all the journals. It's a sucker punch, but it will honor this agreement and get the jump on them on the way out."

"Do you know where the journals are?" Nathan inquired.

"And the Authored Books."

Kayla and Nathan glanced at each other.

"I don't like it, but it may be our only chance," Kayla conceded with a growl.

"Julianna is already teaching from memory anyway. And the third journal has been a long time coming. A little while longer won't make much of a difference. But if we allow them to have it, then take all of them, plus the Authored Books, it's a bigger blow," Tommen pressed.

"He has a point," Nathan said.

Kayla fixed Tommen in a stare like a bear trap. "You think you can pull this off?"

"I do."

Her expression turned unreadable. "I'm not going to lie to you, Tommen, I don't know how much I trust you. But I'm also very conscious of the fact that this was what we needed all along, a mole on the inside, close to Rifun. That level of undercover requires a certain amount of deception and trust. We'll get the journal and hand it over. Afterwards, you deliver all three journals and all the Authored Books to us."

"Sounds like a plan."

"Good. I'm going to arrange a meeting on Tacaga. If I don't see you before the battle, stay safe. Both of you."

The last bit sounded more like an afterthought, as though she were addressing only Nathan and decided to include Tommen merely out of formality. She left the pavilion without another word and without looking back. The men watched her leave, then stared at the door a minute or two afterwards.

"She's always such a joy to work with," Nathan commented sarcastically.

"More and more sunshine every day since Micaiah's been gone," Tommen agreed. "Was she here when I called you?"

"No, she showed up half a second after I hung up. But, given that you weren't planning on her being here, I assume you were preparing for a normal session. Do you still want to continue?"

"Might as well. I came all the way out here."

"I won't force you. And like I said, if you don't want to talk to me, I can arrange—"

"No, it's fine. Just..." Tommen rubbed his face. "I'm just ready for all this shit to be over with. And even then, I don't know that it will be. Today the third journal, tomorrow, who knows? It's always something, you know?"

They spoke for the better part of an hour and then some, though it did little to make Tommen feel better. He'd always assumed that therapy was about identifying problems and working through them. Like physical therapy, it took time and patience and things might not always get put back together one hundred percent, but there was always an end date, a graduation, a day when patient and doctor shook hands and went their separate ways. This psychology thing, though, it didn't feel like that, or it didn't feel like that right now. It felt like an ongoing thing, as if he might never be able to work through his problems and get back on his own two feet, but would be dependent on the shrink for the rest of his life, helpless without it. When did he get to walk away?

"What are you going to do now?" Nathan wondered as they walked back to their cars.

Tommen shrugged. "Right now I think I'm going to head to the precinct and tell my dad what's going on; he deserves to know. And if he's able to get to the meeting on Tacaga, so much the better. Other than that, I guess the only thing I can do is wait."

Nathan nodded slowly. "A good thing to do. Don't get yourself overly excited, but don't neglect yourself either. You know battle is coming, and you know what is expected of you. Start now by mentally preparing yourself. You've seen battle before already; you know the sights, sounds, smells, everything that comes with it. Do what you can to protect yourself from it. Meditate, pray, do whatever you need to do, but don't go into the battle green. Do you understand?"

Tommen nodded. "Yeah. I understand. Is Andrew going to help with the key?"

"He'll be there, yes. Don't worry about it; you just get to the Wheel when you are able. Remember what we discussed. And remember to prepare yourself. You are patient number one. Always."

"I got it. Thanks."

They went their separate ways, Nathan to wherever he went, and Tommen to home. He didn't really mean to since he still wanted to talk to his dad, but it was habit. He gave the house a quick once-over, then texted his dad.

"Where are you?"

"On the side of the road in banjo country. Where are you?"

"Home. Do you have a road, crossroad? I have information that's really important."

His dad gave him the nearest approximate address, but he hadn't been lying when he said he was in banjo country. The Appalachians were home to the highest proportional poverty rate in the nation, and a lot of homes had no electricity or running water. But dammit if they didn't have a lot of guns and a great deal of mistrust for the government, everything from the feds to the local cops. His dad may as well have been a sitting duck with a huge red, white, and blue target painted on him. Nevertheless, Tommen tracked him down and pulled off the road in a blocking maneuver. Some things they didn't teach in driver's ed, but he understood them long before he got his license.

"Can you even be out this late unattended?" his dad wondered as he Banded and got in the passenger seat.

"Can't be too high of an offense if I just let myself in the cop car," Tommen rebutted.

"Touché. All right, does this big pot of information have anything to do with a meeting on Tacaga in a few hours?"

"How did—?"

"Little white bear sent me a message about five minutes ago. But she only said there was a meeting. Didn't say what it was about. Care to enlighten me?"

"Rifun has a plan of attack against the Borelians. Kayla's agreed to cooperate. Me and her are going to be sent after the third journal."

"Ah. Well, that would explain why she wanted me there, seeing how it involves you. What are the details?"

Tommen did his best to take an hours-long meeting and shorten it to a few paragraphs, the evening news version as it were. His dad listened patiently, expression grim but stoic. Even when Tommen explained everything as best he could, Walter remained silent for several minutes.

Finally, "Well, at least they're working together and it sounds like a halfway decent idea." His body language betrayed a deeper personal struggle, between defending humanity from the Borelians and allying with the one who would have destroyed them without a second thought merely a year prior. Tommen had the same misgivings. His dad went on, "They'll be going to Tacaga to make the announcement and round up their little followers from the colony planets, pad their companies with expendable grunts."

"What time is the meeting?" Tommen asked.

"Three in the morning. I told Kayla I might be a little late."

"You want me to get up to take you?"

"With you involved, I want you there. I want to hear more. You've been put through hell multiple times; I don't like the idea of you being coerced into going to the closest thing to hell itself this side of the grave. If there was a way I could go instead of you, I'd take it. If there was a way I could get you out completely, I'd do it. At the same time, I think you are being wiser and more cautious than I would be or would have been if our positions were reversed. For that, I give you credit."

"Thanks, I think."

"It's a compliment. Take it. Any timeline on when they plan to march off to battle?"

"No. If they're going to Tacaga to round up their allies from the other human worlds, they'll need time to sort them into their companies or whatever. We might have a few hours, up to a few days. I don't know."

"All right. Well, they'll want to strike quickly at any rate, keep the momentum moving forward."

"Makes sense."

"Do you have a plan on how you're going to break into Hell's temple?"

"We have the semblance of a plan, but a lot of it is going to be improv. Not a lot is known about the temple, what it looks like, the layout, any of that. We're kind of shooting blind."

He could see his dad did not like the sound of that. Tommen didn't much like the idea either. Problem was, he'd volunteered for this shit. Well, at least he would have Kayla with him, and as long as her anger was directed the Borelians and other adversaries and not on him, he felt pretty okay.

"All right," his dad grunted. "Well, not much we can do here on the side of the road. I'll see if I can't get off a little earlier so we don't miss too much of the meeting."

"Yeah." Tommen exaggerated a nod and looked around. "Huge crop of criminals out this way, I can tell. Hey, how'd that party go over the weekend? Eli was pretty quiet, Will is still pissed at him, and no one is saying much."

Now his dad laughed, more out of relief at the change of topic than anything. "Oh, I imagine so. Lucky for your friend, he was cleaner than a new penny when we got there. No drinking or drugs on or anywhere near him, but a lot of his so-called friends weren't so lucky. He dodged a bullet; now hopefully he's smart enough not to get in front of the gun in the future."

They chatted for a few more minutes before Tommen decided he needed to get home and get some sleep before heading off to the meeting. He got out of the cruiser, dropped the Band, and made for his car, turning around in the road and heading home. He didn't get half a mile before he saw flashing lights in his rearview mirror. He pulled over, thinking that his dad had something to tell him—whether about the meeting or because he might have had a taillight out, he wasn't sure—but the cruiser cruised on by. Tommen saw the ghostly outline of his dad talking on the radio. Back to work, then.

He arrived home and pulled in the garage. He couldn't really say if he did anything else that night; if he did, it obviously wasn't too important. He couldn't even remember having any dreams or nightmares before being shaken awake. It wasn't a violent shaking, and the worst that happened was a skyrocketing of his heart rate and blood pressure. Only his dad, then, with little desire to have to restrain him. Again.

"What time is it?" Tommen mumbled, rubbing his eyes and fighting his blankets to sit up.

"About quarter after three," Walter answered, stepping back.

"Oh. Okay." Tommen yawned. "Got off work early, did you?"

"Just a little. I punched out not five minutes ago. Come on, up and at 'em. We'll go to the meeting, and if we get back in time, I'll Band you before you go to school."

Tommen nodded and yawned again. He stood, stretched, grabbed his hearing aids, then took a quick shower before Banding to finish his morning routine, but without the schoolwork—yet. By the time all was said and done and they were ready to leave, it was twenty after three or so. Way too early, if anyone wanted his opinion. But then, such was the way of things when trying to coordinate the schedules of half a dozen worlds. Maybe it was the middle of the day for all the rest of them and only the Earthlings were being inconvenienced.

Whatever the case, he got them to Tacaga, back in the usual spot. The guards were new, he saw, probably his age. They let them through without much hassle, but they stared at Tommen, as if they couldn't believe that he was an example of what a non-engineered teenager looked like. He couldn't tell whether they were impressed or repulsed, and he wasn't even sure how he felt about the unwanted attention. Sure, all the Tacagans stared and-or sneered, but maybe he felt uncomfortable because they were his age. Maybe he was overthinking things. He really didn't want to think about this.

"No escort?" he wondered when they reached the other side and his dad procured a couple of bicycles.

"Not since the Borelian attack. They're diverting resources to more important things than just undesirable people. Things like, oh, I don't know, survival."

"Everyone's got priorities."

Nevertheless, they did not cause any mischief, simply rode to the nearest train station, politely turned over the bikes, and got on the train. Tommen wasn't big on public transportation, but it was a pretty nice ride without a bunch of Secret Service cronies crowding in around them, just waiting for them to try something sinister like looking around and maybe making eye contact with the other patrons.

They arrived at the governmental building and disembarked. Walter passed by the elevator and headed down another corridor. Even before they entered the room, Tommen heard the voices of the other leaders.

"What do you want me to do?" he asked before his dad could open the door.

"At this point, just listen," Walter answered. "If there's a plan, then there's a plan. I wouldn't presume to dissuade either Kayla or

Rifun from whatever they have their minds set to. Let them argue it out with the other leaders; I'm only here for information and to be kept in the loop."

"Understood."

They entered the room, neither sure what to expect. For one, all of the leaders were there. Toros and Milay from Tacaga; John and Andrew from Aleis, with Nathan as their guest, apparently; a giant and a dwarf—Tommen could not remember their names—from Sakaria II; two men and a woman—again, whose names Tommen could not recall—from Dorigis; Kayla and the Wolf brothers, Logan and Blake, with their allied leaders, Sifura and others whose names and races Tommen did not readily know, save for the D'Bok; Sem and Lin from Vin Lay; and Rifun and several of his advisor generals representing the militaristic side of the First Order of the Akari.

Sides had apparently already been taken, though it was tough to decide the winner. Vin Lay had already sided with Rifun, and Aleis now joined them, as promised. The Dorigisi looked disgruntled as they stood by Rifun; the vote from their world had probably only squeaked out the majority. But the Sakarians remained staunchly with Kayla, Hlohi, and her allies. As for Earth, Mi Chin had gone with Rifun, though she looked about as thrilled as the Dorigisi. Tommen wondered whether she had been more influenced by superior military strategy or similar philosophical views as her Vin Lay peers. Meanwhile, the Tacagans did not take a side, instead standing back and watching, unenthused. They were probably just waiting for the phone call to tell them they were free from being associated with the others in the room.

Everyone stopped to look at Walter and Tommen as they walked in the room.

"Sorry, are we interrupting?" Walter asked innocently.

"You're late," Milay said sharply.

"Well, we can't all be powerful leaders. Some of us work for a living. Please, carry on."

Whatever conversation or, more likely, argument they were

having, the appearance of the two men and the sarcastic remarks seemed to act as a stumbling block to the passionate train of thought, and the tensions deflated in a stunted sort of way. Tommen followed his dad to the wall opposite the Tacagans, putting Kayla's side on their left and Rifun's on their right. If a fight broke out here, there would be four referees waiting to call.

Oddly enough, the fighting itself did not seem to come from either Rifun or Kayla, or at least not from one to the other. Rather, it seemed to be the rest of the leaders who had a problem. The Sakarians felt as if they were being put on the frontlines because they were weird and different—and, in all honesty, they were, but it was a compliment, not an insult, though they didn't believe it. The Vin Lay had a philosophical problem with the armies being divided as they were, pushing for the Order and the Akarin to work together and balance their forces. Aleis, being only farmers and fishermen by trade, pushed for medic designation, ready and willing to treat both armies, regardless of Order or Akarin. The Dorigisi, despite siding with Rifun, wanted to lead the assault on the shipyard; true, their experience was more in the realm of sea-going vessels, but some among them did have spaceship talent and there were none more qualified or more willing to hijack a Borelian spaceship and do some damage.

Tommen found it all very fascinating, really. Forget Sun Tzu and reading ancient tomes; this was a real-life war tent where battle was being planned out. Well, it would be planned out once the measuring contest was over and everyone came to terms with the fact that Rifun and Kayla were kinda sorta maybe working together in a loose way to basically accomplish the same goals. No mention was made of the hostage negotiations or the journal except to mention that Kayla herself would be leading the charge on the Borelian temple. The way they spelled it out, it was something to placate her supporters. Rifun might be the tactical mastermind, but Kayla would be the heroine on the ground, leading the charge. Of course, this brought up suspicion of treachery, and Tommen couldn't stop himself from stepping in and assuring them that all was well; Kayla would be perfectly safe and was most definitely capable of defending herself.

He was largely ignored.

While all of this was going on, he tried to keep an eye on Andrew and Nathan, wondering if there might be some sort of cue to look for, some way of knowing whether their plans had changed as far as going to get the key. They gave away nothing. Hell, they barely even acknowledged his existence. It was as though they'd never even met.

After a short time, the Tacagans sent for food and drink, evidently weary of entertaining their guests and their hostility.

"I shall be glad to be rid of this," Milay hissed, quiet enough that she wasn't making her disdain obvious, but loud enough that everyone heard her anyway.

"Don't worry," the Dorigisi woman told her, meeting her like a couple of rich Hollywood cats ready to fight. "The after-party of our victory will be held on Dorigis. I'm sure you wouldn't be interested in sharing the victory or having drinks with us or anything."

"I'm sure we wouldn't."

Tommen sat against the wall to eat his food, knowing that both actions would do nothing to help his growing fatigue. His dad spoke to Kayla and others and generally made nice.

"So, is war as exciting as the Army makes it out to be when they visit your school?" Rifun asked, sitting about five feet away from him, crippled right hand awkwardly holding his plate, uncoordinated left hand deliberately bringing food to his mouth.

Tommen did not look at him as he shook his head. "It's a lot more complicated than I thought. I mean, I always figured that with large armies, you know, two armies, one battlefield, leading the charge for Narnia and for Aslan."

Rifun chuckled. "Hardly. Modern warfare is much more complicated than that. It's not ten thousand men storming the battlefield, it's ten groups of a thousand men scattered around the countryside, taking small towns and cities, fighting back and forth for days. We'd be doing the same thing if Brelix were more hospitable. In all reality, taking your entire army in for a single charge is a desperate and stupid thing to do. You never want to advertise your numbers, your strengths, your tricks."

"Then why do it?"

"Because we don't have much of a choice. Kayla's been doing very well, sending in her spies and assassins and small forces, but we have to follow it up somehow. She's the surprise right hook; now we have to deliver the uppercut before they can recover and prepare for the follow-up. If we're lucky, we catch them by surprise, devastate their shipyards and their temples, get out before they can really retaliate. Hide in our little holes and prepare to try again."

"Think it will work?"

"We're about to find out."

Rifun finished off the last of his food, then stood and slowly got the meeting back in order.

With food in their bellies and no one dead, planning went a little more smoothly after that. Rifun again gave the speech on Brelix's atmosphere and the length of time they had to get in, do some damage, and get out before suffering permanent damage themselves. It was about the only thing which got unanimous agreement and support. Whatever their internal quarrels, it wouldn't matter if they were all brain-dead at the end of the day.

Then came the actual strategic planning. The plan itself hadn't changed, but the lineup of the troops was a little different. The Aleisi were permitted to be the medics, provided they cared for all wounded, human and non-human alike. The Aleisi, Puritan Amish Pacifists, agreed. Tommen tried to catch Nathan's or Andrew's eye, but got nowhere. The Sakarians would be divided up. The dwarfs among them would fight with the Krydik and Sifura and the other non-human Krydik allies on the outskirts of Ancrath, the initial assault to get their attention. The giants would go with the Dorigisi and companies of the Order to the shipyards. If possible, any Dorigisi with knowledge of spaceships would commandeer said ships and use them to wreak havoc from the air and engage any Borelian ships that descended to give aid. A special detachment of Dorigisi troops would also accompany select Krydik warriors to find and destroy the remaining Council and Great Admirals and any Holy Men of War they could find—arguably the most dangerous mission as they would be far outside of Brelix and have zero backup. Vin Lay would accompany the Order troops attacking the temples.

And as far as anyone knew, Kayla would just be leading the charge on the temples, and Tommen would be somewhere in the mix. No mention was given of the journal.

Food was again called for. Tommen checked his watch. Shit, he had to get going to school. He nudged his dad in the ribs and showed him.

"Go ahead and go," his dad murmured. "You obviously know what you're doing. I'll fill you in on anything pertinent."

"What about you?"

"There are more than enough people here who can give me a ride home." He indicated Kayla. "Go on to school. Have a normal day."

Most parents told their kids to have a nice day. Do well on tests. Have fun with friends. Don't feel up girls in the hallway. Don't get in any fights. But for the two of them, the phrase was to have a normal day. Anything that happened, be it fights or feeling up a girl, as long as it didn't involve aliens, Time, or anything that would get someone thrown in an asylum, was considered normal.

Tommen hesitated, but nodded and quietly left the room. No one stopped him or even seemed to notice; he wasn't accosted by security, and he decided to just open a portal right there and go home. Why bother with a show of riding the train, then riding a bike, then crossing the bridge, and all that garbage? It was nice and polite when coming into the city, but when leaving, he just wanted to go home, and the Tacagans wanted him gone.

He wished his dad had come with him so he could Band and get a few more hours of sleep, but no such luck. Grudgingly, he packed his backpack and grabbed a quick breakfast of eggs and toast before running out the door. Becky was running a little behind and was still chomping on a bagel as she hurried out to the car and hopped in the backseat.

"Sorry, I kind of overslept," she said, pulling the seatbelt around her as Tommen made his way back into the street.

"No worries," he told her. "I've been up since, like, three o'clock, anyway."

"Insomnia?"

Battle plans, actually, but that's a pretty far-fetched answer for you. "Ah...nightmares. My dad kind of had to shake me awake. Gently. He's had to restrain me before, if he's too rough on the wake-up call."

He couldn't see her face, and he wasn't sure he wanted to. "I'm sorry. Wasn't yesterday your shrink session?"

"Yeah, but...I mean, it does help, with the waking part of things. I don't really have control over the nightmares, though."

"That's too bad. I'll pray for you about it, how does that sound?"

"I'll take all the help I can get. And while you're at it, tell the Big Guy to stop sticking His little Tommen voodoo doll. It hurts. Fine, we're all sinners and don't have much of a say, but there are a few people I can think of who could use a little comeuppance, or at least a good shakedown."

Becky sighed dramatically but did not say anything to that. Instead, she commented on a string of good weather that was supposed to move through the area in the next week and would hopefully mark a definitive turn toward summer, at least enough to clear the roads and sidewalks and give people hope that spring would return. Tommen agreed that it would be nice, but wildly predicted at least one more big storm before winter really gave up for the season.

They swung around to the Shaw house, but it was only Will and Sydney riding today.

"Brother sick today?" Tommen asked, backing out of the driveway.

"No, he rode the bus," Will answered. "We kind of had an argument."

"About the party last weekend?"

"Yeah. Dumbfuck went to it and the cops raided it. Found drugs and alcohol, the usual things at a party that size, you know. Well, your dad was one of the ones there, apparently arrested some of his friends. Eli's all bent out of shape, thinks you snitched and got them arrested, ruined their lives."

"Um, I did snitch on him, the whole party."

"I'm not saying it's a bad thing. I told him he shouldn't have gone and that he needs better friends. Well, he's pulling the hypocrite card on me. I guess it's fair, but I mean, I've learned my lesson. Sucks balls that I had to lose my sight before I learned, but I learned. I was kind of hoping he would have learned, too. He just got lucky he didn't get caught with any drugs or shit on him, otherwise he'd be up to his eyeballs in trouble, right there with his friends."

"Some people only learn through experience," Becky said, shrugging. "What's your mom think?"

Will shifted position. "Well, that's the thing. She doesn't know. She thought he was going to a sleepover at another friend's house. Got dropped off home early because the friend got some kind of weird 'stomach bug.' I told him that if he wants me to keep his secret, he's going to find new friends and stay clean. Well, he's clean already, for the time being, but he's going to stay that way."

"Is he finding new friends?" Tommen wondered.

"His current so-called friends are in heaps of trouble and spend their non-class time in Layman's office or at home under house arrest, so he's pretty alone right now. But I do hope he finds new friends. He needs 'em before he ends up in a worse situation than me."

Tommen elected to stay silent on the matter. His thoughts were suddenly filled with Ryan, his foster brother from Hell from way back when. Sometimes Tommen wondered whatever happened to Ryan, if he was in jail, in a gang, dead in a ditch, or if maybe he'd turned his life around. He'd never gone looking and probably never would, but occasionally he wondered about it.

They arrived at school, just another Friday. Mid-chapter quiz in Spanish, chapter test in Algebra, classroom day in English, presentation day in Pop Culture, and the last round of editing before turning in their first completed stories on Monday in Creative Writing. By all accounts, normal.

He and Mrs. Perez had come to a sort of understanding since the last test where she'd had it translated into Welsh. Mutual respect between adversaries, that's how he chose to view it. He'd appreciated the Welsh test, and he told her so, but that hadn't stopped him from correcting some of the grammar and vocabulary mistakes and informing her that her translator friends had used South Welsh whereas he spoke North Welsh. About the same difference as English as spoken in New York versus Alabama. But hey, he couldn't let her get any ideas that she'd won.

And so it went. Test in Algebra, classroom day in English. Lunch was different just because Eli decided not to sit with them. Becky invited him over, turned up her annoying charm to an eleven, and still got shot down with what appeared to be some molten hot words. Tommen couldn't hear exactly what was said, but he didn't miss how Eli looked at him several times. Clearly he'd been mulling this over for a while.

Becky returned to the table, unsure just how to take the encounter. She was accustomed to people bending to her will. Rarely did she meet anyone with a will as strong or stronger than hers.

"Dumbass is going to get himself in a heap of trouble," Will growled.

Tommen was ready to say something but got distracted as his phone went off. Becky easily took his place in the conversation while he checked his phone. It was his dad.

"Home now," the text read.

"Did the war start prematurely?" Tommen texted back.

"No, they've decided to hold off until they get the annoying Borelians out of their way. Besides, we may have bigger problems."

"How much bigger can you get? It's an assault on the Borelians."

"Believe me, I know."

"What's the problem? Where or who did it come from?"

"Dermos and Geros, of all things."

"You're joking."

"I wish I was."

"Must be a serious problem, then."

He could easily imagine his dad sighing. "Yes, I would imagine so."

"Okay, so did Kayla or Rifun mention when they're leading the charge?"

"At the time, they said twelve hours, so that would make it about ten hours from now."

Ten hours, and it was eleven o'clock right now, which meant nine o'clock tonight. Give an hour for the initial assault and the shipyards and stuff, maybe two hours, that made it eleven o'clock. Humans could only survive six hours on Brelix, and seeing how the battle was only meant to last long enough to milk the element of surprise and retrieve the journal, that meant the latest he would be up was five in the morning. That left him enough time to get home, and for his dad to Band him before he went to work. All was well.

It was fantasy, pure and simple. War and battle was not so simple; he'd learned that during the fortress siege. Just the complexity of the plan itself demanded a longer battle, waves of troops, one company relieving the last so they could recover from just standing on Brelix, never mind any injuries they might sustain. If he even made it to work in the morning, he wasn't going to complain about anything he was asked to do. He didn't think he complained about much now, but if he did, he was going to stop.

"Okay," he answered finally. "Ten hours. Are you working tonight?"

"It's Friday. Of course I'm working."

"I know you don't like to, but can you meet me in the Wheel?"

"Now? The shield is still in place; I can't get there on my own."

"No, later. Me and Kayla and Nathan and Andrew are going to get the key to the temple."

"And you want me there as a lookout of sorts?"

"Something like that, yes. And...just so I can see you. Before I go."

"Yeah, I'll be there. What time?"

"I'll text you to let you know."

"Do it as soon as possible so I can try to not be in the middle of something."

"Understood. Thanks, Dad."

"No problem at all. See you later."

When Tommen was thirteen or fourteen, he'd gotten it in his head that he was going to go into the Army, or maybe the Marines, and be a career soldier. Put in twenty or thirty years, lots of medals and commendations, lots of men under his command who looked up to and respected him, maybe do some consulting work for the White House or the Pentagon on matters of state and strategy, then retire with a nice pension and the satisfaction of a life well-lived.

His dad had never discouraged his fleeting dream, and there had been a bit of pride involved that Tommen had moved on from Ryan's antics and wanted to make something of himself, especially in such a noble venture. But there had also been a touch of fear involved, Tommen knew, that his dad could lose his one and only child.

Well, it was shortly after that dream fizzled out—he'd tried to keep up a strict diet and fitness routine only to be sidetracked by pizza and television—when he, Eric, and Varad discovered the forbidden pleasures of alcohol and marijuana. Then it all went straight to hell.

Now, having lived through one battle and heading straight into another, to speak nothing of everything else he'd survived before then, Tommen was glad he'd let that dream go. War was not heroic, and battle was not romantic. It was bloody and messy and terrifying. There was no thrill of the chase, just a breathless panic to make it from one safe spot to another and to hope that you're aiming for the right person when you do stupidly stick your head up over the wall like a Whack-a-Mole. Tommen had recently adopted the belief that if everyone was exposed to war at a younger age—real war, not poster propaganda—then most war might be avoided out of sheer terror. Or else it might cause more wars...out of sheer terror. People were stupid and unpredictable, and some days the best he could hope for was the ability to fulfill his no-kill vow, which seemed increasingly naive the closer he got to this next battle.

As if to mock him, both a Marine and an Army recruiter had set up little tables in the lobby outside the cafeteria. They handed out trinkets to the masses, marketing brochures to the mildly interested or the somewhat considering crowd, and step-by-step instructions to those juniors and seniors who were seriously interested but didn't know where to start and maybe weren't old enough to sign the dotted line just yet.

Tommen figured that if he was going to do something even remotely similar, he'd become a cop like his dad. At least then there were more clearly defined lines of right and wrong, and there was a justice system to help sort it all out, protect the victims and give the innocent a chance to go free. It didn't always work like it was supposed to, but it was better than the haze of battle.

Nevertheless, he perused both tables, picking up notepads and pens and lanyards and whatever other little goodies were laid out.

"Ever thought about the Army?" the recruiter asked him. He was easily a head shorter than Tommen.

"Um...at one time, long time ago," Tommen answered. "Before this happened." He indicated his hearing aids.

The recruiter simply nodded and watched him go. Tommen felt his ears turn bright red as he hurried away, meeting up with Becky at her locker half a second before the bell rang to send them to fourth period. It was a surreal feeling. He was just going along, minding his own business, about to go to Pop Culture to give a presentation and Creative Writing after that, and he'd be spending his night in battle in a temple on Brelix, half a galaxy away or even more.

Things that only happened to him.

"So you got the goodies, too," Becky said, indicating first the freebies he grabbed from the recruiters, then the freebies she managed to swipe.

"Did they try to talk you into joining?" he wondered.

"Oh, please, I wouldn't let them say no to me. Just imagine how useful I could be. I'm below most people's line of sight, so while the terrorists and the Army are shouting at each other and insulting each other's mothers, I just sneak up and sever the bad guy's femoral artery. Boom. War's over in six months."

"I don't think that's quite how it works."

"Yeah, the recruiter said that, too." She shrugged. "Whatever. Macho gotta macho, I guess. Can't let the dwarf girl get all the glory. I'll see you after school."

They went their separate ways. Presentation day was pretty standard, and the whole routine of the class had become pretty dull, which wasn't a bad thing necessarily. That just meant that everything was a predictable, set pattern. Mondays were always the same, Tuesdays were always the same, and so on; the only thing that changed was the decade.

Creative Writing was simply an editing day. Once the final edits were made, they had the whole weekend to polish up their short stories to turn them in first thing Monday morning. Their next unit was simply called "Chapter One" where they would have to write a story as if it were the first chapter in a book. Tommen wondered if he could get away with using the prologue from his first Authored Book. All he'd have to do was back-translate into Welsh to say it was his own, then submit the final work as his translation. Would that be considered plagiarism? If the book wasn't on the market yet, and wouldn't be until 2017, Reisig would never know the difference. But would some kind of holy wrath fall upon him from the Author? Would she be offended, or amused? Maybe he'd just stick with translating the stories he'd already written.

The bell rang for the end of the day. Will said he was going to ride the bus and do things around town, which left just Tommen and Becky in the car.

"Do you have to get home right away?" she asked as they neared her house.

"Depends on how long you want to keep me for," he replied, glancing in the rearview mirror.

"Mm...long enough to cook a hot dog or two?"

Dr. Polski was Jewish, so he didn't eat normal pork hot dogs, and his mistrust of modern food processing practices meant he didn't trust the "all beef" hot dogs either. Mrs. Polski was Catholic and so ate only fish on Fridays, but even so, she didn't like hot dogs of any form. So there were no hot dogs to be found in the Polski residence, except, Becky said, the one between Tommen's legs. Given that he was going to be running off into battle in less than six hours, Tommen was more than happy to oblige.

"Leaving already, Casanova?" Becky wondered, still lying naked on her bed while Tommen picked up his clothes.

"Well, I hate to fuck and run, but I do have to get home before my dad leaves." It wasn't entirely a lie.

"Guess I'll see you Monday, if not before." She got off the bed and approached him. "But before you go..."

For a long minute, he forgot what he was doing and why he needed to leave so quickly, and the best he could manage was a strangled groan as she did him again orally.

He couldn't even really remember when or how he got home except that he walked in the door to his house and almost ran straight into his dad.

"You know, if you really think you're starving, you can always buy your own food," his dad told him, a glint of amusement in his eye. "You don't have to raid the Polski's fridge every time we're low on snacks."

Tommen's mind went a thousand different directions at once, but all he said was, "Why would I do that?"

"Uh-huh." His dad let him through and shut the door. "So

what's the plan for tonight?"

"Survive."

"I gathered that. How about specifics?"

"I go to the fortress tonight. Once Sifura and the others lead the first wave of attacks, Kayla and I go to the Wheel to meet Andrew and Nathan, and we're going to get the key to the Borelian temple. Once we do that, we return to the fortress and wait for our signal. In theory, me and Kayla won't be doing much fighting until we actually get to the temple and go after the journal."

"Well, it's a nice theory, anyway."

"I know."

Walter folded his arms. "And where do I come in? I'm too damn old to fight on the battlefield, but sentry work, I can do."

Tommen nodded. "Yeah. Kayla will go to the Wheel first, but I'll make a detour home to let you know to meet us. Once you give the okay, I'll find you wherever you are, open the portal, and we'll all go together. We'll just have to see what happens after that."

"Fair enough." His dad sighed. "All right, I guess I'll see you tonight."

"Yeah. Guess so."

The only comfort either of them got out of it was the fact that they were both aware of the battle, both aware of Tommen's part, both aware of the danger. There were no secrets this time around. This time, they were both in on it, in some way. Tommen was fighting and Walter was more of a lookout, but they were together.

It did little ease the rock that had lodged itself in Tommen's gut as he headed down to his bedroom, collapsing onto his bed. The next thing he knew, he was waking up in a panic, sure he'd missed something. He felt good and rested, but he would have had to have slept more than six hours to—

"Easy, kiddo. Only me."

Tommen turned to see his dad in the doorway. A Band, then.

"I'll see you tonight," was all his dad said before turning and heading out. Tommen heard the door open and close, and then all was silent. It was only four-thirty.

After several long minutes of sitting on his bed and trying to collect himself, Tommen went out to the kitchen and made himself a light dinner. He didn't want to eat, but knew he should, at least a little bit. He might be able to scrounge up something from the fortress cafeteria later if he really got hungry.

He watched a little TV but couldn't say what the show was or what it was about. He tried to do his homework, but could hardly focus for more than a minute at a time. As his clock ticked six-thirty, he gave up and decided to just bite the bullet and go to the fortress. He just had to keep reminding himself that he wouldn't be on Brelix longer than six hours and that he would be home in less than twelve. As long as he held onto that belief, he could probably make it through the night.

But as he emerged from the portal room into the first floor of the fortress and saw the standing armies—both Order and Akarin—Tommen was suddenly hit with the gravity of the situation. These were two armies who, less than six months ago, had faced off against each other on the battlefield and over a big red button that could have killed all of them in a second. Now they were—well, they weren't united per se, but they were willing to work together for a semi-common cause, anyway. For the Order, it was about the journal. For the Akarin, it was about buying their freedom. But they were both going up against the Borelians, everyone acutely aware that some fates were worse than death.

They were outmanned, outgunned, and Tommen was going to walk into the heart of death itself to steal...a book.

He got sick. He didn't visit the fortress often enough or for periods long enough to know where the bathrooms were, so the best he managed was a quiet corner. He threw up once, twice, offering up everything he'd only just eaten and then some extra stomach fluid on top of that. He flinched at a hand on his shoulder but could do little more.

"Tommen."

Eyes blurry from tears, he could only just make out a glass of water being held out to him. He took it wordlessly, washed his mouth out, drank, washed his mouth out again, then drank until the glass was empty. Then he blindly took a cloth to wipe his face. When everything was clear again, he found Kayla watching him.

"Fuck," he whispered and looked away.

"I don't blame you," she told him. "Not everyone is cut out for war."

"Why did I volunteer for this? Rifun even told me that I was done; I didn't have to fight this time around. But I pressed him. I wanted to."

"It's the will of the Author. You remember what we agreed."

"I know, I know. But even then, why do I have to be the one to get it?"

"Because it was what you believed you had to do at the time. And you still do. To maintain Rifun's trust. I know it's scary. I'm not too enthusiastic about it either. Few here are, but this is necessary. Anything we want to achieve—be it the journal or freedom—we have to go through the Borelians to get it."

Tommen rubbed his face and sat against the wall. "I know. I talked my dad into coming with us to the Wheel as backup kind of sentry duty, just to make sure we don't attract unwanted attention from the Grandfathers and such."

Kayla nodded. "Not a bad idea. Come on. Let's get you cleaned up and find you some kind of armor and weaponry."

Chapter Thirty-One
Beware Trojans

Walter really couldn't say that it was worthwhile to stay on Tacaga after Tommen left. He certainly wasn't planning on fighting. His days of battlefield glory were long past; he'd been relegated to the easy stuff, like being a Time-talented cop on an Unengaged world, chasing after Runners with abilities so nascent that they may as well not have existed. All this charging into battle against foes who were deadly at just a touch and whose leaders were just as if not more Time-talented than him, that was too far beyond him, and his knees agreed.

The only information that he deemed pertinent was the timetable. The plans themselves were already solid; now it was a matter of making sure the right troops got where they needed to be at the right time. That meant that the Sakarians had to go home and divvy up their troops, the Dorigisi had to wrangle all of their space-qualified pilots, the Aleisi had to gather their medical supplies and practitioners, and so on. Then they were to assemble in the Order fortress in twelve hours. When there were objections, Rifun had only to point out that his army was making up the bulk of the main fighting force, the fortress could accommodate the entire army for a short period of time, plus it had food, water, and medicine available, and it wouldn't be disrupting any Unengaged societies—he looked at Sifura and her ilk as he said that.

Few were pleased with the arrangements, but it made sense. Rifun made a quick trip to the fortress with the other leaders, enough to get them acquainted with the fortress so they could hopefully open a blind portal there later. Walter could see Rifun's advisor generals had words and concerns, but they would not voice them here. Then they returned, no worse for wear.

"You may come at any time," Rifun told them. "But we move out in twelve hours, with or without you."

The meeting concluded shortly thereafter, but even then they could not immediately leave. The Tacagans always had to have the last word, and Milay and Toros blocked the door.

"Before you leave and go rushing off to save the universe," Milay began snidely, "we have a gift for all of you. Please, don't get the wrong idea. Consider it a parting gift, from us to you as our last day together, our last day of being human and being associated with you."

"The Borelians will come after you as surely as they will come after us," the Dorigisi woman said sharply.

Milay gave her a "bitch, please" look. "I think not. At any rate, take the gift. What's the expression? Don't count the sails on a free ship?"

Walter figured that was the Dorigisi version of not looking a gift horse in the mouth, though he wouldn't say he didn't have his own misgivings about a free gift from the Tacagans. If it wasn't a specially-crafted insult to each of them, it wasn't going to come without a price. They already owed a lot to the Tacagans. Hell, the Tacagans were finally gaining their autonomy, it sounded like. What more could they want?

The door opened and some servant or secretary or lackey brought in an ornate box which he handed to Toros. While the man handed one gift to each delegation, Milay explained, "We have only a small number of these—" Lie number one, Walter figured. "—so you will only get one per world. You may display them prominently or give them to whomever you choose. They are small shield generators, similar to the technology used to protect your worlds. The larger shields, as you know, had to be calibrated according to each individual world. Because these are not so sophisticated, they are hardly impenetrable, but they will buy you time in the event of attack. Their range is a dome approximately five hundred feet in diameter. They prevent not only portals from being opened, just as the larger shields do, but any use of Time at all. But you can also invert them and make it so you can use Time and even open portals anywhere in that five hundred feet. Useful for your Time agents who may not wish to call for a taxi every time they need to go to the Wheel."

"What's your price?" Kayla asked, turning over the device in her hands.

A few years back, one of his night lights had gone out. While in the store, looking for a replacement, he found little click-on, click-off lights. Like the clapper lights, but with less chance of incidental use. Some of them had timers on them, and Walter had gotten half a dozen of them, figuring that he could save some money by only having the light on while he was going to sleep without keeping it on all night. Plus they might prove useful in a power outage. Problem was, if he woke up in the middle of the night and the lights were off, he still panicked. So he went back to the regular night light. But he still had the little battery-operated click lights in case of power outage emergency.

The devices the Tacagans gave out looked very similar to the click lights, maybe four inches in diameter, two inches tall, softly curving dome with symbols and buttons around the outside he could not read or begin to understand. He handed it back to Mi Chin who would decide how it got used on Earth.

"We also recall that you decided to move your meetings to Dorigis," Milay went on, ignoring Kayla's question. "How is that going?"

"We would have been there today if Kayla had not beat us to it and called a meeting here," one of the men said, an enormous Scandinavian with unusually dark skin and long, black hair. "I expect our victory party will be held on Dorigis."

"Don't bother wasting paper to send us an invite, even as a courtesy."

"We won't, don't worry."

Milay gave a mocking bow to all of them and Walter saw

Rifun shift his stance noticeably. "Thank you for including us in your plans and doing business with us. We appreciate the opportunity to at last be free of you."

"Don't let the door hit you on the way out," Kayla sneered, pushing past her and Toros and leaving the room, Wolf Clan and her allies in tow. Dorigis was the next to leave. The woman and one of the men were small and so only rudely bumped the Tacagans in the shoulder, but the big man caused them to stumble off balance. The Tacagans were visibly irritated for only a moment until they regained their balance and could recover their snooty attitudes, though they stepped aside so the giants of Sakaria II did not do them worse damage. The Aleisi and Vin Lay left without much flourish.

Only the Earthlings and Rifun remained. Mi Chin headed out first, ignoring the Tacagans completely. Walter followed after a moment, and Rifun and his advisor generals were the last ones out. Walter heard them stop and speak to the Tacagans in low tones before leaving and heading down the corridor, catching up to the rest of them at the train station.

"What was that about?" Walter wondered.

"What was what about?" Rifun asked, his tone suggesting he wasn't about to tell and to just buzz off. Walter obliged.

They got on the train. Apparently, the group and its circumstances of arrival were of enough concern that security had been called back in to escort them out of the city. Because of the genetic engineering and lack of forged comradery from the first time around, it was difficult to say whether this was the same crew as before.

There was one notable exception—well, two notable exceptions to this, and that was Dermos and Geros. Dermos, the newest peacekeeper and the only one who had shown any signs of conversation and friendship. Geros, the veteran peacekeeper who just couldn't be made to give a damn anymore. If he wanted to talk to the outsiders, by God—or...chance?—he was going to do it; he was secure enough in his beliefs that he wasn't going to be swayed by overused slogans and catchphrases or pithy gotcha questions and debates. He wasn't a friend per se, but friendly enough.

That was on a normal day. Today was quickly shaping up to be anything but normal, and Dermos and Geros were no exception. Walter might have said that they'd gotten a reaming from their superiors and so that was the reason for their silence. That could very well have been part of it, but experience and body language said otherwise. Dermos had that look of a young man who was dying to say something but was unable to do so because he knew he was in hostile territory and didn't know how to go about it. Geros had that look Walter knew he sometimes got, when he was dying to say something but was unable to do so because he was in hostile territory and he had to work out how he was going to say it without actually saying it, looking for a workaround.

As per usual, the start and end of the train ride was unremarkable and imperceptible to the riders. One minute they were sitting down waiting to leave, and the next, the doors were opening again to let them off. It didn't hit Walter until they were disembarking that this was the last time he would ride the completely-efficient train. He wasn't coming back to Lip, or Tacaga itself at all. Theoretically, he could come back if he got a portal ride with Tommen or any Akari-bearer, but he had no reason to, and the Tacagans probably didn't want him back anyway. Might be that they put up a "No Humans Allowed" sign on their front door just as soon as they were granted racial autonomy.

But there was still that unusual feeling of walking away from something for the last time. Walter slowed his steps just a touch so he could look around a bit, but the crowd of humans and the wall of Secret Service blocked his view. Well, he was never much of a metropolitan man; he'd never felt at ease, even when he was a rich man in London. Charleston was about the most he could really stand. Maybe once he retired, he'd settle down in his next life, buy himself a cottage on a lake with fish and forest with game.

He shook his head as if to clear it, taking a bike and pedaling along with the others, as if on some Tour de France training ride. He couldn't retire just yet. It might give him more time to devote to fighting the Borelians, but he wasn't about to become the kooky old man down the street who wore a tin foil hat and yammered on about aliens. Work helped keep him sane, anchored in the real world, the same world in which billions of people lived peacefully, blissfully ignorant of the impending Borelian threat. He couldn't retire until that was all said and done with at least.

And in less than twelve hours, they would find out whether it would be all said and done with. There would either be a period of peace or else the Borelians were going to go absolutely nuclear ballistic, in which case all of humanity was screwed. And no matter what the Tacagans said about being granted autonomy, as former humans and the ones who aided humanity in the war to such a degree as to install shields that would prevent the Borelians from attacking via Time portal, they would still be targets, maybe even first on the hit list. At the same time, if they were intent on separating themselves, Walter wasn't about to make the Tacagans and their foolish arrogance his concern. Besides, they were more technologically advanced; they could probably hold their own. Maybe.

They reached the bridge and dropped off the bikes. Walter had a moment where he forgot what he was doing, only because he got distracted by the Sakarians on their bikes. The dwarfs had been given children's bikes, which made a lot of sense. But the giants, even getting the largest bicycles available, still looked like grown men riding a toddler's tricycle, and they had elected to jog about halfway through the ride. It was amusing in its own right, but there was an element of pity there as well, considering it was the best the Tacagans could manage for them. Oh well, it was the last time they'd all be here, anyway.

The peacekeepers had no final words of wisdom or warning, and the guest humans started across the bridge without ceremony, though Walter hung back for just a moment. Snobbish denizens or not, Lip was still a magnificent city to behold and the Tacagans really had achieved great things. He was just about to move, when Geros spoke.

"Walter."

He turned. Both Geros and Dermos approached. The older man looked more resolute in what he had to say, though there was a certain subtle current of nervousness in his body language. Dermos didn't even both trying to hide his anxiety and he cast uncertain glances toward the rest of the peacekeepers who were slowly moving off.

"Yes, Geros, what can I do for you?" Walter wondered, unsure where this was going.

Geros shook his head. "Not what you can do for me. What I can do for you, what you can do for yourself. You're an old-timer, a lot like me. I heard that you're a peacekeeper like us, on Earth."

"Peacekeeper, policeman, the fuzz, yes."

The old peacekeeper nodded. "You and me, we've seen things, heard things, felt things, and as much as they follow us, they teach us valuable lessons throughout our lives."

"Yes...?"

"Keep your eyes open. And watch your back. All you humans. The Governors have been up to something, and I don't believe the attack here was entirely an accident, especially the damage done to the basement of the governmental building." He went on before Walter could speak. "Word gets around. Something like that gets our attention, as you might imagine."

"Are you saying it was staged?" Walter wondered, his voice going soft so no one could hear. "What about Ehani, they were attacked at the same time."

"I don't know what to make of it or what to tell you. And I'm not about to go accusing my Governors. I think we can both appreciate that we don't control the laws; we only enforce them." Walter grunted in agreement. "But as much as that's true, my first duty is to the safety of the people of Lip. Your first duty is to the safety of the people of your city. I'm not telling you what to think, only to be on the lookout. Possibly for treachery or a surprise attack."

Walter nodded. "Understood. I appreciate the warning." He

looked at Dermos. "And you?"

Geros chuckled, the first almost-human thing he'd ever done since Walter had seen him. "As I said, I'm not about to go against my Governors, and he needs supervision on his first escort."

Loopholes were wonderful things. Walter thanked them again, wished them well, and headed across the bridge. He stopped about thirty steps in and looked back. The two men were getting a talking-to from their supervisor. Dermos looked like a scared little mouse, but Geros maintained his composure; he was too old to give a damn about the jawing coming from a man half his age.

Walter continued on along the bridge. Halfway across, he ran into Rifun.

"I assumed you might need a ride home," the long-haired man said nonchalantly, leaning on the railing and looking at the river thundering below.

"Everyone else appears to be busy doing your bidding except you," Walter told him.

"Delegation. I already sent my advisors ahead to begin making preparations. But if you want, I'll leave you here until someone notices you're gone. Might not happen until Tommen gets home, but that's assuming he goes straight home and doesn't spend the afternoon with his girlfriend. Then you would be late for work and that's not going to look good to a supervisor who already doesn't like you very much."

"All right, all right, I get the picture."

They continued walking, garnering stares from incoming traffic. Visitors. Tourists. Neanderthals.

"So what did your peacekeeper friends have to say?" Rifun inquired.

"Geros and Dermos, the friendly ones, if there were any friendly ones. Mutual respect, one old policeman to another," Walter answered.

He didn't mention the warning about treachery just for the simple fact that he couldn't exclude the possibility that Rifun had something to do with it, had an in on some sort of betrayal. Whether it was against the Tacagans solely, in league with the Tacagans against the rest of the humans, or, in some convoluted way, in league with the Borelians against Tacaga or the rest of humanity, Walter really couldn't say. But he couldn't just dismiss the gut feeling he was getting. He also couldn't tip off Rifun that either he knew or that he'd been warned about it. If it was against Tacaga, well, the snobs could deal with it themselves. If it was against the rest of humanity, then his first priority was his son and branch out from there. He certainly wasn't going to pretend to be John Wayne or even Micaiah.

Whatever the case, Rifun did not say anything more about the conversation and carried on in silence, his expression and posture saying that he was already mentally charging across the Borelian battlefield. Walter did not bother him.

The young guards on the far side of the bridge stared at them as they went past and offered an uncertain "Good day." Walter heard part of a low conversation as they debated whether that was a proper thing to do when it was Neanderthals involved, or if they should have just ignored them. Judging by the arguments, they'd been having the debate for some time now. Then they were out of earshot.

Rifun opened a portal into Walter's living room but did not go through himself, and as soon as Walter was home safe and sound, the portal snapped closed. A lot of business to attend to, then. Wars took up so much of one's time.

Walter harrumphed into his recliner and leaned back. Not a good idea as he broke into a yawn. He glanced at the clock. Eleven o'clock, so Tommen would be going to lunch pretty quick. Groaning, he got up and retrieved his phone.

"Home now," he texted.

"Did the war start prematurely?" Tommen replied a few minutes later.

Not necessarily, but that didn't mean things weren't going to get interesting. Why did wars have to be so complicated? Why couldn't it really be as simple as two armies, one battlefield, one side wears white, the other side wears black, and once the evil king or queen falls, that's it, end of terror. None of this betrayal and backstabbing and alliances and negotiating and uncertainty. Yeah, humans versus Borelians was pretty cut and dry, but where did the Order and the Akarin fall in this? What about the Tacagans? Why were all their strongest allies enemies among themselves? Why were they all wild cards in their own right? Why couldn't this be simple, dammit?!

He and Tommen texted back and forth for a short time. Neither Rifun nor Kayla had made any mention of retrieving Richard's journal from the Borelian temple. Everyone knew the temple was one of the main targets, but the journal mission was kept in strict confidence among the Order. Tommen outlined the basic plan for retrieving the key and getting the journal, theoretically an easy-in, easy-out with minimal fighting. Walter had his doubts. The Borelians were primarily atheistic, which meant that those who were religious likely defended their beliefs with a special kind of fervor, and invading forces were a pretty good excuse. Even for the nonreligious Borelians, the temples represented a major part of their history and identity, so they were unlikely to just stand back and watch.

Eventually, they came to an agreement on a plan. Well, it sounded like Tommen and the others already had a plan, but they needed a sentry. Maybe "needed" was too strong a word, but Walter wasn't about to turn down an opportunity to help his son in any way possible, especially when it came to something of this magnitude. He couldn't fight on the battlefield, but observe and report was something he was well-versed in.

"What time?" Walter wondered.

"I'll text you to let you know."

"Do it as soon as possible so I can try to not be in the middle of something." There was nothing worse than writing a speeding ticket only to get called away in the middle of it to go save humanity from Borelian slavery.

"Understood. Thanks, Dad."

"No problem at all. See you later."

Walter set his phone on the end table next to the book he was currently reading, reconsidered, picked it up again and poked around until he managed to set an alarm. Four hours wouldn't be much, but it was better than nothing, and there was no way he was going to leave his recliner again without a little sleep under his belt.

He no sooner closed his eyes than he jolted awake at the sound of the alarm going off. Sitting up and rubbing bleary eyes, he fumbled with his phone until he could punch off the noise. Dammit, he was too old for this. Still, it was better than nothing, and he hauled himself out of the recliner to the bathroom.

It was strange to consider, sometimes, the way that Time affected the body's aging. He'd been hovering around fifty years old for quite some time now. With the usual cycles of gaining and losing weight, styling of his mustache, and working out in the sun, he'd managed to pass under the radar from about forty to fifty-five years old here in Charleston. He might even manage to squeak it out until sixty, if he really had to. In that time, he'd obtained any number of small wounds and scars, from cutting himself while slicing potatoes to accidentally getting a bite or a claw from an angry cat to his knee injury last summer. Each and every time, he'd healed completely the wounds he could get away with healing completely, and others he'd merely helped along here and there.

But no matter what, the scars always remained. Some were more noticeable than others, depending on the severity, but they were there, criss-crossing his body like tally marks on a prison wall. He had a scar on his left thigh where he'd been stabbed in a bar fight. He had a ring of scars on the front of his right shoulder where someone had stuck him with a broken glass bottle. If he turned to look in the mirror, he could see scars where he'd been beaten with whips and sticks by the police and the guards in prison.

He sighed and pulled on his undershirt. Time did not heal all wounds, it seemed, no matter how much of it one used on himself, no matter how many years one put between himself and certain terrible events. He considered the mark on his thigh, twisted white flesh that, only a couple years ago, gushed blood because of a poison bullet. Time did not heal all wounds. Sometimes it only gave the infection a chance to fester. He pulled his up pants and tucked in his shirt. Then he strung on the belt and began loading it with fifty pounds of goodies.

Heading back out to the living room and kitchen, Walter could see Tommen's car parked in front of the Polski house. He glanced in the fridge. Well, it wasn't third-world-country level of empty, but it was a little sparse. Nevertheless, he made himself a quick ham sandwich, enough to get him through his shift. He could eat more, but really he just ate for the taste of food, so he could taste something other than his toothpaste. Rarely was he ever actually hungry. More mishaps from Time, he supposed, though he'd heard that those Time Agents who suffered from accelerated aging had to eat twice as much, if not more. Walter shook his head and swallowed. His waistline had enough problems as it was; he didn't think he'd be able to handle that.

He finished his sandwich and rinsed the saucer. He had just pulled on his boots when he heard the garage door open. Tommen switched out the cars. Walter went to the door and opened it, almost running into his son.

"You know, if you really think you're starving, you can always buy your own food," Walter said. "You don't have to raid the Polski's fridge every time we're low on snacks."

Tommen grinned cheekily. "Why would I do that?"

"Uh-huh." Walter took a step back and Tommen slipped inside, sitting down and taking his shoes off. "So what's the plan for tonight?"

"Survive."

"I gathered that. How about specifics?"

Those were sorely lacking, even as Tommen tried to make it as detailed as possible, though whether it was for Walter's sake or his own sanity, he didn't know. Two years ago, Tommen would have had all the bravado he needed to convince himself he was invincible and could take on the Borelian army all by himself. These days, he'd settled into his quiet little place in the universe, fully aware that he was a mere mortal, humbled and distraught from past battles, forged in fire and calmly resolute when he knew he had to do something (though where he got the idea that only he could retrieve the journal, Walter did not understand), but not seeking trouble in order to prove his macho might, instead seeing a psychologist in order to deal with what troubles had already found him.

As he wrapped up his short explanation, Walter folded his arms. "And where do I come in? I'm too damn old to fight on the battlefield, but sentry work, I can do."

Tommen nodded. "Yeah. Kayla will go to the Wheel first, but I'll make a detour home to let you know to meet us. Once you give the okay, I'll find you wherever you are, open the portal, and we'll all go together. We'll just have to see what happens after that."

"Fair enough." His dad sighed. "All right, I guess I'll see you tonight."

"Yeah. Guess so."

At least this time they were sort of in it together. Rifun wasn't holding either one against the other, wasn't springing this on either of them like a bad party. This time, everything was out in the open where the two of them were concerned. It was small comfort, but Walter would take whatever he could get in order to protect his son.

Right now, that meant helping him out a little. It had been a short night, a long morning, followed by all the fun of high school; Tommen was practically asleep on his feet. Walter followed him down to his room. Tommen flopped on his bed, asleep within seconds without even meaning to. Walter Banded him and gave him a good seven hours or so. The teenager wiggled and stirred a little before jumping into a panic and nearly falling off the bed.

"Easy, kiddo," Walter said gently. "Only me."

Tommen got himself flipped around and righted and looked at him. For a moment, he looked confused, and then it all came back together.

"I'll see you tonight."

And he left. No spectacle, no flourish, no mention of nightmares or meeting in the Wheel or the impending battle. If Walter could take any comfort in this, it was that Rifun valued the journal like an art collector valued the Mona Lisa; he was fully vested in getting the journal, which meant he had to keep Tommen safe. It was in his every interest to ensure Tommen stayed clear of danger all the way in and all the way out. Coupled with the fact that Brelix was largely inhospitable and they had to wrap things up as quickly as possible, by the time Walter got home from his shift, Tommen would already be back home in bed. All would be well.

Of course, this only left Walter wracked with guilt that he couldn't help. He was going to be back out in banjo country catching up on his paperwork while his son infiltrated a temple located in the black heart of Hell. It just didn't feel right. Now that all the secrets were out there, he felt as though he ought to have a bigger part. But unless he wanted to join Rifun's cult, the best he was going to manage was being an outsourced, minimum wage security guard. Observe and report.

He went outside and started his car, backing out of the driveway and carrying on as if nothing out of the ordinary was going to happen tonight. He was going to go to work. His son was going to stay home, do his homework (maybe), and raid the fridge before going to bed. In the morning, Walter would get off work and return home to go to bed. Tommen would get up a little bit after that to go to his job. Later on, Walter would be up again, puttering around the house until he left for work. Just the weekend routine. Nothing unusual there.

It left a bitter taste in his mouth, and Walter nearly choked trying to swallow it, making the turn onto the road leading to the precinct. He almost wished tonight would be a crazy night, just so he could stay busy with other people's problems, so he didn't have to sit alone in the dark with nothing but his thoughts and a mountain of paperwork to keep him company.

"Evening, Kate," Walter greeted on his way in.

"Walt," Kate replied, coldly formal.

He punched in, topped off his thermos, and checked the assignment board. Well, good news was, he wasn't exiled to banjo country. Instead, he got cast out to an area with half a dozen trailer parks littered across the hillside. Some of the people were totally normal, very decent people who just fell on hard times or couldn't quite make that leap into middle class. Then there was everyone else, and they usually fell into two groups: the old timers who just wanted to brew their moonshine and smoke or chew their 'baccy, and those who were the epitome of the term "trailer trash." Dirty, messy, didn't care for themselves, didn't care about others, living on welfare, dealing drugs, and causing mischief because they were unemployed and bored.

Friday night? Things could get interesting.

What was more interesting was what, or rather who, was missing from the assignment board.

"No Vin tonight?" Walter wondered, approaching Kate's office and knowing full well he could be opening a ferocious can of worms.

Kate did not look up as she replied, "Vin is taking some time off."

He raised a brow. "Is he coming back?"

"That remains to be seen."

She gave him a look that told him not to push his luck and to stop asking questions. Walter took the hint, said he was going to get moving, and left the area. He traded greetings with some of the other third-shifters before grabbing a set of keys and making his way out to his cruiser for the night.

He didn't even make it out to his patrol area before his first catch. Say one thing for the mountains, the roads through them were very hilly and curvy, and anything could happen. Any corner could hide a cop, as the speeders well knew. Why they continued to speed anyway was always a mystery to Walt, and he handed out a ticket, hardly half an hour into his shift.

His second adventure was more prolonged and came about as he was cruising along the road where most of the trailer parks branched off. He actually happened on the scene about sixty seconds before it came in over the radio. This time, instead of a mere speeder, it was a full accident. One of the trailers was having a raucous party and, in their infinite, drunken wisdom, decided to bring out the ATVs. Unlike some neighborhoods, where the adults usually had the decency to keep their partying away from their kids, in this park, the kids were the passengers on the ATVs. The worst part was, they were totally innocent; all they knew was that Mommy and Daddy were having fun and laughing and playing games and, maybe, finally paying attention to them.

While out running around, two ATVs, both operated by drunk men with child passengers, had gone out into the road. One was hit broadside by a car, and the other hit the car broadside. To make matters worse, the driver of the car, while sober, was not belted in. People went flying every which way and vehicle pieces created a debris field all across the road, down both ditches, up the other side, and into the trees.

As Walter called for backup and half a dozen ambulances, he had a strange sensation wash over him, that for some strange reason, he fully expected Laura to come rolling up on scene, demanding to know which patient was worst off so she could cart their ass to the hospital. But that was silly, because she was gone. She'd moved back to Minnesota. She'd left him. She wasn't coming back.

He shook his head and did his best to contain the scene, fully aware that his backup was easily ten to fifteen minutes out. It wasn't just about rendering crisis care, but keeping the drunk family and friends away from the scene as well. This was going to be a cluster, but when push comes to shove, human life takes precedence over scene integrity.

He went to the driver of the car first. A young woman, maybe thirty years old, partially ejected through the windshield; the only reason she hadn't gotten farther was the sudden shift in momentum when the second ATV hit the passenger side of her car. She was hanging around the A-post, front half through the windshield, back half through the driver's window, bawling her eyes out, complaining of head, back, and hip pain. Walter fished for a marker from one of his pockets and wrote a number 1 on her forehead. Then he moved on.

The driver of the ATV who'd hit the side of the car was now lying across both front seats, unconscious, bleeding from the head, though he still had a pulse. His breathing was bubbly and Walter could see dark fluid dripping from his mouth. Surprise of the century, none of the ATV people had been wearing helmets. He got a number 1 as well. He'd had two small children for passengers, one boy, one girl. The girl had gone up over the windshield and rolled off the hood of the car. She was scared and crying and just said everything hurt. Walter gave her a 2. The boy had been catapulted over the car, hitting the top once before landing on the other side. He was unconscious but had a good pulse and was breathing. Nevertheless, he got a 1.

As for the ATV that had been hit by the car, the driver had caught it square in the driver side headlight and launched a good twenty feet down the road. He was howling about his shoulder, his back, his hips, his leg. Walter couldn't speak for anything but the unnatural bulge in the man's left thigh and prominent bruising. He, too, got a 1.

The child passenger was nowhere to be seen in the light of the remaining car headlight or the cruiser's many lights. Later on, Walter would only say that God was looking out for the family in that he made it to the child before they did. The girl was no older than six or seven, lying, twisted and face down, in the ditch. Walter felt for a pulse and found none. As he rolled her over, he knew instantly that there was no hope. Her head flopped loosely from her spine and her whole left side, especially her head, was crushed, little better than a bag of popcorn. She'd taken it full-on from the grill of the car. Sighing, Walter took his marker and wrote a 5. As he looked around, he saw the fire truck pull up and block the road, leaving just enough room for an ambulance to get through a minute later. Their scene lights lit up, momentarily blinding Walter.

As the paramedics grabbed their cot and made their way into the scene, he got their attention and motioned them over.

"What do we got?" the lead, a middle-aged man, demanded.

Walter just gave a small shake of the head. "Nothing at all. Got a spare sheet on you?"

Both medics looked at the broken child. The second medic, a young woman who might have had a child of similar age at home, sucked in a breath and held it. The man silently handed over a blanket, and Walter gave them a rundown of the rest of the injured.

He climbed out of the ditch just as Kate pulled up in her cruiser and got out. Suddenly the scene was flooded with people, Walter realized. Firemen doing their best to control the crowd, medics running here and there with their patients, and Kate. She spotted him and made a beeline.

"What happened?" she asked.

"Drunk," Walter answered numbly. "Riding the ATVs. Came off the trail here. One hit broadside by the car, the other hit the car broadside."

Kate studied him. "What's the tally?"

"One dead. Six year old girl. My guess is, dead on impact. Best she could have hoped for."

"Shit." She put a fist to her lips. "Fucking shit. Where are her parents?"

"I don't know." He looked around at the crowd, appearing and disappearing in the trees. "Suppose we should start asking around."

Kate nodded. "Guess so."

After questioning the crowd and sifting through a number of drunk answers and conflicting stories, they got their answers. The girl's uncle had been the one driving the ATV. Her dad had been driving the second ATV—the unconscious man lying across the front seats of the car—along with her older sister and male cousin. Her mom had been back at the party making out with a neighbor. By the time she was tracked down, she had passed out drunk and naked in that same neighbor's bed. Using some vague almost-truth about her being in danger of choking on her own drunk vomit, Kate and Walter managed to get her on the way to the hospital via ambulance.

"When she comes around, I want a warrant," Kate said as they walked away. "Negligence and child endangerment. Hell, charge both of them with negligent homicide. The uncle, too. Shit, go after everyone at the party."

Walter nodded grimly. "I'll make sure the fax machine is stocked with paper."

They returned to the accident scene to find the state cops and the highway patrol had arrived and were enthusiastically taking charge. A fatal accident was one thing. A fatal accident where the dead person was a child of six years, that was enough to bring out the best and worst in every cop.

They introduced themselves, talked about the accident, took extensive notes, ten miles' worth of measurements, and a movie's worth of pictures. By the time everything got wrapped up and the road was reopened, it was easily ten o'clock.

"Come back to the station with me, Walt," Kate said, the friendliest she'd been in several weeks.

He did not argue with her, and he followed her back to the precinct. She motioned for him to follow her into her office, which he did, silently shutting the door behind him.

"Did I do something wrong tonight?" he asked.

"Go home, Walter," she told him, leaning against her desk and nearly sitting on it.

"But I still have—"

"Go home. Go home and be with your son." She went on before he could speak. "I don't care how tough you think you are. You saw a six year old die. You found her. You saw her. You touched her. Go home for tonight. I'll talk to Dean in the morning and see if he can't get the CISM counselor in tomorrow for you." She put up a hand. "It's not a suggestion, Walt. You know that."

He frowned. "I know."

"Exactly. And you know why. I'm only going to tell you once more tonight. Go home."

Walter sighed but nodded. He'd no sooner put his handle on the doorknob than Kate spoke again.

"I know I've given you a lot of shit about this whole debacle with Vin, but you're a damn fine officer, Walt, and you did good on that scene tonight."

He did not reply, simply left her office, punched out, and went to his car. Only when he was about halfway home did he consider that Kate's idea of going home to be with his son was different than what was actually going to happen.

Walter pulled over on the shoulder and sat for a long moment. He'd seen a lot of death, and for the most part, it didn't faze him a whole lot. But this little girl was different. In a way, it was almost as if she were his little girl. Little Victoria. Dead at someone else's hand and him powerless to prevent it. On top of that, his son was about to go running off into battle. For as much protection as he was allegedly going to have, there was no good way to control battle that Walter knew of, and anything could happen, any accident could befall Tommen. Where would he be then? He couldn't stop the war. He couldn't stop Tommen from going; he wasn't sure he would want to if he could. But all the same, where did he fall in this? What was his purpose now?

Walter wasn't sure where he stood on the whole Author business, but the thought lodged itself in his mind now. Tommen had Books, Micaiah had had Books, Rifun claimed to have Books. And all books had lead characters, the one the story centered around. Usually it was one or two, maybe a few more. But then there were the supporting characters, those who existed only to fill in the world around the main character.

What if he was only a secondary character? What if he just wasn't that important? What if he was only good for an object lesson about making poor choices, and that was why all of this was happening? Sure, God may love all of His creation, but did the Author? What was he to make of all of this? Truth? Hokey religion?

He didn't know how long he sat there on the side of the road, but the next thing he knew, his phone was ringing. It was Tommen.

"Yeah?"

"Dad, you free for a bit?" Tommen wondered, sounding not a

little harried.

"Uh, yeah. Yeah, I am. I'm just heading home, actually."

"Home?" Pause. "You didn't get fired, did you?"

"No, nothing like that. Listen, I'll be home in a minute. If we get a chance, I'll tell you about it."

"Okay. See you in a bit."

Click.

Walter waited several seconds more before tossing his phone in the passenger seat and pulling back onto the road. He Banded and made it home in no time at all. He walked in the door and found Tommen waiting in the kitchen, dressed in some kind of strange armor.

"Don't ask," Tommen told him around a bite of peanut butter toast.

"Okay, I won't," Walter said.

"Why are you home? What happened?"

So he gave an abbreviated version of events, talking about the accident, what happened, how everyone was drunk and drinking and ATV-ing don't mix.

"Who died?" Tommen cut in, finishing off the last of his toast.

Walter faltered, but finally answered, "The six year old daughter of one of the drivers."

"And you found her."

"Yeah."

"DOA?"

"Dead on impact is my guess. Best she could have hoped for."

Tommen nodded silently. "Got the whole weekend off or just tonight?"

"Just tonight. They're going to try and get CISM counselors into the office in the next day or two."

"Okay." Pause. "You feel up to coming with us to the Wheel?"

Walter raised a brow. "Sentry duty? Cakewalk."

"If you're sure."

"I am. Let's go."

He could see his son was still unsure. In a way, it was both embarrassing and infuriating. He didn't want to need help, and yet here he was. Five years ago, he would have followed the orders to go home just to be polite, even as he knew he could shake it off pretty easily. Now, though, he followed the orders with only minimal resistance, taking it as a relief to go home and get some rest, even if he hadn't been doing a lot of physical work. Tonight might not have been so bad, except...Victoria. Somehow, deep down, he knew that if Victoria had grown up, that was what she would have looked like. Innocent, perfect, with fine brown hair, dark eyes, soft curving nose, thin lips, bright smile, petite, if all limbs, maybe not riding ATVs and getting into that kind of trouble, but adventurous nonetheless.

His thoughts flickered back to the sensation that had momentarily dazed him as he called for assistance, that feeling that Laura was going to show up. He couldn't explain it. Damn, he was getting old. He didn't know how much longer he could do this.

When he finally came back to himself, he found Tommen studying him intently.

"Are we waiting for something? For Kayla?" Walter asked.

"Waiting for you, honestly," Tommen murmured. "You sure you're okay to do this?"

"Yeah, absolutely. Come on, let's get on with this before you have to go running off into battle."

It was a second or two before Tommen assented and painstakingly opened a portal to the Wheel. Walter stepped through, momentarily stunned at the feeling. He hadn't been to the Wheel in a while, had almost forgotten how awful it felt to get there, the air sucked from his lungs, the strength from his limbs. As he came back around, finding himself on all fours in the portal room, he recalled Tommen's explanation that the Wheel of Time was the center of all black holes. It sounded ludicrous, but then, wouldn't everything about Time sound ludicrous to people who lived securely with the belief that they were alone in the universe?

He got to one knee, them pushed himself to something

resembling a standing position. Beside him, Tommen stumbled through the portal and forced it closed. With his strength and attention divided, he fell to his face on the floor. Sighing, Walter went back down on one knee and put a hand on his son's back. Tommen mumbled something into the floor.

"What was that?"

Tommen lifted his head. "I said I'm fine."

Walter raised a brow but said nothing, just got to his feet once more and eventually helped Tommen to stand as well. They looked around.

"So, are we supposed to wait for Kayla here or is there a rendezvous?" Walter wondered.

"I think she's supposed to meet us here," Tommen said. "Honestly, I'm not a hundred percent sure."

"Don't worry, I'm here."

Kayla's voice preceded her appearance as she crossed the portal room to meet them. "Seeing how the coordination wasn't completely nailed down, I figured it best to just wait here for you. Andrew and Nathan have already gone ahead." She looked at Walter. "Are you joining us, then?"

"I'm just here as a lookout," Walter told her. "Make sure nothing happens to you guys while your backs are turned."

She dipped her head. "Fair enough. Good to have you along. Let's get moving."

Chapter Thirty-Two
The Heart of a Black Hole

For a short time, while Kayla got Tommen outfitted with armor and weaponry, it was almost easy for him to push aside the thoughts of war. It sounded strange, but he managed to equate the armor with going to a Halloween party, assuming that party didn't blow up. But overall, easier than the alternative. Maybe because the armor did not resemble anything the U.S. military was currently wearing. Maybe because it felt a lot like cosplay, or maybe they were going to go out and reenact famous battles from history. Judging from attire, the era was probably going to be Japan, the time of the samurai, assuming they took fashion advice from seventeenth century pirates.

Brelix was dark and very unstable, littered with highly active volcanoes and trembling with earthquakes. Most of the land was dark and rocky, and Ancrath was a city built of stone. Even the small stretch called the Fertile Lands which surrounded Ancrath were dark with rich volcanic soil. According to intelligence, Ancrath was entering its winter season, about late October or early November by comparison; the harvest was in but it wasn't full-on winter yet. Furthermore, they would be attacking in the early morning hours. When the call had finally come and Sifura led her armies in the initial attack, it was about three or four in the morning, comparatively speaking. Because Brelix was bigger and had a slower rotation, it would stay darker longer, giving the attackers the advantage.

Only then did reality come crashing back down on Tommen as he, Kayla, Andrew, and Nathan made their exit. Kayla, Andrew, and Nathan went straight to the Wheel, but Tommen headed home first. He called his dad, then stuck some bread in the toaster and got out the peanut butter. Getting costumed had left little time for eating, but he didn't want to stuff himself because he knew he would only get sick on it later.

He managed to push aside his own dread for a little while longer as he talked to his dad and learned of the hell he'd already gone through that night. Tommen knew his dad was tough and weathered some things better than a lot of the guys at the station, but he also knew that every rock got worn down eventually. Death of a little girl, son about to run off to war, his own personal demons, Tommen knew his dad was feeling it. But, hey, let's go piss off some Hands and a few Grandfathers.

Nevertheless, his dad insisted, and the two of them went to the Wheel, meeting up with Kayla and starting out on their secret mission. Tommen had never felt more conspicuous, even when he'd returned from Sifura's world with the hasax and had escaped the Grandfathers' clutches by the skin of his teeth. Maybe because at that time, he had only been using the Wheel as a bridge, just trying to get through from one place to the other. Even in defying the Hands, the Wheel was just a meeting place, like any given Starbucks.

This time, though, they were going to that Starbucks with full intent of burning it down. Andrew and Nathan had been mum on the specifics, but they assured him that once they started playing with the Core of the Wheel and once the key was removed, everyone would feel it. Everyone would know. And someone, most likely the Grandfathers, was going to come running. Which was where Walter came in.

"Do they have to do a full Rebuild, or just enough to get the key?" Tommen wondered as they entered the main Wheel.

"I don't know," Kayla answered, and her tone sounded sincere. "I'm not a Builder. But I don't think it would kill them to do something about this awful steampunk thing they've got going."

"So if Rifun wasn't able to do much more than a little redecorating, what's the difference between what he did, turning everything into freakin' Shakespeare and a little bit of Africa in the corner, and a true Rebuild?"

"Redecorating is just that. Redecorating. Changing the desktop theme, as you put it. When the Hands changed Shakespeare into steampunk Shakespeare, even they only did a little redecorating, probably because they had little desire to call in another Akari-bearer for a Rebuild. The fear was too great. Rebuilding is taking the dimensions themselves and relayering them, completely restructuring them. Like I said, I'm not a Builder, so I don't know the specifics."

"If the Wheel is the core of the black holes, then messing with that has got to have ripple effects throughout the entire universe."

"The more changes, the more waves, I would imagine. Power and responsibility and all that."

Tommen thought back to Chandler's story about the different Rebuilds. Which one was it? The Second Rebuild? Where the Author herself destroyed the Wheel and sent shockwaves so powerful it fucked up entire planets and species. Shit. Had there been some sort of cosmic rainbow afterwards, where the Author promised to never fuck up the universe like that again? Had there been any arks involved to save some people at least?

"If the Wheel is the core of the black holes," his dad began thoughtfully, "then how did it get here in the first place?"

"The Wheel isn't just the heart of the black holes," Kayla said. "It is the heart of creation itself, hand-made by the Author."

"But black holes suck things in. Seems like it should spit things out, if that's the case."

"Perhaps, or perhaps it is the wisdom of the Author that makes it so it requires a little effort to get here. Or maybe there are other reasons for it that have been lost to history. All things fall into legend eventually."

Moving through the Wheel, Tommen felt more than saw that there was a certain level of anxiety present in the crowds, from the lowest marketplaces to the Auctionhouse lobbies. He had a hard time placing the familiarity of it except maybe to compare it to the feeling around sports stadiums or college campuses. Something was brewing in the American subculture. Part of it was born of fear in the wake of shootings and bombings taking place across the country, and part of it was born of fear and frustration and political ideology as polite discourse turned into rabid mobs intent on bullying their way into office, or bullying others to stay out of office or keep them from speaking on college campuses.

This was a bit like that, not the tension before a mob, but the anxiety of the rest of the people, the calm, rational, law-abiding people. They wanted to hear the speaker, they wanted to have a civil debate, they wanted to be politely engaged in affairs or else just go about their business. But what about everyone else? Was everyone else so like-minded, so civil? Was there someone here ready to start a mob? Could there be a shooter in the midst of the crowd? Could there be a bomb? What would happen then? How would I react? Where do I go? Who do I tell? Who is here with me that I have to make sure is safe? And as the time of the event draws nearer, when a hugely-anticipated game begins, when the speaker comes out on stage, that anxiety grows. Some are completely oblivious and some are more paranoid, but the undercurrent of anxiety increases and people wonder just how safe they really are.

Looking around, the Time Agents were a lot like that. Oh, marketplaces were packed and transactions were occurring at the speed of Time, but there was a subtle nervousness running through the crowd. And why not? The Zero Hour Revolution was still pretty fresh in the mind. The Borelians were conspicuously absent from the Wheel. The Cult and the Akarin had had a bit of a falling out and the Akarin, the saviors of the Wheel and the Time industry, had lost. Now the Cult was rumored to be going after the Borelians. Humans were going after the Borelians. Rifun Ndolo was both. Rifun was alive and well and reputed to be leading both sides with the help of Kayla, the wife of the former leader of the Akarin. Despite reports that he had said he wasn't going after the Time industry again, and evidence that Kayla was hardly a willing accomplice, was there any reason to not be skeptical of his claims? Was there any reason not to think that the

Time industry wouldn't face some repercussions?

"Do you think they know something is about to happen?" Tommen murmured.

"You feel it too, then," Kayla stated. "I don't think feeling has become knowing yet."

"No," Walter said. "They know. In fact, they're waiting for it."

"What makes you say that?"

"Call it a hunch, a police instinct."

Tommen knew better than to argue with his dad's police instincts, and he ratcheted up his own vigilance, keeping his head constantly on a swivel.

They made it through the marketplaces no worse for wear, and without being stopped by any Hands or Grandfathers. Kayla led the way, doubling back through a couple marketplaces, just to make sure they weren't being tailed. When Tommen asked who, other than the Grandfathers, would be tailing them, seeing how both the Order and the Akarin had a vested interest in their mission, she refused to say. After a few times back and forth, she appeared satisfied that they were clear to continue. That did not mean that it would be an immediate straight line as she took them on another detour or two before finally ending up in the Archives.

"It makes sense now," Tommen stated as they crossed the lobby and stood on the balcony overlooking the Archives. "This is the fold, where all the dimensions come together, layered one on top of another, almost infinitely."

Kayla nodded. "The truth tends to do that, bring reason to chaos. It doesn't make it any easier to look at, though."

"It's an optical illusion. You might know the answer in your head, but your eyes can only process so much." Another revelation hit him. "That's how Rifun was able to redecorate the Wheel, despite having no Building experience."

"His blindness."

"Yeah. You know about that?"

"I read his Books."

Tommen nodded. "He can't literally see this, but his brain can process it, pick it apart into its pieces. That's how he was able to pull it off, make it look like a Rebuild even if it wasn't. An optical illusion for the rest of us who didn't understand."

"Precisely."

"So we have to get past the optical illusion into the mechanisms. We have to find where all the folds come together, which is where the Core of the Wheel is hidden."

"That's right."

His dad shook his head and rubbed his eyes. "I'm lost in all of this." He went on before Kayla could speak. "Honestly, at this point, don't bother trying to explain it to me. Maybe save it for after you guys get home safe and sound. For right now, I'm just your bodyguard. I'm just here to make sure no one sneaks up on your backside while you're playing with the fabric of creation."

Kayla nodded, her expression reverting back to cold resolve. She turned on her heel and started off down the balcony into the Archives, Tommen and his dad trailing. How many times had he walked through these stacks, never understanding just where he was, never realizing that he was jumping through the folds that held the dimensions together. Looking around, the stacks all appeared innocent enough, but looking out into the atrium revealed the fine lines, the folds, to those who knew what they were looking for, like cracks in a pane of glass that could only be seen at a certain angle. How had he missed them, all the times he was here looking for the answers and they were right in front of him? What else had he missed?

They moved through the stacks, going deeper and deeper into the Archives until Tommen was sure they were completely lost. Briefly he wondered what the map would show, if he brought one up. Then he wondered how the Archives were able to have a map if the whole place was folded into several different dimensions. Then he wondered, if, knowing that, the Archives could have a map, why the rest of the Wheel couldn't also have a map. It would certainly make things easier.

Kayla slowed her quick pace as they wove here and there

through stacks, finally ending up at a spiral staircase, a chain across it with a small, digital sign displaying "Employees Only" on it. How quaint, Tommen thought. Then he considered that where there was, or there was supposed to be, several more floors below them, and everything was very well-lit, this particular staircase descended into darkness.

"This leads to the Core?" Tommen wondered.

"No, this leads to the employee break room. Down the hall is the Core," Kayla answered, her tone making it difficult to judge her seriousness. She looked at Walter. "Can you whistle? Like, loud, shrill, ear-piercing, make dogs howl and children cry?"

"Sorry to say, I don't think I have the talent. But if we have any trouble, are gunshots loud enough?" He indicated the gun still on his belt.

"They just might be."

"You want me to stand here?"

She shook her head. "No. Too conspicuous. I want you to watch the stairs without being an obvious guard."

Walter nodded. "The undercover cop. That's great, but I'm still in uniform."

"No one is going to know what it's for. Besides, as long as you're just perusing the tablets for information, you could be here for any reason. Who is going to tell you what the dress code is for the Archives, hm?"

"Yes, ma'am." He glanced at the nearest row. "What section are we in, anyway?"

"Hell if I know. Can you do it?"

"I expect so." He looked at Tommen. "Be careful. I don't know what's going on, but like I said before: few causes are worth dying for. Rifun's isn't one of them."

Tommen managed a lop-sided smile. "I know. I'll be careful."

Walter looked back at Kayla. "Keep him from doing anything stupid and make sure he doesn't hurt himself."

"I can only try," Kayla said, sighing dramatically and giving

Tommen a look. Then she grew serious. "But we're on a timetable. We have to get moving. Anything happens, we'll be listening for your gunshots. Don't wait for us, and don't come down. If we hear shots, we'll get as close as we can before trouble, then we'll just bust out using a portal. Get yourself to safety. We'll come back for you."

"Roger that."

Kayla made a motion. "Come on, Tommen."

Tommen obeyed, ducking the sign and casting one last look at his dad before following Kayla down the stairs into the darkness.

It was almost like a mini-portal in itself, like wading through freezing, chest-deep water. His breath came in short, ragged gasps and every muscle in his body tightened, sending currents of pain racing up and down his left arm and he once involuntarily made a full fist, forcing his stagnant fingers to move past their points of comfort. He clenched his jaw and told himself to just put one foot in front of the other.

Suddenly, his feet felt warm, or warmer compared to the rest of him. As he descended, his legs and hips also began to feel warm, just like walking into a room with the furnace on. It wasn't until his chest and abdomen broke the thermal threshold that his muscles released and he sucked in several breaths, sitting down on the steps and cradling his left arm, flexing his hand as much as he dared, stunned by the pain more than debilitated by it. He felt hot and cold and pins and needles all at once. Kayla knelt on the steps just below him.

"You okay?" she asked.

"Fine," Tommen answered quickly, the pain subsiding as swiftly as it had come. He stood. "Fine. Let's go."

She did not argue, merely turned and continued the descent. He followed, keeping his arm close to his body.

When they finally touched down, it was in a circular room about fifty feet in diameter with one room off to Tommen's left and five hallways branching off in multiple directions. The overall feel of the room was how the main portal room used to look, back when it was one big room and not multiple smaller rooms, a dark, sci-fi feel to it, with metal and electronic-looking panels all around. Tommen half-expected to see a Klingon walk around the corner.

"What is this place?" Tommen wondered.

"Employees only," Kayla answered. "Honestly, I've never been down here before this. Down one hall is where the Scouts bring all new information for coding and processing to be made or added into tablets. Down another hall is where the secretaries work on the translators and the language software, keeping it all up to date. That room there is, as I said, an employee break room, of sorts. A couple of the halls, I'm not sure. But one of them is supposed to lead us to the Core."

"Which one?"

"This one," a new voice said.

Tommen had a hard time making out the man's features as he walked down the hall, but the voice he was pretty sure belonged to Andrew; it was hard to tell as the room had strange acoustics. Kayla headed toward him, but Tommen stayed a step behind. Shit was about to get real. Sure, they'd all come to the Wheel and sneaked into an employee only section like a group of mischievous hooligans, but as soon as they went down and started to play with the core of the Wheel, the fabric of creation, there was no walking about from that. There was no "oops" or undo or anything like that. Once that process started, they were committed.

"We must hurry," Andrew went on, turning and starting back down the hall. "We're running out of time. The second attacks are about to begin, and we have to be ready to go. Nathan is already waiting and ready."

"How many Builders does it take to do a Rebuild?" Tommen asked. "Or even just to do...whatever it is you're going to do?"

"One is all it really takes," Andrew answered amiably enough. "But the more you have, the easier it is, as long as you're all on the same wavelength. In the stories from the old days, Builders who entered a class together took a binding oath to work with each other as a team, though they used the word 'coven' up until the fifteenth century when the word became more synonymous with witchcraft. It was a group of five to ten Builders, though six and eight were most common. They were tasked with becoming so in tune with each other that if they were called upon for a Rebuild, they would move and work as a single unit. Builder covens who were acrimonious and out of sync could do terrifying damage to the universe if permitted to work. Fellowship was key.

"Unfortunately, it has fallen out of practice, and these days, two or three is the best we can hope for, and even then, while the Builders may be friendly, it is nowhere near the level of the old covens, and our work is mediocre at best."

Andrew sighed. Tommen glanced at Kayla who did not react.

What, then, had the Wheels of old looked like? What defined the greatness of the old Builders? Was it beauty, turning the Wheel into the Garden of Eden? Was it simplicity, making it as easy to navigate as possible, maybe even possible to map it? Was it complexity, folding the dimensions down and making them as compact as they could be? Was it defensive capabilities, making the Wheel impossible for the likes of Rifun to conquer, or conquer easily? Was it some other standard that determined whether the work was superb or sufficient?

There were no rooms in the corridor that Tommen noticed, and at the end there was only another spiral staircase leading into darkness. Andrew went first, stepping down confidently. Kayla made a motion for Tommen to go, which he did, and she brought up the rear.

The first staircase had been like wading through water, difficult in its own right, but generally easy to do as long as one had good footing and any kind of leg strength. This time around, it was like pushing through tar. It was heavy, sticky, suffocating, and almost impossible to move through.

"Be careful," Andrew said, somewhere in the murk. "Always be conscious of your steps. It's a long way down to the Core. And don't forget to breathe."

So they really were going to the Core, and all it took was going the way of the sabertooth, caught in a tar pit and preserved for a thousand years. As the blackness swallowed his legs and chest, Tommen found himself instinctively holding his breath, waiting for something cold and wet to touch his neck, lap up against his mouth and nose. Again, his chest tightened. He opened his mouth as if he were drowning and trying to call for help, and he fully expected to swallow something, be it water or tar. Nothing came rushing into his throat to suffocate him, but the pressure against his whole body was bad enough.

Be conscious of his steps. He couldn't even remember how to step. He couldn't remember how many steps he'd taken. He couldn't see anything, dammit. The only thing that really anchored him to space and time was his hand on the railing. He focused on that, told himself to just take one more step. His feet felt like lead weights, and he didn't lift them so much as he scuffed them along each step until they fell to the next one down. The farther down they went, the worse it got until he was pretty sure he came to a standstill.

Wasn't there supposed to be an ancient, undead army down here, or even a couple zombie guards? Where were the booby traps, the puzzles, the riddles, the fake treasures hiding the real treasures? He hadn't even seen or felt any spider webs. Where was that decision of life and death, where the entire adventure and the entire future of the world hung in the balance? Oh, yeah, Andrew and Nathan were those heroes. They were the ones messing with the Core. But he and Kayla would be charging into the temple.

In that moment, Tommen decided he didn't mind the tar and the murk and the darkness. He forced himself to suck in a breath. This was still ten times easier than whatever they were going to face in the Borelian temple. The more he contemplated that, the easier it was to move, or maybe it only seemed that way. Maybe his fear was propelling him down the stairs. The only reason he knew he wasn't falling down the stairs was because his head was still upright. Or he thought it was. In the Wheel, anything was possible, including walking on the ceiling.

He paused briefly, but he couldn't hear either Andrew or Kayla. Andrew might already be down and waiting, but there was no way Kayla could have passed him. So they were all sticking together, right? Maybe it was just the darkness playing tricks on him. Maybe there was some sort of psychic forcefield in play, so that only the worthy adventurers could pass into the core of the Wheel. That sounded pretty adventurous, right?

Andrew had mentioned that it was a long way down to the Core. What he failed to mention was that the "long way down" was less about the stairs themselves, and more in reference to the distance between the last step and the floor. The tar had no sooner released Tommen to breathe than he was falling and landed hard on a solid floor. If he'd had any air in his lungs, it was gone now, and he just managed to instinctively roll away before Kayla landed on top of him.

He lay on his back and looked up at the stairs, only the bottom two visible from his position; the rest were swallowed in darkness. Then he realized that he could see the stairs, though the whole atmosphere was like that of watching TV on a big screen in a dark room. He coughed, picked himself up, and turned.

The Core of the Wheel took dozens of shapes at once, an optical illusion that changed shape every time Tommen tried to pin something down. First, it was like a bunch of strings coming from all corners of the universe, amassing into a huge ball of light in the center. Then it was a piece of cloth with a mind-numbingly intricate pattern. It changed yet again, this time strings on a musical instrument, humming and thrumming with life. Then another change, a computer grid, but not in 2D, or even 3D, but somehow in 5D, accounting for Time and Space.

Tommen went to his knees, unable to look at it straight on.

"Welcome to the Core of the Wheel," Nathan greeted, patting him on the shoulder. "This is where black holes meet, where dimensions fold over themselves and create this little pocket of mindfuckery called the Wheel of Time."

"You hid the key in there?" Tommen breathed.

"Yes," Andrew said simply. "Now we're going to get it out."

"How do you do that?"

He stood on legs more unsteady than a newborn calf. They stood on a platform, complete with a polite safety railing, looking out into the light. When Tommen dared approach the edge and look over, he didn't see light tapering off into mere darkness; he saw infinite. He saw everything stretching on forever, to the far corners of the universe still expanding. Nathan pulled him away from the rail and got him to sit with his back to the core.

"Best not to look at it for too long," he cautioned gently, though his voice sounded distant to Tommen's ears. The Core of, not just the Wheel, but creation itself. An optical illusion too complex for the human brain to handle. He hardly noticed when Kayla sat down beside him.

"Keep it together. We're here on a mission." Her words sounded as much for herself as for him.

"It will be best for you to sit there and wait while we do the work," Andrew said behind them. "We'll call you when the key is ready to be retrieved."

Tommen stood drunkenly and turned. "No. I want to watch."

Andrew frowned, approached him, and sat him back down, facing away from the core. "Tommen, when the Author chooses an Akarin to become a Builder, that person must spend weeks, even months in prayerful meditation. The studying and the workload is unbelievably intense; it makes the Marines look like dodgeball at recess. The whole Building course, with or without the covens, is a decade long. Part of it is because of the seriousness of the power, but it is also building mental and psychological fortitude to face this sort of magnificence. And even I am still in awe. Tommen, you would not survive."

Tommen rubbed his eyes but did not respond.

Andrew sighed. "Obviously, you felt the resistance coming

down the stairs. For non-Akari-bearers or simply those of weak will, it causes them to turn back. For those who have the strong enough will to make it down here, well, you need Gravity to get back up. Few have that. But between that and the sheer beauty of the Core and how it will destroy a person's mind, why do you think there are no bones down here, no rotting skeletons? Because they always fling themselves over the side, trying to touch it. They always die. If we let you watch, you will go mad, and you will throw yourself over the edge. We won't be able to save you. Neither will Kayla." He opened his mouth, closed it, opened it again. "Please, Tommen. Stay here. We will call you when we're ready."

"Why can't you grab the key, then?" Tommen asked, finally finding his voice. "Why are we here?"

The not-quite-an-Amish man stood. "You'll see. And don't worry too much. There will still be a show for you as well, even with your backs turned."

Tommen couldn't quite explain the sinking feeling he got as Andrew walked away. He'd been dumped by multiple girls in school, watched his dad die in his arms, intentionally opened up a portal into a black hole and had been certain of his own death, and yet that all seemed to pale in comparison to being told that he couldn't watch Andrew and Nathan manipulate the Core of the Wheel. It was complete and utter rejection, as if being rejected by the Author herself. Was that what was going on here? Was she rejecting him, bringing him all this way only to tell him, nope, sorry, not getting in on this one. Was Kayla having similar thoughts?

She sat, kind of a brooding expression on her face, staring at nothing in particular, knees drawn up to her chest.

"Do you really think we'll hear gunshots down here, if something happens upstairs?" Tommen found himself asking.

"I don't know," Kayla admitted after a minute of silence. "But if the Core really is that mesmerizing and that deadly, I don't think we'd be in much danger."

There was some truth to that, Tommen supposed. With his

back to the Core and his eyes on a dark, invisible wall, his thoughts were returning to normal, though he was still sorely disappointed that he wouldn't be able to watch the Builders work their magic. He'd come all the way here, prepared for just about anything, and been told to sit on the sidelines. He couldn't even watch. He couldn't even find it in himself to be truly upset, or at least not much more than meager disappointment.

"Think it'll be this easy to retrieve the journal?" he wondered, nudging Kayla in the ribs.

"I hope so," she said, scoffing as she shifted position, straightening her legs. "We could have this whole thing wrapped up within the hour if that's the case."

That certainly held an appeal. He was no Cinderella, but if he could be back home and in bed by midnight, hey, that sounded pretty darn good. And not having to do any fighting or other running for his life, even better. He might just survive this war with his sanity in tact. Ha ha, yeah, right. He'd end up as battered as any soldier coming home from Iraq, except he would never be able to talk to anyone about his battles.

He chanced a glance over his shoulder, keeping his eyes on the floor until he found shoes, then followed them up to the faces of the Builders as they prepared to do their work. Nathan was a good shrink, and Tommen could forgive him for the deceptive identity. But that's all he was, a shrink. For as much as Tommen knew that returning soldiers didn't want the glory and the romantic impressions that most people heaped on them involuntarily, he also knew that there was a certain comfort in being valued, in being thanked, by family, by friends, by a random stranger on the street who could never understand. But he would never get that.

He looked back at his shoes.

"With any luck, this will be your last battle," Kayla said, putting a hand on his shoulder.

Tommen sighed and shook his head. "No. It won't be. Because after this, I'm walking away. And that's when the war really begins."

She opened her mouth to say more, but Andrew spoke behind them. "We're ready to begin. We're going to make this as minimally invasive as possible so as few people upstairs notice. Hopefully it will buy us more time down here if someone does come to investigate, but it means a smaller window of opportunity to grab the key. As soon as we tell you to hurry up and grab it...hurry up and grab it. One of you, both of you, I don't care, but it has to be done quickly. And at all times, when even remotely possible, do not look directly at the Core. Understand?"

"Understood," Tommen and Kayla answered simultaneously.

Tommen could imagine Andrew nodding and looking at Nathan. "Good. All right, then, here we go. Let's get this over with."

While Tommen was naturally curious about what was going on, he did not dare look back. He did not need to as the whole room was suddenly lit up.

Tommen was a big fan of starry night pictures, the ones that were almost always photoshopped or edited in some way with billions of stars, the Milky Way a bright purple, the sun setting in ribbons of color, the moon huge. He was also a fan of fireworks and pictures of fireworks, glittering colors and patterns against a black backdrop.

The light that filled the room was the best of both worlds. First, there were huge swaths of color stretching all around the room, a sunset painted on every wall, and yet curtained with a darker overtone so that innumerable multitudes of stars could sparkle, each just a tiny pinpoint of light but having the power of the sun. So stunning was the display that Tommen reached out his hand, unsure if it was a flat projection or a 3D experience far outmastering any IMAX theater or planetarium. Some of the stars began to move and pop and burst into more streamers of color, just like fireworks.

Then the swaths changed from late dusk to early dawn, from reds and purples to pinks and yellows. The stars did a dance, swirling about the room in a dance that was uncoordinated yet more beautiful than any professionally choreographed maneuver. Tommen might have said he even heard music in the background, directing the stars in their unknowable step. They slowed and finally stopped, and the color bands turned to blues and greens. The stars were less visible now, and Tommen had to strain to see them. There were no more fireworks, but the little pinpricks of light seemed to twinkle in some kind of rhythm which he could not readily discern.

All of a sudden, the colors disappeared and the whole room was plunged into blackness save for ribbons of gold and silver fireworks threading their way here and there and everywhere, racing around the room like snakes. At first, the movements appeared to be random, but the snakes moved faster and faster until they blazed nearly solid trails of gold and silver in loops and full circles around the room. It wasn't until a second or two later that Tommen realized the snakes had stopped moving, but their trails had been burned into the blackness and still glowed. All the light had been drawn behind him so that it was as if the sun and moon shone together in the sky, if such a thing were possible. His shadow stretched long before him, and even that was mesmerizing in its own right as a gold trail streaked across him, from hip to shoulder.

Gingerly, he reached out and touched the gold trail with his index and middle finger on his right hand. As soon as he made contact, searing pain ten times hotter than the fire had ever been shot through his fingers, his hand, rattled his wrist and momentarily paralyzed his arm and his entire right side. He opened his mouth, but could not scream, could not even find breath enough to gasp.

The silver and gold snakes were released again to zoom about the room, and a silver snake cut across his shadow again, this time across his abdomen, just above his hips, giving his shadow something like an honorary Turitian war band. He reached out for the silver trail with his left hand, same fingers. A tiny voice told him it was a bad idea, but it was distant, like a memory of his mother telling him not to do something. Unimportant.

This time he did gasp in pain, but it was not fire that made him cringe this time around. This time, it was as though he'd touched ice cooled all the way down to absolute zero, instant frostbite, instant flesh death. His burned arm screamed in agony as it never had before, and his whole left side went numb with cold. It took more effort to withdraw from the sensation, and when he did, he felt as though he'd already gone to war and come back. And to think he still had to go out and fight.

The snakes were called again to shine like moon and sun, leaving glittering trails all around the room.

"Come grab the key!"

The voice was distant, but in reeling from the pain of the gold and silver, Tommen had reclaimed that little bit of his mind that would react to commands. He fell over trying to turn around and get up, and tripped over his long, gangly limbs and unusual armor a second time, ungracefully half-sliding, half-crawling across the floor, getting closer to where he hoped the voice was coming from. But at least he'd kept his promise to avert his eyes from the Core for as long as possible.

He bumped into the railing with his head, grunting and clambering to stand up. Taking a breath and semi-consciously telling himself to look up only long enough to grab the key and run, he rubbed his eyes fiercely and looked up.

If the optical illusion had been mind-numbing before, it certainly had the potential to knock dead any who looked upon it for too long. It wasn't just about looking through a microscope at cells or DNA; it wasn't about postulating the makeup of an atom and wondering what lay inside. There, sitting between sun and moon, was creation. An atheist might call it the Higgs-Boson or God particle, a religious person might call it the first point of creation, "Let there be light." But there was no mistaking the fabric of creation, the thing from which everything came into being, infinite and wondrously complex and maddeningly simple, the imagination of God Himself. If there was an Author, fine, but this was the first-ever recorded sighting of the mind of God, Tommen was sure. And all who looked upon Him would surely die.

"Grab the key." Andrew's voice was distant, almost

superfluous, but something about it caught the last pieces of Tommen's mind before they were lost forever.

He blinked.

The pinpoint of creation, he saw, was surrounded by something noticeably dark. He blinked again and saw it had a noticeable, definite shape. That shape was a key, or a key of some form. Something began reaching toward it, and he realized it was his hand. What would happen if he touched the Core? Would he drop dead, turn into a pillar of salt, be severely injured or maimed in some other way, or would nothing happen?

Then the key was in his hand. As soon as he took a step back from the railing, staring at the key and quite certain that this was not the thing of majesty he'd just beheld, there was a flash of light, a thunderclap so loud Tommen may as well have been in the thunderclouds to hear it, and then he was flying.

As he was lifted into the air, he looked around, stunned at how everything, even him, moved in slow motion. He saw the air itself bend with the shockwaves as creation closed in on itself, reverting back to its state as merely the Core of the Wheel. He watched the floor and walls, solid metal capable of taking huge blows without ever showing a scratch, wobble as though made of rubber. The core writhed in a cacophony of colors with billions upon billions of stars twinkling and shining even as fireworks exploded in another sea of glimmering color, the ultimate grand finale of any show.

Then the stars and the fireworks settled down. Then Tommen felt his body touch ground. Then time returned to normal and he fell ass over teakettle for probably fifty feet before coming to a stop. Every part of him hurt and his mind pulsed with a migraine, eyes feeling ready to explode just like the numerous fireworks he'd just witnessed. The room around him had returned to the big TV in a dark room vibe. Slowly he got up on his hands and knees and got sick for the second time that day, spilling bits of peanut butter toast.

"You all right?" Nathan asked, patting him on the back. "It's a lot to take in, and for a minute, I'd wondered if we'd lost you."

"That was magnificent," Tommen whispered, his voice small.

"It is. You can see now why we take our job so seriously, why it takes so much preparation, and why the Author herself chooses her Builders."

Tommen did not reply to that. Nathan helped him to his feet. About thirty feet away, Andrew was helping Kayla. Tommen wondered how she had fared during the show, if she had even moved when the Builders called for them to grab the key. But perhaps some things were best kept to themselves.

As Nathan moved off to speak to Andrew, Tommen glanced at his hands. They looked pretty normal, or what was normal for him. Right hand, perfectly fine, no trace of gold. Left hand, burned and only partially functional, no trace of silver. Maybe it had all been an illusion, just part of the show. At any rate, if the floor was any indication, he certainly hadn't gained the Midas touch. He let his arms drop to his sides and he approached the rest of the group.

"How much of that would the Wheel have felt?" Kayla was asking, her voice sounding as if she'd gone to the dentist and gotten numbed up.

"Hard to say," Andrew said, expression grim, arms folded. "Whatever the case, we should go back up the way we came, retrieve Walter, and return to the fortress. Tommen, you have the key?"

Tommen produced the key. The shape was somewhere between a modern house key with precise cuts, and an old, worn skeleton key. There were engravings all around it, but he couldn't for the life of him say what it read.

"Good. Keep that close. Show it to no one. And more importantly, speak nothing of what you have seen here."

"I don't even know what I have seen," Tommen blurted.

"Even better. Trying to describe it will only make you sound insane, and I'd be willing to bet that once we go back up, you will have forgotten most of it anyway. It's how your brain protects itself. Are there any questions?"

Tommen thought about asking about the silver and gold and

his hands, then decided against it. It had all been an illusion. He knew it. They knew it. He didn't want to sound like a complete moron. So he let it go. The Builders nodded.

"All right, then," Andrew said. "Going up."

The use of Gravity felt so strange, so...petty, compared to the things he'd seen in the Core. He'd literally witnessed the power, the intelligence, that had conceived of Gravity. Something that everything in the universe was subject to in one way or another, and Tommen had glimpsed a time and place where it was just part of God's imagination. For them to manipulate Gravity was like playing with Lincoln logs and calling the little buildings houses and forts. Like the Marines compared to dodgeball at recess.

Going up the staircase was much easier than going down. In fact, they had no resistance whatsoever. No tar, no murk, no suffocation, just walking up the stairs. As they did so—still in total darkness, that hadn't changed—Tommen's eyes relaxed, no longer threatening to pop out of his skull. He closed his eyes and found that where he had expected to be assaulted with memories of grandeur and the beauty and the splendor and things he could not name in English, Welsh, or any language he knew or half-knew, he had only fading memories, as if from a dream. He knew he had witnessed something beyond description in this world, but it was fading now. He could recall the battle in the Akarin fortress more clearly. By the time they reached the top of the stairs, he had only the knowledge of what had happened, but no memories of what actually did. He patted his pocket. Feeling the key brought a short burst of light and memory, but that, too, faded quickly. But at least the key was real.

No one confronted them as they made their way back through the employees only section, and their ascent to the main Archives was unhindered. Going through the darkness of the staircase again, Tommen felt the weariness leave his limbs. He wasn't fully restored to battle-fighting strength, but he didn't feel like falling over either.

When they emerged, Walter was waiting for them at the top. He was not under direct assault, but Tommen could read his body language well enough to know he was expecting something. Company was coming.

"What happened down there?" he asked lowly.

Tommen opened his mouth to answer but could find no words. For one, he knew he could never describe what he had seen. For two, he couldn't even really remember what he had seen. Andrew saved him, saying, "We got the key. How much did you feel up here?"

"A bit of an earthquake," Walter answered. "Knocked a few tablets off the shelves, unbalanced me, and there was almost like a...a ripple effect, that went through here. I don't know how to describe it except as a ripple, like disturbing a puddle of water, but through the air, visible, but I don't know how that could be. I just as soon assumed you were responsible."

Andrew nodded. "Aye, that was us. If we're lucky, any patrons around here will dismiss it as something weird, maybe report it. Worst case scenario, the Grandfathers come swarming in to figure out what the hell happened."

"We best make ourselves scarce from this area, then."

It was a worthwhile idea, and Kayla led the way, having regained her usual confidence. She took them along a more direct route to the lobby. Several other Archive patrons were speaking to the attendant, complaining of the earthquake and other strange things. The attendant promised that the secretaries were on it and the Grandfathers would arrive shortly to conduct their own investigation. Kayla did not stop to give them a piece of her mind. While it might be useful in the short-term, to make their group sound just as pissed as all the other disrupted patrons, it would prove detrimental in the long run if and when the Grandfathers identified four of the five of them as known, self-proclaimed Akari-bearers of one faction of another. Walter would just get lumped in, guilty by association, whether or not he was running with the factions or had any talent of his own.

"All right, Walt, let's get you home, and we'll go run off to war," Kayla said.

"No," Walter said.

The group stopped and looked at him. He shook his head. "No. You go off to war, battle, whatever you need to do. I'll stay here and watch for the fallout, see if anything comes of this. If the Grandfathers or the Hands take any kind of action, you don't need to come home from war only to walk into an ambush. I'll keep an eye on the Wheel until you get back."

"Walt, the shields are still up," Kayla said. "You'll be trapped here. What if they identify you with us and haul you in?"

"I'll only be prevented from returning to Earth or the human planets. The good news is, you've managed to secure some allies for us, and their world is not so protected."

"Sifura's world," Tommen stated.

His dad nodded. "If anything happens and I have to flee, I'll go there."

"Sounds like a plan," Nathan said.

"All right," Kayla agreed after a moment of unsavory consideration. "But take some of your own advice and be careful."

"Yes, Mom," Walter said.

Kayla and the Builders headed off, but Tommen stayed behind just a moment longer. Awkwardly, he put his hand out as if to shake his dad's hand, but Walter pulled him into a full embrace.

"Because I didn't get to do it last time you went charging into battle," his dad said, voice strained. "You take care of yourself. I want to see you sprawled out on your bed by morning, got it?"

Tommen grinned and wiped away a tear he told himself was strictly from anxiety over the battle. "Bright and early."

He turned and hurried after Kayla and the others, checking about every twenty feet to make sure he still had the key. The armor was growing heavy and his stomach yearned for food after having only bites here and there and then throwing it all up. He caught up to the others as they exited the lower marketplaces and made for the portal room.

"Wait, are you going into battle with us?" Tommen wondered, looking at Andrew and Nathan.

"Unfortunately for you, we are not," Nathan answered. "We're part of the hostage negotiation."

"Oh. Can I ask you something, before we go into the fortress where eavesdroppers could be everywhere?"

"I don't see how the Wheel is much better, but go ahead."

"Is it possible to Build outside of the Core? Like, could you go to any planet and just start playing with stuff?"

"Not exactly," Andrew answered sagely. "Building is a gift from the Author, and she chooses her Builders with care. You can study all you want, but if she doesn't give you the ability, you're not a Builder. You would be just as susceptible to the mesmerizing effects of the Core as anyone else. Similarly, she can take it away if its use is not in her will. So while it is possible to Build just about anywhere, it is easiest to do it in the Core, to touch Creation directly, and its use is ultimately up to the discretion of the Author."

Like Chandler and his visions of the future, or his occasional travels between dimensions, Tommen thought. Out loud he simply said, "Oh. Okay."

"Here we go," Kayla said, her voice strained as she opened a portal to the fortress.

Tommen stepped through, and the first thing he noticed was that he had virtually no issues. A little off-balance, a little spike in the headache, but nowhere near as traumatic as normal. Was it simply because his recent experiences made portals look small by comparison? It was the only thing he could come up with, though the rest of them did seem to be affected by the normal side effects. Maybe his mind was already half-gone from the experience and he didn't even know it.

Kayla forced the portal to close, nodding once to the guard who was overseeing all portals opened and closed during the battle, and they walked out into the main atrium where the bulk of the army still awaited orders to move out. Few, if any, knew of their little side quest to the Wheel, or if they did, they did not understand the full scope of what it meant for the battle at large. Nevertheless, most or all of the gathered troops knew that as soon as their little band of heroes returned from the Wheel, shit was about to get real.

They started up the staircase. From above, Tommen could see the divisions in the army. Half the room was First Order. The other half was human and Akarin. Then they were divided into battalions, companies, and so on down the line. No sooner had he spotted the humans than orders were shouted and the great war machine began moving, primarily human and Akarin. Of the humans, primarily Sakarians, easily spotted with their unusual sizes, and the Dorigisi. This was the force sent to attack the shipyards, and they looked eager to do so.

With the army currently occupying the first floor, Rifun had taken up temporary residence on the second floor, normally home to the lower soldiers currently awaiting orders to move out. He again wore his Borelian battle gear and was presently arguing with Julianna in low tones. Tommen, who was at the head of the little band of heroes, stopped and motioned for the others to do the same.

"It's a bad idea," Julianna was saying. "Your place is here, what if something happens?"

"Then it's a good thing my little bodyguard will be close to hand. My place is out there, on the battlefield, leading my men, leading by example. You stay here and read and study and learn and teach. I can't sit in an office any longer, pretending I am a general who only leads from his desk. A warrior's place is in the field of battle."

"But your—"

"I've already taken the meds. I will be just fine. Besides. It's a battlefield full of Borelians. Who is going to know the difference?"

Julianna did not look pleased, looked ready to either start ordering Rifun around or else just rip his head off and save everyone the trouble. After a long couple of minutes where the two faced off like a couple of cats challenging for territory, she backed down, muttering something Tommen didn't catch. Rifun also said something in a lower voice.

Tommen took the opportunity to walk up and make their

presence known. Neither Rifun nor Julianna tried to hide that they'd just been arguing, and though neither volunteered any information as to its subject, Tommen could easily guess.

"Good, you're here. Slight change of plans," Rifun began. "I will be going with you."

"With us?" Kayla questioned.

"Yes. I will be with my men, forging a path into the temple, and then I will go with you and Tommen to retrieve the journal."

Well, if that didn't just throw a wrench into things, Tommen thought. Then he considered that it really didn't matter. The four of them had already agreed to give Rifun the journal. Let him parade it around a bit, then once the partying was over and everyone was passed out and hungover, steal the journals and the Authored Books. That didn't stop him from glancing nervously at Kayla who met Rifun head-on.

"What, you don't trust us?"

"I have no reason to, darling," he told her.

Tommen could easily imagine Kayla as a bear, hackles raised, ears laid flat. "You think I would just abandon my people? I'm doing this for them, not me."

"So we're on the same page, then, excellent. Don't worry, I'll keep my end of the bargain. You can be Moses and free your people at the end of the day."

"What's to keep you from stabbing me in the back?"

Rifun moved his right hand and put the gap where his two fingers should have been in the spot where she'd stabbed him only three months ago. "You have my word of honor."

"Your word means nothing."

"Well, regardless of your opinion, that is what is happening, and you better come to terms with it because I predict we'll be moving out in..." He pretending to check an invisible watch. "Less than ten minutes. Maybe less than five. Come on, then, I'll introduce you to our security detail."

"Security detail?" Tommen wondered.

"They'll be in charge of getting us to the temple safely. After that, everything is up to us."

He took the two of them back to the first floor, maneuvering through the ranks to the front, and only then did Tommen really consider that they were the next ones to leave. Some would go before to clear the way and some would come after, but they were still the next ones to run onto the battlefield. Oh, shit.

Their security detail was a group of eight, all of them seasoned veterans of battle and the Akari, or the Order's version of it. Rifun informed them that he would be in the initial charge, but would drop back to join the temple crew. The unit did not question, did not betray any personal thoughts. They simply accepted their Faharoa's decision and promised to do their very best. Giving Tommen and Kayla a last once over and a brief word of encouragement which Tommen hardly heard, Rifun moved up to the frontal assault. They were not so stoic and were clearly thrilled to have their leader with them, leading them into battle against their ruthless foe.

"I should have gone to bed instead," Tommen said in a small voice.

"You and me both," Kayla growled in agreement.

Then the portal was open and they were charging through.

Chapter Thirty-Three
Shifting Pieces

Walter understood a thing or two about how to read a crowd, and how to read people. He knew a thing or two about investigations, how they were generally conducted, and how people were supposed to react. Depending on the situation, people could be horrified, disgusted, amused, or just generally curious. Someone who did not display the same general emotional or physical reaction as the group at large was either mentally impaired or else had something to do with the incident at hand. Usually those people were a little too eager to want to help out and might come off as pushy.

In the case of some weird, unknown incident in the Archives, the mood had started off as cranky that normal operations had been interrupted, the stillness of the library rudely broken. That had quickly melted into curiosity as the secretaries and the Grandfathers arrived to conduct an investigation. Walter had never seen the Grandfathers conduct an investigation—at least, not as a bystander—so he could honestly say that his curiosity was genuine.

Listening to Kayla and the others, the Akari was the Author's gift to the worthy to bend all of creation, not just Time, but Matter and Energy as well. Walter had no reason not to believe them, after everything he'd seen. The Time industry was the paltry, secularized version, merely a shadow of the Author's power, a bag of party tricks to impress and control the weak-minded. But looking at the Grandfathers now, he wondered if there wasn't just Time in that shadow, but hints of Matter and Energy as well. Called Time, maybe called special abilities reserved for the highest-trained Time Agents, but shadows of more than just Time. After all, Harvesting had side effects more akin to Matter manipulation, the changing of one's DNA, acquiring new traits; the Time Capsules were merely a side effect which the Merchants exploited.

Walter racked his brain but could come up with nothing in the realm of Time that he knew of which might actually help the Grandfathers determine what had happened in the Archives. Maybe they could use some Time sense to say when it happened, but to touch the folds of the dimensions and trace it all back, looking for epicenter as it were, that was far beyond mere Time.

In a way, Walter was almost ashamed at himself for not seeing it sooner. Maybe it wouldn't have been a belief in the Akari or anything, but to be so blind to the power that was out there, the power that the higher Time Agents wielded, and to know now that those who wielded the Akari—whether the Akarin, the Cult, or any other group was up for debate—had ten times that ability. It was the difference between watching TV on an old, static-riddled black and white television set, and watching TV on a brand new high definition, ultra crystal color, whatever the latest fad was in TVs.

To think that Tommen, as only an Apprentice Timekeeper, probably wielded more power than him, a Captain, because he was simultaneously an Apprentice Akari-bearer. Or, he supposed the proper term was Novice, according to Kayla or someone, but still, an Apprentice only.

And how much of that had Tommen learned from him? How much of anything had Tommen learned from him? How much teaching had Walter really done for his boy? Maybe if he'd done more, a lot of this pain could have been avoided. Maybe the warehouse never would have happened. Maybe Tommen would have held different beliefs that would have better prepared him for everything that was to come. Instead, he seemed to have been spirited away by Rifun and Micaiah and Kayla and learning under everyone but his own dad. Walter rubbed his face. Even Teo seemed to have done a better job with Tommen than him.

What could he do about it now, though? He stood on the

Archive balcony and watched the Grandfathers from a distance, tracing the dimensions, taking notes, apparently the standard procedure for scene investigation really was standard across the universe. Walter didn't know what had transpired down in the Core of the Wheel, but his son had been part of it. Different than defying an official ruling of the Hands, Tommen had helped to do something that confounded the Grandfathers, upset the Time industry, could get him executed if caught. And Walter had...what? Played bouncer? Checked to make sure everyone who entered the premises had the appropriate stamp on their hand? Sure, he could have fought a secretary, maybe wrestled with a Grandfather long enough to warn them and buy them time, but it all seemed so silly now. The four of them had been playing with the threads of Creation. How did you stop something like that? Tell them very authoritatively to stop or else he'll say stop again? Threaten to arrest them? Almost as silly as the idiot suing God.

On the upside, though, no one came to interrogate him. No one picked him out in a crowd, surrounded him, said he was going to take a little ride, and tossed him in an unmarked van. No one held up a Wanted poster for his son or Kayla and asked if he'd seen either of them. He was one of the last to leave the balcony, but by no means the last one. He went back into the Archives, getting just a little closer to the investigation scene, but not enough to arouse suspicion. He picked out a tablet or two and pretended to read, all the while keeping one eye on the Grandfathers.

Nothing of interest really happened, or nothing he understood. It was almost like being a rookie cop again, watching the veterans dance with choreographed precision and wondering just how they got it all done. Hell, even as a veteran detective himself, he still wondered how it all got done, especially knowing now that there was no choreographed grace to be found anywhere on a crime scene. The events earlier that night had been proof enough of that. He put the tablets away.

He'd only just stepped back on the balcony when there was a shift in the movement of the Grandfathers. Walter recognized it as the

"Let's wrap this up and get out of here" movement of the dance, or something similar to it. But where that dance Earth-side took half an hour or more, the Grandfathers managed to wrap up theirs in five minutes or less, flying out of the Archives with inhuman speed. Walter only caught snippets of conversation among them as they blew past him, something about taking it to the Hands and exiling and ruling and alliance and a number of other words that didn't seem quite appropriate to a scene investigation and which put up little red flags in Walter's mind.

Still, he betrayed nothing except a little disgruntled annoyance at their rude and hasty exit. He went to another part of the Archives and read for another five or ten minutes before leaving. He didn't need to be seen as though he were following the Grandfathers, after all. He just needed to keep a general eye on things.

Nothing was on fire and no mobs met him when he exited the Archives. With exception of the anxious undercurrent running through the crowd, business carried on as usual. Mingling with the crowds in the marketplaces, he heard very little about anything weird happening in the Wheel, and little or no mention of the Grandfathers beyond their usual duties. Walter couldn't decide if it was comforting that no one took notice and no panic had started, or worrying that no one took notice and they would be caught completely unawares if something happened. His penchant for optimism was wearing thin.

After a time, the hustle and bustle of the market crowds started to wear on him, and he decided to make for the second most likely place to hear juicy gossip: The Food Court. He grabbed a small salad, then sat to listen and observe.

This venture proved more fruitful as he heard much more about the Archives here than in the marketplaces. Most of it sounded like idle gossip. Moms and dads and groups of friends in a shopping mall lightly discussing interesting news with little or no true, professional, well-thought-out insights or verifiable facts. It was just something to talk about to sound somewhat abreast of current events, the latest fascination, the latest fad, the latest fear, the latest frustration.

As far as the general mood of the crowd went, the news from the Archives started out as more of a fascination. "Hey, did you hear about that thing? Yeah, so weird."

Generally speaking, Walter was just fine with this assessment of the situation. It was something that had happened that was unusual, out of the ordinary even for the Wheel of Time, but little more. It would circle around and eventually die, making way for the next unusual thing. The problem came when he knew that if it was something the Hands wanted to exploit, they knew how to stoke the fire.

In mainstream America, such a thing was typically accomplished via social media, posting and sharing and resharing. Outrageous thoughts, outrageous videos, outrageous everything, something that demanded attention and reaction, sweeping across the nation and even around the world at the speed of a click.

In the Wheel, this was accomplished the old-fashioned way: espionage and moles. Certain tables here and there in the Food Court would have just the right conversation at just the right volume with just the right words and phrases overheard to spread to the next table, playing on both emotions and the unreliability of the telephone game. By the time Walter was able to discern a change in the mood of the crowd, the instigators were long gone, or else already moving on to another area to start a new enraging conversation.

Pretty soon, the incident in the Wheel was no longer just an intriguing incident on the evening news, but a fearful attack by the Akari-bearers—the Grandfathers had not yet determined whether it was Order or Akarin—to bring about the downfall of the Time industry. This line of thinking stoked the fuels of the fear fire as denial was the first thing to come out. No, no, no, the Time industry was safe. The Wheel of Time had stood for as long as anyone could remember and had operated the same way for centuries. It may not be flawless, but it was safe; it was familiar. It couldn't fall. Could it?

What if it did? Sure, sure, Unengaged civilizations might not be overly affected, but what about those who were Engaged? It could cause severe economic and political upheaval such as had not been seen since, well, a little over a year ago with the Zero Hour Revolution. Some of those worlds were still being tossed about in uncertain economic storms with high unemployment among its Time Agents and little trust or investment in the Time industry. And that wasn't even getting into the politics.

And then there was that whole massacre thing. Time Agent numbers were way below what they were pre-Revolution. If there was another coup, one that not only involved military execution but casualties from the destruction of the Wheel itself, would there be any Time Agents left to sustain the industry?

Who wielded such power anyway? Was it Rifun again? He'd been successful once, and he had defeated those who had defeated him. If he managed to defeat the Borelians in the rumors of this new endeavor of his, what was to stop him from conquering anyone and anything he wanted? Even if not him specifically, the power that the First Order had to wield in order to accomplish such a thing was astounding.

And what if it wasn't the Order? What if it was the Akarin? Some had escaped and were now seeking to exact revenge against the Hands who had banned them as surely as they had banned the Order, spit in the faces of Time's saviors. Or maybe the Order and the Akarin were allied now, as certain rumors seemed to suggest. With their combined power, going after the Borelians, maybe the Time industry really was in jeopardy.

There was also an undercurrent of fear targeted at humans specifically. A nothing race from a nothing planet had suddenly taken center stage. A human led the Order. A human was rumored to lead the Akarin. A human had been the False Zero Hour. Humans were not running and hiding from the Borelians but taking the fight to them. Perhaps they were more powerful than anyone realized, and no one had taken them seriously until it was too late to do anything about it.

On that line of thought, the next wave of emotion filtered through the crowd as fear turned to frustration. Anger. How had things gotten so out of control? Why were these groups allowed to run rampant to the point where they'd amassed such power as to be invincible, capable of mowing down the Time industry at a whim? The Time industry prided itself on being a business with no involvement in the political or religious affairs of the species it serviced, but at what point should they be made to take some responsibility, take some action? Millions, maybe even billions of people depended on them for their lives and livelihood, and they were content to look a threat in the face, shrug, and turn their backs?

The Time industry could function just fine on its own; the real problem was outside influence, and the biggest one came from those who called themselves Akari-bearers. No matter what the problem was, it always originated with them. Every major problem, and especially every Rebuild seemed to involve them in some way. If they weren't around, there would be no problems with Time. It might not have been so bad if it were a religion confined to the normal temples and shrines and other methods of worship and prayer, but this seemed to be a religion rooted in Time, even spilling into unthinkable concepts like Matter and Energy manipulation. It could not exist apart from the Time industry.

It had to go.

In the space of maybe an hour, Walter had watched the crowd move from idle gossip to a subconscious, unanimous decision to somehow be rid of all Akari-bearers. It wasn't really the crowd that thought this; it was the Hands imparting their will on the crowd. Then the crowd would come to them asking for something they were already prepared to give. Oh, they might put on a show of resistance and make weak arguments, but they would cave and carry out whatever dastardly plan they'd devised even before getting the crowd riled up.

Nothing good was going to come of it, say it that way. Walter debated whether he wanted to leave now and report his findings, or wait to see what more might come of it in the next hour. If the Hands managed to turn a crowd that quickly, either the crowd was already subtly hostile to begin with, or else they were pushing for something much bigger much faster, and Tommen and the others had delivered the catalyst to them on a silver platter.

Walter stood and got himself another salad, telling himself that if something didn't come up before he finished the salad, then he would head for Sifura's world. Problem was, he wasn't entirely sure where to go. If there were half a dozen different peoples coming together to rally behind Kayla and go after the Borelians, they had to have a common camp somewhere, somewhere to take the wounded, make up battle plans, and address inter-tribal disagreements. He just couldn't imagine where that would be because he'd never been to her world before.

He found himself back in the Archives after finishing his salad, looking through maps of Sifura's world, trying to determine where likely camping locations might be. Somewhere central to all the peoples and as hospitable as possible to as many as possible. Wildcats from the desert, fish from the sea, birds from the air, they all had to converge someplace; even if it was only a short camping trip, they all wanted to be as comfortable as possible.

He figured his best bet would be a small lake-slash-oasis on the northern edge of the desert. A small mountain chain tapered off into the region just to the north, with thick jungle to the east and northwest, open plains forming a ribbon between the western jungle and southern desert. No guarantees, but if he was trying to get a number of different tribes to stay in the same general location while catering to a multitude of species-specific needs, that looked like a good place to start.

Nevertheless, he scanned the maps and made notes of several other viable locations, memorizing the coordinates for each and dreading the blind portals he was going to have to open. With any luck, he would be right on the money on his first try. Yeah, right. Lip was the size of Texas and he'd still managed to touch down in the river the first time around.

Walter replaced the tablets and made for the exit, pausing only once to glance toward the atrium. An optical illusion, each tessellation just another dimensional fold, all culminating at a point deep down in a dark corner reached via spiral staircase and sectioned off with a little sign reading, "Employees Only." It was almost hilarious, something one might read about in a novel, perhaps. And yet, Walter wondered if this would all be captured in a novel of some form, a future Authored Book. He shook his head and decided he didn't want to dwell on it too much at the moment. There was a war going on. Once his son was home safe and sound, then they could talk philosophy.

He meandered his way through the Archives, walked the stretch along the balcony, crossed the lobby, and emerged into the Wheel at large.

Immediately upon entering the main Wheel, Walter knew something had happened, that something he had been waiting for while doing research. The crowds were still moving, but now they all moved in a single direction, toward the Seat, the Amphitheater. It wasn't a stampede, as if the Hands had called for some sort of emergency congress, where something terrible had happened and everyone tuned in on the TV to see what the president had to say about it. Rather, this was exactly the product of the rumors the Hands had started in the Food Court. People were afraid and frustrated and now they were moving toward the Hands for answers. Likely the Hands had announced some sort of open session at just the right time to get the crowds to approach them.

Walter melted into the crowd and followed, listening to the din of conversation. The fear and frustration was less specific here; either the group at large did not understand what was going on or else the conversation had devolved to such a point where the specifics no longer mattered and it was all about emotion. He held out hope that it was the former, but experience had taught him to take nothing for granted and always assume the worst.

As it was, there was almost no mention of the strange incident in the Archives, though there was plenty of talk about how isolated the Akari factions were. If they were so powerful, why had the Hands let them continue their operations? Banning them was great, but that was only assuming that the banned groups would listen. Their power had won the Wheel once; what if they tried it again? Something had happened and something was going to happen. Was the Time industry prepared to respond? The Timekeepers seemed to be ill-prepared for an attack, and last time, the Grandfathers had turned on them. Were the new Grandfathers truly loyal? If they were, were they prepared for anything?

So many questions swirling around the throng, and still Walter let himself be carried into the Amphitheater, occasionally maneuvering his way through the crowd to get as close as possible in order to hear whatever the Hands were going to say. The message would eventually work its way through the crowd, but Walter wanted to hear everything from the Hands themselves.

He had a brief thought that, in a place so technologically advanced, they should have at least invented some sort of broadcasting system to get the message out there without relying on the inaccurate renditions of the audience. But then, there was a certain advantage to such unreliability, wasn't there? The uncertainy, the conflict, the confusion.

Shuffled in the crowd, Walter had a brief notion that he ought to get to the outside. It was his police instinct kicking in, the ability to better assess and control a situation from the outside where he could get a better view than simply arms, legs, and bodies, all stuck together in the middle. Taking a breath—and not liking some of the smells that entered his nose and mouth—he began forcing his way perpendicular through the crowd, heading for the edge. By the time he made it and could breathe again, the Hands had assembled.

It was a bit like crowd control on any of the college campuses back home, except slightly less violent. On the campuses, mobs rioted over speakers with whom they disagreed; once a thing of note, now an uneasily common thing. In the Wheel, the good little Time Agents were too dependent on their ruling body to know true tyranny when they saw it. The Hands had instigated the fear and outrage that infected the crowd. They had called the meeting at precisely the opportune time to stoke those fears and so bend them as they saw fit. And now, who knew what would happen?

With Sifura gone to the front lines, Walter would have expected to see only fifty Hands up there. It was close enough to fifty-one to look appropriate without giving away that one Hand was missing. Instead, there were far less than fifty Hands. In fact, he only counted fifteen. Sweeping his gaze over the crowd, the rumor mill was already moving. Having one or two Hands absent was unusual, but not uncommon. Hands from Unengaged societies had an appearance to keep and so might miss a meeting here and there. But to be short thirty-six Hands? Something was definitely up. Walter found himself thanking God or the Author or whoever that the Time dampening field had been disposed of; if he had to make a run for it, he could. It wouldn't be fun, but it was better than being trampled or taken back to the black cells.

He looked at the Grandfathers, trying to gauge their reaction. While a few shifted nervously, most appeared somewhat resolute and watched the Hands intently, so there was a good chance they were in on this as well. Wonderful. He scanned for his exits, but there was only one. He studied the crowd, looking for anything unusual. From his vantage point, he had only to unfocus his gaze and look at it as a single sea of color. From there, he would pick out points of movement, watch where the ripples came from. Those would be the ones fueling the fire and driving the crowd. The fearful crowd would run; the vengeful mob would attack. He needed to find the perpetrators.

He found at least three of them, one in the center close to the Hands. If he had to guess, this was a plant by the Hands. The ripples in the crowd were too calculated, too evenly spaced, too perfect. There was another toward the back of the crowd on the far side, though a plant was unlikely. The ripples were too wild, too much fire too soon. If the crowd listened, it would erupt before the Hands made their move. Then there was a third, closer to his side, a little closer to the Hands than the one in the back. Also unlikely to be a plant. The movements were soft, hesitating, and when Walter brought everything back into focus and picked out the person at the center of the ripples, they were small and alone and obviously afraid. Nevertheless, this could be the most dangerous one of the three because there was no telling what would happen if it got spooked.

It wasn't until later that Walter would consider that from his vantage point, others might mistake him as being in on the whole conspiracy, but in the moment, he was looking out for his own safety, just doing what he'd been trained to do.

Eventually, the crowd quieted from the initial shock of having less than half the Hands present to address them, and they waited eagerly, a flock of sheep waiting for the butcher to comfort them.

Walter paused and considered whether it was really fair to blame the Hands. At the last proper elections, all or almost all of the Hands had been butchered. Now that same enemy was back and more powerful than ever, going after the only force in the universe yet to be subdued. If they did that, what was there to stop him from turning his sights back on the Wheel, really? His word? The Hands were operating in fear and unfocused anger as much as the crowd standing before them now. The problem was, Walter knew well where that fear and rage led, and it wasn't to a perfect utopia. Freedom and security and all that.

At long last, once the crowd had quieted as much as it was going to, one of the Hands stepped forward. It was in that moment that Walter realized the Zero Hour was nowhere to be seen. Having a Hand or two missing, fine. He could accept that. Having more than half of them missing, cause for concern, but he might be able to suspend his disbelief long enough to see what was going on. But not having the Zero Hour present for a meeting of such vital importance, no matter how short the notice, was unthinkable. Alarm bells rang in Walter's head and he double-checked to make sure the Time dampening field was not reinstated. When he was satisfied that it was not and he could use Time freely, he told himself to just stay put. At the first sign of treachery, he could still leave. He would leave.

Nevertheless, his brain was assaulted with horrifying

memories, all jumbled together. Beaumaris cells, the black cells of the asylum, they ran through his mind like a poorly edited movie, and ran together so that he couldn't tell which was which. He closed his eyes, took a breath, told himself to stay in the moment. He had to stay vigilant. He had the ability to leave. He didn't have Micaiah with him this time to hold him up if he had some kind of nervous breakdown. But he did have a son he needed to get back to, no matter what.

When Walter clawed his way back to the present, he found that he had missed whatever introductions and formalities the Hands had seen fit to still go through. With only fifteen of them up there, it was a decidedly quicker affair, anyway.

"No doubt you are all gathered here because of the incident that happened in the Archives," the addressing Hand stated.

Even if the incident itself couldn't have been staged by the Hands, the reaction had been, and they were still intent on controlling it. That was their launching point. Paranoia, no matter how great or how compelling, wasn't always enough to move to action, but one little spark was all that was needed to set off a gas explosion.

"After a thorough investigation by the Grandfathers—" Which took all of...an hour or so? On the other hand, even social media was faster with their investigations and quicker to condemn. They executed people within an hour of allegation, so one hour from the Grandfathers wasn't a huge leap, Walter supposed. "—it has been determined that it was an attack on the Core of the Wheel."

The Hands masterfully let that sink in for a moment.

"As some of you who have been around a long time know, the Time industry has maintained a civil relationship with the Akarin. They alone possess the ability to Rebuild the Wheel when decimated by evil forces. Unfortunately, they have become one of those evil forces and have attempted to turn against us. In being conquered by the Cult of the Akari, they have allied themselves with a great foe of the Time industry, one that we, unfortunately, are unable to defend against by ourselves."

Again, a masterful pause, letting the news and its implications sweep over the crowd.

But then, Walter was forced to wonder just what the Hands planned to do about this perceived weakness. The Time industry was made up of thousands of species with unique strengths and talents. It wasn't a country or an army in and of itself; if anything, it was simply a business.

"The Time industry as a single entity, a single business, is corrupt, petty, inefficient, and weak," the Hand went on. "Even now, three of the Hands have gone to the Akari-bearers to fight in their campaign against the Borelians."

Three? Walter knew Sifura was out there, but who else?

"If the Time industry is to survive, we must become more than we were. Because the Akarin can no longer to be trusted to help us in our times of need, we must fortify ourselves against them. To that end, we, as your Hands and former Hands—" So it was a voluntary thing for thirty-six Hands, the most powerful figures in the universe, to just step down? "—have forged an alliance."

Walter felt his muscles turn to water and his stomach churn as five figures walked onto the stage. Three of them were Borelians—a gray, a purple, and an unknown color—and Walter was willing to bet that at least one was an Admiral, the second a Councilman, the third a Holy Man of War, one from each of the governing bodies and all that was needed to hold Brelix together in the event of severe political and military turmoil.

The other two were Milay and Toros from Tacaga.

"The Borelians served the Time industry loyally for many decades but were deceived by Rifun Ndolo and the Cult of the Akari and later betrayed," the Hand said, gesturing toward the horned figures. "Their own strength was used against them, and they have been attacked and decimated by the Akarin as well, butchering their leaders in shadows and veils, leaving them nearly helpless." Then he gestured to the Tacagans. "Once a colony planet, the Tacagans were held hostage by their own human home world unless they helped build weapons and shields against not only the Borelians, but the Time industry itself, making their world impenetrable. With the Akari-bearers able to break through those shields and conduct secret, powerful operations, they have multiple safe houses on the human worlds."

Walter studied the crowd again, desperately hoping they would see through the charade. But the crowd watched with rapturous attention, waiting to hear how the Hands were going to save them.

"But in their courage, the Tacagans have undermined their human forbearers. A small remote device that, if activated, will shut down those shields."

So that was the reason for the gifts. That was how they really worked. Oh, they probably did what the Tacagans advertised as mini-shields and temporary inverters, but just a flip of the switch and the main power assembly shut down, leaving them helpless.

But more than that, all the months of planning for battle, the research in the lab, the attack, Do Chien's death, the Tacagans had been right there, with everything but the neon sign reading, "Traitor." Less than twenty-four hours ago, Rifun and Kayla had spelled out their entire attack on Ancrath. The strategies, the goals, the intents, the companies, the forces, the allies, the firepower. The Borelians would be ready and waiting—had been ready and waiting. The armies would have walked into an ambush.

Walter felt a strong desire to flee—somewhere, anywhere—and make sure Tommen was safe. If he wasn't in the first wave of attack, maybe word had gotten back and he hadn't gone at all.

"And so, in an effort to maintain the security and integrity of the Time industry," the Hand continued, "we have, after much consideration, decided to restructure ourselves and how we do things—before it comes to another coup or war." Yes, surrender is always a nice option, too. "Many Time Agents will not see much change and are free to go about your business normally." One of the best ways tyranny succeeds, by telling the common man that he will not be affected. "And you can rest assured that the Borelians will protect the

Time industry from the Akari-bearers. The Tacagans will maintain the technology needed to defend us from all threats, great and small. Together, they will work to keep us safe from both the Akari-bearers, and the humans who began this whole mess."

So the Hands weren't completely stupid; they still knew the Borelians were a huge threat. But that was where the Tacagans came in, with their technology to stop them if need be, whether it was shielding or medical research and the cure for the toxins. And to help spread the propaganda against the evil humans and Akari-bearers, both of whom they detested.

Overall, Walter wasn't entirely sure what was going to fundamentally change. The Time industry had a whole army of secretaries dedicated to keeping the technology of the Wheel up and running. The Grandfathers were in charge of the justice system with the Timekeepers being the cops.

"In the coming months, you will see changes in the Wheel. The Borelians will again take charge of the Grandfathers and serve as faithfully as they once did. The Grandfathers themselves will now be in charge of all training and recruitment of Timekeepers and Harvesters. We Hands will oversee the Merchants and the secretaries. As for the Tacagans, they will be working on two major projects. They will begin work on technology that will completely shut down the Akari-bearers' power, or else unlock it that all may learn. Second, they will also begin work to disassemble the Core of the Wheel and reform it so that we are no longer dependent upon those who deviate from the core mission of the Time industry and turn against it."

Basically, they were militarizing the Time Agents in order to destroy anyone who wasn't them and set themselves up as the sole powerhouse in the universe for Time. The Borelians were going to train the grunts while the Tacagans developed the required weaponry, and while all of that was going on, the Hands were going to step back and manage strictly the economy, the funds needed to pay their future army.

So much for the free market, Walter thought. At least if one didn't like doing business with the Time industry, so to speak, they had other options. But the game of Monopoly had been going on for quite a while now and the players were getting irritated; it was time to ramp it up to an eleven and dominate the market.

There was one comfort in all of this, and that was that this had all happened before. For the longest time, Walter had dismissed the Akari in general and found its followers to be more like that little church on the corner populated only by grandparents and their little grandchildren. Now they'd come roaring to the forefront of the mind and the Hands didn't like it. Every time the Akari-bearers made themselves known in any fashion, the Hands tried to beat them down. This latest iteration was as unlikely to result in the total destruction of any faction as any of the previous attempts.

But that didn't mean that some people weren't going to die in the process. And Walter was desperately hoping that Tommen wasn't one of those.

Of course, everyone thought they were above average intelligence, too. It was just statistically impossible.

With these new revelations, Walter watched the reaction from the crowd. Fear, puzzlement, but overall positive. There had been a problem, and Big Brother Hand had offered a solution. Something different. Something to make the big scary problem go away, never considering that the real big scary problem was the one there on the stage.

He also considered that he was off to the side, at a good vantage point to see most everything, and he could be seen. He was human. Humans were not well-loved right now. As quietly as possible, he slipped down to the edge of the crowd and made his way toward the back of the room, to the exit. Down among the people, he could only just hear the Hands speaking, and only about one in three words clearly enough to piece together what was being said, or what he thought was being said.

Basically, there were going to be a few new rules, and a few rules given new emphasis. First, there was to be no mention of the

Akari or its followers—any follower from any faction, didn't matter—except in formal business. Second, any information about the Akari-bearers was, depending on the training and skill of the people, to be either pursued or turned over to the proper authorities. Third, all Akari-bearers and humans were banned from the Wheel. Period. Violation of that particular zero-tolerance rule would result in immediate arrest and a blind date with a Borelian, probably of the green inclination.

Then Walter was out of the Amphitheater and back in the main Wheel, and it was a surreal experience, like walking out of a movie theater and realizing that you actually lived in a world different from that of the movie. Life had carried on normally while you were laughing, crying, or practically falling forward out of your seat in total rapture waiting to see what was going to happen next. Then you get out and immediately get a headache as you try to adjust to the light change, your bladder announces its intentions to embarrass you in public very quickly, and the same teenager who served up your bucket of popcorn is still at the register serving up a bucket of popcorn to someone else. Then you go out to the car and carry on with your day.

So it was with the Wheel. Nothing was on fire, no mobs were overturning tables, no one even held a sign protesting something. All was completely normal. Oh, but word would get around soon enough, and then it would be open season on humanity. Walter did not want to get caught in the middle of that. He got his bearings, turned in a direction, and started toward the portal room. As far as he knew, he couldn't get home, but he'd said he would try to locate Sifura's people, and that was what he would try first.

He got to the portal room, found a quiet spot and an open slot, and stopped. Closed his eyes. He knew the general coordinates, knew basically what he was looking for. Blind portals were no fun on a good day, and they were less fun under pressure. Despite the proclamations that had just come from the Hands, he tried to tell himself that he was in no immediate danger. Humans were banned, yes, but it took time for word to get around; the polite procedure was fifty-one hour notice waiting, that time between an order like that being given, and the punishment being enforced, to give time for everyone to get the memo. That was just how intergalactic mail worked. Furthermore, no one had pointed to him and ordered him to be seized. And on that note, he was in the portal room trying to get home. He was obeying the order to not be in the Wheel.

He didn't exactly go into a tranquil, zen, meditative state, but he calmed down enough that a portal flickered to life. It was on a bare hillside somewhere overlooking a forest. In the distance, a vast desert. But he also saw the glittering lake and what might have been a village. Or a campsite. Taking another calming breath, Walter willed his portal closer to the lake, but the best he got was in the forest nearby. Well, it was still a shorter walk, and he had his gun on him in the event he was attacked by a wild beast.

Walter stepped through the portal, pleasantly surprised to find the weather rather spring-like, about what Charleston would smell like in the next month or two, with the smell of new growth in the air. Flowers, leaves, fresh pine. He got to enjoy this for about three seconds before his allergies kicked in and he sneezed. Damn it all. Just couldn't escape those allergies anywhere, even on an alien planet. Apparently even alien pollen didn't agree with him.

With only the knowledge that the lake and the suspected camp was to the south, Walter picked a direction and started off. He didn't make it a quarter of a mile before he was picked up by a scouting party of a race he did not know. In a way, they kind of resembled the Cowardly Lion from the Wizard of Oz, and only the gravity of the situation stopped him from snickering. They did not have translators, but he knew the routine well enough, he supposed. Come quietly and you won't be harmed. Much.

At the very least, he'd gotten it right on the first try. The war camp had been erected around the lake, each race to his own habitat, or close enough for comfort. The D'Bok in the forest, the Gin Jor in the mountains, the Rupi in the foothills, the Xur in the desert, the Ouin in the water. The only one he didn't officially know was the Cowardly

Lions around him now, but if he remembered correctly, a race called the Da Leio had elected to stay behind in order to safeguard the camp and its warriors.

The camp was a magnificent thing to behold, spread out around the lake, a quarter million strong. It was not uniform by any means, but the mixing of different races lent it a certain beauty. The mountain-dwellers had more rocky shelters or just staked out a claim in the open under the stars. The forest and plains dwellers had earthy shelters of sticks, leaves, and mud. The desert nomads had simple animal hide huts that could be moved at a moment's notice. Similarly, the weapons reflected the owners' environments, be it stone and iron knives from the mountains, wooden bows and stone knives from the forest, or bone everything from the desert. Each one according to his culture and history, making the whole thing a beautiful mosaic, in Walter's mind.

He was also pleased to see that whatever differences they normally had, they were willing to set them aside for a common goal. He watched multiple trade transactions, wooden bows for iron knives, one type of meat for another. He watched an Ouin dive under the water, then return a moment later with a small pouch of what might have been oysters, which he traded for a basket of fruit.

But there was something else about the camp, an element that hung over the lake like an angry thundercloud. The tents set up were a quarter million strong, but the camp itself was quite empty. Here and there, Walter caught sight of someone in a tent, resting, covered in bandages. He jumped once at a snarl that turned into a squealing series of painful yips. A breeze rustled the grass curtain of another shelter, revealing an exposed bone being set and stitches prepared.

Walter was taken to a more permanent-looking shelter built of wood and stone. The leader of the Da Leio escort went in to speak, returning less than a minute later and motioning for Walter to enter. The escort left; either they were unconcerned or else the leaders inside were unconcerned.

He'd only seen the leaders of the various tribes once or twice, knew next to nothing about their social or political structures, and as far as he was concerned, they all looked pretty well alike within their tribes. But if these were the same leaders he'd seen on Tacaga, he didn't hold out much hope for the rest of the tribal army. The hut was dim and he could only make out three leaders, the D'Bok, the Gin Jor, and the Rupi.

"Walter Forbes," the D'Bok leader acknowledged.

"I suppose my warning is going to come a little late," he sighed.

"Sadly, yes. The Borelians knew we were coming. The Tacagan faction of your human tribe. They betrayed us."

"I know." Walter looked away, licked his lips, ran a hand through his hair. "Do I dare ask what happened?"

He was no expert in the body language and mannerisms of the offspring of a komodo dragon and a bear, but he thought it was fair to say that the D'Bok was rather upset. And why not? He carried a steel sword on him. Considering the rest of the group still had bone, maybe iron or some other weaker metal, he was one tough warrior in present company.

"The Borelians knew exactly when the attack was to take place, because it had already been spoken of. We attacked the designated locations around the city, their main roads and their floating carriers. Perhaps we had some element of surprise, perhaps not, but after our first wave of initial attack, the Borelian army appeared. Umwa—" Probably the Ouin. "—led the attack on their floating carriers, their 'ships' as they were called. Un Dai—" The Gin Jor. "—and Ipi—" The bird-like Rupi. "—led the attack on the southeasternmost road, where it is hilly and rocky. I led the attack on the main road at the southernmost point. Sifura took the next road to the west. One of your Sakarian warriors led the attack on the next western road."

The D'Bok shook his head. "The Borelians were not surprised. They were not unprepared. They were not merely a sentry team. We had but two advantages. First, they did not have the Magic. Time, as Aklaq called it. I still do not fully understand it, but she claims it is a powerful weapon, and I could only take her word. Our second advantage came in that the Borelians did not understand how we fight, our attack patterns. They did not understand the Ouin connection to the water, the Rupi to the air, the Gin Jor to the rocks, the D'Bok to the forest, the Xur to the open desert. I cannot speak for your Sakarian faction, though I heard they did well also, in those first moments.

"After we had begun to establish ourselves, the Borelians sent another wave of warriors. Some of these did have the Magic. The only reason we did not perish to the last man was because of Aklaq's Akarin reinforcements. Then the battle turned into a tide of Magic and sorcery, things we did not understand. We tried to help as much as we could, but the Borelians themselves were difficult enough to kill. Aklaq warned us of their toxic skin. I did not believe it until I saw it for myself."

Again the leader paused, though his frustration now turned to shame. "We could not hold ground. The Akarin bid us flee. None of us wanted to, but we had no choice. The Akarin had rescued us, and only they were a match for the sorcery, Magic for Magic. But in helping us, they had taken more forces away from those sent to destroy the flying birds."

"Do you know what happened to those who attacked the shipyard?" Walter wondered.

It was the Gin Jor who answered. "We had the advantage of high ground. I did not understand what I saw, but maybe you will. I saw where they lay their great metal birds. I saw the Akarin and the Order and your Sakarian and Dorigisi factions attack, trying to kill Borelians without damaging the birds so they could still fly. The next thing I know, all but one of the birds are in the air, flying around like angry bees. Some were heading toward us. We, too, were overwhelmed in the rocky hills and were told to flee. We took the chaos of the flying birds to escape to a safe spot to return here. All I know is that some birds began attacking each other. Others went into the city. Some flew low over the battles over the roads and began attacking. The last thing I saw before returning was two or three more birds descending from the clouds."

Walter rubbed his face and eyes. So someone had to have warned Rifun about the ambush, right? Or had everything just been moving too quickly? The boulder had been pushed over the crest of the hill and now it wouldn't be stopped.

"Did anyone see anything regarding the attacks in the city? Did you see them come through or what?"

The three leaders glanced at each other, but no one had anything.

"What about Sifura? Or the Ouin leader, Umwa? Where are they?"

"Sifura was seriously wounded in her battle," the D'Bok leader said levelly. "She is being treated as we speak. We wait for word. Umwa's attack was the only one that one might consider successful as they had the greatest advantage in the water. They followed orders and are carrying on their attack as long as possible. It has been speculated that because the Borelians do not rely heavily on their wooden 'ships' that they may gain a foothold there."

Well, it was something anyway.

Walter took an even breath. "And what about your men? You went out a quarter million strong, or so I heard."

The D'Bok's voice went so soft as to be nearly inaudible, and full of shame. "And so we come back only a quarter of what we were." Two hundred fifty thousand. Down to just over sixty thousand. "Every tribe has been decimated. Every faction dwindled to almost nothing. Some, perhaps, extinct in only a few generations."

Walter closed his eyes. Damn.

The D'Bok went on, "Your son brought an alliance between the human and Xur and a tentative friendship between human and D'Bok. Aklaq came again asking for help and opened our eyes to a world larger than anything we could have imagined." He shook his head. "No more. Perhaps, in its natural course, we could have joined you in the stars one day. But this? All of us, our way of life has been decimated because of you, because of humans.

"We will not declare war on you because, honestly, we have no way to reach you, and we are inferior to your Magic. And it is my understanding that you are unable to get home without help from your Akarin friends. You may remain here under the common laws of hospitality until your friends come to get you. But after that, we ask only that you never return."

Chapter Thirty-Four
The Temple of Tujor

While Brelix itself was generally considered to be rocky and barren, riddled with earthquakes and covered with more volcanoes than a teenager has pimples, it did support its own unique type of vegetation, most of it squat and hardy against pretty much any and every kind of weather. It tended to taper off along major fault lines and in the higher elevations around mountains and volcanoes.

Ancrath itself was situated in a somewhat hilly area. The foothills of the fault line mountains to the east created rocky ripples in the landscape that met with ancient water-worn dips and rises and somehow birthed a city that was a bit like old European cities, with narrow, winding streets that moved with the landscape rather than cutting through it in perfect grids. As powerful as the Borelians were, they were as yet unable to tame their earthquakes and volcanoes. The only major stretch of land that had been intentionally razed and leveled and developed was the shipyard for their spaceships to the east of the city.

Ancrath was bordered on the west by the ocean, having miles of jagged, dangerous cliffs. The ocean only extended halfway across the city's northern border, but the bay sculpted into the landscape was much friendlier. Because of the planet-wide rule that mining and other intentional drilling was prohibited, which included underwater dredging, building up a small harbor had been an engineering feat. Finally, to the south was the only major, industrial agriculture on the entire planet, and it was still less impressive than Nebraska having a bad year.

As for the city itself, it was the core of Borelian society, despite only having two million people (the planet having a total population of roughly three to three and a half million, and less than a tenth of the total Borelian population throughout their colony worlds). It was the epicenter of military and government goings-on. Everything that happened in Ancrath was official business, and its straight, angular, no-nonsense architecture reflected this. There were children in the city, but only because both parents worked for the government. There were some casual cafes and restaurants, but only because the young people were required to do some sort of public service to learn to work and take orders before going into mandatory military service. There were a couple parks, even, but only because the military units conducted regular drills and demonstrations. With such poor vegetation, these parks more closely resembled overgrown parking lots than a true outdoor recreational area.

It was by no means a war-torn dictatorship with barricaded streets and armed personnel on every street corner and air raid sirens and bomb shelter notifications, but there was very little real cheer. The variety of Borelian skins provided the color against the dark, stony backdrop, not flower beds. A majority of the Borelian population in and around Ancrath was between forty and sixty, in human years, and there was enough brass in any given crowd to build several statues.

For the average Borelian born on Brelix, Ancrath or anywhere else, childhood was spent learning the history and glory of Brelix, always preparing them to be good little soldiers, ready and willing to enter the force upon reaching adulthood. All initial military training was done on Brelix, nowhere else. After graduating, the new recruits would do time on any number of colony worlds. After a certain number of years, they were given the option to leave, to start a family of their own, and to work in civilian life, most often in industrialization plants making weapons or other military necessities, or for the government. In working for the government, the soldier would continue to train and increase in rank as long as he was directly consulted. The comparable forty to sixty year old soldiers were grizzled veterans of war and highly regarded. But after a time, they would be given the chance to retire, to take up ownership or management of a particular plantation, to oversee its production and slaves, and to develop Borelian culture in their spare time. Art, music, culinary masterpieces, all came from the elders.

Upon death, a Borelian, regardless of his religious beliefs, would be taken back to Brelix to be given over to Tujor in a ceremony as grand as his military rank. The body was burned down to the bones, then the bones were taken, bleached, and decorated with jewels and other expensive items, then arranged—not just as a skeleton, but in abstract arrangements, usually more than one—and hung as art. Some were kept by the family, others sold as casually as nice stained glass or decorative dreamcatchers, the power of the warrior watching over a household, a mystical talisman. Those warriors of the highest rank and most prestige had their bone spirits hung in the temples or the governmental building. The priests of Tujor would take the smaller bones of burned priests and make full robes out of them. If requested, a soldier could have his bones scattered and given to certain people, a commander giving his bones and his spiritual power to the men who had been under his command.

Most of it was superstition of course, as a great majority of Borelians were atheists. Still, the ceremonies were ancient and almost sacred within themselves, and the bone spirits made pretty art to decorate a room.

Bone spirits were also hung in the sleeping quarters and work rooms of slaves, to watch them and keep them in line, to come to life and pursue a slave if he tried to escape. Some slaves wore bone jewelry to show which family they belonged to, the designation etched into the bone itself. A slave wearing bone jewelry, as opposed to any number of other, far more painful ways of declaring a slave, was said to show loyalty, that he could be trusted to work on his own and do his job well. Few of the slaves in Ancrath garnered this level of trust; most often, they were in Ancrath because they were new and needed a crash course introduction to Borelian society and how things were going to be from now on.

So it was to some advantage that the temple attack team opened a portal right into the primary auctionhouse in Ancrath, about two miles south of the Temple of Tujor. For one, no one expected it and so the team got the jump. For two, upon realizing that there was an attack going on, fresh slaves made wonderful allies once freed from their chains, and many did not need to be told even once to attack their captors. Some of the slaves turned out to be their own allies from the attack on the roads outside the city—Xur, D'Bok, Gin Jor, and the like—captured and turned over to the auction block right away. They were weary from the initial fighting and a secondary beating on the way to the block, but they would continue to fight as long as they could. All they needed was a weapon and a direction to go.

Stumbling through the portal into the chaos, Tommen's first thought was not terror and the need to run and hide. Rather, he likened the scene to a bar fight, like the ones from old Western movies where everyone's punching each other and cracking chairs and bottles over heads. The big difference, well two big differences. First, old Western bar fights were obviously staged, obviously choreographed. This was not. Second, no sheriff was going to ride in with his deputy and just put a solid stop to things.

But that didn't mean that Rifun and Kayla weren't effective at wrapping things up pretty quickly. It was the first time that Tommen had actually seen either of them fight in open combat. Kayla was truly a grizzly, huge, ferocious, taking everything by force and brute strength, of which she seemed to possess more than he might have given her credit for except by Akari augmentation. She used knives, glass, chains, guns, whatever was on hand, stabbing one Borelian in the face not once, not twice, but four times before whirling and opening up another Borelian's throat in a spray of blood, spattering it on her face and drenching her clothes. But she wasn't like a maniac who just enjoyed the killing. Tommen could see in her stance and in her gaze as she paused for just a moment that she did everything because she felt it was absolutely necessary. In this instance, it was.

Rifun, meanwhile, preferred the ninja approach to things,

referring Tommen to a book called *Five Rings*. He spent only a few seconds of attention per enemy, making his kill in three strikes or less, always just enough, never with any real flair or excessive sprays of blood. In the whole time they spent in the auctionhouse, he did not use his revolver once, but preferred swords and knives. If he did use a gun, or something similar, it was one he took from a dead enemy. Why waste his own precious ammo when there were guns with plenty of ammo just lying around?

Both of them used their version of the Akari skillfully, and the whole fight was over in about five seconds. Tommen hadn't even lifted a finger, but was content to hide behind his little security detail and let them defend him. If Kayla wanted to fight, that was her choice. He was just here for the journal.

Most of the freed slaves were returned to their own worlds, though a few declared that they would stay and fight as long as they could. With about a dozen of them together, they quickly formed a squad, chose a leader, and jogged out into the street. Rifun and Kayla did not stop them.

"All right, it's about two miles north to the temple complex," Rifun said, deliberately slowing his breathing. "We buy time for Kayla and Tommen to get the journal, then unleash hell."

The general idea was to take over a small building close to the temple, then use a Fast Band to simply bypass the fighting, cause some damage, retrieve the journal, do some more damage, then release the Band to provide a little more challenge for the troops and open a portal back to the fortress. The signal would be given, saying that their goal was complete and the army was to do as much damage as possible on their way out.

That was the plan. And as Rifun enclosed their force in a Fast Band and they started off north toward the temple, everything seemed to be going according to plan. The city had largely grown silent and the temple was visible even from the auctionhouse, a pyramid with some kind of relief or statue spiraling around it.

Their jog was interrupted by a blitz attack from the west, a full unit of Borelian soldiers barreling into them from a side street, its commander using his own Band like a battering ram. When the two Bands collided, it was like glass on glass, and both of them shattered, causing everyone to stumble.

Tommen didn't see much at first, but he was pretty sure the human body was not supposed to bend backwards like that as Rifun went to great lengths to avoid being touched by the sudden assault. Kayla was saved by the fact that she used a Slow Band to slow herself down. A few members of the team, however, were not so lucky, and Tommen was suddenly faced with the very real possibility of having to fight. That was bad enough, but he had no clue how to fight a Borelian. How did you fight someone you couldn't touch or really get close to?

He was jolted back to reality as a knife was thrust into his hands. The blade itself was probably a foot long or better and the handle was a little awkward, clearly not meant for human hands. But it would do, and not too soon as one of the Borelians fixed its gaze on him and started forward, raising its gun-like weapon.

Instinct kicked in as much as some of the training his dad had imparted to him, and as Tommen dodged to one side, he also moved forward, putting up a Fast Band and getting within striking range.

In a way, it was surreal, and Tommen pulled up short before he could shove the knife in the Borelian's throat. It wasn't that he had any illusions of reciprocated mercy if he chose to give it, but to have an enemy so perfectly at his mercy, it almost didn't seem right. And then there was his no-kill vow. He had come up with this plan of everyone fighting the Borelians, and he had begged to come on this mission. Was he stupid or what?

Only reflexes kept him away from the Borelian's murderous grasp as it or someone else in the group sliced through his Band. Tommen pulled a semi-limbo as the Borelian lashed out first with a fist and followed it up by swinging the gun around, taking a step back and looking for a shot. Tommen put up another Fast Band, this one less than absolute, and managed to stick his knife in the Borelian's bicep. The alien snarled in pain but did not slow down, though its grip on its gun faltered. Tommen used the opportunity to drive his elbow into the Borelian's elbow, loosening the gun which he then confiscated, twisting it in the alien's grasp until he got a clear shot and pulled the trigger with the Borelian's own finger. He made a mental note not to touch his face with his hand, and he wondered if the gloves really were as water- and oil-proof as Kayla claimed.

Tommen knew that a lot of the head shots on TV shows were greatly softened, made to look about as harmless as a chest wound or a leg wound, just a little hole in the skin. In reality, though, the skull was pretty darn fragile and so was the squishy brain matter it protected. He could only say he was thankful not to be in the indirect line of fire and so get covered in alien brains. Nevertheless, his stomach lurched and he fought to keep himself upright and not let his guard down.

Elsewhere, Kayla had three dead Borelians at her feet, and Rifun managed to get two in such a position so that they ended up shooting each other. The rest of the team had been scattered, singled out, and the Borelians were slowly chipping away at their numbers.

Tommen turned around and was nearly impaled. Instead of limboing, he dived forward into a somersault, but it was poorly executed as he was more worried about keeping his own knife and new gun away from his body, plus trying not to touch himself with his gloves anyway. Nothing worse than doing the enemy's job for him. When he came back up the second Borelian was still advancing but was sorely unprepared for a sudden full body blow. Tommen couldn't even register it until he saw that their sudden saviors consisted of half a dozen Dorigisi, three Sakarian giants, and four Turitians in full armor, no streamers to be found.

Despite the turn of good fortune and the fact that most of the assaulting force was taken out in the surprise, there was still work to do and reinforcements would likely be on the way. Nevertheless, once the last Borelian was dispatched, the group took a moment to catch their breath.

"Well, you certainly are a welcome sight," Rifun said to one of the Turitians, breathing heavily.

"Our plans have been betrayed," the Turitian said, its voice slightly marred by its helmet.

For half a second, Rifun stopped breathing. He cast a momentary glance at Kayla, then looked back at the Turitian. "What do you mean, they've been betrayed?"

"The Tacagans sold out, allied themselves with the Borelians and the Hands of Time."

"How do you know this?"

"One of the spaceships was damaged when we attacked the shipyard," one of the Dorigisi said, "but we entered and started pulling information anyway. We found the general notice in the computer."

They'd spilled their entire plan in front of the Tacagans. The Borelians knew their numbers, their strengths, their strategies, everything. They would be waiting for them at the temple, Tommen was sure. Light-headedness washed over him and he took several deep breaths.

"The good news," the Turitian went on, "is that we were able to commandeer four of the six ships. Once the other two are dealt with, the pilots will fly over the temple and the governmental building and take out as many enemies as possible."

"I don't think you're going to have just two ships to contend with," Kayla mentioned, pointing to the sky as hazy gray objects quickly turned into the outlines for spaceships descending into the lower atmosphere. Then they broke through the clouds and zoomed over the city.

"Rest assured. The pilots will do their best. They will wreck the city on their way down if they must."

If I'm going down, you're going with me philosophy, Tommen figured.

"If our plans have been betrayed, we must fall back," one of the commanders said.

"We may never have another opportunity," another said, one Tommen recognized as one of the advisors from the many planning meetings. "We should do as much damage as possible while we're here."

"We'd be slaughtered."

"Death is always an option."

Rifun put a hand up and both men fell silent. He gave both of them a stern regard. "If you're afraid, run now. And pray I don't catch up to you later." He roamed among the Borelian bodies, taking their guns and ammo and other weapons and distributing them among the group, Tommen included. "The full temple attack force will be arriving shortly, if they're not there already. We continue that way. We expected that by this point, they would have some kind of mobilization of their forces, and that is how we shall navigate this sudden turn of events." He glanced back and forth between Tommen and Kayla. "We are still going after the journal if at all feasible. Just understand that we won't be following a polished yellow brick road."

He did not wait for a response, simply headed off. The now larger security detail fell in behind and beside them, Tommen and Kayla safely in the middle. They didn't get a hundred feet before they all hit the deck as two spaceships flew low over the city, probably would have been in its streets if not for the sheer size, although the wing of one of them clipped a building, bending steel and sending stone crashing into the street.

If Tommen ever had any inclination to go spaceship shopping at the local car, er, ship lot, he couldn't say that he would have any clue what he would be looking for as far as style and functionality, but the Borelians seemed to have found a dealer they liked. The ships weren't the little one-man pods as seen in old B-movies, but neither were they hulking whales like the Enterprise. Rather, these seemed to be the perfect size for small planetary operations, enough for a crew of maybe...a dozen? How many people did it actually take to crew a small spaceship? Well, in all honesty, these were probably just little passenger vessels to get the soldiers on and off the ground quickly without having to land the whale. Fast and maneuverable, certainly easier to conduct everyday operations from simple observation to blasting the hell out of your own ships because they'd been commandeered by the enemy. And there was no lack of firepower, either, as they quickly discovered.

Even before they reached the temple complex, it was evident that the main attack force was already there and engaged in heated battle.

Rifun had been right; the center temple, the Temple of Tujor, was massive. Tommen had maybe envisioned some kind of church, maybe one of those mega-churches that saw ten thousand attendants for three different services. He had not been expecting to see the Great Pyramids of Giza looming overhead.

From one end of the complex to the other was as big or bigger than the entire WVSU campus, including all the sports fields, six small pyramids arranged symmetrically around one larger pyramid, each with a carved figure snaking its way around to the top. The one on the largest pyramid faced to the north, but as Tommen looked at the others, he realized they were all the same. All dragons. The smaller ones on the Facet temples each loomed over something at the very peak, something to represent that particular facet. Money, pleasure....

Money is the only pleasure in the world.

Good old Titik. He'd known all along.

But even that fleeting thought was dismissed as Tommen Banded and really looked at the dragons. While the smaller ones all had certain variations, he was willing to bet that, even though it faced to the north and he could not presently see its face, he knew exactly what the dragon on the Temple of Tujor looked like. In the dim light, Tommen could also see that each of the pyramids was covered in bones, the Temple of Tujor covered in bones decorated with what might have been precious stones and other valuable things. During the day, it was probably a glittering masterpiece.

Any advantage the Borelians thought they had with advance knowledge of the attack was quickly negated by the temple attack. No self-respecting army danced out in the open if they could help it, but neither did they want to get trapped in a confined space. And as much as they pushed against the forces of the Order, simple strategy and limited use of Time could not give them the advantage they needed.

Rifun led the way around the outside of the complex, heading north where Tommen bet the entrance to the Temple of Tujor lay. Another advantage the Order possessed was the ability to circle around the Borelians. Clearly whoever had come up with the Borelian surprise attack strategy had not been thinking things through. Probably had never read Sun Tzu, Tommen thought wryly.

As they reached the Order forces, Rifun slowed down just a touch, enough to let his men know he was there, give them a pat on the back, let them know they were doing a good job, boost morale, boost courage, and on to battle and glory! Tommen glanced at Kayla who looked about like she had when she stabbed Rifun: stoic, resolute, uncaring that she stood among her enemies so long as the leader died.

Several of the advisor generals were gathered at the north end, the north Facet temple, whose icon the dragon held represented...victory, maybe? Regardless, they were directly facing the entrance to the temple.

"All right, what are we looking at?" Rifun asked.

"Welcome, Faharoa," one of the generals greeted. "We regret to say that our plans—"

"Have been betrayed. This I know. I have been so informed. But I'm not willing to give up so long as we have a fighting chance. We need that journal."

"Of course, Faharoa."

"So, what are we looking at?"

"Difficult to estimate the numbers, but few wield any sort of Time abilities. Getting in should not be a problem."

Rifun frowned. "That's what I'm worried about. I don't like bait. But on the other hand, that's what portals are for. Any idea what the inside looks like?"

"If it's anything like these smaller temples, when you go in, it will open up into a main atrium with a great statue in the middle, both art and engineering as it is structurally necessary. The whole interior is circular in shape, with altar-like constructions at all compass points and on each side of the center statue, and there are enclosed corridors around both walls leading to a large library-like room at the rear. There are also stairs along the walls in the atrium leading to a second floor balcony. Things could be different in the Temple of Tujor, but I would imagine that the basic layout is the same upon entry."

"Understood. Do you think your men can hold it once we get in?"

"You would not have chosen me as your general otherwise."

"That's what I like to hear. All r—"

He was cut short by the deafening sound of an aircraft coming out of the speed of sound, followed by the shrill shriek of a car needing a serious brake job. Two spaceships appeared in the sky, high up to start, but heading directly for the temple which spiraled into the air a good five hundred feet or better. One ship was in pursuit of the other, firing wildly. Several blasts ripped open the ground in the temple complex, shaking the pyramids, blasting small rocks, and filling the air with heavy black dust. The pursuing ship abruptly ceased fire, but the lead ship wasted no time in taking it up, making a beeline for the largest temple and firing madly.

Huge chunks of stone rained down over the complex. Tommen threw his arms over his head as the group scattered, each person looking for some kind of cover. There was a thunderous crash as a flying boulder struck the dragon at the top of the smaller temple and more boulders came tumbling down. Many got clear, but not all, and nothing remained of them as they were driven into the rocky ground like tent spikes.

The spaceships zoomed overhead, clearing the temple complex. The pursuing vessel again opened fire. The lead ship banked to the right, toward the governmental building, and flew off.

The whole attack had lasted less than twenty seconds, yet it felt like an eternity. Tommen's heart hammered in his chest, his ears rung like gongs, and his whole body shook violently. His stomach churned, his lungs heaved, and he wished desperately to go home.

Dust hung in the air, and with the gloom of night, visibility was limited to about two feet. Only the vague shapes of the pyramids lent any sort of helpful landmark for orientation. Not far away, Rifun was slamming a clip into his recently acquired gun.

"We're not going to get another opportunity like this," he declared. "We move now."

Tommen jumped as something grabbed his arm, but it was only Kayla. They fell in with the security detail and began running. He didn't know where, exactly, as his mind was spinning, and he could only trust that the men knew what they were doing. He could hardly see, and his thoughts were muddled, but his hearing aids faithfully pushed all sound into his ears, whether he wanted to hear it or not. Running, breathing, shouts, grunts, snarls. Only now did Tommen appreciate just how big the complex was. This wasn't just a mad dash for safety, this was taking advantage of chaos and running across an open field that, under normal circumstances, was not a smart maneuver.

Then there were shots, screams of pain and rage, roars of battle as enemies engaged. There was light coming from somewhere off to the side, like a flare, increasing the visibility to about ten feet, the pyramid just a hulking shadow in the dark. When he looked up, Tommen could have sworn that the dragon slithering around the pyramid looked down at him with glowing ruby-red eyes, maybe even moved to get a better look and make damn sure he knew that the Shadows were alive and well.

No god or author can help you here, little one, the dragon whispered in his mind. *Here, there is only shadow.*

Tommen's heart twisted, but he did not dwell on it for long before his feet suddenly went out from under him. Kayla's hand slipped from his grasp and he landed on his face on what amounted to concrete. He felt skin tear but he was unable to cry out. He couldn't even say what had caused him to stumble except maybe his own two feet. Gradually, he picked himself up and tripped again. Stairs. There were stairs here. Only three, he clumsily found out, but between the lingering dust and the shadow of the temple, he was all but blind. He couldn't see Kayla, couldn't see the Order forces, couldn't see Borelian forces either. He couldn't even really see his hand in front of his eyes.

That was no matter for getting inside, because he found the door easily enough with his face, almost the same way he found the ground. Two massive stone doors constituted the entrance to the temple. One was open; he knew this only because of the different air currents and the sounds of battle. It still looked dark inside, which meant he could get hit with friendly fire as easily as move about freely. Knives of anxiety stabbed through his chest. He patted the pocket where the key still lay. Chandler had told him that he would certainly find the journal and that he would have to make a choice on handing it over. That implied that he would live to see the dawn. But in the middle of a dark battlefield, not knowing where his friends or his enemies stood, that promise seemed a distant memory. Taking a breath, he made his way inside.

Immediately, he was met with blinding light. He put his hands up to shield his eyes until he became more accustomed to it.

The temple was bathed in golden light, though the black stone remained staunchly black, as if absorbing the light, stealing it away. The layout was as described, a circular atrium with a great dragon pillar in the center. Corridors ran to his left and right, a second floor balcony acting as the ceiling to those corridors. At the far end of the atrium was a great arch, perhaps fifty feet tall, leading into another room too dark to make out, but Tommen figured it must be the library-like room.

Around the central pillar and around the room were, indeed, altar-like structures, each one slightly different, each used for four heinous purposes, Tommen was sure. And everywhere he looked were bones. Hanging from the ceiling, hanging from the walls, carpeting the floor. The only thing that remained untouched was the dragon itself. As he watched, the dragon pillar suddenly moved. Stony bones and joints creaked and cracked as the statue came to life, slithering down off a stone pedestal. Huge feet with dog-sized claws hit the ground, and the bones crunched underneath. As the dragon moved, the stone rippled and melted until it formed scales, spines, until the stone itself disappeared and all that remained was the dragon, a lion in a cage meant for a house cat.

"Welcome to my home, little one," the dragon rumbled. "I congratulate you on making it this far."

"This isn't real," Tommen stated. "There's war and battle going on. There's nothing here."

"Of course there is. There is me." The dragon lowered its head to look at him. "I know why you're here. You intend to steal from me. I already foiled one part of that plan, moving my little pawns around the board and forming new alliances. But the other part I decided to do in person as it were. I can't let you destroy the work I've spent the last two centuries perfecting. There is one way you can get out of this, return home safe and sound. I will even give you a ride there on my back, and you can tell the world that you flew on the back of, not just any dragon, but the dragon. And lived to tell the tale."

Tommen shook his head, the only part of him that would move. "No. I can't do that."

"Why? Because the little man told you so? Quite frankly, I think I'm being rather generous, giving you this chance at mercy and freedom instead of roasting you alive for that little dynamite incident."

Tommen swallowed nervously. "This isn't real. It can't be."

"All you have to do," the dragon went on, "is take the key to the altar and walk away. I won't make you sacrifice an animal or take any kind of oath or vow. Just put it down and walk away."

Before either could say more, the vision flickered once and then vanished, leaving Tommen in almost total darkness. After a moment, a thousand candles lit at once, throwing light and shadows every which way. Something grabbed his arm and he was hauled to a safe corner, just inside one of the corridors, by Rifun.

"What?" he asked. "But—"

"A neuroelectrical projection field," Rifun said roughly. "The same one they use in the Wheel for reviews. Shows you what you want to see, what you expect to see. Worshipers of Tujor expect to come and meet with the god of death. Well, the priests couldn't arrange that on a truly spiritual level, so they went with the next best thing. Technology."

All around the temple, dazed Order soldiers had been taken by surprise by the Borelians but were now recovering and making a comeback.

Tommen looked at Rifun. "But then, how did you—? You aren't affected by it."

The man shrugged. "I can't see what's not there. The most it will do is give me a headache as my eyes and brain try to reconcile the two. Those of you with in tact brains are much easier to fool."

"That's how you were able to look at the Core of the Wheel and not go insane."

"Precisely. Now then, we just need to find Kayla and get this show on the road. You have the key?"

"Yeah."

"Good. Keep it close. We're going to need it."

Rifun spotted Kayla on the far side of the pillar. Commanding Tommen to stay put, he reloaded and slid out of hiding. He didn't get farther than that as the whole temple rumbled, as if from an earthquake. Fighting came to an awkward pause. Tommen briefly recalled that a Borelian's horns were extremely sensitive and could detect the earthquakes that frequented their world. Judging by their expressions, this was no earthquake.

He'd no sooner thought it than he heard the regular, methodical blasts from a spaceship. It started as a low rumble, then grew to the volume and frequency of a machine gun belonging to the Jolly Green Giant. Rocks and dust dislodged inside the temple and tumbled to the ground. Then there was a direct strike, and another, and another, straight up the north face of the pyramid. Inside the temple, stone rumbled and creaked, and Tommen half-expected the dragon to come sliding off the pillar to defend its home and followers.

Instead, the pillar cracked and began to slide. Another string of direct hits saw the dragon's head and one foreleg come sliding off, breaking off the pillar and crashing to the ground below, killing a dozen or more. Tommen coughed and waved some of the dust away from his face, but it did little good.

As the assault from the spaceships died down, fighting resumed, albeit cautiously at first. The pyramid hadn't collapsed with the breaking of the central pillar, but that didn't mean it could hold up well to another such direct strike.

Tommen watched and waited, uncomfortable at how the fighting was beginning to spread out and make its way toward his position. He breathed a sigh of relief as he saw Rifun and Kayla appear from behind the toppled statue parts, making for the corridor. They skidded to a stop briefly as more loose pieces fell from the pillar.

Then Tommen saw something he could not initially comprehend, and he stood, shouted, and pointed before he could fully realize what was happening. One of the advisor generals—one he would later realize was one of the two he'd seen Julianna speaking with earlier—had come up behind in pursuit of Rifun and Kayla, raising both knife and gun. Fearing he was aiming for Kayla, Tommen sounded the alarm. But as the two turned and brought their own weapons up to bar and deflect the attack, the general merely pushed Kayla to the side and turned his attention on Rifun.

"What is this?" Rifun demanded, just close enough for Tommen to hear. Considering the sounds of battle, they were closer than he was really comfortable with.

"In the heat of battle, working with one who has already tried to kill you and another of questionable loyalty, who's going to know?" the general said. "Then we will have a real leader in place, and we will get back on the right track."

The general was a big dude, some large species Tommen did not have a name for presently. He could have crushed Rifun with a well-placed blow from one massive arm, but Rifun was no fool. Tommen wasn't quite sure just how he did it, but he managed to subdue the general long enough to turn his attention to Tommen and

Kayla.

"Go! Find the journal! I'll take care of this!"

Kayla did not argue, but Tommen could not move. He watched as David took on Goliath, using the Akari in ways Tommen would not have thought possible, bending Gravity to make the general's blows weaker, using Magnetism to deflect his attacks, and a whole host of other maneuvers Tommen did not understand. He flinched as Kayla touched his arm.

"We have a mission to complete," she hissed. "If the Author still thinks he needs to live, she'll make it happen. Otherwise, let's go."

For a long moment, Tommen kept his gaze fixed on the duel. In another movie, that would have been the epic, climactic battle, where leader and traitor general face off. Maybe this was Rifun's movie, or his Authored Book, anyway. Maybe it had nothing to do with Tommen. But why write a Book for a traitorous blasphemer? Didn't that go against everything the Author stood for? Or was it simply recording history?

He was jerked from his thoughts by a literal jerk, Kayla tugging him deeper into the corridor, away from prying eyes and the throes of battle. Behind the thick stone, even the sounds of battle felt farther away. Tommen took several breaths, sure that his racing heart was echoing in the long, dark corridor. They ran into the darkness until they could no longer see each other, then stopped to kneel and catch their breath.

"Okay, Tommen," Kayla huffed,. "We need to find the door that key goes to. What do you know?"

In the darkness, his look of surprise went unheeded. "I have no clue. Didn't Andrew or Nathan tell you?"

"Why would they tell me? You're the one going after the journal."

Tommen rubbed his face and sighed. "Okay. Okay, okay, okay. Keys go to doors and locks on things. I don't know about you, but I haven't seen too many doors or treasure chests around here. If it's something the priests have to get to regularly, it's probably not exactly hidden. If it's something they could have afforded to forget about for a while, it's not exactly obvious."

"Because that makes heaps of sense."

"No, no, hear me out. The Borelians probably didn't have a special vault just for the journal; they had no idea what it was or even that they were going to get it, so it's probably not going to be hidden in the walls or anything. At the same time, if they thought it was valuable, they must have a treasure vault hidden around here somewhere. Accessible only to those who need to get in, but easily accessible in case of attack and they have to clear the hell out."

Kayla was silent for a moment, then said, "I haven't seen any priests running around. Have you?"

"Find the priests, find the treasure vault. Find the treasure vault, find the journal."

There was shuffling in the darkness as they both clambered onto weary legs and aching feet. Kayla put a hand on Tommen's shoulder. "Normally I wouldn't condone this, but this is the Borelian temple of death we're in. Loot the shit out of it. Put some money in your pockets."

Tommen stifled a laugh, strangling it into a small snicker. He cleared his throat. "Well, I don't know my way around this place too well, so we might just have to do a quick sweep. Maybe we'll get lucky and find another staircase marked 'Employees Only.' "

Kayla snickered at that one. They adjusted position so that she led the way with her weapons while Tommen meekly followed, hand on her shoulder. The corridor was much longer than he gave it credit for, viewed from the main atrium, but after a while, he began to question whether they were even on the same floor. He didn't feel any pronounced steps, but a gradual, curving slope he might believe.

"Can I ask you something?" he wondered.

"I suppose," Kayla sighed.

"Why go through the hassle of attacking? I mean, why not take the humanoids, Disguise them as Borelians, and just send them in like casual tourists or worshipers? Incognito stealth mission."

"You would have to ask your fearless leader about that one. But I think the answer is as simple as the fact that this mission is as much about causing damage and fear as simply retrieving the journal. Rifun wants to make a point. The Borelians were upset that he broke their contract; he's trying to show that he's not going to take their punishment lying down. Honestly, I'm not a hundred percent sure. But it sure might have made this bit easier."

"What do you make of the betrayal by the Tacagans?"

"I was pissed at first, but then I wondered whether I really expected anything less."

"You don't think it's just another grand plot twist by the Author to keep her readers interested and us flailing about in uncontrollable plot and circumstances?"

"Oh, I imagine it's a thrilling enough plot twist, but as much as she is in control and could write world peace at any time, that doesn't make us exempt from the consequences of our actions. It would be like turning off gravity so we didn't hit the ground and die after intentionally jumping off a building."

"So then what's the point?"

Before either could say more, Kayla stopped and Tommen bumped into her. He hadn't realized it until just then, but there was light coming from up ahead and faint voices drifted their way.

"I think we found the priests," Kayla murmured.

"What do we do now?" Tommen hissed.

"We take your idea and run with it."

"What idea?"

He found out soon enough as Kayla quickly Disguised him as a blue Borelian. It wasn't a perfect job as the genetics and appearances wouldn't overlap perfectly, but in dim light with armor on and a few scuffs and scrapes and scratches in the Disguise, it should pass well enough to get them close. Kayla made herself a pink Borelian Disguise.

"Obviously we don't secrete the oils," Kayla said softly as she touched up the Disguises and observed her handiwork. "So you have to compensate by acting the part beyond any reasonable doubt."

"How about I let you lead?"

"That was going to be my next suggestion."

Once she was satisfied, Kayla stood back, rolled her neck—her horn imagery vanishing for just a moment as it brushed her shoulder—then slapped on an expression that was very reminisce of Isthim. Tommen simply took a breath, did his best Tyler Freeman impression, and nodded for her to lead the way.

The corridor continued to curve and the light got brighter. They did not hurry, but they moved quickly, with a purpose. No longer trying to sneak up on the vault, they let their footfalls echo. The voices in the corridor ceased, but Tommen did not hear anything to indicate that someone was trying to escape. Either there was nowhere to go, or else there was a force waiting for them.

They ended up in a room about twenty by twenty with a ceiling that hovered just over the head of Tommen's Disguise, and he prayed it wouldn't falter. All around the room were doors, simple man doors; Tommen counted twenty doors total, but only nineteen were open. In the middle of the room was a wooden table with nine Borelians around it, each wearing a robe made of bones and adorned with jewels. Tommen could see every priest was armed just as well if not better than the soldiers upstairs, but they were more concerned with filling a box on top of the table.

"What are you doing?" Kayla barked irritably.

"Saving the icons and artifacts," one priest answered. "As we are—"

"How long does it take?! There's a battle going on upstairs and the pyramid is ready to collapse if there is another direct aerial assault. Then where will we be?!"

"Apologies, ma'am," another priest answered. "We'll just finish up."

"Well hurry up! What about that one?" She gestured to the door still closed.

"That door is missing its key; it hasn't been opened for decades."

She drew a long knife-sword. "Then I'll force it open."

"No!" All the priests moved toward her but stopped just short. One said, "Please, do not defile the door. It would defile the temple itself."

"The temple is being defiled by the pirates who hijacked our ships and are set to topple the pyramids. Is that what you want instead?"

"The pyramid is merely the altar to Tujor," a fourth priest said softly. "It can be rebuilt. But all of this, this is the heartbeat of the god of death."

"Dead men don't bleed," Kayla growled. "But live ones do."

She cut down five of the priests before the other four could react. Moving out of reflex rather than conscious choice, Tommen drew his knife and hacked down two more opponents. The remaining two had only just drawn their weapons when Kayla was on them. The whole skirmish—it wasn't even good enough to be called a fight—lasted less than a minute, and the two of them stood in the middle of a small room with nine dead Borelian priests at their feet.

"All in a day's work," Kayla said, shedding her Disguise and leaning over the table, removing her helmet. Her hair was wet with sweat, face flush with effort. Tears were streaming down her face, more from exhaustion than fear. She sniffed and wiped her nose.

After a bit of effort, Tommen managed to be rid of his Disguise. He was still shaking. Looking at the bodies around him, smelling the blood and knowing he helped with their demise, he got sick.

"Tommen, the next time you go to the dentist, he's going to accuse you of being bulemic," Kayla told him.

He spit once to clear his mouth. "I can't help it. I can't do it. I can't...look at it. I hate smelling it. It's just..." He offered up a gunky string of stomach fluid. "I'm not a soldier. I can't even pretend to be one in my mind anymore. In the heat of the moment, I act on instinct, not calculated training."

"I know. Not everyone is cut out for battle." She straightened. "But you volunteered for this. And look where we are. We are in the heart of a Borelian temple. We made it. We can grab the journal and go. Our mission is almost complete. No more death. And look." She put her shoulder against the box of treasures and heaved it over. "Pay day."

He rubbed his face. "I guess so."

"Come on, Tommen. Live a little. Take home a souvenir or two. Take one home for your dad. Find something nice for Becky."

After a minute of collecting himself, he approached the box and its spilled contents and cautiously started pawing through it. Most of the contents were stone icons. Many were dragons or parts of dragons. Some were similar to the icons at the top of the other pyramids, representing the other facets of death. Some were carvings of various body parts, horns, hands, feet, and some he didn't want to think about. Some were carvings of various weapons. All of them offered up in some fashion for the god of death to bless for victory in battle or else a warrior's death, perhaps for fortune elsewhere, for strength or speed, or any number of things Tommen did not want to dwell on.

But there were other things in the box as well, such as more bones, these ones arranged in abstract art formations. Each one had at least one bone, usually the biggest, that was etched with some kind of writing. It was not a lot of writing, so Tommen just as soon assumed that it was the name of who the bones belonged to, who they had been as a living person.

There was also a handful or two of precious stones of all sorts, many of them small enough to adorn the smaller bones or convince a delighted woman that her new fiancé had money to blow, and sapphires and emeralds looked to be the favorite, with some diamonds mixed in. Picking through, Kayla found a couple topaz and a handful of semi-precious stones like aquamarine and polished granite. Tommen took a generous helping of stones and a few gold—or what looked like gold—coins and stuffed them in a pocket. Hopefully he wouldn't be stopped and searched upon return to the fortress. On the other hand, how was he going to explain where he'd gotten several thousand dollars' worth of jewels? His dad would understand, but would the pawn shop?

Well, it was no matter. He'd figure it out later. In a way, he felt guilty about looting a temple, even if it was a Satanic temple, but then again, maybe not. The Borelians did not believe in forgiveness or mercy, and he doubted the dragon would have felt that much better about him not looting the temple after all the other damage they'd done, so what was a few meager rocks?

Once they'd pawed through and taken everything they wanted, they stood back from the table and faced the door that remained locked. Battle and spoils were great, but they still had a mission to complete.

"Got the key?" Kayla asked.

Tommen swallowed and fussed around in his armor for the secured pocket where the key still lay. He brought it out and held it up in the light of a dozen or more candles. He glanced at Kayla, but instead of fear, he found himself having another geeky moment that he was finally having his Indiana Jones moment, where the mystical, ancient door was finally unlocked and the treasure recovered. Given that the rest of the doors were open with little flourish, he was fairly confident that there would be no booby traps here. Nevertheless, they each stood to the side as he inserted the key and gave it a turn.

The lock ground a bit but did not fully click. Well, so much for a smooth, dramatic reveal. Frustrated, Tommen wiggled the key, turned it, forced it, rocked it back and forth, all the while tugging on the handle. After much tugging and grunting, he felt the lock click and the door give. In the next second, he felt the ground meet his ass as he stumbled back a step. But the door had budged, and that was all that mattered. He got back to his feet as Kayla felt for a purchase, and together they tugged and pulled at the door until it reached a point that was no longer rusted from decades of sitting and it swung open. Kayla hit a wall and Tommen tripped over one of the bodies, but the door swung wide open. There were no poison arrows, no huge boulder, no toxic gas, just a dark room that smelled very, very old and musty. It was enough to make Tommen cough a little, but no more.

Kayla grabbed a candle and, cautiously, they peered inside. It certainly didn't look like anything too spectacular, more like a pantry with shelves running along each wall. The book was not set on a pedestal with mysterious light shining down over it. Rather, they had to go digging through more icons, more bones, more jewels of which they pocketed a generous amount. There was the addition of scrolls and texts in this particular vault, so Tommen figured they were at least on the right track.

"Got it!" Kayla cried. She'd disappeared halfway into a shelf, reaching for the very back. Now she emerged, covered in dust and cobwebs, but holding a very familiar-looking journal. She undid the leather strap, snapped the Imprint, and opened it up. Flipping through the pages, she nodded. "This is it. This is Richard's third journal."

Tommen felt relief wash over him and he leaned back against the shelves, sighing contentedly. "Okay." He rubbed his face. "Give it to me and let's get out of here."

Still less than enthusiastic about the hostage agreement, Kayla grudgingly surrendered the journal to Tommen who tucked it away in his armor. It was bulkier than the key had been, but hopefully he wouldn't be running around in the battlefield with it for too long. When it was secured, he nodded and said, "Okay, let's get out of here."

"Agreed. This place gives me the creeps."

This time, knowing more or less what was up ahead, they moved quickly back through the corridor, almost running except for the weight of the armor, and Tommen did figure out that the corridor was a very gently sloping curve. How deep they actually went was up for debate, and without understanding the properties of the stone and its natural soundproofing, he was unable to judge based on the sounds of battle, either.

Going down the corridor, the sounds of battle had been slight because of the aerial attack, and had vanished quickly in the darkness. Coming back up, the sounds of battle were louder than ever, echoing down the corridor before any light could penetrate the gloom. Kayla slowed their approach to little more than a sneak, Tommen following close behind so that he envisioned something very close to Shaggy and Scooby-Doo tiptoeing in a line down the hallway of a haunted house.

"Aw, shit," Kayla hissed.

"What?" Tommen whispered.

"The Borelians let us in, but they obviously counted on us not being able to get back out."

"What does that mean?"

"It means," a new voice said, "that the paltry force we encountered coming in was just to draw us in. The Borelians circled us after that."

The new voice belonged to one of the generals, the second one Tommen saw speaking with Julianna on the staircase. He was just visible as a black shadow against a gray backdrop. Gradually, the three of them made their way toward the end of the corridor where the light was a little more flattering.

"What's the plan?" Kayla asked.

"Our force was told to stay behind until you returned with the journal. I was just coming to make sure you were even still alive and worth fighting for. We're all that's left. Everyone else is dead or gone back to the fortress."

"And Rifun?" Tommen inquired.

"Already gone back to the fortress. We're just waiting on you. Do you have the journal?"

"We do," Kayla answered before Tommen could deny it.

The general nodded once. "Excellent. I'll rally my men and we'll open a portal home."

Something about this wasn't right. The first advisor had attacked Rifun directly. Now the second was saying Rifun had returned to the fortress and they all had to go. Very plausible, but knowing what he did, someone about it sounded fishy. Still, he did not voice his fears aloud until the general was gone, shouting orders and fighting his way to get to his men.

"You shouldn't have said that," Tommen stated.

"Why not?" Kayla asked.

He relayed his suspicions, starting with Julianna's conversation with the two generals on the staircase. He finished with, "I don't trust them. I don't think Rifun returned to the fortress, or not as he would have us believe. I don't think it's a good idea to go with him or his men. Just...call it a hunch, but something's up."

"There's always something up when it comes to the Order," Kayla said lamely.

Tommen shook his head. "No, you're not listening. Fine, you hate Rifun. I get it. But that has nothing to do with this. Julianna is up to something. I think she's trying to get rid of him."

"More power to her."

"Really? You'd rather have her in charge?"

Kayla did not respond to that, though Tommen could see she was not impressed by his argument. "Please, Kayla, we have to leave."

"I gave my word that I would return and free the Akarin."

"You made that deal with Rifun, not Julianna. And if she's done something, you think she's going to honor that agreement?"

For a long moment, she did not respond. Then she smiled. "I think she will. And I might have a plan. Just follow my lead and hang onto the journal no matter what. It's still a point of leverage for us."

Tommen nodded uncertainly but could not say more before the traitorous general and his small unit returned. They ducked into the corridor, two remaining at the mouth to bottleneck the Borelians and hold off the attack.

"We need to go back to the fortress," the general commanded, hardly even looking at Kayla or Tommen. "Duka! Portal!"

"No, wait!" Kayla jumped in. "We can't. Not yet."

"Why not?"

"Because there is one more thing Tommen has to do. Rifun gave him one special command he had to fulfill after he got the journal, before returning to the fortress. He wouldn't tell me, just said it was a short secret mission."

"What is this secret mission?" the general asked, swinging his head to look at Tommen.

"A secret one," Tommen answered. He took a breath. "I didn't tell you because I didn't know the battle was going to go this badly and because I'm—"

"A coward. I am well-aware." The general grunted. "But you're no fool, either. Very well. You may pursue your secret mission. Where is it?"

"Not here. You have no reason to guard me. You can leave."

Tommen quickly called up a portal to Sifura's world, anywhere on her world, knowing his dad would be waiting for him somewhere.

"I also have no reason to trust a traitor," the general said. He grabbed Kayla's arm and opened his own portal to the fortress. "So I'll just take her with me as insurance. I don't think you hate each other as much as you would have us believe."

Then they were gone, disappeared into the fortress portal. Tommen stared at the empty space where they had been, snapping back to reality as the Borelians began charging into the corridor. Then he just backed up and forced his portal closed.

One Borelian warrior managed to tumble through the portal with him, and they landed where else but the Red Desert, the heart of the Xur people's territory. The Borelian was stunned and uncoordinated, apparently never having had to fight in sand. Tommen was shocked at the change in weather and temperature, but he recovered faster, Banding so he could throw off his heavy armor and boots and rush the enemy soldier.

The Borelian brought its long gun up, but Tommen was already within range. He grabbed the rifle and shoved it back into the Borelian's chest. It loosened its grip and Tommen thrust it again into its face. The Borelian went down into the sand, sliding down a small slope. Tommen merely whipped the rifle around so the muzzle end was facing the soldier, then pulled the trigger. The Borelian came to a stop at the bottom of the slope and did not move.

Tommen sat down heavily right where he was, long gun still in hand. The sun beat down mercilessly, no different than his last vacation here. At least this time around he wasn't racing the clock. Well, in a way, he sort of was. He had to find the camp, hopefully find his dad, and return to the fortress to figure out what the fuck was going on.

He closed his eyes, unsure if this would work while he was awake. He felt the Energy of his position, there in the desert. He felt the Gravity, the Heat, the Light, the forces of the planet and the forces acting on the planet. Then he willed himself to find his dad. It still sounded strange, traveling along the Energy of a place like some sort of spiritual ventriloquist, throwing his consciousness instead of his voice.

Images flashed through his mind of a lake and a mountain and a forest and a desert, all converging into a camp full of strange creatures. It lasted no more than a second, but it put Tommen on his back and he opened his eyes, colors swirling in his vision, a headache blossoming in his brain.

North. The camp was north. He knew that, but couldn't quite say how. Sighing, he picked himself up and stumbled back to where his armor lay. He certainly didn't want to wear it, but he didn't want to just leave it either. He fished out the journal and kept that close to hand, then bundled up his armor awkwardly in his arms and focused on opening a portal. He had only half a dozen images and feelings about the camp, and he hoped it would be enough. After a second or two, a portal sputtered to life, showing the edge of the desert, mountains straight ahead, a forest to one side and plains on the other, and a lake in the middle. Grunting with effort, he stepped through.

The camp was not far away, and he was intercepted by a Da Leio scouting party within five seconds of walking through his portal. In a way, they reminded him of the Cowardly Lion from the Wizard of Oz. Once they determined he was not a threat, they were happy to escort him to the camp. They tried to carry his armor as well, but he did not give it up, afraid of what oils might be on it and not wishing to harm them. They delivered him and his stuff directly to a shelter made of wood and stone. But his first thought was not about speaking to the leaders. Rather, it was on the human man who waited outside the shelter.

Neither of them said a word as Walter pulled his son into an embrace. Despite the threats still looming over his head, Tommen felt only relief. His legs felt weak and his stomach felt empty, but he was home. He'd returned from behind enemy lines. Everything was going to be okay now.

"I didn't know if you'd make it," his dad said, hastily trying to beat down the soft emotions and become serious again. "The Tacagans have allied themselves with the Borelians—"

"We know," Tommen said. "The Turitians and Dorigisi found the announcement in one of the spaceships in the shipyard. It was a surprise, but we could prepare for it."

"You could. But..." His dad sighed and looked around at a camp pitched for a quarter million but housing only a fraction of that. "They couldn't. The leaders would like to speak to you if possible."

Tommen nodded and poked his head in the sturdy shelter where the five leaders sat in a circle. Another, smaller wave of relief flowed through him when he spied Sifura. She appeared to be thickly bandaged in multiple areas, but she was conscious and appeared to be in good spirits. She saw him and motioned him forward.

They gave him a similar account to the one they told Walter, about their surprise being taken away from them, the mind-boggling losses they'd suffered, and their request that humans never return or other interfere in their affairs. When Tommen glanced at Sifura, she just gave him a long cat blink and looked away, saying nothing. He was hurt, but he understood. They had to look out for the welfare of their people. Leading tens of thousands to the slaughter was hardly the quality of a good leader, especially when it was still debatable whether the battle overall had been won. Nevertheless, Tommen thanked them for their sacrifice, promised he would do his best to ensure all humans knew not to interfere, and left the shelter.

"Did you get the journal?" his dad asked levelly.

Tommen nodded. "Yeah. We did." He picked up the gear. "And I got a few souvenirs to take home." He sighed. "I guess I should get back to the fortress. Something's fishy and I need to find out what."

His dad shook his head. "Not right away. You look and smell terrible. You're tired. Everyone from the battle is going to be tired. No one's going to notice if you take a shower and a quick nap before addressing the masses." He continued before Tommen could protest. "And if something is going on, you're going to need a clear head."

Well, there was that. Still, Tommen didn't like feeling as if he was abandoning Kayla. Hopefully the fabled secret mission could cover him for a few hours while he got a nap in. Reluctantly he nodded, then turned his attention away from the fortress and toward home.

Chapter Thirty-Five
New Alliances

Tommen came flying out of a nightmare and found himself in gloomy darkness. Panic set in and he hopped to his feet. The floor was cold stone and goosebumps broke out over his arms and the hair on his neck stood on end. His chest tightened, couldn't breathe. He started walking, almost running, fear nibbling at his heels. He ran a hand through his hair, turned, stared at the cave wall, then took off running, deeper and deeper into the cave until he was consumed by total darkness. Small razor rocks cut into his feet, but he hardly noticed as he came to a stop. The darkness was as comforting as it was frightening, but in the stillness of the cave, he could hear echoes of battle. Shouts, snarls, screams, cries, weapons and injuries, victory and defeat, the realization that something had gone horribly wrong, they'd been betrayed, their movements were known to the enemy, had to fall back, nowhere to run.

He paced back and forth, one wall to the other, deeper into the cave and then back again, right up until faint light touched the shadows, and then turn back to head deeper. He still couldn't breathe and he was covered in sweat that froze to his body in the cool cave air. Still he paced until he was so cold he could hardly move. He leaned against one of the walls, knowing it was a bad idea but unable to tell himself to stop. He pushed off from the cave wall and started walking. His mouth dropped open in a silent gasp as his toe struck something solid, a sharp rock. He went down to all fours. With his body nearly hypothermic now, the impact hurt all that much more, and he was unable to completely stop himself from smacking into the ground with his face, and that, too, was rather painful.

He got his legs under him and sat. He dropped his head into his hands but could do little more. He could not scream. He could not weep. He still could not breathe. All around him, the wind in the cave echoed with the sounds of battle. In the darkness, his eyes played tricks on him, showing him friends and enemies, combat and cowardice. He did not move for any of it. It wasn't real. Couldn't be real. And yet it had been, at least some of it.

In the heat of battle, it had all felt like some terrifying dream, even as he'd known it wasn't. There was no waking up, no extra lives, no do overs. Battle was one chance to get it right. He either made it out or he didn't. He'd made it out, but so many hadn't. He could not conjure up anything or anyone specific, except maybe the tribes who had been decimated. He was just so exhausted. He couldn't pinpoint any one thing that occupied his mind presently. Hell, he could hardly even remember his own damn name.

Gradually, he forced his limbs to cooperate and he drunkenly made his way back the way he came, or the way he thought was right, anyway. Soon enough he was rewarded with a lightening of the darkness. A minute later, he saw a pinprick of light. That pinprick grew until it became a small fire. That fire illuminated stone shelves on the wall, handmade cabinetry, a washbasin, more pots and jars than a ceramics shop. A pot had been hung over the fire, and there were several rugs laid out around it at a safe, responsible distance. Across the fire, sitting on one of these rugs, a man watched him.

Approaching the fire, the warmth brought feeling back into his body in the form of pins and needles and awful squeezing and compression. Once the initial shock was over, his muscles turned to water. Ten feet from the fire, he went to his knees and crawled pathetically over to the wall of the cave, maybe ten or twelve feet from the fire. He leaned his head back and closed his eyes.

He may have slept, or it may have just been one of those things that just happen in dreams with no explanation. When he opened his eyes, he was naked except for his boxers. Chandler knelt beside him, a pot of warm water at his side and a warm rag in hand. Even if

Tommen had wanted to push him away or tell him to stop, he couldn't. He had no strength left, no energy, no will. And besides, the warm water felt pretty good.

As gently as if he were holding a newborn kitten, Chandler took the rag dipped in the warm water and wiped him down. It was not a sponge bath or a full scrub with soap or oils or any of that, just a slow, methodical wash, from neck to waist. Tommen looked on passively, watched as dirt and blood slid to the floor and seemed to disappear. Chandler worked in smooth, even strokes, down his chest and both arms. Even Tommen's burned arm did not protest the warm water treatment; in fact, it seemed to welcome it. He did not fight as Chandler gently pushed him forward to wipe his back. Then he moved the large pot of water, still clean despite the number of times the man had dipped his rag which also remained mysteriously clean, down to Tommen's feet. Then he moved down and continued the process, starting at the hem of his boxers and working his way first to Tommen's knees before going to the lower legs. He made Tommen bend his legs so as to get the back, then had him straighten out again. Finally, Chandler washed Tommen's feet, and Tommen watched as the cuts he'd sustained from the small razor rocks deep in the cave healed before his eyes. The blood washed away and the skin knitted itself back together until it never even happened.

Finally, Chandler dipped the rag one last time and held it out to him. After a moment of consideration, he took it and wiped his face. His arms fell limply back to his sides. Then Chandler took the rag and laid it over a stone near the fire to dry. He took the remaining water in the pot and poured it methodically over the hot coals and stones around the fire, filling the cave with steam.

Tommen did not know how long he sat there in the haze, but when his mind came back from its wandering, he saw Chandler sitting on his usual rug facing the fire, legs crossed, eyes closed, murmuring something he could not hear. Weakly, Tommen moved and tried to sit up a little straighter against the wall. Chandler stopped murmuring, probably praying, opened his eyes, and looked at him. He untangled himself and stood. He disappeared in the steamy haze that still filled the cave but was slowly dissipating. A moment later, he reappeared with Tommen's clothes. He held them out and Tommen took them after a moment to gather his will enough to move his arm. Still he did not redress right away.

"Why did you do that?" he asked, his voice sounding distant.

For a long moment, it looked as if Chandler wouldn't answer. Then, "It needed to be done." He turned to his spot by the fire and resumed his praying.

Tommen did not move right away. His hands moved before his brain could catch up and he found himself putting on his undershirt followed by his T-shirt. Gradually he stood and slid his pants on one leg at a time. Last was his socks and shoes. Briefly he wondered whether the motions were necessary. If he was still dreaming, he should have been able to just dream them back on, right? Oh well, didn't matter he supposed. Besides, the normal motions were kind of nice.

Gingerly, he approached the fire and sat on his normal rug. He watched the fire, looked at Chandler, watched the fire, looked at Chandler. The haze was beginning to clear up and Tommen could see the sweat streaming down the man's face as he prayed. Only when the haze cleared completely did the man open his eyes.

"What do you pray for?" Tommen wondered.

"I pray for the Creator's will to be done, that many will look upon this and understand," Chandler replied, not looking at him.

Tommen studied the rocks in front of him, stared into the hot coals and the fire leaping from them. "What am I supposed to do now? I didn't anticipate any of this."

"You do exactly as you are supposed to do."

"And what is that?"

"The Author will show you when you get to that point, as long as you do not try to be the author yourself."

"Will Kayla be all right?"

"What have I told you before?"

Tommen sighed. "No one dies."

"Do you doubt it?"

"In the middle of battle, it's hard to believe it."

"I know." Chandler did not move, but his expression softened. Finally he looked at Tommen. "Are you hungry?"

After a moment of thought, Tommen nodded. He didn't really feel hungry, but it had been a while since he'd eaten and battle required plenty of energy. Slowly, Chandler got to his feet and retrieved a couple of bowls. This time, the stew proved to be a chunky, meaty stew with very little broth. It was more of a cut up beef roast with gravy. Some potato and carrot chunks provided a taste and texture contrast, and several herbs and spices brought an otherwise bland mixture to life.

"Do you know what happens after this?" Tommen asked.

Chandler shook his head. "One-way doors make it difficult to know, and the Author has not shown me anything. This one thing must happen before anything else."

"Great. A one-way door and I have to walk through it."

"Do not be afraid. The Author will always work it out in the end."

It felt small comfort, and Tommen finished his stew in silence, helping himself to a second bowl though he didn't really feel like it. Mostly he just wanted to go to bed, get a good night's sleep, wake up to an alarm, and head off to the job site for ten hours. No battle, no Borelians, no Order, no espionage. Just the guys, the tools, and a project coming together. He finished the second bowl of stew and set his dishes aside.

"What happened here? While we were in battle, were the Whites also fighting?"

Chandler gave him an unreadable look. "Fighting what? As you yourself said, Shadows will not fight Shadows. They simply let their pawns do the dirty work and they sweep up the pieces." He shifted position. "And yet, there was a bit of a scuffle at the border. The Whites took no chances in ensuring the Shadows would not try to cross. Perhaps they were looking out for the few true Akarin who were also fighting on Brelix."

"Well, we could have used a few more of them."

The man did not reply to that, just finished his own dinner, then took all the dishes to the wash basin. Tommen watched him. Chandler returned.

"Thank you," Tommen said, staring at the rocks around the fire.

"For dinner?" Chandler questioned.

"Well, yes, but also for sticking by me, showing me the way. And the washing, I guess. I still think it's a little weird, but you were right, it needed to be done. I don't know what it did, but it was good anyway."

Chandler nodded. "It was good. And while I appreciate the gratitude, you should be thanking the Author. I may not always be here to guide you, for I am but a man, a character in a book."

Tommen looked sharply at him. "What are you saying? Do you not have a lot of time left or something or—?"

"No, no. We will yet have time together. But it may not always be so. Do not rely on men to guide you, no matter how good they may seem. Even I am not perfect. But the Author knows what she's doing."

Tommen still didn't like the thought of losing Chandler, but he kept his mouth shut. Both men shifted position by the fire and stared into it. Chandler spoke first, still looking into the flames.

"It's time to wake up now."

Tommen blinked and looked up, asking "What?" even as he realized he was looking at his dad.

"Up and at 'em, kiddo," his dad said. "I Banded you, so it's still early enough to hit the fortress before going to work. If you want."

He glanced at his alarm clock, initially confused. Gradually, the events of the last twelve hours sorted themselves out. He sighed and sat up, rubbing his neck. He was still a little sore, but not nearly as battered and beaten as he'd expected to feel. Guess Chandler's ritual washing did him some good in the real world, too. He stood. "I'm going to shower again."

His dad did not stop him. While Tommen intended it to be a quick shower, the warm water again reminded him of the wash, and he lingered a minute or five longer than planned, but by the time he stepped out, he felt almost normal. The battle in the fortress had left him feeling fractured. This time around, he felt almost normal. Not perfect, as a fleeting memory whether called or uncalled could make him break out in cold sweat and strangle his ability to breathe, but better.

He returned to his room and got dressed, choosing clothes he expected to wear to work, telling himself that he was just returning a book to the library and would be heading to work afterwards, something almost normal. He found the journal under his pillow, right where he'd left it. Not the most brilliant of hiding spots, but at least he would have known if someone tried to steal it. He put it in a small bag and slipped that over his shoulder. Just returning a book to the library. Maybe having a fight with the head librarian, but just returning a book. Then going to work.

Out in the kitchen, his dad was cooking up some eggs, sausage, and bacon. Despite still being full from Chandler's stew, Tommen accepted a plate and munched away on the food while pulling on his work boots. They'd come out of the box a perfectly unblemished tan. Now they were gray and white and black and scuffed and one of his laces had to be retied after accidentally getting sliced in half with a razor blade. But they were normal. They slipped on his feet comfortably, settling right into his wear spots.

"Is there anything I can do from here?" his dad wondered. "Do you want me to come with you?"

Tommen shook his head. "I don't want to give Julianna any more hostages than she already has. As for helping from here, just be home when I get back. That would be the biggest thing."

"Will do."

He finished off his breakfast, grabbed the bag with the journal, stood, opened a portal to the fortress, and stepped through.

He was not immediately arrested or assaulted. No one grabbed his bag and ran off with it. No one even seemed to notice he was there. In fact, there was no one else in the portal room period. Remembering Rifun's comments about scrambling the Energy in the portal room, he did a quick feel of the Energy in the room. He'd had no trouble opening the portal and nothing really felt different. Maybe it was just him. Maybe everyone else was still sleeping off the battle. Maybe the Order had been decimated as badly as the tribal armies and the quiet was just going to be a thing for a while.

Rather, it was a bit like the time he'd come to the fortress and there had been an Akarin uprising only just before his arrival. The difference was, with the uprising, those who had crowded eagerly into the atrium had been Order members of all divisions: Artists, Philosophers, Soldiers. This time around, it was only the soldiers, and, it looked like, only those who had actually been in the battle. They were grimy, dirty, grungy, dusty, bloody, and God Almighty did they smell. Tommen felt bile rise in his throat, but he beat it down. He was not bulemic and the smell certainly wasn't as bad as some he'd encountered.

And anyway, his attention was taken by those on the staircase, who seemed to be looking down upon the soldiers as if from a stage. The most obvious figure was Julianna, and Tommen could feel her cold shoulder even from the back of the room. On either side of her were two of the generals, and if he had to hazard a guess, they were the ones she'd been speaking with on the staircase that day. One had attacked Rifun, and the other tried to lure Tommen and Kayla back to the fortress for unknown purposes. But if the one who had attacked Rifun stood up there on stage now, what had happened to the Faharoa?

In a way, it was rather unsettling to think of Rifun as being defeated. Like the Borelians, the man was just unkillable. He just would not go down or stay down. Who was this new force who could depose him? Only Julianna and her scheming mind.

They were the only three up there on the makeshift stage,

though there were a few guards at the base of the staircase. Clearly Julianna had learned from Rifun's mistakes and elected to remain apart from the crowd.

Tommen looked around, trying to read the overall mood of those in attendance. Aside from being exhausted, there was also an air of intense frustration, even anger. Problem was, they could have come from any number of things, from the battle itself, from being betrayed, from losing friends, from whatever she was saying or going to say up there. They might be agreeing with her in their frustration or they could be disagreeing with her and ready to strike again out of their frustration. There was just no way to know. And knowing that, Tommen decided to make himself scarce and just listen for a minute or two.

"The Tacagans not only turned their backs on their own people," Julianna was saying, "but they allied themselves with the very ones we were fighting against. And furthermore, with the Hands of Time, creating a nearly unstoppable force. I say nearly because we all know that their strength comes only from their numbers and paltry Time abilities." She sneered at that and Tommen saw a subtle ripple of agreement slip through the crowd. So they were on her side.

"But even the Borelians had less than this by themselves. By themselves, they had only numbers. They barely even had Time. Even with knowledge of our plans, we were still the greater force! We had great numbers, fearless warriors from many races, many factions, many peoples! We had not only the Akari but the Author's blessing as well! We had a noble mission!"

Now the ripple turned into a small wave as heads began bobbing.

"And still we lost."

Nods stopped cold and there were some reluctant grumbles. Julianna's gaze burned through everyone she touched, and Tommen was afraid she would pick him out. If she saw him at all, she gave no indication, instead returning to her passionate speech.

"This is not the first time we have been so let down, losing to a lesser foe. In the Wheel, one lone Akarin managed to cage you, cage us, in our own castle while he devised a plan to end our reign before it could truly begin. If that mission had been conducted properly, there would have been no need to attack this fortress and lose even more men. And even though that was still successful in the end, there was yet a traitor who sold out our allies and saw them punished for helping us. Now we come home from battling another lesser enemy, failures once more.

"Was it our numbers? No, for we have fought against even worse odds and won. Was it our power? Of course not, for we wield the greatest power! Was it our faith? Surely not, for we fought under the banner of the Author, seeking Richard's third journal. We even extended mercy to the Akarin, and they fought honorably beside us. So then, where did we go wrong?"

Julianna paused there and the gathered crowd grumbled amongst themselves. Still no one seemed to notice Tommen and he did his best to make himself hidden from Julianna's piercing gaze, hiding behind several very large aliens. Pressing himself against the back wall, he slid along it toward the sub-level stairs, making sure not to move too quickly. Unusual movement in a crowd would be more telling than wearing hunter's orange. He halted his movements as Julianna began speaking again and the crowd quieted to listen.

"Each of you here," she said gently, "fought nobly. You have been into the maw of Hell itself, battling the universe's most feared beings. You knew, even before the treachery, that there was every chance you may not return. You could have died. You could have been sold into slavery. And yet, each of you also lost someone. A leader, a mentor, a friend, perhaps even a family member. There is nothing that can be said to ease the grief or bring them back. But how many more of them would be here today if there had been even an ounce of care?

"No man can control the battlefield entirely. No man can control his enemy entirely. Else there would be no such thing as war. But an army is only as good as its leader. And there are certain qualities expected of leaders, especially those who command the lives of hundreds of thousands. You. Which is why I submit to you today that Rifun Ndolo, the man we have called Faharoa, Second, only to the Author herself, is unfit to be leader of the Order and must be held accountable for all who died senselessly on the battlefield, not only today, but through all of his blunders, even the Zero Hour Revolution."

The gate to the sub-levels opened up and Rifun stepped forward. He was not bound or shackled in any way; Tommen could see that the guards who walked on either side of him still deferred to him somewhat, or else deferred to his power. Right now, everything was up in the air, and no one knew who or what to believe, let alone say or do. He walked confidently through the crowd that had parted, most of them with open mouths and uncertain expressions—not that Tommen was any judge of alien body language. He made for the stairs with an air of quiet power and control, walking up the stairs as if going to meet some celebrity host on a talk show, ready to discuss the latest political outrage.

Tommen did not miss the look Rifun gave Julianna as they faced each other on the stair. Despite being higher up, she still only met him eye-to-eye at a polite, conversational distance. His posture and expression said that he now understood everything that was going on, and God help her if he was able to get his hands around her throat. Tommen half-expected him to Band and try it now. But now was not the time or place. Maybe there never would be a good time or place. As long as Julianna still had supporters and as long as Rifun had this hanging over his head, any assassination attempt, even if successful, would inevitably come down on his head and divide the First Order.

Tommen was not the only one walking through a one-way door this morning. Problem was, if everyone here was faced with their own door, how did they keep from tripping over each other on the other side? He closed his eyes and took a breath. Do only what was expected of him. The Author would show him what to do.

"Rifun Ndolo," Julianna started again, "you are unfit to be Faharoa of the First Order. Your battle plans have failed time and again and you have cost thousands of lives unnecessarily. We have gotten nowhere except running around in circles, attacking anything that moves. This time around, we were betrayed and still you insisted on the attack, rather than listen to your advisors to fall back and plan again. The Borelians managed to surprise us and wiped out more than half of all the forces fighting on the ground. Your stubborn determination has seen failure after failure. Even when one of your own generals turned against you, you were unable to defend even yourself before a mysterious, previously-unknown medical condition destroyed you and made you vulnerable. And how much more vulnerable did it make your army once you were unable to lead?"

So that was how Rifun had been defeated; his own body had betrayed him. Well, it was only a matter of time, Tommen supposed. Still, it felt a little unfair. Even more considering Julianna had known for a while about Rifun's seizures.

But what Tommen hadn't quite expected, and what Julianna evidently had not expected at all, was a sudden, smaller uproar of support for Rifun. Tommen couldn't make out everything, but someone said something about how she had fled for her life when it was only a few men pursuing her and that she wouldn't last five minutes on the battlefield. Someone else pointed out that she'd been gone for over a century and had no say in how things went. Another person declared that even when Rifun and Cassius had been gone into the Time Trap that they'd still managed to lead better than her. And a fourth person, who looked like a staunch veteran of multiple wars, declared that Rifun had as good a track record as any leader could hope for, even better given the circumstances of both "losses." Rifun was the successful general and had every reason and every right to lead the Order.

Suddenly the soldiers in the room seemed divided, though Rifun's fan club was decidedly much smaller. Julianna had been working the rumor mill for months now; she had at least three-quarters of the soldiers on her side, and probably most if not all of the rest of the Order. She was Richard's wife, the natural successor and an even more natural leader. Like the carrot leading the donkey.

"The goal," she interrupted, her voice carrying across the entire room, "was not to conquer the city of Ancrath. We can accept that because of the toxic atmosphere which would have killed everyone eventually. But the goal was to retrieve Richard's third journal. Your men had it in their hands and were returning when the traitor Tommen Forbes—who has betrayed us and the Akarin multiple times and cannot be trusted, yet you keep him close to hand at all times anyway—ran off with it. Was he betraying us?" She lowered her voice menacingly. "Or were you?"

"I have the journal!" Tommen shouted, raising a hand so all turned and could spot his general location. He pushed his way through the crowd until he reached the path from the sub-level to the staircase. Glancing at the guards on either side and at the base of the stairs, he approached sheepishly. "I have the journal."

The choice whether to keep it to yourself or give it to the Shadows, Tommen thought, sweat sliding down the back of his neck.

Stiffly, Julianna nodded to the guards and Tommen was permitted to approach. Every step he took was more laborious than he thought necessary, as if the murkiness of the stairs leading to the Core of the Wheel had been somehow transferred here. He felt all eyes on him. Again. Here he was, notorious traitor, again in the spotlight in the aftermath of battle. He needed to stop doing this shit. It was going to get him killed one day, he just knew it.

Julianna's gaze was cold enough to warrant the use of the Kelvin scale, and Rifun's expression was such that, had he been an actor, he might have been in the running for James Bond or maybe Jason Bourne. Tommen felt like a little kid, caught in an argument between Mommy and Daddy as they screamed at each other in Divorce Court.

"Prove that you have the journal," Julianna commanded.

Tommen dipped his head meekly and slid the pack off his shoulder. Moving slowly, deliberately, his dad's police officer wisdom kicking in and warning him to make no sudden movements, he unzipped the bag, opened it wide, and brought out the leatherbound journal. Unsure which one to hand it to, he stood there between them and opened it himself. He wasn't sure which one did it, but the Imprint was unlocked and they both pored over it.

"It is the original," they both declared after a moment, about the only thing they agreed upon thus far.

That brought a whole new wave of division from the gathered soldiers. Rifun's fan club proclaimed victory and demanded his release, some even calling for Julianna's arrest or exile. Meanwhile, Julianna's supporters continued to declare failure as a general and a leader, stating Rifun had been passive and aloof. If he'd acted more quickly, done this, done that, blah, blah, blah. As with all catastrophes, the fallout inevitably made everyone an expert in everything. The greenest grunts were suddenly endowed with decades of experience and wisdom, enough to call out the flaws in the plan, but only afterwards.

"I have never attempted to usurp you," Rifun told Julianna. "I have always remained loyal to the Akari, the journals, the Author herself. If anyone here is a failure and a traitor, it's you."

And so the lines were drawn. The First Order of the Akari could only have one leader, one Faharoa. On the one hand, Rifun, the general who had led multiple campaigns—his success or failure subjective between his supporters and deniers—and had led the Order itself while Julianna was still trapped in the in-between dimension. On the other hand, Julianna, the wife of Richard who had been around at the inception of the journals, who had been faithfully teaching from them, who had spent countless hours tending to the sick and needy and the common Order member on the street, who had been slyly working the rumor mill so as to turn the tide against Rifun.

The crowd below had gone past the polite audience now. For the moment, they were still shouting fruitlessly at the people on the staircase, but it wouldn't take much for them to turn on each other. With the sides intermixed and nothing to distinguish one from the other, it would be a bloodbath and each side would eat itself as surely as take down their perceived enemies.

Problem was, there was no good way to resolve the situation otherwise. If they went based on merit, Rifun had only military merit to give while Julianna had only humanitarian merit; the First Order was supposed to survive on both somehow. Difference was, Rifun did not have any kind of overseer appointed to take care of the humanitarian needs of the Artists and Philosophers, while Julianna already had her loyal generals. She controlled probably three-quarters or more of the entire Order sympathies. Furthermore, Rifun had gone to great lengths to free Julianna from the in-between dimension; there was no way he could justify killing her. He was at the distinct disadvantage here.

"I think the crowds have spoken," Julianna declared. "You are no longer wanted here."

"Fine," Rifun said shortly. "Guess I'll just take my little traitorous minion and leave."

"Excellent. But not before he hands over the third journal to me."

Tommen swallowed. He was definitely the child in this divorce. A chill snaked down his spine as the two faced off.

"Tommen, give me the journal," Julianna ordered.

"Don't do it," Rifun cut in. "She can't do anything about it if you don't. Not like she has any kind of military prowess or battle experience whatsoever. What would she know about the hardships of war?"

Julianna smiled, the fine lines on her face twisting grotesquely, and the winter breeze that came from her made Tommen want to run and hide. "I may not know too much about war on the open battlefield, but I do know a thing or two about leverage." She looked at one of her generals and made a motion.

The general made some sort of deferential gesture and started down the stairs. The three of them watched him cross the path to the sub-levels and disappear into the dungeons, a couple more guards falling in behind him. Tommen knew who they were going for a minute before they reappeared.

Like Rifun, Kayla had not been bound or otherwise restrained, and she walked with her head held high. She regarded everyone in attendance with an icy stare, reserving her own Kelvin glare for Julianna as they met on the staircase. Below them, the crowd lapsed into an uneasy silence.

"Bitch," Kayla said.

"Whore," Julianna replied. She looked at Tommen. "So then, this is how it's going to go. You give me the journal and they both go free."

"Give me the journal," Rifun interrupted. "Julianna dies and Kayla goes free. And the Akarin. Even I am not so cruel as to force them to suffer at this woman's hand."

"Give me the journal, Tommen," Kayla told him. "They fight it out between themselves, we take the opportunity to rescue the Akarin and steal all the Books and the other two journals."

"Yes, please do," Julianna said. "It would probably be the only thing that would reunite us here today."

"I have the rights and the success of the military," Rifun declared.

"And I have the rights of succession," Julianna countered. "I am Richard's wife!"

"And I am his general."

"And I am sick of listening to you two bicker," Kayla snarled. She grabbed the journal out of Tommen's hands and threw it mightily off the staircase into the crowd. "Fight it out yourselves!"

Immediately the crowd erupted into chaos. It was less like an organized battle and more like a bar fight. Tommen saw the journal once as someone picked it up off the floor, and then it vanished as the person had their throat cut and the journal seized and tossed about. Tommen did not resist as Kayla took him by the hand and started running up the stairs.

"Come on," she said breathlessly. "You're going to show me where the other journals and the Books are."

Before anyone could organize a serious pursuit, she painstakingly opened a portal and they slid through, collapsing on the other side.

The room was small and dark, lit only by a red emergency light so that Tommen could just barely see his hand in front of his face and could untangle himself from Kayla. He squinted his eyes against sudden light as Kayla pushed open a door. It took a second for him to realize that this was the secondary portal room on the eighth floor, off Rifun's quarters.

"Okay, where are they?" she asked, crossing the informal living area and slipping into the office.

"I knew where they were before he redecorated," Tommen said uncertainly. He noted her exasperated look. "Hey, there's been a lot going on lately and Rifun wanted this place to look more professional. I don't know where he moved shit."

"Start searching then. If he wins, he can redecorate again. If he loses, he won't miss anything."

So they set to work on ripping the office apart looking for the Books and the journals. Tommen managed to stay more or less on task, but Kayla got distracted as she discovered seemingly endless wells of information. She took some papers and folded them up, stuffing them in pockets.

"Once we're done here," Tommen said, flinging open several drawers, "what about the Akarin?"

Kayla nodded. "The chaos should last a sufficient length of time to break them out."

"What about the big red button?"

"If someone uses it, then I don't think we'll really notice until we find ourselves on the other side. I don't intend to use it, though. Not today. At least not before the Akarin are freed."

"What happened to you leaving them and all that?"

"They're only a shadow of what they were, now chaotic, lost, leaderless. I will help them as much as I can."

"Once you get them out, where will you take them?"

Kayla paused in her search. "I don't know. But they can't stay here."

It was the best and only plan they had. Unlike the last few, this one was completely inprovised. Tommen's heart raced and he always kept an ear out for anyone running up the stairs or trying to sneak in through the emergency portal room. At least on the part of the stairs, being on the eighth floor was suddenly a distinct advantage. Any advancing soldiers would lose steam somewhere around the third or fourth floor. They'd be crawling up over the last stair onto the eighth floor, panting, hands on their knees, one finger up asking for a minute to recuperate before launching an attack.

"There's nothing here," Tommen said, opening up the last cupboard and drawer. "I swear they were up here."

"This is only the office," Kayla reminded him. "Time to go rummaging through his sock drawers."

It felt a dishonest thing to do, like breaking and entering or petty theft. Still, Tommen followed Kayla into Rifun's living area and began pulling open drawers. In the process of searching, he did engage in a little petty theft, taking some of the cash he had stashed away, among other things. Hey, like Kayla said, if Rifun won, he could always get more. If he lost, he wouldn't miss it. He might need it, but he wouldn't have time to come get it. and Tommen would consider it payment for private investigative services rendered, among other things. Bodyguard, minion, student, those sorts of things.

"Found them!" Kayla exclaimed, throwing open a cabinet to reveal all of the Authored Books. They looked as pristine as ever, as if they'd come fresh off the printing press. "Help me with these. Take them to the portal room."

He did so, and the two of them got all the Books to the portal room in one trip. From there, Kayla opened a portal into a small stone room, likely on Hlohi, pushed the Books through, and closed the portal. Once they were safe and sound, she visibly relaxed, breathing a sigh of relief and taking a minute to lean against the wall. "There. That's done. They're safe." She nodded, mostly to herself. "Okay. Now for the journals."

Their pace was far less rushed, though they did still make a hurried search of the rest of Rifun's room. They opened every cabinet, every drawer, left no sock unturned, and still could not find the journals.

"Where could they be?" Kayla whispered.

Tommen folded his arms. "Reconstruction was finished a week or so ago, so all the levels are in tact, including the Archives. The Akarin used to keep the Authored Books on display in the Archives. Maybe Julianna did the same thing since the Archives are under the control of the Philosophers. Her priests, so to speak."

"It would make sense. Only one way to find out."

They walked out onto the staircase cautiously, but the sounds of fighting were still distant. Elsewhere, curious onlookers—Artists and Philosophers—watched, unsure as to just what was going on. Moving stealthily down the staircase, Tommen saw, as they got closer, that the fighting had not passed the second floor. It was still wildly uncoordinated and more like a poorly choreographed bar fight, but it wouldn't be surprising them on the fifth floor any time soon. With all the higher officers, seemingly on Julianna's side, down in the fighting, Tommen and Kayla slipped by the sixth floor largely unnoticed.

No one stopped them from entering the newly-renovated Archives, though they did get plenty of stares. Tommen wouldn't have been surprised if a little messenger was dispatched to inform Julianna of the strange activity, and he said as much to Kayla who agreed.

"We'll just have to make this quick, then," she murmured.

Walking through the new Archives was extremely disorienting. He hadn't spent a whole lot of time in the old Archives, but be remembered coming here during the fortress battle to save the Authored Books. The Archives had had a certain layout, a certain feel to it, something comforting and familiar. Now everything was remodeled and rearranged and neither of them quite knew their way around. After a few minutes, both of them were equally frustrated, knowing that, if someone had alerted Julianna to their presence here or if she suspected it and sent a small force anyway, their time was running short. And they still had to free the Akarin.

Tommen rounded another corner and was rewarded with a welcome sight, though the delight didn't last long.

"I found the display case!" he said in a loud whisper, half-expecting a librarian to shush him for speaking too loud.

Kayla appeared a moment later. It was a different case than the one used for the Authored Books. This one was smaller, understandable since it only had to house three books. Those three books were presently missing.

"Shit," Kayla hissed. "That can only mean that—"

"Looking for these?"

They turned to see Julianna standing there, her loyal generals on either side of her, plus several more soldiers behind them. She held all three journals.

"I admire your spirit," Julianna said. "I admire your loyalty. But it can only take you so far in the face of imminent destruction."

"Yeah?" Kayla drew a knife. "Tell your dogs to stand down and let's me and you have a little discussion about imminent destruction."

The scarred woman grinned, handed the journals to one general, then drew her own knife from a concealed pocket in her dress. It was the same one Kayla had used to stab Rifun. Then she drew a small vial of fluid from that same pocket, dabbing several drops of an oily substance on the blade.

"Borelian poison loses its potency very quickly, I'm told, even with climate-controlled environments," she said lazily. "Good thing it's only been a couple hours. But even so, you still won't be able to survive once I cut out your heart."

She looked like she might have been ready to say more, but Kayla did not give her a chance, instead launching herself for the first strike.

Tommen stood back, one eye on the women, one on the soldiers in case they decided to come for him while the women were distracted. They did not come for him. They did not interfere in any way, either to help Julianna or hinder Kayla. Rather, they stood back as a patient, if intrigued, audience. Tommen had seen catfights before in school, but that was nothing compared to this.

He would say one thing: Julianna was a much better fighter than he would have given her credit for, even fighting in a dress. She moved almost as a woman possessed, twisting and whirling and lashing out with the speed of a serpent. She gave Kayla a good run for her money. But where Kayla was a battle-hardened warrior, she'd also been in battle recently, and she was tired. Tommen could only watch in utter disbelief as, in one fluid movement, Julianna blocked a would-be fatal stab, knocked Kayla's arm to the side, then slid around behind her, pulled her hair and head back, and put the knife to her throat, the oily blade hovering just over skin.

"Well now, this is a bit familiar, wouldn't you say?" Julianna asked, breathing heavily. "Is there anything you'd like to say before I send you to see your husband?"

Kayla grinned and chuckled. "I will still be better off than you."

Tommen couldn't stop a shriek as Julianna pressed hard and drew the knife across Kayla's throat. His shrieking died down as the blood suddenly turned black and the Disguise dropped just as readily as the body. For a long moment, they could only stare at the alien, plated in rock like a Grunjor, yet not a Grunjor. Tommen was the first to speak.

"Jali," he stated. "She was a Builder, one of the Akarin."

Now it was Julianna's turned to snarl in rage. Tommen forgotten, she swept out of the Archives, her loyal pack of hounds following.

Once they were gone, Tommen approached Jali, crumpled on the floor. Even if he understood Feeling and how to control its use on others, there was no point. She was gone. Tommen took an even breath. She'd no doubt done this willingly, traded places with Kayla for some unknown reason. Had she expected to die? Probably not. She had a daughter at home, and a son with a really good one-two punch.

Would either of them know how their mother died? Would they think it noble, think her a hero? Had they known that she returned? Did they know what her mission had been? Had she been fighting on Brelix?

But none of it matter now, he supposed. She was dead. Unless he wanted to be the one to take her body home...

Five minutes later saw him stumbling out of the Archives with Jali's body on his back. He wouldn't die himself to get her home, but he would try his damnedest. He had to use Gravity just to hold her one-ton body, and he had to pre-plan every move he made and adjust his Gravity tracks to match, or else he was going to be crushed under her weight.

He made it to the third floor before he had to lay her down and take a rest, as well as look to see what was going on and how he was going to get out of here by himself, never mind with this load.

There was no fighting on the second floor anymore. On the first floor, the fighting had turned into cover fire to allow for a retreat. Along one wall, Tommen could see the sub-level gates were open and a path was being viciously defended to allow the Akarin to escape. He could not pick out any familiar faces, but his path looked pretty clear. Maybe if he just came off as non-threatening, trying to fulfill some kind of humanitarian mission, he could fall in with the Akarin and get out.

It wasn't much of a hope, but it was a reason to keep moving. Planning out and structuring his Gravity tracks, Tommen again hefted Jali's body and started down the stairs. He stopped again when he reached the second floor, planning his route of escape and calculating his chances. The Akarin were still moving, but there weren't that many in the sub-levels. Likely once the last one was out, their defenders would begin to fall back and the clear path would close.

Determined to not stop for anything and not abandon Jali unless he absolutely had to, Tommen took a breath and set up as many Gravity tracks as he could in advance, anchoring them against himself so they were less likely to wobble and break and he would have an extra second to dump his load before it crushed him. Telling himself to just keep moving and not look around, not stop for anything, he took off down the stairs.

It was a bit of a bad idea on his part as it was akin to racing down a steep hill; eventually, your legs would get away from you and you would fall, most likely on your face, snapping your head back and breaking your neck. He managed to slow himself down before he touched down on the first floor, nervously feeling his Gravity tracks waver and Jali's body take on some extreme weight before it evened itself out and all was right again.

No one appeared to notice him as he made a mad dash for the wall until he reached the tail end of the escaping Akarin. The last one out through the gates was Kayla, helping an injured man who was unable to walk. They paused as they saw each other. Finally Kayla jerked her head down the path. Tommen nodded. Together, the three of them hurried along the path as best they could, Kayla with an injury, Tommen with a body.

Every so often, Tommen's dad had to do a personal security detail for someone important. It wasn't anything major like the United States President or Congressmen or anything like that, as those people usually had their own security. For Walter, sometimes it was for the mayor or someone on the city council. Sometimes it was for a prominent speaker on a college campus. Sometimes it was for high profile suspects who were in the middle of a trial or who had received their verdict. Everyone wanted to ask questions and get in the know, and Walter's job was to keep them from getting too close, too pushy, or too violent.

Running along the wall on the first floor of the southwest stair, Tommen felt how he figured those important people must have felt, at least to some degree. Crowds, crowds, people everywhere, shouting, yelling, trying to get close to him, trying to hurt him. As predicted, being the last ones out, the defenders began falling back and the attackers closed in from behind. Still, the portal room was within sight, and his short Gravity tracks remained stable, so long as no one noticed them and tried anything.

They reached the portal room, the defenders blocking the doorway, forcing the attackers into a bottleneck situation. Finally able to stop and breathe for half a second and actually look around, Tommen was stunned to find Rifun there in the portal room, opening up portals left and right for all manner of Akarin species. Kayla handed off her injured companion to someone of like species, then turned to Tommen. Her expression softened when she saw Jali across his back.

"Oh, sweet Jali," she whispered, touching the woman's stony skin. "I told her not to do it, to think of her kids. But she was always a woman of duty. And great Faith. Far greater than I could ever dream of." She looked at Tommen. "Thank you for bringing her body down. I know it wasn't easy."

"That's great and all," Rifun interrupted, opening the last few portals for the last few Akarin, "but there is still a mob out there that wants to kill us all."

Kayla sighed but nodded. "I will go with you, Tommen, to take her back to her family."

"One portal to Tuqa, coming up," Rifun said irritably, sweat dripping from the end of his nose as he less than gracefully ripped open another portal.

Kayla faced him. "I still don't trust you, and don't expect the Akarin to come running at your beck and call." Tommen could almost see her pride bulging in her throat as she swallowed it. "But I thank you for helping us escape, for sparing us."

"Get the hell out of my hair," Rifun told her.

She gave him a smirk, then motioned for Tommen. Together they stepped through the portal.

Less than an hour later, they sat in the living room of a very sorrowful Tuvak family, listening to the woman's daughter wail inconsolably while she did whatever funeral rites and preparations their culture demanded. The men had their own part of the rituals and rites to perform, and tradition demanded they did it with shrouds and masks of varying importance and significance, all of which was lost on Tommen. Despite telling them they would leave them to mourn in peace, the family demanded that the two of them stay, to share her last moments during the rites, as tradition demanded.

Kayla recounted a tale of heroic battle. Jali had indeed been on Brelix, one of those assigned to protect the tribes from any Time-wielding Borelians so they had a fighting chance. She told of the switch, made in the depths of the sub-levels, of the woman's courage, knowing that her death was very likely, especially if she were discovered. Kayla finished her tale, then handed it over to Tommen who had been the one present when she died.

Tommen had been told often that he was a good storyteller, and he supposed it was true when it came to speaking of fictional things. Anyone could tell a lie. But he'd never been gifted with such artful storytelling when it came to the truth. He told what had happened, about her bravery in stealing the journal, defying both Julianna and Rifun and leaving the outcome of the fight up to the Author. He told about their escape to the top floor where they rescued the Authored Books. He told about the Archives, her challenge to Julianna, the fight that ensued.

He told Jali's family that she had died in defiance of tyranny, with the glow of courage and the certainty of her purpose in her eyes. He tried to make it convincing, for her daughter's sake, because he sure as hell didn't believe it. To him, Jali had died the same way he might expect anyone to die, with a little fight left in them, that little hope that someone would save them, and then the quiet certainty and realization that it wasn't going to happen. But he did not say that part out loud.

Once he was finished, the funeral rites wrapped up quickly, all meaning and significance lost on the alien visitors. Then all but the immediate family was instructed to leave to make way for the final rites and the departure of the soul. As far as Tommen was concerned, her soul had already departed, but what did he know? He'd never been dead. Still, he respectfully followed the others outside.

"Your part now is complete," one of the extended family

members told them. "If you wish to go home, you may do so."

Kayla dipped her head. "Thank you for allowing us to be part of this."

"Thank you for bringing her home," another family member said graciously.

They said their goodbyes and walked off a short distance, just so they didn't feel as though they were still intruding or making a rude exit.

"I don't know what's going to happen now," Kayla said. "Everything seems to be changing all at once and in extreme leaps."

Tommen nodded. "Guess we can only take it one day at a time."

"I expect I will see you again in the future. Until then, take care of yourself, and look out for your dad, too."

He thanked her and watched her leave. A second later, he opened a portal back home. With a last look at Jali's family still lingering outside, waiting for some invisible cue, he turned and left.

Epilogue

"I thought that was your handwriting on the note," Rifun said as Tommen walked up the slope toward the caved-in entrance of Forbes Cave. He managed a dry chuckle, but his posture was in no mood for jokes as he took a drink from his thermos. "Come to join me at last?"

"Hardly," Tommen told him. He held out a large manila envelope.

Rifun took it cautiously, opening it up and examining the contents. He brought out three passports, several hundred dollars in cash of various currencies, a smaller envelope, and a folded piece of paper. He unfolded it, his expression twisting into something that Tommen could only describe as emotional but trying not to be. He then peeked in the smaller envelope, enough to confirm its contents but not dwelling on them. Rifun huffed a sigh and slid everything back in the envelope, securing the clasp.

"I know you were looking for the Books and the journals," he said. "Why save this? More to the point, why give it to me when you have to imagine the leverage potential behind it?"

"Julianna will come for you eventually," Tommen told him. "Think of this as a chance to get a head start on her."

"Far away from you, I imagine."

"I've forgiven you for what you did to me. I don't know that anyone else has or ever will. Call it a gesture of good faith."

Rifun stared at the envelope a moment more and sighed, his hands dropping to his sides. "I suppose I always suspected someone would try something. Maybe a splinter group of soldiers, maybe the

Akarin would inspire something in the Order, I don't know. But looking back, while it all makes sense, I still can't put the pieces together in my mind. It's almost as if I can't see them clearly." He took another drink.

Tommen dug out an orange script bottle and shook it. "It's because of these. And that." He nodded to Rifun's thermos.

"I don't understand."

"Tarka root is a mild depressant, similar to alcohol, maybe marijuana. On its own, it's probably good for your seizures, to keep them in check. But these—" He shook the script bottle again. "—are not the pills you think they are. They're not Versed. They're Dexedrin, an amphetamine, an upper. One of the worst things you can do is give uppers to someone with a seizure disorder. So you drank your tea to stay ahead of it, mixing uppers with alcohol. Your brain was so fucked up you couldn't see straight even if you had your sight. On top of that, tarka root loses its potency when exposed to air, so every time you opened your bag of powder, or just opened your drawer and exposed the solid root to air, it was less and less effective. By the time the battle came around, it was almost completely useless, leaving you medicated only by amphetamines. It gave you the strength and willpower to go through with the battle, but the social and political damage within the Order had already been done, and uppers plus seizure disorder means you were a ticking time bomb for a drop, which was exactly what Julianna's minion general was waiting for."

Tommen could see the realization crossing Rifun's face, and the man said quietly, "I got my own medication from a pharmacist who is also a Time Agent and Order sympathizer. But he was loyal to Julianna the whole time."

Without so much as a grunt, Rifun hurled his thermos at the side of the cave. Being cheap plastic, it cracked, and black liquid began leaking out, staining the snow.

"Take the money and run," Tommen said. "I don't know what you believe, but whatever you're looking for in this life, I hope you find it. Without needing to kill anymore."

Rifun did not reply, but one hand went to his revolver, faithfully on his hip. Tommen turned his back and walked away, fully expecting a bullet to take him in the back or back of the head. It never came, and had he looked back, he might have seen the last of the threads breaking and dissolving into thin air.

He was free.

Author's Note

Synchronization was probably one of the most fun TCW books to write just because of how much stuff comes together, about the Order, about the Wheel, about the Akarin, and it all comes together with an explosive battle and grand betrayal.

Bringing back the Xur and the D'Bok and some of the other species was remarkably enjoyable, and pairing them with the various human groups and even other alien species was more fun than I thought it would be.

Unfortunately, the hardest thing about it was keeping the battle on Brelix within a reasonable scope of knowledge. Tommen has demonstrated very well that he is a coward, so having him running around all of Ancrath and taking on legions of Borelians wouldn't fit his character at all. His mission was only one small part of the battle, something most of the people were not even aware of. Kayla might have been better-suited for such a task, but she was roped into helping Tommen, and Rifun wanted to make sure the journal got found, or so he thought.

And so, in the space of a mere 301,000 words, Rifun has finally been deposed. Julianna rules the First Order, the Akarin are scattered, and the Hands, Borelians, and Tacagans have forged a rather unholy alliance.

But wait! There's more!

The Chivalrous Welshman isn't done yet. Or rather, his enemies aren't quite done with him, and the most dangerous ones find Earth's defenses laughable. Now Tommen is fully exposed, no longer able to rely on the safety of Time and the justice of the Grandfathers. Nor can he call on the Akarin for reliable help, or use Rifun's fascination with him as a shield among wolves.

As we march into the home stretch of *The Chivalrous Welshman* with only two books to go, personal vendettas begin to lash out from the shadows. Earth itself may be protected for the time being, but that doesn't mean the consequences of Tommen's intergalactic adventures can't find him. And he isn't the only one who's facing the consequences of his actions.

- Brooke

www.ingramcontent.com/pod-product-compliance
Lightning Source LLC
Chambersburg PA
CBHW030551310726
48979CB00011B/2116/J

* 9 7 8 1 9 5 3 1 1 3 2 8 3 *